THOSE WHO GIVE

a novel by

Rosemary Cania Maio

Rosemary Cania Maio

**1stBooks Library
Bloomington, Indiana**

ISBN: 1-4033-1950-2 (e-book)
ISBN: 1-4033-1951-0 (Paperback)
ISBN: 1-4033-3360-2 (Dustjacket)

Library of Congress Control Number: 2002105706

This book is printed on acid free paper.

Printed in the United States of America
Bloomington, IN

1stBooks - rev. 10/04/02

Acknowledgments

Excerpts from "Love in Armor" reprinted with permission of Scribner, a Division of Simon and Shuster, from *A Kindly Contagion* by Walter Toman; copyright © 1959 by Walter Toman; copyright renewed © 1987 by Walter Toman.

"Footprints" a poem with multiple versions and authorship claims, including a version by Margaret Fishback Powers © 1964; one by Mary Stevenson © 1984 with a claim she first wrote her version in 1936; and many ubiquitous claimed but not copyrighted and unclaimed versions, one of which is used, in part, here.

"Quality" from *The Inn of Tranquillity* by John Galsworthy, © 1912, now in the public domain.

Special thanks to Diane Uttley of the Bernard Shaw Information and Research Service for identifying Shaw's age of disillusion quote as originally written for a paper read to the Fabian Society on October 16, 1891, then published in "The Impossibilities of Anarchism, the Anarchist Spirit," *Essays in Fabian Socialism*, Constable, © 1949.

Special thanks to the 1st Books Production, Technical, and Cover Design staffs for facilitating the frustrating journey through the editing process. These skilled professionals made this book possible.

for Sam and Kate

Thesis: Give, and it shall be given unto you; good measure, pressed down, and shaken together, and running over, shall men give unto your bosom. For with the same measure that ye mete withal it shall be measured to you again.

Luke 6:38

Thesis: Those who give have all things. Those who withhold have nothing.

Hindu proverb

Contents

PROLOGUE

Educational opportunities for females were scarce in the United States in 1800. Latin Grammar Schools catered to boys and only aristocratic boys at that. Girls were expected to receive training in social graces, domestic activities, and needlework at home. If a girl worked diligently at her samplers, she could learn numbers and letters, and then, if she were so inclined, expand that knowledge to simple reading and arithmetic. Not many were so inclined. The word *brain* was a non sequitur after the word *female*. Young ladies of aristocratic birth practiced their curtsies, improved their postures, and met no greater challenge than the order to stitch their French knots neatly. The most carefully worked sampler was a disaster if a flip to the back revealed a tangled mass of threads.

Miss Elizabeth Peabody, born in 1804, would have been destined to a life of thimbles and silver serving spoons if not for the education she received in the private school run by her mother. While the education of females was generally scoffed at, the Peabody girls did quite well for themselves. One of Elizabeth's two sisters married Nathaniel Hawthorne, the other, Horace Mann.

Elizabeth deferred marriage in favor of teaching, her first attempt at age eighteen in Boston. Boston was a hub of progressive education, inciting and stimulating diversification of methods and facilities. In 1824 Boston's English High School was the first of its kind in the United States. In 1826 Boston audaciously established the first high school for girls. The response was overwhelming. So monumental, in fact, that the school was closed two years later. Too many girls were fighting for enrollment. The school could not be expanded. It was far too costly.

In 1827 Massachusetts passed a law requiring a high school in every town of five hundred families, with a course of study including United States history, bookkeeping, algebra, geometry, and surveying. Towns with populations exceeding four thousand were required to add lessons in Greek, Latin, history, rhetoric, and logic. Influenced by this atmosphere all her life, Elizabeth got her chance to contribute to it years after the inception of high schools. At the other end of the spectrum. In 1859 when she was fifty-five years old, Elizabeth learned of a new concept in education being practiced in German-speaking communities. Emanating from Europe, Friedrich Froebel's *kindergarten* was first attempted in the United States in Watertown, Wisconsin, in 1855. Elizabeth was interested in the new theory that focused on the child as an active being. Book learning, senseless at so young an age, would be a natural outgrowth of the directed self-activity of the *kindergarten*. Through play, games, stories, nature study, and motor activity, the child would discover inherent capabilities and interests as well as develop social cooperation.

In 1860 Miss Elizabeth Peabody established in Boston the first English-speaking private *kindergarten* in the United States.

Hannah Irene Boesch attended Miss Peabody's new school in 1863. Little Hannah didn't know it at the time, but she had descended from a long line of females interested in more than domestic activities. Her maternal grandmother had been negotiated into the ill-fated 1826 attempt at a public high school for girls by Hannah's great-grandmother. Hannah's mother had been educated in a Female Seminary. Irene Boesch was thrilled with the progressive concept which was the foundation for Miss Peabody's school and couldn't wait to enroll her daughter. And so Hannah got her start in education. She was destined to devote her entire life to its goals.

At sixteen she enrolled in the Fourth Massachusetts State Normal School for training in the art of teaching. It was during those years that Hannah decided her place was in the high school. The fascinating new procedures of the Oswego Movement made up her mind. Edward A. Sheldon of Oswego, New York, finally made it big with the new teaching methods he had been pushing for years. Oswego graduates were commissioned to train new teachers all over the United States. Eager to learn, Hannah traveled to Oswego for instruction in oral and objective teaching.

The movement advocated the elimination of recitation and memorization as the mainstays of classroom instruction. The function of the teacher, therefore, changed from overseer to instructor. Faced with the duty to motivate awareness and reasoning, the teacher needed new skills including a much more extensive knowledge of subject, an ability to plan and organize lessons in advance, and the skill to devise appropriately ordered questions to direct students along the road to wisdom.

The teacher as "school-keeper" paled in the light of such challenges. Getting the student to think, to reason, to use his senses for observation became the new quest. Hannah left Oswego infused with the fervor of the movement. She could now do what she felt she had been born to do: she could now truly teach.

When she left Oswego, Hannah traveled with other graduates carrying the Oswego message, recruiting disciples in Massachusetts,

New Hampshire, Vermont. More and more women were replacing men in the classrooms of the country. Hannah finally took her place among them, itching to put into practice the procedures she was selling to others. Her last tour took her into upstate New York to an area still clutching to old techniques and traditions.

She liked the community despite its archaic views on education, and she settled there in 1880, needing to find roots somewhere, intent on revolutionizing the system. Hannah Irene Boesch possessed all the idealism, all the spunk, all the stamina, all the training, all the intelligence that could possibly be hoped for in a young woman of twenty-two. Her attributes served her well in her teaching and in her carefully orchestrated rebellions. She was to fight many good fights for over fifty years.

Progress was slow in a town that preferred to shield itself from the rest of the world. Money was scarce and people resented being taxed for education. The school district encompassed a vast rural area that viewed "book-learning" as useless in a world of physical labor. When Hannah started teaching, the district was ignoring the 1874 compulsory attendance law.

As the years passed, she made her mark again and again. She was instrumental in revising curriculum, establishing departmental instruction, and enforcing compulsory attendance, though she came to regret her crusade to gather up truants and herd them into the confines of the school. She found herself stymied by the disruption they created. Bodies could be legislated into any form of control, but minds were another matter.

And so new programs had to be developed. Technical training. Manual skills. Special instruction for children with speech defects, physical handicaps, and mental deficiencies. Special classes for non-English-speaking children. The abnormal, subnormal, and yes, the paranormal. By 1930 there was a national outcry among educators for differentiated classes to respond to the needs of the gifted child.

We spend our money and expend our efforts to recognize and fulfill the needs of the sub-normal child and offer nothing to those at the other end of the scale. The gifted child, whose future worth to society is immeasurable, is being neglected. Our gifted children must provide for our future. We need leaders for our democracy! We need minds that can successfully compete with the rest of the world in the fields of science, industry, art, education, religion, and the trades.

The schools were faced with the demand to successfully educate the truant, the incorrigible, the deficient, and the gifted.

The burden was impossible to shoulder, especially in a district with little concern for the costly development of specialized programs. But Hannah argued anyway. Hannah argued and pushed and prodded for small changes for so long that she eventually created a network of attack that became her avenue for progress.

It was at age sixty-seven that Hannah Boesch fought the biggest fight of her career. The rumblings of a new trend in education caught her ear. It seemed to her to be the only way to allow for individual differences, to create special environments fulfilling the varying needs of students. It seemed reasonable to release students from the childish atmosphere of the elementary school after grade six instead of after grade eight. Placing them in an intermediate situation for grades seven, eight, and nine would be in the interests of training for the demands of the last three grades. School districts all over the country were replacing the old eight-four system with the new six-three-three set-up. Thousands of the new "junior" high schools were being built and staffed. Hannah had grown accustomed to being years behind the rest, but at her age she decided she couldn't afford the wait.

In 1925 she began the slow, arduous process of persuasion. Her network carried her from other teachers to church groups to women's clubs to government officials. She prodded and pressured, charmed and cajoled, begged and badgered until she expanded small town minds to accept change and be willing to pay for it.

Even in her sixties she was a gutsy lady, her diminutive figure belying her strength. Adversaries misread her as a weakling only once; when provoked, she shed the delicate outer skin to reveal the casing of a warrior. She slowly swayed public opinion to her way of thinking, appealing first to other women, building an offensive line. The men fell into agreement once they were convinced that the idea was theirs. But the biggest challenge awaited.

There had to be a new school. The old high school would suffice as the intermediate "junior" high, but a new building was needed to accommodate grades ten, eleven, and twelve.

The city fathers wanted to use the existing school for both the junior and senior buildings. Split it down the middle. Renovate. Add a

xiv

few rooms. Chop up the larger rooms. Surely there was a way to avoid the cost of a new building.

Surely, Hannah patiently pointed out, there was no sense in pouring money into an old building that would soon be too small to house the number of students assigned there. Renovations would be costly and worthless in the long run. If the community wanted to enhance educational opportunities for its children, this was a proven way to do so. If the community wanted to change to a six-three-three system, which they said they did, facilities and staff would have to be provided. She cited statistical evidence, brought in knowledgeable speakers, and pounded away at public meeting after public meeting.

At one point she lost her temper with their parsimonious thickheadedness and insular attitudes, called them old fools with no brains and stomped out of the meeting. But nothing deterred her attempts completely. She bounced back again and again, hammering the same theme, for three years.

The old high school was first used as a junior high in September, 1928, when the new senior high was dedicated. Hannah's efforts would have been in vain had the project been stalled much longer. The shock of 1929 was looming on the horizon, along with successive years of misery and want. Hannah and thousands of teachers like her would teach without pay during those years.

When the school for grades ten through twelve was ready to be dedicated, the city council met in secret session to determine a name. The first to be placed in nomination was James Joseph Conklyn.

He was, after all, the mayor and as such deserved recognition. The school was built during his tenure in office, and as leader of the town and all it endeavored to accomplish, his name should be emblazoned forever as a symbol of the freedom and wealth of opportunity that America, the land of the free, the home of the brave, provided. The council was preparing to proclaim unanimous support for the mayor when a meek but steady voice rose out of the wilderness to audaciously put a crimp in the flag-waving.

Hannah Boesch? Hannah Irene Boesch? The fellow obviously didn't wear the trousers in his household. How absurd to name the school after a woman when there were so many perfectly good men around worthy of the honor. However, in the interests of democracy and a good laugh, the name was allowed to be entered for consideration. The laughter ceased when the votes were counted.

Could it be? Could it be true that exactly half of this august assemblage voted for Boesch? What began as a social gathering rapidly degenerated into a cock fight. No one knew for sure who was voting for the woman. But it became sport to hurl accusations, the more colorful the better. Insults and innuendoes flew, tempers flared, and nothing escaped scrutiny: politics, religion, wives, children, annual income, annual outgo. A second vote produced the same totals. So did a third.

The fourth vote settled it. Still split right down the middle, tired of the shenanigans, and ready to compromise, the group settled down to lick its wounds. Both sides proclaimed victory and accepted defeat. Of no mind to rekindle the brouhaha, the city council quickly solved the next problem by resorting to the neutrality of the alphabet.

Boesch-Conklyn Academy would outlive both Hannah Irene Boesch and The Honorable Mayor James Joseph Conklyn. The future would add floors and wings, four gymnasiums, three cafeterias, playing fields, a stadium, science labs, shops, and other trappings of progress.

Hannah knew that she planted a perennial. In the end she looked back with a deep sense of fulfillment. She was proud of her accomplishments, proud to be a teacher. The one deep incision into her pride came late, late enough in her life, when she was almost through with life anyway. Had it come earlier, the hurt may have warped her, paralyzed her enthusiasm. As it was she swallowed the hurt in the waning years of her life. But, try as she did, she never forgot. Nor did she forgive. Hannah Irene Boesch went to her grave cursing the illogical, unfair, insulting stupidity of that despicable hyphen.

BOOK ONE: October 23, 1980

Four Women and A Machine

Alyssa Matthews pulled into the parking lot at 7:20 a.m., looked at her assigned spot, muttered "Oh, shit" to herself, shifted the car into park, opened the car door and grabbed the push broom she had stashed on the back seat. Her parking space was once again a kaleidoscope of broken glass. As she swept the fragments into the grass, she wondered where she might buy a pooper scooper. Effie was seeking a faster easier way to dispense with what was becoming a morning ritual. She had never even seen the device so popular in large cities where laws prohibited dog droppings on sidewalks. But if it scooped up poop, wouldn't it scoop up glass?

She pitied the poor fool who had to mow the lawn. Sparkling bits of jagged color dotted the grass, promising to become a maintenance man's nightmare. The proverbial buck would grind to a halt in the rotary blades of a reconditioned John Deere.

The morning was bright and warm, unusual for late October. Heavy, somber winter clothes were still packed away in dark closets, the initial frantic search for them postponed until the first blast of cold. Located a few miles south of Old Forge, the area shared the frigidity of its record-breaking dips below zero. Lifelong inhabitants accepted the certainty of severe winters with resignation and courage that was sometimes beyond the comprehension of newcomers to the area.

Alyssa's lavender-flowered dress, a vestige of summer, highlighted her femininity as well as the morning's splash of sun. The delicate attire also caricatured the presence of the broom. Alyssa's slight figure was as incongruous as those housewives of commercial fame, elegantly clad while mopping the kitchen floor. Blessed with a hardy spirit, Alyssa Matthews had survived northern New York winters all her life. A long hard winter makes spring so much the sweeter, she was fond of saying.

Struck suddenly by the absurdity of the scene, she started to giggle. Halloween was approaching. Maybe she would wear black and carry the broom to classes. It might jolt a few kids into a reaction. Getting their attention was the first step, after all. Some of them were still on summer vacation. One boy had told her just exactly that when she asked him why he had done no work at all in almost two months. "I'm not ready to do any work yet," he said firmly. "I'm still on vacation. Maybe by Thanksgiving ..." She hadn't laughed at that. The first third of the course was critical. The boy was missing her carefully-laid foundation. Unless he could build his own later on, a feat accomplished by very few students, the whole structure of the course would lie in pieces at his feet. And she couldn't catch him up when he decided three or four months down the road that he wanted to pass English. Individual attention was a thing of the past, devoured by the last contract.

Three more cars pulled in and parked two rows down. No glass there. Too open for a late night beer party. Alyssa good-naturedly suffered the inevitable jibes from her colleagues as they passed. They too attempted to tolerate it all with a shake of the head and a laugh. There might be a whole brigade of brooms before winter set in to discourage outdoor parties.

Alyssa made quick swipes with her broom, wishing she could have some semblance of luck with parking. It was simply a case of rotten luck last year when her car fell prey to Fat Ferdy, a three - hundred pound sophomore who indiscriminately wreaked havoc in the parking lot as an expression of his displeasure with one of his teachers. At first, school officials were hard-pressed to prove Ferdinand's guilt. He carried nothing on his person that could have caused such cavernous dents in the hoods and trunks of six ill-fated cars in the parking lot. The mystery cleared when an astute guidance counselor trained in the eccentricities of youth suddenly theorized that the means of assault wasn't on Ferdy's person because it was Ferdy's person. He had merely lowered his devastating derriere onto the light-gauge aluminum and it buckled under his colossal physique. Car designers intent on decreasing weight for fuel efficiency never anticipated the vengeance of a Fat Ferdy. Rumor had it that he executed a few bumps and grinds to accentuate the depths of his displeasure, but no eyewitness ever substantiated the charge. After the guilt was accurately assigned, Ferdinand's future was secure. He became the object of a frantic search for remedial aid. There had to be programs of assistance for students with problems like Ferdy's, other than free lunch?

"Hey, Matt, that a new means of locomotion?" Jason Haywood locked his doors and strode over. Somehow Alyssa had been initiated by nomenotomy within weeks of her first year at Boesch–Conklyn. She was fortunate; first-year teachers sometimes lose more of themselves than just a few letters.

"It's loco and it's motion, all right," Alyssa countered. Then she focused on his vehicle, a bright yellow 1974 Corvette. "How do you dare park that here, Jay?" It was the color of the sun, she thought, if it had a name it would be Phoebus. He leaned over. "Sheer

3

arrogance," he said with an assumed air of confidentiality, "and an abiding faith in the benevolence of youth."

Alyssa laughed. "I think you'd better get in out of the sun, Haywood. Your brain is rotting."

"Actually, my second car is," he said ruefully. "It's getting a new transmission today, and I'm too far off the beaten path to car pool. It's just for a couple of days." He shrugged his shoulders and lifted his arms in a gesture of helplessness.

"I hope your luck is better than mine," Alyssa called after him as he made his way into the building.

Alyssa parked her car and gathered books, papers, and thermos from the back seat. Two brightly colored folders at the top of the pile triggered a frown. Senior research papers. Both failures. She had spent two frustrating and discouraging hours grading them the night before. She could not justify passing them. How college-bound seniors could submit such inferior work was beyond her comprehension.

Once she entered the building, she headed straight for the main office to check her mailbox. She pulled a handful of papers in various sizes and colors out of it, adding to her pile of things done and things to do, maneuvering to maintain control over slipping papers and sliding books. The handle of her blue thermos was firmly clasped by one finger. Effie had disposed of one without a handle long ago, and years of experience had perfected her balancing act.

She remembered to grab a sign-in/sign-out sheet for homeroom, said a cheery "Good Morning" to secretaries and to Harry Bassard, who was unlocking his office door, and left the main office. In the hall she ran into Haywood again. "How's the contract going, Jay?" she asked. "That last memo didn't say much."

"There wasn't much to say," he answered. "It's slow, very slow. Every time we meet we go forward one step and back three. They don't want to give at all, just take. And I don't think the membership would appreciate more work with less pay."

Alyssa's eyes flashed anger. "You must be kidding. What do you mean? How much more can they expect us to do?"

"Plenty. They're at the point where they would lay off the rest of us if they could possibly get away with no teachers at all. Money, as the philosopher said, is tight."

"What about our requests?"

"The English department? Mattie, look, all I can tell you is that we're holding firm, we're trying like hell, and it's going to take some time. That's all."

"Have you even mentioned our problems yet?" she persisted. "I know you have to think about everyone from kindergarten on up, but please, Jay, don't forget us. We were the sacrificial lambs for the last contract. I never thought the day would come when I would be willing to cut someone else's throat for my own benefit, but the last three years have made me selfish. Nobody cared about us three years ago. And I don't give one damn about anyone else's problems right now. The distribution of work is lopsided around here anyway. I only want a break so that I can go back to teaching the way I know I should. English is the backbone of the whole system and — "

"Stop, Mattie, please! You don't have to lecture me about it!" He was good-natured with his interruption, but not entirely without pique. She was not willing to give up, however; she was bristling with determination.

"You have a copy of our report?"

"Yes," he said firmly, "and so does the rest of the team."

"How about the other side? Do you have enough copies for them? If not, I'll run them off for you as soon as — "

"No, no, don't do that! It isn't necessary. We've got all the copies we need. And we'll do all we can. I promise."

"We need more than that. You've got to ram this down their throats, Jay. Make them see what has happened to us. Nobody around here cares. We submitted that report to Bassard a year ago. He said we were dealing with negotiable items that he had no control over. But there was plenty that he could have done if he wanted to."

She took a breath and he asked the question he already knew the answer to. "What do you mean?" She unloaded. "Show me in the contract where it says that phys ed teachers, industrial arts teachers, and department chairmen should not be assigned study hall and homeroom duties. Explain to me why some history and foreign language teachers have only four classes —"

Jason Haywood, sports car enthusiast extraordinaire, went into overdrive. "Now you're talking crazy, Alyssa! That's the kind of thing I've been hearing for months from the other side of the table." She was not impressed. Besides, she was on a roll. Someone was listening.

"You missed my point completely, Jay. Why can't we be relieved of something – anything! during the day? Bassard could have taken homeroom off our backs, or study hall. It never bothered me that people come here to sleep or socialize every day. But it bothers me like hell now! I can't keep up any more. I wrote part of that report, you know. And it got away from me. I lost my objectivity. Became too

5

emotional. But I made a mistake when I said that no one has expired from the strain. I was wrong about that. Not one of us who cares about what we do is teaching the way we know we should; it's a subtle form of death, but it is death. A slow, painful giving up of the spirit. If we don't —"

He stopped her in mid-sentence once again. "Okay, Mattie, okay. I understand, really I do. I know where you're coming from. Many of us feel the same way. I promise we'll handle it the best way we can." He was making signs to another colleague, obviously anxious to be on his way. The conversation ended with misgivings on both sides, the union member steeped in thoughts of right and wrong, the union negotiator consumed by thoughts of reality.

Alyssa continued down the hall to B building, passed by the cafeterias, gyms, and study halls, entered C building and climbed the stairs to the fourth floor. Along the way she thought about what she wanted so desperately: four classes again; two preparations; sanity; control; time. Why wouldn't anyone understand?

She unlocked her classroom door after blindly unsnapping her school key ring from the left snap inside her purse; this was done after she snapped in her home and car keys on the right side. Once inside the room, she locked the two research papers in her filing cabinet for safekeeping, her fear of losing or misplacing student work a constant reminder to lock things up. On the top of her desk she dropped the rest of what she was carrying, then extracted her mail from the pile, along with her thermos, then locked the door again and walked down the hall to the faculty room.

One of many such havens scattered around the sprawling complex, the fourth floor faculty room had its usual early morning crew. Staff gravitated to the most conveniently located room. This one had become an English department refuge years ago. Alyssa opened the door to a familiar scene: a body was lumped in a chair by the window, reading; and Bonnie Mason was cursing at the duplicating machine, which was spitting blank sheets of paper all over the room.

Bonnie quickly hit the stop button, wailing in frustration. "When did this damn thing die? It worked yesterday fourth period!" Alyssa responded with the warning everyone knew and loved: *Stay away from these machines the first thing in the morning. They will ruin your whole day.* Of course Bonnie knew that and of course Alyssa knew what Bonnie would say next: *I had to type this test last night and I need it first period.* None of this, however, had any effect whatsoever on the woman sitting by the window; she turned the page of her book and read on.

Bonnie released her ditto master from the machine and flew out the door, almost colliding with Jean Tevarro. Still fuming over the glass in the parking lot, Jean hardly noticed Bonnie's haste. Having no affinity for brooms, Jean resentfully kicked the glass out of the way. She had served on the Ad Hoc Committee for Parking Management, so she was just disgusted with the whole business. The committee of five teachers had deliberated over seven months to develop a lengthy and comprehensive report on conditions including vandalism, usurpation of spaces by student drivers, hazardous bottles and nails, and poor maintenance. It was Jean who pointed out in her own colorful way that the potholes were large enough to swallow her rear end in one gulp. The committee compiled a twenty-four page report with documentation laboriously gathered from other teachers, counselors, secretaries, anyone who parked in staff lots. There were plenty of horror stories, including the saga of Fat Ferdy. Among the committee's suggestions: Patrol the lots. Resurface the lots. Plow them before school hours during the winter. Discipline students who break parking rules.

The committee submitted its report when classes resumed after spring break. Jean knew she would get pressured into typing the final draft because she was the English teacher on the committee. Her usual response to that was: We all got college. Do it yourself. But this was important to her for personal reasons and she wanted the report to be perfect. Her only problem was time, finding the time to type twenty-four pages. Spring break was late in the year, she felt guilty over waiting to submit a report that was finished weeks ago, but that was the first chance she would get. It didn't much matter, though, when the report was submitted. It was totally ignored, except for a request for assigned parking in all lots. Drivers were greeted with parking stickers the following September; no member of the Ad Hoc Committee for Parking Management was in attendance when parking decisions were made over the summer.

Jean was furious. She demanded answers. What she got were the usual put-offs: there was no money to resurface (But you recondition the playing fields every year! she said); there was only one plow for all the schools in the district (Can't it come here first since we open earlier than any other school? she asked); patrols were out of the question unless teachers would consent to do it voluntarily (Jean's reaction to that exceeded the boundaries of polite conversation). The committee had been a smokescreen; she felt like a fool for expecting otherwise.

Alyssa poured herself some coffee from the blue thermos, took one look at Jean and stated the obvious, "You're in a black mood this morning."

Jean grunted. "I'd like to take all that glass out there and shove it down Bassard's throat."

"You were on the parking committee, weren't you?"

"Yes, and never again. Never again will I give that bastard the sanction of 'a faculty committee.' He gets everybody working their asses off, does what he planned to do anyway, regardless of the committee recommendations, then claims that he has faculty support. He'll never use me again."

"I'm surprised you got caught at all, Jean. You've been around long enough to know the score. I learned to keep a low profile long ago. If you don't, you end up doing committee work all year and kissing your classes good-bye."

"They caught me in a moment of weakness," Jean explained. "I had just replaced two tires that were punctured beyond repair; I was so aggravated that I forgot how things are. I won't forget again."

The woman sitting by the window kept turning the pages of her book. Jean stared at her sourly, then started looking at her mail. Alyssa was doing the same, sifting through the usual stuff. She red-circled names of students in her homeroom, classes, and study hall that were listed on the sign-in/sign-out sheet because she would need that info all day. She threw out an impassioned plea to require her students to join a book club. It was one of many she received throughout the year; her response was automatic now. She ditched them all; no time anymore to collect money and organize orders. When she read the latest order issued from central office, she stared in disbelief. "They must be kidding," she said. "Have you read this yet?"

"No. Let me see." Jean reached out for the notice, then returned it after a glance. "Oh, no surprise. Didn't you see it splashed around in the press last night? CYA at its finest."

Alyssa looked at the notice with contempt: All teachers are hereby notified that it is now school district policy that all students will receive daily homework assignments in all courses, and that teachers will collect and review all homework on a daily basis.

Jean raised one eyebrow. "Does it give you the impression that teacher has been steeped in luxury all this time and is finally being made to get off her lazy ass and do some work? I'm sure that a segment of the community is reading it that way. What the hell is teacher doing if she has to be forced to collect homework?"

Alyssa felt shell shocked; and she felt a need to exclaim what both of them knew. "I don't give homework every night. There are always times when it isn't justified. And kids have changed. So many do not care about losing points because of homework. And some courses are not geared for homework that can be collected and returned every day, anyway. How do you collect a reading assignment? Or a research paper on a daily basis? I fail to see any reasoning at all in this!"

Jean raised both eyebrows. "I just gave you the reasoning! It looks damn good in the newspaper! And it's one more thing that we can be held accountable for. Nobody wants to know what we do, just what we might not be doing. Can you see the home ec department taking home six classes worth of homework every night for 'review'? Can you see us doing it, on top of everything else?"

Alyssa shook her head and deposited the notice in the circular file; it was one more insult added to a long list of injuries. She glanced over at the woman sitting by the window, engrossed in her book. No concern over central office edicts there. No mail to sift through either, it appeared. Alyssa's box was always stuffed to the gills. She continued to sort through the small stuff: notices for homeroom students, a request from the nurse with a list of names, two requests for assignments for students who were out sick. She would take care of it all during the day. A third request for assignments made her bristle. One of her students would be out of school for the next two weeks. Family trip to Florida. Advance assignments were requested. It was district policy that such requests be honored. She knew, however, that it was a mighty rare student who actually did any of the work assigned while on vacation. But she was required to supply it anyway.

When Alyssa picked up what she thought was a drop slip, she moaned, causing Jean to look up from her own pile of mail. Though it was the color of a drop slip, the drop slip was an add slip. "Dear God," Alyssa said, "this is number 27. The slip is dated 10-21, so she should have shown on Tuesday. And what the hell do I do with her now? The course is half over. I can't give her private lessons on how to write a research paper."

"Who is it?" Jean asked.

"Gayle Fine."

"It doesn't ring any bells. Maybe she's new to the district."

9

Alyssa nodded. "Or a change-of-heart code one. By law we're obligated to take anyone until age twenty-one. Did you know that?"

"Sure do. Last year I had a sophomore who looked at least forty. He had failed sophomore English four times and was taking all three levels at once."

"Did he make it?"

Jean laughed. "Hell, no. No matter how I tried, I couldn't get him to write a sentence with a subject AND a verb in it." Alyssa suddenly had a thought. "He wasn't, by any chance, Peter Cavanaugh?"

Jean indulged in a small smirk. "The very same gentleman and scholar. What did he do, or I should say, what didn't he do for you?"

"He signed into my seventh period 2R class the third week of school. He was truant two days, ended up in ISSR, then was out sick. I caught him in class long enough to assign books and give him the lowdown on course requirements. He looked at least thirty to me and terribly out of place. I told him if he attended class and submitted some work he could certainly get through the course. He showed the next day with no books, put his head down on the desk and slept all period."

"That's his *modus operandi* all right," Jean confirmed.

"But wait. You haven't heard the best part. I went to see Ann Brady about him. I wasn't about to put up with his dozing off; sleeping in class gets contagious. By the time I saw Ann, Mr. Cavanaugh was cutting class again. Ann told me she would see what she could do, and from the way she said it I could tell she's been doing for this kid for a long time. A few days later I found a drop slip in my mailbox. But it was for a lateral move — 2R with a different teacher. I went to see Ann again to find out what was going on. Not that I minded losing the kid. He would have had me running all year, and I've got enough of those types. But I was curious to see how he managed to bend the rule on lateral moves. What clout could he possibly have had?"

Jean was curious too. How in the world did he manage to change teacher? She began to understand when Alyssa gave more details. "He also changed period. That was his strategy. He brought in a note requesting early dismissal because of a job and changed to a second period class." Alyssa paused for effect. Then concluded: "With Al Rentsen."

Jean grinned. "Well, Peter Cavanaugh will finally pass sophomore English. And the whole mess was all your fault anyway. You said two nasty words to him, *attendance* and *work*. But his worries are finally over. Uncle Al will take care of him."

10

Suddenly remembering the presence by the window, Alyssa nodded and rolled her eyes at Jean who assumed a "who cares?" expression. Focusing once again on the add-slip-that-looked–like-a-drop-slip in her hand, Alyssa wondered if this was indeed a returning code one. A code one was a drop-out. Drop-outs were supposed to be sad, tragic reminders of educational deficiencies. They didn't fail; the system failed. Realistically, however, each one signaled the loss of one body and a mountain of work. Fewer students meant fewer papers to grade, fewer records to keep. Even Alyssa, who had always welcomed new students, now looked resentfully at add slips and thankfully at drop slips. She now noticed something else. "Hawkens forgot the student number again, so I'll have to hunt that down today," she complained to Jean.

She would add the new name to attendance records, grade book, and seating chart, taking pride in carefully noting dates and codes of entry or departure; Effie had a reputation for keeping accurate and detailed data. Student numbers, therefore, were a critical necessity. The nine-digit demons became the vogue when the district, along with the rest of the civilized world, went computer. If she didn't get Gayle Fine's numerical identity before the next time grades were issued, she would have to do it then. The student number had to be added next to the name on computerized grade sheets. She learned her lesson about letting numberless new students pile up. It only hap-pened once; she had spent hours grading the last papers in the marking period, then averaging for the report card grade, then filling in bubbles with a number two pencil, only to have her grade sheets rejected because of missing student numbers. She had to run from office to office ferreting them out. She joined a chorus of voices complaining about the extra work load that arrived with computers, but there was no stopping the wave of the future.

Thinking about Gayle Fine as number twenty-seven in her senior class, Alyssa asked, "How many seniors do you have, Jean?"

Jean hesitated, then said as matter-of-factly as she could, "Five."

"Five," Alyssa said flatly. "Five?" Alyssa said incredulously. Her shock was too severe for exclamation.

"Yep," Jean said with a Cheshire-cat smile. "Count 'em on one hand. Or one foot if you'd care to remove a shoe." Her ecstasy was overflowing.

Alyssa was mystified. Jean Tevarro was not of the breed to harass and intimidate students the first week of school in a concentrated effort to encourage mass transfers. It was a tried-and-true technique used by some to decrease class size.

11

Scaring the hell out of 'em worked best in elective courses not required for graduation, courses that could be dropped easily. English was not an elective, and so a student had to transfer. Mass transfers were finally stopped when administrators noticed how cockeyed class size was becoming. Effective teachers were bombarded with students fleeing from incompetents or first-week ogres. Alyssa had experienced the invasion, bitter that those who did little work to begin with would be required to do even less. But her heart went out to the refugees signing into her classes. When a class total hit thirty, she was thankful for the contract limit on class size and turned others away.

Now it was more difficult for a student to change teachers. A few silently suffered along until January, their patience strengthened by the knowledge that a sympathetic guidance counselor could then hide a transfer under the guise of new scheduling for the second semester. Some found other ways to bend the rules: requesting early dismissal, making massive schedule changes, taking advantage of faculty infighting, moving to a different track, kissing ass, playing politics. But it was students blessed with concerned and, more important, screaming parents who found themselves whisked out of the clutches of their tormenters in incredibly short order.

Alyssa suddenly had a theory. "What period, Tevarro?" she asked.

"Aw, you guessed it. By a quirk of scheduling, I've joined the ranks of the privileged few. It's heaven, Alyssa. All five of them work like hell. We've already had some fantastic discussions. I was worried at first that it would be deadly, but the kids are just right. And they work on their own just beautifully a few days a week which gives me a chance to grade papers. I know I'm gloating, but I'm going to enjoy it while it lasts."

"I envy you," Alyssa said. "my seniors are third period, and you know how seniors love morning classes. There isn't a chance in hell that I'll ever get fewer than twenty-five research papers to grade."

Jean went on to say that her senior class was eighth period. Alyssa knew it had to be in the afternoon and the extremely small enrollment made excellent sense for the last period in the day. By eighth period any self-respecting senior was two hours gone. Seniors petered out by fifth period. Afternoon classes for seniors were notoriously empty, morning classes overflowing. Seniors badgered counselors to schedule physical education and English, the only courses many of them needed for graduation, early in the day. Senior year was a time to relax, to enjoy, to make some money to fund the relaxation and enjoyment. No amount of coaxing could convince a senior that laziness begets laziness. No amount of reasoning could convince a senior that educational opportunities beyond high school require self-discipline and solid study habits, traits that need fostering during the senior year. No amount of screaming could convince a senior that twelfth grade might be worthy of notice.

In addition to students interested in The Great Escape senior year, there were those holding down jobs through sheer necessity. Middle-class America, fighting the world's biggest inflationary monster since Louis XIV, was sending every able-bodied family member to work just to maintain financial solvency. More and more high school students were pounding the pavement looking for work and the government, satisfying the symptom instead of curing the disease, worked feverously to create more minimum-wage jobs. Schools ended up where they always end up: in the middle of a messy situation. Required by law to educate students through the senior year, and also required by law to allow students the personal right to early dismissal, schools had to mutilate themselves to fulfill yet another demand from society.

Alyssa was reflecting on these conditions. "It amazes me how few seniors take a full schedule of classes. I took six courses right through senior year. I didn't think it was a sin to graduate with more course credit than I needed. In fact, I saw senior year as an opportunity to take some elective courses."

"Attitudes have changed," Jean said. "My own daughter shortened her schedule senior year. I fought with her for months over it, but I couldn't get her to change her mind. She took double English and double gym, graduated in January with minimum credits, and took off for college. The whole thing scared me silly. I thought she was too young to be shifting her life into high gear. But she did all right. Dean's list all the way. She's in law school now."

"I guess it's like anything else," Alyssa said. "Some make it and some don't. Do you teach the poem 'Opportunity'? It's not the condition of the sword that matters, it's the person wielding it." Jean nodded consent. Alyssa continued, "I guess what really bothers me is what all these new trends are doing to us. Scratch that 'us.' You've caught the fluke of the century."

"Well, for a semester anyway. It won't last but I'll make hay while the sun shines."

"Speaking of hay, I cornered Jason Haywood this morning and I think I rattled his cage a little too violently. Nobody expects fury out of me."

13

"Are they getting anywhere?"

"Who knows? All I got out of him was 'it takes time' and 'we'll do all we can.' And he told me, in so many words, that it was heresy to suggest a fairer distribution of work."

The woman sitting by the window shifted position with what seemed to be little loss of concentration. Jean, however, was visibly disgusted at Alyssa's last statement. "But it wasn't heresy three years ago?" she said.

"Of course not," Alyssa answered. "Don't you remember? It was about time we were assigned five classes like everybody else. My stomach turned every time I heard that statement. The gross ignorance of it still makes me sick. We didn't have a chance. The rest of the membership wasn't about to vote down a satisfactory contract because we were getting screwed."

"I told Haywood once that they would have accomplished something if they had lessened the load for another department. And that increasing ours was a step into the Dark Ages. But I told him that before I found out what they gained by selling us out. Release time for union reps costs the district plenty, you know."

Alyssa did know. "I suggested to Jay this morning that shop, phys ed teachers, and department chairmen be given homeroom and study hall duties. Maybe we could rotate those assignments."

Jean started to laugh. "My, my, Mrs. Matthews. That is heresy you're preaching."

"I suppose it is. But if they hired an extra teacher here and there the shop and phys ed people wouldn't have to teach seven classes, the home ec girls six, and the business department lord–knows-how-many. There's the rub, right? If they hired a few more English teachers, we could go back to teaching four classes. Fat chance."

Jean was about to respond when the door flew open to reveal a furious Bonnie Mason. Her blonde hair limp and lifeless, the usually delicate lines of her face contorted into an ad for *The Grapes of Wrath*, Bonnie stood before them close to tears. Her odyssey to find a friendly duplicating machine had taken her from one faculty room to another. Scattered at diverse locations in the sprawling complex, the rooms challenged physical stamina when it became necessary to navigate from room to room. Bonnie encountered long lines at two machines, but her spirits rose when she finally reached the last room and spotted one duplicator not in use. Exhausted by the long-distance run, strung out from stress, pressured by the warning

14

bell signaling five minutes to homeroom, Bonnie Mason missed the obvious.

"Now what do I do?" she moaned, holding the ditto master up with two fingers, dramatically displaying the destruction. Chewed as though it had been attacked by a ravenous animal, its purple ink smeared into the grotesque forms of a Rorschach test, the master could never produce the ninety copies Bonnie needed.

"All right, calm down," Alyssa said. "It isn't hopeless. Make another master from the black copy. I'll run down to unlock your homeroom."

Bonnie's frustration deepened. "I couldn't make a black copy."

They all knew why. "Out of order," they said in unison. The only machine of its kind in the school, the zerox copier was used and abused so often by so many that it was out of order more often than not. Getting that black copy for future masters wasn't easy.

Bonnie was in trouble. She knew the consequences for reneging on a test date. But Alyssa wasn't out of ideas yet. Effie had been awakened and Effie never failed to come through. "All right, what kind of test is it?" Alyssa said calmly.

"Vocabulary," Bonnie answered.

"Sophomores? Regents?"

"Yes."

"Good. I have class sets of those. Let's go to my room."

Bonnie was torn. "No, Alyssa, I can't do that. You've given me too much stuff already. I feel like an incompetent nincompoop, I can't even make copies."

"So you think the rest of us can? This is hardly the time for pride. Besides, when your files are as fat as mine, I fully intend to raid them."

Bonnie smiled. "Okay, Mom, whatever you say."

Alyssa's hazel eyes danced with mirth. "And stop calling me mom. I've told you before, I may look old enough to be your mother, but it was biologically impossible when I was five."

"I don't see why you and Jeff don't adopt me. I've suggested it enough times."

Alyssa and Jean both laughed. As much as Bonnie tried to hide her figure under bulky sweaters and loose dresses and suits, she still exuded a voluptuousness that is natural to some women. This time the running joke with Alyssa ended with Alyssa saying: "Not on your life. I'm not competing with those boobs in my own house!" All three women broke into laughter as the homeroom bell rang. All three gathered up paraphernalia and pushed through the door to greet the day.

The woman sitting by the window remained. Erica Vetterly turned another page of her novel, oblivious to the call to homeroom. She had trained a student to take homeroom attendance, and he was doing a better job than some of the so-called professionals in this loony bin. There was no need for her to start work for another twenty minutes. And then she only had to direct another student to start up the film projector.

Jason's Fleece

Reality, thought Jason Haywood, nobody wants to face reality. He had been on the team three years ago. It was his first experience negotiating and he observed most of the time. What he saw made him sick. Dollars and cents. That was what every item was reduced to. It was the first time the Board hired professional negotiators and they were determined to be worth their fees. The union had been backed into a corner. There was the usual press: the union "issued demands," the district "offered proposals." Teachers were wild-eyed maniacs only interested in personal gain; Board members were concerned citizens responsibly trying to hold down the tax rate. Enrollments were on a steady decline and costs had skyrocketed. School districts all over the country were paring budgets and the most costly items, buildings and staff, were under attack. Dollars and cents.

Alyssa was right. The English department had been placed on the sacrificial pyre, had been the final offering held back until the ultimate compromise had to be made. Settlement came quickly after the district gained the right to cut staff in its largest department. Dollars and cents. And look what the membership gained: a three-year agreement, a six percent increase per year, relief from bus duty for all grade levels, release time for union reps. Give and take, parry and thrust. They had been dangerously close to a strike vote, and the Board's hired thugs were immovable. And why not? Their paychecks weren't in danger, and their children were in private schools. How long could the luxury of four classes last anyway? If it hadn't happened three years ago, it surely would happen now, because that fight had been cake compared to what they were up against this time.

In the last three years the Board had closed five elementary schools, eliminated driver education, laid off hundreds of teachers, all social workers, three out of four psychologists, and all elementary guidance counselors. School nurses suffered a change in job description from "nurse teacher" to "nurse" which allowed their salaries to be cut in half while their duties remained the same. The change came four years after the district forced them to take courses without compensation to earn the "nurse-teacher" designation.

The Board threatened to cut music and art sections, and then did when no one of consequence protested. All school libraries were ordered to cancel magazine subscriptions and to stop buying books. Sports were severely curtailed, initiating the first significant public response. Booster clubs kept the sports programs afloat. Bus routes were shortened and sometimes eliminated. And still taxes went up.

Each time a new money-saving measure was announced, a sore festered in one segment of the community and people banded together to exercise their constitutional right to protest. But the committees were self-interest groups: parents whose children had an interest in music or art thought it obscene to fight for football and hockey once the music and art programs were mutilated; parents faced with providing transportation after bus service was denied voiced no objection at the loss of social workers. Nobody cared much about the libraries' problems after driver ed was abolished. The libraries had plenty of books. Driver ed credit lowered insurance rates. Again and again the sores festered and oozed and ran blood. Then they scarred over.

Dollars and cents. Save, save, save. Conserve energy, increase productivity, use good business sense, and keep those taxes down. That, thought Jason Haywood, was the mentality they were up against. Assure the public that the kids weren't suffering, promote the biggest lie of the century, and slash the hell out of everything.

He had read the English department report. It was an impassioned plea for mercy. But the negotiating table was no place for impassioned pleas and never in the history of organized labor had it been a place for mercy. There would be ice in hell before the Board would agree to lighten the English load and hire more teachers. And what if by some miracle it did? What an uproar that would create, he speculated wryly. Why hire more teachers when the money could be used to reinstate driver ed or varsity track?

His heart understood Alyssa Matthews, but Jason Haywood had learned at his first negotiating session that the heart is alien to those surroundings. The English department's report was in his briefcase; in fact, he hadn't yet shared it with any one else on the team. He wouldn't waste anyone's time, time was far too precious to spend on hopeless causes. Chances were excellent that the English department's report would never again see the light of day.

The Hairy Bastard

Harold E. Bassard knew what everybody called him. It all started the day he entered school as a child. Had he initially enrolled in school as H. Eugene Bassard, he would have been called Gene instead of Harry, and probably would have missed out on all those fun times at the hands of his tormentors through the early grades. But it toughened him up, and he had a much better experience later on because he developed survival skills at a tender age. At least that's what he theorized as an adult. And he knew that spending all of his working life in a school meant that the name-calling wouldn't end until he retired. And it wouldn't end then. Even then he would be remembered over coffee in countless homes, over beer in countless bars, over dinner in countless restaurants. Countless reminiscences in countless minds. Rote legacies, the unfathomable accolades and condemnations of every teacher, every administrator, pronounced after the fact, in retrospect, colored by age and experience, verdicts handed down by jurists deaf and blind to all pieces of evidence save one: their own personal experience with the defendant.

After ten years in the classroom, Harold E. Bassard tired of teaching the same thing year after year. He hated grammar, despised spelling, loathed vocabulary. Administration looked appealing then, an opportunity to escape lesson plans and tests and a rigid schedule. So he took courses in administration and applied for the first opening that came along. By the time he was forty-three, he had eight years' experience as assistant principal, which gave him the courage to apply for the job he wanted from the beginning when it went up for grabs. Actually it was easy to get. He was male, he was a homegrown success story, he knew the right people, he had the right attitude.

When school opened in September, 1980, Harry Bassard had been principal at BCA for ten years. He was fifty-three years old and was counting the days to retirement. Every day he unlocked his office door wondering what new crisis would arrive. And how he would rationalize it away. Smoke bombs, fire crackers, false fire alarms, bomb scares, drug raids. He had explained them all away. And what he could avoid explaining, he kept carefully hidden: the students caught fornicating in a stairwell, the male teacher caught attempting to seduce his male students, the female teacher caught growing marijuana. Whenever the school gained public attention, it was Harry

Bassard who suffered the glare of the spotlight, Harry Bassard who was under fire. And Harry Bassard was wearing down.

Each school year demanded more and more from him. Nobody was satisfied with existing conditions; students were constantly forming committees to complain and demand; staff morale was at an all-time low, school bureaucracy at an all-time high. Most of what everyone bitched about was beyond his control. He couldn't do a thing about staff cuts or computer sheets. And he was a little tired of listening to wailings about workloads. Nobody put in more hours than he did. Twenty years out of the classroom, Harold E. Bassard had become the compleat administrator.

On October 23, 1980, he entered his office to face one more day in the countdown to age 55. Sitting at his desk, he scratched the full beard that he had grown to compensate for his bald head. He would live up to his sobriquet one way or another; he hadn't totally lost his sense of humor. As he scanned his appointment book, he became aware of a flashing light on the corner of his desk. He picked up the phone receiver and pushed the button that connected him with his secretary. "What is it, Brenda?" he asked.

"A Mrs. Conneally," Brenda answered. "And does she sound hot!"

"I never get the cool ones. Put her through." Harry waited for the connection, then said pleasantly, "Hello, Harold Bassard here, Mrs. Conneally. How can I help you?"

The woman was spitting nails. "I want my daughter's English teacher changed immediately!"

Harry tensed for a fight. He bristled at such requests, especially when made in that tone of voice. "I'm sorry, but it's not school policy to change student schedules because of teacher preference. If we allow one to do it, the whole place will be moving around all year. Perhaps a conference with the teacher and counselor will address your concerns." He used the usual approach but had a feeling it wouldn't work. She was too incensed to begin with. But he certainly couldn't buckle immediately; he needed to know much more. She gave it to him with both barrels.

"Mr. Bassard, I've already tried that route. Since the first week of school I've badgered the counselor to do something about this situation. The teacher claims she's too busy to return my calls during the day and that she doesn't get paid to make calls on her own time. I'm losing my patience with the runaround. I simply cannot accept the possibility that my daughter will learn absolutely nothing in her English class this year."

Harry was on to the truth, but still he proceeded to wiggle into what might turn into an opening for negotiation. He very slowly and very carefully outlined all the possibilities for remedial aid. Also, Mrs. Conneally's daughter could pick up progress report forms every Friday so that her academic status could be reported by all her teachers. Plus, the girl's homeroom and study hall teachers could be notified of her special needs and enlisted to help. And he would personally see to it that a conference would be scheduled with all concerned parties in attendance. He ended by saying that he believed this would be a much better approach to the problem.

But it wasn't working and he knew why. He hadn't yet acknowledged her problem. Still he had to hold firm. He remembered too well the domino effect of lateral changes. Besides, huge numbers of students disliked their teachers for every reason imaginable. So Harry tried again, this time suggesting a "trial period." That was when Mother showed her stuff.

"Look, I've been begging the counselor since the first week of school, and she finally got fed up with me and suggested that I talk with you. If I had known sooner that I needed your approval, I would have called you sooner. My daughter has been through all the 'trial period' that she is going to go through. This is no frivolous request because my daughter doesn't like the color of her teacher's eyes! My daughter's future is at stake and I don't really expect you to be as concerned about her as I am. But I want you to know that at this point I am truly desperate. If Beth Ann comes home with one more story about that woman's incompetence, I will be going over your head with my complaints. Beth Ann has always been an excellent English student and I will not sit by and watch her waste an entire year with Mrs. Vetterly. I'm not the type to threaten, sir, but when it comes to the welfare of my children, there's no limit to what I'd do. If you don't intervene in this, I'm going to the next Board of Education meeting to ask why we're paying teachers to show movies and play games. Don't doubt that I'll do that and whatever else it takes to get my daughter a decent education."

Well, she had to go one way or the other, Bassard thought. Back down or fire up. Not only did she fire up, she also spoke the magic words; it was all *open sesame* from here. "I'm beginning to appreciate the nature of your concerns, Mrs. Conneally, and I admire your willingness to go to bat for your children. I've been known to do the same for my own from time to time. Please give me a few days on this. What year is your daughter?" He had already written her name on a note pad.

There was an audible sigh of relief, then: "She's a sophomore. Regents level."

"Okay. I'll speak to her counselor, let's see, that's Ann Brady, isn't it? Ann is an excellent person to work with, I hope you realize her hands were tied."

"I have no complaint with Mrs. Brady. In fact I have little to complain about except Mrs. Vetterly. Beth Ann is doing well with all her other teachers. She's having trouble with math, but that's her fault and she has been using the progress report once a week. Mrs. Vetterly gives her 92 every week and Beth Ann can't figure out why. She hasn't taken a test or handed in a shred of work since school started. I know there are students and parents who like that just fine, but we do not. Other than that, Beth Ann is adjusting well to the high school."

"Well, we try to make the transition as easy as possible. I'll speak to Ann about a possible change of class for Beth Ann. I can't promise you anything because I don't know if there's another class with a seat available the same period that your daughter now has English. I'll have Mrs. Brady get back to you as soon as the details are worked out. You should understand that other changes in Beth Ann's schedule might be necessary. And of course you must remember that if and when a change is made, Beth will have to keep very quiet about it."

"Of course, Mr. Bassard. Thank you so much for your help."

Harry ended the call with another soothing "Mrs. Brady will get back to you," then dialed Ann Brady's number. "Good morning, Ann. I just spoke to the mother of Beth Ann Conneally. You could have warned me."

"What's to warn, Harry? Erica is a walking time bomb." She wanted to add, why the hell do we protect her? but she knew why. Erica's protection was everybody's protection. "Anyway, Mrs. Conneally has been calling me twice a day since the first week of school. I kept giving her the line about school policy, but it never dented her persistence. I had to refer her to you. She was ready to go public. So what do you want me to do?"

"Give her what she wants. I told her you'd get back to her as soon as you figure out a way to do it. And continue to handle these requests in the same way. We can't let changes get out of hand again."

"You're telling me. Between computer errors and course changes, my change slips are threatening to break through the ceiling. There might be a problem finding her a seat, though. Let me run a quick check."

"Who else teaches sophomore regents?"

"I'm looking for my list, Harry. When is all of this going to be available in a split second? So far these computers have done nothing but slow me up. Here it is: Courtman, Matthews, Mason, Rentsen, Vetterly, Whittsley."

"Try Matthews or Mason first," Harry instructed, "then Whittsley or Courtman. Stay away from Rentsen."

"Give me a little credit for brains, Harry. I wouldn't plunge the girl from the frying pan into the fire." Harry spoke a quick apology, then asked for an update in a few days. After he broke the connection, he pushed the button for Brenda. His appointment book showed three sets of parents waiting in the outer office for conferences to readmit their suspended children to classes. The two girls and one boy had been guilty of excessive truancy, smoking in the lavatories, and spitting at a teacher, not necessarily in that respective order. Harry was ready with his lecture on respect, responsibility, and self-discipline. He gave it in duplicate and triplicate every day, aware that some offenders would reappear in his office until the school was relieved of their presence through some legal procedure. "Has my first appointment arrived yet, Brenda?" he said into the receiver.

"Yes, sir," Brenda responded. "But Jim Cote is out here to see you. He says it's crucial to see you now. He looks awfully distressed, Harry."

Well, of course, Harry thought. If they aren't hot, they're at the very least distressed. Brenda knew two adjectives; he would suggest she get a thesaurus. "Send Jim in first, Brenda, then the parents, one couple at a time, when Jim leaves." What tragedy could have possibly befallen the biology department? Jim Cote was never anywhere but in his room at this time of the day. The antithesis of Erica Vetterly. It was a dark and stormy day when Harry had to deal with problems from both ends of the spectrum.

Impeccably dressed in a vested gray business suit, Jim Cote stood before Harold Bassard looking nauseated. A slightly green tinge visited his face, a shade almost in harmony with one thin strip of chartreuse in his multicolored tie. Jim believed that a teacher should look the part, set a good example; his suits reflected his conservatism, his ties announced his lively spirit. Because he taught elective courses — his specialty was genetics — Jim Cote enjoyed teaching highly motivated, capable students. His kids weren't troublemakers, they weren't truants, they weren't mentally deranged.

23

How then could he explain what he had just seen in his room? How could it happen to him? He was fairly certain that no one could hate him enough to do such a thing. And he was horribly embarrassed to have to tell anybody about it. He supposed that he shouldn't take it personally, but what other way was there to take it? He wished Bassard would ask him to sit.

"What's up, Jim?" Harry asked.

Jim brought his left hand up to straighten his already perfect-looking tie. His hand remained there, positioned slightly below his neck, in a gesture of reticence. It looked as though he needed to choke the words free from his throat. "Ah, ... I, ...ah, that is . ." he fumbled.

"Spit it out, Jim, I've got a busy schedule this morning." Bassard swiveled around in his chair, grabbed a cigar and lit it, oblivious to Jim Cote's already queasy stomach.

"All right, but I've got to sit down," Jim said. "And would you please blow that smoke the other way? I'm a little green around the gills."

"Sure, Jim, sure. Just get to the point." Teachers. Everything's a catastrophe.

"I unlocked my door this morning at about 7:45 or so. I was a little later than usual because I needed to run some copies and I had to stand in line forever, it seemed. I wasn't happy about being that late because I like to make the room available to students who need a place to study early in the morning. You know, Harry, we don't provide enough opportunities for students to be students. But I don't care if they talk, either, because they need a place to do that too. I don't care if they talk quietly even after homeroom begins, as long as they don't get rowdy and loud. Kids who want to study should be able to, and we all need to hear announcements. The PA system in my room isn't the best. I'm really very understanding, I try not to be unreasonable, I'm ..."

Jim took a breath and Harry seized the opportunity, "Everybody knows you're a good, kind, compassionate teacher, Jim. I've had an order in for more copy machines for two years, and the PA system is lousy in a lot of rooms. Someone will be looking at it next week. I'm sorry I can't give you better answers, but that's the way it is. Anything else?"

It wasn't exactly the scientific method he was using, Jim knew that. He would try again. "When I walked into my room this morning, I ... ah... I saw ... ah ... I saw something that shouldn't be there."

24

Bassard started puffing wildly on his cigar, deriving no small measure of satisfaction from the increasing density of smoke building around Jim Cote's head. The man was an avowed non-smoker and he deserved a little discomfort for his infernal stalling. "WHAT did you see that shouldn't be there?" Bassard asked, cigar clenched between his teeth.

Jim took a deep breath. "Excrement," he said.

Bassard almost swallowed his cigar. He leaned forward in his chair. "What? What are you telling me? Excrement?"

"Excrement. Feces. Call it whatever you want. I opened my door this morning and there it was!"

Excrement, Bassard thought. Feces. Goddam technical jargon. Why is it so hard for some people to call shit shit? But he began to feel guilty about the smoke. "All right, Jim. Try not to think about it. I'm sorry you had to get sick to your stomach. We'll get it cleaned up and I'll announce over the PA that dogs are not allowed in the building. Damn kids have to be told everything every year. I do remember something of this sort happening a few years back. I guess we'll have to pull the rule out of mothballs. The more things change, the more they stay the same, eh? Go on back to your homeroom, I'll send a custodian up."

Harry reached for his phone, started to dial, then noticed Jim's blank expression. He stopped dialing and replaced the phone receiver on its cradle.

"It wasn't a dog, Harry."

What was it then? A mouse? A rhinoceros? Or should he have said a canine?

"It couldn't have been a dog. Unless the kids who have managed to steal master keys are training dogs to use them. That room was locked from the time I left last night until the time I unlocked it this morning. Besides, it's not animal feces."

Harry couldn't believe what he was hearing. "Look, Jim, the rooms are cleaned every night. Maybe the custodian is bringing in a dog. That would explain everything. How can you be sure it's not from an animal? You didn't hang around long enough to put it under one of your microscopes. So what are you suggesting? Are you suggesting that it's human?"

"I'm afraid so."

"That's ridiculous."

"Harry, dogs don't climb to defecate."

"And people do?!?!"

"Not necessarily. It was probably placed there after the fact."

25

Harry Bassard shoved his cigar into an ashtray. Now it was making him sick. After the fact? Placed there? "Where is this ... this ... excrement?" he asked.

"On the top of my desk," Jim answered.

The Apartment

"Are you sure you won't need these today?" Bonnie asked, still feeling guilty.

"Of course not," Alyssa said. "I'm not finishing those lessons until next week. Just have the kids write answers on their own paper. The key is in the folder. I'm not giving you very much, Bonnie. It's an easy test, basic matching and multiple choice. I used to create some real brain twisters, but I haven't had time since we changed the vocabulary book."

"I had a real beauty before it was demolished. I planned to share it with you, that's how good it was. But it's not totally lost, the rough draft is next to my typewriter. There's always next year."

"How about if I use it next week?"

"I'd like that," Bonnie said, her face brightening. "I'll retype it tonight."

"No. Not tonight. Tonight I have something else for you to do." Bonnie's puzzled expression encouraged her to continue. "Are you still looking for an apartment?"

Bonnie said yes and went on to explain that her rent was exorbitant and other costs were keeping her in the poorhouse. "I'd love to get out before winter sets in. The heat kept me at poverty level last winter and that was at a steady sixty degrees. I've had no luck finding something better."

"I think I found it for you. It's the apartment Jeff and I lived in before we bought our house. Mrs. King called me last night looking for a new tenant. She doesn't like to advertise. And she never did want to make a fortune, just enough to help pay expenses. She loves her home and wants tenants who are clean and non-destructive. It's an attic apartment. Well, sort of. I don't want to spoil your first impression with too many details. Jeff and I loved it there. I think it will be perfect for you."

"Did she say what the rent is?"

"One hundred a month. Including heat. Jeff put in a separate gas water heater and the electricity is split, so you'll have a separate utility bill every month. But you'll be warmer than sixty degrees this winter. Mrs. King likes it warm and cozy. She must be close to eighty by now, bless her."

"Where do I find this piece of heaven on earth?" Alyssa wrote the information on a 3x5 card she extracted from the pile she kept on her desk for quick notes and reminders. Then she told Bonnie that Mrs. Alexander (Dorothea) King was expecting to see her new tenant today. "Call her from school to arrange a time."

"I can't thank you enough for this." Bonnie was elated.

"The way I see it, she needs you and you need her. I'm simply making the connection. Oh, you'd better call her after lunch. She does volunteer work in the morning."

"And she's eighty?"

"Eighty going on twenty."

The Indictment

Paul Haust stood in front of his mailbox and wondered if the fire he felt in his brain was visibly pushing steam out of his ears. The executive order that he held in his hands was the latest in a long line of whiplashes that he, as department chairman, was obliged to administer. He didn't know how much more his people could take. He had fought long and hard on this one, and now he knew he had lost. What he wanted was one last rip-roaring blast at the son-of-a-bitch who let this happen. For Paul, "bastard" had become too hackneyed, thus too mild, a sobriquet.

But his door was closed, he was "in conference" with Jim Cote, Brenda said. Safe in his inner sanctum commiserating over the needs of the biology department, no doubt. Paul Haust wished he had the pull with Bassard that other department heads had, but Paul Haust couldn't bring himself to revere Bassard's bottom. He simply could not play the game. Instead of fawning, Paul fought. Instead of crawling, Paul stalked. Instead of submitting, Paul rebelled. And instead of winning, Paul lost. Bassard saw to it every time.

The only reason Paul wanted to see Bassard now was to thank him for nothing, to commend him for his cowardice. The order was irreversible, but Paul needed to unleash the fire in his brain, to spew it back at its creator. But Bassard was busy with other things.

Paul stormed out of the office and headed for his domain on the fourth floor. He moved the way he always moved: fast and furious. He caught Bonnie in the hall, then moved into Alyssa's room and was taken aback by the order and quiet. "Do you beat these kids, or what?" he asked.

"No, Paul, they came to me this way," Alyssa laughed. "And I'm grateful to whoever trained them last year."

"I just came to tell you that there's a meeting tonight. It's crucial for everyone to be there."

"Now what?"

"Can't get into it now. Just be there right after school."

"The resource room?"

"Yes. And spread the word, I may not be able to contact everyone between now and then."

Alyssa shook her head in agreement as he flew out the door. He left her with an uneasy feeling, but that was nothing new, he always seemed to be in the process of chewing nails. She hated emergency meetings. Good news can always wait.

Emissions

Jean Tevarro's gynecological difficulties began at the tender age of nine when she awoke one morning with excruciating pain. Her first bloodletting occurred later in the day while she was learning to multiply fractions. Feeling the wet between her legs, she was horribly embarrassed and asked permission to use the bathroom. Old Miss Titleman bristled at the girl's poor grammar, gave her a lecture on the proper use of "can" and "may," and sent her back to her seat. They were in the middle of a lesson. By the end of the lesson, blood was trickling down Jean's leg. She had certainly seen her own blood before from the usual cuts and scrapes of childhood. But this was different. She hadn't fallen, hadn't cut herself that she knew of. And the pain, the pain that she felt earlier came back. Sharp, pulsating stabs of pain that made her double over. She burst into tears, but didn't dare move.

Old Miss Titleman's eyes widened in her wrinkled, leathery face. It couldn't be. It was abnormal. The girl was too young. But there it was, threatening to sully the floor. She had to protect the rest of the class from knowledge of such things. The other little girls, still innocent. And the boys, the boys! "Go to the nurse! Immediately!" The taut lines in old Miss Titleman's face constricted in disgust. She watched the wretchedly sick little girl run from the room, then quickly returned to business. There was no harm done; it all happened too fast. No explanations were required.

The nurse dredged up a bit more compassion, first calming the child, then instructing her in the proper use of a belt and pad. Jean's hysteria returned when the nurse suggested a return to class. She was having trouble understanding that what was happening to her was natural and nothing to be ashamed of. If it happened to everyone, then why did Miss Titleman get so angry? No dear, the nurse said, not everyone. Just girls. Then Jean was really confused. Why just girls? And wasn't Miss Titleman a girl?

It was getting too complicated for the nurse. It was time to call Mother. Mother moaned something about wretched fate and something more about Jean's being shackled to the whims of her body at so young an age. Mother had been dreading The Talk from the day she gave birth to a daughter. How could she now tell that daughter she was a woman at the tender age of nine? Mother knew it was cowardly, but she couldn't figure out what to say, much less how to say it.

Jean spent a few years feeling very much the outcast. She was miserably ill every month and had no idea why. She didn't dare ask questions and resigned herself to the agony. At least she knew it would stop. Eventually her girlfriends became afflicted too and she felt not quite so alone. She was in the eighth grade when she began to piece together information she gathered from dirty jokes the boys were fond of telling. And some of her girlfriends were more worldly than she. One of them, in the habit of singing "once a month, every month," to the tune of a popular commercial, made her realize that not everyone suffered the way she did. Getting her period was akin to the bubonic plague; she could never refer to it in terms of the lighthearted Campbell Soup song.

The more she grew, the more she suffered. And the more she became involved in life, the more she learned to do it encased in pain. The world didn't schedule itself around her menstrual cycle. Twelve to fifteen hours of steady pain put her out of commission every month, but she took exams, she made appearances, she did what she had to do. She wouldn't be a slave to her body.

As she made her way through college, she listened to assurances from doctors and other women that once she had a child the wrenching pain would subside, the Red Sea would part, she would menstruate quickly and painlessly like "normal" women. For years she thought she was abnormal, a blight on society, the demands of adulthood compounding her distress. She did not enjoy being quarantined for two days out of every month, even though the rest of the world seemed to think so. She knew the score. Employers didn't want women who would need time off for pregnancies, much less for monthly sickness. When she married Dominick Tevarro, Jean looked forward to having children. They were wildly in love and they both wanted a large family. Better health would be a bonus.

But the miracle of birth was not accompanied by the miracle of normalcy. Not with the first child, or the second. Or the twins. Or the fifth. Jean learned to enjoy pregnancy as a merciful alternative. Labor pains were at least productive and at worst less severe than what she was subjected to every non-pregnant month. She nursed her babies, even the twins, to further avoid the misery reserved for the female of the species. But she couldn't nurse forever. And she couldn't adequately raise more than five children. After all of it, Jean Tevarro was still in pain "once a month, every month," and she laughed when she heard other women discuss "flow." The word didn't quite make the grade. "Hemorrhage" was more like it.

When The Pill hit the market, she gave it a try, not for its intended use, but to regulate the hemorrhaging and eliminate the pain. It was miraculous, but, she soon decided, not worth the side effects. In six months she had high blood pressure, twenty extra pounds, and a diminished libido. While The Pill didn't do much for her physical health, it gave her considerable emotional support. American women began to speak freely about themselves and about their unique problems, no longer willing to accept old taboos and stigmas. Jean learned that she was not alone, she had been foolish to label herself "abnormal." She owed no one an apology for being female.

On the morning of October 23, 1980, Jean was forty-five years old and still hemorrhaging. Even the combination of a jumbo tampon and a hospital-sized pad did little to quell her fears of saturation. She would never forget the terror of the first time. It was period number three-hundred-seventy-two, she had already survived through twelve hours of pain, and she meant to make it through the day and catch up on her sleep that night. Luckily the cramps started after school the day before. So she wouldn't have to call in this month. Sometimes the curse hit on a weekend; that was best of all. Like it or not, that was the way she had to live. How could she take two days off every month? And students can be incredibly crude when faced with teacher absences. One foul-mouthed fellow thought it appropriate to ask her if she was "on the rag" once when she was out sick. Jean, being Jean, was more outraged than embarrassed. She pursued the joker relentlessly, first demanding a definition of the phrase, then explaining slang and substandard English, along with manners and respect. I don't ask you embarrassing questions, do I? She had him blushing in no time.

When she rose to leave the faculty room, Jean felt a sudden gush and cursed the fact that the tampon lasted a mere thirty minutes. As she walked down the hall still joking with Alyssa and Bonnie, she was worried about the staying power of the pad. When she unlocked her door, she was greeted by an odor that turned her already scrambled insides. She took one look at the top of her desk and saw the source of the stench. She controlled the urge to vomit and quickly locked the door, ordering her homeroom to wait in the hall until she returned. She asked a student to circulate a sign-in sheet for attendance in case she didn't get back in time. Then she began the trek down four flights of stairs and across two buildings to the main office, giving thanks every step of the way that she was in the habit of wearing black slacks when she had her period. Wouldn't old Miss Titleman be proud?

Jean arrived at Bassard's door just as Jim Cote was leaving. Brenda was not at her desk, so it was easy for Jean to slip past Jim and close the door. "Harry," Jean said, trying to catch her breath, "you're never going to believe this. There's a pile of shit on the top of my desk."

The Cafeteria

It was situation normal in the cafeteria. Groups of students were scattered all over the large room. Two chess games, three card games, and scores of conversations were in progress. Homework was being started, finished, copied, compared, cried over, ignored. Books were changing hands, hands were changing rooks, and bodies swarmed together and apart, together and apart, like ants around an ant hill.

There were four separate homerooms located in the cafeteria. Bonnie's occupied the square of tables nearest the door. She screamed for her kids to sit down as soon as she entered the room, thankful that someone had unlocked the door, which was usually her responsibility. Two of the other teachers assigned there also called for order; the fourth hadn't arrived yet.

Bonnie set her books and papers down on a table and prepared to take attendance. She had to scream again to quiet the room down enough so that she could hear herself think. Taking attendance under these conditions was quite the challenge, even with the procedure Alyssa taught her. For one thing, the cafeteria tables never had the same number of seats, so an alphabetical seating order was impossible to maintain. Any seating order, in fact, was difficult to enforce; too many students in too large a room. She often got caught recording an absence, then spotting the student gossiping with someone in one of the other homerooms.

The noise level began to rise again, but Bonnie was too busy pulling and marking cards to concentrate on anything else. The morning announcements were filtering softly through the box on the wall over her head, the sounds barely above a whisper. Bonnie used the PA system to explain irony to her classes: it wafted a gentle breeze of sound in the large rooms and blared you out of your seat in the small ones. Situation normal.

Bonnie was in her third year of full-time teaching, her tenure year. The district had given her just enough part-time work during her first five years out of college to keep her hope alive for a full time job. She was on call to sub for three of the five years, hopping from school to school every day, her assignments ranging from first grade to auto mechanics at the high school. Then she spent a year teaching fourth grade math to eighth grade students, filling in for a teacher on leave. After that she went back to per diem work. She hated every minute of it. She hated feeling incompetent and unprepared. She hated babysitting. The kids were never fooled when she was placed in a situation she had no training to control; the district was sloppy with assignments, and often followed the "warm body" theory. But she survived and she persisted. The insecurity was maddening, but once she established a reputation as a good English sub, she was in demand and enjoyed more assignments in her field of expertise. So she waited for her own classes, her own students, her own chance to prove herself an educator. There were times during those years of instability and humiliation when she would have switched careers, but no opportunity arose, and going back to school to train for something else was out of the question. She was too far in debt; she had to work. She would not return to her family a failure in need of support. She would waitress if she had to, it was honest work. Her father's words rang in her ears every time she felt frustrated and disgusted with her meager subsistence. He gave her the lecture for the first time when she was fifteen.

"Why in God's name do you have to go to college?" he rampaged. "High school will make you smart enough to get married and have babies. And you're too damned good-looking to settle for just any man. Smarten up, girl! Pick a winner! You've got what it takes to snare yourself an easy life! Don't be a fool. Let the homely girls go to work. Thank your lucky stars you're female. Men can't do what you can do. I work day and night to make life easier for you and your mother. And that's my duty and I accept it. You've got to find yourself a man who thinks the same way. Now I don't want to hear a word more about this college foolishness."

As she made her way through high school, Bonnie spoke a number of words more, causing the lecture to be delivered with colorful modifications. She cringed every time she heard it and shuddered spasmodically once when the lecture ended with what her father evidently thought was the saving grace of his theory. "Look at your mother," he said. "Look at your mother if you need proof!" And with that he sealed his daughter's resolve. Bonnie had been looking at her mother ever since she had developed the maturity to really see her. Mother was beautiful, intelligent, energetic, and bored. And one day Mother took Daughter aside to advise her to escape the paper doll existence that Father was trying to bully her into.

Bonnie knew she was alone with her dreams when she left the comfort and security of her Maine home to attend college in New York State. The only remnants of home that she carried with her were her mother's love and good wishes, furtively offered the day she

36

left. There would be no support from her father, financial or otherwise. Bonnie fought hard not to hate her mother as well as her father, reasoning that her mother had chosen her own path and was now saddled with it. What good would a revolt do either of them? Why should they both suffer in poverty? So Bonnie took out loans and worked as many jobs as she could find. She watched every penny, wore the same clothes for four years, and didn't eat lunch because it wasn't included in the cheapest meal plan.

When she graduated she possessed a bachelor's degree, temporary certification to teach, a 3.8 cumulative average, and an $8000 debt. Luckily she could defer payment on the debt for five years. Enough time to get some stability in her life. She was raring to go, spitting fire, oozing enthusiasm. She had worked and sacrificed and scraped and suffered and the payoff was near. That was the promise when she decided to train to be a teacher. There were plenty of jobs for teachers; teachers were notoriously mobile, hopping from district to district in search of better working conditions, salaries, and benefits. Districts all over the country were competing to attract the best teachers available. But while Bonnie was in college, something insidious was happening out in the world of budgets and contracts and student population, something beyond the perception of would-be teachers like her. Thousands of starry-eyed students, preparing themselves for disappearing jobs, would become thousands of starry-eyed graduates applying for positions that no longer existed. Thousands of fresh, excited minds would have nowhere to go.

Like all the others, Bonnie was bitter with the feeling that she had been duped. But she couldn't allow herself to wallow in her bitterness; that would mean failure and failure would make her father happy. She had traveled a long way down the road to independence and she would persevere. If she wanted to stay in the field that was teasing and tormenting her, she had five years to take thirty graduate hours to earn permanent certification. She continued to waitress to supplement her subbing, which paid twenty-two dollars a day two or three days a week. She managed to pay for the $3000 worth of graduate courses as she took them; she bought a clunker for transportation, rented a two-room apartment, and still skipped lunch. She supplemented her high school wardrobe with name brands she bought at factory outlets. She was determined to survive.

At the end of five years, she was permanently certified to teach and joyfully accepted an appointment in her subject area at BCA. It was a lucky break. They had to pay her more because of the graduate hours, but her subbing experience counted for nothing. She hadn't subbed enough each year to qualify for a boost on the pay scale. The one full year in math would eventually translate into retirement credit, but it didn't count otherwise; it was out of her certification area.

Eleven years and $11,000 worth of education after she left home to make her own way in life, Bonnie Mason was still struggling financially. But now with great hope for the future. She finally had a slot of her own in the system. A firm grip on her own destiny. Her tenure year, the third year of her English assignment, was the key to her future. Tenure would provide the stability she craved. She would finish paying off her loans, then move on to improving the quality of her life. Climbing the pay scale would help her cast off the nightmare that haunted her asleep and awake, the nightmare of submitting to her domineering father.

In her tenure year, Bonnie felt better about the career she had chosen. She saw teaching as a chance to nurture the growth of other human beings. The frustrating years of subbing had driven that tenet from her mind, but once she had her own classes, her own chance to prove herself, the belief returned, stronger than ever. Nevertheless, on the twenty-third day of October in the year of Our Lord one thousand nine hundred eighty, Bonnie Mason whispered her version of the Floater's Prayer as she took attendance in her homeroom in the cafeteria of Boesch-Conklyn Academy. *Please, Boss, give me a room of my own. Anything, anywhere. It's not that I'm ungrateful. I know I'm lucky to have a job. But isn't it time for me to get a room? A room of my own, Boss?* Whenever the prayer popped into her head, she had to fight feelings of guilt. Being out of a job was still too fresh an experience. Tolerating the confusion, the inconvenience, the frustration of floating from room to room every period of the day was the price she paid for being low man on the totem pole. Actually, her situation had improved dramatically in three years. She now hustled around to four different locations during the day. When she started working full time, it was seven.

Maniacal Morning Minutiae

In the beginning and for the beginning, Man created the homeroom. When God had His chance at creation, God, in His infinite wisdom, chose to dispel chaos. Man, given His opportunity, in His finite foolishness, selected alternative B.

When Man created the homeroom, He simultaneously engendered the homeroom teacher, a multi-talented personage responsible for all areas of minutiae. Difficult enough to pronounce, minutiae are even more difficult to keep under control.

Homeroom attendance records were legal documents verifying students' presence in or absence from school. Affidavits were signed and notarized at the end of each school year, affidavits pledging the accuracy and insuring the culpability of each homeroom teacher. Alyssa Matthews was never comfortable signing that affidavit. It wasn't her own efficiency that she doubted; Effie had carefully honed her method through the years, making accuracy a natural by-product. What bothered her was the underlying threat of a system demanding that she take full responsibility for variables that were well beyond her control.

The unwieldy system was plagued by loopholes large enough for a broad range of imaginative abuses. Sometimes students wrote their own excuses to cover absences or had a friend write them. If the handwriting remained the same throughout the year, the chance of recognizing forgery was almost nil. Sometimes students didn't bother to forge excuses, choosing instead to forge absence slips. The slips, written by the homeroom teacher to validate absence, were based on the explanation offered on the excuse submitted. Pads of slips periodically disappeared from desk drawers and filing cabinets. Forging an absence slip became necessary when a bogus excuse would undoubtedly be caught by an alert homeroom teacher, or when the pressure of a classroom teacher demanded immediate action.

Some students slipped in and out of school so often that they beat the system simply by wearing it down. And some parents would tell eager lies to cover up what everyone involved knew was an illegal absence. Viewing the school as an adversary, these parents considered it a holy duty to protect their offspring. Some felt joyfully powerful when bucking authority, vehemently asserting that Johnny was home sick in bed even when an irate administrator protested that he just saw Johnny hotfooting it away from school grounds. Variations on the theme of masking truancy were clever and copious. Ranked alongside discipline, attendance was an ever-present thorn to teachers and administrators, a thorn that splintered and grew, each new particle drawing strength from the base, widening and lengthening to produce its own progeny, twisting and gyrating to reach monstrous and grotesque proportions.

For in the beginning, Man also created The Law: Attendance required from age five to age sixteen. And The Corollary: In the event of insufficient progress, attendance allowed until age twenty-one. And The Warning: All of the above determines State Aid. Thus and so, the bottom line forced attendance record keeping to scale the list of priorities, scrambling over other duties with ease, peaking arrogantly, autonomous and intimidating.

When Alyssa started teaching, she saw homeroom as just another duty that every teacher had to endure. There was no choice in the matter, tolerating non-instructional duties was part of the deal. Well aware of the tales of terror emanating from pre-union days, she was thankful that she couldn't be required to teach seven classes, coach a sports team, act as faculty advisor to a club, police the lunch line, and supervise the loading and unloading of buses twice a day. Homeroom and study hall were crosses to bear, but tolerable ones in view of others historically borne by teachers. As the years passed, homeroom time was cut from forty-five minutes to thirty minutes to twenty minutes to ten minutes, the extra time added to the instructional day. Alyssa, whose primary concern had always been her classes, was glad to get more class time. But something was happening to homeroom in direct opposition to diminishing time.

Through the homeroom teacher, administrators found elusive truants; counselors contacted students about schedule changes, the PSAT/NMSQT, SAT, remedial reading and math, competency exams, scholarships, and college applications; the nurse scheduled physicals and eye-and-ear examinations; the librarian repeatedly attempted to collect overdue materials; the Student Association conducted polls; the yearbook staff collected money; the Red Cross collected cans of food; the Homecoming committee distributed ballots to elect a queen; the junior class voted on a prom theme, the senior class on a ball theme; clubs solicited new members; other teachers assigned detention, threatened students not reporting to study hall, requested the return of texts from students who had dropped or transferred out of courses after books were issued, and sent students to the in-school suspension room. Distributing schedules in September and January, the homeroom teacher struggled to answer questions about code changes because that information was not readily available. The homeroom teacher assigned twenty lockers to thirty students, begged and badgered and threatened for the return of health forms requiring a parent's signature, distributed report cards, signed honor and merit roll declarations, delivered requests for schedule changes to the appropriate administrator's office, distributed student handbooks with an accompanying reading of sections 3, 4B, 6, and 12, herded the crew to assemblies with customary care to funnel them into assigned rows, and, each and every day, the homeroom teacher performed the function for which the whole thing was originally intended.

Identical attendance records for each student in each homeroom were kept on two cards, a small one sent to the office to compile the daily list of absentees for the whole school, and a large card kept by the homeroom teacher as a permanent record. Both cards had to tell the same tale with identical markings and codes. Alyssa couldn't bear the thought of transferring the record for the entire year from the small card to the large card in June. For each student in the homeroom? Twenty-six-seven-eight-nine or thirty times? One hundred eighty days each time? During exam week? No way. So Effie devised a system to organize the mess and fulfill the obligation each day.

She assigned each student a number from one to thirty according to the alphabetical listing of names in the homeroom. Then she numbered both cards, front and back, and the seating chart, as well as envelopes for filing excuses. When an administrator requested all the excuses for a student (or, worse yet, just one) she could access them in a second if they were all together in one envelope. Only once, years ago, had she been caught unprepared by such a request; she had to use valuable time going through all the excuses for the entire homeroom. She had to wait a while to implement a filing system, however, because her homeroom for years was in the cafeteria. The envelopes were born the first year she had access to a desk, even though it was someone else's desk. She begged the use of one drawer. It was pure joy to be able to grab the appropriate envelope when a request came through for excuses, even though the envelopes were in a drawer that was in a desk that was in a room that she had cause to enter only once every day. If the request came through while she was teaching in that room, God was in His heaven and all was right with the world. If it came through at another time, she ran laps until she could gain entrance without disturbing another teacher. The Floater's Prayer was on her lips for years.

When she moved into her own classroom, Alyssa instituted the number system. Effie was delighted with it from the beginning, and now it made the homeroom period almost long enough. When in numerical order, the small cards were also in the alphabetical seating order of the homeroom. Alyssa could fan through them quickly to determine who was absent. In the first weeks of school, before she matched names with faces, it was critical that students sat in assigned seats. Once everyone became familiar and relaxed, she could easily spot a stray and return a card that would have erroneously recorded an absence. The biggest annoyance, however, wasn't strays; it was tardies, students who were late for every reason the human brain could conjure up.

Each absence was recorded with a slash, a half-chevron, in the appropriate box for the appropriate day on the back of the small computer card. It was at this point that Alyssa's numbers paid off. Once she marked the small cards, she used the numbers to locate corresponding large cards and quickly marked those as well. She had the procedure skillfully under control, but if that were her only attendance duty during homeroom, the ten minutes would have been slashed to five.

"Mrs. Matt, I left early yesterday, but I forgot to sign out. My mother wrote me an excuse. Is that okay?" Alyssa looked up to see Sharon Newcombe, a waif of a girl with wide innocent eyes and a naivete that was sometimes charming, sometimes maddening. Then Alyssa looked at the excuse, reflecting on the fact that she had heard this tune before. Sometimes the tone was changed, sometimes the tempo; sometimes it was embellished, other times it was austere. But the melody and the refrain remained inviolate; in essence it was the same old ditty.

"Look, Sharon, you are a junior. You know the rules. You must sign out if you leave the building for any reason, even if you forget your note. You can't come and go as you please and then cover yourself the next day. I'll believe you this time, but don't ever do this again."

Sending the girl to an administrator would only prolong the inevitable. Issuing detention meant fishing out a detention slip and filling it out in addition to two attendance cards and an absence slip. Hoping that the warning would discourage future reoccurrence, Alyssa grabbed her pad of absence slips and wrote the girl's name and grade and the date. She checked the date of absence on the excuse to be sure it was accurate, then noted it on the absence slip.

Often she had to note or correct the date on the excuse itself to avoid future confusion.

"Sharon, you left at 11:00. Did you return?"

"Yes. For eighth period. My mouth was still numb but I had a test."

"As long as it wasn't speech class, Sharon, the condition of your mouth wasn't relevant."

Sharon wasn't at all sure how to react, but Mrs. Matt was smiling, so she smiled in response. Alyssa noted the return time on the excuse, then finished marking the slip, writing "dentist" after "reason for absence," and adding "ex. 11:00, ret'd 8th per." at the bottom. She signed it and handed it to Sharon Newcombe whose starring role in the dull little comedy was terminated. Alyssa wasn't so lucky. She had to play out the final act. She found Sharon's small card, number 16; noted the date, times of departure and return and reason for absence on the front; marked the little box on the back; then flipped through the large cards (Effie kept those mercifully clipped in a notebook) to number 16; noted the date, times of departure and return and reason for absence on the back; and marked the larger box on the front. She wrote a note to notify the office and filed the excuse in envelope number 16. Sharon Newcombe's numbing experience the day before was finally and officially a matter of record. But as the curtain closed, the ingenue was mentally preparing encores. Miss Newcombe had been dropped off in plenty of time to attend both seventh and eighth period classes. She had spent seventh period in a first floor lavatory, gossiping with friends. But now her seventh period teacher would never know. And so what? It was only study hall.

Four more notifications of partial absence were waiting for Alyssa's attention. They had been part of the stuffing in her mailbox. When properly channeled, such excuses allowed compilation of a daily sign-in/sign-out sheet. Secretaries typed the data at the end of each school day and then stuffed mailboxes to get the excuses to the proper homeroom teachers. This attempt was sometimes thwarted by students stupidly or cleverly unaware of homeroom number or teacher name. Excuses sometimes arrived days late or not at all, further complicating the morning procedure and more significantly, widening the margin of error. Sharon Newcombe could have accomplished her deception easily enough in a variety of ways. But part of her story was true: she had forgotten her note.

At the beginning of the year the faculty had complained about the "new procedure developed to disseminate sign-in/sign-out information." The sheets were typed and then posted in three separate class offices. It took only a few days for consensus that the information was inaccessible stuck on three bulletin boards in three different offices. So then the sheets were posted in the main office. It took a few more days for consensus that this wasn't much better. Why couldn't everyone get a personal copy? Well, of course that was possible. What stymied Alyssa was the decision that the faculty would have to pick up their own copies every morning; if the excuses were stuffed in the mailboxes, why couldn't the sheets be put there? But that was not to be, so she added that duty to her morning routine; Effie had to have accurate data.

She positioned the sheet for easy reading, focusing on the four red circles she had already made around familiar homeroom names. If she was lucky, the four excuses in her mailbox would correspond with the names and the information on the sheet. She read the first excuse. Mark Nettleton, excused at 2:00 for a road test. She checked the sheet. He didn't come back. She wrote out his absence slip, found his number 14 small card, noted the date, time, and reason for absence on the front, marked the back, flipped to his number 14 large card, noted the date, time and reason for absence on the back, marked the front, then filed the excuse in envelope number 14 and called him to pick up his slip.

Next excuse: Roberta Ossinski. Excused for a dental appointment. No times on the excuse. Times on sheet: out at 12:30, in at 1:52. Write times on excuse. Write absence slip. Find number 26 small card, note date, times, reason for absence on the front, mark the back. Find number 26 large card, note date, times, reason for absence on the back, mark the front. File excuse in envelope number 26. Call Roberta to pick up slip.

Joseph Natte. Please excuse for family reasons at 10:45. Check list. Aha! Returned at 2:50. Write return time on excuse. Write absence slip. Find number 12 small card, note date, times, and reason for absence on the front, mark the back. Find number 12 large card, note date, times, and reason for absence on the back, mark the front. File excuse in envelope number 12. Call Joe to pick up his slip. But wait a minute. Returned at 2:50?

"I hate to pry, Joe, but why did you return ten minutes before the end of school?"

"Had to. Football practice."

"Uh-huh, I knew there had to be a good reason." Some rules, she thought, can't even be crimped.

The last excuse belonged to Giacomo Nucciovannichi, number 20. He had been absent from homeroom the day before, so Alyssa found his small card in the green envelope used to send the computer cards to the office everyday, It was explained on the excuse and verified on the sign-in sign-out sheet that he arrived at 9:00 after blood tests. She marked his tardiness on the back of the small card, noted the date, time, and reason on the front, flipped to the number 20 large card, marked the front, noted the date, time, and reason on the back, and filed the excuse.

"Come and get it, Jack." She called him to her desk while still writing.

"You could get it legally changed, you know," she said, referring to his name. The first time she tried to squeeze it into the small space on an absence slip, he told her with a grin that "Jack Nuccio" would suffice. They still joked about it.

"No way," he said. "I make people I don't like write the whole thing out."

Alyssa made a comment about the possibilities of lengthening her own name for the same purpose and, because she still had to take this day's attendance, grabbed the pile of small cards, all now in numerical order because she had returned those cards she had already worked with as she finished with each one, fanned them, found three absentees in addition to Annette Nieully, whose card was already out because she had been absent the day before, pulled the additional cards, marked them, found the large cards using numbers, marked the large cards, placed the four small cards in the green envelope, returned the other small cards to the pocket in the homeroom notebook for safekeeping, along with the pad of unused absence slips, closed the notebook and slipped it into the desk drawer she reserved for homeroom materials.

She looked at the clock. It was still an hour ahead, but an almost-perfect hour. She had a couple of minutes to herself. Heading for her filing cabinet to get out materials for first period, she was aware of a body entering the room. Annette Nieully sauntered over, excuses already in hand. Alyssa fought to control her anger. If the girl wasn't absent, she was late. If she wasn't late, she left during the day. Annette Nieully bounced in and out of school enough to warrant the undivided attention of one entire homeroom teacher.

"Nettie, why can't you get here on time in the morning?" Alyssa left the filing cabinet to pull out homeroom materials all over again. She pulled Nettie's card out of the green envelope.

"Here's my excuses," Nettie said, throwing two bits of paper on Alyssa's desk. Please excuse Nettie's absence on October 22 for family reasons. Please excuse Nettie's tardiness this morning because the alarm didn't go off. Alyssa wrote the slips, marked both cards, and bit her tongue. There was no way to stop Nettie's flagrant disregard for the rules. Not as long as she supplied excuses. And her source was inexhaustible. *Please excuse Alyssa from homeroom because she finds it to be demoralizing, insulting, and a waste of precious time.*

The bell rang. In the midst of the stampede, the green envelope was whisked off the desk by Alan Nathan, appointed to this duty because of his reliability, to be delivered at just the right moment to the proper office. Cards were not accepted before or after the five minutes between homeroom and first period class. Alan Nathan had once neglected to pick up the envelope because his card was one of those in it, and Alyssa had to send a student from first period class. The student returned with the cards and a nasty note berating her for her irresponsible disregard for the rules. Rather than waste valuable class time on her defense, Alyssa waited for her free period to plead her case. But no excuse was acceptable, and she left the office feeling like a felon on parole. She also decided that the next time the cards were late, she wouldn't send them at all.

Two Tardy Terns

The multi-colored Volkswagen putt-putted its way out of the McDonald's parking lot. It coughed and wheezed its way down city streets as if it were apologizing for its curious appearance. It was a mobile junkyard, resplendent with motley color — one door silver blue, the other garish green, the trunk lid sunny yellow, the hood bravura red. All remaining metal was rather neutral in contrast, a murky blend of dull orange and brown, primed for future uniformity.

"This car embarrasses me," said the young man to his friend the driver.

"So take the bus," said the driver.

"That's a bigger queer job than this car."

"So shut up. I don't think the bus stops for breakfast either."

"Nah. I asked once, but the driver wasn't game. Said he had a schedule to keep." The passenger chuckled. "I'm sure glad I don't." Then the young passenger looked at his watch. "We're late," he said matter-of-factly.

"Well, if you could have limited yourself to two breakfasts, we might have made it. You blew that girl's mind ordering a Big Mac at eight o'clock in the morning."

The car suddenly swerved to avoid hitting a bump, but hit it anyway.

"I like gettin' a rise outta people — hey! slow down, will ya? My head can't take this abuse."

"What time is it?" the driver asked.

"Twenty-five after eight. Don't worry about it. We only missed homeroom."

"I've got a test first period," said the driver, "and old man Axelrod will give me the business but good if I'm late. And he doesn't give make-ups."

"Okay, Einstein, but it looks like you're going to have to double park."

"The last time I did that I got towed," the driver said, looking frantically for space that just wasn't available. He quickly shifted the car into reverse, made a fast exit from the student lot and zoomed into the faculty lot.

"You won't get towed out of here?""Nah. Nobody's ever in the end spots. Jason told me. He's trying to get me a parking sticker. Then I can park here all the time without being conspicuous."

47

Rosemary Cania Maio

The passenger rolled his head back and laughed. "In this thing you want to be inconspicuous? Why don't you start by painting it all one color?"

"Haven't got the scratch, man. My boss won't give me any more than twenty hours a week. And my mother hustles every penny I make to the bank for college. I'm working on my brother to sand and prime the rest of it. He works in a gas station. Then maybe I can convince my mother to let me get it painted. I don't know. She's tough."

As the driver pulled his keys out of the ignition, the passenger ripped two pieces of paper out of a notebook. Both students wrote furiously, then exchanged papers.

On his way out of the car, the passenger stopped dead and let out a long, low whistle. "Now *that* is a motor vehicle," he said, staring intently.

"What?" asked the driver, looking in the direction of the stare. "Oh, yeah, that's Jason's. He took me home in it once. And he let me drive it last year."

"You're kidding," said the passenger, eyes wide with envy. "I'd sell my mother for a 'Vet." Lack of a marketable product meant little to him.

"Jason wouldn't be interested. He's got more women on the line than Hugh Hefner. But I might be able to talk him into letting me take a drive later." The driver of the multi-colored Volkswagen was enjoying the look in his friend's eyes. "Meet me in front of his room after first period. I don't have a class second period. Maybe we could take it then."

"I'll be there," said the 'Vet lover, not at all concerned with the fact that he had a class second period. "And don't worry about it. I'll write you another excuse. My excuses are always a success."

"Don't worry about it," the driver mimicked. "Is that your philosophy on life?"

"Sure. Worry will give you pimples and ulcers. Besides, what can they do to you around here? Nobody gets forty lashes. Hey, toughen up, man. We're seniors, now, remember? We got certain rights and privileges."

The driver of the patchwork VW shook his head in agreement, but still moved very quickly down the hall. Every minute counted. If he was too late, "The Axe" wouldn't let him take the test. Signing in wouldn't take very long, and he could take the short cut to the room and stop at his locker after first period.

When he opened the door to the senior office, the driver of the VW felt his heart sink in his chest. The office was empty. The secretary who was supposed to serve his needs by accepting his excuse and writing a late slip wasn't there. After an eternally long three-minute wait, the young man told his friend, "I'm not waiting any longer. I'll give the excuse to The Axe and come back here later."

"Okay, but I'm staying. I always follow the proper procedure." He sat in a chair next to the desk. "That way I don't have to worry about getting into trouble."

The owner of the VW saw the joke and laughed. Then he fled through the door and down the hall, praying that he wasn't too late. A zero on a unit test would destroy his average.

The young man sitting in the senior office looked at his watch, then at the clock on the wall. It wasn't concern that made him do it, but boredom. He noticed the discrepancy, carefully pulled the stem, and reset the watch. Sometimes it was fast, sometimes it was slow. This particular morning it was ten minutes slow. He had a beautiful digital watch at home, but he wouldn't wear it to school for fear that it might be stolen when he had to remove it during gym or pool classes. And he took gym or pool every day of the week. He had cut so many classes during his sophomore and junior years that he had to make up the time or risk graduation. But that didn't worry him. He was a happy-go-lucky fellow who did what he absolutely had to do only when he absolutely had to do it.

Once he pushed his watch ahead ten minutes, he looked around for something to read, spotted the rack of college catalogs, looked through them and extracted those from community colleges. He knew he was an academic disaster, but he wasn't as stupid as everybody thought. He liked to work with his hands and he loved working on cars. Nobody imagined that he was thinking about his future, but he was. When the time came, he would do something about it. Until then, he had other things on his mind.

Orphean Song

Alyssa's first year of teaching had not been extraordinary. The mold is cast with an exhausting blend of excitement, enthusiasm, relentless physical and mental activity, and sleepless nights. By the end of September that first year, she knew she had to see the doctor. The fatigue that she had no patience for was so severe she thought it might have been mononucleosis. She'd never been so tired in all her life, and she needed all the energy she could muster. When lab tests showed her blood to be better than the average American female's, she was relieved. And not too surprised at the doctor's suggestion that she might need more than four hours sleep each night. Mind over matter, she told herself. Just keep pushing. You're not sick. Keep that adrenaline flowing. You can sleep all you want in July.

The pace was brutal, but she had to keep at least one day ahead of the kids. As a new teacher she had absolutely nothing to fall back on. She had never taught any of the literature; some of it she had never even read. Attempts to learn her schedule before school started had been futile. She wanted to get a jump on lesson plans during the summer. As it was, she learned early that little was done for the convenience of the teacher.

The first day of school hit her with the force of a hurricane. She opened her assignment folder in total dismay at the conglomeration of numbers and names. No one offered help in decoding the information, and she hated to impose on the time of others with questions. Fiercely independent, she figured it all out for herself. Common sense told her that the codes above each list of names had to indicate class level and period and room number. And it didn't surprise her any to find out that she was in six different locations every day. She expected to be a floater; first-year teachers could never even hope for a room. She was surprised at her assignment of classes: three regents-level sophomore classes and one class of regents-level juniors. A first-year teacher with no non-regents students? How lucky could she get? She later realized that the juniors were all repeaters. They had all failed the regents exam at least once, some of them two and three times. But she could handle that, it made them a challenge. She did come to wonder, though, why that class was scheduled eighth period when everybody was tired out. Those kids were at a disadvantage to begin with. The department meeting followed the distribution of assignment folders, and Alyssa found some ready help there. Mary Gregory, department chairman, Alyssa's teacher senior year, gave Alyssa and Beth Whittsley and Hank Courtman the run-down. The three novices would commiserate with each other often during the year, finding solace in their common bond.

Alyssa noted curriculum requirements for the courses she was teaching, found out which books were required, where they were stored. Which chapters in the red grammar book? the blue grammar book? Which vocabulary book? Two? One for sophomores, one for juniors. And they buy those? In the bookstore. But they haven't been ordered yet? You need numbers? Numbers for vocabulary books by next Wednesday. And review books for juniors? Second semester.

Short stories, novels, poetry, plays. Compositions, literature questions, use of the library, reference books, reading comprehension, spelling, grammar. Lesson plans, seating charts, tests, quizzes, study guides, assignment sheets, study hall, homeroom. And the daily requirement to be interesting, relevant, motivating, equitable, physically attractive, and emotionally stable. All the preparation was worthless if she couldn't present her material effectively.

The challenge was overwhelming and she met it. Exhaustion had no place in her life, no bearing on her sense of commitment. Alyssa knew that with patience she could handle the daily routine, the duties, the preparation. She endured the insulting absurdity of having no room and no desk by working out of one drawer in one filing cabinet in one faculty room. As her materials grew, she carried home what the drawer couldn't accommodate. She used folders to keep class work organized and at her fingertips. When a student wanted to make up a test, she found the test where she put it the day it was given, with the absent student's name on it, in the folder for that period.

She was the grand wizard of organization, always looking for new ways to be efficient, new ways to fulfill non-instructional duties. Because it was and would forever be those duties that diminished the time and energy she needed for teaching. And, in those early years, it was her teaching that worried her.

College sharpened her mind and awakened her spirit; it deepened her love for literature; it gave her instruction in evaluative techniques, models for test construction, methods in classroom learning. But college, with all its theory, college, with its feeble attempt at experience called student teaching, college didn't teach her how to teach. At the end of her student teaching, Alyssa had no more idea of how to be an effective teacher than a car salesman has of how to make cars. And she knew it. And it frightened her.

She could evaluate literature, she could devise tests; she was an excellent speller, a fairly decent grammarian; she loved words for what they could accomplish; she viewed reading and writing as the two most essential skills a human being can possess; she had the will to teach.

But could she? Could she instill understanding, trigger thinking, inspire the will to learn? She had doubts about her judgment. Was she expecting too much or too little? Were students failing because her tests were too difficult or because she hadn't presented the material clearly enough or spent enough time on instruction? She agonized over every test, every paper, evaluating herself more sternly than her students. Doubts of her own capabilities, her own skill, her own effectiveness plagued her. She made a secret pact with herself that if she turned out to be a poor teacher she would give it up. The classroom was too influential a place to be run by the shoddy and weak. And her vision of work in those early days (when work is often perceived as a vision) was suffused with an aura sparkling with necessary ingredients: commitment, dedication, achievement, satisfaction, fulfillment.

She learned how to teach that first year. She learned that she could be the vehicle through which her students learned, that she could get through to them. The progress of some of them thrilled her. The lack of progress in others upset her, but she came to understand that some students would fail in spite of her attention, in spite of her careful work, and so she avoided the self-flagellation that could have destroyed her early on.

Somewhere along the line she also dropped a condescending attitude that would have eventually undermined her influence, for students know when they are being looked down upon and resent the implications. She realized that the condescension was the result of her own limited circle of friends in high school, that it grew out of her shock at finding students with little or no motivation, students extremely deficient in basic skills. Some of them were practically illiterate. And in regents level classes.

How could a human being exist without possessing some proficiency in reading and writing? While it threw her into further shock to admit it, many get along very well, live happy and productive lives, without benefit of language skills. Not everyone, she reasoned, is a good English student. Not everyone loves to read and write and spell. She would give them all she could in the hope that occasionally along the way she might touch a life or two. Her acceptance of stark reality put the first chink in her armor of idealism. It also caused her to see kids first as people, then as students. And that was the first milestone in her career. As the years passed she became fond of telling friends that she'd never had a severe discipline problem. She would say it wonderingly, in awe of the incredible fact, not pausing long enough to remember that golden moment in time when she rejected condescension in favor of respect.

She ended her first year astounded by what she had accomplished, what she had learned, how she had grown. But more than that, she felt a pervasive humility. It was consuming, this career she had selected. Influencing the minds of others, the highly impressionable minds of youth, was a responsibility that she could never take lightly.

Even though she wasn't physically there, she couldn't wrest her mind from school that summer. She had spent most of every vacation during the year on schoolwork, either grading papers, typing, or getting a jump on future lesson plans and reading. As the year progressed, she set aside projects for the summer. Sometimes she wasn't satisfied with first attempts at tests so she made note of changes for the future. Sometimes she had to hand write dittoes for lack of time and she typed those out during the summer. She sought out additional grammar exercises because some chapters in the grammar books just didn't supply adequate drill. She typed fifteen pages of study questions for *A Tale of Two Cities* because she found time only to compile and hand write them during the year; she would never, in all the years following, be satisfied with distributing anything that was handwritten. The clean, clear precision and formality of a typed page appealed to her sense of organization and style, even though she typed with two fingers and every page took close to an hour for her to complete (Learn how to type! she told her students). She revamped her poetry unit because she wasn't satisfied with it.

She filled a corner of the bedroom with books and cardboard filing cabinets and Jeff wondered aloud when there would be no more room for him in their small attic apartment, unaware that his observation would one day well into the future extend beyond their physical surroundings.

Alyssa opened her assignment folder the second year with the assurance that experience provides and the fear that the system perpetuates. Non-instructional duties would be easier, but would she be able to use the materials for class that she worked so hard on the year before? Would there be different classes, new preparations?

Rosemary Cania Maio

She was low man on the totem pole, along with Beth and Hank, and could expect anything that senior teachers didn't want. She held her breath, tried to slow her pounding heart, flipped quickly past homeroom and study hall lists, and scanned the tops of the four sheets indicating her class assignments. English 2R ... English 2R ... English 2R ... she was thrilled, she could use the materials she had and, even better, expand and enrich her program. She had some ideas on how to better teach vocabulary and she wanted to combine book reports with literature questions, so that one would complement the other ... But the last sheet. Would it be English 3R? She wouldn't mind if she had repeaters again, but maybe it would be a regular class. What if it was 2NR or 3NR? New preparation. Tough kids to handle.

She looked at the sheet. She couldn't stop looking. She wanted to kiss it, wave it over her head, screaming, at what she saw. English 2S. It was scholarship. *Scholarship!* In her second year of teaching? Unheard of. Didn't you have to work ten or fifteen years before you were rewarded with a scholarship section? How could she possibly be placed among the elite so soon?

Then she knew what must have happened. It was a mistake. It had to be. Sorry, Mrs. Matthews, but you really are much too young, too inexperienced for the responsibilities of a scholarship section right now. Don't you agree? Why, look at the rest of the department. Many good teachers with more years still haven't taught scholarship. Maybe a few years down the road ...

That was it, all right. It couldn't be otherwise; it didn't make sense that older teachers were overlooked.

And then, suddenly, she knew it was true. Mary Gregory, sitting a few rows away in the large auditorium, was craning her neck to catch Alyssa's eyes. When the connection was made, when Mary Gregory wrinkled her nose and winked in that omniscient way of hers, Alyssa knew it was true.

She looked down at the list of names and her spirit soared. They were hers. She had worked hard and well and someone took notice. And the human spirit will thrive, will soar among the seraphim, when someone takes notice.

She revved into high gear to prove herself worthy of Mary Gregory's trust, to prove herself capable of meeting this new challenge.

In later years she would tell newcomers to the English 2S curriculum that it was the most demanding course the department offered. The new preparation called for constant attention.

Excitement bubbled up in her when Mary dictated course requirements: *A Tale of Two Cities, Silas Marner, The Bridge of San Luis Rey, A Separate Peace, To Kill A Mockingbird, Our Town, Julius Caesar, The Merchant of Venice.* Except for *Tale* and *Silas,* all were new preparations for Alyssa, and even the two novels she had taught the previous year to regents sophomores could not be presented in the same way to scholarship students. She had to come up with something more challenging for those two novels as well as study guides, quizzes, tests, essay questions for the others. After she read the others and prepared daily lesson plans. Researching information and developing evaluation meant multiple trips to the library and to the department resource room to find criticism and evaluation. Symbols, themes, allusions, character analyses, history, plot structures. And that wasn't all. Mary's dictation didn't stop with novels and plays.

There was another vocabulary book ("Please let me know exactly how many you'll need by next Wednesday, so that I may order them. There's a surplus from last year in the bookstore and my head will roll if I order too many again.") which Alyssa would have to key, and the course called for more extensive use of the red grammar book. She had used that the year before with her juniors, but those plans were hardly suitable for scholarship sophomores. There was a new short story book ("That also has to be ordered for them to buy, and don't forget the totals for the regents vocabulary book and *Tale,* which is for all four classes.") that Alyssa found to be stimulating and challenging, college-level in scope. Two new poetry books rounded out Mary's outline of the course.

That was the year Alyssa increased her own vocabulary with the more difficult scholarship vocabulary book. She devised a methodical, effective unit on phrases, complete with instruction sheets, work sheets, drill sheets, quizzes, and tests, a unit that could be taught in twenty-minute segments day by day in conjunction with one of the works of literature. For she realized early on that she would be dealing with literature all year to get through it all. Everything else would have to be skillfully interwoven; each week her lesson plans for that one class were a masterpiece of organization as she scheduled literature, vocabulary and/or grammar, depending upon the difficulty of each unit, and spelling. She fit in instruction on writing skills and reading comprehension, and searched out additional exercises on analogies, those devious devils that test vocabulary, experience, reasoning, and the ability to recognize and match relationships. Analogies showed up on all kinds of formal tests; her students needed help with analogies; what if they got a teacher junior year who didn't bother with analogies, how would they get through that section on college boards?

That was the year Alyssa learned how to teach lyric poetry, so much more difficult with its sophisticated prosody, its obscurities, and its passion, than the narrative poetry she had taught her regents classes the year before. That was the year she did further research on *Silas* and *Tale*, and began to compile notes on content and style for the other six major works. She discussed the mysteries of fate and death with *The Bridge of San Luis Rey*; adolescent psychology, peer pressure, and man's capacity to create evil with *A Separate Peace*; the destructive influence of prejudice, the constructive influence of love, the parent-child relationship, and injustice born of hatred with *To Kill A Mockingbird*; she enjoyed for the first time spreading the central message of *Our Town*: Emily's death is not the tragedy, the tragedy lies in her realization that she did not fully appreciate life when she had it, and so we are reminded that every minute particle of life is precious, that the greatest of all tragedies is to live and not to love or appreciate life.

That was the year Alyssa expanded her Shakespearean repertoire, which included only *Macbeth* from the year before, with the politics, treachery, and scrambling for power in *Julius Caesar*, (a play she recognized as eternally universal, for what government exists without its Caesar, its Cassius, its Brutus, its Lepidus, its Antony?) and with the controversial usurer, the beautiful and clever lady, the pound of flesh, the three caskets of *The Merchant of Venice*.

That was the year she delved deeply into the realm of short fiction. The anthology, *Short Fiction Craftsmen*, was a compendium of the best by the best: Chekhov, Poe, Steinbeck, deMaupassant, Mansfield, Crane, Bradbury, Updike, Melville, Camus, Hawthorne, Joyce, Porter, Irving, Harte, Bierce, James... She reveled in intricate plot structures, fascinating characters, points of view, themes, allusions, symbols, and the added attraction of parody and allegory. Investigate slowly and carefully, she told her students again and again, develop an awareness, then strive for understanding, and appreciation will follow. Look, look at this word, this phrase, this sentence, this paragraph, this entire work of art, this character, this theme, and marvel at the skill that created it.

That was the year that Alyssa Matthews first experienced the ultimate satisfaction that teaching can provide, the awareness that one's work has inspired others to excel. Her scholarship students, highly motivated to begin with, returned to Alyssa all that she selflessly gave to them. And, because of experience, she was more effective with her three regents classes. It was a beautiful year, in spite of the volume of work, in spite of her daily recitation of the Floater's Prayer, in spite of homeroom and study hall duties.

She was delighted to find the same schedule of classes her third year — three sophomore regents, one sophomore scholarship — and she spent that year enriching her materials, adding, modifying, typing, filing. Her request for a filing cabinet was finally honored, and though it was located in a room she inhabited only one period a day, she was thankful. Her files were growing larger than her bedroom.

Her fourth year began with a jolt when she saw her class lists: English 3R . . English 3R ... English 3R ... English 2S. While she had some materials from her first-year class of repeaters, she felt the pressure of a new preparation. Placing the materials for 2R in the bottom drawers of her filing cabinet, she made room for new folders, for the latest chapter in the saga of her training. She would move faster with regular regents juniors than she had three years earlier with repeaters. As she looked over what she already had to work with, she was dissatisfied. She had learned too much in three years to be content with first attempts.

The fifth year retained the three regents junior classes, but changed the 2S assignment to 3S. Junior scholarship. Even better than sophomore scholarship because juniors were more mature, more receptive. And, Alyssa reasoned, any student who could get through the sophomore scholarship curriculum successfully was bound to be one hell of a junior. And in those days she was right. She put aside the mountain of 2S materials and spent the year building 3S. All of it except *Macbeth* was new. The emphasis was on American literature and the text conducted a survey from colonial times to the mid-twentieth century. Interwoven with that was a unit on drama including *Antigone, Oedipus Rex, All My Sons, Death of a Salesman, Macbeth, The Emperor Jones,* a unit on the essay as literature, a unit on biography and other types of non-fiction, and the usual vocabulary, grammar, spelling, reading comprehension, and writing. She was in awe of her 3S students that year. She thought she had seen the epitome of excellence with sophomores, but her juniors truly outdid themselves, especially in writing. She read papers that reflected sensitivity, depth of thought, and creative flair. Writing, she always said, good, effective writing is the product of agonizing, gut-wrenching work. There is nothing easy about improving your style of writing. There is a great deal of frustration, a constant crumbling of paper and wringing of hands. But the harder you work, the better you'll get.

Year six brought with it a full schedule of scholarship classes — two 2S and two 3S. For a moment Alyssa felt like a pig, but the moment passed quickly. Having a wide base for both courses, she was able to concentrate on areas that bothered her. The 3S course offered no instruction in spelling beyond the chapter in the grammar book which students already covered in the 2S course. So she incorporated *20 Days To Better Spelling* into one semester, even though it meant typing out twenty tests. The essay unit for juniors also needed to be updated. While she had no intention of eliminating the classic examples of Bacon, Montaigne, Lamb, et. al., she decided that the genre would impress students more if she also included contemporary examples, so she found and duplicated essays on a wide range of topics from editorial pages and magazines.

She updated reading lists for both courses, and devised book reports geared to make her students think, react, respond, not just copy summaries from book jackets. She developed an independent study unit for students who needed even greater challenges than the scholarship curriculum provided.

She collected money to order *Literary Cavalcade* for all four classes, hauling the magazine from the mailroom every month to her classrooms because it offered excellent literature on both professional and student levels, word games, and advanced grammar exercises designed as preparation for college boards.

She had the time of her life, exhaustion an integral part of it. Now and then she would collapse for a day or two, just long enough for her physical self to be energized by her indefatigable spirit. She couldn't bear the thought of a sub messing up her lessons. Indeed, she never expected a sub going in cold to be able to do what she could do in her classroom. And the longer she was out, the further behind her very tight schedule became. More than once she went to school sick because a sub would have undoubtedly made a shambles out of intricate plans, or been unable to get a scheduled test out of a locked filing cabinet, or been too scatterbrained to keep track of a really important writing assignment due that day. By year six Alyssa started to notice the pattern of her yearly illnesses. She was sick every fall, either in October or November, and then again in March. Colds mostly. Hacking, sneezing, stuffy old-fashioned colds. Eventually she didn't even see the doctor, just called the office for her "usual": antibiotic, cough syrup, decongestant. As the years went on she asked for them by name: sumycin, phenergan, ornade. She always remembered what the doctor told her the first time she saw him. If her blood was better than the average American female's, she could certainly survive the common cold. And so she pushed on.

Her full schedule of scholarship classes extended into her seventh year. By that time she had been around long enough to get a room of her own and enjoyed the luxury of having all her classes and homeroom in one location. How much easier it became to haul books and show films and gain access to her files. But the '75-'76 school year was destined to be the peak from which there is only one course of travel.

In early March, 1976, Mary Gregory had to have a mastectomy. By the end of April she was back in school to see her students through final exams. In the middle of May there was the incident with the black student. Mary let it be known that she had been planning to retire from the beginning of the year anyway, and made a very quiet exit in June.

It broke Alyssa's heart to see her go. Mary was her courage, her inspiration, her model, her teacher. The place would never be the same. It was truly the end of an era. Two other older teachers left that year, and three the next, and one the year after that. The Old Guard was passing the torch. And the new generation was fully capable of taking it up. It's up to us now, Alyssa and Beth and Hank agreed.

It wasn't ego, then, that made Alyssa see herself as indispensable. It was self-confidence, an overwhelming belief in herself, a belief born of achievement. As the years passed, mastery of the subtleties of her craft had fused with her mastery of curriculum. She learned that methods and assignments are tricky — what works well with some classes isn't at all effective with others. She learned that flexibility is the most valuable trait a teacher can possess and never hesitated to modify plans, relegating her sense of organization to second place when it came to the best interests of her students. She learned that every class, because it is a group of individuals randomly comprised, has a personality, a character that is in some respects controllable and moldable, but in others viable and sometimes volatile, and that interaction within any particular class is dependent upon many factors.

She could teach and she finally knew it. She knew it the first time she faced a class with plans hastily concocted in her mind between periods, her original plans mangled by an announcement over the PA. She knew it when she made mistakes and admitted her own fallibility in deference to the truth, when she learned to say "I don't know" always followed by "But I'll find out," both statements accompanied by the thrill of having students interested enough to stump her. She knew it when she began to see her students go on to success in college. She knew it every time a face brightened with understanding, every time a mind expanded with knowledge, every time she demanded excellence and got it. She knew it when the reputation she wanted to establish from the very beginning began to filter through the school via students. Mrs. Matt was tough, but she was fair.

Her apprenticeship had demanded much from her, and she by no means felt that she knew all there was to know about teaching, but the novice had evolved into the craftsman. She had learned her Orphean song.

Mary's retirement effected a change in Alyssa's classes, an inevitable change. Paul Haust was appointed department chairman and his first crusade was to distribute scholarship sections to as many teachers as possible. Alyssa, knowing what joy and satisfaction those classes provided, could hardly disagree with sharing the wealth. Sometimes the only thing that keeps a teacher going is that one bright spot during the day. And so she willingly gave up the ideal schedule, fully aware that she really had no say in the matter. Paul had so gallantly asked her permission to do what he had every right to do without even her knowledge that she respected him from that day forward. And he promised that whenever possible he would give her any overflow of scholarship sections. In her eighth year, then, Alyssa went back to three 2R classes and one 2S class, which was reminiscent of her second year of teaching.

It was difficult to go back to regents classes. She had forgotten the tedious repetition, the constant pounding required. She had been speeding along on a supersonic transport and it took some time to adapt to a stagecoach. But she didn't worry much over it. She had adapted so many times over the years that she was beginning to feel invulnerable. There wasn't much she couldn't do if she set her mind to it. It was a remarkable attitude after only eight years experience in a field that abounds with change, with disruption.

But Alyssa's experience had been unique in the annals of beginnings. New teachers are historically assigned a full schedule of the bottom of the barrel, a practice that quickly sours many right out of the profession before they can wait out the misery and discouragement. Alyssa never traveled that route. No, she would habitually tell anyone who asked, kids haven't changed, students are what they've always been ...

For eight years she worked hard and her work brought her immense satisfaction. But in the ninth year everything changed. In the ninth year she, along with everyone else in the department, opened an assignment folder filled with five classes and three preparations.

Intelligentsia I

"You're not following directions. Read them again." Alyssa whispered the warning to a number of students. Each was visibly shaken at the thought of almost losing points foolishly. The teacher knew she should let them make the mistake and learn the lesson in the most memorable way, but her compassion had a way of overriding her feelings of practicality.

It was one of her crusades every year. Prepare them for life. I don't care what you're doing or when you're doing it, train yourself to follow directions. You can mess up a math test, reduce a new thirty dollar sweater to the size of your little sister's Barbie Doll, ruin your favorite pair of designer jeans, kill yourself or someone else with too much medicine, waste time, effort, and money if you ignore or misinterpret directions.

She continued her journey up and down the rows, checking papers, making quiet comments, then sat at her desk to work on plans for the next week. Eyes scanning the room every few minutes, she invariably recognized roving glances, suspicious stares, desperate attempts.

"Please keep your eyes on your own papers." She said it firmly but objectively, directed at the class as a whole. Never named names unless it was so bad she had to move a seat. Offenders got the message. Everybody got the message. What she wanted was for the cheating to stop, whatever form it took, however it was attempted. And she knew what to look for. She had seen it all one time or another.

Eyes shaded by one hand to mask furtive stares to the side. Notes hastily or painstakingly written on desk tops, hands, arms, books, notebooks, tissues, backs of chairs, anything mobile and accessible.

Entire tests showing up on the wrong desks, names not matching faces, as the result of perilous exchanges. Occasionally a really reckless soul would hide one or more pages of notes under the test paper.

One young lady, usually an excellent student, sat on her notes and read them between her legs. Alyssa was so embarrassed herself that she waited to collect the test, gave it a zero, and explained why in a note at the bottom. The girl turned scarlet when the test was returned. Explaining that she didn't get a chance to study the night before and panicked, the girl promised never to cheat again. "Why didn't you tell me?" Alyssa asked. "I would have given you a break. Your work is always in on time. You're always prepared for class. We all screw up once in a while. But cheating is not the answer." It was a risky concession, even when made after the fact. If word spread that she was soft, she would be bombarded with excuses on test days. Balancing the dictates of her heart with the dictates of her head usually gave Alyssa more work to do, but the way she saw it, if she gave a student a break, that student was given an opportunity to learn when he had not, to work when he had not. Learning was the key. But even potential learning didn't stop her from refusing mercy to the chronically irresponsible.

Distinguishing between the sporadic and the potentially chronic was not always easy and occasionally her kindness was abused, which disturbed but did not deter her inherent sense of compassion. She was not in the business of destroying little children, pouncing on them, claws extended, to rip their eyes out.

She had experienced teachers like that herself. Women making a Hollywood spectacular out of focusing everyone's attention on the villain, while screaming vindictively, waving the sullied paper in the air for dramatic effect, then wrathfully ripping the contamination to shreds. And men, inwardly delighted at catching a culprit, conducting a lengthy, cold-hearted, icy-toned, torturous interrogation. Alyssa shivered at both methods. She had no taste for making students squirm. Even when she caught one red-handed, she removed the notes, replaced the test with a fresh one, and made the student take the whole thing over again in the time remaining in the period without any visual aids. She did it quietly, certainly looking disgruntled, but with an ounce of mercy. Everybody knew what was going on anyway. She tried to discourage cheating without creating animosity, which would surely inhibit learning for the rest of the year. And the cheater was allowed to fail with at least some of his dignity intact. While cheating certainly was attempted by students in all ability levels, Alyssa worried most about it in her honors classes.

Pressured by parents and peers, barely able to function under the weight of schoolwork, sports, music, student government, church and civic affairs, clubs and puberty, accelerated students sometimes rivaled Evel Knievel in taking chances to get those high grades they were born to get. Especially sophomores. The hot shots of junior high were accustomed to inflated grades. Some teachers in the junior high, teachers free of SAT's and The Final Evaluation, were known to grade strictly on effort, a nebulous area subject to sham and trickery.

No wonder that sophomores were in a state of shock when those once easily acquired grades went only to *la creme de la creme*.

As she looked up once again to survey the room, Alyssa saw thirty scholarship bodies, but only sixteen scholarship minds. In the past three years she had seen scholarship students actually fail the course, which made no sense since they could have easily passed in a regents section. The department was in an uproar about it. Paul had met with scholarship teachers over and over again.

It was during one of those meetings that Alyssa pointed out the once–famous-but-since-forgotten unwritten rule: scholarship students had to maintain at least an 80 average to remain in a scholarship section. Mary Gregory insisted on it. "God Bless that old lady," Paul had said. "She knew what she was talking about."

But the classroom had changed since Mary Gregory. Students developed rights after she retired, and parents developed egos that needed filial sacrifice.

And the great minds directing the ebb and flow of education in the United States decided that every student was created equal, that egalitarianism was rightfully the new banner hoisted over every edifice of academe, that freedom and equality superseded the arbitrary existence of standards, that comparing the work of one student with the work of another was sinful, that students should be coddled and cooed into taking substantive courses while fluffy electives were created to satisfy credit requirements.

Colleges started screaming about freshmen who couldn't write a decent sentence, much less a coherent paragraph, and at the same time created courses in the intricacies of Captain Marvel and dropped foreign language as an entrance requirement.

Academic freedom and the call to give students what they liked rather than what they needed almost reduced education on all levels to blithering idiocy. Even the elementary schools joined the madness, going wild with a media blitz, hauling carousel projectors and cassette players into classrooms the way military equipment was dropped on the beaches of Normandy.

It *was* war. War against tradition, war against the old way. War against pencil and paper, chalk and board. War against rote learning, memorization, drill. War against forcing students to sweat and toil to learn. How much more enjoyable a lesson was when presented on a large screen in colorful animation.

Learning is bliss! It needn't be drudgery! Enjoy! Enjoy!

And a generation of students passed through and graduated unable to read and write, spell and think.

Stop! said the generals of the army. Maybe it is important for a student to learn multiplication tables. Maybe it is important for a student to know that words can be broken down into syllables. Maybe it is important for a student to write in order to learn how to write.

Stop! Retreat! Go Back!

And the army followed the command. Back to Basics became the hue and cry. Back to readin', 'ritin', and 'rithmetic.

That made Alyssa Matthews chuckle. She had never left. "I'm an old-fashioned teacher," she told parents every year at open house. She said it for the first time when she was twenty-one and she never deviated from that simple statement of her philosophy.

But being an old-fashioned teacher didn't supply her with old-fashioned students. And scholarship sections would become prestigious collections of fancy names and lofty IQ's. Somehow interest and motivation, hard work and its attendant commitment to sacrifice and suffering were no longer required attributes of the scholarship student. He was there because he had every right to be. And if he failed, it was most likely teacher's fault for demanding too much of him.

For some scholarship students there was no pressure at all from home, and for others the pressure was astronomical. Some students would go through any means of dishonesty to get those exemplary grades to show mom and dad. For them, the grade was everything, and it took a few years and some maturity before they realized that high grades were nothing more than hollow numbers when the knowledge that they were supposed to reflect had never been attained.

Alyssa was in the habit of teaching the course so that only exemplary students received exemplary grades. To do otherwise was a fraud and an insult to her and to the small number of superior students that kept her spirits up. She felt overwhelmingly frustrated with the new breed of scholarship student, the type that felt he owed nothing to his own education, the type that sat and did nothing, expecting plaudits in return.

And there would always be that segment of the old breed, the type that stretched himself so thin that he gasped his way through school and cried real tears as he argued violently that a 98 should have been a 99.

The number of genuine scholarship students, students willing to work, meeting one challenge in anticipation of the next, students eager to learn, with above-average ability and average humility, was dwindling every year. Ironically enough, class size was doing the exact opposite.

Alyssa finished jotting in her plan book, fitting in parts of speech with *Silas Marner* and vocabulary. She checked pages in all three books to project assignments accurately. Then she looked up once again and saw most test papers face down on desks. She took a stroll around the room to be sure that it was possible, then announced, "Those of you who have not yet finished have five minutes to do so."

A few heads swiveled to check the clock and the teacher returned to her desk pleased that the vocabulary test took only fifteen minutes. There was enough time remaining for her to return the five-page papers they wrote on *Tale*. If the test had taken longer, she would have allowed them to work on the next vocabulary lesson. For a fleeting moment she thought of doing that anyway. It would give her a chance to start grading the vocabulary tests.

But she was too excited at having the time to get those papers back. Some students had done an exceptionally superb job. She wanted to see those faces light up. And others had put little time or thought into the assignment and had handed in work that was mediocre, superficial, juvenile, or otherwise totally or partially unsatisfactory. They needed to know that she would not accept such work from scholarship students.

Alyssa unlocked her filing cabinet and lifted out the stack of papers belonging to first period and hoped that her fifth period class would be as speedy with the test so that she could return their papers also. Then she could get the senior research papers that she collected yesterday into some kind of order. The filing cabinet was bulging, but it was the only thing she had that would lock securely.

Alyssa made sure that she had all the first-period papers and the dittoed sheets that she had prepared while grading them, locked the filing cabinet, and deposited the pile she was carrying on her desk.

Suddenly there were some mighty excited students in the room. "You finished grading those already? It hasn't been a week yet!" whispered a girl sitting in front. Alyssa smiled and nodded her head, eyes dancing. The girl's paper was one of the A's. Alyssa leaned over and whispered back, "I give you time limits, don't I?"

Returning student work within a reasonable period of time was an absolute necessity to Alyssa Matthews. How could a student learn from his mistakes on a test if he couldn't even remember taking the test when it was returned? How could a student improve his writing on the next assignment if he was not aware of the mistakes he made on the last assignment?

And when students realize that teacher is organized, conscientious, and not afraid of hard work, how can they complain when she expects those attributes in them?

Alyssa loved surprising classes with a speedy return of their work. But, oh, how difficult it had become to do so. She had graded close to sixty five-page papers in five days. And she evaluated written work with a fine-toothed comb.

"Okay, folks, time's up. Check to be sure your name is on your paper and send 'em up!"

The room came alive with activity and word spread quickly that the papers were ready to be returned. Alyssa dropped the tests on the top of her desk, picked up the pile of dittoed sheets, and started to distribute them, counting out six for the first row at the far right of the room.

"I always start over here," she remarked to the students in the front desks of those rows, "I'll have to try to remember to swing left once in a while. It's not fair to those guys." She gestured to the other side of the room.

"What's this?" asked one of the students. He thought he was getting his paper back.

"You'll see in a minute," Alyssa said. Then, when everyone had a sheet, she explained. "You're looking at your mistakes in spelling, punctuation, sentence structure, grammar, capitalization, in short, a representative sampling of the mechanical and grammatical errors in the papers you are about to get back. It was a lot of extra work for me to put this together and run it off for you, but it's worth the effort if you learn from your mistakes. I want everybody's attention focused on the first sentence, and I want you to make corrections and take notes as we go along, then save these sheets for future reference. You've noticed already that there certainly are no names here. This is not meant to point a finger at anyone. What I want is for all of you to learn from each other's mistakes."

The teacher then proceeded to deal with each item first by reading it, then by asking the class to recognize and correct errors as they appeared. She filled in instruction on errors that no one recognized or corrected. Mistakes ranged from the foolishly simple to the sophisticatedly complex, from misspellings to misplaced modifiers, from capitalization to diction, from pronoun case to parallel structure, from subject-verb agreement to fragments and run-ons. And every bit of it was essential to good writing. Alyssa Matthews had never succumbed to the theory that form doesn't matter, that what a student writes is superior to how he writes it, that good ideas compensate for poor expression. Hogwash. She went right into orbit when she read a paper filled with spelling and/or grammar errors. One of the papers on her desk drove her wild with *A Tail of Too Cities.* That was the night Jeff seriously considered dousing her with cold water to cool her off.

The paper on *Tale* was traditionally the first formidable writing assignment Alyssa made her intelligentsia struggle through. She intentionally made the task difficult and demanding,

"We're going to spend the year improving your abilities to use the English language effectively, accurately, creatively, and maturely," she told them the day she assigned the paper." We study grammar not as an end in itself, but as a means to mature writing. How can I instruct you in subject-verb agreement if you can't pick out a subject and a verb? How can I expect you to use objective case pronouns as objects in your sentences if you don't know which pronouns are in the objective case and how to recognize a direct object, an indirect object, or the object of a preposition? How can I tell you to use a possessive case pronoun before a gerund if you don't know what a gerund is? Don't ever believe that studying grammar is a waste of time. For years now, some people have been saying that and trying to pull grammar out of the curriculum. A great many teachers despise teaching grammar. Well, you're stuck with one who loves it. The first step in mastering any skill is to become familiar with the tools of the trade. The master carpenter starts out by learning how to use a hammer, a saw, a square, a chisel. The master writer starts out by learning the rules of grammar. And spelling. And punctuation.

"I also expect that you will work this year to improve sentence structure. For some of you, this is where the sweat and tears come in. Because some of you still think it's quite satisfactory to express ideas the way you expressed them in sixth grade. But it's not satisfactory. It's nothing but juvenile to compose every single sentence with a subject followed by a verb. I'm going to expect that you make a valiant attempt this year to vary your sentence structure, to express your ideas in more effective ways. I also want you to work to improve diction, that is, choice of words. This is another area for sweat and tears. We are all terribly lazy when it comes to diction. We use the same words over and over again because it's just plain easy to do so.

"We're too complacent or too hurried to come up with other words that are more effective or more accurate, words that are familiar to us but not readily available because it takes time and thought to dredge them up. If you spend the time and stretch your brains a bit, you'll be surprised at the extent of the vocabulary you already have but never use. The vocabulary that we study this year will give you additional fuel to fire up your writing, but, once again, only if you work at it. If you never use any of those words, they're useless to you even if you score a one hundred on every vocabulary test. I had a professor in college — I can't even remember his name, but I'll never forget what he said one day about words — he said that there is a word or a phrase in the English language to express every shade, every nuance (that's any subtle distinction) of meaning that the human mind can possibly conjure up. The tough part, of course, is finding the word or phrase. But rest assured that it exists. The deficiency is not in the language; it's in us.

"I'm still learning vocabulary. I still struggle to find the right word, to express myself in just the right way, to make sure that what I write is a reflection, an accurate reflection, of what I want to say. The best writers in the world struggle with expression. Don't ever fool yourselves into thinking that it's easy. When I was your age I used to go through whole pads of paper just trying to write an opening paragraph that I could live with. I'll never tell you that it's easy. But I'll guarantee improvement if you'll work with me for the rest of the year.

"Now is the time for you to start. There's too much to learn to put it off until senior year. I have seniors who can't write a complete sentence currently trying to write a research paper. They are frustrated and annoyed because I informed them that style of writing counts. I want better things for you people. I want you to get rid of the baby fat now. You are exceptional students and exceptional demands will be made of you, demands beyond the fundamental requirement to stop making foolish errors and accidental mistakes. Demands beyond sentence structure and spelling and punctuation. Because I want to go on to the challenging stuff — original evaluation, creative writing, critical thinking.

"Train yourselves to care. If you concentrate on good writing, you will eventually develop good habits and a mature style. If you start now to develop your own personal style of writing, you'll be prepared for any kind of writing assignment when you hit college. You'll have a choice of topics for this paper and you'll realize when you see the list that I want evaluation out of you, not plot summary. I want original thought and careful assessment, not a rehash of the plot or a regurgitation of what I've told you in class about the characters and themes.

"This is not the kind of assignment that can be done overnight," Alyssa warned. "On the other hand, if I give you two months I know you'll put it off for seven weeks. So you have two weeks. This paper is due on October 17. At the beginning of the period. If it comes in any later than that, you will be penalized. Don't plan to take that day off. If you aren't here, I'll expect you to send in your paper. Deadlines are for everyone. I have an obligation to be fair to the people who are on time."

As it turned out, she had good luck on the day the paper was due. Most of them were in on time. And now, five days later, she returned them by moving around the room very quickly, handing them out individually to nervous students. "When you get your paper, read through my comments very carefully, then read a neighbor's paper. I'd like those of you who didn't get A's to read an A paper. I'll be circulating to answer questions."

The room was quiet for some time as students concentrated on Alyssa's comments and suggestions. When students began to compare papers, Alyssa began to circulate. "Is my evaluation accurate?" she quietly asked one student.

"Yeah," the student answered sheepishly. "I didn't start it early enough. I only had two nights to work on it. I guess I put it off too long. I thought it was gonna be easy."

"I warned you, though, didn't I?"

The student nodded his head the way students have for centuries, acknowledging the fact that he had not heeded a warning.

"Can I write it over?"

"No. You'll just have to do better on the next one." Alyssa was not thrilled with the denial. She considered rewrites to be a valuable learning experience for students, but she had all she could do to grade papers once. "Next time I want to see your outline and your rough draft a few days before the paper is due. We'll go over them together and try to work on your problems. But I won't nag you. It will be up to you to arrange a time when we can get together. Fair enough?"

The student agreed and Alyssa moved on, hoping that he would indeed have the initiative to seek personal attention, all the while wondering when she was going to find time to give it to him.

She stopped at another desk. "All your hard work paid off, didn't it?"

The girl was beaming. "I wrote this over so many times I wanted to throw it away the day it was due. I hated it by then."

70

"That's not an unusual reaction," the teacher said. "Don't be discouraged by it. At least you know you've got what it takes to write well. Keep struggling with it. Eventually your style will even out and you'll be able to wrestle primarily with reasoning and content. You won't have to worry quite so much about expression. You may have to guard against never being satisfied with what you write. That may always drive you crazy, but that's what pushed you this far. You'll have to learn to accept that about yourself and not let it get you down. I'm sure that right now you're glad you didn't ditch this piece of frustration. Why don't you let someone read it? It is a model paper."

As soon as Alyssa moved away, the shy girl was bombarded with requests. She hesitated only a fraction of a second, then exchanged papers with another student.

Alyssa moved to the next row. The room had become noisy enough for her to speak with one boy in relative privacy. "It's difficult to write this kind of paper on a book that you never read, isn't it?" she said softly. Some students were moving around to read papers, which emptied a seat directly in front of the failing student. Alyssa sat.

"You wrote more than I did," the student said.

The teacher shrugged her shoulders. "I can't help it. I get involved when I read papers. I laugh, I cry, I grit my teeth. Sometimes I wish I had the writer next to me to kiss or to choke. I guess you know which of those categories you fit into." She paused, hoping for some kind of response, but when none materialized, she went on. "I always try to say something positive about a paper so as not to totally discourage a student, but you made even that impossible. So what do we do now? Do you have any suggestions?"

Still no response.

"Can you do better than this? I have no idea if the work in this course is too difficult for you, or too much. Is it that you can't do the work, or that you won't do the work? Either way you shouldn't be here. You haven't passed a thing yet, and I'm worried about you."

"I'll try harder," the boy said with a shrug. He obviously just wanted her to go away, so she did.

Famous last words, she thought. She had already notified his parents that a change to regents might be the best thing to do, but the parents never responded. And they had to sign before a change could be made.

A voice interrupted her thoughts. "I don't understand what's wrong here," the student said. Alyssa looked, then said, "Read that sentence out loud."

71

"After the trial, Mr. Carton takes Darnay to a tavern where they can dine."

"You just read what should be there. Now look at it again and read what is there."

The girl began again, but more slowly this time. "After the trial Mr. Carton takes Darnay to a tavern wh- oh! - were they can dine."

"Sometimes we get too close to our own writing and that's what happens when we proofread. We read what we mean to say instead of what's actually on the page. I know that you are beyond the stage of confusing 'where' and 'were,' so the error isn't serious. It's just a matter of proofreading. That's why I suggest that you have someone else proofread for you to catch silly things like that."

"It was really stupid of me," said the girl. Alyssa could see that she was close to tears, that the inconsequential error was not the problem at all.

"Don't beat yourself over it. Even professional writers have editors, you know! I love perfection, but I love a flawed student who learns from his errors even more."

Alyssa paused, knowing that what she was saying was the absolute truth, but still not pointed enough to soothe the fears of this youngster. Her head was bowed, and Alyssa couldn't leave her this way. "You're not satisfied with your grade, are you?"

The girl shook her head, then raised it. She was fighting to hold back the liquid brimming in her eyes. "I worked so hard on this!" she said. "I spent hours and hours. And I never got a B before. My mother's going to kill me."

"As I explained the first week of school, a B paper is better than average. It's solid, it meets requirements, it's well-written. When you get a B out of me, you've done a good job. An A paper has something extra, something beyond basic requirements, something special. It might reflect exceptional style or technique, original evaluation, or excellence in some other area. There has to be something special in the form and/or the content before I'll give a paper an A. Have you had a chance to read an A paper?"

"Yes," the girl said, her eyes widening. "I couldn't believe it. I couldn't even understand some of it."

"Well, don't worry about that. Your special excellence needn't be like anyone else's. I don't want you discouraged. I know you work hard. Just don't quit on me. Get used to the competition. It will never go away as long as you're in school. And it really gets fierce in college. There may always be students better than you forcing your grade down to a B. It's a nasty fact of life. I always resented it as a student. That's right! I got my share of B's and C's because other students were brilliant and I was not. We can't all be valedictorians, you know."

"Do you think I'll ever be able to get an A?"

"Yes, I do. I think you've got what it takes to do anything you set your mind on doing."

"Will you help me next time?"

"You bet." Alyssa winked and moved on. She stopped in front of a student who was sharing jokes with a neighbor. "Hey. Shakespeare," she said. "I really enjoyed your paper." The student turned, his face radiant. "But I didn't work that hard on it!" he said. "I can't believe it!"

The teacher smiled knowingly. "Some people are naturals. But don't let this go to your head. You might blow the next one. I'm curious, though. How long did you work on this?"

"A couple nights for a few hours. I wrote a rough draft and copied it over. That's all."

"Well, you're a young man with a rare gift. There's a vitality, a spark in your writing that I haven't seen from a student in a long time. It's in the way you construct your sentences, the way you phrase your ideas. Did you notice that I allowed you a couple of fragments because I knew that you wrote them intentionally for effect. You have developed a taste for words and for expression. There's always room for improvement, of course, and I expect that you'll soar with the eagles this year. You're really in shock over this, aren't you? Nobody ever told you this before?"

The boy shook his head. "Hell, no," he said.

"Well, let's leave the devil out of this," she laughed. "Have you ever had an assignment like this before?"

"No," the boy said, carefully omitting the nether regions.

"What did you think of the assignment?"

"It was tough. It made me think."

"Ah, so it was a challenge."

"Yeah, I guess so."

"Then you did get involved, even though it was only for a few hours. Evaluation comes easily for you. And somehow you developed this marvelous style of writing. Do you like to read?"

"Heh- I mean, yes. I never stop. I finished this book in a week."

Alyssa suddenly knew all the answers. "And your mother started taking you to the library when you were four," she stated.

"How'd you know that?"

"I have a crystal ball. And I've always believed there's a correlation between reading and writing and thinking. It's a pleasure having you in class. And I meant what I said about your first book in my comments. Think of me some day when you're writing your first dedication. Or your second, for that matter." She patted the still-stymied student on the shoulder and glanced at the clock. Her sixth sense told her that the period was almost over.

"Okay folks, return to your seats. I'm going to hand out folders. Put your papers in your folders and send the folders up again. Do this quickly. There isn't much time." The folders passed hand-to-hand down rows, were ritually stuffed, then passed back up again.

Alyssa believed in folders as a method of organizing and storing student work, as a way to check student progress or lack of it. Folders were now department policy. They had become more than a mere record of student performance. Folders were now the first line of teacher's defense. Bulging folders were proof that teacher was working hard.

As the bell rang and the class filtered out of the room, Alyssa gave permission to a few students who asked to take papers home to show parents. "Don't frame it, please!" she implored. "I have to have it back tomorrow for your folder!" Feeding those folders was like trying to satisfy an insatiable beast.

As Alyssa issued her warning, her mind flashed images of Bonnie's latest dream. Everyone had roared at the account, but the laughter had only glossed over chilling possibilities. What would it be like to face parents, guidance counselor, and administrator with an empty folder? With no proof other than your own word? What would it be like to produce a folder with blank sheets of paper in it? What happens when teacher has no defense that will stand up in court? Would Bonnie's dream come true? Would teacher be buried alive in a manila grave?

While she once encouraged students to show papers to parents and one year required it, now she allowed only those students who asked to take papers home. Because chances were excellent that those students would return the goods. Alyssa recognized the feeling that accompanied her every move lately. It was fear. Pure, unadulterated fear. The pressures of accountability were omnipresent, enveloping the whole school in a hazy black film. No one could peel the film away. It rested on the outer layer of the skin and slowly seeped its way to vital organs.

Alyssa knew she was afraid. Afraid of the gruesome scenario of being placed on the docket. Indicting teachers had become the way of the world. She told herself to fight it. Fight it before it consumes you, before it mushrooms into paranoia. Then you won't be any good at all. And so she pushed the fear to the back of her mind and battled every day to keep it there.

As students began arriving for second period, Alyssa realized that she had better get a move on. She discouraged further conversation with some of her still-lingering students by locking the folders in her filing cabinet and gathering her grade book, attendance book, seventh and eighth period folders containing spelling tests that she wanted to grade, and study hall folder.

Then she flew out the door, still entertaining questions from a student whom she had designated a "clinger" the first week of school. She lost him to his next class halfway down the hall, muttered a prayer of thanks that she could rest her brain for a few minutes, continued through the hall, down two flights of stairs, across three more corridors, down two more flights of stairs, heard the second period bell ring, and cursed her own stubbornness at wearing three-inch heels with a dressy dress.

She was on her way to the assignment that was the most detestable part of her day. But that fact didn't slow her down any.

The Mad Shitter

When she left Bassard's office, Jean knew she needed another pad to soak up the massive evacuation of her insides. She stopped at the nurse's office where she kept an emergency supply. It occurred to her to use the nurse's bathroom, but a student was in it. Time was passing quickly. Too quickly. The first period bell rang. Jean shoved the pad into her purse and fled to class.

Her first period class was locked out of the room. She couldn't leave them in the hall disturbing other classes very long. And she was giving a full period test on *Macbeth*. She hoped, as she hurried back to her room, that no one had tried to do her a favor by unlocking the door. Harry had asked her to keep quiet about the excrement.

Poor Harry, Jean thought. They couldn't pay me enough to put up with the shit he puts up with. Or the excrement. Curious that Harry used that word. Finesse isn't his strongest trait.

And his request had been unnecessary. Jean was not about to sensationalize the sensational; there was one very sick person running around, maybe more than one. Poor Jim Cote, she thought, he must have died, taken it personally. He was such a nice guy, a real gentleman, a teacher with a heart, soft spoken, a teacher with a lifetime commitment to learning, his own as well as his students'.

Jean knew Jim Cote held one doctorate in his field and was working on another. Why he remained in a high school was a mystery to most people. But Jean had spoken to him once about it. It was right after he earned his doctorate, when rumors were flying that he was leaving for some professorship at a big university. Nobody was quite sure which university, and Jim was mum on the subject, which caused the rumors to multiply and flourish. He wasn't reclusive, he just thought that his plans were private. Which made him a perfect target for gossip. Nobody ever asked him anything. It was much greater fun to speculate. Eternal ignorance is eternal bliss to gossipmongers.

Not one for malicious speculation, but sincerely concerned over the possible loss of one excellent teacher and friend, Jean cornered him one day and asked. It was a remarkably simple question and she had no intention whatsoever of spreading the answer. The vultures could hover forever as far as she was concerned.

Jim's answer didn't surprise her. They had begun together, she and Jim, and they had exchanged philosophies more than once over the years. Their minds ran on the same track, in spite of the fact that they taught in different disciplines. Jim Cote had no desire to leave the high school regardless of plenty of offers.

More pay with less busywork on the college level.

More pay with fewer frustrations in industry.

More pay with more prestige wherever he cared to go.

Except he didn't care to go. Thanks, he told them all, but no thanks.

He liked what he was doing. He enjoyed teenagers. They were fresh and alive and still in awe of the world. He wanted to work with brains, not hardware; a microscope meant nothing to him without the questioning eye of a student peering down into it.

Once he became department chairman, Jim Cote devoted his afternoons to restructuring the existing curriculum. Then he developed a program of independent study for students of exceptional ability, students destined to excel in the scientific world. He cared for them himself, nurtured them, prodded them, challenged them, all the while anticipating the pride he would feel when he set them free. And, once he became department chairman, Jim Cote indulged in the other luxury that accompanied the position. He scheduled his own classes.

Unlike other department chairmen, however, Jim kept a homeroom. But only after negotiating a rotation for the rest of the department. Each year he took the homeroom duty from a different teacher on his staff. And his people loved him for it. For them, relief from homeroom duty was a small nugget of gold, even if it materialized only once every nine or ten years.

Their hopes for further relief were dashed when Jim wouldn't volunteer for the other non-instructional duty from which chairmen were exempted. He drew the line when it came to study hall. That was a hopeless waste of an entire period; his time was too precious to spend in foolish babysitting.

In the midst of his very satisfying career, there was only one source of aggravation, and Jim Cote knew he asked for it. The condescension he was subjected to when he visited colleges was maddening.

Eager to keep up with changing curriculum trends, lab techniques, and new research, he traveled two or three times a year to schools all over the country. He usually did it in conjunction with family vacations because the district wasn't interested in funding what it called "frivolous activities" and applying for sabbatical time was too political for him.

Whenever Jim entered a college classroom, whenever he spoke with a college professor, he felt the unmistakable attitude. The air was rife with it.

High school teachers are morons, intellectually inferior insects in the educational hierarchy, incapable of scholarly thought and ambition, quite content to pander about with trivialities.

In his own low-keyed, self-disciplined way, Jim managed to transmit his brilliance at every stop without ever mentioning the doctoral prefix he had earned after years of hard work. And he usually ended his visit by politely refusing a job offer, which positioned him perfectly for his favorite parting shot: if all the good teachers are gobbled up by colleges, what kind of student do you think you'll be getting here? the scientific mind isn't hatched full grown at age eighteen, it evolves slowly and painstakingly for that number of years, the evolution directed and nourished by teachers, first grade teachers, fifth grade teachers, tenth grade teachers. What caliber students would you have to work with if no one trained them for you, if no one awakened their minds and sharpened their intellects for you?

Jean knew about Jim's periodic defense of teachers. "I staged another coup for public school teachers," he would proudly tell her. And she would smile at his choice of words, thinking all the while that a coup does not a revolution make.

She decided to hunt Jim down later in the day. Maybe he would feel better if he knew The Mad Shitter hadn't singled him out. The Mad Shitter. Jean shook her head and rolled her eyes. She was getting just like the kids, tagging everything.

The hall was empty when she reached the fourth floor. Except for her class. Thank God. They were assembled in front of the locked door.

Well, it's about time! you're late! no test! no test! where've you been? no test? why's the door locked? not enough time! no test? no test! I have to leave early! there is too not enough time! aw, c'mon ...

Jean succeeded in calming them, then ordered all to the auditorium. "Quickly and quietly, please, classes are in session. Sit every other seat, every other row. Now go. Fast. You're wasting your own time."

As they mumbled and grumbled their way down the hall, Jean unlocked the door, entered her room, and quickly closed the door. She held her nose with two fingers and walked to her desk, trying to avoid looking at it. But it couldn't be helped. The tests were in a desk drawer. She found them quickly, along with her records, and headed for the door. It opened before she got to it, and she jumped.

The custodian voiced an apology for startling her. He stood there, shovel in hand, wondering how in hell he got stuck with the crap. He didn't see the pun. His sense of humor was long gone, a victim of his job. He had worked in the schools for twenty-five years and every year was worse than the last one. He wasn't happy when he was transferred to the high school, it meant he was on the bottom again. After twenty-five years. And this was what the bottom meant. Shoveling shit.

"Yoo wone nee dat," Jean said, looking at the shovel, "take da hole blodder, I wone be yoozeen id."

Suddenly the custodian burst into laughter.

Jean's fingers were still firmly pinching her nostrils together. When she realized how absurd she looked and sounded, she too started to laugh. Still protecting her olfactory organ, she honked a request for open windows.

Then, feeling like a stock character out of *commedia dell'arte*, she lifted her head for comedic effect. "God-da go," she enunciated majestically, "stew-dants way-ding."

She ran out the door and all the way to the auditorium, where she listened to moans and groans from students not pleased at having to take a test on their knees. Teacher couldn't manufacture too much sympathy. She was trying to figure out when on God's earth she was going to get to a bathroom.

She sat on the edge of the stage to keep an eye out for cheating and prayed there wouldn't be too many questions to make her get up. Somehow she felt safer sitting. Gravity and all that.

Back in Jean's room, the custodian was still chuckling. He could remember a time when he laughed his troubles away, a time way back when life wasn't a heavy burden to be borne every working day. A time before he allowed life to imprison him with worries and cares.

What was it the wife was habitually telling him?

You'll never have to worry about laugh lines in your face.

Well, wouldn't she be surprised. He had laughed so hard his eyes blurred over. It wasn't the first day of the rest of his life, to be sure. But it felt good, so very good, to laugh. Especially when hauling shit, he thought. And he laughed again.

The Multi-Media Mogul

The last bit of film wound its way around the take-up reel. A large white square was left on the screen in the front of the room, the screen no longer a source of entertainment. Some few minds had ceased to be entertained long before anyway. Those minds were asleep in heads cradled in folded arms on desk tops.

Erica Vetterly closed her book, walked to the front of the room, switched on the lights, then walked over to the projector and flipped the button to turn it off. The film ended ten minutes before the end of the period. Erica wondered how she had forgotten that this film was short. She made a mental note to waste the time at the beginning of the next period, so that the film would run until the bell. Always better to blow time at the beginning than to have them restless at the end. It wasn't that she had anything to say to them at the beginning or at the end, but at least at the beginning she could arrive late or fiddle around with attendance.

The one thing Erica Vetterly did religiously was take attendance in all her classes. She was no fool. Her classes were her job. The first and, it usually ended up, the last demand she issued to her students was that they attend class. She needed physical shapes to justify her existence.

"Bill, rewind that film for me, will you?" she said to a boy sitting next to the projector.

"Sure," the boy responded. "Hey! We gonna see films all year? I'm getting tired of it."

"Just one more for now. We'll start it tomorrow and it'll run for five days. It's *A Night To Remember*. Ever hear of it?"

"Nah. What's it about?"

"The sinking of the Titanic."

"Oh. What's that?"

"It was a ship, Bill. A huge luxury liner that was supposed to be unsinkable."

"But it did, huh?"

"Yep. Tune in tomorrow for the details."

"And all next week?"

"Four days next week."

"Then what do we do?"

"Oh, I don't know. I haven't thought that far ahead yet. Maybe we'll do some library work."

"Work? Wha' d'ya mean, work? You said at the beginning of the year that we wouldn't have to do no work, just watch movies, read, and be here."

"That's right, Bill. Now you think about it. What might I have you do in the library?" The boy's face lit up with sudden understanding. "Now stop asking questions and rewind that film for me. I have to run it again third period."

"Yes, m'am, will do," Bill said.

Two Gulls in Search of the Sea

The young man waited for his friend in the midst of the surging flux of bodies that flowed in clumps through the halls between periods. Lockers were slamming shut with the sharp hollow sound of metal hitting metal; a girl passed him screaming epithets at a cohort running ahead of her; scores of students passed, laughing, talking, hurrying, dawdling. The young man didn't see much more than a blur, and heard little of the harsh cacophony around him. He was too involved with his own thoughts.

He was disgusted with himself. If only he had realized that he was twenty minutes late before he walked into that room. He wouldn't have gone in at all. Old Man Axelrod had been furious. How did he expect to take a full period test in twenty minutes?

But that wasn't the worst of it. The Axe really went into orbit when he read the excuse. Late because of family reasons, it said.

Only family was spelled "familie."

The young man had been mortified. He could still feel the embarrassment creeping up his neck and around his ears as he relived the scene.

The class was busy, heads were down, minds concentrated on the test. But it was, to be sure, mock concentration. Even the desks and chairs developed ears when Old Man Axelrod set his sights on an illegal absence and demanded to know "Just who wrote this excuse?"

His own hide at stake, the young man didn't feel it too large a sacrifice to assert adamantly that his mother had only an eighth grade education. Her reputation was a small worry compared to the crisis at hand. She didn't have to pass Axelrod's course. It might have worked if there hadn't been that other thing.

"Hey, man, you dead or alive?"

The closeness of the words startled the young man, who looked at his friend with a wry smile, "How long have we known each other?" he asked.

"What do I know? Four, five years. Why? You wanna have an anniversary party?"

"Anybody ever tell you you're a lousy speller?"

"Yeah. All the time. Never bothered to do anything about it. So who cares? Listen, have you talked to Haywood? Can we get his wheels?""Not yet. We'll do it in a minute. I want you to learn something first." The young man took his pen and wrote in block letters on his palm. "This," he said with a smirk, "is how to spell my last name."

"Yeah. Well, sure. What'sa matter? Didn't I … ?" He looked closer at the word. "I blew it, didn't I? Hey, man, I didn't realize, ya know? I'm sorry, I really am. I mean, it wouldn't matter much to me, getting caught. But you get all bent outa shape. And it's my fault. I really feel bad about this. I'm just a screwup."

The young man looked at his friend and saw the contrition in his eyes. He was a good friend in spite of his spelling problem. "Not much escapes The Axe," said the young man.

"What'd he do?" asked the friend.

"What I told you he would do. Wiped my ass all over the room. But I can't do much about it now. I'll try to see him after school. Don't worry about it." The young man smiled and slapped his friend on the shoulder. "See, I'm beginning to believe in your philosophy. C'mon. Let's see Jason. I can use some fresh air."

Within minutes the two young men were racing out of the building with the key to the bright yellow Corvette. Jason Haywood remembered what it was like to be young and adventurous. Life imposes restrictions all too quickly. Make hay while the sun shines. Take thy fair hour, Laertes.

He didn't even tell them to be careful. Of course they would. What he might have been mildly concerned over was the one key. Lord knows where he lost the other one. And he just couldn't find the time to have a copy made, what with school and negotiations and his active social life. He just couldn't remember everything. Well now he'd get his extra key. One of the boys had a brother who worked in a gas station

Jason began his lesson on the privileges and responsibilities of the private citizen in a democracy comfortable with the thought that he would have to write an excuse for both boys when they returned. He could do it with a clear conscience. The honest truth was that they were running an errand for him.

The Study Hall A Second Period Extravaganza
(NOT The Study Hall: A Second Period Extravaganza)

> I traversed the corridors of doom bewildered by the temerity of spirit forcing me onward, ever onward, through the consumptive ebonied mists, beyond the streams of deliquescent darkness, past the intermittent scintillation of blinding phosphorescence, the inexorable consummation of the labyrinth yawning to encompass my substance, my very soul. Surveying the hated hollowness, I cursed the compulsion that necessitated my diurnal descent into its depths.

Alyssa arrived at her study hall two minutes after the bell rang. Joe Axelrod, "The Axe," as he was not-so-affectionately called by his students, was already there. Erica Vetterly hadn't arrived yet. She was anywhere from ten to fifteen minutes late every day. The place was chaotic as always, students still refusing to accept the fact that this was study hall and not a free-for-all. Trying to figure out who was supposed to be there and when was still a confusing and frustrating experience. Even the responsibilities of homeroom paled under the glare of study hall attendance-keeping and supervision.

Initial study hall lists in September had been largely erroneous masses of names. Alyssa had stared in horror at the two hundred names on her list, dreading second period the first day of school. It turned out to be worse than her wildest nightmares. Axelrod's list showed two hundred names also. The room, which was the school's only gymnasium when Hannah Boesch taught classes there, was bursting with bodies. Students sat on chairs, desk tops, each others' laps, and the floor. They were enjoying the party and looking forward to its continuation. Alyssa was sickened by the sight, repelled by the disorder, disheartened at the thought that a great deal of time, energy, and patience would have to be spent to remedy the situation. But it couldn't be helped. She would not sit there every day and watch them play. And if they worked quietly, she could get some work done too. The only ounce of salvation, the only dram of mercy that she saw that first day was Joe. Joe Axelrod was a gift from God.

Each teacher running a study hall was faced with the decision of chaos or control. Either let them socialize, thus destroying the purpose for which the time was theoretically intended, or muzzle their mouths and leash their bodies, thus sanctifying those holy intentions. Both methods were insanity, of course. Even the chaos had to be reduced to the level of a reasonable roar, not an easy task once the reins were slipped. And the control had to be maintained. Both methods were a direct route to a peptic ulcer, the former swift and uncomplicated, the latter slow and torturous.

Sometimes the teacher opting for control would have to put up with chaos because all study halls were immense, causing assignment of two or more teachers. Establishing quiet in one portion of the room while the rest of the place ran wild was impossible. Alyssa had suffered through that situation before. When she saw that Joe was co-hosting the Study Hall A Second Period Extravaganza, she breathed a sigh of relief. She and Joe shared the same philosophy. No talking. No fooling around. Study. As in books. Or sleep. As in bored or lazy. But no talking. Let the poor fools interested in getting an education get some work done.

Alyssa and Joe, adamant about running a study hall like a study hall, agreed on one other matter that first day: they needed help. It took the entire period for students to sign attendance sheets, which Joe delivered to the office as proof of enrollment. He requested that another teacher be assigned to help with supervision. It would take time, he was told, so make the best of it.

The first week was hell. There was nothing to do but let them talk and play, with an occasional command to keep it down. Alyssa hated every minute of it. It was a colossal waste of time. Hers and theirs. For a few days she attempted to call roll, careful to read names of only those students assigned for those particular days of the week, trying to read across computer sheets accurately, enduring catcalls and foolish comments. But it was hopeless. The only way to keep valid attendance was to assign seats. She stopped calling names and went back to circulating sign-in sheets. More than once she entertained the rather delicious notion that she could play the farce for what it was. Give up. Plenty of others had long before this.

Gym and pool classes, science labs, and the opening of the library took large numbers out of the study hall the second week of school. It was also during the second week, in a moment of reckless abandon mixed with a large dose of disgust, that Alyssa and Joe compared lists. Joe had heard some other teachers talking about it, a quick check wouldn't hurt, and- well, the saints be praised! that sneaky ol' computer must have had the hiccups! About a third of the names were the same. Things were looking up. The two of them were responsible for the whereabouts of only, let's see, four hundred minus ninety-seven makes three hundred and three. Now THAT, said

Alyssa, is progress. And if we put our heads together, maybe we can figure out a way to eliminate a couple hundred more ...

Her wild imaginings were interrupted by a ringing phone. Although the sound was muffled, it was coming from somewhere in the room. But where? Everybody's attention was diverted by the game of search and find, a game providing raucous pleasure to spectators as they hoot and holler while players make utter fools of themselves.

The ringing continued.

"Oh my god," Alyssa said. "It's up there." Joe, thinking she meant above the old basketball net - nothing was too absurd for him - looked up.

"No, Joe, not there. THERE!" She pointed to a spot next to the entrance, above the sunken gym floor, beyond the rows of amphitheater seats. "Do you see it? Next to the door? The cord! See the cord?"

He saw it all right. What he saw was the distance one of them would have to travel every time the phone rang.

"Somebody covered the phone with something," Alyssa said. "Just the cord is visible." She scurried across the gym floor, up the flight of stairs, over to the phone. There was a ratty old sweater covering it. She lifted the sweater, then the receiver, and breathed a gasping "Study Hall A." To nobody.

Fully aware of the consequences if she descended again into the pit, Alyssa replaced the receiver and waited for the callback. It came almost immediately.

"What's the matter? Can't you people answer your phone?" Bob McGuinness, Assistant Principal for Discipline of the Sophomore Class.

"We had to find it first, Bob. This is Matthews, what-can-I-do-for-you?"

"Oh, hello Matt! How are you? I haven't seen you at all this year!"

After a few more amenities were dispensed with, Bob gave Alyssa names of two students he was tracking down for truancy. Repeating the unfamiliar names under her breath (she would have to remember to grab paper and pen next time), Alyssa returned to Joe with the first of many requests for attendance records. Required to determine whether each student was reporting to study hall and, if so, when, or, if not, when, they scoured sign-in sheets for the rest of the period. It was relatively easy then, in the second week of school. But as the year wore on, complexities of time and place would make the job oppressive.

During the third week, Erica Vetterly showed up. Well, not exactly "during," more "at the end of." TGIF, the clarion call of the proletariat, would never be amended to TGIV. Rather, the appearance of her hawkish nose and vulturous mouth, along with a body bearing a rudimentary resemblance to extruded metal tubing and an attitude reeking of alienation, prompted a variation of theme that she had wittingly and unwittingly nurtured through the years: ONIV. Oh-no-it's-Vetterly was the non-verbal response, the hushed exclamation, the flicker of feeling, the facial contortion, every time she made contact with animate objects beyond age eighteen. Those objects knew she fostered a pleasant relationship only with her students, the effort to keep them lazy and slothfully content a yearly insurance policy promising low premiums and astronomical dividends.

Not having received a study hall assignment, she had been hiding out in the hope that she wouldn't get stuck at all. When Bob McGuinness finally found time to ferret out help for the two teachers in Study Hall A, second period, he checked the master schedule and noticed Vetterly's two free periods. One of them was second period. He wrote a note and put it in her mailbox. Monday morning.

She read the note, ripped it into pieces, deposited the proof in the nearest wastebasket, and forgot about it. At the very least she would postpone the assignment for a few days. At the very most the bureaucratic labyrinth would obscure the entire matter, which would get her off the hook entirely.

After starting the third week with no help in sight, Alyssa and Joe made their third request for another teacher. Wednesday morning.

Bob McGuinness saw red rats. He had a feeling this would happen, he knew he should have seen her. Her defense now was predictable: she never found any assignment in her mailbox. Bob McGuinness made his way past the line of students waiting for verbal reprimands and the two sets of parents waiting for scheduled conferences, and scoured the school trying to track down the elusive bitch. He found her in the library ordering films like a hypochondriac filling prescriptions.

"Mrs. Vetterly, may I have a word with you?" he whispered, exercising more self-control than he was feeling. He would tell her and that would be it.

"Why, of course, Mr. McGuinness. How could I survive without the wisdom of your words," she whispered back sharply, well aware of his mission, enjoying the redness creeping up his neck. Her waspish tongue might make him think twice before assigning her duties in the future. But no such luck now.

"Seeing that you choose to ignore written instructions, I'm giving them to you verbally. Because you did not receive a study hall assignment with your original schedule, I am now giving you a study hall assignment. You will report to Study Hall A, second period, immediately and until further notice." Then he unclenched his teeth, turned on his heel and stalked from the room.

Erica neglected to report the next day and was sorely tempted to round out the week, but decided that she had pushed things far enough. When Alyssa and Joe saw her descending the stairs fifteen minutes into the period on Friday, they exchanged quick glances of disappointment. Vetterly was worse than nobody.

The seating chart took days of figuring. After giving Erica fifty names, Alyssa was still short seats. She juggled names, days, and seats until she covered a sheet of paper with little boxes and notations. A student assigned to the study hall on Monday, Wednesday, and Friday, MWF on the computer sheet, could sit at a desk assigned to another student on TR, Tuesday and Thursday. She went through the list, giving seats to students appearing every day first, then to students assigned MTWR or TWRF or MTWF or any other variable of four days, then all combinations of three days — MTW, TWR, TWF, MWF, et cetera — then doubled in combinations of two days, and added the very few one-day appearances last. It was the only way to fit one hundred bodies into forty-eight seats, no, forty-seven seats she realized when she checked the count. No desks were provided for teachers, so she had to move a desk and chair to the front for herself. She had three rows with twelve desks, one row with eleven. And her seating didn't work until she extracted ten names of students who had never shown at all. She hoped that they had had schedule changes that she had just never been notified of. If not, she would have to rotate them daily into seats of absentees. At any rate, they were names she had to check on.

When she was satisfied that she had drawn as accurate an account of attendance as possible, Alyssa was ready to cage the beasts. It was an appropriate metaphor considering the response she provoked.

You gotta be kidding, they told her. What the hell is she doing, they asked each other. We ain't gotta do this. Shit, I don't wanna sit here. Who does she think she is anyway? What is this, a prison?

Recognizing the verbal abuse as a shock reaction to sudden shackles in lieu of freedom, Alyssa ignored it. Responding to it would only have dignified it anyway, and she felt too good about finally instituting order. The party was over.

She walked the four rows calling out names every day for five days because of the complexities involved and because they were in the fourth week of school. The seating chart was organized to show clearly which days each student was required to be in study hall. Some seats would be occupied by only one student, some seats by two or three students appearing on different days. Moving down each row of twelve seats, Alyssa seated only those students assigned for that day. She repeated the procedure the next day to pick up those students not required to appear or just absent the day before, double-checking those she seated previously as she went along. She did the same thing for three more days. Theoretically, the procedure should have taken care of everyone. But they were too far into the year. She missed students who were chronically absent, students who were in the library, or in the computer room, or making up tests, or involved in some other activity somewhere else. There was no way around it, she would have to catch them as they showed.

A few students came in waving add slips while she was seating the others. They went from one teacher to another and received the same order from all of them: go back to be rescheduled, we're full here. The three supervisors agreed that it was worth a try even though they had no authority to turn anyone away. The worse consequence was a reprimand and a reminder that they had no choice in the matter. But the kids didn't return. It occurred to Alyssa that they could easily hide out somewhere instead of returning to counselors in search of another study hall. Counselors figured that they had assigned a study hall; how would they know if a kid was turned away? The kid would never return the add slip. The odds were excellent that he could get away with being on no one's study hall list, and if his records were not subjected to a check, he could do what he pleased second period. The key to success was to keep a low profile, to avoid getting caught. Alyssa felt sure that it was happening, and she didn't care. If the counselor ever checked his copy of the student's schedule, it wouldn't mean much if he didn't have an add slip with her initials on it. She wouldn't be responsible if she hadn't signed anything. She noted "no room" on add slips in her mailbox and returned them to counselors. It was an elaborate game of shuffle and hide, counselors and teachers constantly at odds, counselors obligated to fill schedules, teachers anxious to minimize class size, both teams conscious of the only rule of play: Protect Yourself.

By the end of the fourth week of school, the Study Hall A Second Period Extravaganza was as organized as it could be. Joe also seated his students quickly and efficiently with his deep assertive voice and serious commanding demeanor. There were few audible complaints on his side of the room. Erica's students, purposely lumped in the middle, sat where they pleased within the boundaries of her four rows. It turned out to be a qualified blessing that she arrived late every day. By the time she clomped down the stairs, Alyssa and Joe already had the place settled down. It took a few detentions and constant reminders to get Erica's crew in the middle of the holding pen, but her students soon realized that the other two keepers would ride herd over them in her absence. That revelation, coupled with the well-known fact that Mrs. Vetterly didn't take attendance, promoted the inevitable: by Christmas her section would be sparsely filled.

On October 23, 1980, study halls at Boesch-Conklyn were as controlled as they could be in a society that was consuming itself with demands for personal freedom. The quest for human rights, civil rights, employee rights, employer rights, fetal rights, gay rights, women's rights, men's rights, equal rights, bedmate-without-benefit-of-marriage rights, rights flagrant and rights obscure, rights right and rights wrong eventually permeated every level of academe.

At BCA student rights were made a prime concern on that fateful day in May, 1974, when a young man showed up in Bassard's office to protest his suspension from school for refusing to wear a shirt to classes. Bassard would have turned the sophomoric senior around in short order had he not appeared with reinforcements, that is, his father and, as the SS arrogantly announced, MY LAWYER. By the time the three crusaders for freedom left, Bassard had learned a valuable legal lesson: Tread carefully when Johnny threatens to sue. In the interests of human rights, civil rights, student rights, personal rights, et. al., state law prohibited public schools from enforcing any kind of dress code. Thus the Age of Jeans, the Era of Shorts, Sweatshirts, Tube Tops, Halter Tops, No Tops, Hats, and Diaphanous Blouses was upon us all.

With a great deal of disgust, Harry Bassard informed the complainant who happened to be Jean Tevarro ("But it's not even warm yet!" she said. "What does he plan to do in June? Drop his pants?") that she would just have to tolerate the hirsute view because the SS had every legal right to offend her. "What about my rights?"

she asked. "Forget it," Bassard snapped. "Or do you want to drag this stupidity through court?"

The SS returned to classes, his bare bosom doubled in size, his father's words ringing in his ears. "We're going to beat the bureaucracy on this one! They can't tell you how to dress!" Jean found his attitude more distasteful than his appearance and, in an effort to get him as far away as possible within the legal confines of the classroom, moved him to the back of the room. She waited for a charge of discrimination for that bit of strategy, but it never materialized. Probably because the kid liked his new neighborhood. The girls on either side of him admired his biceps.

While the school was under continual pressure to enforce discipline, the law of the land was working itself into a tizzy to ensure personal freedoms. Offenders' rights had to be protected too. And so every rule, every regulation, every disciplinary treatise had to be subject to appeal. And the appeals procedure was built with minute, exquisite care. The victim shouldered the burden of proof; the accused looked for an out among the complexities of his legal defense, overshadowing the victim as a candidate in the rights department.

When that young man won the battle to bare his chest, he did it at the end of the first year of The Open Study Hall, that grand testimonial to student maturity, that great experiment that failed immediately but took five years to "phase out."

The crowning achievement of a committee of student leaders, open study halls were instituted in a blaze of good intentions, idealism, ego, and faulty reasoning. College students are allowed to use their free time as they see fit, the committee explained. Why can't high school students be given the same opportunity to prove themselves responsible? What better way to teach responsibility, to foster maturity? Give us a chance and we will make you proud. Give us a choice and we will do the right thing. Realistically speaking, some will weaken and choose entertainment over study, but they will learn from their mistakes, and experience, after all, is the best teacher. Allow us the freedom to learn for ourselves, the freedom to grow, the freedom to make our own decisions, to be responsible for our own actions. We are aching to prove ourselves! Give us the opportunity!

It was a pip of a student committee, one of those groups composed of surnames that pillar and sometimes pillory the rest of the community. Armed with weighty nomenclature, lengthy research on the existence of the experiment in other school districts, and youthful zeal, the committee was indeed impressive.

The idea was presented at a Board meeting in a spectacular display of persuasive expertise that rated a two-page spread in the newspaper. The committee had done a superb job, an inordinate amount of work. Weren't young people capable of marvelous things? How refreshing to see youthful enthusiasm and concern directed toward constructive endeavors. Teenage troublemakers were overshadowed for once by a corps of articulate, intelligent, progressive leaders-of-men. Everybody loved it. Everybody who had any influence in the matter, that is.

The opposition didn't have a chance by virtue of its nature: why should teachers and administrators be allowed to block progress? They were split into two camps anyway, one supporting the idea as a means of ducking study hall supervision, the other opposing it as contrary to human nature. The split in the ranks summarily dismissed opponents as old-fashioned, negative pessimists.

The plan was overwhelmingly approved. The committee, successfully satisfying their obsession to leave a mark on the old alma mater, took their bows, graduated, and moved on to enrich college campuses all over the country. They never witnessed the mischief and mayhem that they engendered.

In a flurry of related activity, the high school was given "The Campus Look." A few rolling hills covered with sod, a few full-grown trees, an adorable little pond, some shrubbery, and a romantic network of wood, stone, and wrought iron walkways, bridgeways, and sitways with three symmetrically-positioned gazebos was the architect's design for the transition from depressing to inspirational. It is a shame that students must strive to be creative, must struggle to learn, in a depressing environment, the architect told the school board. *This*, he said, directing his four-foot pointer to the easeled sketch of heaven, *this* is the kind of environment our young people deserve. *And*, he added with a flourish that punctured the bottom of the cherub adorning the peak of the middle gazebo and caused the whole celestial concept to teeter precariously, *and* what we have here is *functional* as well as aesthetically pleasing. *Such* a lovely place to *have lunch*.

There was some grumbling in the community over the external renovations. Some people wondered long and loud how landscaping could improve college board scores. Some people had the audacity to express a concern over the cost of the project. They were the fools, of course, because the money was not coming out of local taxes. Absolutely not. The district qualified for a federal grant and the money could be used only for external improvements. Other districts were finding ways to use that money, why not this one? A few people were frustrated enough to point out that tax money is tax money is tax money, but they constituted a mere whimper in the midst of a chorus of stentorian voices.

People react and respond to controversial issues according to individual sensitivities based on age, sex, social status, intellectual capacity, educational training, idiosyncrasies, job status, mental stability, physical well-being, experience, and a host of other external and internal stimuli. Public interest died away as soon as the project was done. CONSTRUCTION:CRITICISM = COMPLETION:APATHY.

And everybody was in such a tither over the outside, which, of course, was highly visible, that nobody remembered to look into what was happening on the inside, which, of course, was nobody's business anyway. Highly-trained, well-paid professionals had that situation under control. Indeed they did. "The Campus Look" was designed to be the perfect adjunct to the plan for open study halls.

Intense work over the summer solved problems of logistics and implementation. Supporters of the concept included representatives from all staff levels. Teachers, counselors, and administrators struggled to foresee and then make provisions to eliminate as many problems as possible before school opened. Some wrinkles would have to be ironed out later, but the fewer the better.

Faculty orientation was scheduled during the general meeting before the first day of classes. The pros optimistically sanctioned, the cons pessimistically condemned the possibility of success. The pros, blessed with a slight edge in the matter, were tired of the constant barrage of "what if's." The cons sensed doom.

Everybody was assured of the existence of rules. Students had to decide where they wanted to go, get there by the time the bell rang, and stay there all period. They could not wander the halls. They were required to maintain reasonable, responsible behavior in each of the four study halls regardless of classification. They were to report to study hall only during those periods when they were assigned to study hall. Lunch periods were not study hall periods. During lunch students had to remain in the cafeterias. Students were expected to use their time wisely, to blend study moderately with relaxation.

The student body was notified during assemblies the first week of school. Cheers were heard in the neighboring town, as far north as Reykjavik, and all the way to Ushuaia. A migrant worker, startled by the sudden roar coming out of nowhere, scurried up a tree in the Salinas Valley.

OPEN STUDY HALLS! Freedom! Freeeedom! What to do and where to go. Where to go and what to do. I'll meet you ... Can you get out of ... We're meeting in ... Get there in time for ... So what, I'm cutting math ... Don't worry about it, there's no attendance ... Mike has plenty of white slips ... Will he be there? ... Don't start without me ...

Study Halls C and D were outfitted with juke boxes, soda and candy machines, and a cooler for ice cream. Study Hall B contained sofas, easy chairs, card tables, and TV. Study Hall A retained its ordinary desks and chairs, looking forlornly naked compared to the other three. It was the quiet study hall, the place to go to study.

By Halloween Study Hall A was a huge mausoleum. But Study Halls B,C, and D were unqualified successes. Teachers volunteered to chaperone activities according to personal taste. The entire faculty was encouraged to "mingle," to "socialize," to take advantage of the opportunity to enjoy an informal relationship with students. Teacher-student rapport could only improve. But there were teachers who held out, who wouldn't be caught dead or alive in one of those mammoth "holding pens." The pros were still smug. When the novelty wore off, they said, students would slowly filter into Study Hall A.

Thanksgiving came and went, Christmas rolled on by, January exams crept up stealthily and passed (though few students did), Easter breezed on by, then exams again. Through it all, Study Hall A remained empty. More teachers taught summer school that year than ever before in the annals of education. It didn't look good for the pros. And the cons were changing their tune from "what if" to "we told you so."

The inherent weakness of the plan was reluctantly acknowledged: high school students are not college students. And what a pity, Jean observed sardonically, since all college students are models of moderation, self-control, and maturity. Level-headed, responsible, and God-fearing, loyal, hard-working, and brave members of society are they all.

Because it was just plain too much work to go back to scheduling everybody into study halls again, the plan was continued for a second year. It just hurt too awful much to scrap all the work already done. And it was too embarrassing to admit defeat. Besides, maybe the first year was a fluke, an aberration. Maybe things would straighten out if given a chance.

But not much changed. Students still fought over which soap opera to tune in, which tune to play on the juke box, and who was cheating at cards. Black students marked their territory in Study Hall B and dared anybody to enter their turf. A few young entrepreneurs made a fortune taking bets on football, baseball, basketball, hockey, and anything else that moved. Custodians still complained bitterly about the squalor. Teachers still screamed about excessive truancy, a few brave souls risking life and limb to pluck out a truant from the midst of his friends and escort him to the class he was cutting. There was just no control, no accountability. And that observation finally tolled the death knell for open study halls. Because public schools are accountable, public schools are responsible for the whereabouts of students during the scheduled school day. Parents calling the school to locate their children were becoming disgruntled with the school's inability to find and extract students from the nooks and crannies of the building. Understandably, school officials want to avoid, at all costs, telling a parent no one knows where his child is.

Thus, while they should have been severed with a machete, open study halls were gently "phased out." It was deemed to be too psychologically offensive to yank away suddenly a privilege that students already had. Each succeeding year, incoming sophomores were denied the privilege until the school purged itself of The Grand Escape to Freedom. The phasing out took three more years.

By September, 1978, the entire student body moved from no study hall scheduling at all to rigid scheduling. Students were once again required to be in a certain place at a certain time every period of the day. But the germ of personal freedom was still making its way through the body of education. Because of excessive truancies in physical education classes and a state mandate that set minimum attendance quotas required for graduation, it was decided that the only way to make gym classes palatable to all was to give students a choice in selecting activity units. The casual observer, had there been one around, would have noted that for eons some students have hated physical education, that some students hate math, or English, or history, and that life is filled with irritating obligations. In the absence of a casual observer, however, the school established its Elective Program for Physical Education.

Students reported to the gyms *en masse* to sign up for units they could at least tolerate, which resulted in thirty-seven sections of calisthenics and two sections of trampoline. Physical education teachers, who enjoyed teaching units that required a bit more strenuous activity, became auctioneers and carnival barkers.

95

Eventually types and numbers of sections had to be limited, thus closing out students from popular units and forcing them to select from what was left.

Because students were given the right to select softball over golf, gymnastics over volleyball, square dancing over tennis, physical education teachers spent days signing them up, compiling lists, and distributing the info to study hall teachers. Study hall teachers then spent days figuring out who was supposed to be where and when. Perhaps it would have been possible for everyone to remain sane through it all if the lists appeared once every semester. As it was, the lists changed every six weeks. Every time a student changed his gym unit, he changed his study hall assignment. The lists came through during the second or third week of each six-week period. A few times they didn't come through at all.

Study hall teachers, not to mention counselors, were wild trying to keep track of attendance. The havoc lasted two years. It was finally decided that the complexities weren't worth the privileges, that students were still cutting gym classes anyway, that they could survive their educational experience without physical education electives, and that the tail was wagging the dog.

A disciplinarian at heart, Alyssa Matthews never supported open study halls. She volunteered for duty in Study Hall A and maintained her classroom standards regardless of those students who chose to be irresponsible. If they wanted to pass with her they had to study. A large segment of the faculty felt the same way. Rolling with the punches is a fact of life for teachers; so is getting bruised by the process. The only thing Alyssa did enjoy during those years was the respite from study hall record keeping.

When traditional study halls were reintroduced, teachers as well as students lost some freedom during the day. And the work for teachers was multiplied by the gym elective procedure. Alyssa, who wouldn't have minded returning to study halls as they had been prior to the open study hall debacle, went crazy along with most everyone else trying to keep accurate attendance. She kept asking why things had changed so, why couldn't study halls be reasonably controllable as they were in the years right after she started teaching. She hadn't changed. She always believed in study during study hall. It really wasn't so much to ask, was it?

On October 23, 1980, Alyssa was still asking. Open study halls were gone, gym electives were gone. But something remained. Some residue from all that frenzied effort to pacify and satisfy students, to grant them their inalienable rights in the absence of personal responsibility, to forfeit authority. It was an attitude, a consciousness. And on October 23, 1980, the air was thick with it.

My psyche reeled as I fought to maintain restraint under the incessant yet intermittent battery of abuse, the iniquitous assault abrading my weary spirit. The tongues of inquisitorial fire were malevolently designed for singular, divergent invasion of the flesh. I shrank from the first pricklings of pain, cognition dictating the eventual extension of pinpoints into a flaring web cauterizing the flesh from my bones, exposing the rawness below. The means of the torture was horrifyingly clear: I was being flayed - layer by layer - flayed - flesh excoriated by a demonic process, for while the source of my suffering appeared to be externally ignited, it based itself within - WITHIN - I WAS BEING FLAYED FROM WITHIN - FROM THE VERY DEPTHS OF MY SOUL - I WAS THE PERPETRATOR AND THE VICTIM.

"Everybody sit down, stop talking, and get to work." Alyssa's voice boomed out over the sea of swarming bodies.

"Okay, folks, the bell rang!" bellowed Joe, announcing the obvious.

Why, oh why, do they have to be told every day, thought Alyssa. Every damned day we come in here and scream the same thing. Lord knows we'll never come in and tell them to break out into an orgy. They know that. And still, every day, every goddamned day …

"Stop talking and get to work! That goes for everybody!" Alyssa set papers on her desk, but waited to sit until the talking stopped.

"Terry, turn around. Sue, stop talking and get to work," she said firmly. She still needed to check her seating chart for most names, but there were a few that were burned into her brain.

When the place finally settled down, Alyssa sat at the student desk that was entirely too small to accommodate her materials. She liked to leave the study hall folder open with the seating chart and attendance sheet showing. She needed to make notations all period. But if she left the folder open on the desk, there was little room to grade papers.

She pulled out the seating chart and her attendance sheet, labeled a new section with the date and started matching bodies in seats with names on the chart. She was always especially careful to look only for students assigned on any one day of the week. Occasionally she caught herself listing a student as absent on a day of the week when that student wasn't even assigned to study hall. It was an easy mistake to make. There was a student coming down the stairs. Everybody looked up. The noise started up again. "Stop talking, please," Alyssa said. If she allowed a murmur, the murmur would turn into a roar within minutes.

The late student handed Joe a pass and sat down, causing a few ripples on that side of the room. "There's no reason to start talking," Joe said. And his side of the room quieted down again.

Alyssa was halfway down the first row on her seating chart when she noticed that the boy assigned to the fifth seat was sitting in the sixth seat. She had changed him back twice already. She made sure that she wrote the name of the student who was assigned to the sixth seat on her list of absentees and went on, aware of noise on the other side of the room.

Joe was up and walking toward the two students making the fuss. He sent one back to the middle section where he belonged. Alyssa recognized the boy. He never showed up with anything to do and furtively wandered around the room until caught and sent back to his seat. Erica never bothered to say anything to him, though he was her student.

By the time she reached the end of the second row, Alyssa had written fifteen names of absentees and was watching Greg Prevost's hand signals and facial contortions with increasing displeasure. She watched him waste time in study hall every day. What bothered her was that he was failing her first period class. He was one of the new breed of scholarship students.

"Greg, stop clowning and get to work," she said. "Sue, turn around and STOP TALKING."

Joe was up again looking as if he were ready to kill. Erica's wandering minstrel was at it again. The boy made the mistake of trying to badmouth Joe and ended up back in his seat holding a detention slip.

Alyssa finished her list of absentees. Twenty-two names. Then she went through the absence slips students had left on her desk at the beginning of the period, noting reasons for absence after names on her absence sheet for previous days. There were also passes for Thursday, Oct. 23, in the pile, so she noted locations after some of the names she had just written.

There was twittering in the back of the room. "If the talking doesn't stop, I'm going to move seats," Alyssa said. They didn't know that changing seats would be more agony for her than for them. Alyssa looked over the attendance sheets with a knowing eye. Besides the ten students that never showed up at all, there were plenty of other names that appeared over and over again with no slip or pass to legalize absences. She would have to report them "to the appropriate administrator" soon. But not right now, she decided. She had two sets of spelling tests to grade for her afternoon classes. While she could never maintain the concentration necessary to grade compositions or other written work during study hall, she could manage spelling tests and objective tests. She could manage, that is, with fewer distractions.

"There is entirely too much noise in this room. There are people here who are interested in getting some work done. SO PLEASE STOP TALKING."

The room quieted down again, just in time for Erica Vetterly's entrance. Every step she took down the stairs and across the old gym floor bounced off the walls and echoed a nerve wracking shriek. She sat at her desk and opened the morning paper.

Alyssa started grading her tests. Mary Ann Bruson was up and walking to the front of the room, accompanied by smacking and sucking sounds coming from various locations. When she reached Alyssa's desk, she whispered for permission to go to the bathroom. It was one privilege that Alyssa couldn't bring herself to deny anyone. Joe had announced no pass privileges the day he assigned seats, and Erica left her pass on the corner of the desk for students to use at will. Alyssa liked Joe's method best, but opted for the middle road. It was impossible to tell who was stretching the truth, some students used the pass to wander around, but she would never forget the little girl who slumped in a heap on the floor after asking for a pass to the nurse. Alyssa hadn't refused permission, she just hadn't written fast enough. The girl had gone into sugar shock, the nurse later explained.

Mary Ann took the pass and traveled the width of the room to the stairs, visibly embarrassed by the animal noises and more smacking and sucking sounds accentuating the beat of her clomping clogs.

It was too much for Alyssa. "Stop that foolishness this instant!" she shouted. Joe got up to walk his beat. Alyssa rose to walk hers. By the time they finished traveling up and down the rows, the inferno quieted down again. Alyssa went back to grading her spelling tests.

A student delivered the library sign-in sheet to Joe. He checked off his students then carried the sheet to Alyssa. She matched names on that sheet with names on her absence list, crossing out and noting "L" for each student who was not really absent, but in the library.

Noise in the back of the room again. Alyssa got up, walked back and calmly gave two boys the lecture on study hall manners. When she turned her back to begin the long trek to the front of the room, one of the boys gave her the finger, causing the immediate area to go into convulsions. Alyssa looked back and the laughter subsided.

By the time she reached her desk, the phone was ringing. It was her turn to answer it so she kept on going across the room and up the stairs, grabbing her study hall folder on the way. The ratty old sweater was still covering the phone; it did wonders to muffle the sound. The request was for a student with an unfamiliar name. Alyssa went down to check with Joe, then Erica, then returned to the phone with the news that no one had ever heard of the kid. She covered the phone with the sweater and returned to her spelling tests.

Mary Ann Bruson returned and another girl took the pass.

Alyssa went back to her spelling tests.

Angela LoGuasta was up, book in hand, heading for Sue Carson. Angela stopped on the way to giggle with Greg Prevost, shot a wave to a bored cohort across the room, paused to shove Mike Allen's books off his desk, and quickly sat next to Sue just as Alyssa's head popped up at the explosive sound of the books hitting the floor.

The phone was ringing again. Joe got up to take his turn. Alyssa watched as Mike Allen scooped up his books. There was a period of restlessness which she ended with a terse, "All right, quiet down." She returned to her spelling tests. She said nothing about the books because a reaction would have only prolonged the disturbance. Books, pencils, and pens hit the floor so often that an angry response was disproportionate to the offense. Nine times out of ten objects flipped and flopped inadvertently. At any rate, if teacher flew into a rage, any number of falling objects would periodically disturb the peace. Even when her patience was thin, Alyssa concentrated on maintaining a controlled level of authority devoid of hysteria. Some students make a career out of provoking nervous teachers to explode. Using age-old techniques, these students don't care about getting into trouble. Besides, what they do certainly doesn't constitute felonious assault. How ridiculous teacher looks after the fact, trying to convince anyone that pencil-tapping, foot-thumping, gum-cracking, or such subtle acts of defiance as dirty looks or mumbled obscenities are worthy of capital punishment.

Joe returned with two names. "McGuinness wants attendance on these two, pronto," he said. "They're both in his office now. Are they yours?"

Alyssa looked at the names. They were hers. Two out of the ten that never showed. She wrote a note to that effect and sent it to

McGuinness via the student who was returning with the bathroom pass.

She went back to her spelling tests. She wasn't doing very well with them. She was only half-way through one class.

A student requested use of the pass. She told him the pass was out, he could use it next, and returned to her spelling tests.

Angela and Sue were getting loud. Alyssa looked up and asked Angela to return to her seat. "We're studying. Why can't we study together? What is this, a prison?" Angela said sarcastically.

"You're using that book as an excuse, and we both know it. NOW MOVE!" Angela's face contorted with disgust. She slammed her book shut and stomped back to her seat, making as much noise as she could. Other students twittered as she passed. As soon as Alyssa lowered her head, Angela leaned over to whisper to the boy next to her. "STOP TALKING," Alyssa said vehemently.

The phone started to ring again. Knowing that hell would freeze over before Erica got up to answer it, Alyssa took her turn again. And she was getting impatient. Fed up with all of it. When she reached the phone, she took the receiver off the hook and left it dangling.

As she descended the stairs, she saw the party that was brewing in the back of her section. Erica's wandering minstrel was engaged in animated conversation with one of her boys. Joe had already given the little bastard detention.

By the time she reached the back of the room, Alyssa was shaking with rage. "YOU!" she said, pointing to the wandering troublemaker, "GET BACK WHERE YOU BELONG RIGHT NOW!"

The entire room was silent. She didn't realize she was screaming.

"AND YOU!" She pointed to the student with the overactive middle finger. "HOW MANY TIMES DO YOU HAVE TO BE TOLD TO SHUT UP? THIS IS A STUDY HALL. YOU HAVE NO RIGHT TO DISTURB OTHERS WHO ARE TRYING TO WORK."

Alyssa probably would have calmed down rather quickly had the boy taken her tongue lashing the least bit seriously. But he was laughing. Head rolled back, body bouncing with the joy of it all, he was having the time of his life.

Still screaming, Alyssa asked the obvious question, straining to keep her hands away from his neck. He stopped laughing, took a deep breath, and wiped the moisture away from his eyes. He was bored now with the whole scenario.

"Aw, go fuck yourself, lady, and leave me alone," he said.

Alyssa was momentarily stunned. Then she wanted to slap his face.

"GET OUT!" she told him. "GO TO IN-SCHOOL! NOW!"

He slid out of his seat and ambled out of the room.

Alyssa returned to her desk, still shaking, and looked for an in-school suspension form. It was the first time this year she had need for one. She knew she didn't carry them around, but she looked among her papers and folders anyway.

By the time the period was over, Erica's wandering minstrel attempted to take up residence once again in Joe's section. Joe grabbed the kid by the collar and sent him to the in-school suspension room also.

"I'm sorry I made a spectacle of myself," Alyssa told Joe at the end of the period. "I've never lost control like that before."

"How long have you been teaching?" he asked.

"Twelve years," she answered.

"That's quite a record, young lady," Joe said, his head tilting to one side. Then he added: "And may I welcome you to the planet Earth?"

> The hour had come. The subterranean sepulchre once again spewed its dreary denizens, incarceration terminated by a phantasmagoric reverberative knell. My hour of deliverance had come. But I felt no joy, no particle of relief, no sense of freedom: I was filled with a terrifying and all-consuming dread, for I could focus on only one unalterable certainty: THE COMPULSION WOULD UNMERCIFULLY RETURN — I WOULD AGAIN DESCEND INTO THE PIT.

Interlude

Carpeting has to be subjected to a lengthy, persistent battery of abuse with no intermittent care before it will give up the ghost. The carpeting in the fourth floor faculty room started giving up its life a year after it was installed and immediately abandoned. The school's one vacuum cleaner never left the main office level. Five years later the wall-to-wall disaster, its colors faded under layers of filth, seemed to be begging for a release from its confines and proper burial. Dust and grime had slowly eaten away its fibers. It was unraveling. Right down the middle of the room.

A bit at a time the carpeting was inching its way out, but at least it had found a way out. The inanimate objects resting on top of it would be there forever: the ancient davenport with its twisted frame and thin cushions, the two chairs with torn upholstery and loose arms, the solid wood tables, once covered with protective glass, then stripped bare by a thief, now succumbing to neglect.

On each table there rested a lamp. And each lamp, when originally placed, must have been the proud finishing touch to the decor of a comfortable and attractive room. Now, under yellowed shades, the lamps were merely ignored along with the rest of the furnishings. It had been at least a century since either lamp housed a light bulb.

The room was lit by huge, bare fluorescent tubes attached to the high ceiling. Located in the middle was a large rectangular table surrounded by sturdy classroom chairs. No one sat anywhere else, even though upholstered furniture, holes and all, offered more comfort. Well ... almost no one. Occasionally a brave soul wearing old clothes would wander over and sit down as gingerly as possible so as not to raise too much of a dust storm. Jean did it once when she felt a particular need to sit on something soft. She made the mistake of leaning just a mite too heavily on one arm. Hers and the chair's. Hers held, but the chair's gave way, and sent her sprawling.

From its ugly drapes to its tattered window shade to its dried out, creaking door, the room was a monument to neglect. Dirt was encrusted on woodwork and in corners, the solitary sink bowl stained yellow from water passing through rusty pipes, the toilet seat dotted with splash. But in spite of its condition the room was seductive in its appeal. It was sanctuary. There were no students there.

"Do you think it would do any good if we petitioned to have this room cleaned?" Bonnie asked Jean.

"It's worth a try. When did we do it last with no results?"

"Last spring. And as far as I can see, the same dirt that was here in June is still here."

"Write something up and leave it on the table to be signed. I'll take it to Harry myself with a threat to call the board of health. There's no doubt that this place would be condemned. Wouldn't that be embarrassing?" Jean looked at the closed door at the back of the room. "Is somebody in there?"

"I don't know. It was closed when I came in. Try knocking."

Jean knocked and heard a voice that said, "Be right out."

"Do you have to use the facilities?" Jean asked Bonnie.

Bonnie said no and Jean breathed a sigh of relief. She had attempted between first and second periods to "use the facilities," but her efforts were thwarted by a long line. Her students had worked beyond the bell first period, and she hadn't wanted to risk too much time hunting for an unoccupied faculty bathroom elsewhere. So she went right to the fourth floor bathroom, closest to her next class. When the second period bell rang, she was third in line and couldn't wait ten more minutes. That is, she couldn't keep her class waiting ten more minutes. At the end of second period she decided that she had better get to a bathroom or the halls would be running red. She was two hours beyond sopping.

The door opened and Alyssa walked in. She set her books on the table, then lit up a cigarette. Her hands were trembling.

Beth Whittsley came out of the bathroom, and Jean ran in.

"Would you care to sign this?" Bonnie asked, looking up for the first time at Alyssa "What's wrong, Matt?" she said. "You're shaking."

Alyssa inhaled deeply, then released the smoke from her lungs in a long, steady stream. It was her first cigarette that day, quite an accomplishment, she was usually on her tenth by third period. She was waging a campaign to cut down, to smoke only during lunch and her free period. She knew she was a nervous smoker, and that she could harness her habit with some willpower.

She looked at Bonnie. "What have you got there?" She read the petition: We, the undersigned, respectfully request that the fourth floor faculty room be thoroughly cleaned before one of us needs exhumation. Then she signed her name under Bonnie's, smiling slightly at the imagery. Leave it to an English teacher, she thought.

Deeply concerned, Bonnie asked her question again. It was most unusual to see Alyssa's even keel disturbed. "Oh, I'll be all right,"

Alyssa said. "I flew into a rage last period and I just need a few minutes to calm down."

Beth Whittsley looked up from the petition. "During class? What happened?" She too was startled at the thought of rage in Alyssa Matthews.

"No, no," Alyssa said. "Play time. Study hall. Some kid told me to go fuck myself and I reverted to a screaming idiot. Hell, I was screaming at the top of my lungs before the obscenity."

"I've had kids tell me that and worse," Beth said. "Don't take it so hard, Matt. It isn't the end of the world."

"I know," Alyssa said, thinking that Beth really didn't understand what was bothering her. "It's just that I never lost control like that before."

"You always have been somewhat of an anomaly. Christ, Alyssa, you had to blow sometime."

"As long as you get back to normal fast," Bonnie said. Then she added, continuing the mock consternation, "Who else is going to listen to the rest of us bitch and moan?"

"That's me, all right," Alyssa smiled weakly. "I'm your typical shoulder. A regular Hetty Pepper." Noticing some confusion over the reference, she added, "O. Henry, 'The Third Ingredient.' I used it all the time with my regents classes until I finally got so frustrated at their inability to see the humor that I stopped. It's impossible to force people into thinking something's funny. Kids are too dense or maybe too shallow to see that kind of humor, I guess. Maybe it's just too dated. I don't know. All I know is I gave up with it. It exhausted me."

"At any rate," Alyssa continued, "I work at being cool, calm, and collected. I hate arguments, I hate confrontations. Because I know what I'm like when I'm angry to the point of hysteria. I lose all my faculties. I can't think, I can't speak rationally, I turn into a maniac. And I hate myself that way. So I developed a calmness that is much more functional than hysteria. And it's served me well. Until today. Today my seams burst. I wish I could drop a bomb on that study hall. I despise it."

Alyssa pressed the stub that was left of her cigarette in the cafeteria bowl that served as an ashtray and lit another. She knew she was chaining and would have lit the second with the first to make it official if she had thought of it in time.

"I'd decimate mine if I could," Beth said. "I've got one girl that I'd like to put through the wall. Angela LoGuasta. And she's no angel. She's got a nasty disposition and a nastier mouth."

"I've got her too!" Alyssa exclaimed. "Second period. She lips off at me every day."

"Well, she's with me third period."

"No wonder she's a beast. God knows how many times a day she sits in study hall. Two periods in a row is bad news. Have you tried detention?"

"Sure. But she just gets meaner."

"Yep. That's been my experience too. And I can't see sending her to ISSR where she'll be waited on. Kids like her enjoy a trip to vacationland."

"Speaking of vacationland," said Beth, "I found a note in my mailbox this morning from McGuinness. It was one of his famous 'see me immediately's,' front-and-center, pronto. I always feel an urge to click my heels and salute when I'm standing in front of that man's desk. Someday I'm going to send *him* a note to see *me* immediately. I wonder how long it will take him to show."

"I wouldn't hold my breath waiting," Bonnie said.

"But you might mention that maneuver to Jean," Alyssa interrupted further, "she usually does what the rest of us dream of doing. I think she'd get a kick out of that one. But go on, sorry we interrupted." Alyssa almost knew what was coming. She never had trouble with any of the administrators and she knew why. But she had heard many a horror tale from others.

"Needless to say," Beth continued, "the trembling subordinate hustled her bustle front and center. And do you know what he had the nerve to ask me to do? He wants me to agree to transpose nine detentions into one day in ISSR for a kid who's been nothing but a pain in the ass since the beginning of school. I've been tracking this kid for weeks and finally caught three truancies. He's the one I kept checking on from your homeroom, Bonnie."

"Ah, yes," Bonnie said, "and you aren't the only one on his tail. I've had requests from his other teachers for his attendance records."

"And Bob wants you to cancel the detentions and put him in ISSR instead," Alyssa said to Beth. "That's pretty sneaky, isn't it?"

"And you know, Matt, he almost caught me. But I didn't agree right away, I told him I'd think about it. And the more I think about it, the more it stinks."

"Why sure," Alyssa said, "nine days of after school detention is much more painful than one day in one room with assignments and lunch delivered. That kid must have really cried the blues to Bob. Either that or Bob knows the family."

"Oh, he does," Beth exclaimed. "He made no bones about that. And the dear boy has a job after school. So I asked Bob to ask the kid why he didn't think about the consequences when he was cutting my class. He's been absent fifteen days already, and I was lucky to catch him at all. He's clever. But I kept with it. And now McGuinness wants *me* to give *him* a break. Ever wonder when it's our turn?"

"Don't do it, Beth," Alyssa said. "That's not the purpose of ISSR. Besides, if you agree, that kid will be running to Bob all year for diaper changes. Of course, it's hard to know just how far Bob is willing to go with this. You might have Bassard to worry about. If the parents call Bassard, which Bob might instruct them to do, Harry might put the pressure on you."

"I know," Beth said resignedly, "all the rhetoric that our disciplinary actions can't be overturned by anyone is nothing more than a huge trick. There is no flagrant reversal. Just pressure to get you to change your own decision. Lord help you if someone decides to take on the kid's defense. I went through a classic case of it last year. I refused to take homework from a kid who was chronically truant. He decided to hand in a paper six weeks late and I wouldn't take it. The kid went right to Bassard who informed me that I had to take the paper. I'll never forget what he put me through. All of a sudden, I was the culprit. Could I prove the kid was truant? Had I sent home notices of absences and progress reports? Bassard put me on a merry-go-round and wouldn't let me off until I accepted that paper. I simply got tired out running back and forth to his office trying to defend myself. While the kid sat back and waited.

"Even when I proved truancies, I didn't have a leg to stand on because school policy dictates that we are required to supply make-up work to truants. In the end, everything was my fault because I hadn't sent the proper forms home at the proper time. When Harry threatened a parent conference, I was at the end of my rope. The whole thing had become so twisted, so blown out of proportion, and the deck was stacked against me."

"Of course," Bonnie injected, "the parents would have claimed that it was your fault they never knew the kid was truant because you never notified them of absences."

"And naturally," Alyssa added, "if they knew, if they only knew, they would have done something about it. You didn't have a chance, lady. So you took the paper?"

"Yes, as humiliating as it was. The kid was cocky as hell, and had every right to be, I guess. And you know, I was terrified to grade that paper. It was perfectly horrible, but I passed it. I was afraid I'd end up on that merry-go-round again …"

The third period bell rang, interrupting Beth's metaphor.

"What are you going to tell Bob today?" Alyssa asked Beth.

"I'm going to refuse. But if he decides to fight me, I'll give in fast. I've learned one lesson about life around here. They'll wear you down to nothing if you let them. Kids, administrators, parents. I'd pass out from shock if I ever heard a word of thanks or praise from anybody."

"Just a small pat on the back would be nice occasionally," Alyssa said, "Not a brass band, but just the clear, concise tinkling of a bell."

"That's beautiful," Bonnie said.

"And completely out of context. C'mon. We're late." Alyssa shoved the remainder of her cigarette into the cafeteria bowl in an attempt to extinguish its glowing tip. But she succeeded only in bending it in half, snuffing out part of its fiery glow. A small part of the tip continued to burn, sending a thin trail of blue-gray smoke into the air.

"You know, Matt, I thought when I started teaching that I was set for all my working life. I don't think that anymore." There was a tinge of sadness in Beth's voice.

"I know what you mean," Alyssa agreed.

"There has to be something better than this," Beth continued. "But we've got too many years invested to get out now. I think our eventual pension would amount to around twelve dollars a month. We've got to make at least twenty years or lose almost everything."

"Eight years to go, Beth."

"And I hope I make it. Every year gets worse. There's got to be something better than this."

"Hey, you two are lucky," Bonnie piped in as they parted in the hall to go to separate classrooms. "Seventeen years and I'm getting the hell out too!

Emission Control

Jean Tevarro wiped the blood from her fingers with pieces of stiff, barely absorbent toilet paper, wondering when budget cuts would eliminate even the stiff stuff. No, they couldn't do that. Toilet paper is a basic human need in a civilized society. They couldn't stop supplying toilet paper. Could they? There was a time when pads were available. Insert a dime and crank. The machine was still on the wall. Empty.

It all depends on one's definition of basic human needs, Jean thought, and one's status when one passes judgment on the needs of others. And finances. If we can't afford to buy it, then you don't need it.

She pulled a tampon out of a zippered compartment in her purse, peeled away the protective paper, and inserted the tip. She was so wet that it slipped in easily. The clots that were passing out of her body had completely saturated the tampon she removed as well as the pad. Her panties were also stained, along with her slacks. But at least the black slacks didn't herald her condition to the world.

She hated the thought of wearing bloodstained clothing for the rest of the day, but she didn't store slacks in the nurse's office. At least the new pad would separate her clothes from her body to some degree. She found the sanitary pad in her purse and saw that it wasn't very sanitary any more. Pens, pencils, and the usual dregs of a woman's purse had soiled it considerably. She wrapped some toilet paper around the pad. It wasn't an unusual maneuver; she used the method whenever she was compelled to keep using a soiled pad. It would have to do until she could get back to the nurse's office. At least she had stemmed the tide. As she pulled up her slacks and tucked in her blouse, she looked in disbelief at what had come out of her. Maybe the doctor was right. Maybe a hysterectomy was the only way to stop it. Yearly D and C's didn't. Queer word, hysterectomy. To cut out what? Hysteria?

She pushed the handle to flush the toilet and waited to be sure that everything disappeared. When she realized that a second flush would be unnecessary, she let herself out of the cubicle. Everyone had left. She washed her hands quickly and attempted to dry them with brown paper that was even less absorbent than the toilet paper that was crinkling to mold itself around the pad between her legs.

She slid her materials off the table top and scooted out the door, glancing quickly at the clock. She was late, but not that late. And her third period class could take care of themselves in a pinch. They were scholarship juniors and in every way deserving of the title.

A Teacher's Prayer

The brisk walk back to her room afforded Alyssa Matthews a chance to regain her composure after the outburst in study hall. The quick stopover in the faculty room allowed her an opportunity to talk about what had happened. She knew she needed to talk about it, to unburden some of the embarrassment.

She knew she shouldn't be, but she was embarrassed by it. The more she tried to divert her mind from what had happened, the more her thoughts returned to that hell-hole of a place, and centered on her irrational screaming in the listening silence.

She played the scene over again, this time with herself reacting calmly and firmly. She could have avoided the confrontation and protected her reputation. If only she had. What is it going to be like in there now? Now that they know they can provoke me to hysteria?

Alyssa Matthews acknowledged the futility of trying to reverse time and found solace in what had become over the years her bastion of strength, her personal prayer: *Study hall doesn't matter. Homeroom doesn't matter. Hall duty doesn't matter. My classes matter. I'm here to teach. I've never had a severe discipline problem in any of my classes. I'm here to teach. I'm here to teach.*

She had only minutes to clear her mind and she was accustomed to the cleansing procedure. *My students deserve the best I can give. If something upsets me, it makes no sense to take out my anger or frustration on them. They should not feel the brunt of my humanness.*

And she would harness her mind, manipulate her nature, to accommodate her primary goal. *Study hall doesn't matter. Homeroom doesn't matter. Hall duty doesn't matter. Nothing matters except my classes. Nothing.*

When she walked into her room third period, she threw her head back as if she had walked blindfolded into a brick wall. The heat was stifling. It filled every space in the room like some kind of monstrous blob trying to wrest control over every inch. Breathing was a chore, very close to an impossibility.

Some students had already opened all the windows in the back of the room to let some of the heat out. Others were fanning themselves with notebooks. One student asked why the heat couldn't be turned off. Another asked why it was on to begin with. Alyssa gave her stock reply. If she requested that the heat be turned off, it would be off forever, or until she cajoled a custodian to turn it back on again.

The thermostat on the wall, the brand-new one with the impressive-looking locked cover, was a joke. It regulated nothing. The heat was either on or it was off. Indefinitely. She had requested that it be on the week before when the temperature dipped and the room was uncomfortably chilly. A custodian did something violent to the heater in the back of the room, and the heat came pouring through. She wasn't about to get it turned off for one day of freak weather, then have to bother the custodian again to beat it back to an active life. Besides, by the time she harnessed a custodian, the day would be over.

One of Mary Gregory's first suggestions was, "Befriend your local custodian," and Alyssa had, but she was also smart enough to realize that too many "urgent" requests would risk his goodwill. Still, she knew the price of an uncomfortable classroom. While she was able to push herself to perform while sweating profusely or shivering uncontrollably, expecting kids to do the same was just not practical. Very often she modified her plans as an act of mercy. How valid is a test taken in such conditions? Can the mind function at full bore if the body is in pain? What happens to the functions of the brain when creature comforts are suspended?

She knew the reactions, she had seen them time and time again: lethargy, inattention, poor performance. Even superior students are affected by physical discomfort. We're all human. Aren't we?

The student who asked why the heat was on to begin with asked his question a second time. He was used to getting answers from his third period teacher. This time, though, she was avoiding any.

Cerberus

She saw him standing in her doorway as soon as she crinkled out the door of the faculty room. Her classroom was only three doors down the hall, which allowed her an immediate glimpse of his brown suit, his administrative form in the shadows.

He stood there, clipboard in hand, one shoulder leaning against the open door, right foot crossing left and casually balanced on its toes. He seemed to be deep in thought, concentrating on whatever was clipped to the piece of molded plastic he held in his hand. Jean knew she was making enough noise in the empty hall at least to raise his head. He was obviously waiting for her.

Janus, she thought.

No, Janus she could handle.

Cerberus. Cerberus was more like it. Radical, liberal, conservative.

Which one today? or this morning? or this minute?

He didn't look up until she was standing directly in front of him. As he lifted his head, his right arm also lifted as if head and arm were connected by a string running under his suit jacket. The arm directed itself to a shirt pocket, then reappeared with a sixth appendage, a gleaming gold pen, personalized yet impersonal.

His body drew itself up to rigidity with a little bounce, the lines of authority pulling him taut and unyielding. His pose, his demeanor, his raised brow, his cold stare, all were indications that a sans-trial verdict was about to be read.

Jean beat down the impulse to walk right by him and into her classroom. He'd only follow her in. Better that he played administrator out in the hall.

"Observing today, Dan?"

"Don't try to evade the issue, Jean. Are you always this late to class?"

"What kind of question is that?"

"The logical one, don't you think? The bell rang, the hall is not exactly overflowing with people, your class is in there waiting."

Jean peered through the doorway. A few students were talking quietly, a few were studying. "That's what they're doing, all right. Waiting. Aren't they extraordinary?" She looked at him brightly.

So she wanted to banter, did she? a little verbal swordplay? Well, he was accomplished in that area himself. She wasn't going to get away with this so easily.

"*How* they're waiting isn't the issue, either," he said, shaking his head a bit and raising an eyebrow. Then he used his gold appendage to record his acute perception. "The very fact that they *are* waiting is the issue. And you know it. And so I will again ask you the logical question: are you always this late to class?"

"There is not a shred of logic in your question, Mr. Dannemore. But there is a great deal of assumption in it. You have already decided that I am *always* late to class. Why have you not considered the possibility that this is an isolated occurrence?"

"Is it?" Ah, she was going to be easy to snare after all.

"Yes, I have three classes in a row in the morning. It's difficult to fit in bathroom privileges sometimes. Think back. Try to remember what it's like to have three classes in a row." As she spoke, she watched the gold appendage bounce and slide, bounce and slide, its gleam threatening to blind her. "Or did you never have to cross your legs in pain, Mr. Dannemore?"

He looked up at her then, in contempt. He liked women soft and pliable, frilly and feminine. This one was prickly and mouthy, entirely too bold for his taste. And he knew what she was trying to do. And she wasn't going to get away with it.

"I would appreciate it if you would keep a civil tongue, Mrs. Tevarro. And an honest one. This is not an isolated occurrence, and you know it. Stop evading the issue and give me the truth."

Jean was instinctively aware that the students in her classroom might have caught on to what was transpiring in the doorway. She felt an urge to end the foolishness quickly. What could he do to her for being late anyway? He would undoubtedly write it up and file it in her personnel folder. So what? She was about to tell him to do just that and leave her in peace. But he had gone too far. If he wanted to lock horns ...

She lowered her voice, "Don't accuse me of lying, Dan. I might consider it if the stakes were high enough, but this piddling shit isn't worth the effort."

He noted the word with a sense of purpose.

"Careful, Jean, you're very close to insubordination. I know it's difficult for you, but try to weigh your words carefully."

She looked at him with new understanding.

Then she spoke slowly and emphatically, the level of her voice no longer a concern, "YOU. CAN. TAKE. THAT PEN. AND STICK IT.

SIDEWAYS. WHERE. IT. DOESN'T. FIT. DAN. There, was that easier for you to get down? Sorry I left out the ASS, but I'm trying to be a lady."

He smiled then. A little corner-of-the-mouth twitch. He had the situation well in hand. "You're not a lady and you are a liar," he said. "Unless the person who called me to complain about your first period class was lying."

"My first period class?"

"That's right. Your students were locked out of the room well into first period this morning. Are you denying it?"

"Somebody called you to complain, huh?"

"Yes." Let's see you wiggle out of this one.

"Anybody I know?"

"I can't tell you that."

"Of course not. Didn't expect you to."

"Please remember that the complaint was made against you. The teacher who complained had every right to do so."

Jean nodded her head toward the closed door across the hall. "Was it Al Rentsen? Were they disturbing his magic act? Or does he have a few new card tricks?"

"You know we can't require students to be on time if teachers aren't. You're avoiding the issue again. Were you or were you not late to class first period?" With a flash, he readied his gold appendage. "I only want the simple truth."

Jean stiffened. She had known all along what he wanted. "Sometimes, Dan, the truth is not simple. Or is that concept too complicated for that pea-brain of yours? Don't answer. Don't say a word. Don't even write. You can write to your heart's content when I'm finished because when I'm finished you'll never forget what I've said.

"You are a pompous fool too caught up in your own importance to see beyond your own self-righteousness. You enjoy raking people over the coals whether they deserve to be or not. The only thing that matters to you is the wielding of your power. You want the issue, now that you've dredged up the decency to clarify it? You want the truth? Well, you're going to get it, buddy, in spades.

"I was late for first period for reasons known to me and Harry Bassard. I promised him I wouldn't talk about it to anyone and you don't even fall into that category. If you're terribly desperate to fill in the blanks on that clipboard, ask Bassard to explain. I am now late for class because you have decided that your top priority for the day is to brand, harass, and intimate me into submission. Previous to this criminal investigation of yours, I was in the bathroom. I was in the bathroom because I was soaked with blood. I have my period. If you do not believe me, for you are a stickler for accuracy, a champion of truth, if you do not believe me, I will be glad to show you proof. Tell me, Mr. Dannemore, do you need to see a bloodied pad in the interests of truth?"

She didn't wait to hear the answer she could see.

"And please use some maturity when you write this up. The word is 'menstruate.' It's more difficult to spell than 'shit' or 'ass' so use a dictionary." She left him standing in a crimson aura of rage as she walked into her classroom and slammed the door shut.

She stood there, with her back leaning against the door, and took a deep breath. Once again she felt a surge of wetness between her legs.

The room was strangely silent.

Then the silence split.

It took her a second to realize that her students were applauding.

Elder Statesmen

Seniors. Alyssa Matthews never wanted to teach seniors. She never had the slimmest desire. Sophomores and juniors were enough of a challenge. Then sophomores and juniors were enough of an accomplishment because they were a continual challenge.

The department already had its master teachers teaching seniors when she started working at BCA, and the policy was continued until those teachers retired and a program of senior electives was instituted. The electives came after Mary Gregory left, mostly because she was not too keen on the idea. It wasn't that she thought the old ways were always best. She simply felt that the complexities attending such an innovation would rise up and create more problems than the innovation was worth. And she was right. Oh, how right she was. But no, she was living in the past, holding on to antiquated philosophies, refusing to modernize. When she retired, proponents of the program got their way. Seniors would have the opportunity to choose their poison.

The senior elective program was exciting to many staff members who viewed it as an opportunity to specialize, to research into areas of personal enjoyment, to break out of the monotony of teaching the same thing year after year. A large part of the department was infected with the excitement of course selection. Sharing what he loves is the ultimate, consummate joy of the teacher.

Under the able direction of Paul Haust, the department worked a magnitude of extra hours to develop twenty-five course outlines and a special curriculum catalog with course descriptions, objectives, and requirements. Locating appropriate texts was the most tedious job teachers faced as they spent time hunting through scores of book catalogs to determine what was available at reasonable cost. While the work was above and beyond the demands of their normal work day, they researched and planned and typed with little ill feeling, for the work was directly related to teaching. And for many, it was a labor of love. When the program went into effect, the labor of love was instantly tarnished by frustration. Mary Gregory's prophecy was fulfilled.

Students did not familiarize themselves with requirements before signing up for classes and counselors balked at the extra duty. Some students never bothered to pre-schedule at all, choosing to wait until the first week of school when they could hop, skip, and jump from course to course to see what was easiest to pass. Why waste time reading the curriculum catalog?

Some seniors managed to avoid attending any class for days because it was so easy to claim that they were in line to see a counselor. Teachers received original class lists that meant nothing because students dropped and added so frequently. Beginning instruction on the first day was an impossibility; beginning during the first week became folly. Once again, scheduling was the culprit reducing an ambitious program to a shambles. Scheduling and human nature

Not willing to be beaten at the sound of the gun, the department fought its way through the debris. Teachers of juniors assumed the duty of educating the future seniors in the intricacies of senior electives. Requirements were tightened; students had to enroll in courses commensurate with ability. The regents student could not slide through easy courses. At least, that was the theory.

While most problems were ironed out over time, the scheduling dilemma would remain indefinitely. Because some classes fill to capacity, closing out interested students, while others remain empty. Because ability levels are tenuous. Because students are students. Because all bodies have to be stuffed somewhere, anywhere, regardless of ability or interest or motivation or desire.

Even after the department's attempt to prepare students for the program, senior elective teachers found themselves facing radically heterogeneous classes. Complaints that students were not able to do difficult work or that students were misplaced for any reason went unanswered. Or those complaints bounced off that concrete wall of scheduling that announced: He Has Nowhere Else To Go. You'll Have To Put Up With Each Other.

The purity of heart that accompanied the creation of senior electives was soon blackened by practicality. The drudgery of keeping records on hopscotching students, the frustration of fighting with counselors and administrators over scheduling, the adamant refusal to lower standards in spite of heterogeneous grouping, soon drained the enthusiasm that sparked the program. Discouragement ran high in the department as teachers recognized that the system was beating them down when the only thing they were trying to do was improve it.

And at that time, the system wasn't done with them yet. As Paul Haust watched his staff dwindle, he saw what was in store for all of them. When the number of teachers involved in teaching seniors no longer corresponded with the number of senior sections, he had to enlist every member of the department to handle the load. And so the system dealt its final blow. The entire program was evaluated and reorganized, some courses were dropped, and some teachers were forced to teach courses they had absolutely no interest in, courses that were written by others. Sharing what he hates is the ultimate, consummate agony of the teacher.

Paul brought Alyssa into the program when he had to blitz everybody into it. Alyssa was not overjoyed; in fact, she was more than a little frightened by the thought of seniors. Not seniors as students, but seniors *per se*. She had heard it more than once in the faculty room.

Pressure. The year Bassard called in Mary Gregory because so many seniors had failed final exams. "What are you doing to my seniors?" he raged.

Pressure. The year all teachers of senior English were required to explain and defend every failure.

Pressure. Seniors must graduate. In spite of themselves. And teacher had better see to it.

The course that Paul gave her included instruction on writing a research paper and study of the works of William Shakespeare. In one semester. She immediately decided that ample time could be allotted to the writing of a paper, but she would have to hammer the Bard into a thimble to do him any justice at all.

Alyssa took on seniors the year the fifth class was added. She was still teaching sophomore regents and sophomore scholarship, so seniors presented her with not only another roomful of students, but with a third preparation as well.

From day one she knew that seniors needed at least twice the amount of time and energy she was able to devote to them. She assumed that the demanding and difficult course would draw only the best students, students willing to work, students with at least average reading and writing abilities. It took her exactly two days to see that her assumption was idiotic at best.

The first time she taught the course she was amazed at what senior elective teachers were tolerating. "They're in and out of there like ping pong balls!" she told Jean. "And I've got kids who never read a word of Shakespeare. How am I supposed to get them through *Hamlet*? And what about the ones with no plans to go to college? Why in the world are they in a course that requires the drudgery of a research paper?" Jean welcomed her to the club, informed her that initiation lasted forever, and Alyssa settled in for a long membership. She soon realized that easier courses filled up fast and her course, along with many others, was a dumping ground for the unscheduled. So she did what she always did; she switched to emergency power, activated her make-the-best-of-it mentality, and surged full speed ahead.

Concentrating on the differences among her students, she steered the course to the middle of the road. She wouldn't lower standards, but she compensated by giving intense classroom instruction. It was exhausting, but it gave everyone an equal chance to pass the course, regardless of ability. How proud she was that she was getting non-regents students through Shakespeare! Some of them couldn't pass a quotes test to save their souls, but they could express basic understanding and show accurate familiarity on an essay test. Why shouldn't they be exposed to great literature? She knew she could get anybody through the course if he worked hard enough and if she worked hard enough. A little voice inside her poked through her persistence every now and then saying, "Don't do it. Let them fail. You'll only get more." But the voice was faint and she squashed it quickly. Every semester the class grew.

It also necessarily came to pass that students on the other end of the scale, exceptionally bright students, had to be weeded out. While she could adequately challenge them with the research paper, they yawned through her teaspoon approach to Shakespeare. Not able to change that approach because the bulk of the class needed it, Alyssa instead tactfully suggested that the one or two superior students move on to one of the accelerated courses the department offered. It broke her heart to send them away to be enjoyed by another teacher, but how could she accommodate their needs too? She had too much to deal with already.

The job would have been easier if all her seniors could write reasonably well, could read with average comprehension. But that just wasn't so. The temptation to rant and rave over inadequate instruction by previous teachers dulled as soon as she realized that some of her own previous students were reappearing in her classroom as seniors. They were as poorly prepared as others. Only she knew that she had given the instruction. She knew she taught the material.

Can any one teacher be held accountable for what a student doesn't learn after he studies his own language for eleven years?

How many teachers does it take to convince a student that he is required to write complete sentences, and how many more to teach him how to do it?

She had said it herself so many times over the years. They absolutely refuse to learn this. They've had it over and over again. Every year since first grade. And they never learned it. And they're not about to learn it now.

As she gave instruction on the procedure for writing a research paper, she agonized over the lack of basic writing skills. It's time to pay the piper, she told them. Now you're supposed to apply what you've learned about your language. If you haven't learned anything, you're in trouble. They were in trouble, all right. She would then spend twenty minutes lecturing on the importance of precision and organization, only to entertain the question that invariably sent her into orbit. "Does spelling count?"

There were times when they pushed her to the brink of madness with their lackadaisical attitude. She had to push and pound, push and pound, first to get them to accept requirements, then to get them to remember. Because every time she graded papers, she saw the same mistakes, the same attempts to fool her. Even after she gave fair warning that yes, she would count words if she had to; yes, she would check to see if references were actually used in the paper; yes, she would count the number of times references were cited in footnotes; yes, she would check for plagiarism; yes, yes, yes, proper forms were required for footnotes and bibliography, note cards and rough draft would be handed in with the final paper, all papers had to be typed, all papers were to be proofread, typographical errors were not acceptable, the due date was carved in stone.

When she saw the precision of form and the depth of content that she struggled for weeks to elicit, she was elated, not only with the combined accomplishment, but also with the fact that good papers took only fifteen to twenty minutes each to grade. Each poor paper raised her blood pressure for forty minutes to an hour.

But still, still they fell back into old ways, still they taunted her with foolish attempts to complete weeks of work at the last minute. One student tried to mask an unacceptably short paper by creating margins larger than the text. Another turned in eight sparsely filled note cards as evidence of lengthy and intense research. Still another copied information verbatim and submitted a paper that reeked of plagiarism, never once considering the fact that the discrepancy between his own style of writing and that of professional writers would highlight his guilt. On and on it went. Padded bibliographies, incorrect form, poor organization, insufficient research, inadequate footnotes, poor expression, grammatical errors, spelling errors. On and on and on.

True, she kept her sense of humor through most of it. The paper that innocently announced "the octopus has four foot long testicles" had her rolling on the floor as she tried to decide which error to attack first. But the comedy never did outweigh the frustration or the tragedy.

Pop Quiz

Alyssa took attendance, marking Jeannette Jadhone and Rita Olivetti absent. Both girls had been in class the day before. Neither had turned in a paper. She double-checked then triple-checked the roll because students were no longer sitting in alphabetical order. Seniors think themselves too mature for assigned seating. Once she matched names with faces, she allowed them that small concession, even though it created the need to triple check.

She called Curtis Holbert up to the desk. He had been absent the day before. "Do you have a slip?" she asked. If he produced an absence slip showing a legal absence, she would have to take his tardy paper without imposing a penalty. She didn't like the idea - faking a legal absence was too easy - but she was teaching in a public school. One look at him told her that she wasn't going to be placed in that position at all. He held no paper. In fact, he offered no excuse. He said: "My homeroom teacher was absent today and the sub was too late to write excuses, so I don't have one. I'll bring it in tomorrow."

1. Is the student telling the truth?

    1) Yes, he is. The entire statement is pure fact.
    2) No, he is not. The entire statement has been fabricated.
    3) Yes, he is. But partially. The homeroom teacher was in fact absent. However, the sub was not late. The student did not provide the sub with an excuse for his full-day absence, therefore the sub did not write out an absence slip.
    4) Yes, he is. But partially. The homeroom teacher was in fact absent. The sub was indeed late. The student, however, had not been absent the day before. He had merely cut his third period class to avoid the embarrassment of not having completed his research paper.
    5) Yes, he is. But partially. The homeroom teacher was in fact absent. However, the sub was not late. The sub had plenty of time to recognize the student's excuse as a forgery and has since referred the matter to the appropriate administrator.

6)

7) Yes, he is. But partially. The homeroom teacher was not absent. In fact the homeroom teacher did write an absence slip, but the student lost it between first and second periods.

8) No, he is not. The homeroom teacher was not absent. The student had cut the day before. He has a forged absence slip in his pocket but chooses not to show it to this teacher.

9) None of the above, but I'm leaning toward # _____.

10) All of the above, except # _____.

2. Will the student bring in the excuse tomorrow?

1) Of course he will.

2) Of course he won't; he already tried that and the sub caught him.

3) Of course he will, but it will be forged.

4) Perhaps he will; it remains to be seen.

5) None of the above, but I've got a nifty answer of my own. (Please write your nifty answer in the space provided on your answer sheet. Please remember that nifty answers should also be brief, as space is limited.)

Alyssa steeled herself for the next question. He had to know it was coming. "Where's your paper? It's already a day late and you've lost ten points."

"I don't have it."

"That's obvious. When do I get it?"

"You can't take points off. I was absent yesterday."

"Why? It would help if I could see an excuse."

"I was sick."

"Oh, I see. Well, Gordy Schatzen had a music lesson yesterday, but he delivered his paper to me anyway."

"He wasn't sick."

And neither were you. "A lot of people worked their tails off to get that paper in on time. Is it fair not to penalize you for being late?"

"The student handbook says we get two days for every day we're out to make up work. I want my two days."

Alyssa Matthews felt the stirrings from second period all over again. This time, though, she was determined not to lose control. She knew what she was up against. She made the effort to speak evenly.

"You've had eight weeks to work on that paper. What makes you think that you can get special dispensation just because you were absent the day it was due? I warned everybody about that."

He held his ground. "I told you, the student handbook. You can't do anything about it. I know my rights."

The stirrings started to rumble. She thought of the day she checked note cards and he had only three, the day she gave an open-book test on bibliography form and he failed it, the entire week she spent giving help with rough drafts and he never produced one. The rumble subsided. It was a desperate attempt, but he was not going to get away with it. Period. She could not let him further his plan by taking every third day off until he finished his paper. That possibility was very much in the offing if she gave in now.

"No, Curt, you are mistaken. You do not have the right to be irresponsible. That rule applies to short-term assignments, tests, and quizzes. Had you done the work required right along, one day's absence for any reason would not have prevented you from handing in a paper, from sending it in yesterday, or at least showing up with it today. I will not accept your reasoning. I suggest that you make every effort to get a paper to me tomorrow. I'm not accepting papers after that. At ten points a day, papers handed in on Monday already failed."

He looked at her, his composure not at all shaken, and said, "Your interpretation of that rule is wrong, totally wrong. I know. I've been through this before." Then he smiled. "Give me a pass to go to the office and I'll bring back some verification for you. It won't take long."

She should have told him to go on his own time. But when she thought of it, it was too late. She had already given him a pass.

3. Read each of the following statements carefully. Decide if each is TRUE or FALSE.

1) The student is clever.
2) The teacher is correct in assuming that the student is trying to hoodwink her.
3) The student deserves to be commended for his offer to help the teacher by gathering information to solve the problem.
4) The teacher is wrong to allow a previous experience to interfere with her handling of the student.

5) The student should not be condemned for demanding his rights.
6) The teacher's control is admirable.
7) The kid's a bum. What I want to know is what are those two girls up to?
8) The teacher is not allowing for individual differences.
9) The student's control is admirable.
10) The teacher lacks compassion.

4. Which of the following is the BEST way to resolve the conflict?

1) The teacher dictates a resolution.
2) The student dictates a resolution.
3) The teacher and the student negotiate a settlement.
4) The conflict is resolved through mediation.

ESSAY

Discuss this confrontation in terms of fairness, justice, and truth. Be very careful in your assessment, for you should avoid contradicting any of your previous answers. Your discussion must deal with fairness as it applies to this particular situation, justice on this same level, and truth as a basis for the two.

Rated X

In the midst of the raucous applause, Jean Tevarro walked to her desk and unloaded her books. She took attendance with a quick look at the back of the room. Three empty seats. No one absent.

She stood there in front of them, then, in the growing silence, and met the stare of twenty-seven pairs of eyes.

She loved this class. Looked forward to it every day. There was something magical in its composition, in its blend of talkers and listeners, the facile and the cautious, the idealistic and the practical, the naive and the worldly. She had been trying to make use of the diversity in novel ways, trying to sharpen existing abilities and promote a crossing over. Draw out a few more listeners, get them to react, to share. Pull back a few talkers who needed to learn how to listen.

Creating a climate for the constructive exchange of ideas is an arduous task, and, in some classes, an impossibility. Jean knew that this class had potential. If she handled them right, they could learn a great deal from each other, all twenty-seven of them. And once she determined her goal, all twenty-seven of them were permanent fixtures in her mind in school and out.

She never even considered starting the day's lesson. So, she thought, this is what is known as pregnant silence. They shouldn't have witnessed that foolishness, but they did. Hear the silence roar.

"I hope you're not waiting for a cute little curtsy," she said. "This isn't exactly Academy Award night. I'm having a bad day and you think it's reason to applaud?"

"That was fantastic!" said one boy, a student with an impetuous nature. His utterance was followed immediately by a chorus proclaiming much the same opinion: "You sure told him" and "He deserved it" and "How could he do that to you?"

After someone made the astute observation that it was the first time all year that teacher was late to this class, the crowd immersed itself in personal accounts of injustice suffered at the hands of authority. One girl proclaimed herself the victim of unfairness because she had to serve one day's detention for being one minute late to another class. Someone else was even later than she, but the other student forged a slip and got away with it.

Jean let them go on, let them skim some of the emotion off the top, before she interrupted to direct the discussion to the substance contained in all of them. She cut in fast when the girl with the detention story ended her narrative with a curt, "Who the hell does he think he is, anyway?"

"Sorry," she said, "that language is not acceptable in this classroom."

The rejoinder was in every face.

"I know I just used it. But I'm not particularly proud of the fact. You weren't supposed to hear it either. Just because you did doesn't give you the right to use profanity in this classroom. I'm authority here and I say no foul language. Not from me, nor from you."

Now how do you like that?

They didn't. And they proceeded to say so.

Why not? Everybody talks that way when they're familiar with each other, when they're relaxed. Don't we have that kind of relationship? You let us speak our minds, why can't we use mild profanity as an emphasis?

She volleyed back and forth with them, first shooting holes in their rationale, then toying with her adamant assertion that she was authority, hoping to elicit a response on that level. But they weren't nibbling at the bait. Instead they insisted on pursuing the lesser topic.

"All right," she finally told them, "is this what you're after?"

She moved to the blackboard and wrote four very large block letters. When she turned around to face them again, she was pleased to see the reaction she wanted. Her plan could have easily backfired.

"Well, isn't this what you have in mind?" she asked. "Tell me, how long would it be before we'd come to this?" She gestured toward the four chalked letters, but didn't pause long enough to allow a response. She knew what one might be, and she was determined to squash it before it was verbalized. "And don't try to tell me that it wouldn't necessarily come to this, that marijuana doesn't always lead to heroin, that if I give you an inch you won't take a mile. Don't try to tell me, much less convince me, that some of you wouldn't sink to this level of language eventually because I've heard many of you use this word. 'Go get your fucking books' you say to each other. How about 'Hurry up and go to your fucking locker' or 'Did you take that fucking test!'. The word is common among students, isn't it? You hear it in movie theaters all the time, you hear it in the halls of this school every day. Do you really want to hear it in this classroom?"

Some students shook their heads from side to side, others gave little physical evidence of mental processes. "What's the matter? Everybody fall asleep?"

Loud and clear, a voice popped out of the middle of the room. "Please erase it." The voice belonged to a girl who usually sat quietly, one who kept her opinions to herself because she hadn't yet developed enough confidence to express them. She felt intimidated by some of the other students, afraid that they would chop her to pieces if she dared to disagree. She had never been in a class like this before. She found it invigorating, but still hesitated to open her mouth. And she was thankful that Mrs. Tevarro never put her on the spot, never tried to force her to respond.

Jean's pulse quickened when the girl made her firm request. She had been waiting for the breakthrough. After the first report card grade, the girl had explained her reticence to become involved in discussions. She thought her grade should have been higher and that her lack of participation was lowering it. Jean explained that that was not the case at all. She knew the girl well enough by then to realize that what was going on in her brain during discussions was far superior to what was coming out of some students' mouths. Take your time, she told the girl, don't feel pressured. Join in when you feel comfortable doing it. And if that's never, so be it.

Please erase it. Jean looked at the girl and saw that she was good for more than three words. "Why?" she asked. The girl never hesitated. "Because I don't like it. I don't like to hear it in the halls, or see it in the bathrooms. I especially don't like it up there. Please erase it."

"I'll be glad to," Jean said. "And thank you, Michelle, for saying what a lot of people were thinking." She picked up an eraser and wiped the word away.

A boy spoke. "Well, I don't think it's all that awful." A girl agreed. Another boy chimed in support. "Yeah, what's the big deal anyway? It's used so much it doesn't even mean anything any more."

Jean saw the color rising in Michelle's face. Don't fail me now, kid. If you clam up, I'll have to take up the gauntlet. Nobody else is willing to. If I do, it won't be the same. Come on, keep going.

"Are you saying that it's okay to do something wrong just because everybody else is doing it?" Michelle stiffened in her seat. "I don't agree with that at all. I think it's offensive to use that word. I don't use it, and I'd rather not hear it, so I stay away from people who do. I feel sorry for anyone who has become so comfortable with that kind of language that he honestly thinks it doesn't even have meaning any more!"

The boy who made the statement bristled. "And who do you think you are to feel sorry for me? That happens to be my opinion."

Rosemary Cania Maio

"I'm sorry," Michelle said, "I didn't mean to pass judgment on you. But don't you see? You were trying to do the same thing. And we're both way off target, anyway. Profanity means different things to different people. Should it or should it not be allowed in this classroom? That's the issue here."

Another girl spoke up, then another, then a boy. Soon most of the room was involved. Jean listened to the reasoning, some of it good, some of it not so good. She listened beyond points at which she normally would have cut in, because Michelle and her supporters were giving the other side some spirited opposition. When the two camps seemed to reach impasse, Jean spoke.

"Some of you have very strong feelings about this," she said, "and some of you are arguing for the sake of arguing. I respect your feelings and I hope that everyone gets so deeply involved next week when we discuss poetry."

Everyone laughed and she continued. "The decision in this matter is not yours to make. It's mine. If you think I'm pulling rank on you, you're right. If you don't like it, it's too bad. I have no control over you outside this classroom. But while you're here you can expect me to try to influence your behavior and your beliefs.

"There was nothing good about the language that I used a while ago, nothing to be admired, nothing to emulate. It's the language of the ignorant, used by the educated in times of anger or frustration or laziness. You may be comfortable using that language with your friends, with your families, or with strangers. I'm pretty free with it myself at times when I'm not even angry or frustrated or lazy.

"But you will not use those words in this classroom. I will not use those words in this classroom. We're all here to learn to be better than that."

She paused a moment to let her words sink in. It crossed her mind that she should have thought to close the door during the confrontation with Dannemore. She'd be giving a nice safe vocabulary test right now.

"By the way, I haven't forgotten your test. You'll get it tomorrow." She knew which students had been attempting to prolong the discussion simply because they hadn't studied. "Now," she said, "I still want to know why you greeted me with applause today when you've never so much as thanked me for all the terrific lectures I've already delivered this year."

They laughed again and she began to maneuver them along the path that they had thus far ignored. Mr. Dannemore had every right to question me. I *was* late. What was it that irritated me and caused all

130

of you to take my side? How do people react when they're backed into a corner? How might you react? Can you understand and accept the fact that others may react differently? How can people with authority best use that authority? What part do emotions play in any confrontation?

As the discussion lengthened, Jean managed to encourage one student to stop and think before he blurted, and to give verbal support to another student who faltered out of shyness. At an appropriate time she directed their attention back to the detention story. Exactly how unfair was that detention? Did the teacher know the other student forged a slip? Would you give the teacher that information? Would it help you any if you did? What's the real gauge of fairness? Does that teacher give detention to everyone who's a minute late without a pass? Then what's the real gauge of fairness? She worked hard to pull the word out of them. Finally someone said it.

The discussion inevitably meandered to Jean's physical condition. Some of the girls blushed. So did some of the boys. Once a few comments were made, the blushing subsided, embarrassment was replaced by objective interest, and twenty-seven adolescents and their teacher discussed a subject that few adults handle maturely in mixed company.

Jean noted the striking fact that the room never separated into two distinct male/female factions. As feelings surfaced, she was pleased that she didn't have to referee a battle of the sexes, that she had little trouble keeping the discussion on a basic plane of human understanding and concern.

Embarrassment crept in now and again and had to be dealt with carefully. Jean didn't want the discussion to end with questions unanswered and views unexpressed. She couldn't allow them to become enmeshed in the quagmire of embarrassment. How could she thereafter convince them that all human concerns are worthy of intelligent discussion? At one point, thanks to TV commercials, the discussion turned to sanitary napkins and douches. Everyone agreed on one thing: they hated those commercials. Then one of the boys wanted to know "just what is that douche thing?". Someone asked him why he hadn't learned that in health class. The boy explained that he was saving health for his senior year. So Jean explained as tactfully as she could, privately reminding herself that all else is suspended when a student sincerely seeks an answer.

By the end of the period, Jean had one last question to throw out for consideration. "You thought it was terrific that I resisted authority. Yet you have accepted my authority over you. Why?"

She asked the question fully confident that they would work through to the core of the answer. They didn't disappoint her. When the bell rang, Jean issued another reminder: nothing will interfere with tomorrow's test!

She spoke with a few students individually as they left the room, knowing that they would continue discussion in small groups during lunch. She overheard Michelle telling another student, "You've got to do more thinking and less talking," and wondered if she might have to come down hard on her some day soon. The transition from lamb to lion might have been too successful, too intoxicating.

When the room was finally empty, Jean sat on a student desk and stared out the window at the glaring sunlight. She mulled over the challenge she faced with her third period class. As a whole the class was like any other class. But she couldn't take the easy way out and deal with them as a whole. She had already allowed their individual natures to awaken, to emerge, and to clash. No easy way out now. Just good old-fashioned hard work. The thought excited her. She hadn't sought out new materials in years. But this class awakened her spirit.

As she left the room to go to lunch, she thought about the scene with Dannemore. What constitutes extreme provocation? A gold pen and an attitude? She could see it all in her personnel folder. When asked a simple question, the teacher responded with gutter language, for example ... The only good thing about it all was that it happened so quickly. Jean Tevarro decided that she was glad about one other circumstance as well. She decided that she was glad she hadn't thought to close the door.

Who's Gayle Fine?

The teacher sitting in the back of the room nodded her head and smiled encouragement to the young girl standing in the front. The young girl was noticeably nervous, her hands shaking slightly around the note cards she held.

Just begin, sweetheart. The first few words are the hardest. You'll find courage as you continue. I graded your paper during lunch yesterday because I knew it would be excellent. It was and so are you. So take your time and work your way out of this anxiety. You're going to be just fine. That's right, get started, hear the first earth-shattering, heart-pounding, isolated sounds of your own voice bounce off the walls. See, it's not so bad after all, is it? Not bouncing off hard walls at all, but being absorbed by warm flesh. That's right, look at me when you need courage. Your friend is trying to make you laugh. I want to kill her too. Just don't look at her and she'll tire of it. Concentrate on what you have to say, don't break your pace.

Go on to the next card. Good. You did that beautifully. Smooth transition. Your voice is leveling off now, you're gaining confidence. Everyone is listening to what you're saying, even your silly friend. Your audience is captivated. And you're not shaking anymore.

The teacher leaned forward, elbows resting on the top of the desk, hands framing her face. She used a nod, a smile, an appropriate grimace, any facial expression necessary to relay her unspoken message: You're doing fine. Keep going. Calm down. I'm pleased with your mere attempt to do this. Anything more is pure delight.

The teacher knew that for most students the entire experience was pure agony, that the very idea of speaking alone for ten minutes was torture of the worst degree. There were times, though, when she wondered if her suffering outweighed theirs. But still she required the activity because the experience was too valuable. She required that they cover the substance of their research findings and share personal experiences. She wanted them to learn from each other's mistakes and triumphs.

The teacher was still smiling when the young girl in the front of the room completed her report with a sigh of relief and a look that said, "That wasn't too painful after all, especially now that it's over!"

The teacher was thankful that one more survived the ordeal. Only once, years ago, did she have to think fast to save a girl who froze solid as soon as she got up to speak. Not a word would come out even when the girl was allowed to sit at her desk. The teacher, not happy about giving the girl a zero, started asking questions. Then the class, in a beautiful burst of human support, started showing interest by asking more questions. The girl slowly thawed and lived through the report. Oddly enough, the girl enrolled in a speech and drama course the next semester. The teacher just shook her head in amazement.

The young girl in the front of the room invited questions and discussion grew around her report.

Just before the bell rang, the teacher commended the day's speakers because they were the first to bite the bullet. Students had randomly selected numbers the day before because it was the only fair way to determine who would speak when; Alyssa checked the list of numbers so that she might remind students four, five, and six to be ready tomorrow. When she saw that Curtis Holbert was number four, his number picked for him by another student the previous day, she notified number seven that he wouldn't have the weekend to prepare as he had planned. By the end of the period Curtis Holbert was still nowhere in sight.

And Gayle Fine hadn't shown at all.

A Slice of ISSR

The in-school suspension room was the end of the road for disciplinary action within the confines of the school. Theoretically the room was the savior emerging out of the multitude. It gave teachers the immediate option of ridding their classrooms of disruptive students without time-consuming referral to administrators. It allowed student and teacher to work together toward an acceptable agreement on proper behavior in the classroom. It allowed the school to keep its problems to itself and boldly announce: We have discipline firmly in hand and we are educating while we discipline. Aren't we the clever ones? It kept more students in school for attendance purposes. Out-of-school suspensions were public costly reminders of the school's failure to do its job. The ISSR was a severe blow to students who actually enjoyed being sent home.

Theoretically the room and the option were well worth the planning, well worth the implementation, well worth continuance. When used as originally intended, the in-school suspension room was a victory for humanism, a vehicle for learning, a raging success. What better way is there for settling disputes than by thoughtful compromise, by rational communication, by constructive interaction? What better way to teach self-control, responsibility, and respect?

The theory was noble in its pristine state, but subject to decay just as all educational policies are, for all educational policies must necessarily blossom within the framework of the human factor. Theories are always pure and chaste before people get their pragmatic way with them. The in-school suspension room was pitted by impurities from the very beginning, in spite of continual attempts to educate everyone on its proper and effective use.

Teachers were warned that the room was to be the last resort after a series of lesser attempts to enforce discipline. Still, some teachers sent students as a punishment for failure to complete homework assignments, and some teachers with low boiling points sent students indiscriminately without a moment's thought to other alternatives.

Students were advised that the room was not punishment at all, but an opportunity for them to think about the behavior that sent them there and to devise a written plan for the modification of that behavior, an acceptable plan the condition of their release. So some students decided that the room was an excellent alternative to attending classes and made a game out of provoking teachers to send them there. Referral to ISSR saved many a student from taking many a test and insured the availability of make-up time for tests and assignments in all classes. ISSR, then, became a familiar haunt for some students and infamy for others.

Administrators demanded that faculty and students strictly adhered to the rules, then proceeded to pass judgment on referrals, pressuring teachers in biased attempts on the behalf of students. Sometimes all three dynamics were in play: administrators abusing their power, teachers misusing the privilege and students manipulating the process. But still, still, in the final analysis, the room was vital. When used for its intended purpose, when used with temperance and care, the room justified its existence.

At the end of third period Alyssa Matthews once again thought about the boy she sent to ISSR. She had packed him neatly in one corner of her mind so that she might function normally with her seniors. Once her seniors left the room, the boy popped out again, laughing and sneering. At the end of third period Alyssa Matthews was more than a little anxious to bury herself in the faculty room for lunch. She had absolutely no desire to see that boy ever again. She didn't have to worry about making peace with him as a foundation for his future learning. He wasn't in one of her classes. She had enough classroom students to worry about.

Damn that study hall.

If only she had kept calm. She could have issued detentions. Now the kid was waiting it out, probably dozing comfortably, and she had to finish what she started. With the faculty room door ten steps away, she was obligated to sprint down four flights of stairs and across two buildings to fill out a form. *The* form required to keep the kid in limbo. Only she had no desire to keep him there. He was missing classes. His teachers may have already received notices to send the day's assignments. His teachers would be inconvenienced, she was not only inconvenienced but exasperated by the whole situation, and the kid wasn't bothered in the least.

The facts had been clear to Alyssa Matthews for a long time. The more the reins were tightened on students, the more they choked teachers. Every single disciplinary move required follow-up. Teachers had to keep checking or detentions might never be served. Teachers had to supply work for students in ISSR. Teachers were required to provide make-up work for proven truants.

A stringent rule was enacted to discourage truancy: Four illegal absences from a full-year course or two illegal absences from a semester course constituted sufficient reason to deny credit for the course. Teachers enthusiastically applauded the rule as a deterrent to truancy. The district finally adopted a policy with some teeth in it. The applause diminished rapidly as teachers realized that the policy was merely nipping at students and gnawing at them. Because teachers shouldered the burden of proof. Teachers had to fill out forms, check homeroom attendance, daily sign-in/sign-out sheets, and attendance in other classes. Teachers had to spot forged slips and excuses. Teachers had to supply detailed documentation to parents and administrators and hope that one or the other or both wouldn't come to the aid of the student with some arbitrary defense. Once the rule was enacted, teachers became truant officers. Gathering data, notifying parents, convincing administrators, proving truancy – all of it became an integral part of the instructional day.

Alyssa decided that she would avoid the paperwork and the follow-up by extracting a quick promise that he would behave in study hall in the future, then send him on his way. He must have calmed down by now, she reasoned to herself, imagining the use of a tranquilizer gun. Besides, he wasn't doing anybody any good in ISSR. She grabbed some papers to grade during lunch. More spelling tests and the vocabulary tests from first period. The room was rapidly filling with students. No, she told one of them, I'm not a substitute, just a leftover from last period. Your teacher will be in soon. Please don't wrench the windows open like that. It makes it very difficult to close them afterward. I don't know why it's so hot in here. Please don't horse around in front of that window, it's a fire escape. Someone could easily fall out and it's a long way down.

She could see that what she said meant little to them. They would do as they pleased when she left. So she left, hoping that their teacher would arrive before they did damage to themselves or to the room.

As she trekked briskly down the hall, she became aware of a body running to catch up with her. She turned and smiled at a familiar face. An astonishingly clear and pretty face when the being behind it decided that the world was full of joy. A muddled, dilapidated, scowling, or defiant face when the being behind it found the world filled with other things.

A Filling of SOS

The only absolute Alyssa could identify in the being was fluctuation. The girl was monumentally moody, her temperament influenced by limitless sensitivity. She was clawing her way through adolescence, a victim of her own intensities. Alyssa had pulled her through many a crisis, sometimes by offering advice, sometimes by just listening.

The girl had begun the year by showing up every morning during homeroom. The teacher didn't have time for amenities much less serious matters during homeroom. At first the girl was upset: Does this mean we can't talk anymore? The teacher was soothing: Of course not. Come see me whenever you want. Except during homeroom, the girl corrected. Except during homeroom, the teacher repeated.

After that the face appeared at least once a day, every day, at times other than during homeroom. Sometimes when the face presented itself for no other reason than to emit a fleeting hello, the teacher knew that the girl was merely reassuring herself that Mrs. Matt was still around, still available, just in case life became unbearable.

While she had helped students with personal problems often enough before, Alyssa never experienced one quite as omnipresent as Cassie Quimly turned out to be. Alyssa slowed her pace. "Good morning," she said. "How's life treating you today, Cassie?" She could have skipped the question. That face. That maskless face.

"Life stinks."

Alyssa smiled. "That it does. On occasion." They walked a few steps. "What's making life particularly smelly today?"

"Everything," Cassie growled.

"That covers a lot of territory. Do you want to go into detail now or wait until you feel like talking?"

"Now."

"All right. We'll have to find a place other than the hall."

The only available possibly-private spot was the resource room. Every classroom was being used. Alyssa just hoped that no one was in the resource room.

They were in luck. Only stacks of books would be privy to this private conversation. "All right," Alyssa said after they both sat, "spill it." "I'm on restriction again."

"For what?"

"I'm failing English."

"How can you be failing English? You did so well last year!"

"I don't like Mrs. Whittsley."

"Why not?"

"She's not like you. She doesn't explain things the way you do. She goes too fast and she yells too much." Oh, Lord, Alyssa thought, even when I succeed I fail. It's such an old, tired story. Why do they have to love teacher to learn? I was no different. Why do humans have to prepare themselves for life, make decisions that critically affect the future while engaged in a roustabout with acne, puberty, and self-image, while battling a universe filled with sinister forces, be they real or imaginary. Adolescence. Blah!

"What do I have to do to get you to knock me off that pedestal you've so conveniently plopped me on?" Alyssa asked. "You're using me as an excuse to dislike Mrs. Whittsley. Do you understand what I'm saying?"

"You were the best teacher I ever had. I learned more from you in one year than I've ever learned from anybody else."

And it's doing you a world of good now, isn't it? Alyssa thought. Idolatry is too soothing to the passionate mind. This cannot go on. "What you learned last year was the result of your work and your intelligence. I may have inspired you to do your best, but the fact remains that *you* followed directions, *you* studied, *you* learned. And *you* can still do all that. I happen to know that Mrs. Whittsley is an excellent teacher. Don't scowl at me like that. It's the truth. Maybe if you'd stop wishing you still had me, you might be able to see it. Have you listened to one thing she's said this year?"

"No," Cassie said petulantly.

"Then how can you blame her for your problems? Learning is a two-way street, you know."

Cassie lowered her head and looked at her hands which were fumbling with the pages of a book. She lifted a corner of the book's brown bag cover and started to tear it back slowly, ever so slowly.

The teacher became determined. She had seen signs of this kind of showdown for some time. She knew what was materializing all along, but could never get a firm enough grasp on anything to arrest the inevitable. At last the growth was large enough to destroy. "Cassie, I can't take you by the hand and lead you for the rest of your life. I don't teach juniors any more, but even if I did, I think I would refuse to have you in my class again."

The bowed head popped up, eyes filling with tears. Alyssa was accustomed to student tears. Time and time again she allowed that form of human reaction to surface and expend itself. Go ahead and cry, she'd say, and then we'll try to work it out. Cassie Quimly had cried before. And sometimes just sharing her tears was the only remedy she needed. But not this time.

Alyssa spoke through the tears, directed her words beyond the ravaged face. "You're too dependent on me. I'd like to think that these sessions are preparing you to take care of your own problems some day. I won't be around forever. Do you plan to run home from college to complain to me about some professor who rubs you the wrong way?"

A tear brimmed over onto Cassie's cheek. "Well, of course not," she said.

"Then stop complaining about Mrs. Whittsley. Start listening to her. Don't expect her to be me because that is an impossibility. Can't you accept the fact that teachers get nervous and angry, that they are sometimes caring and sometimes indifferent, that they have good days and bad days just like everybody else?"

"You never have bad days. You never yell at anybody. I was never afraid to go to your class. I wanted to go."

Just ducky, Alyssa thought, but I'm a freak, child. You'll never see it, but that's what I am. A freak. "I have bad days, too. I just work hard to hide it. Tell me something. Do you think it would be sensible for me to expect all my students to do excellent work all the time?"

"No," Cassie said, "I guess not."

"Then why do you expect all your teachers to be what you think they should be? Mrs. Whittsley has her own methods of teaching and her own personality. You know, sometimes I think that my methods aren't very effective. I tend to be too soft and I know it. Maybe Mrs. Whittsley tends to be too hard. But we are both what we are, and neither one of us can teach any other way. All of my students don't adore me the way you do."

Cassie wiped her eyes with her hand. "That's not true. Everybody thinks you're great."

"Baloney," the teacher said, "you don't know all my students. If I'm so stupendous, why do I have so many students failing? I've got more than my share, believe me. And what did I try to teach you last year about making sweeping generalities?"

Cassie smiled weakly. "You said not to."

"Do you remember the scene in *To Kill A Mockingbird* when Atticus tells Scout that it's really impossible to understand another person without climbing into that person's skin and walking around in it?"

"Yeah," Cassie said, "it's in the beginning of the book."

"Yes, it is. And do you remember the circumstances?"

"Scout was having trouble with her teacher. She didn't want to go to school."

"We discussed that scene at length last year, Cassie. Didn't you learn anything from it?"

"I guess I forgot."

"Well, would you kindly remember? Would you kindly try to understand Mrs. Whittsley before you decide you hate her guts? And would you try real hard to understand yourself?" Cassie nodded in agreement. "I haven't been trying very hard."

"Ah, the dawn," the English teacher said, "the dawn in russet mantle clad."

"That sounds like Shakespeare."

"Glory Hallelujah! Shakespeare it is. From *Hamlet*."

"When do I get to read *Hamlet*?"

"Senior year."

"It's your course, isn't it? Will you- I mean, you won't refuse to let me in, will you?"

"I'll think about it. Right now it doesn't look as though you'll ever be a senior. Not if you don't clean up your act. Have you started *Macbeth* yet?"

"Mrs. Whittsley said second semester."

"So you heard her say that, did you?"

"I never thought I'd like Shakespeare, but I really got into it last year."

"If you thought *Caesar* and *Merchant* were good, wait until you read *Macbeth*. The witches, the prophecies, the reversal between Macbeth and Lady Macbeth. Ambition, guilt, remorse, treachery, murder, slaughter. The sleepwalking scene, Banquo's ghost, the bloody daggers, the water imagery, Macbeth's famous 'Tomorrow, and tomorrow, and tomorrow' speech. And the porter scene when the porter imagines himself doorman at the gates of hell. It's comic relief really, but it comes just after Macbeth murders Duncan, the king, when Macbeth begins his own journey through a living hell to an eternal one. And Lady Macbeth is absolutely fascinating. She attempts to become the personification of evil, but crumbles under the weight of it all. Oh, Cassie, it's a magnificent play. I miss teaching it. You're going to love it."

"Will you help me with it?"

"Absolutely not. You'll get your help from Mrs. Whittsley. By next semester you'll be used to it because right now you're going to promise me that you'll start listening to her and doing your work. Because if you don't, you will continue to fail.

"I want you to change your whole attitude. Don't ever refuse to learn again because you don't like your teacher. I don't care what the subject is, or who the teacher is. It took me a long time to learn that, Cassie. I went through high school like most students, refusing to work for teachers I didn't like. College finally opened my eyes. If you think you've had eccentric teachers here, wait until you get to college. It occurred to me that my distaste for a teacher resulted in nothing more than my own punishment. Who suffers, Cassie? The teacher? Or you? Who ends the year no further ahead? Who doesn't learn? Who isn't prepared for the final exam? Who fails?

"I want you to start thinking about yourself, about your education. Accept Mrs. Whittsley because if you don't you will fail. Do it for you because it is very important for your future that you pass English. Now promise me that you'll give it a try."

"Okay, I'll try. I'd sure like to get off restriction."

"This, you thickheaded wonder, is the way to do it. And maybe then you won't be such a grump all the time."

"I can't wait to get out of high school. Then I'll be too old for restriction. Boy, my mother just won't quit now."

"Oh, you poor baby. My mother used to ground me if I walked in the house five minutes past my curfew. And my curfew was eight o'clock on weeknights and nine o'clock on weekends. I never liked it either, and maybe she was too strict. But now I understand why she worried about me; I don't expect you to understand, you're not old enough. But you can at least consider the fact that your mother disciplines you because she loves you."

The girl responded with the blankest of looks.

"Has that never occurred to you? Do you think she puts you on restriction for kicks or what?"

"I guess not," Cassie said. "It's only when I do something wrong."

"Or when you don't do what you're supposed to do."

"Yeah. I still don't like it."

"You're not supposed to like it. If it makes you feel any better, Cass, adolescence is notoriously miserable. Have you decided what you want to do after high school?"

"College."

"I know that. For what?"

"I want to be a teacher."

"Oh no you don't." The response was immediate and emphatic. "The one thing you don't want to be is a teacher." Please, Lord, spare this one. She hasn't the foggiest notion what she's in for. And she feels too deeply.

"But I like kids," Cassie said. "I love to babysit."

"Teachers are becoming extinct." Alyssa said." There are no jobs. And there's a lot more to it than meets the eye." You want to be just like me, only you don't know the facts, child, and I don't think I can make you see them. Liking kids is no help at all; in fact, it's one big liability. "Well, you still have plenty of time to think about it. Right now I think you'd better get yourself some lunch. I have a few things to do this period also. Just remember your promise and let me know how you're doing."

Cassie repeated that she would try, thanked Alyssa for her time, and walked slowly to the door. She was waiting for Alyssa to join her. The teacher knew and didn't get up. At 11:00 a.m. she was physically and emotionally spent. Cassie would have to make her way to lunch alone. The teacher needed a couple of minutes to rest her brain. "There's one more thing I'd like you to do before you go," Alyssa said. "Please rearrange that miserable face into a smile?" Cassie did and left.

She's a classic, the teacher thought, my very own leather-bound classic. Alyssa continued to think about Cassie and about Beth Whittsley. It had been easy to defend Beth; she was one of the best teachers in the department. But some teachers made it damned difficult to tell a student that he was to blame. Thank God Cassie didn't have one of them. And Mom, dear old restriction-loving Mom. Alyssa never met the woman. For all she knew, dear old Mom might have horns and a tail. Those are the chances you take in this business, she thought. Chances, always chances.

The Second Slice

Alyssa mulled over Cassie Quimly all the way to her previous destination. When she arrived at ISSR, the girl was whisked out of her mind in short order. Alyssa Matthews stood in the doorway and stared.

The room was empty.

She felt her nerves start to shatter, her heart start to pound. Where the hell was he? Did they release him because she hadn't filled out the damn form fast enough? She couldn't just let it go. She pushed on to the main office to see Bassard about it, to try to get some answers.

And she hoped that he was there. If not, she'd be running again, possibly all afternoon, chasing down all the bastards.

The Greek Way

CHARACTERS: BONNIE, English teacher
                    LAINIE, Business teacher
                    JEAN, English teacher
                    JOYCE, French teacher
                    ALYSSA, English teacher
                    CHORUS of twelve citizens

SCENE: A room. A large window taking up two-thirds of the back wall. Ugly drapes are hanging precariously at each end of the window, both sides sagging at the top where hooks have become disengaged from the crooked rod. To the left of the window, a door. When the door is opened, a sink and toilet are revealed. In the middle of the room, a large table, an updated Sophoclean altar surrounded by six heavy wooden chairs. On top of the altar, vessels for libations to the gods: a hot pot, a blue thermos, a red plaid thermos. Between the window and the altar, a davenport resting against the left wall. From the looks of it, it needs to rest. Two hard chairs directly across from the davenport. Upholstery frayed with a gaping hole or two. One chair has an arm in a sling. Filing cabinet nestled between the chairs in phallic simplicity. Two terminal tables fit in where space allows. Ancient lamps with yellowed shades squatting on tables.

Carpet: Dusty. Musty. Dead. Autopsied.

On the left side of the room, in front of the main altar, a duplicating machine sprawled atop a smaller altar. Underneath are stacks of paper, reams of it, and two or three gallon tins of copy fluid. The room is glaringly bright, what with the fluorescent lighting and the colors on the walls. One wall is red, two brilliant orange, one sunny yellow. Very little natural sun filters through the window. The ceiling is dark, dark blue, almost black. A large painting hangs on the wall over the davenport. It is a swirling mass of red and orange. Maybe a comet, maybe the sun, maybe a state of mind. Maybe none of the above. Maybe all.

The women are dressed rather ordinarily. BONNIE, in loose-fitting skirt and jacket, also wears fashion boots, twentieth-century cothurni. JEAN wears black slacks and white blouse; LAINIE, brown slacks and coordinating sweater; JOYCE, powder blue sweater and skirt; ALYSSA, lavender-flowered dress. Each CHORUS member is completely covered in black. Black body suits, skull caps, gloves. Blackened faces. In stark contrast, each wears a white blindfold and earmuffs, a break from tradition. In keeping with tradition, the CHORUS reflects public opinion, twelve citizens offering commentary, counsel, judgments, verdicts.

AS THE CURTAIN RISES, LAINIE is standing in front of the duplicating machine; BONNIE is standing to the right of the main altar, holding books. She has just arrived. JEAN is seated at the main altar, her arms extended, hands positioned on the red plaid thermos. All are frozen in time. The CHORUS, also frozen, is scattered in groups of two or three all over the stage. They may individually assume any posture and may be grouped under the altar, on top of the filing cabinet, on chairs, on top of the window sill, in front of the curtain before it rises, hanging from the ceiling, in any space not taken by other animate or inanimate objects. When the CHORUS speaks, either collectively or as individuals, it does so with appropriate choreography. Movements are slow and deliberate, timeless and universal, and may be individual or collective.

The first sound heard is the steady budda-BUM, budda-BUM of the duplicating machine. It speaks its monotony thirty-two times. Then the women come alive.

BONNIE: All right, who fixed the machine?

LAINIE: Thirty-six, thirty-seven,
               Me!
               Thirty-eight, thirty-nine ...

JEAN: Isn't it nice to have a mechanic
               Around the house?

BONNIE: But it's too late for me. Where were you
               When I needed you, Laine?

LAINIE: -nine, fifty, fifty-one,
               When?
               -two, fifty-three ...

BONNIE: This morning when I gave up on this one
               And ran my legs off. I used the machine
               In C building,

LAINIE: Sixty-one, sixty-two, sixty-three,
            Sixty-four, sixty-five.

            (She hits a button to stop the machine.)

            Oh no, that one's hopeless.

BONNIE: I know. I learned the hard way.

LAINIE: I tried to fix it the other day,
            But I ended up covered with fluid.
            The damn stuff burned a hole through
            My favorite sweater and smeared eight
            Fingers worth of nail polish.

BONNIE: That's what destroyed my master this morning.

LAINIE: Did it get chewed up?

BONNIE: Badly. I had to throw it out.

LAINIE: Well, this one's working now.
            It was just an adjustment. For some reason
            Every fifth sheet still slides through blank,
            So allow for that when you're counting.
            Maybe some day
            I'll figure out how to fix the counter.

JEAN: Have you seen our petition?

LAINIE: No.
            What exercise in futility
            Are we involved in now?

            (She laughs, reads, laughs, signs, laughs, laughs,
            laughs ...)

JEAN: Do I detect a note of sarcasm?

LAINIE: Oh, you do, you do!
            If we don't clean this table,
            The coffee stains get moldy.

(BONNIE walks toward the window. Pulls it open.)

JEAN: It got awfully warm up here
Since this morning.
Or is it me?

BONNIE: The heat's on! Didn't you
Notice it in your room?

JEAN: Come to think of it, it was a little
Warm in there last period.

LAINIE: Why the hell is the heat on today?
It must be close to seventy degrees outside.

JEAN: For the same reason that the heat
ISN'T on
When it's twenty.

(BONNIE picks up a brown bag on the window sill,
then drops it quickly, pulling back in disgust.)

BONNIE: Oh my God. OH MY GOD!
My lunch
Is crawling
With ants!

JEAN: Why did you put it there?
We deal in certain absolutes
Around here:
Grades are issued every six weeks.
Attendance is taken in every class.
Exams are given in January and June.
There's no such thing as a lost exam.
We always get ants when it's warm.

BONNIE: But it's been cold.

JEAN: Not today.
Get with the program.

(LAINIE calls out from the sink where she is filling the hot pot with water.)

LAINIE: I've got instant soup and some crackers. Join me.

JEAN: Make sure you run that water long enough
                 Or you'll be drinking rust.

BONNIE: Thanks, I'd love a cup of rus-er,
                  Soup.

(LAINIE sets the hot pot on an altar and plugs it in.)

JEAN: How about getting rid of
                 Your ant-infested lunch?

BONNIE: I'm not touching it.
                  Why spread the ants?

JEAN: You mean you haven't noticed
                 The little buggers
                 Crawling on the rug?

LAINIE: Stop it, Jean, you're making me itch.

BONNIE: It'll be cold again soon
                  And they'll go away.
                  Hibernate, or whatever ants do.
                  This is just one last fling.
                  Indian Summer doesn't last forever.

LAINIE: Unfortunately,
                 For us and the ants.

BONNIE: I know.
                  I dread winter this year.

JEAN: They're predicting a lot of snow.

LAINIE: So what else is new?

BONNIE: Wouldn't it be grand if we could just

149

Pole vault over winter,
Fly from October to May
In one fell swoop?

JEAN: Stop wishing your life away.
You're too young
To wish your life away like that.

LAINIE: Look who's talking.
I seem to recall a little something
You're fond of saying
Every day of the week.

JEAN: Is it June yet?

LAINIE: There.
Isn't that wishing your life away?

JEAN: Touché.
But I'm an old lady
And there are certain privileges that
Come with age.
Still, I used to wait until
March or April to say it.

LAINIE: When did you start this year?

JEAN: The first day of school.

BONNIE: Hey! Maybe I should pick up that bag
With two fingers and drop it on Bassard's desk
With our petition.

JEAN: Ah ... no. Not today.
He's had enough trouble today with
Droppings on desks.

LAINIE: What's that
Supposed to mean?

JEAN: Nothing.

BONNIE: Since when
            Do you say anything
            That means nothing?

JEAN: Since now. Forget it. Forget I said it.

BONNIE: Then I should do it?

JEAN: Do anything you want,
            Brave one.

BONNIE: God, what if
            They were cockroaches?

LAINIE: Would you please get off
            The creepy crawlies?
            I don't want to be looking
            For extra meat in my soup.

BONNIE: I wonder where Matt is,
            She's usually here by now.

JEAN: And Joyce. She's in school.
            I saw her this morning.

LAINIE: The water's ready, Bon.
            Do you have a cup you can
            Make your soup in?

BONNIE: No, damn it. Wait!
            Maybe there's one left over from last year.

            (She checks the top drawer of the filing cabinet
            and pulls out a ceramic mug with a broken
            handle.)

            Here's one ... wounded, but willing to serve.

JEAN: You'd better scrub it. The treasures
            In that drawer are ancient.
            Probably carrying bubonic plague.

151

(BONNIE carries the cup to the sink and starts maneuvering faucet handles.)

BONNIE: How come this powdered soap
            Takes your skin off,
            But it won't touch the stains in this cup?

LAINIE: Speaking of soap, whatever happened to
            The bar soap I brought in?

JEAN: You didn't nail it down.

            (BONNIE returns to the main altar to make her soap ... rust ... SOUP!)

BONNIE: That sink must be a hundred years old.
            It isn't easy to mix
            The hot and the cold when they're coming out of
            Separate faucets.

JEAN: So what's to mix?
            There isn't any hot.

BONNIE: Son-of -a-gun.
            All this time I thought I just didn't wait
            long enough for it
            To get to the fourth floor.

            (BONNIE sips her soap ... soup ... SOP!)

LAINIE: There.
            Isn't that soothing? Nothing like hot soup
            To cure what ails you.
            Have some crackers.

JEAN: You sound like my mother.

LAINIE: Or any mother.
            And what's that you're drinking?
            Tequila?

JEAN: It should be,

The way I feel. But it's not.
It's soup.
My insides are mangled today.
It's plug and mattress time.

BONNIE: I'm due in a couple of days myself.
            I guess that's why I'm so jittery.
            Do you get miserable before?

JEAN: Hell, no.
            Vicious. I get vicious.
            I want to kill
            Anything in sight.
            Attack.
            Pillage.
            Destroy.

LAINIE: Sounds about right.
            I'm on the verge of tears
            Every minute
            For about a week.
            If my husband looks at me sideways
            I cry.

JEAN: Do you try to fight it?

LAINIE: All the time.
            But it's hard.
            Easier said than done, anyway.

BONNIE: I get depressed sometimes.
            But it's the swelling
            That drives me mad.
            I can hardly wear shoes. In fact,
            That's why I'm wearing boots today.
            They give more than my shoes.
            Regardless of the warm weather.

JEAN: I read somewhere that even the depression
            Is purely physical.
            Water builds up on the brain,
            Just as it bloats the rest of the body.

Rosemary Cania Maio

> Taking a diuretic helps.

LAINIE: I didn't know that.
I always feel so guilty
After I explode over nothing.
My husband never could understand
Why I become so sensitive.
And I don't think it will help much
If I tell him it's water on the brain.
Maybe I should try water pills.

JEAN: Your doctor never suggested them?

LAINIE: I never complained to him
About the bloating.
Haven't seen him
In five years anyway.

BONNIE: Not even for a pap smear?

LAINIE: I hate those stirrups.

JEAN: That has nothing to do with it.
There isn't a woman alive
Who enjoys the experience.

LAINIE: Well, I've been thinking about
Making an appointment.
My husband
Is getting tired of my moods.
I'm impossible to live with for a week,
Then flowing for a week.
That's half of every month.
He thinks he suffers.
He should be on my end of it.
I told him that once,
But it didn't make any difference.

JEAN: How I wish every man on earth
Could go through it once.
Just once.
All of them together.

154

What a scenario that would be.
Send them all off to work
With their insides gushing out,
With stabs of pain splitting their guts.

BONNIE: Clots and cramps,
Pads and plugs.

LAINIE: And then looking forward to an encore
In twenty-eight days.
Good old Eve sure did a job on us,
Didn't she?

JEAN: She just suffers the notoriety
Of being the first.
Adam was just as weak, if not weaker,
For succumbing to her. Right?
What I want to know is
Why didn't God inflict some
Eternal punishment on men
After Cain killed Abel?

LAINIE: Now there's a good one
For the theologians.

JEAN: Theologians, hell,
Can't you figure it out?
Women's lib is a few billion years
Too late.
Helen Reddy was not only presumptuous,
She was wrong.
God's a man.
There's no doubt about it.

LAINIE: Have you notified Gloria Steinem?
I mean, what chance have we got
If the Big Boss is against us?

JEAN: Oh, He's not against us.
Or maybe He is.
I don't know, and I suppose
I shouldn't complain.

The man in my life is kind and thoughtful.
I can't help but think, though,
That he's an exception.
I had a run-in with the rule this morning.
I was late to class last period because
I was soaking through everything and
Absolutely had to change.
Dannemore was waiting in my doorway.

BONNIE: Oh, no, I live in fear
Of seeing someone waiting in the doorway
After the bell rings.
What kind of mood was he in?

JEAN: Ugly. Sneaky, underhanded ugly.
Normal, actually, for him.
Making secret notes on his goddam clipboard,
Sneering in that self-righteous way of his
As if he'd caught me chewing on the Apple.
Someone lodged a complaint, or so he said,
So I explained that I have three classes in a row
In the morning and had to use the bathroom.
That should have been enough,
But it didn't satisfy his thirst for blood.
So I offered to show him some.

BONNIE: Literally?!?!

LAINIE: You didn't tell him …

JEAN: Yes, I'm afraid I did.
I stopped making apologies for getting my period
Years ago. Neither man nor woman will ever again
Embarrass me over it. His face turned red,
Not mine.

BONNIE: My God, Jean, where do you get the nerve?
Lord knows he deserved it,
But I could never be that bold.

LAINIE: Me either, but I love it!
He came right into my classroom a few weeks ago

156

And started yelling at me over something.
What the hell was it? I can't even remember,
That's how important it was ... Oh, yes,
Now I've got it. I blocked it out.
He wanted to know
Why I wasn't reporting to study hall.
He stood there and reprimanded me
In front of my class.
I protested that I certainly was
Reporting to study hall.
Then he ordered me
To see him later to straighten it out.
Come to find out, he never noted in his records
That he changed my study hall
The first week of school.

BONNIE: And the jerk was looking for you
            In the first assignment.
            It figures.

LAINIE: Oh, how apologetic he turned
            In the privacy of his office.
            I thought of inviting him for an encore
            In front of my class, but I was so upset
            I just wanted to end the whole thing
            And forget about it.
            I'm thrilled that you gave him a dose
            Of his own medicine, Jean.

JEAN: Well, he made me angry, and I'm not in the habit
            Of swallowing my words,
            Even though my big mouth
            Gets me into trouble sometimes.
            I'm glad I did it, though I doubt that it will
            Change him even a tiny bit.
            I suppose the thing that disturbs me most
            About Danny-boy
            Is that he never ever confronts a man.
            Here I go again: poor abused womanhood.
            But the fact remains
            You'll never see him walk into a man's classroom
            Reading the riot act.

BONNIE: You know, you're right.
            There was a ruckus in the hall the other day
            During fifth period.
            My kids were trying to concentrate on a quiz,
            So I looked out,
            Expecting to see students from lunch
            To chase away.
            But there were no students, there were three men:
            Courtman and Rentsen,
            Both have classes that period,
            And Dannemore. All were laughing and talking.
            I can't imagine that he was telling them
            To get back to class.

JEAN: I've seen him walk right by noisy classrooms
            If the missing teacher was a man.
            He knows he can intimidate women,
            But the men tell him to go to hell.

LAINIE: Well, he won't try to intimidate you any more.

JEAN: Don't bet on it.
            I'm a little intimidated right now.
            There are too many subtle
            Forms of revenge around here,
            Too many ways they can get you,
            Subtle and otherwise,
            For me to feel smug.

BONNIE: Did I ever tell you what he did to me last year
            When I sent two boys to his office
            For fighting in class?

JEAN: I don't think so.

BONNIE: You'd remember if I did.
            The boys were more rowdy than violent.
            They just needed a talking to, I thought.
            Dan talked to them all right.
            He told them they should behave
            Because I was the nervous type.

JEAN: Excellent reasoning.

BONNIE: And I was nervous because
I hadn't found a man yet.

JEAN: You're kidding.

BONNIE: Those boys couldn't wait to relay the message.
I was livid.
Not to mention embarrassed.
My two fighters never fought again
Because they found a better form of entertainment.
Luckily they tired quickly, I only suffered
A couple of months.
Are you tired today, Miss Mason, or just horny?
Are you really mad at us
Because we failed the test,
Or is it because you're horny?
What's the matter, Miss Mason?
Didn't get it last night?
I had to grit my teeth and handle the whole thing
As if it was a colossal joke.
If they ever realized it bothered me ...

LAINIE: A woman without a man is like a
Horse without a saddle.

JEAN: Did you ever tell Dannemore
That your marital status
Has nothing to do with this job?

BONNIE: Hell, no, what good would that have done?
And I'll never send another student to him, either.
That's probably part of his strategy anyway.
Alyssa told me
When I first stepped foot in this place
To handle my own problems.
I had to learn the hard way.
Besides, I'm the token spinster.
At least once a week somebody asks me
Why I'm not married yet.

I should start to get creative with answers.
Maybe next time I'll say I'm not interested
In men any more and might try women.
Or Saint Bernards.

JEAN: Don't be surprised
If that's the next rumor regardless.
This whole place was in a tizzy
When you were dating Haywood.
People had you two
Living together, secretly married,
And more than one nasty mind
Was counting months.

BONNIE: The token bachelor and the token spinster.
What a pair.

JEAN: Interesting that single men are bachelors
And single women are spinsters.
What a mean, wretched, nasty-sounding word.
Or, if you like, pick old maid or divorcee.
Semantic discrimination.

BONNIE: Are we back to Eve again?

JEAN: What's that you're working on, Lainie?
It looks like a crazy crossword puzzle.

LAINIE: This mindboggling masterpiece
Is the State's latest attempt
To drive us to the brink of insanity.
I have to keep a chart like
This for every one of my students
To record progress toward competency.
Look at this. For Typing I there are three levels:
Level two
Level three
Level four ...

BONNIE: Why isn't it levels one, two, and three?

LAINIE: Don't ask stupid questions.

This is from the almighty State.

JEAN: And only the Almighty knows the answer.

LAINIE: For each level there are three problems:
Level two
    Problem one
    Problem two
    Problem three
Level three
    Problem one
    Problem two
    Problem three
Level four
    Problem one
    Problem two
    Problem three

BONNIE: That's better.

LAINIE: And for each problem there are three forms:
Level two
    Problem one
        Form A
        Form B
        Form C
    Problem two
        Form A
        Form B
        Form C
    Problem three
        Form A
        Form B
        Form C
Level three
    Problem one
        Form A
        Form B
        Form C
    Problem two
        Form A
        Form B

```
                    Form C
            Problem three
                    Form A
                    Form B
                    Form C
        Level four
            Problem one
                    Form A
                    Form B
                    Form C
            Problem two
                    Form A
                    Form B
                    Form C
            Problem three
                    Form A
                    Form B
                    Form C
```

BONNIE: That's worse.
Unless, of course, it was B, C, and D.

LAINIE: A student starts at level two, problem one, form A.
If she fails,
She goes to level two, problem one, form B.
If she still fails,
She goes to level two, problem one, form C.

BONNIE: And if she can't pass after three tries
At the same kind of problem,
There's little hope.

JEAN: My, my, what we will go through
To eliminate failures.
It's the paper equivalent
Of a cat-o'-nine-tails for the kid who cares,
And a long-running cop-out
For the kid who doesn't.
The State claims that it's insuring competency
With rigid standards and individual attention,
And teacher is pulling her hair out.

BONNIE: Christ, Lainie, every kid is at a different level
           All the time.

LAINIE: Ergo these charts, which, by the way,
           Are my creation.
           Cute, isn't it?
           And there's more.
           Typing II has levels five, six, and seven.
           Level five has problems one, two, and three
           With forms A and B for each problem.
           Level six has problems one, two, and three
           With forms A and B for each problem.
           Level seven has problems one and two
           With forms A and B for each problem.
           I have to spend a week out of every month on this
           And keep these charts and folders all year.
           I've had to eliminate part of the curriculum
           To fit in all this extra activity.
           I feel like I'm on a trolley to the madhouse.

BONNIE: And I thought we had competency problems.
           I wouldn't want to have to keep track of all that.

LAINIE: It's murder, believe me.
           And every time a new set of problems
           Arrives from Albany,
           I fly into a rage. They don't know
           What the hell they're doing.
           Mistakes are everywhere,
           In the problems, in the directions.
           And the kids don't help at all.
           If I don't beg and badger,
           Some of them would never bother
           To reschedule when they fail.
           I have to give make-ups
           Whenever I can grab a kid during the day.
           I can't waste too much class time with this crap.

JEAN: There's always the specter of the noose, hanging,
           Ready to be tightened around your neck.
           Tell me something, Lainie.
           Do you ever wish

163

You had gone into secretarial work?
Instead of this rat race?
A nice quiet office somewhere. Think of it.
Typing, filing, paperwork.
About one-third of what you're doing now
If you eliminate the kids
And the papers to grade every night.
No kids to worry over, to push, to tolerate.
Hell, even a not-so-nice, noisy office
Would be less hassle, less commitment.

LAINIE: I never thought much about it.
I always wanted to be a teacher.
I saw something ... I don't know ...
Noble, I guess it was, about teaching.

BONNIE: Doesn't everybody start out that way?

LAINIE: I suppose so. All I ever needed
Were a few topnotch girls
To keep me fired up.
But I'm getting fewer and fewer excellent students.
I haven't got a one this year.
It's discouraging
To beat your head against the wall all day
And end up with nothing but bumps on your head.

BONNIE: Something has happened to student attitude.
Even I can see it,
And I haven't been around
As long as either of you.
Kids don't want to give that extra push any more.
They're too involved in figuring out
How to slide through gracefully.

JEAN: I wish I had other skills to fall back on, Lainie.
At least you're trained to do something else
If you should ever decide to.

LAINIE: Oh, God, I'm so rusty.
But I should be able to build up my speed again.
When I graduated from college,

I could take shorthand at 130 words a minute.
Believe me, that's wicked fast.
And I was typing 110 words a minute
With accuracy.
My typing teacher told me
She never had a student type
Beyond 125 words a minute,
So of course I had to do it for her.
I jammed the machine.
But I did it.

JEAN: And to think that somebody once said,
"He who can, does. He who cannot, teaches,"

LAINIE: I've heard that before.
Who said it?

JEAN: George Bernard Shaw.
He was, many think, a brilliant man.

LAINIE: Well, I think he was an idiot.

(The women freeze. The CHORUS comes alive,)

1st CITIZEN: I hated school, I hated books, I hated teachers'
Dirty looks.

2nd CITIZEN: Me too.

1st CITIZEN: I hated reading,
Hated math,
I wanted out,
An' got out fast.

2nd CITIZEN: Me too.

1st CITIZEN: I counted minutes endless minutes
Endless hours endless days.
Whata useless worthless waste.
Endless minutes endless hours
Endless days...

2nd CITIZEN: Me too.

1st CITIZEN:
I won't force my kids
Ta go through that hell.
Freedom comes at sixteen
An' I tell 'em that.
I'm happy enough
Ta use my back.

2nd CITIZEN: Me too.

1st CITIZEN:
All that crap 'bout learnin'
Never did me no good.
Who cares 'bout fancy numbers?
X's and Y' s?
Two plus two makes four.
Four take away two makes two.
Why do I need any more?
Who cares 'bout fancy words,
I don' need no fancy words here.
The boss ain't never yet asked me
Fer a fancy word.

2nd CITIZEN: Me too.

1st CITIZEN:
I feed my family, pay my bills,
Got no problems.
I'm happy even though
I hated school.

2nd CITIZEN: Me too.

1st CITIZEN:
I'm happy I tell you …
Satisfied.
What mores there to life
'Cept going to work every day
And havin' a beer on the weekend.
It's 'nough for me, it's 'nough!
It's the wife she complains.
Not 'nougha this, not 'nougha that.
The kids need shoes.
The kids need clothes.

The kids need, need, need.
The bills are high.
The house is old.
Sometimes ...
Sometimes I hate the wife and kids
The way I hated school.

2nd CITIZEN: Me too.

1st CITIZEN: I'd make more money if I could,
I like to give my family things.
Not just what they need.
I'd like to give 'em what they want.
Me, I don' need nothin', I don' want nothin'.
But my family, well, that's somethin' else.
It ain't my fault I'm doing this, it ain't.
Lotsa people hate school.
It ain't my fault I'm doing this
Just 'cause I hated school.

2nd CITIZEN: Me too.

1st CITIZEN: I never had a teacher good 'nough
To make me like it.
Ain't that what they're suppose to do?
Make ya like it?
Ain't that their job?
They was all boring, dull, and mean,
Waitin', just waitin' to see me fail.
They loved it they did when I failed.
Well, I dint dis'point any of 'em.
Who cares 'bout history anyway?
Dead people and all them facts.
Mem'rize this and mem'rize that.
Who cares 'bout dead people and wars?
Who cares?
Who cares how the resta the world talks?
Waste a time.
I'm never gonna talk with no foreigner.
My daughter she comes home
Sayin' all these weird words.
For what?

167

She ain't never
Gonna talk to no foreigner neither.
It's just a goddam waste a time.
That's what I think.

2nd CITIZEN: Me too.

1st CITIZEN: Still ... maybe ...
Nobody ever made me care.
Maybe if they gave some time to kids like me
Insteada always to the smart ones.
Boy, they like the smart ones.
And the ass kissers.
I ain't smart and I ain't no ass kisser.
Wouldn't ya think
That somebody woulda made me care?

2nd CITIZEN: Dunno.

1st CITIZEN: Whadda 'bout you?
You been working here almost forever.
School was bad even a hunnerd years ago?

2nd CITIZEN: Yup.

1st CITIZEN: You survived all this time
Without no big education.
When ya gonna retire?
Ain't it 'bout time?
'Cause when ya do, ya know,
I won' get laid off no more.

2nd CITIZEN: Soon.

1st CITIZEN: Well, hooray fer you.
An' hooray fer me.
I'll feel better then.

2nd CITIZEN: How old're you, boy?

1st CITIZEN: Twenty-two.

2nd CITIZEN: I know this is a waste of breath,
I was twenty-two once, so I know.
Don't spend the next forty years doing this.

1st CITIZEN: Forty years?
Forty years?
I use to count the minutes.

2nd CITIZEN: Me too.

3rd CITIZEN: Did you see the evening news?
Those damn teachers are at it again.
They want another raise in pay.
And you know what that means.
Well, I can't afford it.
They make a fortune already.
A fortune.
And for doing what, I ask you.
For doing what?
Handing out papers?
Giving tests?
Talking?
Assigning homework?
It wasn't very long ago when I was in school.
The way I remember it, I did all the work.
What could be easier than a teacher's job?

4th CITIZEN: They watch while students sweat over tests.

5th CITIZEN: They only work a hundred eighty days a year.

6th CITIZEN: They talk about nothing all day.

7th CITIZEN: They only work a hundred eighty days a year.

8th CITIZEN: They teach the same thing year after year.

9th CITIZEN: They only work a hundred eighty days a year.

10th CITIZEN: They have all summer off. All summer!
Who else has all summer off?

3rd CITIZEN: Hell, they don't work,
                    They play a hundred eighty days a year.
                    You want to be a kid again? Be a teacher!
                    I just want to know, if they have it so tough,
                    How do they find time to sell cars?

4th CITIZEN: And paint houses?

5th CITIZEN: Sell real estate?

6th CITIZEN: And run restaurants?

7th CITIZEN: Sell vacuum cleaners?

8th CITIZEN: And work in stores?

9th CITIZEN: My barber is a teacher.

10th CITIZEN: So is my TV repairman!

3rd CITIZEN: And they've got the nerve to want more pay.
                    It's disgraceful, that's what it is.
                    The rest of us
                    Have to scrimp to make ends meet.
                    Why shouldn't they?
                    It isn't fair that my taxes should go up
                    To give them money for luxuries.
                    I will not pay any more.
                    In all my years of schooling,
                    I had only one good teacher.
                    Only one who cared about me.
                    The rest went from bad to worse.
                    Do you remember old B. O. Baxter?

4th CITIZEN: Fashion Plate Farnsworth?

5th CITIZEN: Nervous Nellie?

6th CITIZEN: Chesty Powers?

7th CITIZEN: Nearsighted Singleton?

8th CITIZEN: Bad Breath Bumply?

9th CITIZEN: The Crying Nun?

10th CITIZEN: The Duck?

3rd CITIZEN: Remember Shakey Shivers? He was a real Mental case.

4th CITIZEN: And The Beauty Queen?
I wonder if she ever did pose for *Playboy*.
She sure had the body for it.

5th CITIZEN: My friend said he saw the issue!
He said it sure looked like her
Even though her hair was a different color.
Hell, she could've changed that.
And she was, like, ten years younger.
So it could've been her. Yessir,
It probably was her.
That's what my friend said.

6th CITIZEN: You remember how we used to harass
That jerk we had senior year?
And he never knew
We were making a fool out of him.

7th CITIZEN: Yeah, remember when we told him
There was an emergency call for
Him in the office
And he ran all the way down there?
And while he was gone we skipped out!
Ah, those were the days ...

8th CITIZEN: Remember how we used to get to
Old Lady Lipply?

9th CITIZEN: She cried so easy she must have had
A faucet in her head.

10th CITIZEN: And we worked the handle!
Yessiree, those were the days.

We sure had some good times.

3rd CITIZEN: I had a teacher once who

4th CITIZEN: Failed me when I deserved to pass!

5th CITIZEN: Sent me to the office for talking when I wasn't
The only one who was talking!

6th CITIZEN: Embarrassed me to tears.

7th CITIZEN: Hit me!

8th CITIZEN: Pulled my hair!

9th CITIZEN: Put gum on my nose!

10th CITIZEN: Lost my test and made me take another one.
I failed the second one
But I know I passed the first one!

3rd CITIZEN: I was at a PTA meeting last week
And we were discussing what we should do
With some extra funds we'd accumulated.
One of the mothers suggested
A gift for the teacher.
Well, I tell you, I was appalled!
The teacher gets paid doesn't she?
That's what I said, the teacher gets paid.
Well.
Come to find out …
The mother who made the suggestion
IS A TEACHER!
Now how do you like that?
Just how do you like that?
Do they stick together or
Do they stick together?
It's disgusting, simply disgusting.
Don't you agree?

11th CITIZEN: My potential for academic excellence
Was a combination of inherited traits

Passing through generations of genius
On both sides of my family tree.
There was brilliance in my genes
From the moment I was conceived.
Coupled with inbred intelligence,
A constant exposure to probing
Developed my extraordinary mind.
I was miles above other students,
And always towered over my teachers.
I never had a teacher who could offer me
A sufficient challenge.
They were always so involved
With the average and the dummies.

12th CITIZEN: That was my educational experience
During my pre-college years.
Then later I found some college professors
Seriously deficient in intellectual prowess.
When I reflect on it all, I invariably
Reach the same conclusion:
Whatever I learned, I learned myself
Through my own drive and direction,
In my own way.
No teacher ever made a difference
Or even a small contribution
To the development of my intellect.
Oh, I thought so along the way, as a child.
Every now and then I had a teacher
Who was entertaining or witty or clever,
A teacher I liked.
Most of the time
I merely tolerated their stupidities,
Played their little games,
And kept my mouth shut.

11th CITIZEN: I was a precocious child and as such
Found my advanced intelligence
Constantly thwarted, trampled on
By teachers obsessed with uniformity.
And nothing has changed in the schools.
My children are gifted; they are experiencing
The same treatment.

Teachers still stifle creativity
And reward mediocrity.
Students are pigeonholed and labeled
To fit into the system.

12th CITIZEN: When the system should mold itself
Around its brightest stars,
Adapt to fulfill the needs of the gifted,
Even at the expense of lesser minds,
Minds that will never
Amount to anything anyway.

11th CITIZEN: I say if a student doesn't want an education,
If he's too disruptive or too stupid to learn,
Then throw him out.
Get rid of the brainless.
Make way for the elite.

12th CITIZEN: It's time for a revolution in the schools.
It's time for teachers to be held accountable
For the progress of their students.
It's time for special programs for the gifted.
They've been ignored long enough.

(The CHORUS freezes. The women come alive.
JOYCE enters carrying a pile of books and papers
that would weigh down Atlas. She drops the pile
on the main altar and pushes it to the side.)

BONNIE: How about using a grocery cart?
I thought English teachers
Carried a lot of books around,
But you've got everybody beat.

JOYCE: I can't help it!
I lost my room when I went on leave.
Don't have any kids, girls.
You get maternity leave,
Then you get screwed to the wall
When you come back.

LAINIE: It's your department, isn't it? Staff cuts?

JOYCE: I suppose so. All I know is
I went on leave a French teacher
And now I'm teaching Spanish and Latin.

BONNIE: They cut your French position?

JOYCE: And told me I'd pick up the slack in Spanish
And replace Agnes Martin.
Or be laid off.
Agnes was one hell of a Latin teacher.
They pressured her into retiring
Because she wouldn't teach
The overflow in Spanish.

JEAN: A language teacher is a language teacher is a ...

JOYCE: Except I don't know any Spanish
And my Latin is horrible.
I spent all summer teaching myself
So that I wouldn't be a complete fool in class.
But I still have to rely on notes.

LAINIE: Which isn't very impressive to students.

JOYCE: If they ever catch on that I know little more
Than they do, I'm a dead duck.
Thank God I have mostly first year classes.
My one second year Spanish is driving me crazy.
I hate feeling unprepared and inadequate.
I hate it.
I'm a good French teacher, but Lord knows
What kind of reputation I'm building now.
There's only so much I can do,
I can't devote every minute when I'm home
To schoolwork.
I have a husband and a baby to take care of.

(There's a knock on the door.)

That's mine. Kid making up a quiz.

175

(She hunts through her mountain of books and papers, pulls out one sheet, and goes to the door. She opens the door, instructs student, and returns.)

JOYCE: I figure if I can hold out long enough
There will be a French opening.
How I loved teaching French.
In the meantime I'm stuck.
I go home at night so frustrated
I could tear the house down.
But I need this job.

JEAN: Whatever happened to the days when women
Could choose
Between staying home with their kids
Or going to work?
There's no choice any more.
Today kids mean you have to work.
Haven't we come a long way baby?

JOYCE: It broke my heart to leave my daughter.
The babysitter saw her take her first step.
I'd love to be home with her.
But who can make it on one pay these days?
My heat bill alone devoured us last winter.
Taxes keep going up.
My refrigerator blew last week
Two days after my washing machine broke down.
So if they tell me I'm teaching Hindu next year,
I'll spend the summer listening to Hindu tapes.
I've got no choice,
I need this job.
I'll survive it.
What's really pathetic is the gigantic ruse.
What they're doing to me is nothing
Compared to what they're doing to those kids.
Maybe if people knew why their kids aren't getting
A decent education …

JEAN: Do you really think it would matter?
After all, the Board

Is only trying to keep taxes down.
You're only getting half of Agnes Martin's salary,
And they didn't have to hire a Spanish teacher.
You're saving the district a bundle.
Who cares if you know what you're doing or not?
Besides, that's your problem,
Isn't it?

JOYCE: Every minute of every day.
But it just isn't in me
Not to care.

JEAN: And that, my dear,
Is what they're counting on.

(The women freeze. The CHORUS comes alive.)

1st SEMI-CHORUS: Wasn't she great?

2nd SEMI-CHORUS: And wasn't he?

1st SEMI-CHORUS: I worked for her …

2nd SEMI-CHORUS: He made me see …

1st SEMI-CHORUS: She was so kind …

2nd SEMI-CHORUS: He nurtured me …

1st SEMI-CHORUS: I loved that course,
Surprisingly,
Because of her …

2nd SEMI-CHORUS: I found my way,
Courageously,
Because of him …

1st SEMI-CHORUS: Wasn't she great?

2nd SEMI-CHORUS: And wasn't he?

(The CHORUS freezes. The women come alive. ALYSSA enters. The phone rings. BONNIE answers it. JOYCE opens a bag and pulls out a sandwich. ALYSSA heads right for her thermos, unscrews the top, pours her coffee, lights a cigarette, then drinks.)

BONNIE:	Faculty room. No, she's not here.
JEAN:	You look as if you're going to Inhale that cigarette whole.
BONNIE:	I think she has a class this period.
ALYSSA:	I just checked on a kid I sent to ISSR this morning ...
BONNIE:	Oh. Well, you might try the library.
ALYSSA:	... and he's not there ...
JEAN:	Who released him?
BONNIE:	Oh. In that case I don't know where she might be.
ALYSSA:	... Bassard suspended him.
BONNIE:	What do you mean?
JEAN:	What'd he do?
BONNIE:	Look, she's not hiding in the filing cabinet If that's what you mean.
ALYSSA:	He was obscene with me in study hall And worse in ISSR.
BONNIE:	We aren't harboring any fugitives.
JEAN:	Worse?
ALYSSA:	He told me to go fuck myself ...

BONNIE: Okay, you're forgiven.

ALYSSA: ... and he couldn't keep his filthy mouth shut In
            ISSR ...

BONNIE: Yes, if we see her, we'll send her down. Good-bye.
            (BONNIE slams the phone receiver down.)

ALYSSA: ... he asked Annie Brady
            If she was masturbating
            Under the desk.

JEAN: Oh, Christ. And she's alone down there
            When she relieves Tom.

LAINIE: Kids even know the damn terminology today!
            And worse yet, they're anxious to use it!

ALYSSA: No, no. That was my vocabulary.
            Sorry. I'm so shook up I can't think straight.
            Or maybe it's that I can't think twisted enough.
            He asked her if she was playing with herself
            Under the desk.

            (Joyce, who has been chewing very slowly, puts
            down her sandwich. Her eyes are wide, her facial
            expression even wider with disbelief.)

JOYCE: That's disgusting. With any vocabulary.

ALYSSA: Then it got progressively worse,
            If you can imagine it.
            Ann's down there shaking like a leaf.
            He went on quite colorfully, I guess.
            I tried to miss most of the gory details.

JOYCE: Did Annie phone for help?

JEAN: There's no phone in ISSR.

JOYCE: That's right. I forgot.

179

Tom doesn't want to be bothered
By the phone constantly.

LAINIE: Can't blame him for that.
Everybody would start calling
To dictate assignments.

BONNIE: What did Annie finally do?
Were there any other kids
In there with her and the pervert?

ALYSSA: Three other boys
Who started to join in on the fun.

JEAN: Wonderful. By that time poor Annie
Must have had visions of gang rape.

LAINIE: They shouldn't allow a woman in there
Even to relieve Tom. He'll bust heads
If anybody gets out of line, but let's
Face it, how much can a woman do?

JOYCE: Isn't that what we're fighting for these days?
Equality?
The libbers would crucify me for this,
But I don't want equality if it means
I have to do what men do.
Why do they think it's such a big accomplishment
For women when the man stays home
And the woman goes out to work?
So what if they reverse roles
If the roles remain the same?

JEAN: That's part of the distortion that
Men and women have created around the
Whole concept of women's liberation.
The purists merely want women to have
Freedom of choice, as much freedom to
Direct their lives as men do.
But even that very noble idea
Is inherently distorted.
Because most men are as trapped as women.

It's insulting and degrading and unfair to women
When a man and a woman
Are equally qualified for a job
And the man gets it just because he's a man,
Or when a man and a woman
Are doing the same job
And the man gets a higher salary
Just because he's a man.
You can't blame women
For trying to right those wrongs.
Unfortunately the basics have been bowdlerized
By men clawing to maintain their privileges
And by women interpreting equality
To mean superiority.

LAINIE: Bowdlerized?

JEAN: From Dr. Thomas Bowdler.
            In 1818 he published
            An expurgated Shakespeare.
            To expurgate is to remove
            All obscene or otherwise objectionable material,
            Usually from a book.
            Bowdlerize is synonymous with expurgate.
            Maybe I didn't use it right.
            What do you think, Matt?

ALYSSA: Because Dr. Bowdler had the colossal nerve
            To expurgate Shakespeare, his name was given
            To a process that reeks of censorship.
            Therefore, to bowdlerize is stronger, more
            Negative,
            Than to expurgate.
            That's my feeling for the word, anyway.
            I think you used it in a most interesting way.
            You could have said the basics have been
            What? Mutilated?
            Mutilated would have worked.
            But somehow I like bowdlerized.
            It's more thought-provoking.

JEAN: I think you're right.

Mutilated is ... safe.
It's a safer word than bowdlerize in that context.

BONNIE: How about manipulated?
Not as effective as mutilated, maybe,
But still it's ...

LAINIE: Would
You
Girls
Save it for the classroom?
What the hell happened to Annie?

JEAN: Sorry, Laine, it's in the blood,
So to speak ...

ALYSSA: Annie waited in the hall
Until she caught someone to stay with the animals.
I think it was Roger Lifts, he patrols the halls a lot
Even during his free period.

JOYCE: He wouldn't if he had any papers to grade.

ALYSSA: It's a good thing he was there, Joyce.

JOYCE: Oh, I know.
Slap my mouth.

ALYSSA: Annie ran to Bassard's office,
Praying all the way that he was there.

LAINIE: And Harry suspended the whole crew?

ALYSSA: Yes. I guess he was furious.
I just talked to him. Say what you will
About Harry, there are
Some things he won't tolerate.
He's got a vicious job down there.

BONNIE: It is good to hear of some support from the top
Once in a while.

ALYSSA: Well, the fact that the animals
Started lipping off at him
Probably had something to do with it, too.
And when I think that I started it all
By sending the little twerp there in the first place,
My one and only referral ...

JEAN: He certainly justified it, don't you think?

ALYSSA: I guess so, but it sure is hard on the nerves.

JEAN: Why are you lighting another cigarette?
The last one's still burning in the ashtray.
Calm down, please, before you run out.
Then what will we do with you?

LAINIE: Would you like some soup, Alyssa?
I've got another packet.

ALYSSA: Thanks, no, between the caffeine and the nicotine
I should make it through the afternoon.

JOYCE: You really should eat something.

ALYSSA: I don't eat lunch; I eat a good breakfast,
But I never could eat here.
I don't mind at all,
And I keep my girlish figure.

BONNIE: How can you run around this place all day
Without refueling?

ALYSSA: I always have.
Mom.

BONNIE: Oh no you don't.
We aren't going to reverse roles.
I couldn't hack it.

LAINIE: By the way, who called earlier, Bonnie?

BONNIE: Brenda.

Bassard's hot on Erica's trail.
I had a hard time convincing Brenda
That we weren't hiding her out.

JEAN: Brenda gets overzealous sometimes.

LAINIE: Bassard puts the pressure on her pretty good.

ALYSSA: I'm sure Erica has a class this period.
One of her kids transferred into one of my classes
A while ago.

JEAN: So they can't find her, huh?

BONNIE: No. Brenda checked the library.
I don't know where else she could be
With a class
If she's not in her room or in the library.

ALYSSA: Maybe she's got them
In the gym doing calisthenics.
She doesn't exercise their minds any.

JEAN: Or maybe she's not with them at all.

LAINIE: Would she have the nerve?

JEAN: Erica is one large nerve.
I saw her in the parking lot before I left my room.

JOYCE: When? This period?

JEAN: Yes, m'am. She was getting into her car.
Why not? It's a gorgeous day.
Think of all the errands you can run
On a double lunch period.

ALYSSA: And her fourth period class
Gets conveniently lost in the lunch crowd.

JOYCE: She's playing with fire; if anything ever
Happens to one of those kids when they're

184

	Supposed to be in her class, She'll get crucified.
JEAN:	Kindly remember that Christ was innocent. It'll never happen to her; not Erica; To one of us, maybe, but not to her.
ALYSSA:	Jean's right; Erica's been getting away with it For years; she'll never get burned.
BONNIE:	At least Harry's after her.
JEAN:	So what? What can he really do? Take her to court? Do you know how difficult it is To dismiss a tenured teacher? The publicity alone would kill Harry And bury the rest of us alive. Everybody already knows that teachers Do nothing all day. Given the perfect example, the public Wouldn't hesitate to stone the rest of us. What irony; like it or not, we're blessed That Erica gets away with it. And she'll get away with it Forever or until she retires.
ALYSSA:	Whichever comes first, Probably the "forever." Why retire when you're getting paid To do nothing?
JOYCE:	Sometimes I wonder if tenure is worth it.
LAINIE:	Are you crazy? It protects all of us, you know.
ALYSSA:	Don't ever believe that this district, Or any district, for that matter, Would hesitate a fraction of a second To replace teachers at the top of the pay scale

> With rookies at a fraction of the salary.
> Especially today
> With austerity budgets and school closings.

LAINIE: How would you like to lose your job
Because you stepped on
Somebody's
Influential toes
Or because some administrator doesn't like
The way you part your hair?

ALYSSA: And then there's always good old-fashioned
Nepotism.

JOYCE: I've barely got a job now; sometimes I wish
They'd just fire me; then I'd have to find
Something else.
This hanging on for dear life is for the birds.

JEAN: There are a lot of teachers, good teachers,
On the outside looking in these days.
Maybe they are the lucky ones.

BONNIE: My tongue is hanging out for tenure
And Vetterly abuses it every day.
Was she ever any good?

ALYSSA: She must have been
Or she never would have been
Tenured to begin with.

JEAN: It's easy to fake it for three years.
We're all actors, aren't we?

BONNIE: Hell, I'm not faking it.

LAINIE: None of us faked it either, Bon.
It's just a difference in people.

ALYSSA: Erica would have been a lousy anything.
Besides, who knows what standards
She had to maintain

Way back when?

JOYCE: You wonder, though,
How she survived all those years.
We all get observed.

JEAN: And you know what a farce that can be.
You're not getting the drift here, Joyce.
Erica is what she is.
Nobody bothers with her any more.
She's a sore that has to be covered.
That's all.
She'll never be cured,
She'll never be surgically removed.
She's just there.
Scabbed over.
But there.

ALYSSA: You girls have never had to listen to her, either.
Her "philosophy" is enough to make you vomit.
She really thinks she's right
And the rest of us are idiots.

LAINIE: Oh, we've got one or two in our department ...

JOYCE: So do we ...

JEAN: That's why she never flinched this morning, Matt,
When we were talking about
Rentsen and our workload.
It never bothered her to get a fifth class; in fact,
She told me once that she wasn't at all concerned
About class size.
Large classes mean job security, she said.

ALYSSA: Large classes mean job security.
The old bitch,
That would be her attitude.
She does the same thing
No matter how many kids she has.

BONNIE: Hey! Remember that in math?

187

Zero times ten is zero and zero times a million is still ...
ZERO!

(BONNIE opens her class attendance book and starts turning pages, removing paper clips, and jotting with a pencil. LAINIE cleans up the mess from the soup, JOYCE finishes her lunch, JEAN drinks the last of her soup and returns her thermos to its spot on the main altar, then she heads for the bathroom. ALYSSA empties the ashtray, lights another cigarette, and begins to grade spelling tests. LAINIE and JOYCE begin to attack piles of papers also. There's a knock on the door, JOYCE says, "That's mine," and gets up to retrieve the quiz from her student. Then she settles back to grading papers. The women freeze. The CHORUS comes alive.)

1st SEMI-CHORUS: I never had a teacher I liked.

2nd SEMI-CHORUS: I never liked a teacher I had.

1st CITIZEN: He was the worst teacher I ever had!

2nd CITIZEN: What!?!? He was terrific!

1st SEMI-CHORUS: I always had teachers I liked.

2nd SEMI-CHORUS: I always liked teachers I had.

3rd CITIZEN: He was the best teacher I ever had!

4th CITIZEN: Are you crazy!?!? He was a real jerk!

1st SEMI-CHORUS: I never had a teacher I didn't like.

2nd SEMI-CHORUS: I never liked a teacher I didn't have.

5th CITIZEN: Her class was the greatest!

6th CITIZEN: Her class was a bore!

1st SEMI-CHORUS:	I always had teachers I didn't like.

1st SEMI-CHORUS: I always had teachers I didn't like.

2nd SEMI-CHORUS: I always liked teachers I didn't have.

7th CITIZEN: She was too easy!

8th CITIZEN: She was too hard!

9th CITIZEN: She was just right!

1st SEMI-CHORUS: I had a teacher once
Who said I'd never get through college.
Well, I showed him!

2nd SEMI-CHORUS: I had a teacher once
Who said I'd never get through college.
Well, maybe I would have
If he had taught me something!

10th CITIZEN: He was so unfair!

11th CITIZEN: If it wasn't for him,
I never would have graduated!

12th CITIZEN: Who? Him?
He was a nondescript nobody.

1st SEMI-CHORUS: I had a teacher once
Who said I was perfect for college.
The damned fool!
I should have gone to trade school.

2nd SEMI-CHORUS: I had a teacher once
Who said I was perfect for college.
I was.
And he had nothing to do with it.

FULL CHORUS: Isn't it a pity,
Isn't it a shame,
That public education
Is trickling down the drain?

189

Rosemary Cania Maio

1st SEMI-CHORUS:

The school bus, the school bus,
Get out from behind the school bus.

2nd SEMI-CHORUS:

Taxes, taxes,
Save to pay the taxes.

1st QUARTER-CHORUS: What? Another book?
You've got to buy another book?

2nd QUARTER-CHORUS: What's wrong with the way you talk?
You tell that teacher
There's nothing wrong
With the way you talk.
No kid of mine is a dummy.

3rd QUARTER-CHORUS: Your teacher is a ninny,
Your teacher is a farce,
Tell him to take that chalk of his
And stick it up his arse.

4th QUARTER-CHORUS: Were you the only one?
Or one of two or three?
We've got a case
If the whole class failed.
We'll get her casket built and nailed
If the whole class failed,
If the whole class failed,
But not if you were the only one
Or one of two or three.

1st SEMI-CHORUS:

The school bus, the school bus,
My kids can't take the school bus!?!?

2nd SEMI-CHORUS:

Teachers, teachers,
Save to pay the teachers.

FULL CHORUS:

Isn't it a pity,
Isn't it a shame,
That public education
Is pouring down the drain?

(The CHORUS freezes. The women come alive. JEAN exits from the bathroom. BONNIE, who is flipping pages with a vengeance, becomes more and more frustrated as she jots then erases, jots then erases.)

BONNIE: This rotten book.
            It's obvious that the people
            Who manufacture this thing
            Have never used one.

(ALYSSA looks up from her spelling tests and lights a cigarette.)

ALYSSA: What's wrong? Let me see what you've got.

BONNIE: Here, before I throw it out the window.
            I put the first six weeks in with no problem,
            But who ever has a problem
            With the first six weeks?
            I can't figure out how to fit in
            The rest of the semester
            So I won't have to flip pages to count absences.

ALYSSA: I've done that often enough. Flipping pages
            A hundred and fifty times
            Every six weeks
            Is a real pain.
            At least you have the brains to do this in pencil.
            I used a felt-tip when I tried to set up my book.
            I put in all the names and tried to match the dates
            On facing pages to correspond with
            The report card periods.

BONNIE: Yeah, that's what I'm trying to do.
            It isn't working.

ALYSSA: And here's why.
            You're doing the same thing I was doing.
            Only I had to throw out my first attempt
            And write names and codes all over again.
            You can just erase the dates.

191

Here, look at my book.
You have to eliminate the long vacations entirely
To get it to fit, and then it still doesn't at the
End of the semester.
I just added those few days in this section.

BONNIE: Oh, I see!
But your pages are so neat.
They don't cover half the names
When they're flipped over.
How did you manage ...

ALYSSA: You can't separate the ends at the perforation.
Forget the perforation.
You have to cut each page with scissors ... here.
But be careful that you have
Enough pages for each class
For the entire year.
I've made that mistake more than once
And had to start all over again with another book.
And watch out for your seniors;
You need to keep a full page
So you can write names for the change second
Semester.

BONNIE: Wait a minute, you're losing me.

ALYSSA: Just pull these paper clips. This is my senior class,
First semester with names.
This full page has no names yet, but it's ready
For the new crew second semester.
If you cut this page,
You'll eliminate the space for names.
It's not exactly a tragedy,
But I like to keep my classes in order in this thing.
It's confusing enough
Without having my third period attendance
After my eighth period.

BONNIE: I agree.
Okay, I understand that now.

ALYSSA: The other thing to remember
Is not to cut the last page
Of the first semester
Because you need to fit in the last few days.
Luckily, that Wednesday, Thursday, and Friday
Will be exam days and there won't be any classes.
Now, to get this section out of your way
For the second semester — I haven't done this yet
Because we haven't gotten there yet, but this is
What I plan to do — fold this section over.
See what I mean?
Fold it where you would have cut it. Then
Clip it to the other pages
And you're ready for second semester.

LAINIE: Don't tell me you've got the second semester
Plugged in there already.

ALYSSA: Yes, I do.
I like to get all this busywork out of the way early.
I hate to have to fumble around all year with it;
Once I get the dates set, I also plug them into
My plan book for the year.

JOYCE: My God, how neat your book is! What are all
These pretty little x's?

ALYSSA: I never thought of them as being attractive.
I guess they are at that.

LAINIE: You would create an aesthetic attendance register,
Matthews.

ALYSSA: Well, I used to draw a line through vacation days
And through students who transferred or dropped,
But the lines got lost in all that fancy gridwork.

LAINIE: You're right. It's confusing.
It's hard to tell which little boxes
Are blocked out when you use lines.

ALYSSA: And I live in fear of

193

Marking the wrong kid absent,
Or the wrong day,
Or the wrong anything.
The red x's fill in each whole square
And reduce the margin of error.
I've found them to be a huge aid to accuracy.
It takes only a few seconds to x-out
Whatever needs to be eliminated.

JOYCE: So you don't keep your grades and attendance
Together?

ALYSSA: I used to, but this works better.
I'm able to section my grades for easier averaging
If I keep them separate from the attendance.
When I started teaching,
I recorded grades and attendance together.
I think everybody starts that way,
Squeezing grades in with attendance
On the day the test or whatever is given.
I finally decided that that was stupid.

LAINIE: It sure is, and so am I.
Do you know what I go through
Trying to average grades
Scattered across two pages,
With the quizzes, tests, and homework
Interwoven?

ALYSSA: Sure, I used to do it.
You have to get
The quizzes and tests and homework
Separated because they're weighted differently,
Figure separate averages,
Then figure the final average.
It's miserable.
But I didn't mean to call you stupid, Lainie.
Everybody's different;
We've all got our own procedures.
What works for me
Might not work for anybody else.

LAINIE: No offense taken; I'd like to try your method.
              Can I see your grade book?

ALYSSA: Sure. It's really very simple.

LAINIE: Look at this. I love it.

ALYSSA: Spelling grades are grouped here,
              Major grades here.
              There's enough room to group anything you want,
              And you can even enter grades for each group
              In different colors
              To make identification even easier.

LAINIE: You use red x's here too.

ALYSSA: That way I don't enter grades in the wrong spot.
              Most of the time, anyway.

BONNIE: Can we get back to the attendance book?
              I'm not sure yet that I have these dates right;
              Did you eliminate Thanksgiving vacation?

ALYSSA: No, because it's only two days out of that week.
              Here, take my book and copy the dates for your
              First class for the whole year.
              Then you can reproduce it for your other classes.

BONNIE: Thanks, Matt, that's a good idea.
              It'll be great not to have to bother with this
              For the rest of the year.

ALYSSA: Just turn pages and clip at the end of each
              Report card period.

JOYCE: May I see that when Bonnie's done with it?

ALYSSA: Of course, and the grade book if you're interested.

JOYCE: No, that I do already.
              I've always kept separate books.
              But I have to admit, I haven't figured out

The dates for the year yet.

BONNIE: Do you know how easy this makes it
             To count absences?

ALYSSA: Just use a piece of paper under each name
             And read across.
             It's easy to keep your own record
             There at the end, too.
             Just jot down the count
             After you tally for each name.

LAINIE: Ah ... do you think I could get in line
             For your attendance book?

ALYSSA: Sure, Laine.

LAINIE: Hey, Jean, aren't you interested in this gold mine?

JEAN: Nah.

JOYCE: How do you keep your records, Jean?

JEAN: You're looking at it.
             This gold mine that you've discovered
             Has been around for some time.
             I caught on to Alyssa two years ago.
             You girls are slow.
             I just wait for the wizard to figure out the calendar,
             Then I tap the mother lode.
             Right, Mattie?
             When did the old brain
             Straighten out the mess this year?

ALYSSA: Oh, somewhere around
             The second week of school.

LAINIE: Pretty good, Tevarro.
             You've got all this already!

BONNIE: I wish I had Alyssa's patience for this kind of thing.

JEAN: Don't need it.
We've got Alyssa.

BONNIE: I'm going down to check my mailbox.
Can I bring up anybody else's mail?

ALYSSA: Please do. I never thought of it
When I was commiserating with Annie.

JEAN: Me too. `

LAINIE: Me three.

JOYCE: Don't bother with mine. I just stopped.

ALYSSA: Why don't you try to get Mrs. King
While you're down there,
Or have you contacted her already?

BONNIE: Haven't had a chance.
I'll give it a try.

(BONNIE leaves. The women freeze. The CHORUS comes alive.)

FULL CHORUS: IT IS THE DUTY OF PUBLIC EDUCATION

1st CITIZEN: To teach good citizenship!

2nd CITIZEN: Proper manners!

3rd CITIZEN: Personal hygiene!

4th CITIZEN: Responsibility!

5th CITIZEN: Values!

6th CITIZEN: Self-confidence! Self-control! Self-discipline!
Self-esteem!
Self-expression! Self-improvement!
Self-knowledge!
Self-preservation! Self-reliance!

197

Cooperation!

7th CITIZEN: Initiative!

8th CITIZEN: Creativity!

9th CITIZEN: Motivation!

10th CITIZEN: Discipline! Discipline! Discipline!

11th CITIZEN: Sex education!

12th CITIZEN: Communication skills!

FULL CHORUS: IT IS THE DUTY OF PUBLIC EDUCATION

1st CITIZEN: To instruct our young people for life!

2nd CITIZEN: How to drive a car!

3rd CITIZEN: Write a check!

4th CITIZEN: Balance a checkbook!

5th CITIZEN: Fill out a 1040!

6th CITIZEN: Write a decent letter!

7th CITIZEN: How to listen! study! talk! read! write! spell! Think! evaluate!

8th CITIZEN: Take tests!

9th CITIZEN: Contribute to society!

10th CITIZEN: Develop an appreciation for music and art!

11th CITIZEN: How to bowl!
Swim!
Golf!
Play tennis!

12th CITIZEN: How to fix a car, change a baby, build a house,
Prepare a meal, make a dress,
Choose a spouse,
Get into college, find a
Job, run for political office,
Shop comparatively, invest wisely,
Live moderately and well,
And
BE HAPPY!

FULL CHORUS: IT IS THE DUTY OF PUBLIC EDUCATION!!!

(The CHORUS freezes. The women come
alive. BONNIE returns. As she walks into the
room, she trips on the rug, just a small
stub-of-the-toe stumble, but enough to make
her bend over to remove a long thread of thick
rug yarn. The more she pulls, the longer the
thread becomes until it finally reaches the far
wall.)

LAINIE: We'll be down to bare floor if you keep doing that.

BONNIE: Somebody's going to get hurt if I don't.
Good Lord, it doesn't want to stop.
This rug is starting to look like the Grand Canyon.
Are carpets supposed to unravel like this?

ALYSSA: Did you get Mrs. King?

BONNIE: Yep. Made an appointment to see the place
Right after school.
From what you've told me,
I'm ready to move in today.
The price is right.

ALYSSA: You're going to love it,
But I fear you've forgotten Paul's meeting tonight.

BONNIE: Oh, damn, I did.
Do you think he'd mind If I missed it?

ALYSSA: Better not.
I think it's important, and he said it won't take long.
Mrs. King will wait.
Is any of that mail mine?

BONNIE: Oh! Sorry.
There's something for everyone,
Even Joyce.

(BONNIE distributes papers in various sizes and shapes.)

JOYCE: Uh-oh.
Greetings from the Board of Education.
I'm afraid to open it.

BONNIE: Nothing as exciting for the rest of you.
Unless your hearts pound
Over the attendance sheet
And the usual heap of excuses.

ALYSSA: Wrong, postage-stamp breath,
There's a small envelope hidden inside my heap.
Wonder what it is ...

JEAN: Looks like an invitation.

ALYSSA: To what? Negotiations?

JOYCE: Oh, shit, 'shit, double shit.

JEAN: My sentiments, exactly.

JOYCE: I was afraid of this.
Not only do I have to teach
What I'm totally uninterested in,
Now they order me to get certified in it!

BONNIE: Courses? You have to take courses?

JOYCE: The fact that I worked my tail off
To get permanent certification in French
Doesn't mean a damn thing

If I'm teaching Spanish and Latin.
I really thought they'd leave me alone
For a year or two, seeing that I'm doing
The district a favor.

JEAN: There's your faulty reasoning, Joyce.
They're doing you a favor. They're doing all of us
A favor.
We're all damn lucky to have jobs,
And we'd better not forget it.

ALYSSA: The district is covering itself
In case some parent wants to know
Why there are
Uncertified teachers in our classrooms.
At least it will be able to say
That you're working toward certification.

JOYCE: This really stinks.
I don't want certification in Spanish and Latin.
But if I don't work at it,
They have every legal right
To fire me.

JEAN: I hope, for your sake,
There's a French opening soon.
That's the only way you'll escape.
If too many years go by, and you do get certified
In Spanish and Latin, you know what they'll do to
you.

JOYCE: Keep me where I am
And hire a cheaper replacement?
I wouldn't doubt it.

ALYSSA: The fact that you're an excellent French teacher
Has absolutely nothing to do with any of it.
It makes me sick ...

JOYCE: I just don't know how I'm going to manage courses
On top of everything else.
I've got to take six hours a year,

And it's too late for this semester.
I'll have to take two courses next semester.
I'll be damned if I take anything over the summer.
Never again will I do
Anything for free over the summer.
And I'm not taking any more work home either.
They pay us for what we do here.
What I don't get done here
Won't get done.

LAINIE: I don't blame you, Joyce. Not one bit.
It doesn't make much sense for them to tell you
You're not qualified after they indicate that you are.

JOYCE: I've been working so hard for those kids.
I'm just beginning to see some progress,
Mine and theirs!
I won't be able to do course work too.
I'll have to let things slide here ...

JEAN: Sure. If you can do it.

JOYCE: That's what really makes me angry.
I have to face those kids every day.
And I have to live with myself.
That is what they're counting on, isn't it?

JEAN: If you're that kind of teacher, yes,
That's what they're counting on.

ALYSSA: And if you're not, so be it.
They really don't care,
As long as their asses are covered.
The law is on their side,
And the public stays dormant.

JOYCE: Maybe there's something in the contract
That could help me put off courses for awhile.

LAINIE: What contract? We haven't got a contract.

JOYCE: Aren't parts of the old one extended?

LAINIE: Sure. Everything but money.
I don't see why they don't give us even our step
Raise.

ALYSSA: Because it's money in the bank.
They're making money on the money they're
Not paying us.
I've got very bad feelings about this contract.

JEAN: So do I.
We're going to have a long wait this time.
Waiting is very profitable for the district.
Especially if they can provoke us into a strike.
Two-for-one is a real money-maker.

JOYCE: Please don't say that word.
I haven't gotten over the last near-strike yet.
Maybe I'll talk to Jason about filing a grievance.

LAINIE: Oh, Joyce, I hate to dash your hopes,
But forget about a grievance.
Especially in your position.
Do you remember when I adopted my son?
We got him at the beginning of May that year.
I took a week off because I didn't think I
Could handle meeting him
For the first time after school
And taking him to a babysitter the next morning.
I really felt the pressures of this job
And the responsibility of getting my students
Through exams that year.
I wanted to be home with my son,
But I couldn't abandon my students, not in May,
Not with exams a month away.
So I stayed with my son a week
And came back to work.
The next year I took child care leave.
In the meantime, Jason notified me that the district
Was in violation of the contract for not paying me
For the week I took off.
I couldn't believe

> That they docked me for that week,
> I'm rarely out for any reason.
> So I submitted a grievance.
> One week before I was supposed to return from Leave,
> I got a call from the Board office.
> I was told that if I didn't drop the grievance,
> My new assignment would be impossible to bear.
> It was a blatant threat
> And it shocked the hell out of me.
> I always knew that this district is rotten,
> But I still don't understand why
> They had to insult and degrade me that way.
> After I came back here to work through exams.
> Was my one-week's pay
> Going to break the district?
> Or do they just enjoy
> This power they have over us?
> Jason was disappointed,
> But I dropped the grievance.
> When I told him why,
> He was furious, wanted to make the
> Whole thing public. Of course, I wouldn't.
> After it all blew over,
> I'd be shoveling coal in the boiler room.
> · Don't submit a grievance, Joyce, you'll regret it.

JOYCE: Well, then, I'm stuck, aren't I?

ALYSSA: There is something you can do.

JOYCE: What's that?

ALYSSA: Take lessons from Erica.

(The women freeze. The CHORUS comes alive.)

FULL CHORUS: School days, school days,
                     Dear ol' bend-the-rule days ...

1ˢᵗ SEMI-CHORUS: Nor in the spring,
                     Nor in the fall,

I never went
To study hall.

2nd SEMI-CHORUS:

I never did my homework,
I never read a book,
I realized that I could lie
To get me off the hook.

FULL CHORUS:

Don't parents have enough to do
Today?

1st CITIZEN:

The only effective way to fight drug
Abuse Is Through
Special Programs In Our Schools.

6th CITIZEN:

Students with learning disabilities have
Special needs that must be
Acknowledged
And attended to Through
Special Programs In Our Schools.

12th CITIZEN:

Students with above-average
Intelligence
Must be stimulated and directed along
The road to success Through
Special Programs In Our Schools.

1st CITIZEN:

Too many people are turning to alcohol
For comfort these days.
Can't something be done about it
Through
Special Programs In Our Schools?

6th CITIZEN:

Isn't it shameful that we segregate
Certain members of society
Because they're physically or mentally
Handicapped?
Isn't it shameful that we set them apart
With no chance for normal living?
Can't we do something
To incorporate them
Into the mainstream of life?

Why not resolve the issue by instituting
Special Programs In Our Schools?

12th CITIZEN:

Our children are our future.
How can we expect America to
Maintain
Her status as leader of the free world
If our children are not being educated?
How can they assume the reins of
Leadership
And direct this country to greatness
If the schools are pumping them out
Unable to read and write?
How can we compete with the rest of
The world
In the fields of science and technology,
Literature, music, art,
If the schools are not producing
Superior intellects?
We must look carefully at the shameful
Performance
Of our schools, determine why we have
Slipped into
Mediocrity, and fight to reestablish the
Excellence
That once was the mainstay of public
Education.
I will not try to deceive you, dear
Friends.
This will not be easy.
We must be willing to work long and
Hard.
We must be willing to sacrifice.
We must be willing to institute
Special Programs In Our Schools
To combat the growing ignorance, the
Widespread
Lowering of standards that mark our
Educational system
With the stain of disgrace.

FULL CHORUS:

It's the school's job.

It's the school's job.
Don't parents have enough to do
Today?
It's the school's job
To cure society's ills, ease its pain,
Supply its frills, expel the bane
Of ignorance.

(The CHORUS freezes. The women come alive.
ALYSSA is waving her fists in the air. One fist is
holding a small piece of paper.)

ALYSSA: I don't believe it!
I'm going to kill this girl,
She's driving me beyond insanity.
She's always late!
Two minutes, three minutes, five minutes,
Or she's absent,
Or she's excused for an appointment.
I'm already sick and tired of writing slips for her.
Don't you think three slips a day is a little much?
I'm sick, sick, sick
Of handling her attendance cards.
She was late this morning
With that sneering smirk of hers,
And now
She's excused at two o'clock for a driving test!

JEAN: Oh, goody, imagine how she'll come and go
After she gets a license.

ALYSSA: She's already got a license.
These excuses.
She oversleeps
And I've got to fill out two cards
And an absence slip.

BONNIE: Most kids learned real fast
How to beat
The big crackdown on absences.

ALYSSA: And these excuses are legitimate,

Written by mommy or daddy
To protect baby's ass.
How the hell are we supposed to teach
Responsibility
Under these conditions?

LAINIE: Are you nuts?

JOYCE: What'd she say?
Somebody call the medics.
The girl's flipped out.

JEAN: Who is this eel, anyway?

ALYSSA: Annette Nieully.

JEAN: Bingo!
You have my heartfelt sympathy, my dear.
I had her in homeroom last year.

ALYSSA: So that's why my homeroom is so well-behaved.
But you couldn't do anything with Nettie either?

JEAN: Heavens, no,
Mommy told me her little baby
Had oodles of problems.
And the excuses kept pouring in.
Put up with it, teach,
You've only got eight months to go.

JOYCE: Somebody should tell mommy
That no employer will put up with the kind of habits
Baby is learning here.

ALYSSA: Now who's flipped out?

BONNIE: How does this girl spell her last name?

ALYSSA: N-I-E-U-L-L-Y.

BONNIE: I think I've got her in study hall.
I've only seen her twice.

> She told me her name was pronounced "Nelly"
> Not "Nilly."

JOYCE: Wait a minute! She's in my
Second year Spanish class.
She told me she pronounced it "Nully"!

JEAN: She told me it was "Nilly,"
I distinctly remember.
How could I forget?
I had to read and repeat it
A few thousand times.

ALYSSA: But how lyrical, how musical,
What poetry!
Nettle-Nilly-Nelly-Nully
Is really an artist at heart.

JEAN: Or a CIA agent.

(The women freeze. The CHORUS comes alive.)

FULL CHORUS: Do teachers live in houses?
Do teachers sleep in beds?
Do teachers snore and sneeze and cry?

6th CITIZEN: Old teachers never die
They just lose their class!

FULL CHORUS: Do teachers pay taxes?
Do teachers eat food?
Do teachers feel and want and dream?
Do teachers have families?
Do teachers draw breath?

6th CITIZEN: Nah.
I had one once who snorted a lot, though!

FULL CHORUS: STUDENTS DON'T FAIL.
TEACHERS FAIL.

1st CITIZEN: So what's the big deal over class size?

2nd CITIZEN:	I was in classes of 45 And I survived it!
3rd CITIZEN:	Class size? Doesn't that depend upon The size of the room?
4th CITIZEN:	Class size Doesn't matter Doesn't mean a thing If the teacher's any good!
FULL CHORUS:	STUDENTS DON'T FAIL. TEACHERS FAIL.
5th CITIZEN:	Why are we allowing such smut in our Schools?
6th CITIZEN:	Did you see some of the words in this Book? I went through the whole filthy thing And circled all of them!
7th CITIZEN:	And look! Look at this disgusting sentence On page eighty-four!
8th CITIZEN:	Get those books off the shelves Out of our classrooms! Protect our children! Those teachers are peddling pornography!
FULL CHORUS:	STUDENTS DON'T FAIL. TEACHERS FAIL.
9th CITIZEN:	Let Each Become All He Is Capable Of Being.
10th CITIZEN:	We must insure equitable treatment For all students.

11th CITIZEN: We must raise standards
And lower the failure rate.

12th CITIZEN: We must require minimum competency
And lower the drop-out rate.

9th CITIZEN: And so it is decreed.
And so it shall be done.
Notify all teachers!

FULL CHORUS: STUDENTS DON'T FAIL.
TEACHERS FAIL.

(The CHORUS freezes. The women come
alive. ALYSSA lights another cigarette,
then opens the small envelope that looks
like an invitation. BONNIE is waving a slip
of paper in the air.)

BONNIE: How can they do this to me now?
These kids aren't supposed to be
Changing classes this late.
Now I've got to catch this girl up on
Two month's worth of work.
The cut-off date for transfers
Was weeks ago.
Why do we have a cut-off date
If it doesn't mean anything?
I'm going to Bassard with this.

LAINIE: Don't bother.
I'm still getting new kids too.
The counselors are still scheduling.

BONNIE: Damn it all.
They put her into my largest class.
She makes the big three-o.

JEAN: You could lie and say you're filled that period.
It's been done before.

BONNIE: I can't do that.

211

Unless the kid's a real problem.
Beth Ann Conneally. Anybody know her?

JOYCE: Oh, she's an angel.
She's in my homeroom.
Never absent, always studying.
Don't worry about a thing,
She'll catch up on the work.

JEAN: Which teacher is she leaving?

BONNIE: Don't know,
The slip shows her leaving math
For my class.
I'll have to find out eventually
To get her grades and folder.
More running around ...

(ALYSSA suddenly says, "Oh, God," rises, walks to the window, and stands there, looking out. The other women watch her, then look at each other.)

JEAN: Mattie?

BONNIE: You counting the ants?

(ALYSSA turns around, walks back, stubs out her cigarette, rubs her face with one hand, then passes the contents of the small envelope to JEAN.)

JEAN: You're smoking too much.
It's bothering your eyes.
Shall I hum a bar or two?

ALYSSA: Forgive me for being dramatic,
But I never expected ...
Here. Read it.

JEAN: "Dear Mrs. Matthews,
Thank you for taking an interest in our son, John, while he was in your Senior English class last

212

year. It has been a long time since he worked for anyone as hard as he did for you and got a positive result - good grades. He was most pleased that you asked him to play his bagpipes and give a lecture about them."

BONNIE: I remember that!
My whole class
Flew out of the room and down the hall
To listen at your door.

ALYSSA: The whole floor was at my door.
The sound was incredible.
Pipes are meant to be played
In the wide open spaces,
Certainly not in the confines of a classroom.
I worried a little about disturbing other classes
When I gave him permission to play.
And, sure enough, somebody complained.
But I didn't care.
You should have seen that young man play,
The pride, the stately walk.
He was magnificent.

JEAN: "Piping, as you now know, is his great love. I meant to write you sooner to let you know how much we appreciated your concern and your skill." Christ, Alyssa, now I'm getting misty.

JOYCE: Me, too. Keep reading.

JEAN: There isn't much more.

LAINIE: It should go on forever …

JEAN: "John is in college now and terribly pleased that you worked him hard to prepare for it. We concur with John that Mrs. Matthews is the greatest. Sincerely, Mrs. William Trackman."

LAINIE: Isn't that beautiful?

JEAN: "P.S. John wants you to know
that he bought a pocket dictionary!"

ALYSSA: The kid couldn't spell to save his life.
He was so bad
And I was so frustrated
That I resorted to teasing him about it.
Mercilessly.
At least I made him care.

JOYCE: I wish somebody would send me
A note like that.

BONNIE: It's your bell, Alyssa.
Remember what you said this morning?
What was it? A silver bell? A crystal bell?

JOYCE: Any bell will do.

JEAN: It's a voice in the wilderness
Is what it is.
I received one of these
Many, many years ago.
It's yellowed with age
But I still read it
Every now and then.
Cherish this, Alyssa,
It's a museum piece.

BONNIE: Well, Mrs. Tevarro,
Since I have your lovely daughter
In one of my classes, perhaps you
Could take the time to ...

JEAN: Forget it.
You know I fought like hell to get
My lovely daughter into one of your classes.

BONNIE: It wouldn't be quite the same, anyway,
Would it?
So tell me, barring that possibility,
How long do I have to wait

For any bell to ring?

ALYSSA: Who knows?
               All I know is
               It took me twelve years.

(Suddenly the room is filled with a voice from the heavens.)

ATTENTION PLEASE!
ATTENTION PLEASE FOR SOME SPECIAL
ANNOUNCEMENTS!
ATTENTION FACULTY!
A SPECIAL IN-SERVICE WORKSHOP HAS BEEN
SCHEDULED FOR …

JEAN: They announced this already today.

… TUESDAY, NOVEMBER 5th …

LAINIE: And as I noted earlier,
               the fifth is on a Wednesday.

… ALL FACULTY AND STAFF ARE REQUIRED TO
PARTICIPATE …

ALYSSA: When was this announced?

JEAN: This morning.

… THE WORKSHOP WILL OFFER PRACTICAL
TRAINING …

ALYSSA: I never heard the announcements this morning.

… IN CONFLICT-RESOLUTION AND
PROBLEM-SOLVING …

ALYSSA: Oh, shit, why don't they leave us alone?

... WITH A SEMINAR ON TEACHER BURN-OUT. CLASSES WILL BE CANCELED FOR THE DAY.

ALYSSA: That's what I was afraid of. Chalk up another day.

JEAN: From what I hear, these workshops
            Are supposed to continue all year.

LAINIE: I hate the damn things.

ALYSSA: I'd much rather teach.

JEAN: I want to know how we can afford
            The instructional time.

ATTENTION FACULTY, STAFF, AND STUDENTS ...

JOYCE: Why do they make announcements during lunch?
            Nobody can hear in the cafeterias.

... THE BUILDING IS TO BE EVACUATED ...

JEAN: What?!?

... IN EXACTLY FIFTEEN MINUTES.

ALYSSA: It's a bomb scare.

I REPEAT, IN FIFTEEN MINUTES, EVERYONE MUST LEAVE THE BUILDING.

LAINIE: Why, in God's name,
            Are they announcing this now?

STUDENTS WILL NOW GO TO THEIR LOCKERS TO COLLECT BELONGINGS, THEN RETURN TO THEIR FOURTH PERIOD CLASS.

ALYSSA: Oh, sure,
            Fat chance.

I REPEAT, STUDENTS WILL NOW GO TO THEIR LOCKERS TO COLLECT BELONGINGS, THEN RETURN TO THEIR FOURTH PERIOD CLASS.

JEAN:	Then what? The halls are already filled with kids Who won't hear the rest of this.

DISMISSAL WILL BE ANNOUNCED IN FIFTEEN MINUTES.

PLEASE WAIT FOR THE ANNOUNCEMENT OVER THE P.A. SYSTEM.

JOYCE:	I'm glad I don't have a class this period. What a confused mess.
LAINIE:	Well, ladies, let's hit the hall, Those kids out there don't know what's going on.
JEAN:	Can't we hide out in the bathroom? Remember that fire drill?
LAINIE:	It was below zero out!
JEAN:	I still laugh over that. We were packed like sardines in there Just in case anybody checked this room.
LAINIE:	And Dannemore did. I saw him through the crack in the door.
JEAN:	If I hadn't put my hand over your mouth, He would have followed your giggling.
ALYSSA:	God, we almost suffocated in there. But it was suffocate or freeze.
JEAN:	What the hell, It's a beautiful day, girls. Erica's out there enjoying it,

217

Why shouldn't we?
Let's herd those kids back to class
And get outside.

ALYSSA: Whatever on God's earth made me think
I could get these spelling tests graded today?

(The women gather up books and papers, all
except JOYCE.)

Hey, Joyce, don't you want your stuff?
What if the place blows up?

JOYCE: It can all blow up with it.

JEAN: Have you forgotten the cardinal rule
Of fire drills and bomb scares?

(BONNIE places her hand over her heart.)

BONNIE: Never leave the premises
Without your records.

JOYCE: Grades and attendance.
I forgot.

BONNIE: Don't let those records burn.

JEAN: Technically, we're supposed to get
Homeroom records out, too.

ALYSSA: Sure.
Who the hell carries homeroom records around?

JEAN: It's still our responsibility ...

ALYSSA: What isn't?
C'mon, Joyce, grab your records
And let's go.
Some kid thinks he's doing everybody a favor.

JEAN: Why do you automatically blame a kid?

Hey, Bonnie,
Did you make more than one phone call
When you were in the office?

BONNIE: Don't get funny, Tevarro.
Don't even joke about it.
You know how fast rumors spread around here.
I can see the headline now:
Tenure Denied to Teacher
Suspected of Bomb Scares.

(The women leave. THE CURTAIN FALLS.)

The driver looked at his companion. "What time is it getting to be, anyway?"

"Almost noon."

"Hell, we've got to get this baby back. Jason might want to go out for lunch."

"Too late for that, man. He didn't say when he wanted it back, did he?"

"Nah, but we can't ride around in this thing forever."

"Too bad, I'm gettin' used to it. Can't we go somewhere and really open it up? Look at that speedometer. They don't even make 'em like that anymore!"

The driver had seen. 130 mph. It did seem a shame to keep it at 35. The passenger kept on talking. He even offered to get behind the wheel himself. What a waste of all that power! When would they ever get another chance like this? The driver finally agreed. It was too much to pass up. He headed the yellow Corvette out of town to a lonely stretch of road. The passenger again offered to drive, and again the driver refused. He was taking enough chances for one day.

The road was long and straight when he started to exert pressure on the accelerator. The speedometer needle edged steadily upward. When it pointed to 80, the road suddenly started to curve to the right and the driver felt an instant of panic, then a flood of determination as he concentrated on the changing line of the road. He gained confidence as the road straightened out again, and the confidence flowed to his foot, pushing, pushing, ever so slowly, pushing the car and himself and his friend to higher and higher levels of exhilaration.

Then suddenly, and for no apparent reason, the panic returned. It sprang at him out of the darkest recesses of his mind like some wild beast. He had a strange vision that the earth was flat and he was nearing the edge. At 95 mph he thought he caught a glimpse of eternity.

His friend was disappointed. He wanted to hit 100. He wanted to be able to say that he had traveled once on land at a speed of 100 mph. The driver said he was sorry, but not this time. This time 95 was enough.

When they finally returned the yellow Corvette to the faculty parking lot, when they finally found Jason Haywood after checking his schedule in the main office and knocking on four faculty room doors, they were not really surprised at his anger. He was right. They had taken advantage. They should have returned before fifth period.

The young passenger handed over the copy of the key to the yellow Corvette after the driver gave up the original. Not even his friend knew that he held back the second copy, that he had paid for two keys while his friend was waiting outside. The young passenger knew he'd never own a Corvette, and he might never even drive one, but it felt good having that perfectly useless key in his pocket.

Intelligentsia II

There was a time when scholarship classes meant few attendance problems. Alyssa remembered commenting on that fact to Mary Gregory. One of the beautiful things about scholarship students was that they rarely missed class, which freed teacher from time-consuming checks, which enabled teacher to forge ahead quickly without worrying over stragglers. There was a time when scholarship students missed only an occasional day or two or no days at all, which meant that teacher didn't have to manufacture different tests, set aside hand-outs, and repeat lessons over and over and over again. There was a time when scholarship students cut very few classes, finding the courage to do so only during the senior year.

It came to pass, however, that even scholarship students discovered the ease and the exhilaration of truancy. And once made, the discovery flourished within the intrinsically human tendency to enjoy doing what is forbidden, to savor flight from responsibility.

The first time Alyssa caught a scholarship student for truancy she was in genuine shock. She imposed the same penalty as for any other student and saw far beyond the individual case. She didn't want to have to question every single absence of every single student, but she knew she would at least have to give the impression that she was doing so. If they thought she didn't care, they'd be cutting class all the time. There was still one good thing about them. Once caught, a scholarship student rarely repeated the crime.

So Alyssa kept a careful, watchful eye on her attendance register. When she thought she saw a series of suspicious markings, she notified parents. Sometimes students fell into the habit of being absent on one particular day every week. Or always on sunny days. Or during the World Series. Sometimes it took an act of Congress to get a student to produce absence slips. Sometimes slips verified only a portion of the actual absence. Did the homeroom teacher really mix up the dates, or did the student forget when he wrote his own excuse? Possibilities were endless.

When she notified parents, Alyssa hoped for a response. Sometimes she got one. And always she guarded against wild accusations. There was always a chance of accusing an innocent, heaven forbid, so she carefully requested parental verification of "absences" not "truancies." She took that stance after listening to a

222

few indignant responses, one of which turned out to be a sham, but that's another of many stories ...

When she entered her room after the bomb scare was over, she knew she would have to wait awhile for all her students to appear. It was too bad that they lost some class time, but she decided that it could come off the end of her lesson plan. There would be enough time for them to take the same test that first period took. Then she would hand back papers during whatever was left. She wouldn't have much time to circulate, though, and she would have to save the sheet of errors for another day.

The thing that disturbed her most had nothing to do with the bomb scare. She hated giving the same test that she gave first period. There was too much time in between. Someday, she thought, somebody's going to do something about teachers' schedules, something more constructive than making sure that lunch and the free period weren't back-to-back. Teaching duplicate sections so far apart during the day was maddening because the time span gave students too much opportunity to cheat. There were plenty of ways to frustrate the cheating, but all the ways involved creation and duplication of varied materials. And Alyssa just didn't have the time to devise, type, duplicate, and key more tests. So she put up with the fact that some of her fifth period students found out test questions and looked up answers somewhere between first and fifth periods. It was a concession that she once would have never made. It was a concession that grew out of five classes and three preparations.

Before she asked her fifth period class to settle down for their test, she looked around the room for Susan Jancucci. She spoke with some students about the danger of calling in a bomb scare - no, it's not a lark, it's a serious offense, would you like your house to burn down because the fire department is busy with a bomb scare or a false fire alarm?- then she saw Susan standing by her desk. She drew the girl aside. "I think your mother is a very wise lady. What do you think?"

Susan Jancucci nodded and smiled. She was really relieved that her criminal activity had been halted. She was not a felon at heart, just a pretty little sophomore intoxicated with the excitement of a new school, new friends, and, she mistakenly reasoned, new freedoms. "My father thought I should call you too," Susan said. "He said I got myself into it, so I should get myself out of it. I'm really sorry. I don't know why I did it. Your class especially. You're the best teacher I've got."

"I know why you did it. Double lunch. I wouldn't mind it myself. There are plenty of days when I'd like to leave and just keep going. But we've both got a commitment here. Don't we?" Alyssa thought about the girl's phone call, her embarrassment, her confession. She had been cutting class. And Alyssa couldn't believe her ears. Jeff had answered the phone, then handed it over with a quizzical look on his face. Alyssa looked down at her half-finished dinner and started talking, it seemed, to the macaroni on her plate.

This one really surprised her. They never really shock me, she told Jeff afterward, but will they ever stop surprising me? She never expected to hear from this one, this sweet, adorable, cute-as-a-button child who was never anything but polite and sincere. Actually, she sent the notice home because Susan's grade had dropped a bit. She added the list of absences because of habit. Effie was habitually thorough.

Then the girl called to confess. The only thing Alyssa Matthews could think about as she peered through the sauce covering her spaghetti was the sheer unpredictability of it all. It was hit-and-miss all the time. Mere skill was powerless against an evasive, capacious, metamorphic bull's-eye. Susan swore on her class ring and all else that was sacred that she'd never cut class again. Alyssa suspended detentions on one condition: Susan had to get her grade up and keep it up for the rest of the year. Once during the period the teacher looked up to see Susan Jancucci in obvious agony over the test she was taking. Lack of discipline had certainly taken its toll.

When the first few finished tests were dropped on her desk, the teacher recognized names of students who always finished first. They were bright, they studied hard. Or were they and did they? Maybe they had friends from first period. And was there only one Susan Jancucci?

The teacher directed her thoughts to other matters. She couldn't allow herself to dwell on uncertainties when there were so many certainties to deal with. And she knew, she knew the consequences of a suspicious mind.

The Nightmare

The call had come at 8:00 p.m. while she was typing. She thought she knew who was calling, so she picked up the phone receiver casually. But the heavy voice on the other end was not at all familiar.

"I'm looking for the Mason who teaches English at Boesch-Conklyn," the voice said. "You have her, sir," Bonnie answered. Any hour of the day, sir.

The voice said, "Are you a Mrs. or a Miss or one of those liberated mongrels?" Then the voice chuckled. Bonnie was two seconds from detonation. "Who is this?"

The voice made a quick assumption, then a tedious introduction. "Just an irate parent, Miz Mason. Archibald Brissonson. You failed my boy and I want to know why. He works very hard. Every night he holes up in his room with a pile of books. I never see him after dinner. He tells me he should have passed. He says you don't like him. Some kind of personality conflict. I want to know what's going on. Your side of it before I go any further with this."

Bonnie had to think fast. Faster than fast. Brissonson. Who the hell—? John? Jack? No. Joseph. Joseph Brissonson. Fifth period, seniors. Joe Brissonson had failed, all right. And royally. But a personality conflict? She had no idea whatsoever that the kid even had a personality.

"My side of it? Mr. Brissonson, I don't engage in combat with my students. We aren't adversaries. And I did not fail your son, he—

"Yeah, yeah, I know. He failed himself. I used to hear that all the time. But they were wrong. I made it through college in spite of their doomsday predictions."

Too bad for me, Bonnie thought, as she conjured up a picture of her classroom with Joe Brissonson in it. "Joe failed because he refuses to bring books to class. Most of the time he sits idle because he can't seem to remember to carry a pen and some paper." Dad was having none of it.

"I can't believe that. Why would he do homework and then forget it? He's not that scatterbrained. He's had some trouble satisfying the damn gym requirement, which is a waste of time anyway, but he isn't stupid when it comes to his academic subjects. I made sure that he'd remain in regents because I know he can do the work. He knows what's expected of him. Now, all I want to know is your end of it. Are you clear with your instructions? Do you grade fairly? Are you out to get my boy?"

As the man rambled on, Bonnie focused on the one student pulled out of the multitude. There was something else about Joe Brissonson that she couldn't quite grasp. And then she had it. "The main reason for Joe's failing was his attendance. He missed some work when he was absent and never made it up. I can't just ignore those zeros in fairness to the rest of the class."

But the man was having none of that either. "What are you trying to pull, Miz Mason? Joseph hasn't been absent. Not once yet this year. I haven't written any excuses and I'm looking at his report card right now. You didn't indicate any absences either. Do you know what you're doing?"

At that point, Miz Mason was beginning to wonder herself. She explained to Mr. Archibald Brissonson that she didn't have her records at home, but would make a thorough check on everything the next day. Attendance, grades, the whole works. She'd just have to get back to him with the information. Mr. Archibald Brissonson gave her until the end of the week. Bonnie never got a chance to thank him for his generosity because he immediately broke the connection.

Bonnie finished typing her test, spent some time with the phone call she had been expecting, soaked in a hot bath, cleaned up her kitchen, and settled into bed with some papers to grade. She tried not to think about Mr. Archibald Brissonson, and she fell asleep around midnight. At 4:00 a.m. she awoke drenched in a cold sweat, a scream congealed in her throat.

It was the same old nightmare, the same terror, the same awakening. For years she had lived with it. For years she had joked about her propensity to dream about everything and anything. A weak mind, an overactive imagination, a frustrated libido. She entertained her friends with the grotesque convoluted distortions that her brain transmitted during sleep. Technicolor trauma, she called it. Wide-screen whimsy. She was still making people laugh. The manila folder episode had been a howler.

But she never told anyone about the nightmare. All the other dreams were sporadic flickerings, impressions left by some experience that her brain found worthy of mention during sleep. And some of the others were frightening. But none of the others repeated. The nightmare materialized whenever she was overwrought, overtired, overanxious, whenever she felt inordinate pressure or the threat of imminent failure. She was sure that the nightmare was a manifestation of the doubts and fears that her conscious mind could arrest and quell, but her subconscious mind gave in to.

When she was in college, she attempted dream analysis, but had difficulty pinpointing specific objects for symbolic interpretation because the nightmare was not within the realm of specificity. It was, instead, a massive generality, a huge void sucking her into its darkness. There was no villain, no voice, no instrument of torture. Her terror was elicited by nothing more than nothingness. She decided that perhaps the threat of the void was the ultimate threat of the unknown, the threat of insecurity, especially when she considered the point in her life when the nightmare began. It was the same old nightmare, all right, ten years later.

As she sat shivering on the bed at 4:00 in the morning, Bonnie's conscious mind focused on Mr. Archibald Brissonson. He was, for all intents and purposes, the catalyst for the resurgence of the nightmare. Because in her mind Bonnie Mason equated him with her father.

Bonnie asked for advice the next day during the bomb scare. She told Alyssa about the phone call and her subsequent check into Joe Brissonson's records. The student had been absent two days and her records showed that he had presented legal excuses for those days. But he never made up the work he missed. Standing in the bright sunlight of that warm October day, Alyssa listened to the story, then attempted an explanation.

She had had a similar experience that forced her to acknowledge the latest in student maneuverings. She had recently spoken to the mother of a failing student, and the mother was quite concerned over her daughter's grade of 68. The comment raised a red flag. Alyssa quickly balanced the phone receiver between her chin and shoulder and flipped the pages of her grade book, thankful that she had returned the mother's call from school or she wouldn't have been able to check immediately. The mother was mighty distressed to find out that her daughter's grade was 58, not 68. Still, Alyssa had doubts as to the student's role in the error. She explained to the mother that perhaps she, Alyssa, made the mistake while bubbling in grades, or perhaps the computer operator did it. More investigation, however, revealed the truth. There was no error. The student had changed the grade.

"It's remarkably easy for them to do," Alyssa concluded. "Report cards aren't cards at all anymore. That computer paper is very flimsy. It's easy to erase, then use a pencil or find a typewriter to change a grade. I told Mother it was commendable that her daughter hadn't given herself an 88, but that didn't calm Mother down one bit. There's one little girl at BCA who will never try to alter her report card again."

The Pact

When the bell rang to summon all into the bombless building, Bonnie decided that she would follow Alyssa's advice. She would talk to the student and try to have as little contact as possible with the father. The student was the major concern. And the way Bonnie described the father, dealing with him wouldn't help anybody anyway.

Bonnie was disappointed when she had to begin her lesson without the body of Joe Brissonson in the room. Her insides started to churn as she wondered what had become of him. The bomb scare and the nice weather must have lured him away. He had to be cutting class. God, Joe, not today, she thought. Your father's deadline is tomorrow. Then he'll roast us both on a spit. Where the hell are you? But Joe didn't materialize among the shapes slowly shuffling into the room. As she watched them enter, Bonnie was aware that most of them would never exceed that slow shuffle through the entire course. She didn't enjoy this class very much. It was a challenge, all right, but not the kind of challenge that teachers dream of.

The course drew mostly non-regents and a smattering of lazy regents students. They always showed up the first week with the idea that the course would be cake. Bonnie stubbornly refused to let the course sink to that level, even though other teachers were teaching other sections like a merry stroll through Romper Room. On this twenty-third day of October,1980, Bonnie had something special to use in class. She distributed copies of a short news article that she had typed and duplicated earlier in the week. It was perfect for class, or so she thought when she first saw it.

Her initial reaction to the piece flooded back and enveloped her with the fury she felt the first time she read the headline: Teacher Runs Red Light. Then she remembered how her anger festered when she first read the article. Sixteen moving violations were listed, some with juicy details. Sixteen names. One offender happened to be a teacher. At first she became defensive, her mind clicking off key words for a letter to the editor. Slanted journalism. Insult by innuendo. Sensationalism. Subliminal manipulation of public opinion. Then she decided that a public reaction would only dignify and enhance the travesty, highlight it even further.

One of her primary goals in this course was to teach students the difference between news releases and editorial comment, objectivity and subjectivity, facts and feelings. But what about this? What about a news release worded to evoke an emotional response? A skilled journalist could influence the opinions of the reader without the reader knowing it. And in news releases. This particular headline was a blatant example of it. To her, anyway. So she decided to use the article in class as an introduction to her unit on slanted journalism and sensationalism. It wasn't as perfect an example as *The National Inquirer*, but she would get to that eventually. Besides, in her opinion, there was more danger in subtlety.

She had shown the article and the accompanying worksheet she devised to Alyssa and was a little disappointed at the reaction from the more experienced teacher. By all means, try it, but, Alyssa warned, be prepared for anything. They might get frustrated with this vocabulary even though you plan to give definitions. They might turn you right off because this whole concept isn't tangible enough to keep their interest. Give it a try. If it flops, you'll just have to backtrack with simpler examples.

Bonnie knew that her lesson was in trouble as soon as she began it. They didn't care much about the definitions of "innuendo" and "subliminal," words they wouldn't even try to pronounce. One student remained interested enough to say that he didn't see anything wrong with the headline. So what if a teacher got a ticket? He knew teachers who did worse things than that. Bonnie tried to explain that the headline would be just as underhanded if the word teacher were replaced by fireman or nurse or plumber.

But try as she might, she couldn't get them to understand. It bothered her deeply, not because her preparation had been a waste of time, but because the concept still eluded them. She would have to find some other way to get the point across. A simpler way. How ironic, she thought. What could be simpler than that four-word headline, yet what could be more complex?

How can people defend themselves against propaganda, against mind control, unless they are at least taught to acknowledge their own vulnerability? Bonnie knew that the students in her fifth period class especially needed to develop such mental processes or they would undoubtedly join the great mass of humanity manipulated by clever politicians, unprincipled journalists, and unscrupulous salesmen, peddling everything from mops to nuclear warheads.

But the class was not a total bust. Five minutes before the end of the period, Joe Brissonson strolled in with a pass. His appearance pulled Bonnie out of the doldrums. She hustled Joe out into the hall amidst considerable hooting from his friends. You're in for it now, Joe, they said. Bonnie shut out the noise by closing the door and looked into the face of the boy as he struggled to get his hands into the pockets of his tight jeans. She had to look up to see his face and, for a split second, it wasn't his face at all that she saw, but another's. Boy? Man? Male? Student? Lover? What? All of the above.

"Your father called me last night," Bonnie said. "He wanted to know why you're failing. Would you mind explaining the personality conflict we're supposed to be having?" Joe grimaced and reddened. "Aw, Miss Mason, I'm sorry. I had to tell him something. Otherwise he's on my ass something wicked. I can't stand it when he gets on my case."

"Is that why you erased the number of absences on your report card?"

"Yeah. Hey! How'd you find that out? He doesn't know that, does he? Boy, there'll be hell to pay if he finds that out. I won't even go home anymore. You don't know what it's like listening to him."

But I do, Bonnie thought, I do. "He said you're in your room every night doing homework. Why don't you ever hand any in?"

"That's how much he knows. My room is the only place in the house where I don't have to listen to him. And I've got a stereo system."

"Headphones?"

Joe shook his head. "Hey, I'm doing some work now, right? I handed in that thing we had to do last week. I'll make it through all right. I always do when the chips are down."

"Joseph, my boy, right now your father is holding all the chips. I don't relish the thought of getting you into hot water with him, and I don't really care if he thinks I'm an idiot, which he does."

"He thinks everybody's an idiot except him."

"Does your mother have a say in anything? Can you confide in her?"

"She died when I was eight."

"I'm sorry, Joe. It's too bad that you and your father aren't closer. He never remarried?"

"Are you kidding? Who would marry him?"

"Your mother did."

"Yeah, I took care a that. Whenever they had a fight they both agreed that I shoulda been an abortion. I heard that a lot when I was a kid. I hadda ask my second grade teacher what an abortion was. She wouldn't tell me."

Oh, God, Bonnie thought. Child abuse comes in all shapes and forms. "Still," she said, "you and your father have been going it alone for a long time. Maybe if you ..."

231

"Too long. Look, Miss Mason, you can't do nothing about my father and me, so forget it."

"I suppose you're right. But I wish I could. I wish somebody could. I've gone through father problems myself. Nobody was ever able to help me."

"Yeah?" Joe said. "You too, huh?"

"Maybe we'll talk about it someday, if you want to. Right now I think we'd better discuss you and this course. The only way you're going to get through it is to do some work. Agreed?" Joe nodded. "And you've got to stop cutting class. Your father doesn't know and I don't see any reason to tell him what you've been doing if you promise to straighten out."

"You'd do that for me?"

"Only if you toe the line from now on. I mean it. If you miss this class one more time before the end of the semester, if you don't do your work, I'm spilling everything. It's blackmail, Joseph, and you can take it or leave it."

"Nah, it's not blackmail. I'll take it. What are you gonna tell old Archibald?"

"I don't know yet. But whatever it is, the only way I can get you off the hook is to take the rap myself. I don't care about that, Joe. I don't care what your father thinks of me as long as you stick to your end of the bargain. You're going to have to work hard to raise that miserable 50 to a passing average."

"Ah - about that 50, I - ah - I sort of - well … "

"You changed it."

"Yeah."

"To what?"

"60"

"Tell me something. Why didn't you change it to 80 as long as you were changing it?" He looked a bit insulted. "Aw, no. That woulda been wrong. I mean, I failed, right?"

"Right. But your sense of wrong is still a little warped. Or maybe it's your sense of right." He smiled, then asked, "Do you think I could maybe do some extra work to really bring it up to a 60, my first grade I mean?"

"We'll see. First I want you to show me that you're going to change your ways."

"I will," Joe Brissonson vowed. "I will, I promise. And thanks, thanks a lot."

The Pariahs

Her color code made it easy to distinguish which folders belonged to which preparation: two red for scholarship sophomores, one black for seniors, two yellow for regents sophomores. She pushed the fifth period vocabulary tests into the right pocket of the red folder labeled FIFTH PERIOD, ENGLISH 2 SCHOLARSHIP. She always placed papers for grading on the right side because the pocket on the left side always contained make-up work. Sometimes during the year the left pocket bulged with paper, but the right pocket was never allowed to become too full. She was almost obsessive about cleaning out that right pocket, whether it held spelling or vocabulary or literature tests, grammar assignments, compositions, or quizzes. The ungraded contents of five right pockets were with her always, but never overflowed onto or into her desk. She had never lost or even misplaced a set of papers in all her twelve years of teaching and she had no intention of ever doing so.

The top of her desk was consistently immaculate. She certainly used the space during class, but at other times nothing remained there except a blotter with a small calendar slipped under one of its corners. Once upon a time after her miraculous acquisition of a desk that was hers and hers alone she courageously stored her keyed and annotated texts in a long line just beyond the fringes of the blotter. How convenient it was to have her books at her fingertips. She loved it when she suddenly thought of the perfect example during class and could merely reach out to get it in her hands. Like a good entertainer, she knew the effects of timing. Then one not-so-fine day her *Merchant of Venice* disappeared. Shortly after that her keyed red grammar was gone. She made a frantic search both times, retraced her steps, considered all alternatives. She never located the books, of course, and she felt as if she had lost two limbs.

She became fearful then. She didn't want the added work of keying two new vocabulary books. Keys were supplied for both books, but printed on pages separate from the text. She had written all the answers where they belonged to expedite her own recognition during class. Even the separate pages of answers weren't as valuable as the keyed books.

And what if her Dickens disappeared? It was brimming over with notes, it had been a part of her since her first year. All of them, all of her books were technically irreplaceable because they contained bits

Rosemary Cania Maio

and pieces of herself scattered throughout their pages. Revelations, explanations, definitions, reactions, tones, moods, even occasional mistakes hastily crossed out or altered by experience, all chronicled on the thousands of pages.

When her grammar disappeared, Alyssa was in luck. She had another keyed copy bequeathed to her by Mary Gregory. She had almost given the book to a new teacher to save the novice some work, but held back because she treasured the book as a lasting reminder of Mary's spirit. The replacement didn't completely negate her sense of loss, but at least it eliminated the necessity of staring down at answerless pages. She wasn't so lucky with the Shakespeare. Bad enough that it disappeared the day she lectured on Portia's quality of mercy speech, she also had to go scrounge around the resource room to find a replacement. All the decent copies had gone to students, and she ended up with a coverless, dog-eared, page-shedding copy for her own use. And when it happened, she hadn't taught the play enough times yet to feel comfortable without her notes.

The long line of books on her desk, she decided, was too tempting. Too many people were in and out of the room all day long. By the time she taught *Hamlet*, all her books had been locked away for a few years. The first time she equated Claudius' "Is there not rain enough in the sweet heavens" with Macbeth's "The multitudinous seas incarnadine," she did it from memory because her *Macbeth* was buried under a pile of other books. It would always be a small irritation, and just another thing to think about, to unlock her filing cabinet at the beginning of every period, to extract the books she needed for that period, to lock them up again at the end, to remember to take those books she needed for one reason or another when she left the room.

One year she had to leave the room every other period. She had four classes that year and no two were consecutive. That year she rationalized that the schedule allowed her time mentally to prepare a fresh start for each class. And at least she had her own room. The next year she was assigned five classes and was startled by the grouping. She had classes first period, third period, then sixth, seventh, and eighth periods. The trilogy at the end of the day was bad enough because it came at the end of the day, but it was even worse because of its composition. Three in a row of the same thing: English 2R. So that time she rationalized that at least she was in her own room, that it would be convenient when she was showing films, that it was only for one year, that she was experienced enough to

234

handle anything. As the year progressed, she realized that she had to psyche herself for eighth period. Immediately repeating a lesson once and maintaining exuberance is easy, but the third time around with no break is horrible. But dreading eighth period wouldn't do her or her students any good. After all, it was the first time around for the kids. So she fought her own boredom in order to give all three classes equal treatment, equal instruction, equal parts of herself, even when the film projector overheated and sent smoke trailing through the room one day during its third consecutive run. She didn't hang around after school the year of the trilogy. She was so exhausted at the end of the day that she left immediately after the last bell sounded.

Alyssa had no say in the scheduling of her classes. Few teachers did. Whatever her schedule turned out to be was tolerable to her because it could not be changed. And always there was someone in a worse fix than she. Like the year Lainie began teaching third period, then had four in a row in the afternoon. Lainie, who was raring to go in the morning, had to put up with the frustration of a slow start every day, and she complained about it all year. It seems, she said, that they find out what would be an ideal schedule for each one of us, then work their hardest to give us anything but.

Alyssa wasn't so sure that there was some devious plot afoot. Instead she reasoned that with so many teachers and so many class sections and so many other variables like room availability and course popularity mixed into the stew, teacher schedules couldn't turn out ideal very often.

The year of Alyssa's afternoon trilogy was the year her lunch and free period were back-to-back, fourth and fifth periods. She loved that because it gave her an uninterrupted hour-and-a-half during the day to take care of papers from sixth, seventh, and eighth periods. She could grade objective tests the day after they were given.

Through her relatively few years of teaching, she had experienced a wide variety of schedules. She was fortunate enough during her first three years to have first period "free." That gave her time when she was an amateur to straighten out her head for the rest of the day, to duplicate materials, to run her homeroom cards to the office herself. As she grew in experience, her free period started to meander through the rest of the day and that pleased her because, like Lainie, she became comfortable with an early start. Each year she would adjust her thinking and her planning to fit a new schedule.

Experience taught her other things: afternoon study halls were desirable because of smaller enrollment; a free period during a lunch period meant no access to counselors or administrators; being free eighth period offered an immense temptation to leave early, which she often did the year she was free eighth period; sometimes the kids were as sluggish first period as they were eighth period; one's room was only available when one had a class in it, at other times someone else was using it and it was downright rude to disturb other classes just because one forgot a pile of papers to grade; one erased the board as an act of courtesy before the next teacher came in, even though one would have to write the same thing later in the day (It's work no matter how you do it, she told Bonnie once. It's more strenuous than it looks to fill four boards with info two or three or four times a day. Dittoes are no bargain either by the time you type and duplicate and file. Even transparencies are a pain because you have to make the transparencies, roam up and down the hall to find an overhead projector with a lamp that hasn't burned out, make sure that someone isn't going to steal the damn machine the first time you leave your room, or, in your case, figure out how you're going to get different machines on different floors because you float, then hope and pray that every room you're in has a screen, then listen to the kids complain that they can't see the screen from the back of the room anyway); one leaves nothing on the top of one's desk that might be inadvertently picked up and carried away by another teacher, or purposely pilfered by almost anyone.

She kept control over her three preparations through careful organization; all the folders in her filing cabinet were thoughtfully arranged for easy access, pulled out and returned with care, to accommodate future needs. When she needed to find something, she found it quickly. Always. Her files were miraculous.

She knew exactly what was contained in every one of her desk drawers at all times. She had it all catalogued in her mind: homeroom materials, the study hall folder, classroom folders, mounds and mounds of classroom tests, study sheets, and other materials that were doled out a little at a time all year, graded work that had to be returned when time allowed, extra copies of this and that, make-up work, emergency lesson plans, copies of progress reports and other notices and notes she sent to parents and counselors and administrators.

She never dealt with the here and now without thoughts of what comes next. She was in constant preparation; she had to be because she was never quite sure how many copies were stored in each of the folders in her filing cabinet. She tried once to indicate a count on each folder before she filed for the next year, but the system didn't work very well because of constant dipping into filed folders for new students or for students who had lost first copies. The only way, then, for her to determine numbers was to pull the folders for an entire unit and count the contents of each one. It was crucial to her to run off sufficient numbers well before she needed materials.

When she saw two scholarship sections in September, 1980, her reaction was a far cry from the excitement and gratitude that bubbled up in her the first time she was assigned a scholarship class. The first thought that popped into her head was that she had run off an extra class set of all her scholarship materials the year before to save herself some future time. But with two sections, thirty copies wouldn't be enough. She would have to run off thirty more of everything all year.

She thought it was peculiar herself, her insistence on planning ahead. She had never been particularly organized as a student, even in college. She procrastinated as much as anyone else then, and she continued to do so in her personal life afterward. She'd wash the kitchen floor next week, or shower in the morning, or shop for groceries tomorrow. But teaching was different. She had to feel that she knew what she was doing and when, she had to feel organized which, in turn, made her feel competent which, in turn gave her the right to demand excellence from her students.

When she had piles of paper waiting for distribution, she felt secure. And she felt victorious. The machines wouldn't get a chance to ruin her plans at the last minute. When she knew that the most conveniently located duplicator was having a good day, she hauled out as much as she could handle during lunch and/or free period and made copies to store for future use. She learned to use answer sheets whenever feasible so that she wouldn't have to duplicate entire tests. Sometimes even that caused more work because students would write answers or graffiti on the test papers, and she would have to make more copies of tests anyway. But most of what she distributed had to stay with students. She firmly believed in the value of study questions and work sheets because she used them not as busywork but as instructional aids. She duplicated those materials all year long. And sometimes a real battle ensued.

There were the days when the duplicator worked beautifully, but paper was not available. Or the times when the duplicator worked beautifully, paper was piled to the ceiling, but not a drop of fluid could be found in any of the four faculty rooms. And then there were the times when she typed on extra sized ditto masters, but only short paper was available, or when only long paper and short masters were around, or when she tried to get copies out of an old master that had long since lost its ink. There was a time before black zerox copies when masters just had to be retyped. Even after the miracle of black copies that could be run through another machine to make dittoes, there were problems. The original had to be exceedingly clear or the process from original to black copy to ditto master would produce student copies too fuzzy to read. Alyssa hated that. She absolutely despised distributing material that was poorly reproduced. She knew that even the best student wouldn't give a glance to information or questions that were difficult to read. She wasn't too fond of doing it herself. How many times the absence list was impossible to read because it was too light or cut off in the middle or afflicted with long white stripes cutting through all the names. It was a waste of time, work, and paper to distribute such garbage.

So on occasion she did what many other teachers did. She learned how to sneak around. It was every man for himself anyway. One acquired whatever one felt was necessary for one's students through any device or means, devious or otherwise. One learned to beg, to borrow, to pilfer, to prevaricate, to punch, to tickle, to torment. If the last can of fluid or the last ream of paper was located in one of the other faculty rooms, it had to disappear when no one was around to witness its removal. If a limit was placed on the number of black copies made on the zerox machine, one needed to duplicate the same thing more than once during the day or avoid documentation altogether. If a working duplicator was suddenly replaced by a clunker, one rallied with friends to locate and steal back the good one.

The entire faculty was accustomed to such activity, such desperation. They were being run by the machines, and they never stopped resenting the relentless tyranny. All four faculty rooms were continuously abuzz with complaints. Everyone was disgruntled over one thing or many things or all things.

At the end of fifth period Alyssa carried both red folders, both yellow folders, and her record books to the fourth floor faculty room. When she arrived, she and Jean decided to migrate for the period because the room had become so warm. They traveled down one floor to the next closest faculty room and, after some socializing with colleagues they rarely saw, started grading papers. Isolated conversations continued throughout the room. Then another teacher walked in. The man started cursing as soon as he entered; he cursed and mumbled, mumbled and cursed, and aimlessly threw papers from one location to another. His text was being changed against his wishes, he was disgusted with the rest of the department, there was nothing wrong with the text they were using, it was an unforgivable waste of taxpayers' money to replace perfectly usable books, types of problems never changed anyway, what difference did it make if the copyright was 1960, they could buy all the books they wanted he wasn't going to use them, he would continue to use the old texts until they rotted no matter what the department squandered money on.

Those interested in the matter hurled words of support and challenge into the air. Then a few barbs were thrown in to relieve chronic cases of boredom or restlessness. It wasn't long before the argument reached thesis level then splintered into philosophies of education, the role of the school in society, the advisability of changing the grade system, and the latest developments of a currently popular night-time soap.

The two English teachers looked at each other and each knew what the other was thinking. The majority of teachers in all disciplines were dedicated and caring. There were math teachers who spent hours after school pounding theorems and formulas into the densest of brains, just for the thrill of seeing eyes widen with the glimmer of understanding; science teachers who labored over weekly lab assignments in addition to everyday classroom duties; language teachers who struggled with the impossible task of teaching a foreign tongue to students who had little proficiency in their own; business teachers who rarely left school without a pile of papers to grade, who fought a losing battle trying to convince counselors that their courses demanded at least normal intelligence, that they were not designed to be a dumping ground for students desperate for credit; history teachers who were plagued with constant pressure to cover more and more material and to develop an appreciation of the past in students with little interest in the present. But the incompetents, the malcontents, the pedants, the dullards were scattered like spots of mold over every department.

The only philosophy was to live and let live or, in some cases, to live and let die. Alyssa Matthews believed in that philosophy. So did Jean Tevarro. It was difficult enough to be responsible for oneself without trying to judge or criticize others. But still, both women knew the facts, both women felt an increasing irritation with the facts and the philosophy.

After the increase in their workload, English teachers had become pariahs. They did not voluntarily serve on faculty committees and often ignored appointments to such committees. They no longer sponsored clubs. The department had once directed and produced the senior play, along with a yearly production in conjunction with the music department. An English teacher once took charge of public address announcements, insuring clarity and precision with instruction in public speaking and requiring students to audition before they were allowed to dispense information. A literary magazine which published students' attempts at creative writing also bit the dust, along with the debate club. The school newspaper lost the involvement of an English teacher and proceeded to print articles marred by grammatical and spelling errors. Alyssa counted forty-seven misspellings in one such issue and stared in horror at FILTHY AND UNSUPERVISED, STUDENTS PROTEST BATHROOM CONDITIONS, the worst of several headlines displaying manglings of the language. It certainly was a fine tribute to the English staff. She wanted to run to the office, check schedules, and pull the editor and reporters out of classes. She wanted to ask them if they had slept through English for years. But she didn't. Because she realized that her anger was misdirected at poorly guided students, and that it wasn't anger at all that she was feeling, but helplessness.

What she really needed to do was take over the newspaper, whip those kids into shape, demand a superior product, instill a sense of pride. She could taste it. She could see the results. But she couldn't do it. Not with eighty-three compositions waiting to be graded, over one hundred spelling tests, forty-five literature tests, and over one hundred vocabulary tests by the end of the week. Not with lessons to plan for the following week and the following month. She couldn't do it. Instead she closed the newspaper and threw it in the wastebasket. She was there to teach her classes, not to cure every ache and pain in the building. And so English teachers became isolated from the rest of the faculty.

"He's got a real problem, hasn't he, poor soul," Jean snickered out in the hall. "I can't stomach listening to that when I've got so much work to do. I had to get out of there."

"I think I drew blood biting my tongue," Alyssa answered. "The bastard doesn't want to prepare new lessons or key a new book. It might cut into his social life. What the hell would he do if he had the number of texts that we work out of?"

"It's a good thing you didn't say anything. Even I keep my mouth shut when I hear stuff like that. They only tell you that it's your fault, you should've picked another subject to teach. I've even heard that jerk brag about the remarkable condition of his plan book. I think he's used the same one since 1950. Can you imagine using the same plans for years on end?"

"Is this October 23rd? Then turn to page 40, exercise 3," Alyssa said devilishly. "We're constantly evaluating the effectiveness and relevance of our materials, I'm on a constant crusade for activities that are different and exciting, and he's complaining about a change in the one text he's used for twenty years. Amazing." The same thought struck them both at the same time. "Have you ever wondered who's the fool?" Jean asked Alyssa. Alyssa said no, she never gave it a thought before, but now, the way things were, she wondered more and more every day.

The two women decided to journey down to the main office to check mail boxes. They did not hear the reaction to their abrupt exit.

"Did those two prima donnas leave?"

"It's too noisy in here for the English department's intellectual ears."

"Then why do they come here at all?"

"I have to unwind during the day. I can't work every minute."

"Better they don't make a habit of coming here. They'll monopolize this duplicator, too. Have you ever stood in line behind one of 'em? They waste more paper. I'd like to know what the hell they're running off every day."

"A good teacher has it in his head. All that goddam paperwork is an excuse."

On the way to the office Jean thought she would continue discussing the dual themes of fools and exciting class activities, so she told Alyssa about the confrontation with Dannemore and the challenge she faced with her third period class. Alyssa's hazel eyes lit up when Jean described her scholarship juniors. The younger teacher had experienced such a blend of students twice before, once with juniors, once with sophomores. "I was so young when I had them," she complained. "I worked like hell with them and loved every minute of it, but I was so young. I know so much more now. I'd give my right arm to have a class like that now." Then she offered to check her files for materials. She had so much that she didn't use anymore, so much good stuff that was lying useless in manila folders. Jean could use it, then tell her about student reactions and performance. She could compare it all with the times when she used the material. How exciting that thought was to her! She never considered that she was replacing the joy of real experiences with vicarious ones, that she needed to relive the past in order to enjoy the present, that she had become so desperate. On October 23,

1980, she was not fully aware of the slow metamorphosis that had begun three years earlier. But awareness was imminent, it was looming ready to descend upon her, ready to consume her and rip her world to shreds.

As they walked the long hall leading to A Building, Alyssa spotted a peculiar item resting on the floor against a locker. They stopped and stared and debated. "You're crazy, Matt," Jean insisted, "it's just a balloon." Upon closer inspection, though, she had to agree that it was something else. All she could say as Alyssa grabbed her arm to pull her away was, "Green? Since when do they come in colors?" Aesthetics, Alyssa told her, progress. Where have you been, woman? Living in a cave? Then she went on to explain that they were also available in an array of exotic flavors. Lemon, lime, strawberry, peach, orange. By the time they reached the main office Jean added banana to the list and they were both convulsed in laughter. The two women often rationalized that while conditions certainly were not ideal, BCA was still not as bad as some high schools. They didn't need police in the halls, they didn't need to be escorted to their classrooms. There would always be fears connected with teaching, fears of student reprisals, fears of parental accusations, fears of unknown catastrophes. But they didn't have to be afraid of being beaten or stabbed or raped like teachers in some big-city schools. They had their problems, any school has its problems, but there were worse places to teach.

The mailboxes were crammed with paper. Alyssa found three requests for attendance records of homeroom students and a response from another teacher regarding the attendance of one of her own classroom students. There was also a pile of study hall notices individually directed to homeroom names, which reminded her that she needed to send out some herself. She had to find out where the no-shows were spending second period.

Jean started chuckling while reading one of the notes in her mailbox. The note was written on the bottom of a sheet of paper after a list of names. "These kids never showed up in study hall," she told Alyssa, "so I sent their names to Dannemore. He's checked for me before. He has more time than I have to do it. But after this morning I'm on his shit list." Alyssa read through his response: Mrs. Tevarro, please verify student study hall assignments with appropriate counselors, then notify students through homeroom procedure, then report to parents using appropriate forms. Thereafter report to me.

"I hope Bob takes care of mine," Alyssa said. "I plan to send him names, that's all. I hate spending time on this crap."

"Me, too. Face it, we just send names to protect ourselves. Nobody goes crazy tracking down study hall kids." Alyssa didn't bother to say that she always did just that. Instead she answered, "After what I went through this morning, I wish more of them would get lost."

"Oh, well, Danny-boy is getting sweet revenge. But the joke's on him. I'm not going through all this over study hall. I don't care if they show up or not." She crumbled the sheet of paper and threw it in a wastebasket.

"You ever worry about being responsible for them, wherever they are?" Alyssa asked. "I'm sure Dannemore kept a copy of that note. It gets him off the hook if anything is questioned."

"Sure I worry. We all do in varying degrees. But if we all did everything we're supposed to do around here, we'd be doing it twenty-five hours a day."

"Step right up and take a chance," Alyssa said in her best carnival barker voice, "five chances for a dollar, try your luck at the wheel of fortune." Then her mood changed as she started to read her own mail. The note was written on an ordinary memo form.

TO: A. Matthews
FROM: L. Broglio
DATE: 10/23/80
RE: Curtis Holbert

Please allow Curtis time to make up work missed because of absence.

That was it. It said no more.

Alyssa hadn't forgotten about Curtis Holbert. She had jotted his name on the list of reminders she kept clipped to the front of her class register. It was the best place for the list because she always carried the register. Effie Efficiency never neglected to return phone calls or run checks; loose ends were anathema to her. Old Effie recoiled in disgust at the mere thought of mouthing those two little words. Effie "forget"? Horrific, horrendous horrors! Old Effie methodically avoided the plague of shame by engaging in constant perusal of her list. The List would save her soul. Old Effie urgently studied and updated The List for better or for worse, for richer or poorer, in sickness and in health, whether it needed it or not. She added items with diligence and determination, and crossed out items with a vengeance akin to the fires of hell. Old Effie copied The List over because it was messy, added some items simply for the immediate pleasure of crossing them out, and filed The List in the same folder reserved for inhaling and exhaling. It was a Holy Trinity of sorts: Alyssa, Effie, and The List.

And so the memo meant an immediate trip to guidance. Jean understood that, said something about hunting down Jim Cote, and the two women split forces and went their separate ways.

Detachments

Sophomores:	Ann Brady A-L
	Dick Ruggles M-Z
Juniors:	Alan Quincy A-L
	Bernie Nuovo M-Z
Seniors:	Allen Hawkens A-L
	Dave Butte M-Z

It was still too early in the year for her to remember which students were assigned to which counselor, especially since she had sophomores in four classes, juniors in homeroom, seniors in one class, and a mixture in study hall. It meant she had to deal with all six counselors and three administrators all year.

She checked the listing of counselors she had written in her plan book the first week of school. For some reason, the information was no longer stuffed in mailboxes in September, so she had stopped by the cluster of offices and asked secretaries for the breakdown. She enjoyed a casual, friendly relationship with all the secretaries, even the one who once refused to take her attendance cards after the first period bell. For all intents and purposes, they kept the ship afloat, they buoyed the bureaucracy. And, as far as Alyssa could see they suffered the most abuse; they took it from administrators, they took it from teachers, they took it from counselors, they took it from students, they took it from parents. No wonder they were a tight little group. They knew everything that was worth knowing and, for the most part, kept it all among themselves.

She was glad she had to see Hawkens. Dave "What-A-Beaut" Butte was impossible to talk with, never helpful, always floating around on some cloud in another galaxy. He had no idea what he was doing, his desk was in perpetual disarray, and he had a reputation for spreading the mess among his unfortunate students. More than one teacher had received notes from him about students they had never even heard of. More than one student had been stuck with classes completely alien to those agreed upon six months earlier. More than one college application had gathered dust among the mountebank's wares, long after deadlines, long after hasty assurances. He was a menace to anything that came within fifty yards of his office.

Alyssa said a silent prayer of thanksgiving for Allen Hawkens, and another fervent prayer that she wouldn't have any big M through Z senior problems for the rest of the year. She exchanged compliments on apparel with the secretary in the outer office and sat to wait her turn after she was told that Hawk was in conference with a student. In fact, both counselors' doors were closed. As she waited, she looked over more of her mail.

TO: Homeroom Teachers
FROM: Guidance
DATE: 10/23/80
RE: Career Projection Data Forms

Wonderful, Alyssa thought. Just ducky. Keep forms for absentees. Statistical purposes. Future programs. What future programs? With what money? This means ten minutes chewed out of first period tomorrow. First period, oh shit, the nurse's list is for first period. Twelve have to go for physicals tomorrow. Has to be done at the doctor's convenience. Pull them out of class. What the hell difference does it make? I'm not allowed convenience. There goes my quiz on *Silas* tomorrow. Damn. It's all ready to go. Told the kids yesterday to be ready for anything Friday. Big joke. Maybe I should have announced names this morning. No, that would have been a mistake. Some would sign in late to avoid the doctor, then have to go next week. Better I didn't say anything. I was right yesterday though, didn't know myself how right.

TO: ALL DISTRICT CLASSROOM TEACHERS
FROM: CENTRAL OFFICE
DATE: OCTOBER 21, 1980
RE: WORKSHOPS ON THE HANDICAPPED

Once again as she read, Alyssa's mind exploded at certain key phrases: least restrictive environment, adapting curriculum, the legality of mainstreaming. Once again her litany began: I can't believe they're really going to do this to us. How are we supposed to give individual instruction to the handicapped? How? How can we handle any more preparation? Any more paperwork? Training is optional now, but when will we be required to do this? Oh, God, what's this? Legal ramifications? What are my legal responsibilities

246

when I am assigned a handicapped student? How much more do they think they can get out of me? I've got over a hundred kids with "special needs" now. Each mainstreamed child means another preparation. Each one. And an acre of worry. Legal ramifications? We can't satisfy the damned state mandates now. It's not humanly possible. Not humanly possible.

The secretary was staring at her. "I just stuffed those. Lou brought them in." Alyssa looked up. "Ever feel as though you're reading your own obituary, Doris?"

"What is it? I didn't read it at all."

"Mainstreaming. They want to make all of us special ed teachers. I don't want to be trained for special ed. Sometimes I think the mentally deranged are out here running things." She folded the notice in half lengthwise, then in half again top to bottom, and handed it to Doris. "Throw this out for me, would you?"

"Glad to. It's printed on pretty paper, anyway. I like this shade of green." She tossed the folded page into the basket under her desk. "Isn't there some way to fight it?"

"Not that I can see. Nobody ever bothers to ask teachers what education is all about. We're supposed to be seen and not heard. The 'experts' dictate policy and the experts have never taught in public schools. It's insane. We have to take orders from bureaucrats, administrators, and legislators. They pass laws and write books and lecture on philosophies of education without ever having taught a lesson or graded a paper. Nobody tries to tell doctors how to practice medicine or lawyers how to practice law. But it's open season on teachers. Education is everybody's whipping post."

One of the closed doors opened. Butte's. Erica Vetterly stood in the doorway, snarled a vicious "You'd better do something about it, and fast!" and slammed the door. She paused by Doris' desk long enough to say, "Make sure that he does, would you? He doesn't know his rectum from his windpipe," then stormed out of the office.

Alyssa watched her go, then turned her eyes slowly back to Doris in a look that said "What the hell —?"

"She's been slamming that door every day for the past week," Doris said. The door's going to hold up, but I'm afraid I'm starting to splinter."

"What's the problem? I didn't think she had it in her to get that excited over a student." Doris smirked. "Not just any student. Her son."

247

"Vance? I had Vance in class. He's a terrific kid. Bright, personable, witty. I loved him. I figured she must have adopted him. He's a senior now, is he? I can't keep track who's where anymore."

"He's almost valedictorian is what he is. But there's a problem with his physics teacher. Get this: Erica wants his teacher changed because the one he has is incompetent."

"Oh, brother."

"Vance is planning to major in physics and chemistry, I guess, so she's all bent out of shape about what a poor teacher might do to his preparation for college."

"And his average, no doubt. Well, from what I know about Vance, he'll survive anything."

"It's still a circus down here when she comes in!"

"But what justice. Vetterly and Butte deserve each other."

Alyssa heard the other door in the office open and turned to see a student leave. "See you later," she told Doris. She walked into the office briskly and sat in the conferee's chair next to the counselor's desk.

Allen Hawkens was a distinguished-looking man with a full crop of perfectly white hair, a rugged angular face, and piercing ebony eyes. He had long ago accepted the change in his job description. The change was unwritten and unspoken. Nevertheless he knew. He dealt with almost three hundred schedules every year. The title of "counselor" had become obsolete, though he advised whenever he could. He enjoyed the closeness he developed with some of his students, but the great majority remained mere names. By the time he finished scheduling and rescheduling for one semester, it was time to do it for the next. The counselor in him was alive and well but living in limbo, having arrived at that address many years ago.

He smiled when Alyssa sat next to his desk because he always enjoyed seeing her no matter what questions or problems she carried. Though the two could have engaged in the familiarity of "Hawk" and "Matt," neither did. He had been "Mr. Hawkens" when she was a student, and while she could comfortably manage an occasional "Allen," she couldn't go as far as "Hawk." She could refer to him as "Hawkens," but "Al" was too frivolous. He had known her as Alyssa Marie Grispelli and she was still Alyssa Marie Grispelli plus Matthews plus a degree plus students that she cared for. She was one of his successes and he was proud of her.

"First of all," Alyssa said as she flipped open her class attendance book and pulled a slip clipped into the third period section, "I need a number. Gayle Fine?"

"Oops." He leaned forward and slid a pile of cards to the edge of the desk.

"Yep, you did it again," she teased. "And you sent me the wrong color slip. At first I thought I was losing someone."

He laughed. "I'm color blind. Sorry I made your heart go pitter patter for nothing."

"Might you have any idea where this girl is?"

"She hasn't shown yet? I was afraid of that."

"She's missed half the course already. Can't you find her something easier?"

"Everything else is filled third period. Do what you can with her, would you Alyssa?"

"Well, sure, but I need a body and a brain to work with."

"There's brain enough in her. It's the body. Getting the body here isn't going to be easy. I thought I had her convinced that if she graduated she might be able to find a decent job and support herself. Her parents are divorced. The father is in Florida and doesn't want her. She was living here with her mother, but the mother ran off to points unknown with a new husband. Gayle is never sure where she'll be spending the night. She didn't want to begin the year at all, and it took me a while to find her. That's why she started so late. I talked until I was blue in the face just to get her to come in to see me. I'll have to try to contact her again. Let me know if she doesn't show up tomorrow and any day thereafter. I've got the nurse involved in this, too. Gayle has a history of blindness."

Alyssa's body jerked. "What?"

"Not the real thing. Well, it is and it isn't. Have you ever heard of hysterical blindness?"

"Yes," Alyssa said. "Lord, what some of these kids suffer. I think about that sometimes when I get aggravated over a kid who's failing. Who knows what he has to go home to every night? Or if he even has a home to go to? How will you find this girl? Where might she be? She can't be sleeping in the park. Or can she?"

"She left me a number earlier in the week. Oh, before I forget again, here's her student number. She lives with her aunt off and on."

Alyssa took the card he offered and copied the number. "That sounds promising."

"Her aunt, ah— her aunt isn't exactly the matronly type. She makes a living by selling herself on street corners."

"Oh, Christ have mercy."

"And in bars. She lives above a bar."

"Allen, this is beginning to read like a cheap novel."

249

"You know what they say about fact and fiction."

Alyssa groaned. "Look, I'll keep you posted on her attendance and do what I can to get her through the course. But you know that anyway. You can't fool me with your 'every other section is filled' routine."

"She needs somebody with a heart, Alyssa," he said softly.

She looked at the number she had just copied, thinking this was the easy part of her mission. "I just found this in my mailbox," she said, handing Broglio's note to the counselor. "It's totally ridiculous. The kid is getting away with murder."

She started an explanation of her side of the story, but he stopped her. "Don't waste your breath. I know exactly what happened. His encores are carbon copies. The original performance was a one-man show three years ago. He managed to get, in writing from Bassard, THE interpretation of the two-days-to-make-up-work-missed–because-of-absence rule. He's been using it to his own best advantage ever since."

"But can't you do anything with his parents? Can't they see what he's doing?"

"Mom produced and Dad directed the premier. No doubt they applaud the encores. Didn't you recognize the name? You didn't, did you?"

"Holbert? No."

"Cynthia Holbert is the first woman to be appointed judge in upstate New York, and Curtis Holbert, Senior, has been on the Board of Education for the last twenty years. The family is well-versed in influence and power. I'm really surprised that you didn't make the connection."

"I don't care about all that shit, Allen. I don't penalize a kid for his family, and I damned well don't grant him favors because of it. It makes me sick when this happens. Oh, I know it happens, I'm not that naive. Somebody should take those people on. You can get away with murder if you're rich enough or powerful enough."

"Don't let it get to you. Nobody can take those people on and emerge from the battle unscathed. That's why nobody does it."

"And justice for all. Did you see that movie? People cheered at the end of that movie. I could watch that ending a million times and still feel victorious."

"At the end? At the very end, when Al Pacino's sitting on the steps of the courthouse? He's on the outside looking in. I got the impression that he'd never get in again. That's a hollow victory, it seems to me."

"No, that's the most glorious victory a human being can achieve, to sacrifice himself for his principles, especially when his principles are noble. The human spirit can take only so much abuse and then it cracks. I admire the person who fights back even at the risk of his own neck, probably because I'm not that kind of person."

"I don't believe in martyrdom," Hawkens said. "The time for martyrs is long past. Today people forget too fast. You can serve your cause far better by slowly chipping away to make your mark."

"So tell me, have you been chipping away at Curtis Holbert?"

"Iron doesn't chip."

"All right, he gets away with it. I swallow what's left of my pride every time he walks into the room, and let him hand in work whenever he damned well feels like it. What, pray tell, am I supposed to say to the two girls who haven't handed in papers yet? They were in class yesterday, but not there today. The paper was due yesterday. Is it now one day late, two days late, or do I, perhaps, owe them time? If they're out tomorrow and Monday, their six days would take them two weeks beyond the deadline, but technically their papers would be only one day late. Maybe I should devote some time to lecturing on this little trick. Or better yet, tell Bassard to schedule assemblies. He wouldn't even have to show up, the assistants are all experts in the 'Holbert Procedure.' And why isn't it in the Student Handbook? There should be a section labeled MOCKERY anyway."

"Calm down, Alyssa. The agreement Curtis made with Bassard three years ago included the kid's promise that he would keep his mouth shut and refrain from recruiting any disciples."

"How nice. You're telling me that I can throw the book at those two girls. I can maintain my standards with everyone else by playing the hypocrite. How am I supposed to keep from knifing that devious little bastard?"

"Self-control?"

"Ah, yes. That for which I am famous."

"If it makes you feel any better, Joe Axelrod was in here this morning bellowing over the same problem. Curtis owes him work too."

"Joe's an old-fashioned teacher, Allen. I've often wondered how he's put up with it all these years. He has no patience for stupidities. At least I started with the stupidities, I know nothing else. I learned how to live with them, though it's getting harder and harder even for me. I joke about knifing Curtis Holbert, Joe might do it. And I wouldn't blame a man like Joe, I'd acquit Joe in a minute."

"He's a good man and a good teacher."

251

"But he still has to knuckle under for the Holberts."

"Just like the rest of us. There will always be Holberts. About all you can do is try not to let it taint you. If it does, you won't be any good to anyone. Believe me, Alyssa, I've been through this before. Ride it out and forget about it."

"It's so unfair, so insidious …"

"Listen to me. Don't dwell on it. Don't dwell on the Gayle Fines or the Curtis Holberts. You won't survive it if you do. There's such a thing as detachment. Stop wondering about Joe Axelrod. That's how he made it through: one fine day he developed a healthy sense of detachment. You don't resort to it all the time or you'll turn into Erica Vetterly. Only during crisis, Alyssa, only when you're shaking with rage or sickened by injustice. I wish the world was made differently, I wish I could tell you otherwise. But I can't. I told you, I've been through this before. If I didn't put up with the Curtis Holberts, I wouldn't be here for the Gayle Fines. Detachment. You've got to learn detachment."

She knew somewhere deep inside that he was right. She knew and yet she felt defiant, for the knowledge was repulsive to her. "You just told me you needed somebody with a heart."

He understood. It had taken him a long, long time to learn. Until finally he realized that he either had to change or get out. She too had to learn in her own way, in her own time. He was trying to spare her some of the suffering, that was all. When he looked at her, he thought of his own daughter.

"Some heart," he said. "Too much heart is no good. Too much heart can destroy you."

"I know enough not to get too emotionally involved in my students' problems," she said.

"That's not what I'm talking about."

"I know."

"Then swallow hard and forget about it."

She would try, she said. She would try to close her mind to the repugnance of Curtis Holbert. She would swallow hard and add another layer of bile to the monstrous thing growing inside her.

In the meantime in the science wing Jean Tevarro smiled broadly and offered congratulations. Jim Cote was sorry he had been forced to make the decision he made, but still excited at the prospect of blazing a new trail. She had found him in his office and made him laugh when she poked her head through the doorway and announced, "All teachers shat upon this morning will receive a compensatory bonus in the next paycheck."

That, he said, was exactly his problem. Or rather, the lack thereof. "I have to get out," he told her. "Next September I'll have four kids in college at once. Harriet never worked because she wanted to stay home with the kids as they were growing up. Now she wants to go back to school for the degree she never finished. I make a decent wage here, but it isn't enough for all that tuition. I finally have to take one of those offers I've been refusing for years."

Jean told him he was damned fortunate to have somewhere else to go. "I'd leave this rat hole in a minute if I could find another job with close to equal pay, the hell with making more. I know what you mean about having everybody in college at once. It's great fun having them a year apart when they're young, but financial disaster when they get older. I can hardly wait for mine to tell me they all want to get married in the same month."

Jim expressed some apprehension at the thought of starting all over again in a new job, and Jean told him that his feelings were only natural. He was resigning in January, and he swore her to secrecy. He had no desire to witness the inevitable bloody battle over the chairmanship.

Jean felt good about Jim's decision to move on because he felt good about it. She was infected with his enthusiasm. After she caught up with Alyssa and listened to her Curtis Holbert tale, after she read the notice on mainstreaming, she felt an odd sense of revenge. "The world does not deserve good teachers," she told Alyssa without mentioning Jim Cote. He's getting out, she told herself, he's getting out and I'm glad because his excellence is wasted here. And damn it all, I'm jealous.

The Plea

They hadn't written a single thing since school started. Nothing in eight weeks. Grammar: Yes; Spelling: Yes; *A Separate Peace*: Yes; Short Stories: Yes; Vocabulary: No, the books weren't in yet; Writing: No, teacher wouldn't give writing assignments when she knew she didn't have time to grade them.

She had to avoid assigning written work somewhere. Certainly not with seniors writing a research paper. It boiled down to either the scholarship or the regents sections. She didn't want to be partial to the scholarship sections, but somehow felt it a greater sin to neglect their need to experience varied and frequent writing assignments. She knew in her heart of hearts that that was wrong, but sugared over her displeasure with good intentions. The regents sections didn't do much writing in the beginning, but she'd catch them up later on.

She thought once or possibly twice about the limited benefits of spending less time grading papers. Maybe it was a good idea to give a paper one cursory reading, slap a grade on it, hand it back, assign another paper immediately, and hope for some improvement. Maybe many hastily written and graded papers did compensate for none at all. Maybe, maybe, maybe ... she would never know, though, because she simply could not grade papers that way.

As soon as she started to read a student's paper she assumed a dual role. Every time she slashed with her red pen, an electrical impulse slashed through her brain. Why, she asked herself, why was this mistake made? How could it have been avoided? Who's responsible? Her eyes darted back and forth from mistakes to names, from names to mistakes. The register that she kept in her head was even more complicated than the one she kept on paper. Who has spelling problems, who's weak in grammar, whose grades are erratic.

No matter what she was grading, she could not refrain from detailed analysis, for she graded with a sense of involvement, with a desire to pinpoint and to understand what might have prompted a student to give a particular answer. What rule of grammar hadn't he learned or just failed to apply? Was there a way to cure his spelling ailment, or was his inability to spell deeply rooted somewhere back in grade school? Was the synonym that he gave for that vocabulary word totally wrong, or did it reflect a shade of meaning that she had never considered? It was more demanding to require students to supply synonyms or antonyms on vocabulary tests. It was much more difficult than matching or multiple choice. So much more demanding and difficult — for them and for her.

When teacher aides were added to the educational scene, she wasn't at all interested. She never would have allowed a teacher aide access to her papers, even if aides were made available in the high school. She felt an intimate attachment to those papers that was impossible to undermine. She wouldn't even allow Jeff to help her grade the objective part of her final exams. First of all, he might make a mistake, the point system was complicated. As it was, she triple-checked every paper to avoid making mistakes herself. Secondly, there might be some leeway with student answers and she had to make those decisions herself. And thirdly, she had to see what kinds of errors were predominant so that she might revise her teaching the following year.

Nobody, but nobody, touched her papers. And written work was by far the toughest, the most consuming. She had to get inside the student's brain to determine what made him react or describe or reason in a particular way. She had to identify, acknowledge, his thought processes before she could accurately and effectively challenge or criticize his reasoning. And many times she had to seriously consider the idea herself in order to offer a sound improvement. She knew she wasn't being particularly helpful when she jotted "Huh?" or "Change this" or "Poor sentence" in the margins. Students needed more than that if they were to learn anything. They needed specifics. And even when faced with specifics, some students demanded debate, so she always felt the pressure of being accurate and equitable in her assessments. Could she refuse credit to the student who took issue with the reasoning that Caesar's arrogance is highlighted by his refusal to heed repeated warnings? We don't view John Kennedy as arrogant, the student explained, and John Kennedy didn't listen to Jeanne Dixon.

More than once she had to explain to a student that his paper was dull not because she wasn't particularly interested in the topic, but because the paper was lifeless due to weak examples or lack of wit or poor expression. Sometimes she wondered herself why she could grade a paper no higher than a C. Those were the most difficult times because she had to give a better rationale than pure instinct.

Every time she set eyes on a paper, she engaged in an intense mental process remarkably similar to the most strenuous physical activity. It was a fact of her life from September to June, and she lectured Bonnie on it once when Bonnie was nervous over a parent conference. Enjoy your summers, Alyssa said, because once September rolls around, your mind is shackled to this place. You're never really free at any other time. Even during vacations your mind will slip back to some kid or some problem. Don't try to fool yourself by thinking otherwise. We're cut out of the same cloth, you and I. Let your mind rest during the summer because it will show no mercy at any other time.

Alyssa Matthews knew she couldn't change. That was why she became involved in the department's attempt to change conditions. When Paul asked her to write a section of the report, she agreed to do it. Everyone knew the effects of the last contract. When she focused on her own situation, she realized what had happened to her. After the first year of the contract, she felt worn, but still intact, still willing to push on. The second year was measurably worse, ending with a gasp for air. The third brought with it disgust, disappointment, illness, depression. Why couldn't she do what she used to do? teach the way she knew she must? She found her answer, or rather, she was forced to acknowledge the answer when she wrote her section of the report.

How uncomfortable she was at first! She had always solved her own problems, made few referrals, few requests for outside intervention; she took pride in being even-tempered and in control of her classroom. Writing that report forced her to admit defeat, compelled her to declare a loss of control. She was crawling for help and she didn't like it. But at least she began to understand why the sense of achievement that once pervaded her spirit in June had been replaced by a sense of survival. The report opened her eyes to the disturbing, unequivocal truth:

The English department at Boesch-Conklyn Academy considers it imperative to notify the principal, the superintendent, and the Board of Education of existing conditions that seriously inhibit if not totally prevent teachers of English from handling the immense responsibility of teaching proper and effective writing techniques. Conditions at BCA have evolved to the point where we find it not humanly possible to spend required time on the grading of student papers; remediation has become an impossible dream.

It is our firm conviction that all students benefit from and are entitled to individual attention, but our efforts are constantly thwarted by our ever-increasing workload. Attempts to help even the most seriously deficient students are becoming impossible. Because of staff cuts and the addition of a fifth class, the numbers we deal with have increased dramatically.

In the 1969-70 school year each English teacher was assigned 80-90 students; by 1974-75 the number increased to 90-120, and by 1979-80 increased again to 120-135. We find it ludicrous that we currently have 50-60 more students enrolled in our classes each year and are under constant pressure to provide individual instruction in writing skills. Even normal classroom writing assignments have become monumental grading tasks when 80-120 papers are handed in at one time. Hasty grading of papers gives the student no remediation and no incentive to improve. We are looking back hungrily to the days when we could assign numerous and varied writing tasks and spend sufficient time grading papers. Even five minutes grading time per paper, when multiplied by the number of papers, results in hours, sometimes days of work, and five minutes is grossly minimal time to correct mechanical errors, constructively criticize, and encourage the student by writing, in many cases, more than the student has written!

The days of 80 students in 4 classes were also the days of only two preparations. We now handle significantly more students in 5 classes with three preparations. In other disciplines this third preparation signals no catastrophe, but we are unique in that an additional preparation adds another mountain of work. Contrary to misguided popular opinion, English 2 Regents and English 2 Scholarship are not the same course with a few extras added for the brighter students. They are two distinctly different courses with additional books, tests, quizzes, assignments, and requirements. Every course in our curriculum requires its own arsenal of books. For example, a teacher preparing lessons for English 2R, English 2S, and one senior elective uses at least TWENTY different books over the course of one school year.

English 2R: Basic Vocabulary for Sophomores
Warriner's Grammar (blue)
Narrative Poetry
A Survey of Short Stories
A Tale of Two Cities
Of Mice and Men
Silas Marner or A Separate Peace
Our Town

English 2S: Advanced Vocabulary for Sophomores
Warriner's Grammar (red)
Modern American and British Poetry

Short Fiction Craftsmen
A Tale of Two Cities
Silas Marner
To Kill A Mockingbird
A Separate Peace
The Bridge of San Luis Rey
Our Town
Julius Caesar
The Merchant of Venice

Seniors: Writing A Research Paper
Hamlet
Othello
The Taming of the Shrew or Twelfth Night

Other combinations of courses for three preparations are no less demanding. And, it should be noted, each teacher considers the availability of additional optional texts in literature.

Other disciplines may require three different texts plus review books for three preparations, but it is the nature of our unique beast that requires us to obtain, distribute, and collect over twenty different titles every year. Except for seniors. Senior titles go out and come in every semester. Quite obviously, we are not speaking of impossibilities here because we are handling this colossal load. We are teaching five full classes with three preparations and not one of us has expired from the strain. We have become experts in juggling a multitude of activities inflicted upon us because "everyone else has 5 classes and 3 preparations "when, in fact, we are inherently and fundamentally more complicated structurally than any other discipline in the school. We juggle vocabulary, grammar, spelling, reading comprehension (still another text we deal with), along with all the varied and sophisticated elements of poetry, short stories, novels, and plays. We throw in the time-consuming responsibilities of homeroom and study hall assignments, along with curriculum revision and the nuts and bolts of everyday classroom activities. Somehow we keep it all moving in a steady rhythm. Our juggling act is marred, however, by our frustrated attempts to incorporate writing skills into the flow. We've lost the luxury of having time to spend on writing. We resent the misuse of our training and our expertise; and we mourn the fact that our enthusiasm is being wasted on a juggling act.

We are fully aware of the financial difficulties facing the district. We know that our current workload resulted from efforts to cut staff to save money, and pleas to alleviate the situation will undoubtedly go unheeded. Indeed, with today's attitude toward "overpaid, underworked" teachers, we are aware of the general sneer that would accompany any request we might make to lessen our load to allow time for writing skills. We recognize the futility of requesting measures that would require additional staff at this time, but strongly suggest that the district consider our plight as soon as it is economically feasible.

In the meantime, of course, students will not be getting the individual attention so many of them need. The State of New York has mandated a minimum level of writing competency for each of our students, and it is physically impossible for English teachers to give adequate instruction to fulfill that mandate.

The ending surprised her; spilling her guts was not a familiar activity and admitting defeat was totally out of character, but at the same time, she felt a sense of relief. It was a relief to release the venom locked inside her, to acknowledge that her Orphean Song had become so discordant and sour.

When the report was totally ignored, it was an education for her because she had sincerely believed that her name on it would carry some kind of weight. She wasn't being egotistical, she merely thought an employer might stop to listen when an employee voiced one complaint in eleven years, especially if the employee were consistently responsible and competent. Didn't it make any difference that *Alyssa Matthews* felt overrun, that *Alyssa Matthews* couldn't keep up anymore, that *Alyssa Matthews* spoke up? Apparently not. If she ever entertained any thoughts that she was special, those thoughts were ground into the dirt. She was nobody just like everybody else. And the entire experience changed her in another way: she was through playing Pollyanna.

She thought once or twice over the summer that maybe, just maybe ... Paul had submitted a list of suggestions for temporary relief, a list that included alternative scheduling, elimination of homeroom and/or study hall duties, and reduction of class size. Maybe, over the summer, something had materialized. But no, all was the same in September. Only one bead of hope remained: the new contract. All the information was given to the union, and the department settled in to wait for the timely arrival of the cavalry.

The Observation

He walked into the room after she began her lesson. She had already taken attendance, signed slips, and settled them down to begin. She was in the middle of a sentence about Gene's mental anguish when the closed door opened and he walked in, walked down between two rows of seats and sat at an empty desk in the back of the room. The kids looked around, watched him move, and became so many sticks of wood. It was a quiet class to begin with; after the alien landed, the desks became so many headstones in a cemetery.

Bonnie immediately panicked. She shouldn't have, she knew she shouldn't have, she had been steeling herself for the intrusion ever since she heard he had popped in unannounced earlier in the week down the hall. Connie Baker was a year younger than Bonnie, and had subbed longer. Connie Baker was only in her first year of full-time teaching as a replacement for a teacher on leave. Connie Baker had been observed on Tuesday, so Bonnie knew it was only a matter of time. Only tenured teachers received advanced notification of observations.

Bob McGuinness sat in the back of her classroom and her hands turned cold and clammy, her vision blurred, and she lost her train of thought. Her tenure year. She had to live through two, possibly three, observations. The number depended upon how much time the administrator assigned to the English department wanted to spend, when he could pull himself away from his office.

Bob McGuinness had never taught English. However, quoth the powers that were, are, and will forever be, does the judge have to be a criminal to pass judgment on the criminal? That was the universal complaint about observations: how can they evaluate what they know nothing about? are they deified upon completion of courses in administration? There were other more specific wailings: What did he expect to find 8th period on the day before Homecoming Weekend? The kids don't have a dress code, why should I have to wear a jacket and tie? I don't sweep the floors, can I help it if the room is dirty? He had a fit because I let a kid go to his locker during class! The kids can read my handwriting, why can't he? He said my flag is tattered and should be replaced. I knocked myself out and all he saw was "a colorful display" on my bulletin board and I didn't even put it there! He thinks my desk should be in the middle of the room instead of in the corner. Can you believe it, he wanted to know why I haven't reported a broken window! You should only know what used to go on in his classroom! How did he manage to write a full observation when he only poked his head through the doorway for two seconds? I had to show *him* how to teach, and now *he's* evaluating *me*! I clearly told him to come in any time but third period, and I'll give you one guess when he showed up. Complaints dredged up the same old themes: Harassment. Farce. Intimidation.

Bonnie hoped that the color hadn't completely drained from her face. She started to lecture again, and, while she was talking, she picked up an extra copy of *Peace*, walked to the back of the room and gave it to McGuinness so that he might follow along. She directed the class to specific lines on specific pages to make her point about Gene. He had built up animosity in his mind, he had created his own evil, he and Finny were adversaries only within the context of Gene's thoughts.

The novel was difficult to teach. Bonnie had discussed it repeatedly with Alyssa, who had taught it so many times that she was almost an authority, a title she shunned because, as she often stated, there are no authorities on great works of literature. There's always more to see, more to learn.

Bonnie went on to the theme of friendship as evidenced by Gene and Finny in the first four chapters of the novel. She had dealt with the tone, reminiscence saturated with fear, of the first half of the first chapter the day before, along with the sharp change in tone with the beginning of the flashback that would constitute the rest of the novel. She had established the background of the novel, 1942, World War II, and the immediate setting, a private school for boys in New Hampshire. She dispelled the notion that the boys were in college. No, she said, high school, a private high school for boys. It's important that you know that. These boys are not much older than you. What they experience in this novel is experienced by adolescents the world over. Most teenagers don't suffer in these extremes, thank God. But if you think about it, if you really think about what is happening in this story, you should be able to identify your own problems as adolescents and, perhaps, deal with those problems more maturely.

She told her three sophomore regents classes the day before that John Knowles had attended Phillips Exeter Academy in New Hampshire and that after the book was first published in 1960, Knowles' mother said that if she knew her son had been so unhappy there, she would have pulled him out. Bonnie used the anecdote to inspire curiosity, and stubbornly repeated it for all three classes even though it bombed with the very first. Maybe she should have saved it for the end after all the tragedy. When she complained in the faculty room about the blank faces, Alyssa suggested that she shelve the story altogether. It was a cute comment on the relationship between authors and their mothers, but the subtle humor was lost on sophomores.

Bonnie had also gone into characterizations the day before: Gene, Phineas, Leper; it was too early for Brinker and Quackenbush; Chet Douglass and Bobby Zane were very minor. She also pointed out the symbolism of the tree, Finny's pink shirt, the Summer Session, and blitzball; the foreshadowing at the end of chapter three, the imagery at the beginning of chapter four. She connected the imagery with the remainder of the chapter which flowed from Gene's suspicions to his perception of the truth and his subsequent shame and finally, to the shocking consequence of his jealousy.

She ran out of time before she had a chance to deal adequately with the theme of friendship, although she knew she had touched on it while lecturing on everything else. She still needed to get them thinking about themselves: How do you feel when your friend outshines you? How do you feel when you know that you always get caught, but your friend gets away with anything? Would you want to have a friend who is perfect? Is Finny perfect? Why does everyone follow Finny's lead? Have you ever heard of the name 'Phineas' before? Why did Knowles name this boy 'Phineas' with no last name?

From friendship she planned to veer off onto the themes of peer pressure and conformity vs. nonconformity. And she had jotted a note in her book as a reminder to mention Knowles' periodical references to the war in Europe, and the boys' perception of that war. Later on she would lecture on the themes of war and peace in depth. Later on she would attempt to instill appreciation as well as understanding of Knowles' magnificent tapestry, his skillfully crafted montage of symbols and themes.

She also made a note because she forgot to point out the effectiveness of the first person narration. Can anyone explain feelings of suspicion, fear, hatred, and guilt better than the person experiencing those feelings? Gene tells the story in retrospect, as an adult. Therefore, he assesses as an adult. This point of view gives the novel a perspective that would be sorely missed had the author decided to write in the third person or in the first person, but as Gene with an adolescent mind, with no flashback, without benefit of adult perception and hindsight. The story is tinted with objectivity because it is told by a man and not a boy.

Today's lesson was to reflect all of those concerns, but she had to change the dynamic from discussion to lecture because no one was responding. She was just getting into Gene's conformity and Finny's nonconformity when McGuinness rose from his seat and walked out of the room. She was just beginning to forget he was there when he tiptoed up to her, handed her the book which he never opened, and made his exit, softly opening and closing the door.

As soon as he was out of sight, the kids relaxed. They knew why he was there, and while he was there nobody made a peep. "Weren't we good?" one girl asked.

"He gives me the creeps," said another.

"I'm glad he left, I have to blow my nose."

"Were you nervous, Miss Mason?"

"Aren't you proud of me, Miss Mason? See, I know when to keep my mouth shut."

"We like you, Miss Mason. We didn't want him to think you're no good."

"How'd we do? Were we okay?"

Bonnie smiled. "You were wonderful." There wasn't much else she could say. A rowdy class was no good. A quiet class was no good. Beauty lies in the eyes of the beholder. And it was a crap shoot. She went on with her lesson. She'd find the observation written up and in her mailbox whenever McGuinness found the time to write it up and put it there. Until then, she'd just have to wonder.

At the end of the period she prepared them for the next chapter: Be ready now for Gene's identity crisis. He can't accept what he is or what he's done. He can't even confess to relieve his tortured soul. He has to bear the burden alone, the destructive burden of massive guilt.

Say What?

NAMES.
Names, names, names, names, names,
First names, last names, middle names, game names,
Given names, taken names, nicknames, gouged names,
Well-wrought names.
So many names that name doesn't look like name any more.
Identity lost in a labyrinth
Of hundreds, hundreds and thousands of names, names, names,
Names, names, names, names, names, names, names.
The polynomial system of nomenclature.

"What do you mean you didn't want to correct me? Your name is uniquely yours and I have no right to mangle it. It's your identity, you should be proud of it, and I have an obligation to learn how to pronounce it correctly. Now say it again for me so I can work on it. Mus-TOP-o-vich. I've been saying Mus-to-PO-vich, haven't I? Well, Mus-TOP-o-vich isn't so difficult, but I'd never know if you didn't tell me. Don't ever be afraid to correct me if you think I'm doing something or saying something wrong. Both of us might learn something. Teachers aren't perfect. I make mistakes just like everybody else."

Mustopovich. Dzyzn. Veronne. Mordecai. Xerxes. Beighton. Frere. Ieue. Marineiri. Marnerelli. Ng. Osczynsky. Rukoff. Mythe. Peliteria. Jancucci. Dyem. Kirgaard. Alyssa was pretty good with names. Remembering them and matching them with faces: fair to partly cloudy. But the sun shone on her ability to pronounce and spell. She would break them down into syllables, allow for accent possibilities, and keep in mind that normal rules of pronunciation are suspended when it comes to peoples' names. A boy once told her, "Never mind, you'll never be able to say it right. It's Japanese." But she insisted and she practiced all year. Both she and the student laughed the day of the final exam when she still couldn't get her tongue and mouth and throat to cooperate.

How could she insist that they pronounce vocabulary words correctly if she mispronounced their names? Every year the surnames were a challenge that she met and overcame. First names were usually easier, though on occasion she bloopered ("Oh, I'm sorry. It's KIR-sten, not KRIS—ten. I wasn't paying close enough attention"). In September, 1980, she looked over her class lists and saw a first name that stumped her: Siobhan. The teacher asked around for help, but nobody knew, so she pronounced it the way it looked, even though she was not comfortable with that pronunciation. It just did not feel right. The sophomore corrected her. The teacher inferred from the student's tone that the student was weary of correcting everybody, so the teacher noted a hasty reminder to herself: She-VAN. The next day while assigning seats she tried again. The student laughed hysterically. The teacher blushed and asked again. Then she got it right: Sheh-VAHN. Siobhan. And what a beautiful Gaelic name it was, too!

The first day of school Alyssa had all her students fill out an information sheet. She hated making them do it for the umpteenth time that day, but she needed ready access to phone numbers and personal data. She also used the sheet to find out how she should be addressing students. Because correct pronunciation was the tip of the iceberg. She wrote her seating charts (in pencil, ALWAYS in pencil) using names that students preferred. The whole procedure was astonishingly complex.

Not all Kathleens prefer Kathy; some insist on Kathleen or Kate. Does Elizabeth like Liz, Beth, Liza, Betty, Betsy, Bets, Babs, or does Elizabeth like Elizabeth? Or is it Elisabeth? Is William a Bill or a Billy, a Will or a Willy, or perchance, is he a William? Is Robert a Rob or a Bob, a Robby or a Bobby or a Bert? Is Patricia a Pat or a Tricia? Antoinette an Ant, a Toni, or a Nettie? What about Nelson, called Bud; Armand, called Army; and Edna Mae, who dies a thousand deaths whenever she isn't called Grace? Who could refuse Annunciata Granini when she furtively asks to be called Debbie? Who could fail to address John as Jack, Charles as Chuck (or never as Chuck, but always as Charlie) and Margaret as Peggy (or Margie or Maggie or Meg)?

"Please don't call me Emerson. Everybody calls me Irv."

"My friends don't even know that's my name. Call me Al."

"I hate my name! Hate it, hate it, hate it!"

"It's not KARE-in, it's Kare-IN."

"Oh no, nobody calls me Terry. My name is Theresa."

"Oh, you can call me Kay, or you can call me Kate, or you can call me Katie, but don't you ever call me Catherine or Katharine or Kathryn."

Rosemary Cania Maio

NAMES.
NAMES, NAMES, NAMES.
NAMES, NAMES, NAMES, NAMES, NAMES.
NAMES.

Sanctuary

As soon as seventh period was over, Alyssa left her room to spend the five minutes until eighth period in the faculty room. She raced out of her room ahead of the kids because she needed a cigarette and a break before the last period of the day. While in the faculty room, she graded the last five spelling tests for the eighth period class and entered grades in her grade book, which she couldn't have done had she remained in her classroom. She left the faculty room bolstered by the thought of "one more to go," a thought she verbalized to a still-disgusted Beth Whittsley who said, her voice dripping with relief, "Take heart, tomorrow's Friday."

The days of the week were a collection of mundane impressions and trained reactions: Monday (the exposition) was sleepy, slow, a resigned prerequisite; Tuesday (the complication) gathered momentum, numbly at first, then with hopeful vigor; Wednesday (the climax) was hump day, drawing energy merely from its position; Thursday (the denouement) was a disappointment, a natural barrier in the flow of things; Friday (the conclusion) was the salvation, the last push of nonexistent energy, the final reward, the promise of nourishing collapse.

"Friday should follow Wednesday," Alyssa said to Beth in the hall. "Who can we see to change the calendar? Thursday just doesn't make it. It's too much of a blow to my psyche."

"Go see McGuinness," Beth said bitterly, "I just gave in to him on that kid I told you about this morning. He'd revel in a little thing like changing the days of the week. If that fails, check the main office. There must be a damn form available."

Peat and Repeat

Her arrival in class was concurrent with the harsh clanging of the bell ringing the start of the last period of the day. She took attendance and keyed some of the chevrons with a "B" for "Band." Members of the marching band had been excused from seventh and eighth period classes every Thursday since school started. Some of those students were failing because of class time missed and work never made up. Paul M. Smith's parents pulled him out of band because he was failing. Paul M. Smith's parents were Edsels in a world of K Cars and Cadillacs.

Afternoon classes were plagued by absences due to medical appointments (You have to take what you can get, doctors and dentists are booked months ahead of time), sports events (Sports are essential to the development of the whole person; students grow and learn within the context of healthy physical activity and the spirit of competition), and music rehearsals (Groups cannot practice as individuals, groups must practice as groups; the study of music contributes to the development of the student's cultural self, to his growth as a well-rounded person; extracurricular rehearsals just don't work because too many students don't show up). Whenever she was up to her ears in frustration over all of it, she felt a strong urge to notify the phys ed department or the music staff that she planned to pull kids out of their classes for a spelling practice or a grammar rehearsal.

At least it was almost the end of the band business. Double practice on Thursday and Friday this week, then no more. She had nine kids in two classes missing work every week. Even though she told those nine kids that they were responsible for keeping up, she still had to manage and schedule make-up work, and she still worried whether or not it would be completed. She tried to avoid instruction on Thursdays, but that was next to impossible, so nine kids automatically missed lectures and explanations, tests or quizzes or whatever.

Was she really supposed to teach it all nine times more at the convenience of nine different students with nine different schedules, including different lunch and study hall periods, varying bus arrivals and departures, and a whole list of extracurricular activities?

She stood in front of the rows of desks holding the spelling tests. She used to require that students write out misspelled words ten times each. It worked out well because, as she told them, "You'll either do it before the test to avoid errors and save points, or you'll do it after the test when you've already lost the points." She wouldn't raise the grade and imposed a penalty if the words weren't written on the test paper and handed back in within the week. Keeping records on the activity was a major undertaking, and she did have to check papers again; it was surprising how many students handed in more misspellings. It worked, though, it worked, but she didn't do it anymore; she could no longer handle the paperwork.

The spelling tests were still in order according to rows, so she was able to shoot them back in thirty seconds and simultaneously pull out papers belonging to absentees. She reserved those papers in the safety of her eighth period folder while she listened to typical student reactions: who studied and failed, who studied and passed, who didn't study and failed or passed, who didn't care either way. It was all there, it was always there attending the return of graded papers: joy, sorrow, shock, dismay, disappointment, resignation, embarrassment, bravado, envy, the whole spectrum of human emotion.

With her hands on her hips, she went into the spiel she had already given to her seventh period class; every day it was peat and repeat and she was good at it.

She moved to the blackboard which she had erased at the end of the previous period. A great deal of dramatic flourish would have been lost had she left the information there and merely pointed to it the second time around. She knew that students got obsessed with copying all the words at once and, in the process, missed all the meaning. The words had to be fed to them a little at a time to preserve the meaning.

"Now take this down if you forgot it, can't find it, or never learned it. And learn it if you don't know it yet!" Like a warrior with a sword she wielded her weapon with ferocious pride, though the weapon she brandished was no more than a piece of chalk.

> I before E except ... except when?
> Except after C
> Or when sounded like "a" as in neighbor and weigh.
> What are other notable exceptions? *The weird foreigner seizes neither leisure nor height.* Good! You must memorize that sentence. It doesn't make much sense, but who cares? Just think, you'll never mix up

seize and siege again! Okay, we'll also add *caffeine, codeine,* and *sheik* to the list of exceptions. How about *The weird foreign sheik seizes neither leisure nor height nor caffeine nor codeine*?

Stop moaning and groaning, it's a well-known fact that the English language has more exceptions than rules. But it's our language, we have to express ourselves with it, and we can achieve some skill if we learn its complexities a little at a time. The more you use these rules, the more they'll become a part of you, until one fine day when you realize that you can spell. One more thing about the IE rule: "except after C" means EXCEPT AFTER C, NOT CH, chief is spelled c-h-i-e-f.

Next: the "seed" rule. What words end in c-e-e-d?

Exceed, proceed, succeed. Excellent.

What one word in the English language (no exceptions here! isn't that great?) What ONE WORD in the English language ends in s-e-d-e?

Supersede! Remember that it's super! It's special! Right?

It's THE ONLY word that ends in s-e-d-e.

How are all the other words with the "seed" sound at the end spelled?

That's right: c-e-d-e. Some examples, please?

Precede (to go before), concede (to give in to), recede (to go back), accede (to agree to), secede (to withdraw, as in *The Southern States seceded from the Union*), intercede (to go between, to mediate, that is, to go between two opposing forces in an effort to settle the dispute).

Next: mnemonic devices. The word "mnemonic" means "of the memory." The art of mnemonics is an attempt to aid memory through the use of certain formulas. You can think up your own formulas to help you remember as long as you're careful not to make the formula more complicated than the thing you're trying to remember. What words did I give you as examples of the use of mnemonics in spelling?

Separate: there's a rat in separate, s-e-p-A-R-A-T-e.

Cemetery: all are at ease in the cemetery, remember all E's.

Assassination: two asses in a nation.

I know they're stupid, they're corny, they're ridiculous, but I don't care, it makes no difference to me that you think I'm loony, as long as you never again misspell these words.

"Now, turn over your spelling tests, keep your notes on your desks, and write these words as I dictate them to you. Yes, Chris, you can use another sheet of paper. No, I'm not going to grade these, so don't get nervous. And don't try to check your notes while you're writing, I'll be moving too fast. We've still got grammar and a short story to cover this period.

1)	chief	11)	succeed
2)	intercede	12)	assassination
3)	weird	13)	conceive
4)	height	14)	foreign
5)	siege	15)	proceed
6)	exceed	16)	ceiling
7)	separate	17)	seize
8)	leisure	18)	their
9)	veil	19)	cemetery
10)	neither	20)	supersede

Now check your work with your notes. No! Wait! First I want you to add one more word: grammar. THEN check your work with your notes." It was an old ploy to trick them into awareness. There were enough grammar books within view. She walked around the room glancing at papers as she passed, making comments. "It starts with a CH, doesn't it? ... Listen to the pronunciation: thay-yer. Can you hear the long a? Thay-yer. Their. Neighbor. Weigh. The sound of long a is EI." Once she got to the back of the room, she remained there. "All right. Let's check 'em over! Lynette, number one please!"

She became aware of a problem as the words being spelled, and after all were spelled correctly, she made one last point: the IE rule applies only when the two letters are pronounced as one sound. It doesn't apply every time you see the two letters together. For example, with *reinstate* and *reiterate* we pronounce each of the letters individually. The r-e is a prefix in those words, a prefix meaning *again*. Anybody know what *reiterate* means? Nobody knew,

271

so she walked to the board, wrote the word, its definition, and while she was at it, also gave them *diphthong* with appropriate notes.

"Next week I want to see some improvement in the spelling grades. I can understand some of your mistakes, but for the most part you're not studying enough or you're not studying properly. It is impossible to learn how to spell a word by just looking at it and hoping for the best. Not too many people have photographic memories. You have to write the words, you have to practice them, you must work at this a little at a time. If you do, you can add to the number of words you know how to spell, and by the time you get out of this place, you'll be able to fill out a job application without misspelling simple words. Do any of you read *Dear Abby*?"

Many of them did indeed and said so. She opened the cover of her blue grammar book where she knew she would find the clipping taped for speedy access. She read, her sense of practicality feeding the conviction in her voice, her sense of practicality feeding her sense of drama. See? her voice said, this is real life, I'm not trying to con you or harass you. This is for real; what I'm trying to teach you is critical, is crucial to your lives. She read, not Plato, not Horace Mann, not Jacques Barzun, not Albert Shanker, not Gordon Ambach. She read:

DEAR ABBY: Today a young woman in her twenties came into my office for a job interview. Most of her application was impossible to read. She misspelled the state we live in and the month she was born. Her verbal skills were not much better. She claimed to be a high school graduate. That's hard to believe. When she left I ripped up her application. It's obvious she needs a job. She is a single mother. I hope this letter will inspire teachers and students to work harder because writing and speaking skills are required even in entry level jobs and employers are not equipped to teach job applicants how to communicate. Signed, CONCERNED IN NEW JERSEY.

She looked at them then, "Enough said. Sign me CONCERNED IN NEW YORK and take out your grammar assignment."

Homework was a worksheet on complements: direct objects, indirect objects, predicate nominatives, predicate adjectives. The teacher felt that the grammar book did not supply enough individual drill, so she added worksheets on each of the four, then on the natural twosomes.

She had begun the year with notes on the eight parts of speech and the uses of each in a sentence. That was the foundation. She laid it carefully day by day and attempted to cement the whole business with worksheets, tests, and quizzes. And, of course, logic.

The only way to understand grammar is to deal with it logically, she told them. First I'm going to give you the bare bones, that is, the parts of speech. Then we'll go on to the meat of the matter. If you don't master the bare bones, you're going to run into incredible difficulties later on. Some of you have been failing your way through grammar for years; I'm offering you a chance finally to understand it. I'm telling you now that it is possible for you to understand it as long as you start now and work with me. Some of you will be struggling through geometry this year. There's a basic resemblance between geometry and grammar: both subjects become more and more difficult as the year goes on. Both subjects build on previously learned information. If you don't learn a little at a time in the beginning, you're going to be lost later on.

The quick review of the worksheet began with the first student who hadn't given an answer for the spelling exercise. That student didn't follow directions, so she repeated them: "Read the entire sentence. Then tell us the subject, the verb, and the predicate nominative or predicate adjective. Remember: if the complement is a predicate nominative, it's a noun and it's interchangeable with the subject; if the complement is a predicate adjective, it's an adjective and it describes the subject. And the verb is ALWAYS linking: either a form of the verb *to be* or a verb of the senses. Now let's try again."

She was pleased with the responses. The few errors made indicated ignorance of fundamental information and she reacted appropriately: You didn't recognize the entire verb; look again. Does it rename the subject or does it describe the subject? Why is it TOTALLY IMPOSSIBLE to have a direct object in this sentence?

"That was pretty good," she said at the end of the exercise, knowing that the worst was yet to come. "Now we have to mix them up. It's relatively easy to pick out complements on a worksheet that deals with only one or two types. It gets harder when they're mixed up."

She moved to the board again and kept talking while she erased to make room for more notes. "But it really shouldn't get harder when they're mixed up, should it? What's the key to all of it? What have I been telling you for the past week?" A student volunteered the answer: the verb. She reviewed the information once again, information that they had already been tested on, information that they all should have mastered, information that she had repeated and would repeat again and again and still again in the months ahead.

"You need this, "she told them. "It's old now, from the first two weeks of school, but you still need to know this and to use it. Later on, when we study pronoun case, you're going to need this information again. You can't take pot shots to figure out grammar, you need a process.

"One more thing. Be sure when you find the verb that you've found the entire verb, or you're going to run into trouble. *Should have been* is the verb *to be*, so it's linking. But *should have been sleeping* is the verb *to sleep*, so it's action. Study the sentence, consider the meaning of the sentence. There are complications to this and we'll figure them out as we go along as long as you're thinking and USING THE PROCESS. Now turn to page 83 in your books."

She waited for them to find the page. "Do the first five sentences of Review Exercise A right now. Listen first, please. Don't follow the directions. Instead I want you to make three columns on a sheet of paper. Use a clean sheet because you'll be finishing this for homework. Label the first column Subject, the second column Verb, and the third column Complement. In the third column write not only the word from the sentence, but also identify what type of complement it is. You can use abbreviations: d.o., i.o., p.n., p.a. And don't forget to look for those indirect objects!" She waited for most of them to finish the first sentence, then made sure they understood directions. "This is what you should have for number one: Subject, custodian; Verb, unlocks; Complement, doors - d.o. Now do the next four."

She patrolled the room, trying to catch mistakes as they were being made, peering down from an uncomfortable height. Whenever she knew she was about to spend some time at a student's desk, she felt an odd sense of discomfort, an impulse that she was barely aware of, but responded to with a bending of the knees and a lowering of the body. Somehow she felt better when the student was slightly above her, looking down, rather than the other way around. The automatic squat was quite fluid and feminine and certainly more ladylike than bending at the waist and thrusting her bottom into an awkward and potentially embarrassing position.

They knew by now that she didn't walk the room to snap the whip or tighten the thumbscrews, that she was out there mingling for a higher purpose. A hand went up and she finished with one student to help another, bobbing up and down, rising and falling like the seats on a merry-go-round. She pondered long and hard sometimes in her attempts to understand what was blocking a student's progress.

"There's no reason for you to confuse direct objects and predicate nominatives anymore. The verb, the verb is the key. And there's a way to check yourself, just like in geometry. If a word is a predicate nominative, it can replace the subject. Look at number one again. Besides the fact that the verb is an action verb, *doors* cannot replace *custodian* as the subject. Are the doors unlocking the custodian? Do you see that now?"

"Don't let a question throw you. Change it into a statement, then go through your steps."

"Of course you can have more than one complement following one verb. Look at the conjunction. Right?"

"How on earth can you find a direct object AND a predicate nominative after the same verb? That's impossible. Isn't it?"

"You never memorized the forms of the verb *to be*. Now you're paying for it."

"No, no. The verb *to have* is not linking, it's action. Think about it: I have ... what? There's always a direct object. You're confusing *to have* when it's used alone as a verb with *to have* when it's helping another verb. You've got to think. Remember to find the whole verb and THINK." Complications. Always complications.

She glanced at the clock and decided that she needed to move on to the last of the day's work. "Finish those for tomorrow," she concluded, "and take out your charts for today's story."

TITLE: Quality

AUTHOR: John Galsworthy

SETTING: London during the Industrial Revolution

CHARACTERS: the narrator
Mr. Gessler

PLOT: Mr. Gessler, a German shoemaker, is in business with his older brother making superbly crafted shoes and boots. The narrator, a customer of the Gessler brothers, visits the shop over a period of years, but not very often because Mr. Gessler's shoes wear like iron. With each visit of the narrator we see another step in Mr. Gessler's slow deterioration. He cannot mass produce his shoes, he cannot change himself to fulfill the demands of the Industrial Revolution. He refuses to compromise his standards because of the pride he takes in his work. He loses half his shop to a firm making factory shoes, then his brother dies, then he dies of slow starvation.

She required that students write a chart for each short story. Your charts will be immensely valuable next June when it's time to review for the exam, she told them. I know it's a lot of work to read a story and complete a chart every night. I know you have other homework. So I'll expect you to at least begin your charts on your own, then finish them as we go over each story in class. Just don't fall behind with them. When we finish the unit I'll let you know when I plan to collect your charts for grading. If you don't keep up along the way, you're going to have an impossible load of work to do at the end. If you complete your charts one at a time when the stories are fresh in your minds, you won't have to write out fifteen charts the night before they're due.

She quickly listed title, author, setting, characters. "Yes," she told a student, "you may include Mr. Gessler's brother, but be sure to make a note that he never appears in the story, he is only spoken of." She also had to repeat the setting because students did not pick it up from allusions and the narrator's typically British speech patterns. Then she had to protest once again, as she had with previous stories, that no, she was not going to dictate a summary of the plot, each student was required to write his own.

The story was one of her favorites. Dealing with the concept of craftsmanship, Galsworthy employed all its finer points. He was a master of characterization, of realism and objectivity. She taught the story the same way she taught any work of literature, with an emphasis on form. Form and content, content and form, each supporting the other, each giving substance and merit to the other, each deathly pale without the other.

She learned early on how students reacted to the story. Some stopped reading as soon as the narrator explained that Mr. Gessler's boots were "made by one who saw before him the Soul of Boot — so truly were they prototypes, incarnating the very spirit of all footwear." Some continued a little further along on the first page of the story to Mr. Gessler's first spoken words, "Id is an Ardt!" and then gave up trying to understand the man's German accent. Some read all the words to the end, but did it while babysitting or during commercial breaks or on the bus or in the cafeteria. Mr. Gessler deserved more than that. Mr. Gessler deserved the undivided attention of the entire universe.

When you read a story, she was fond of saying, think of the story as a huge sack under your feet. As you read, lift the sack higher and higher until your hands are up over your head and the sack embraces you completely. Then, and only then, can you say that you've read the story. And by then you should know what the sack is made of — is it soft and warm? is it scratchy? is it metallic? is it made of sorrow or sunlight or shivers?

She began each lecture simply, with the conviction that fundamental simplicities had to be dealt with first: tracing the basic plot, explaining figures of speech, extolling the virtues of the author, translating Mr. Gessler's delightful (to her) speech. "*The incense of his trade* is the smell of leather," she said. "*Fordnighd* is *fortnight*, a period of two weeks. *Nemesis* was the goddess of retribution or vengeance. When the narrator says *Nemesis fell* he means that he must pay dearly for ordering too many pairs of boots: he has to wait too long a time before he visits the shop again because the boots won't wear out. When he says *They lasted more terribly than ever* he doesn't mean the boots are terrible. The word has another meaning here; it means *to an even greater extent*."

As she spoke she directed students to specific lines and pages. She asked, "What evidence is there that Mr. Gessler is a master craftsman?" After accepting the most obvious answers from students, she pointed the way to another: Mr. Gessler's boots are an extension of himself. The narrator, whenever he walks into the shop, feels as though he awakens Mr. Gessler from a "dream of boots." Mr. Gessler's boots never hurt, never pinch, they fit perfectly. When the narrator mentions a pair that creaked, Mr. Gessler is horrified, but still, his knowledge can meet any crisis. "Zome boods are bad from birdt" he says.

Mr. Gessler takes pride in his skill and in the quality of his product. He remembers every boot, every pair, every difficulty, every triumph. "Do dey vid you here?" he says. "I 'ad drouble wid dat bair, I remember." When the narrator wears a pair of hastily purchased boots, Mr. Gessler says, "It 'urds you dere. Dose big virms 'ave no self-respect. Drash!"

She went on to the next section of the chart. "What's the climax?"
Silence.
Still having trouble pinpointing the climax?
Climax, climax, who's got the climax?
It's no treasure hunt, you can't just poke around blindly. First determine what the conflict is, then decide when the conflict is resolved. What's the conflict? Mr. Gessler against the factory stores. But is it only the factory stores he's fighting? What about the people buying shoes? What part do they play? Who's demanding fast service and cheaper prices at the expense of quality? How many people would shop at Mr. Gessler's store today?

The conflict is between Mr. Gessler and society.

When is it resolved? When Mr. Gessler dies. That's the climax.

Mr. Gessler's. She hadn't reached hers yet. For Beauty and Truth remained on the fringes of the argument.

"Let's look at the end of the story once again. The sales clerk tells the narrator that Mr. Gessler slowly starved himself to death because he spent what little money he had on leather. The sales clerk is rather cold and detached, isn't he? But the narrator isn't, and the reader, who has been under the influence of the narrator, isn't either. The sales clerk is unfeeling, the narrator is shocked and saddened. But there's something else being expressed here too, something in between the objectivity and the tragedy.

"Is Mr. Gessler really defeated? The last words in the story, *He made good boots* are his epitaph. He spent a lifetime making good boots. And he died making good boots. For him there is no other way. For him it would be far more tragic to give in, to compromise his skill, to forfeit his dignity, and live.

"Mr. Gessler's death forms the climax of the story. The conflict is resolved. But the resolution provokes a great deal of thought. Who really wins and who loses? Is the tragedy Mr. Gessler's? Or society's?

"What did you feel as you read this story? What do you feel now? Can you feel the suffering and misery of this man who only wants to maintain excellence? That's his only sin, his only transgression. He works to feed his body, but more than that, he works to feed his spirit. Is it fair that he must lower his standards, he must make inferior boots, or he will sell none? Is it fair that he is destroyed by an impersonal social system that requires him to be less than he is?"

How difficult it was to impress upon 16-year-olds the poignancy of Mr. Gessler's special agony. Difficult and demanding. But she could not ignore her own mandates.

The last section of the chart required a statement of theme. Ask yourself why the author wrote the story, why did he create these particular characters, place them in this particular situation, and resolve the conflict in this particular way. What point about life is the author making? You certainly don't have to agree with what he's saying, but you need to identify his point, his purpose, in order to disagree with it. And when you recognize his point, you have the theme.

"What is the theme of *Quality*?" she asked.

Silence.

She made a few direct inquiries, and referred to the title.

Silence. No response. Nothing.

Barely something. Less than nothing.

She wanted to scream. Or cry. Or rip out a wall. After the intensity of the discussion? After careful instruction on theme and eight previous stories? Nothing?

"Not this time," she told them. "I'm not dictating a word-for-word statement of theme. You think about it. Surely you can explain what the author is saying in this story. What do you think we've been talking about all this time?"

She slammed her book shut and looked at the clock. Two minutes.

"Okay, Chris," she said. "Now!" The crinkled white mass flew across the room and sailed beyond its target. Chris knew the penalty for misses. He retrieved the projectile and plunked it in from a shorter distance.

"That's no big feat," Alyssa teased as he made his way back to his seat. She proceeded to lock up materials she wouldn't be taking home, and crushed the thought that *Quality* was perfect for a writing assignment.

They hadn't written a single thing since school started, but they would. They would when everything else calmed down, when senior research papers were graded and handed back, when the scholarship sections were tired out and needed a break from writing. She'd get to it then. There was more than enough in the curriculum to keep them busy for double the amount of time they had in one school year anyway. They would just have to do other things. She knew the best way to teach writing was to do it slowly over a long period of time, but the best way was no longer practical, no longer possible. Not for her regents classes, anyway. She had to cut back somewhere. Later. She'd pick up the writing later.

When the bell rang she was ready to leave the room but was held up by a frustrated little girl engaged in what seemed to be a lively discussion with three boys. The boys left laughing, but the girl remained. "Mrs. Matt, those boys are driving me crazy," the girl stammered. "They think they know everything! All day they've been telling me I'm wrong and I know I'm right! Isn't *condom* short for *condominium*?"

Alyssa tried with all her might not to laugh, but she simply could not hold it in.

"Now you're laughing at me! All day they've been laughing at me!"

"Listen, sweetie," Alyssa said gently. "*Condo* is short for *condominium*. A condom is a birth control device. Sometimes it's called a prophylactic, sometimes it's called a rubber."

The girl started to spit and sputter. "Ohhhh! I'm going to kill those miserable, lousy, rotten —" Alyssa never heard the rest because the girl was already in hot pursuit of her tormentors.

The room cleared fast. It always did after eighth period. The teacher locked her door and started down the hall, pushed along by the thought that the faster everybody arrived the faster Paul's meeting would end. She wanted to leave, to get out of the building and into the sunlight; it was still a beautiful day.

The hall was filled with students making hasty getaways; locker doors slammed, and some students were massed in small clusters here and there. The teacher issued greetings to just about every third student she met eyes with and passed two girls from one of her classes. One of the girls called her back. "Mrs. Matt, would you settle an argument for us?"

The teacher slowed her pace to walk with them. "I'll try."

"Who's better looking, Starsky or Hutch?"

"Oh, dear. That's a tough one. Do you really think I'm qualified to decide?"

Sure, the girls agreed. And we need somebody to break the tie.

"Well, I don't know. One is so dark and handsome, the other so light and handsome. Really, girls, I don't think I can choose!"

They thanked her for trying. They understood her dilemma.

"Then again," the teacher added, "I also think Dan Rather is terribly handsome and David Brinkley awfully cute."

Who? the girls asked. What new series weren't they familiar with?

"Try the national news."

Aauuggh! A fate worse than death!

The students went their merry way; the teacher veered off to gather up Jean Tevarro for the one activity every teacher loathes with a gargantuan passion: a meeting.

Rendezvous

"Of course, I love you. But loving you is extraneous to these surroundings." She was trying to keep him at a safe distance by stretching her arms forward as far as they would extend. But his arms were moving too, much more skillfully than hers, and with greater purpose. Amidst the giggles and the four arms dancing in the air, the inevitable joining of hands came quickly. Then it became a toss up as to who was the aggressor and who the aggressee.

"No," she said weakly, "please . ." as he brought her hands behind his neck and pushed forward. "Honey, don't ... not here ... don't ..." She thought of that crazy joke: don't ... don't... don't ... don't stop ... and then couldn't say any more because his lips had reached hers and were pressing and opening, his hands traveled the length of her arms and were tangled in her hair, and she was lost in him, in his lips and his mouth and his tongue, in his arms and his hands.

The door knob jiggled and the noise startled her back to reality; she opened her eyes to the glare of desks and chairs, and pulled her head back. The jiggling stopped, but her fear remained. "You've got to get out of here," she whispered. "This isn't my room. Even if it were, a locked door means nothing here." He pulled her close again. "I missed you last night. I couldn't touch you over the phone." And he kissed her again, and she felt her legs weaken, her whole body threaten to yield. Just one more minute, just one, let me feel his touch, let me hold him in peace, without fear, without secrecy. Just one more minute, and then forever.

The door knob jiggled again, this time with a few knocks added. She heard; he didn't. She moved her face to kiss his cheek, his nose, his eyes, then said, "Go. Please. I'll see you later." He backed her further into the room against a low counter and sat her on it. He smiled that radiant smile of his and moved his hands to her hair and then to her face. "Just one more?" She nodded and he moved his lips once again to meet hers. His hands moved from her face to her neck in a long, slow caress, then to her shoulders.

She knew the destination of his hands and couldn't move her own, which were wrenched around the edge of the countertop, to stop them. The spell was too strong, too overpowering; both of them driven by it, drowning in it, mesmerized by its beauty and its force.

Her eyes closed; she saw nothing but him, memory and thought suspended beyond the raging spiral of tactile response. Stroking and squeezing, his hands pushed her beyond reality to the brink of madness, so intense was the pleasure they provided. His lips left hers to follow the journey of his hands, down her throat to the silky fabric of her blouse, to the satiny finish of her skin. With almost no effort at all, he slid the buttons aside, and she, so intoxicated, buried her fingers in his hair, felt the smoothness of it, and the bulk, as she arched her back just a little to further affirm the pressure of his lips.

He knew it hooked in front. The thought suddenly panicked her, though it excited her beyond belief: the point of no return. She summoned all the strength she had left. "No, sweetheart. Stop. We've got to stop. Please." She had to raise his head with her hands.

"I love you," he said.

"And I love you. But you have to leave." She looked down and giggled. "Are you going to be able to walk straight?"

"I'll go to the gym and take a cold shower."

"You devil. But it's all your fault. We aren't even supposed to be acquaintances here, remember?"

"You know the thoughts I have whenever I see you?"

"Think all you want, my love. Here, you'd better wear your jacket." She buttoned her blouse. "At least women don't have to worry about that. Of course, now I have to go to a meeting feeling like I've wet my pants."

He laughed. "The price you pay for love."

"Scram," she said, opening the door. "See you later."

He closed the door, planted another kiss on her lips, and gave her other end a slow massage. Then he left.

She made sure she was all together, picked up her books, then headed for the main office. She wanted to check her mailbox before the meeting. McGuinness just might have written up the observation, and she was anxious to read it.

A Little Cleanser Clears Us Of This Deed

"Why do I always think of The Bobbsey Twins when those two are together?"

"Who two?" Alyssa asked.

"Bonnie and Connie," Jean said. Then she chuckled, "I guess that's why." When they entered the resource room, Paul was pacing back and forth waiting for everyone to arrive so that he could begin. His command of "right after school" meant little, he knew, because of unforeseen hold-ups. Alyssa had waited for Jean because Jean was busy arguing with a student over a grade.

Bonnie and Connie waved them over.

"Look at this rot," Bonnie complained. "He was in my room no longer than fifteen minutes and he thinks he knows how I should be teaching that book, a book he never taught in his life."

"Would you care to take bets on whether or not he's ever even read it?" Jean sneered.

Alyssa looked at the comments on the observation sheet: level of difficulty not commensurate with students' comprehensive abilities, suggest simpler approach to subject matter to promote student involvement and reduce apathy.

"The kids clammed up as soon as he walked in and he interpreted that as apathy. How am I supposed to teach that novel simplistically?"

"You can't," Alyssa said, "it's impossible. *Peace* is too deep, there's too much psychology in it, too much style to ignore. Cool down, this isn't as bad as it looks. In fact, it isn't bad at all, as these things go." She handed the sheet back to Bonnie. "He checked 'good' on everything."

"How could he check 'good' after 'provides for individual differences'? He never saw evidence of that, and then he stuck me with that apathy bit. It doesn't make any sense!"

"Forget sense," Alyssa told her," and look at the bottom line again. It says 'recommend continuation.' It really is the bottom line. That's all that counts with these things."

Jean added: "They feel they need to offer some kind of suggestions for improvement or they're not doing their job. How would it look if every one they wrote was glowing with praise? Then THEY would look deficient. He wasn't in your room long enough to find much to criticize so he latched on to the biggest cop-out there is.

So who's perfect? He has an obligation to be critical, to criticize something, anything. You got away pretty clean, it seems to me."

Connie bristled. "I've been trying to tell her that. He observed me this week too. I had to sweat the whole period with him in the room and he couldn't even wait for me to find his evaluation in my mailbox, he stayed after class to tell me to do something about the dirty words written on the desks! And you know what else he said? That the chalk trays needed cleaning! What is wrong around here? Doesn't anybody realize what we do, how much work goes into every lesson? I mean, sometimes my lessons are disasters, but I still put in a lot of time and energy. Doesn't anybody consider that?"

"Nope," Alyssa said. "That is systematically ignored. You'll get used to it."

"Oh no, I won't," Connie said, "because I'm not hanging around that long. My husband is taking over his father's business and he needs office help. I'm not sticking this out until it's too much of a sacrifice to leave. Once the money gets decent you're trapped."

"True 'nuff," Jean said. "Hey! Was that observation done the period you're in my room?"

Connie grinned. "True 'nuff!"

"Those desks have been like that for centuries."

Alyssa rolled her head back and let out a small shriek. "Aacck! They're mine! Don't you remember, Jean? Two years ago I came in one morning and found new desks in my room and we figured that you got the old ones to replace your even older ones. Remember how I recognized obscenities to identify my old desks?"

"Oh, Lord, yes. The pictures, I remember the artwork."

"You brought in Comet cleanser and we scrubbed one night after school."

"That's right. What's on them now is only two years old. Well, Connie, we can haul out the Comet and the sponges again."

"Not this girl," Connie said. "If that jerk wants clean desks he can scrub them himself."

"Good for you," Alyssa added. "When I started teaching, I thought that was part of my job description, that I was negligent if the desks got dirty. I used to keep an eye out for anybody writing on the desks because I was afraid of being labeled a slob. Everybody was wild over what seemed to be the most important duty a teacher faced: catch the culprit and make him show up after school to scrub all the desktops. That way, all the desks got a periodic cleaning and the teacher who owned the room kept an unblemished reputation.

McGuinness still thinks it's a top priority. I don't any more. Those desks can get so raunchy they sizzle and burn away for all I care."

"But," Jean said with a forced grin, "we are still responsible for the condition of the desks in our rooms. And, frankly my dear, I don't give a damn either."

Bonnie made it an agreeable foursome, then asked, "So you think I should just sign this foolishness and forget about it?"

"You can attach a statement in your own defense if you want to," Alyssa advised, "if you want to put the time into it. I wouldn't bother, though. I'd just sign it. I'm telling you, Bon, I've seen worse."

Bonnie was about to argue that she'd seen better and was used to the best, but Paul appeared to be ready to start the meeting.

Alyssa poked around in her purse and fished out her cigarettes and a round metal portable ashtray. Jean lifted one nostril in a look of disgust. "Well, you gave it to me," Alyssa whispered, referring to the ashtray. "My mistake," Jean whispered back. "There's nothing worse than one who quit!" Alyssa pursued as she lit up.

As Paul began to speak, Alyssa felt Bonnie tapping her on the shoulder. She swiveled in the seat to hear Bonnie's whisper over Paul's booming voice.

"I've been meaning to ask you — do you have a recipe for pie crust?"

Alyssa put her hand up to shield her mouth and whispered back, "Sure, a terrific one using oil instead of shortening so you don't have to go through all that rigmarole with the butter knives."

"Remember to bring it in for me?"

"It's not difficult, but I'd rather show you. We'll have to get together on it."

Bonnie nodded agreement and Alyssa swiveled again to face front. Pie crust? What single girl in her right mind ... ? Bonnie was hardly Miss Betty Crocker Bake-Off. Alyssa kept her thoughts to herself, aware that she'd never ask Bonnie a direct question to confirm her suspicions. If Bonnie had any grand announcements, Alyssa would be the first to know. If Alyssa didn't know, nobody knew.

The Substance Of The Indictment

Paul Haust finished his presentation and waited for a reaction. The stunned silence was broken by Hank Courtman, who seemed to speak for most of the others in the room. "Wait a minute," he said. "I'm not sure my brain is absorbing this. Run it by me again."

Paul took a deep breath; he knew that it was not a lack of understanding that his people were struggling with, that the air was laden with disbelief. He summarized for them. "We are now required to teach the research paper to sophomores and juniors. All levels will receive instruction, and all students will write a paper. We have no choice in the matter. I fought like hell but got nowhere. You know the background on this. We were doomed from day one."

The meeting broke up quickly, teachers clustered in groups of two and three, wailing amidst themselves. Some blamed Paul, some blamed the administration, some blamed each other, some blamed wretched fate. All knew there was no way to reverse the edict, that they would just have to suffer it out, that sooner or later it would die a natural death as all such edicts do.

Bonnie flew off for her appointment with Mrs. King; Alyssa and Jean lagged behind until they were the only ones left in the room with Paul.

Alyssa was incredulous. "How can they do this to us? It doesn't make any goddam sense! How do we fit in eight weeks' worth of additional work for sophomores and juniors? What do we cut out? Novels? Plays? Short stories? Poetry? Grammar? Vocabulary? Spelling? What? What, Paul? I can't even fit in one simple writing assignment for my regents classes yet because I've got so damn many papers to grade.

"Do you know the agony I go through to teach *seniors* how to write a paper? Now I'm supposed to do that with sophomores who can't write a complete sentence yet? And when am I supposed to grade all these papers? It's insane, Paul, it's ludicrous!"

"I know, I know. I can't do anything about it; I'm as disgusted and frustrated as you are over it, and I can't do anything about it." He was trying not to get defensive, trying to control his own frustration in deference to hers. While he had little patience for the constant barrage of discontent voiced by some of his staff, he tapped his reserves for her: she was not a chronic complainer.

"We submitted that report for nothing, didn't we?" she said, spitting out the words. "They must have laughed like hell. Are you sure anybody read it? I just can't believe that they'd do this to us after reading that report!"

"Not only did I hand deliver it, I also spent a few days explaining it. I even put the Board through an extensive review of our curriculum catalogs. Please believe me, I tried to make them see the handwriting on the wall. I obviously failed."

Jean asked: "All this goes back to that group of graduates pressuring the Board last spring, doesn't it?"

"Four," Alyssa said bitterly. "There were four of them. We graduate twelve hundred students every year, and four of them returned to condemn their training. But they got headlines. It's always news when teachers are being attacked. Those kids disgusted me. And nobody raised the issue that maybe it was their fault they weren't prepared for college."

"I recognized two of those names," Jean added. "I had both kids when they were juniors. The amount of work each did would have easily fit into a thimble."

"Did you notice anything else in those newspaper articles?" Paul asked.

"Like what?" Alyssa said.

"It was hidden fairly well, but there nevertheless. The core of the attack was on writing skills, but it wasn't actually the English department that those students found fault with. I've been fighting at upper level meetings for weeks trying to capitalize on that fact. As it turned out, we got screwed along with the history department."

"The history department?" Jean asked.

Paul added: "Inadequate training in writing history papers. That's what the attack boiled down to."

"We have an excellent history department here. They assign written work," Alyssa said.

"But not research papers." Paul put his hands in his pockets and leaned back in his chair.

Alyssa's sense of reason was swelling rapidly. "If a student gets training in writing a research paper his senior year, which is the logical time for him to get it, he should be able to write a paper for history, science, or any other college course that requires one."

Paul smirked. "Cut out the logic and reasoning. And prepare yourself for tonight's headline: All History And English Courses Require Research Paper. Translation: Rest Easy, Parents, Be Not

Afraid. Your School Board Will Mandate Excellence From Negligent Teachers."

"I think I'm going to vomit," Alyssa moaned.

Jean took another stance. "I've just spent two weeks trying to get the concept of a topic sentence through to my three regents classes. They think a run-on is a car accident and three run-ons make a hell of a good composition. It will take at least four months to get a decent paragraph out of some of them. They're juniors and they can't spell and they can't write and they can't read and they won't think. They still need to learn fundamentals, but I'm compelled to suspend all that, I'm compelled to teach *Ibid.* to students that don't understand basic rules of grammar."

Paul shifted in his chair. "I tried to explain all that. Believe me, I ranted and raved, I pleaded and begged. It's useless. I even considered taking a stand as a department. But that idea gave me nightmares. What a headline that would make: Teachers Refuse To Teach."

Alyssa's eyes lit up. "Why can't we supply the history department with a format for writing a paper? A simple one, just the basic procedure with models for footnotes and bibliography?"

"The history department is as disgusted as we are with this. They are not anxious to grade all those papers. No way in hell will they consider doing our job. That's how it was put: they will not dirty their hands with our work."

Jean said, "And you can bet your life that they'll grade those papers on content only anyway."

Alyssa walked to the window and looked out, squinting her eyes against the harsh glare of the sun. "Don't aggravate me. I had a kid submit a paper last year that he wrote for me and for a history course. Half of it was quoted directly; the footnotes, when he bothered to footnote, were a disaster, no page numbers, incorrect form; the bibliography showed fifteen sources, the kid used three, there was a requirement of seven; it was full of mechanical, grammatical, and spelling errors. I spent more time making comments and circling errors than the kid spent writing the paper. I failed it, the history teacher gave it a B. Then the kid's mother came in screaming for my head on a platter." She turned her back to the sun. "I've got all I can do to handle senior papers, Paul."

"It's so goddam nonsensical!" Jean said. "Every kid in the school writing at least two research papers every year. How the hell can the library accommodate all that activity? And they've cut all the aides. I thought the state was mandate crazy. But this beats them all. If ever there was cause to define the word *overkill*, this outshines 'em all!"

Paul moved his head up and down in slow affirmation. "Exactly. You're finally beginning to see the light. The hot potato has been flipped along royally."

"And the buck stopped here," Jean said.

Alyssa folded her arms in front of her body and tensed up, as if she were attempting to bandage falling parts. "No, no, no. Poor choice of verb. Very poor indeed. Shoved. Try shoved. We've had it shoved," she said emphatically, "right up our collective ass." She moved away from the window and sat on the top of one of the large desks. "Ever since I wrote that report, I've had something in the back of my mind. The report forced me to acknowledge reality, something I might not have done consciously otherwise. I've always plugged away in my own little world regardless of what was attacking me from the outside, in spite of the casualties dropping around me. When I wrote that report I shattered my own little world and joined the war. Only it is no war, not really, because in a war there are at least two sides. We're governed by the old snowball-in-hell theory, we can't even form a defensive line. The other side has all the ammunition and feels obliged to bloody us periodically, to maim us with a merciless barrage of abuse, suspicion, and accusation.

"We're being used, grossly exploited to cover everybody else's ass! The State mandated minimum competency when parents started suing school districts because their kids couldn't read and write when they graduated. The Board of Regents was horrified, parents were horrified, school districts were horrified, boards of education were horrified; everybody was enraged and horrified. Except teachers. Because teachers knew why. But teachers weren't allowed to do anything about it, teachers wanted to spend more money, they wanted to do less work! Heavens, no! The omnipotent Board issued a goddam mandate! They created more bureaucracy in Albany to oversee and distribute competency tests. Did anybody notice that the reason students are not receiving an adequate education is that we are overrun with work? Hell, no! The State fulfilled its obligation to the public, what the hell does it care if we follow through with the gut work or not? If we don't, we get strung up, not them.

"And besides the State, we've got our own district on our backs. Every time somebody moans we get another mandate locally. So everybody's happy, everybody's ass is covered, because everybody funnels the shit down to us. We are the bottom line and we are expected to produce whether it's humanly possible to do so or not. There I go again. I've been quoting that report a lot lately. Sometimes I wish I never wrote it. Why did you ask me to write it, Paul? You didn't do me any favor."

He smiled a little. "I saw signs that it was all boiling up inside you; I just thought it would be good if you let it out. And I thought it was about time you became involved in department matters; you've always been the phantom of the opera around here."

"Gee, thanks. Now I'm miserable like everybody else. I can't believe how sensitive I've become, not only to the widespread ignorance of what we do, but also, and more violently, to the shocking indifference to our needs and our problems. I'm overwhelmed by all of it, and I'm insulted. I'm grossly insulted; I feel like chattel, like baggage to be moved around and ordered about without care or feeling. I'm not used to that. I'm a child to chiding."

"Desdemona," Paul said. "An appropriate allusion."

Alyssa nodded and looked at Jean. "Do you feel that way?"

"For a long time. You're just catching up to the rest of us. Welcome to the planet Earth."

Alyssa looked away. "That's the second time today somebody's told me that." She looked back at Jean, then at Paul. "Would you mind showing me the exit? I don't like it here."

Devoid of human flesh, stripped of living things, the hall was like a tomb, unnatural yet natural. As the two women walked, their footsteps echoed against the solitary hardness of plaster and metal and glass. The lights were dimmed in the holy name of Energy; a large container stood sentinel in the holy name of Budget. Something had to catch the drips when the roof leaked. Bits of paper were scattered along the edges of the walkway, paper strewn like flowers along the primrose path. A book lay open on the floor next to a classroom door, its pages ripped and dirtied, its gaping wound befitting the sepulchral surroundings. Alyssa stopped to pick it up, a grammar book, more than half its pages mutilated. She thought of that time when she was walking with Mary Gregory, when they both saw a teacher use a book for a doorstop. How furious Mary had become! how indignant! She thought of that time and closed the covers of the book, in much the same way as one would close the eyes of the dead.

"That one's for the garbage," Jean said. She needed one last trip to the bathroom before they left the building, and Alyssa forgot her thermos, so they were headed for the faculty room.

"I'm afraid so," Alyssa said, piling the book on top of the two research papers she planned to grade that evening. "We don't have enough books as it is, and they're doing this to them." She pulled on the door to the faculty room, but it wouldn't budge. "It's locked already. Do you have a master key?"

"Sure," Jean said as she located her key ring. "Don't you?"

"Never got one. My room key is just for my room."

Jean unlocked the door and swung it open. She shouted from behind the closed bathroom door after she made a beeline. "Do you want to take my master and have a copy made?"

Alyssa didn't answer so she asked again when she left the bathroom. "There's no reason why you shouldn't have a master key," she added.

"I never wanted one," Alyssa explained. "Don't want one now. If anything disappears, nobody can point the finger at me." She dropped the grammar book in the wastebasket, then retrieved it and put it on a shelf. Then she picked up her thermos. "Okay, ready to go."

Jean stared at her. "Why did you save that book?"

"Some parts are still intact. Maybe somebody can still use it."

"You're a real winner, Matthews. And you're paranoid. I mean, we all are to a large degree, but don't you think you're carrying it too far?"

"What do you mean?"

"The key."

"Oh, that. To tell you the truth, I tried to get a master key a long time ago when I was floating and people kept locking me out of their rooms. You know how that goes. Then I tried again because for a long time I was practically the first person in the building in the morning; I used to get here so early that no one else had unlocked this room yet. They kept telling me in the office that no keys were available and none were being made. So I gave up. I heard a few weeks ago that for some reason keys were being made again, so I did request one. Maybe I'll get one, maybe not. So it's not paranoia, after all, just resignation. See? I'm back to my old self, all that meanness I just let out wasn't the real me. I'm an employer's dream, Jean. I do what I'm told and wouldn't say shit if my mouth were full of it. Sorry, that's disgusting imagery, another thing I'm getting into a lot these days. Forgive my increasing decadence."

Jean locked the door behind them.

"Speaking of shit and decadence," Alyssa continued, "did you hear about the pile Joe Axelrod found on his desk this morning? Of shit, that is. I don't think decadence comes in piles. Or does it?"

Jean stopped walking. "Who?"

"Joe Axelrod. I heard about it during the bomb scare. Actually I overheard it; some kids were talking about it behind me on the stairs when we were coming back into the building. I was glad I hadn't eaten lunch."

"I've been guarding my mouth all day, and it got out anyway. Damn it all, there are no secrets in this place."

So you knew about it?"

"From personal experience. The Mad Shitter paid me a visit too, along with Jim Cote. That's three with Axelrod."

Alyssa wrinkled her nose and looked at Jean sideways. "Christ, what next around here? Now we've got to be afraid of finding shit on the desk in the morning. And you've got the nerve to tell me I'm paranoid? Anybody who isn't must have formaldehyde in his veins."

Once in the parking lot, each woman circled her car as a preventive measure. Alyssa threw her daily quota of research papers into the back seat, thinking that she'd have to step up the grading over the weekend or she wouldn't meet her own two-week deadline. Both folders hit the handle of the broom and slid to the floor. She mumbled a curse as she attempted to gather note cards and bibliography cards, which had scattered across the seat and floor, and return them to the right folders. She sensed the presence of a shadow, and looked up to see Jean leaning against the rear fender. "This is why I insist on folders with pockets," she said as she inserted cards "Of course, I still get some in manila folders and then I have to balance them on my nose."

"How bad is it to teach the research paper?" Jean asked. "I've never done it."

"It's hell, pure hell. More misery than teaching anything else you can imagine because of the work and the frustration. And that's before you try to grade them. Then it gets worse. It's the ultimate writing assignment on the practical end of the scale. Don't get me wrong, I've gotten some joy, some satisfaction out of it too. But I had to fight for it. With twelve kids and a lot of time to spend with them, teaching the research paper can be a thing of beauty and a joy forever. But with over a hundred kids and no time, well, you can figure that out."

"Do you think any of Paul's suggestions would work?"

"I think Paul's suggestions are more offensive than the original order. I suppose it's because I'm so deeply entrenched in doing everything the right way. Believe me, it's a waste of time to have a whole class write one paper. I know Erica fell in love with the idea, but I find it repulsive. I couldn't stand the confusion."

Jean shifted position. "You know why Paul suggested it."

"Of course. Anything to make our position more palatable. And anything to protect ourselves. Our tender bottoms are sticking out a mile-and-a-half on this one. Paul's realistic; rather than face charges of insubordination or, worse yet, incompetence, we at least have to appear to be doing what we're told. But I can't do it that way, Jean, I can't water it down to a farce, then teach it like great literature. Either I do it right, or I don't do it at all; I've never taught any other way."

"So you're going to do the whole smear with all your classes?"

"I didn't say that. I can't possibly do that; it's not humanly possible, remember?"

"How about requiring just a page or two of paper? That would cut down on a lot of grading time."

"That stinks too! A research paper is supposed to go into some depth, for God's sake! You know, one of my kids from last year told me this morning that she wants to be a teacher and my blood froze."

"What are you going to do about this research paper thing?"

"Nothing."

"What do you mean, nothing?"

"Just exactly that. Nothing. I am not teaching the research paper to my sophomores. They can take the course from me when they're seniors and need it for college."

"You're getting awfully brave in your old age."

"Brave, foolish, paranoid, insulted, disgusted, resigned, what else? What else am I? I wish I knew, Jean. I wish to hell I knew."

293

The Eyedropper

Paul Haust sat tapping a pencil on his desk. Tap, tap, tap, tappity, tappity, tap, tappity, tappity, tap, tap, tap.

A little at a time. He had to feed it to them a little at a time. Like pabulum. No, pabulum implies nutrition, sustenance. Pabulum isn't at all appropriate. Try poison; that fits.

Who could ingest great quantities of bitterness all at once? It had to be rationed through a tube, the flow strictly controlled. Drip, drip, drip, tap, tap, tappity, tappity, tap, drip, drip ... drip. Use an eyedropper, careful now, slowly, not too much at once or the patient will heave and convulse.

He stopped tapping, flipped the pencil upright, and started listing names in six columns: who taught 2NR, who taught 2R, who taught 2S, who taught 3NR, who taught 3R, who taught 3S. When he finished, all names were written twice, once in each of two different columns. Then the fun began.

He had to decide who would best chair each of the six committees, taking into consideration personalities and reputations for getting the job done. If you want something done fast, give it to a busy man. If you want something done by a committee, put someone in charge who will do the work other members don't do.

2NR-Bonnie Mason 2R-Hank Courtman 2S-Alyssa Matthews

3NR-Connie Baker 3R-Beth Whittsley 3S-Jean Tevarro

Each of the six chairmen was also a member of another committee. Bonnie Mason was also on the 2R committee because she taught 2NR and 2R; Alyssa Matthews was also on the 2R committee while she chaired the 2S committee, and so on. Paul couldn't help that, it was the way they were organized.

Once he established the committees, he wrote a rough draft outlining the duties of each one: curriculum revisions; no, he crossed out *revisions* and changed it to *addenda*. A curriculum section had to be added to each of the six levels, a detailed account of just how they would incorporate the research paper into the year's work.

When he was satisfied with his rough draft, he made a move for the typewriter he had lifted from one of the faculty rooms. The machine was locked in a closet because he was afraid someone would borrow it back. The hairs on his neck still stood straight up whenever he thought about his fury at not being able to procure a simple typewriter without resorting to theft.

Halfway across the room, he decided it could wait, he would type tomorrow. Sophomore teachers had just received the committee lists for final exams, which necessarily assigned all of them to work on questions for two separate exams. Junior teachers were working on a report delineating and supporting objections to the Regents Comprehensive Exam and statewide competency tests. He had just set all that in motion a few days ago, how could he hit them with more committee work so soon? Slow down, fella. The eyedropper, remember?

He unlocked the closet to get his coat and left the typewriter on the shelf. Monday. Monday was soon enough. He would notify them Monday, set a deadline for Thanksgiving. No, couldn't do that, the exams were due the last day of school before Thanksgiving; that wasn't his deadline, that was issued out of the Board office because secretaries had to have time to type. He asked once if they were sure six months was enough.

The week after Thanksgiving then; that would have to do. The junior committees were working all year anyway.

The week after Thanksgiving. That way by Christmas all of it would be in black and white; he would have something to point to just in case; by Christmas the department would be covered. He decided to make a note of the deadline before he left.

295

Dirge Is Another Word For Song

She was like Achilles seeking Hector, with Paris temporarily at bay; like Ajax perishing by his own hand; like Niobe, all tears; like Jason searching for the fleece; like Atlas bearing the burden; like Theseus seeking the Minotaur and Perseus seeking Medusa; like Oedipus stubbornly seeking Truth; like Prometheus stealing fire; she was Helen and Pandora, Athene, Cassandra, Cassiopeia, Calypso, and Electra; she was Calliope and the son of Calliope, begging the return of Eurydice, when even the Furies wept; she was what she was not, she was not what she was. She was Everyman and she was Noman; she sprang full grown out of the head of the Twentieth Century.

The car was under her and around her, but she hardly felt its presence. Part of her was molded into its mechanism, directing passage down familiar streets, that part of her able to function when the button was pushed.

She had intended to run some errands after work, the list was neatly written on a 3x5 index card. Groceries, Jeff's shirts at the cleaners, the phone bill, stamps. But Effie was unconscious, knocked out and sprawled in a corner. Too many other things to think about. Curtis Holbert. Study hall. Classes. Kids. Mainstreaming. Cassie Quimly. Nettie NillyNellyNully. Pie crust?

Connie Baker. How discouraged she is. Where, oh where, are the new people going to come from? Sooner or later they're going to have to hire more teachers, and there won't be any to hire. Can't anybody see that? Heads are buried in the muck. As soon as the field became glutted, they clamped down on restrictions and requirements. No more thirty hours, now they have to get a Masters. As if that makes them better teachers, as if having to do all that additional work and having to spend all that money when they're trying to keep up as new teachers and working at the low end of the pay scale, as if that will make them exemplary teachers. It's insane. You'd have to be crazy to put up with it to qualify for nonexistent jobs. Permanent certification. We always said it was a device to insure enrollment in graduate courses. Poor Joyce. If I had to take courses now, I'd commit suicide; they can keep the extra pay.

Man the scalpels! Full speed ahead! Enrollment is decreasing every year, but my class size increases. More classes, more students; between lay-offs and attrition they managed it, they used

296

the excuse that enrollment is down to increase enrollment. Clever. Fewer students, but even fewer teachers equals more students per teacher. It makes me sick. *No one has expired from the strain.* That report is going to need revision soon.

She made the turn into her driveway thinking about her decision not to teach the research paper to sophomores. It frightened her, rebellion did, yet compliance, the very thought of compliance, violated her.

Wasn't it time to switch to emergency power? time to regroup for the attack? time to meet the challenge head on? the way she had met all the others over the years? Some of the others had been just as infuriating, just as absurd.

Not this time. This time even the emergency generators were spent; too many emergencies had taken their toll. This time the debilitation was too severe, the insult too massive, the absurdity too complete. The ambrosia was turning rancid, the song was sticking in her throat, the tumor was rooting.

Blessed with a curse, Orpheus sealed his fate. She, too, looked back. *It's not humanly possible* ... Unlike Orpheus, she saw what she had no desire to see and gazed with yearning and lengthy solicitude. And Orpheus be damned (which he surely was), she would look again. Again and again she would turn to what had been, until she was lost in it.

Swallow hard and forget about it, the wise man said.

But Alyssa Matthews, the teacher who demanded careful evaluation from her students, the teacher who revered the mind's capacity to assess and reason, Alyssa Matthews who knew no other way to deal with life except through mental processes, Alyssa Matthews could do nothing but think about it.

Cogito ergo sum.

No. For her it was the other way around.

Wunnerwummun

She was about to unlock the front door when she heard squeals and running feet. The child was all of three years old, a beautiful, budding child with the face of an angel.

Childhood traditionally symbolizes innocence, she told her classes when she taught *Peace*. We are born innocent into this world; as we grow we learn fear and hatred, guilt and shame; as we grow we become aware of poverty and evil and injustice; the world sees to it, life tarnishes our innocence, then snatches it away. Evil exists in many forms; when we experience enough of it, we advance, if you want to call it that, from childhood to adulthood, and that is called loss of innocence. Some scholars believe that every piece of literature ever written deals in some way with the theme of loss of innocence.

The child was jumping up and down and tugging on the hem of the lavender–flowered dress. "An Lis!" she cried, "An Lis! Look! Lookit my roos!"

Alyssa turned and sat on the front steps, facing the little girl, who was dancing about wildly like some wood nymph and lifting her shirt and lowering her pants as far as her two small hands could push.

"Look! Look, An Lis!"

Though she was not blood-related to the child, Alyssa glowed whenever she called her "aunt," which she had done, at her mother's insistence, ever since she learned to speak.

"Whatever are you so excited about?" Alyssa queried.

"My unroos, An Lis! Lookit my unroos!" She tugged at her pants and shirt.

"Well, hold still a minute, sweetheart, so I can see what you're talking about." She dropped the research papers and her purse on the step and reached out both arms to catch the swirling child, thinking as she did it that the little girl should always wear fresh flowers in her hair. But fastened securely, as it were. "Now stand still a minute, Sabrina, and tell me slowly what you want me to see."

Sabrina looked up with a smile that would melt an iceberg. Her large brown eyes widened and her head bobbed to accent every syllable, "Look at my un-roos, An Lis!"

Alyssa's eyes followed the child's downward glance. "Aha! Your underwear!

Sabrina tilted her head and looked exasperated. "N0, AN LIS! My UN-ROOS!"

"Don't get impatient with me, sweetheart, I don't have any little girls, you know. Now it looks to me like you're showing off your underwear. I do know that little girls like to do that. And I do think you look quite beautiful. Look at those yummy colors, bright red and blue and yellow. Can you tell your colors yet?"

"Not UN-WARE, UN-ROOS!"

Alyssa's brow deepened with concern. "Oh, dear, this is getting critical. Dumb old teacher doesn't understand, does she? Maybe we'd better bring in a consultant. C'mon, give me your hand, we'll go bother Mommy."

She had her purse slung over her shoulder and the folders cradled in one arm when the light bulb lit. She had seen an ad in a magazine. Not un-WARE, un-ROOS, not underwear, but ...

"Underoos! You're wearing Underoos, Sabrina!"

The sprite started to cavort again in gleeful disabandon. "Yep, yep, yep, arnt dey bootivul?"

"Oh, yes! Yes, they are! And so are you! Oh? There's more? Let me see; no, honey, you shouldn't undress in the middle of the lawn, just raise your shirt for me."

"Look, An Lis. WUNnerwummun."

"Ah, yes, I see. That is her picture, isn't it?"

"Uh-huh. I wanna be WUNnerwummun."

The teacher stared at the bright-colored cloth, then at the three-year-old face. "Are you sure that's what you want to be?"

"Yeah, yeah, yeah!" The head bobbed up and down and the body started swirling again amidst a frenzied chant of "WUNnerwummun, WUNnerwummun."

Alyssa dropped to one knee in the grass and freed her arms of the folders and purse. She caught the moving child and pulled her close. She was a loving child and her arms immediately circled Alyssa's neck.

They looked at each other then, the woman and the child, the woman's eyes filled with love and pain, the child's eyes filled with love and mischief.

"You don't really want to be Wonder Woman, do you?"

"Yep, I do."

"No, you don't."

"I do."

"You don't."

"I do."

"You're a silly goose, you know that?"

The child giggled and buried her face in Alyssa's neck. The teacher squeezed hard, then let her run off.

A Mother and Child Reunion

"I called that school today to beg a favor for your sister and you go and pull this on me. What in hell do you think you're doing? What? Playing big man because you're a senior? Sometimes I think you had more brains when you were in grade school! What's going on? What else are you doing that I don't know about?"

"Aw, Ma, nothing. Nothing else."

"I don't like a liar, Brian. You'd better not be lying to me. I don't care how old you are or how big you are, you're still living in my house and I'm still responsible for you. You're only seventeen years old. Do you want to pump gas for the rest of your life like your brother?"

"You're blowing this way out of proportion. I was late to one lousy class and you're treating me like I'm some kind of criminal. I told you, it won't happen again."

"It better not. That's what I'm telling you, young man. It better not. You've never pulled anything like this before. Not that I know of, anyway. And this is no time for you to jeopardize everything you've worked for. I just can't understand how you could pull something like this when you're sending out college applications. How are you supposed to go to college if you don't graduate?"

"I'll graduate, Ma. Don't worry, I'll graduate."

"Don't you tell me not to worry, Brian. Don't ever think for a second that I'll ever stop worrying about you or your sister or your brother. I started to worry the minute I knew you were in me and I'll stop when I'm dead. That's how it is with children. Someday you'll know, when you have your own."

He looked at her distraught face, and he was sorry, sorry that she was upset because of him, because of something he did. It had always been that way. Bernie never cared much whenever he brought her pain. Bernie was the oldest and he slid in and out of trouble all the time. Oh, nothing really serious, nothing horrible, just little skirmishes all through school. Bernie had a mind of his own, that was all. Ma kept saying that Bernie had the intelligence to be anything, but the will to be nothing, and Bernie was perfectly happy being nothing. It never bothered Bernie that he was a disappointment to Ma and Dad.

But it bothered Brian. Over and over again he vowed that he would never disappoint them the way Bernie did. Instead, he would

301

make up for all of it, he would make them proud. He and Beth Ann, of course. Beth Ann was a natural at making people proud of her. But still, she was a daughter. He was a son and he knew the difference. Bernie wasn't a son to boast about, but he, Brian, would be.

Ma always said "you'll know when you have children of your own," but she was wrong. Brian already knew. He knew his responsibilities as a son, he knew his duty as Bernie's brother.

He saw the hurt on his mother's face and felt guilt at having put it there.

"I don't ever want to get another phone call like that," she said. "I was used to them with your brother, but not with you, not with you. Whatever made you that late this morning? You left the house early enough."

He hesitated, then said, "I picked up Joe."

"Not again, Brian. Even your father's told you that boy is no good. He's no good for you. Can't you pick friends better than that?"

The middle son hesitated again. It used to be so easy to keep them happy. But the older he became, the harder it got. Some things he had to speak up about. Some things went beyond blind obedience.

"There's nothing wrong with Joe. He's got it tough at home. He's not a bad kid. Why do you hate Joe? He's never done anything wrong. He just wanted breakfast, he doesn't get any at home."

"I don't believe it! How can you sit there and defend that kid when you got into trouble because of him! Have you been fooling me all these years? Is there a brain in that head of yours? How can you defend him when you were late this morning because of him?"

"Yeah, but — you don't understand. He doesn't have too many friends and I think he's all right. Hell, the way kids smoke and drink today — you know how many kids are on drugs today, Ma?— you should be thankful I don't hang around with some of them."

"I am, son, I am. I know there's worse, but there's also better. And I want nothing less than the best for you. I'm not trying to make a snob out of you. We're ordinary people. Your father works in a mill, I punch a cash register. We're not exactly snooty upper class. But that boy is influencing you to do things you wouldn't do on your own and I don't like it."

She'd never understand, he decided. He still had control over himself, Joe wasn't an ogre directing his life. Right now, though, there was no way to get her to see that, and she might never see it. One thing was for sure: she'd never accept the fact that Brian was capable of being flawed, that even he needed to escape the straight and narrow occasionally. So Brian said he would cool it for awhile with Joe.

"I don't want to make you feel like a baby," she said, "but I'm giving you fair warning of what I'm going to do. Tomorrow I'm going to call your guidance counselor and instruct him to notify all your teachers that I want to know immediately when you're not in class or late for any reason."

He didn't care. It didn't matter because he wasn't going to mess up again. He told her that and moaned a little over the fact that he would probably fail Axelrod's course the next report card period. He thought it a good idea to prepare her for that. But she had her own announcement to make.

"Mr. Axelrod told me that he would allow you to take another test. He said it's going to be more difficult than the one you missed, but thought you deserved some consideration because it was your first offense. He was really furious but softened up when I told him you've never done anything out of the way since kindergarten. Remember when your kindergarten teacher called me because you wouldn't leave the bathroom?"

He laughed along with her. "I couldn't tell her I didn't make it in time and my pants were wet. I wouldn't come out for anybody but you."

Helen Conneally looked lovingly at her middle child, her second son. She had seen every inch of his body grow, she had seen him crying from hurt and burning with fever, laughing from joy and bursting with pride. She had applied bandages to imaginary wounds and suffered with him to heal real ones. She knew that no one on earth could love him the way she did, could care for him the way she always had. Not a father or a sister or a brother. Not even a wife. It was never her intention to exclude those others from his life, for they played their roles in all lives, but she knew the special and profound attachment of mother to child superseded all others. The cord wasn't severed at birth, it remained forever.

She felt that way about all three. Even Bernie, because she still had hopes and dreams for him. Hopes and dreams for all three. There could be no other way. She was mother to them all. She would hope and dream and worry and plan until the day she died.

The Maid

She saw the house as soon as she rounded the last corner; at least, she saw what she hoped was the house. Her expectations had been hazy all day because of Alyssa's meager description. Nevertheless, she was excited. The rent was unimaginable in 1980. One hundred a month? Including heat? She was paying almost four times that where she had been living for the last seven years. The landlord was in the habit of raising the rent every six months and the place had oil heat. She froze during the winter and paid dearly to freeze. Rent, heat, utilities, gas for the car (poor sick thing that it was) and loan payments kept her very near poverty level, in spite of the fact that she worked. The Working Poor. She heard the phrase spoken again and again by newsmen, and though she didn't consider herself a member of that group, for she had no family to support, she felt an alliance with it. Very often she walked out of a grocery store wishing she qualified for food stamps. Some weeks she was down to twenty dollars for food and gas and naturally the car ate better than she. But she was used to budgeting close, and she knew how to coordinate one new skirt with what she already had in the closet to manufacture at least three different outfits. She bought only on sale and waited for the last markdown with obsessive persistence; sometimes she returned to a store for the fourth or fifth check on price only to find the article she was interested in gone, but that was the chance she willingly took. Better to lose it altogether than pay too much.

Handling money, or rather, most of the time not having any to handle, was a way of life to her. She complained, like anybody else, but she did what she had to do to survive, like anybody else. After all, she had only herself to worry about, she had only her own needs to attend to.

But her life was changing, it was taking another course, veering off from her solitary self. She had someone else to think about, someone else to care for, someone else whose needs she unselfishly attended to. And bless him, he ate like a horse. One hundred a month. Including heat. It couldn't have come at a better time. For the first time since she left home, she'd be able to save some money. In her mind she was already spending the savings.

At a hundred a month including heat she would have moved into dirt floors and mud walls, if even that sort of place were available at such a price. What she was living in wasn't much better, the walls were cracked and dirty, wallpaper was peeling in the bedroom, the toilet leaked, and the kitchen sink plugged solid if a grain of rice escaped down the drain.

One hundred a month including heat for Alyssa's old apartment. Heaven on Earth. Or close to it. It had to be. She couldn't imagine Alyssa living in a dump.

She parked at the curb and stared, not willing to move, wanting to absorb her first impression, let it fill her with the excitement that was growing and growing until she thought she would burst with it. The sun was still shining brightly, though the balmy feel of midday was lost to the chill of late afternoon. She raised her sunglasses to rest on the top of her head so that she might see the house without obstruction, without shadowed sight. She sat in the car and saw her dream fulfilled. All else had fled, she was Pandora looking at the jewel that remained.

The house was magnificent.

Located where it was, in a row with other dwellings, it lost some of the splendor, the aura of splendor, that it would have necessarily radiated had it been situated alone on a hill overlooking a valley with acres of velvet green stretching as far as the eye could see.

Not that it looked out-of-place; the homes around it did not detract from its effect, not in and of themselves, for they, too, were immaculately kept and appealing. Each one, in fact, would have fit perfectly in the aforementioned idyllic setting. Each was proud and stately and serene; each was old and cautious and self-serving.

The street was a Declaration of Success, a Tribute to The American Dream. The American Dream Realized. Long ago. Long, long ago. All who resided there, it seemed, lived happy, comfortable, fulfilling lives. Those who passed by saw security emanating from the elegance, they sensed the presence of money and status, and some imagined the transferal of those elements to their own lives, as if by magic some ancient spell could change the fate of men. Still others, in a class by themselves yet in all classes, passed by with habitual response and, often, purposeful reason — to pause for a moment of nourishing envy and then move on. The street made Bonnie think of the home she left, the home she hadn't stepped foot in since, but still thought of as "home" because she knew no other.

The house at 527 Brickstone Street was externally similar to its neighbors in that it showed the facade the world expected to see. And it was similar in other, more specific, yet just as obvious ways: the large porch extending along the front and halfway down one side; two other smaller porches, balconies really, off the second floor;

white double-four clapboards, white stone quoins, slate roof, one-stall detached garage set back from the house. The front door was framed by typical colonial adornments: arched pediment with dentiled cornice over the doorway, sidelights to the left and right, and beyond the sidelights two pilasters — thin, flat, rectangular fluted columns.

With her first look at the house, Bonnie failed to notice many of its particulars, including the precise number of gables and the abundance of modillioned cornices along the various roof lines and the stone chimneys. She did feel its overall power and effect, though, and she did understand the one striking peculiarity. White shutters. White shutters on a white house. It would have been odd, an error, too colorless on any other house. But not on this one. As she looked at it, she saw immediately and she understood.

It was the glass. There was so much color, so much vibrant, animated color in the glass that the house itself needed none. Indeed, the house itself was forever deprived of any covering save white, for the glass was more permanent than paint; perhaps more permanent than the house.

She left the car and walked the length of the sidewalk to the porch, looking up all the way. Every small window wasn't a window at all but a picture frame holding a painting. The house was a gallery displaying works of art. She couldn't resist; she turned and walked around one side of the house to view what might be displayed there. And she wasn't disappointed. The windows were round and square and triangular, fitted here and there not for practical purposes but for aesthetic ones. Some depicted people, some animals, some flowers, some what she thought were heraldic symbols. She would have to study them further.

But she needed to insure that possibility; it occurred to her that she might be taken for a prowler, even in the daylight. Mrs. King, Alyssa said, was old. Bonnie remembered her manners and walked back around to the front of the house. She admired the rich floraled glass in the sidelights on both sides of the door and the wedges of deep crimson and gold fanned out in the pediment above it. She was about to ring the doorbell when she heard the voices, high-pitched angry voices, shouting.

She didn't know what to do. She wanted that apartment, sight unseen, so badly she could taste it, and yet, how could she ring the doorbell? Something was going on that was none of her business. If only she hadn't had that meeting to go to. That made her late. It could have all been settled by now; she was ready to move in within the hour.

The voices got louder. She decided she'd better leave and call for another appointment. As she turned to step down from the porch, the voices took form and she was aware that the dispute had reached the front door. She turned back and saw two forms in the doorway.

A man who looked to be in his forties, but was actually nearing sixty, pushed the outer screened door open; it wasn't the usual aluminum screened door, but one made of etched and carved wood and, of course, painted white. When the man pushed it open, he did so with such force that it remained open. "You're a stubborn old woman," he hissed, then raced through the opening, past Bonnie without so much as a look, and down the front steps to his waiting car. The stubborn old woman called out, "You're a hateful old man!" and waited until he sped away to break into tears.

Bonnie wished she knew the words to some spell that would allow her to make herself disappear in a puff of smoke. Or turn into a statue. Indeed she would have made an exquisite figure cast in marble.

But she was awkwardly standing there. "Mrs. King, I'm Bonnie Mason. I called you earlier today about the apartment, Alyssa Matthews sent me, but I think I should come back later. Will that be all right with you?" She reached out both hands as a sign of geniality, something she rarely did, but somehow, now, was as natural as walking. The old woman took hold of both her hands, said "It's nothing to be alarmed over, dear. Don't feel embarrassed. I'll compose myself in a minute," and drew her into the house, leaving the screened door ajar, the dual doorway free and open.

Dorothea King dabbed at her eyes with a handkerchief she mystically conjured up out of the air, for her dress had no pockets, and then took a deep breath. "There. I'm fine now." She smiled and looked at Bonnie. "Welcome to my home, dear. My, but you are a tall one, aren't you? Or is it that I'm so little? Those things are so relative, aren't they?"

Bonnie laughed and nodded. "Also faked easily," she said, as she looked down and turned one ankle to the side. "These help to raise you up in the world."

Dorothea King looked at Bonnie's feet and smiled. "Oh, my, how I wish I could still wear boots like those. I did once, you know, and I remember how I felt in them — like a cavalry officer, like a soldier on a mission, but mostly —" She looked at Bonnie's face. "Mostly I felt tall!"

Bonnie laughed again. "You might be able to find a pair with modified heels; you know, not quite as high."

307

"Oh no, dear. My boot-buying days are over. I'd look ridiculous now in them. It's not that I'm too old, it's just that I'm too, let's say, mature. Aren't euphemisms wonderful? There's a time in life when you have to say stop to some things. I'm almost eighty-three and proud of it, but some things are lost to me now. Enjoy life while you can, dear, every second of it. Do all that you want to do, but not out of a fear of death. Do it out of a fear of life."

Bonnie didn't know what to say. She hadn't expected a philosopher, just an old lady, an old grandmother-type, in spite of Alyssa's warning that the old girl was "eighty going on twenty." Weren't people supposed to be senile by the time they hit eighty? Hardening of the arteries or something? Apparently not. Not all, anyway.

Bonnie didn't know what to say, but she knew what she wanted to do; grab her and hug her for dear life. She was beautiful, beautiful in every way, so beautiful that she outdid the effect of the house. Bonnie almost forgot what she was there for, she was so enthralled with the woman, with the impish face and spirit. But Mrs. King didn't forget.

"Come, dear, for la grande tour. First I'll show you the house because I love it so, then the apartment because I'm after your money! And be wary! I'm a cunning saleswoman!"

Bonnie toured the first floor, strolled in and out of rooms, and paused at doorways to soak up the warm, homey atmosphere the woman had created with furnishings and decorative additions. "No antiques, you'll notice," Mrs. King said. "I have no use for old junk. And I do all my decorating myself. I can't imagine calling in someone to tell me what I like or don't like. It's a matter of taste, they say, and I know best when it comes to mine. Why should I eat lamb when I prefer pork chops? If something clashes or looks drab to somebody else, that's their problem, don't you think? They can do what they want in their house, as long as they leave me alone to do what I want in mine. Had a lady friend once who told me to match the pillows with the drapes, that was the latest thing in fashion. Told her I was seriously considering shredding the drapes on the windows, cutting them in strips, sort of like a long fringed affair. Asked if I should shred the pillows too. Poor thing, she left in a huff. Never saw her again. Now wasn't that peculiar?"

Bonnie listened, laughed, enjoyed, but asked no questions and uttered few comments except an occasional "how lovely." Mrs. King talked nonstop, moved nonstop, and delighted her nonstop. She knew very little about decorating, but saw nothing that clashed. And nothing, even to her untrained eye, looked drab.

Besides the entrance foyer, the first floor of the house included a small sitting room (Useless, dear, simply useless. Some day I'm going to get shelving put in here to make a study), a large dining room, a large living room (We used to call this a parlor, but that's old-fashioned now), a modern kitchen with serving area (This is called a nook, a breakfast nook; isn't that quaint? Of course, I take all of my meals here. One person gets lost in the dining room. But when the girls come for dinner, we use the dining room. I enjoy that with the candles and crystal and all), two baths, one full (Nothing like a shower, dear!) and one half (I call this the powder room) and a bedroom which Mrs. King pointed out but never moved toward.

All the floors were carpeted (Hardwood floors are beautiful but not very practical at my age) except the foyer floor, which was slate, and the kitchen floor, which was hand-painted ceramic tile. The baths were completely tiled, floors, walls, ceilings (Just a damp sponge does the trick! Add a little soap and you're Mrs. Clean!). Mrs. Clean, Bonnie thought, definitely lives here.

"I have a woman come in once a month for the heavy stuff," Mrs. King said. "I feel guilty about that, she's almost as old as I am. But I do the everyday jobs myself, I'm not in the grave yet!" Her mood darkened just a shade. "Though some would have me there. Some people think I'm crazy, one person living in this big house. But just because you're one person doesn't mean you have to live in a hovel or in one of those homes for the creaky." Then her mood brightened again. "But I'm not alone, am I? You're here, Bonnie Mason, and that makes two. Would you like to see your apartment now? We'll go up through the foyer, but you'll have your own private entrance at the side of the house. I'll show you that later, we'll leave by that route."

Bonnie followed her up the winding staircase to the second floor and admired the handrail and spindles along the way. The house was almost overpowered by the profusity of wood. All the doorways, doors, moldings, were ornately crafted, carved, curved, thick dark-stained wood. The dining room was wainscoted to the ceiling, every ceiling was beamed, including the kitchen but excluding the baths. Richly grained, the wood was dark and warm.

As she traveled up the staircase, Bonnie felt the shimmering smoothness of the handrail and reached out to the right to touch the raised-panel wainscoting similar, but more ornately carved than that in the dining room; flocked wallpaper extended above the wood, intensifying its depth. The staircase led to one landing, then curved upward to another, and she saw from the inside the windows that had intrigued her before. She wondered why Mrs. King hadn't mentioned them, for some were in evidence on the first floor. She was forming the question in her mind and waiting for a lull.

"You know, dear, in my day we used to call girls like you 'buxom.' Nobody uses that word anymore. Nobody says 'buxom' or 'bosomy' anymore. They have such awful words now. 'Tits' and 'knockers' and 'jugs.' Nothing's charming anymore, everything's so sordid and crass. I used to wish I was built like you, but one day I realized how silly that was. The Lord makes us all different for a reason. Do girls still try those silly exercises and send for miracle creams and potions? We did in my day. We did a lot of silly things. Like wearing boots to feel tall. Anything can be faked, as you said before. Some girls even faked their bosoms. That's one thing I never did, though I'll admit I thought of it. You have to learn to like what you are. There are no miracles."

Mrs. King kept talking and Bonnie kept laughing, straining to keep it quiet as she followed the woman up the stairs. Once they reached the second landing, Bonnie felt disoriented because of the turns.

"We'll pass the second floor," Mrs. King explained, "because it's closed off. If I ever need to offer more rooms for rent, they're available. But as long as I can manage without doing that, I can't see crowding my house with people. I like my privacy, and, I will add, I respect yours. There is one key to this door and I'll give it to you when you move in. That way you'll know that no one can get in from this entrance."

"Where are we?" Bonnie asked. They were standing on the third landing in front of a door and a window. The window, off to the left, was no help because she couldn't see out of it. "I lost my bearings. Does the house have a third floor?"

Mrs. King smiled. "Yes and no. It has a full attic, you see. Are you ready?" She said it as if she was about to unveil the find of the century, and Bonnie responded accordingly. "As ready as I'll ever be."

Dorothea King slipped the key in the door, turned it, and pushed the door open. Bonnie looked in and fell in love, though by this time she was ready to accept rats in a shack.

It was really one large room, almost as large as the floor space of one level of the entire house. The bedroom and bathroom doors were not yet visible. What Bonnie saw when she looked through the doorway was the kitchen, brightly furnished in yellow and white. And she saw furniture, which she had meant to ask about, since she owned none. A large round white wrought-iron table glistened in the kitchen area; it was ringed by four matching wrought-iron chairs with yellow-and-white striped padding. The table top was a thick piece of clear glass. The counter area with cabinets and appliances was not the usual squared-off variety, it was rounded in a semi-circle behind the table and chairs. A set of yellow-and-white canisters sat on the countertop, along with a bowl of fresh fruit, and in the middle of the glass table was a centerpiece gorged with flowers of every type and color.

Mrs. King asked, "Shall we go in?" to give her a nudge, and Bonnie stepped foot in the apartment for the first time. Off to the right she saw the living room area, which was filled with a sofa, two chairs, tables, and a desk. Beyond that, Mrs. King directed her to a door and the bathroom, which, to her delight, housed not only the usual appointments, but a washing machine and a clothes dryer as well. "You can thank Jeff Matthews for the machines," Mrs. King explained. "He figured out a way to get them up here. How I miss that clever boy!"

Once they were back in the kitchen area, she further explained that Jeff Matthews had installed the skylight there and in the bedroom when he and Alyssa had lived in the apartment. "How I love those two children," Dorothea King exclaimed. "They did so much for me when they were here. They were more than children to me, more than children. They were my first tenants, and I've been afraid of any others since they left. But it was time for them to strike out on their own, to live in their own home. It was time . . it always becomes time … sooner or later. But I knew if I asked Alyssa to find someone, I'd be happy with her choice." She patted Bonnie's arm. "And I am, dear, I am. Come, now you see the *piece de resistance*."

She took Bonnie's hand and moved her to the left toward another door. They made a peculiar sight, the two of them, the small white-haired woman leading the tall buxom blonde. It looked like the child leading the mother and yet, how could that be?

Bonnie followed obediently, thinking that the woman could lead her into the fires of hell and she'd willingly go. *Piece de resistance*? Whatever could exceed what she had already seen? Mrs. King started to talk again, and whenever she talked, she stopped moving momentarily.

"Jeff and Alyssa — isn't that a beautiful name, dear? Alyssa. It shimmers off your tongue when you say it. She was like a daughter to me, like a daughter. Not that 'Bonnie' isn't beautiful, it is, of course. But it's, it's more lively, isn't it? It's bonny, lass!" She laughed. "My

Scottish isn't very good. Now what was I telling you? Jeff and Alyssa - oh, yes -Jeff and Alyssa decided that more natural light was needed up here, that's why he put in the skylights. And he fixed the plumbing and the wiring and installed this beautiful kitchen. I don't think there's much that boy can't do. He's like my Alex was, he is. You know that old saying, *Jack of all trades, master of none*? Some men fit that old saying, but some are masters of all trades. My Alex was and so is Jeff Matthews. Alyssa's a lucky girl, a most fortunate woman. So was I, so was I. And let that be a lesson to you, bonny lass, marry a man who knows something! Marry a man for two reasons: one, he's good in bed, and two, he can stop a leak in the kitchen sink!"

Bonnie laughed and squeezed the woman's hand. Mrs. King's eyes were twinkling. "It's nice to be old," she said. "Now I can say anything I want and get away with it." Then the twinkle left. "With some people. There are some who think I'm a crotchety old fool. Maybe I am." She started moving again and her voice deepened. "You must excuse the dramatics dear. Alex always said I should have gone on the stage. Come, it's time for you to see it. It's time for you to meet my Alex, what's left of him anyway."

Bonnie had to sit on the bed, the sight was so unnerving, so completely overpowering. She had never seen anything like it, except in a church, where such windows exist naturally. Anticipating some of her questions, Mrs. King sat next to her on the bed and spoke softly. "It was his final achievement, his crowning glory, though he lived many years after he completed it. The window was commissioned by some aristocrat in France, some man whose name I've long since forgotten. When it was finished, my husband couldn't part with it. There was too much of his soul in it, too much of his heart. He put the man off with some story about poor glass, and eventually sent another window. I remember how excited he was when he went to France to oversee the installation of the second window, how excited he was because it was the second and not the first. He built this entire house for that window and what a time I had convincing him not to put it in a front gable. How proud he was! He would have put his colored glass all 'round if I had let him. But Alex, I would say, we have to be able to look out somewhere. And he would laugh and say that looking out was worthless, that everything of value was in.

"He was tall and handsome and dignified and he worked with his hands. They were exquisite hands, strong and gentle hands, that touched everything in this house. When he died, I wanted to go with him. Women have done that before haven't they? In ancient Egypt or somewhere? How could he go without me? What would he do? I

312

should have been prepared for it, I should have been. He was twenty years older than I, and I should have known. But knowing doesn't prepare you for it either. Don't marry a man older than you are, it hurts too much. He left too soon."

The woman's eyes were filled with tears, though her back was straight, her head uplifted. She looked adoringly at the window, its colors animated by the afternoon sun. "He left and yet he's here. His spirit is here in this house. His love is here." In spite of the tears, her voice became stronger. "While I draw breath, no one will ever mutilate this house. *How sharper than a serpent's tooth is an ungrateful child.* The man you saw leaving, damn his blackened heart, is my son. He would rip this house to pieces with his sharpened claws. Marry for love, my bonny lass, marry for love and don't have children. If you make a mistake and choose the wrong husband, you can toss him away. But you can't do that with children. Find happiness with your husband, don't count on anything from your children."

Bonnie's eyes, too, filled with tears. A few seconds passed, then Mrs. King rose. "Enough," she said, "enough of sadness and pain. The past is gone, the present is passing quickly, and the future remains to be seen. When will you move in?"

"Tonight, if I could swing it," Bonnie said. "But I guess I'll have to wait for Saturday. Is that all right with you?" She knew she would lose the security deposit her landlord held, but she was of no mind to give a month's notice that she was leaving. Mrs. King completed the tour, taking Bonnie to the outside via the side entrance, as she had promised. Then she relinquished all keys to the apartment.

Bonnie looked up from ground level to see the window from the outside before she walked to the front of the house. What exquisite beauty man can create, she thought. She had many questions which she reserved for another time. There would be plenty of time after Saturday. The biggest question, though, loomed in her mind. Why was she in armor? It was unmistakable that the woman depicted in the window was the Maid of Orleans. She was Joan at the stake, flames leaping up around her. But why, why had the artist clad her in armor? That didn't make sense, armor in the midst of the flames.

Love and Deception (Alyssa)

Alyssa bolted upright at the illuminated 7:46 on the digital clock. How could she have overslept? Where was Jeff? Why didn't he wake her? She would miss homeroom altogether. Call the office. Someone had to unlock the door. First period test. Good God, how could she have ...

Her racing thoughts screeched to a halt when she suddenly realized that it wasn't a nightgown floating around her, but a dress, her lavender-flowered dress. It was 7:46, no, 7:47, in the evening. Now she remembered. She had collapsed on the bed at 4:00. Nice nap, she mumbled to herself, then flopped back down to the sanctity of the bed and the warm afghan she had wrapped around her. She wanted to stay there, warm and safe, forever.

She almost dozed off again, but heard Jeff's footsteps on the stairs that needed carpeting. That was how she gave tours of the house: these stairs need carpeting, these windows need to be replaced, that door still needs to be refinished The list of "needs" was lengthy, but she was comfortable with it because the house was solid, the "needs" were mostly cosmetic, and Effie had everything under control.

Jeff entered the room and saw she was awake. "Welcome back to the land of the living. Feel better?" She wondered if the land of the living and the planet Earth were in any way related. "You should've wakened me sooner. Now I'll be up half the night."

He sat on the edge of the bed. "We can use the time together."

She tensed, then forced herself to relax and propped herself up on one elbow. "Kiss, please, before you scold."

He took her in his arms and kissed her. "How do I get you to stop doing this to yourself?"

"Doing what?"

"Don't make me angry. You know very well what. The only time you're rested and healthy is during the summer. You rev into high gear the first week of September and drive yourself into the ground by Thanksgiving. You're merciless with yourself. By June you're a basket case. You rejuvenate over the summer, then start the cycle all over again. I've been telling you this for years and I'm giving it another try: Slow Down. I'd love your undivided attention more than once or twice between September and June. Sometimes I feel like I'm living alone. We used to be pretty inseparable."

"We still are! And you have my undivided attention whenever you want it. Please, honey, don't be upset with me. I just need a little extra sleep now and then, and I don't think I'm completely over that cold I had a few weeks ago."

She said it as if she believed it herself, which she did. He accepted it as if he believed it himself, which he didn't. It had happened before, it would happen again. She was hopeless; he couldn't even imagine life without her, but she was hopeless.

Alyssa Marie Grispelli and Jeffrey James Matthews tied the knot within a month after she graduated from college and he from trade school. They adored each other, couldn't bear being separated even for a few hours, and started their life together penniless, though poverty had little effect on their plans. And why not? They were both ambitious and they both had jobs.

From the very beginning they had agreed: Never let an argument extend beyond bedtime and never take your job home with you. They never had a chance to test the first rule because adversity is predicated on duality, that is, whenever they disagreed, Jeff invariably had to fight with himself or not at all; Alyssa heated up, but she did not fight, and in the interlude of silence they both cooled off.

The second rule governed an equally obscure set of circumstances. You don't take your job home with you; whatever happens there stays there when you leave. Alyssa believed in that as adamantly as any human being could believe in anything, with a passion that was strongly opposed to the piles and piles of papers and books that she carried home every night. And they certainly did, as husband and wife, occasionally discuss their days. But "you don't take your job home with you" meant "you don't go home miserable and cranky and take out your discontent on your spouse." That's what it really meant, and that was an easy rule for her to follow because she wasn't miserable and she wasn't unhappy. That was easy because Jeff was the greatest guy on earth, they loved each other thoroughly, and she slowly mastered a terrific technique that kept him satisfied and allowed her to do what she felt she must without currying his disfavor. She learned to lie.

While he couldn't help but notice her exhaustion, she lied to make it less than it was, for if she admitted to it he would try to stop her from doing what she fully intended to do, exhaustion or no exhaustion. "No, hon, I didn't stay up very late after you went to bed," she would say, then add to herself, "Three o'clock isn't late, it's early, it all depends on how you look at it."

She disguised as much as she could, and while she took her job home with her in the severest ways, she convinced herself that she did no such thing, and was proud of her priorities; the important elements in her life were ordered in the healthiest, simplest manner: Jeff and her personal life came first, teaching second, and everything else had to fight for third. The activities she enjoyed beyond Jeff and school — needlework, yarn work, baking, personal reading, home projects — were fit into her schedule with stealthy care. She felt she was wasting time if she sat in front of the TV with idle hands, so she inevitably worked at something while she watched. "I get tired just watching you!" Jeff would say. "Can't you ever relax and do nothing?" And she would say, "This is nothing! It is relaxing to me! I enjoy it!" And besides, she could crochet an entire afghan within a matter of weeks if she worked on it for just an hour a day while watching the news.

From the very beginning she refused to join any kind of social organization that would require her presence during the week. There was neither time nor energy left after she met the demands of her first two priorities. Her love for crafts prompted her to join a ceramics class one year; she loved every minute of it once she conjured up the strength to get there, but dropped out when she and Jeff bought their dream house because she needed to spend too much time on remodeling projects. She said it herself repeatedly, she wore the statement like a banner announcing her origins and her net worth: I've never been bored five minutes in my entire life.

She wasn't bored and, she knew, she wasn't perfect. There were dark areas in her personality that threatened to overshadow her accomplishments, threatened to drag her down into nonactivity. She was sometimes moody, sometimes depressed when she took on too much and felt the weight of it all. There were times when she was so exhausted that she secretly wished she'd get sick because then she'd have an excuse to crawl into bed and rest. And often, those were the times when Jeff would get on her back, so that she felt pressured to lick her wounds but, at all costs, hide them from him.

At one point she made a startling observation about herself; it was during her "self-evaluation" year, the year she started asking her students to consider the psychological "why's" of literature. WHY does this character act this way? What is it in his personality that causes him to do what he does? Sometimes people DO things because they FEEL things. Sometimes if you can understand how a person FEELS, then you can better understand his actions. You'll be surprised at how this will influence your final reaction to his actions.

Have you ever noticed that I don't immediately reprimand every student who walks into class late? Sometimes I sense that a student is embarrassed or angry himself over whatever caused him to be late. Sometimes understanding is best served by asking WHY?

She taught it long before Cassie Quimly. And as she looked at herself that year, one of the things she observed was the way she began her days. Every morning she awoke with her mind racing, filled with the burdens of the day before she even lifted her body from the bed. By the time she washed her face, she was already beyond her lesson plans, the parent conference scheduled during her free period, and dreading an after-school dental appointment. Her mind was beating her down before breakfast! The psychological activity was wearing her out, draining her energy and her spirit before she left the house! It had to stop. And stop it she did. Once she recognized what she was doing, stopping the enervating process was, to her, the easy part.

She also acknowledged that year the fact that she was a perfectionist and a workhorse, that sometimes she attempted too much, no, that ALWAYS she attempted too much at once. But that recognition she wouldn't do anything about, for that was her substance and her meaning. The barest compromise she could make, when those traits became oppressive, was to take Jeff's advice and slow down. Without him she might have roared into a collision with herself long before; with him she made periodic checks on her speed, slowed from frenzied to frantic, then accelerated again when he wasn't looking.

During the school year, weekends were even more difficult to get through than weekdays. Saturdays were filled with household chores, cleaning, laundry, grocery shopping, cooking. Sundays were for odds-and-ends: visits to let families know she and Jeff were still alive, more household chores, and schoolwork. Sunday was not made as a day of rest, Sunday was made to preface Monday.

As the years passed, weekends took on a character of their own. She wouldn't go out Friday nights because by Friday she felt the toll from the week, she was so tired she couldn't move. She wouldn't go out Saturday nights because she worked nonstop all day to eliminate having to do anything on Sunday. Why go out if she would only fall asleep at 10:00? She wouldn't go out Sunday nights because then she needed to wash her hair, do her nails, concentrate on whatever schoolwork she hauled home, and soak in a hot tub; she called it "getting ready for the week."

Jeff frequently rebelled at their skimpy social life: "We're not eighty years old, Alyssa. Hell, senior citizens get out more than we do."

Whenever he expressed his displeasure, she would suggest they see a movie or go out for dinner. Once she swore off household chores on Saturday because she noticed how much she began to dread the sixth day. If she washed a batch of clothes every night after school and cleaned one room at a time during the week ... It wasn't long before she rolled back into the old routine.

She tried, she really did. She maneuvered and manipulated her life like so much clay; she became adept with the final step. No matter where the rough spots appeared, no matter how they were born, she attacked them vigorously to restore a smooth, glasslike surface.

The first time Jeff noticed that she was sick every year in October or November, he offered the observation that she started school like a maniac, then steadily increased to the level of hysteria. She appeased him with denials and vowed to hide her box of Kleenex. What did he know? The beginning was crucial; there was no other way to begin; the kids had to know that she was what she was: organized, competent, knowledgeable, a firm but compassionate disciplinarian. If she didn't handle them right in the beginning, all was lost. You have to begin by being strict. You can always loosen up later on. But if you begin loose, it's impossible to tighten up later. It was beyond his comprehension. The beginning, the middle, the end — none of it could be taken lightly. She loved him all the more for the concern, but he wasn't a teacher, he couldn't understand. She had to do what she had to do and that was it.

Once she complained to him about a substitute and he said, "Why should you care if they don't call the one you request? You can't do anything about it, so why let it bother you?" Another time when she mentioned something about the condition of her room, he said: "It's not your room, it's the school district's room. At any rate, it's just a room that they're letting you work in. Why should you care about it if nobody else does?"

How could she make him understand? She decided that one has to be a teacher to understand, so she gave up expecting him to. She never did run home every night bursting to spill the day's events, and that fact, coupled with his pragmatism, eventually prompted her to speak of school very infrequently.

Even during conversations with family or friends, she rarely discussed students. While she occasionally volunteered an appropriate but innocuous comment; she never made an issue out of her students, or used them for entertainment or shock appeal or even as simple vehicles to pass the time away.

For that matter, she was never rude enough to correct anybody's grammar either, though she was sorely tempted whenever she saw errors in print. Spelling errors were glaring and irritating to her ("the curse I live with") because she thought that advertising owed at least the right spelling to the public, in view of the fact that the rest of it was hyperbole or outright deception. Couldn't somebody catch "clearence" and "restuarant"?

Now and then, usually when she had time off, Jeff would jokingly suggest that she quit working. She laughed along with him, though she didn't see the joke. She liked a sparkling house too; she appreciated being able to do the laundry at her leisure; she loved to dabble in gourmet cooking when she had time to enjoy the luxury. But she wasn't born to wash floors and fold underwear, to mend the holes in his socks, to sew on buttons, to vacuum and dust. She was driven to do more than that, though she admired and respected women who chose to be home caring for their families. But with no children, she felt no compulsion even to consider that option.

She saw teaching as a near-perfect blend of work and free time. What other job could give her ample vacations during the year and eight weeks of freedom during the summer? To her, the schoolwork that she did during those times didn't count because she did it for herself. And teaching was hers. Her success, her achievement, the daily affirmation of her worth. What would she do after the house was cleaned, the laundry done, the freezer filled? There was never enough time to do it all while she worked, but that sacrifice she was willing to make; the other way around didn't appeal to her at all.

And besides, teaching did something else for her beyond feeding her self-pride and inflating her self-image. She didn't believe in working for nothing; she was good, she worked hard to be good, and she expected remuneration for her skill and her services. Teaching filled her life with a sense of achievement without which a woman like her would have withered and died, and teaching provided her with a much more tangible reward: a paycheck. Never let it be said otherwise; Alyssa Matthews loved her paycheck. And who, among us, can fault her for that?

"Did you check on those pedestal sinks today?" she asked.

"They're three times as much as a normal one."

"Wonderful. We always manage to want the most expensive line, don't we? I suppose it's because you don't have to buy a vanity

319

cabinet with a pedestal sink, so they figure they'll grab you on the money you're saving. One way or another, they grab you."

"Do you still want the sink?"

"Yep."

"Thought so. I told the guy I'd be back."

Alyssa pulled herself fully upright and crossed her legs, Indian-style, striking a familiar pose. "This house is going to break us. Every time we do a room we go over budget because we can't bear to insult the integrity of the house. There are a lot of people getting rich selling 'modern colonial.' How much is the sink?"

"Somewhere between two and two-fifty."

"Christ, is it made of gold?"

"Porcelain, which in sinks is just as valuable, and rare; the good, heavy, old-fashioned kind that doesn't easily chip is rare anyway. The cheap kind wears away if you put a Brillo pad to it. The way you scrub things to hell, you'll put a hole right through one of those in a month. I told the guy I only wanted to buy a sink, not the whole store; then he told me if I wanted the sink in any color but white it would cost a hundred dollars more. Funny fellow."

"I want white anyway, so I can get wild with the wallpaper or the floor. Maybe this weekend we'll start looking through samples. I'll plan on half of my next check for the sink. That's crazy, isn't it? I have to work a whole week to pay for one sink?"

"Are you sure you want it? I can make a vanity and countertop for a conventional sink easily enough. And those are in stock. The guy said he can't order a pedestal until we put half down."

"Independent bastards, aren't they? You can't even change your mind without paying for it. I suppose it isn't his fault, what would he do with a $250 pedestal sink? There aren't too many lunatics like us floating around. Did you ask how long it would take to come in?"

"He said he couldn't tell me that. Maybe two weeks, maybe two months-"

"Maybe two years? Good old American know-how."

"Half the country's out of work, unemployment keeps going up, and it takes a century to get anything. I don't understand it either. Have you checked on our trestle table lately?"

"God, I forgot about it. It's been almost a year. I'll call tomorrow, although it seems to me they would have called if it came in. What do you think about the sink?"

"I think they're maniacs, the sink is grossly overpriced, and their attitude stinks. By the way, I also checked prices at two other places."

"The same?"

"Of course, it's a conspiracy. But I guess we both want the sink, so I'll order tomorrow. Merry Christmas."

"Sure. If it's in by then." She put her arms around his neck and kissed his cheek, delighted with the lovable game he played. If his life depended on it, he wouldn't give her a sink for Christmas. And she, because she was what she was, had already selected his gift, which was on layaway and half paid for. She heard his stomach growl. "Hungry?"

"For you." He pushed her back gently and followed the line of her body with his. He caressed her with his lips and hands and she felt warm, even warmer than before. Both passionate and affectionate, he concentrated not on his but on her feelings and responses. The depth of their lovemaking had grown and flourished over the years. When he touched her, she felt loved; when he loved her, she felt cared for. It crossed her mind that evening, as it had often enough before, that she was fortunate to have found him, this man of pure heart and simple, unshakable devotion.

In twelve years they hadn't tired of each other, or irritated each other to the point of polite toleration, or alienated each other completely. They spoke of it once or twice, the very special bond that they enjoyed beyond the bond of mere marriage. There was something else between them, something mystical and magical, that transcended the usual. At the moment of orgasm, however, they were like all others, drowning in a sea of sensuality, indifferent to the cliché, and content to believe that the rest of creation was superfluous to the flesh and the bed.

He held on to her as if separation meant death. She tightened the grip of her arms as he dropped his head to her shoulder and whispered, "I couldn't live without you, Alyssa." All else became suspended, all else trite and worn and meaningless. But, alas, such moments are brief.

She heard his stomach growl again. So did he, and the bed started to bounce, this time with their laughter. He attempted to get up, but she pulled him back to stroke his groin. "I guess you need a second course!" she teased. He fought her off with a pillow at first, then decided to pretend submission, which did the trick. "I may not be growling," she said, "but I'm starting to wonder how this afghan might taste with, say, a little mustard?"

He suggested that they go out. She said that she would rather not, she was too hungry to wait, she would make something. If the truth were known, the last thing she wanted to do, or very nearly the last, was cook. But if they went out, she'd have to shower, fix her make-up, get dressed again. If they stayed home, she'd just have to shower and slip on a robe. If they went out the drive would take time, the dinner would take time, the drive home would take more time. It was faster to prepare something quickly at home, clean up, spend some time together in front of the TV, then let him drift contentedly off to sleep.

She couldn't tell him she had every intention of grading her night's quota of papers; it would make him angry and he would overreact. She loved him more than anything else in life, but he was so overprotective.

She had figured it all out in a split second. She was wide awake and the night was young after that lengthy nap. Maybe she'd even get a chance to grade the two sets of vocabulary tests she had slipped into one of the research paper folders "just in case."

Her plan ran smoothly enough through dinner and clean-up and TV. But, oddly, it wasn't Jeff who dozed off early; it was she. Despite all her intentions, good or otherwise, she was sound asleep in Jeff's arms by 10:30.

As she explained to him the next day when she woke up with a sore throat: she wasn't over that cold yet, that damn cold she caught the third week of school.

Love and Deception (Bonnie)

She ran her hand up and down his back, across his wide shoulders, down his back again to his buttocks, applying gentle pressure, trying to waken him. He always slept afterward, more from contentment than exhaustion.

The body of a gladiator, she thought, an Adonis. Ulysses must have looked like this. Her hand massaged his neck, fingers buried in the mass of yellow hair. No doubt about it, she thought, our kids will be blonde with blue eyes, little urchins with wide smiles, his smile, his mind-shattering, pulse-quickening smile. She moved her fingers to his ear, then to his cheek and lips, then extended one finger along the length of his nose in loving mischief.

What if she had never met him? What was it that sent her shopping that day in July? Fourth of July sales? That was it. She had waited for the July sales to hunt up a new bathing suit. Never got the suit, used the old one all summer. And what a summer it turned out to be. Because of him.

The carpeting in the shopping mall had fatefully twisted around the heel of her shoe; she had twisted her ankle and landed on her knees. He happened to be nearby. He helped her regain her composure through the laughter and pain; the laughter shielded her embarrassment, she couldn't get up for the pain. They decided later that destiny had thrown them together, that the chapters of fate reserved for lovers were written indelibly, charting inevitable courses.

She saw him often through July and August, dreading the restrictions that September would undoubtedly bring. They slept together for the first time in August, tired of worthless self-control, aching to consume each other's beauty. It was the first time for both of them, but once begun, the lovemaking fed upon itself, the desire never satiated.

September did bring restrictions and secrets. They had to pass without a flicker of recognition in spite of their intimacy. It wasn't easy, but they had to avoid gossip. Just until June. Then they could marry and get on with their lives together. Even then there would be talk, but after the fact it would die down quickly.

She finally woke him up by nibbling on his ear. He raised his head just enough to catch her lips with his, then moved to suck the nipple of one breast. One hand traced the smooth line of her hip while the other massaged the nipple not engulfed by his mouth. She didn't want him to stop, but the time, the time.

"Michael, it's almost midnight."

He moaned agreement, reached up to encase her face with his hands, smothering further comment with his lips and tongue. She couldn't bear it when he seemed to want to devour her. Her body responded with a tingling, a yearning, then a slow, aching sensation that sent her into a mindless vacuum. Only he existed. Until the final explosion that brought with it reality.

"If you don't get out of here pretty soon, you're going to have one hell of a time explaining where you've been."

"I'm studying with friends," he said with a grin, then added," You are definitely a friend, and I plan to study you for the rest of my life. Besides, my mother doesn't check up on me. I've been holding the family together since I was twelve."

Bonnie knew that, he had said it before, but she still had no idea what it meant. He never seemed willing to go further with it, so she never pressed for details.

After a pause he added, "She sleeps nights now." He was suddenly serious, for his mind was flashing old images of death and a young boy, a young boy searching for money to buy food, searching in the absent woman's purse, the dead man's pants, the dresser drawers, the piggybank.

He had briefly spoken of it before, and she knew if she waited long enough he would open up to all of it. She spoke softly, almost reverently. "What happened to your mother when your father died?"

He hesitated just a few seconds. "She went crazy with grief. She was in a kind of coma through the funeral. He died so suddenly, no warning at all. I don't think she would have taken it any better if there had been a warning or a period of waiting anyway. As it was, the shock destroyed her. She went through the motions of the funeral without ever making contact with anybody. From the instant Dad collapsed on the kitchen floor, her mind snapped. Now she says she knew at that instant that he was gone. She stood there clutching a frying pan and a knife with butter on it, staring at him on the floor. I remember toast popping up and my sister Andrea screaming. She was only eight and more terrified of the look on my mother's face, I think, than anything else. I dialed the operator for help, calmed Andrea down, and pried Mom's fingers from the pan and knife. She was frozen in time, refusing to accept what happened. That's what her therapist told her."

"Is that how she came out of it, through therapy?"

324

"Eventually, yes. Two year's worth. I held her hand through the wake and funeral. Relatives poured in from all corners of the earth. I didn't know any of them. I guess funerals make people do things out of guilt or obligation. At the time I didn't understand where all those people came from, or why they bothered. Mom recognized no one, spoke to no one. She just stared at my father in his coffin. And held my hand. I overheard comments for three days about how hard she was taking it, what a brave little man I was, and what a waste it was for a good-looking woman to be widowed at thirty-six. I think they were taking bets in the next room on the length of time before she remarried. I was glad to see them go."

He shifted his body on the bed. "Her shaking started soon after. She was still not talking to anyone. The doctor left his phone number and I called him one night when the shaking finally frightened me half to death. Her whole body would pulse and quake. She had given up control of it. The doctor put her in the hospital and quickly found out there was nothing physically wrong with her."

He paused to sort out his feelings. Then he went on to explain that he had taken over in his mother's absence. He told the doctor that he and Andrea would live with relatives, but there were no relatives nearby. So he became a little automaton, a small manly robot, cooking, cleaning, doing the laundry. Images flashed through his mind again, images of lying at school, carrying grocery bags larger than he was, reading to his sister to get her to fall asleep. He did it for eight months until his mother returned, still weak but resigned. He had always thought mostly about himself whenever he looked back on those eight months, about himself and what he managed to do. Now he looked in the eyes of the woman on the bed next to him and began to see the other side of it; he began to understand what his mother had gone through. Her pain was becoming significant.

"She went through therapy for eight months in the hospital, then, after she was released, for over a year at a clinic. It's been six years now and she still sees a psychiatrist every few months. She told me about a year ago what happened in the hospital. After eight months she finally admitted that Dad died, that he wouldn't ever touch her again. And she released her grief. Violently, from what she told me. A screaming, clawing, wicked acceptance of the truth. And she finally cried." He stopped again, trying to dissolve the lump in his throat. "Is it possible to love someone too much?"

She was suddenly shivering and moved close to him to dispel the chill. The story had touched her deeply and she thought about Mrs.

King, what Mrs. King had said earlier. She had never been in love before this, never slept with a man because she never liked one well enough to sacrifice her self respect. And he was more man than any she had ever met. He cared more for her than for himself.

"I don't know, Michael. If she had loved him less, she might not have suffered so. But then she wouldn't have had that joy that so many people never experience. To shun love because it might bring pain is senseless. The future is out there regardless. I met a lady today whose husband's been dead more years than you've been alive, and she still aches for him. Maybe she did love him too much, maybe your mother loved your father too much, but how do we judge? What's too much? And how do we stop it before the pain?"

Bonnie reached down to the foot of the bed and pulled up a blanket to cover their nakedness; her frugality stopped her from turning on the heat, her frugality and a driving need to stay close to him. They clung greedily to each other, absorbed by that moment in time which jolted them into a vision of the one consequence of love that mortals choose not to consider, the one consequence that is inevitable yet mercifully obscure.

Invincibility returned. For the body existed and the mind responded accordingly. Together they could lick the world, overcome all obstacles, meet all challenges: love, fidelity, devotion would carry them through, the sum of their parts was greater than all things.

"Neither one of us has a father," Bonnie said. "You loved yours and he's dead. I hate mine and he's alive. No. I shouldn't say that, I don't hate him. It's worse than hate, I don't feel anything at all for him. That's worse than hate. I've decided I'm not going home for Christmas this year. It was always useless, anyway, my going home for Christmas. He wouldn't let me in the house. I always stayed with my aunt and my mother would visit me there or we'd spend time shopping or something. I used to wish my mother was strong enough to leave him during the years when I hated him. But she could never live comfortably enough without him. I understand that now; it was very stupid to think she had to make a choice between him and me. When I left I was old enough to eliminate that possibility."

"Have you told them about us?"

"Not yet. And I won't until after we're married. Not that it matters at any time. My mother's happy as long as her boat isn't rocked and my father will wallow in self-righteous disgust when he finds out I'm putting a husband through college. I told you before, he thought I was perfect dumb bait to catch a rich husband."

"I've been thinking about that. Maybe I won't go to college right away, maybe it would be better if I worked a year. I could still take some courses at night."

"Like hell you will. What's the matter, feeling threatened?"

"What do you mean?"

"Your masculinity. Will it embarrass you if I work and you go to school? If that's what you're thinking, you're crazy. I've got an education and you don't; I've got a job and you don't. So I work and you go to school. So what? If your pride hurts too much, you can keep your part-time job, but honey, you're going to be busy as hell with school. I expect you'll want straight A's."

"Do you really think we can do it? Financially, I mean?"

"Of course we can do it! As long as you don't decide to go to Harvard. By the time you start, my loans will be just about paid off. I'm used to setting aside that money anyway, so I'll just keep doing it. And I have a big surprise that I would have told you sooner if you hadn't dropped your pants as you came through the door. I'm moving out of this dump and into a mansion, a very cheap mansion, if you can imagine it." She gave a quick description of the house, Mrs. King, and the rent, leaving out some details purposely. "We're moving to Easy Street! Everything is falling into place for us. There's only one thing that we've got to worry about, as far as I can see. You still haven't said a word about us to your mother, have you?"

He nodded.

"You've got to break it to her. I worry about how she'll take it. Maybe she'll get upset at losing you. That bothers me, and I think you're worried about it too, aren't you?"

"Yes, but we've got to bite the bullet sometime."

"Sometime soon, the sooner the better. She deserves to know; we can't just elope without her knowing it. My family is forever lost to us, I'd hate to alienate yours too. And besides, here's something else to think about. You're under age in this state. She'll have to sign before we can get a marriage license. Unless we go out-of-state. But I don't want to do that; I want her to love me because we both love you. How do you think she'll react?"

"I don't know. I don't think there'll be a problem, but I can't say for sure. I've never even brought a girl home before."

"Well, we can't wait much longer, she might need time to adjust to the idea. What if she's violently opposed?"

"Then we go out-of-state. I don't want to do it either, but if it's the only way, then it's the only way. I can't wait as it is."

327

"Neither can I, baby, but we have to. We aren't the first to feel this way and people have waited longer under worse conditions. At least we aren't sneaking around in the back seat of a car or in sleazy motels. At least we have a sleazy apartment."

"How private is the new place?"

"Very. Better than this. You aren't going to believe your eyes. But what's this sudden concern over privacy? I think you'd take me in the middle of the freeway at rush hour."

"Tomorrow?"

"If you ever do what you did today again, I promise you a knee to the groin."

"Never heard of that one, but I'm game for anything. "He started tickling her.

"I'm serious, you oversexed maniac."

"Oversexed and underloved."

"Bullshit: If anybody walked in on us this afternoon, I'd be fired by now. It's too risky. Promise me it will never happen again."

"Can't control yourself, can you?"

"Hell no, and who can control you?"

"All right, no more at school. Do you know what the kids call you?"

"Oh Christ, Michael, spare me."

"Farah Fawcett with boobs. I laughed like hell the first time I heard it."

"What am I supposed to do, wear gunny sacks to work?"

"You'd look good in a cardboard box. You should get your hair cut like hers."

"That's all I need — the tousled look. I read somewhere that it takes hours to get her hair to look like that, like she just rolled out of bed. I really like it, but I can't go to school looking windswept. The hair will just have to hang in a clump, I'm afraid. Sexy isn't in for schoolteachers. Maybe I'll get horn-rimmed glasses. Do you think that might help the image?"

"Then they'll call you Farah Fawcett with boobs and glasses."

"How about Farah Fawcett with boobs, glasses, and a bun? When I interviewed for a permanent job, I was told that. Of course, he said, you'll wear your hair up. The bastard also wanted to know if I took drugs in college and if I had a steady boyfriend. I wanted to tell him the drug bit was an insult and my love life was none of his business, but I bit my tongue because I wanted a job. That's why we have to play it frigid at school, Michael. Please. Not even a cute little pinch on the ass or even a wink. No recognition at all. They'll have enough to talk about next September without somebody remembering he saw us walking together."

"Okay, teach, you're the boss."

"Now would you please get dressed and out of here?" She watched as he pulled on his clothes, then left the bed herself to lock the door behind him. "And Michael," she said just before he left, "please think about telling your mother about us. I'd like to spend the holidays with your family, so think about telling her before Thanksgiving."

BOOK TWO: Interim Progress Report

FRUSTRATIONS

I

On October 27, Gayle Fine made an appearance halfway through third period and Alyssa spent most of fourth period explaining the course and attempting to give capsule instruction on how to write a research paper. She made it very clear that Gayle would have until the end of the semester to submit a paper and even offered to take it during exam week; she wanted to give the girl every millimeter of hope available. She was particularly kind as she went through the boredom of note cards and bibliography form; the girl was frail, so frail she seemed to be in danger of shattering. On October 27, Alyssa also received the three late research papers. One of them failed.

The week before Halloween skidded along with prescheduled bumps and grinds. All week classes were disrupted by P.A. announcements at fifteen minute intervals calling students for yearbook pictures. There was no way of knowing whether or not students were bona fide members of clubs and sports teams, so whenever a new group was called, teachers stopped in the middle of sentences and powerlessly watched classes dwindle. Kids moved in and out, in and out, all day long, every day for a week. Experienced teachers knew enough to plan very little and expect even less.

It was on Wednesday of that week when the five-page bomb was circulated among teachers in the English department. It went from hand to hand and eventually to Alyssa Matthews. Jean carried it in, dropped it on Alyssa's desk and said, "Read it and weep." Alyssa read, but didn't weep. She was beyond that stage and she was before it. The list of recommendations came from some "Committee on Literacy" and was addressed to the English department. It was five pages telling her how to teach and what to teach. And it was from laymen. It said: Students need instruction in filling out job applications and writing resumes. Students need to learn how to write a business letter. Students need listening skills, which should be taught before anything else. Students need to learn how to converse intelligently on the telephone. Time should also be devoted to public speaking, an art which is lost today. Students need practical instruction for the practicalities in life.

It further said: It is deemed necessary by this committee that every student be required to practice writing on a strictly scheduled basis, that is, every student should be required to complete at least one writing assignment per week, that assignment no less than 150 words. It is the opinion of this committee that students are not receiving enough instruction in writing, therefore the literacy rate is declining. It is suggested by this committee that weekly writing quotas be established to effectively teach writing.

It ended with: Please initial and pass on to the next name listed. If you disagree with any of the content herein, please attach a rebuttal and submit material to replace that which you object to.

Alyssa finished reading and saw that half the department had already signed. She ran down the hall looking for Jean and ran into Paul, which was better. She tried to control the shriek. "Who are these sons-of-bitches, Paul? Do they have to keep adding insult to insult?"

He looked at her glumly. "Initial it. It's a committee of concerned citizens working for the Board with Curt Holbert as chairman."

The name burned a hole through her brain. "If I sign this, it means I agree with it! And I don't!"

"You want to explain why you don't?"

"Can we let them believe this is possible? This weekly quota shit? Who can grade that many papers?"

"I'll ask you again: Do you want to try to tell them that? And before you answer, would you calm down and consider the fact that WE ALREADY HAVE. Haven't we? Haven't we already told them?"

She threw up her arms in disgust.

"Initial it," Paul said. "Initial the damned thing and continue the way you always have. Can't you do that? For God's sake, Alyssa, that's what we always do, isn't it?"

She scrawled her initials next to her name, then handed the papers to him. "Here, you give it to the next puppet, I haven't got the stomach for it. My gorge rises at it, to quote one who knows about such things."

The Committee on Literacy courteously waited for the return of the initialed report, then felt comfortable notifying the press for public release of the details. The newspaper article caused more reaction within the department than the committee paper had. Alyssa read the article and thought about what Paul had said. Continue the way you always have. Big joke. That's what we always do, isn't it? Even bigger joke. We keep signing our names and signing our names. Someday it's going to backfire. Someday we're going to sign one too many times.

She started to laugh. It was absurd to the point of hilarity. Or was it hilarious to the point of absurdity? The more she thought about it, the more she laughed. Jeff asked what the hell was so funny. She shook her head; she kept laughing, but she shook her head, as if to disown the whole business altogether.

The first week in November brought with it the first flakes of snow, playing airy games on Monday, falling heavily and lastingly by the end of the week. The temperature dropped and Alyssa thought of the long, cold winter ahead. She was still not feeling very well; her cold refused to vanish completely. She was in constant discomfort from either a sore throat, a congested head, or the cough which lingered through all other symptoms as they appeared, disappeared, and reappeared. Feeling as she did, she dreaded winter because she felt worse in the cold; she actually shivered when she felt a chill. Thank goodness her room was warm and so was the faculty room. It was study hall that drove a chill through her every day. There wasn't any heat at all; she and Joe had both complained. Erica didn't complain, she just arrived late and left early. Alyssa thought of leaving a number of times, but wouldn't leave Joe alone. And the worst was yet to come. In January she would have to carry her coat and let kids go to their lockers one at a time. Study Hall A was notoriously cold. But it wasn't the worst spot in the school. Bonnie, too, was complaining about the cold and she was in the real Arctic region. Study Hall C was air-conditioned; somehow the heat came on in September and May, the air-conditioning in between.

Alyssa called in sick one day that week in November and, of course, she felt worse the day after. But she couldn't expect a sub to give the afternoon classes their short story unit test because the test was locked up. And she planned to grade charts while the kids were taking the test. So she dragged herself in.

Grading the charts during class didn't appeal to her, but she couldn't do it any other way. There were fifteen charts per student. She ignored mechanical errors and concentrated on content. It wasn't fair to penalize anyone for mistakes in areas she hadn't covered yet, even if she had the time to grade that way. Still, she was disturbed by the writing, the fragments, run-ons, sloppy expression, and poor spelling. She expected that titles, authors, and names of characters be spelled correctly, but, many times, they weren't. She expected accurate and adequate synopses of plots; she expected that students would follow the directions she repeated six or eight times. She expected what she always expected and got what she always got. Disappointment. She scanned the bulk of the charts quickly, but paused to read climaxes and themes, the two sections that gave indication of thought and understanding.

There were quite a few A's and B's and she knew she was grading generously because she wasn't considering mechanics. But some students obviously put a great deal of time and thought into the project. She could tell at a glance who had. Still, though, as she flipped pages she felt guilty and had to keep reminding herself that she was grading generously because she couldn't take the time to grade any other way.

As she handled each set of charts, her eyes darted to the bottom of each page. The themes. The themes were so important. By the time she finished with all that had been handed in (some would be late, some never), she was so frustrated she felt like chewing on the short story book so she could spit it out. The themes. They had reduced the themes to nothing, to less than nothing

No, this isn't the theme, she wrote. What is the theme? Again and again she wrote it, again and again until she grew tired and resorted to question marks. How could they reduce Chekhov's *The Lottery Ticket* to "money is the root of all evil"? How could they do that after she spent so much time and energy explaining Chekhov and his emphasis on psychology, his use of mental rather than physical action in the story?

And Lord, what they did to Mr. Gessler. "Quality is better than quantity" they gave for the theme. Over and over again. "Quality is better than quantity." This is just a cliché, she wrote. What about Mr. Gessler? How can you forget Mr. Gessler? Again and again she wrote it. You forgot Mr. Gessler. Again and again and again until she got tired. Then she stopped. It was too late. She had failed to get the message through.

The kids were set free on Wednesday that week because of the disruptive in-service day. Such days are, at best, disruptive. At worst, they are far more devastating. Alyssa lasted through the morning session. Then she couldn't take any more. Her sanity was being threatened. She had to escape or go mad.

Coffee and donuts were served from eight until nine o'clock to camouflage administrators burdened with the duty of taking roll. At nine the entire faculty listened to a woman define teacher burn-out. She was a perfectly coifed, impeccably dressed woman who knew what she was talking about because she had burned out two years ago. She listed the symptoms: emotional exhaustion, feelings of failure or frustration, decline in self-esteem, increasing fatigue, feelings of indispensability, physical illness, stress.

Here I am, Alyssa thought as she listened to a lengthy explanation of each symptom, an explanation she hardly needed.

She waited patiently for the lecture to end. She knew the symptoms; every teacher in the room knew the symptoms. She and the others were waiting for the cure, the little pill, the injection. What? What to do about it?

The perfectly coifed, impeccably dressed woman devoted the last ten minutes of her lengthy presentation to the cure. It took her that long because she wrote it on the portable blackboard set up for her convenience.

RX: learn to say no, set realistic goals, improve communications with others, improve physical fitness, concentrate on longer periods of relaxation after work, use leisure time to unwind, learn new forms of recreation, do something frivolous once a week.

Alyssa almost laughed out loud. Easy for you to say, lady, easy for you to say. So you burned out, did you? Well, you have my sincere congratulations. Now you're an expert making a bundle writing books and giving lectures. Congratulations. Life gave you lemons, so you made lemonade. Is there room for the rest of us in your lemonade stand? What do the rest of us do? The rest of us who don't want to do something else, the rest of us who just want to teach in peace?

"She make you as sick as she made me?" Alyssa asked Jean.

"Nope. I'm changing my ways. Let's see if I've got it right. Next time a student wants help, I say no; the next time Paul puts me on a committee, I say no; the next time grades are due, I take my sweet time. When I go home from work my family can go to hell, I'm not cooking dinner anymore. I'm taking up tennis and golf and once a week I run nude through the parking lot. How's that? Did I get it right?"

"Why Jeanie, you forgot the one you need to work on most: improve communications with others."

"Stop laughing, Matthews. From what I've heard, we learn to do that this afternoon."

The remainder of the morning session was an introduction to future workshops which were both federal- and state-funded and would run again second semester. The first session was devised to set up committees; subsequent sessions would be scheduled as follow-up to allow interaction among committees and feedback. The first day of the workshops was designed to give intensive training in conflict resolution and to identify areas of future commitment, including staff morale and communications. At the word "committee" Alyssa's mind immediately regurgitated. She looked at Jean, who was thinking the same thing.

"You know what they can do with this crap?" Jean said when the session broke for lunch. "They're not getting me on any committee."

Alyssa agreed. So did Bonnie. Partially. "I don't have a choice, do I? If I don't mind my P's and Q's, I'll be out the door in June. Until I get tenure, they can let me go without giving any reason. I'm stuck. Maybe I can get on a committee that evaporates quickly and quietly."

"Isn't this a little stupid, committees to improve morale?" Alyssa said. "What are we supposed to do, form a pep club or a cheering squad? Hell, the student pep club fizzled out eight years ago."

Jean smirked. "It's the same old story. There's money available for this program so the district is grabbing it. And some people really think it will improve morale. You saw how excited some of them were. I think I'm jealous."

"And there's a split in the ranks already. Did you see it in there? We're right into the pros and cons again. The pros see this either as a chance to play or as a genuine opportunity to change the rotten atmosphere around here. Mark my words, those committees are going to turn into so many social clubs, and any committee with a serious purpose is going to hit up against a brick wall. Christ, I don't come here to socialize, I come here to teach. Nobody sees what would improve my morale."

"Nobody wants to see that, Mattie," Jean said. "We're right back to public relations again. This is going to look yummy in the newspaper. So far this year we're assigning and collecting and reviewing homework every night, we're teaching the research paper to every adolescent body in the place, and we're grading at least one 150-word writing assignment per body per week. And now, the saints be praised, we're learning to resolve our conflicts, to train our sensitivities, to clarify our values, and to improve our rotten attitudes. You can mark my words on this: by the time all this shit is over, somebody's going to decide that morale was miraculously raised from the dead."

"Well, I won't be a part of it. You'd better go along, Bon, it's too risky for you not to."

"That's right," Jean added. "Don't take any chances. You can be replaced too easily. As for me, I'm with Alyssa. Hiding out."

"Wrong. Not hiding out. Sick. I'm calling in sick the next time this stupidity is scheduled. They don't have to pay for a sub and my blood pressure is worth using a sick day. I'm getting mighty tired of being insulted."

Alyssa spent that afternoon working in her room. She put together the two final exam sections for the 2R exam, folded the pages carefully and slid them into her purse so she wouldn't forget to take them home for typing. One page contained the spelling section which she insisted on doing yearly because some other teachers didn't have the patience to do it right. It was tedious to devise ten five-word groups with one misspelled word per group. She didn't mind doing it as long as it turned out accurate. The second page contained ten multiple choice questions on *Tale* that she devised very carefully so that they would test general knowledge as fairly as possible. She tried to avoid questions that might be easy for her students but impossible for students of other teachers to answer. She still had to come up with an essay question on poetry and four composition topics for the 2R exam as well as for the 2S exam (except the essay question was on short stories), but she decided to finish up the objective sections for the 2S exam first. For that exam she was writing the spelling section and the complicated grammar section which was fifteen sentences, each with a portion underlined, with alternatives offered to alter one, two, or possibly no errors in the underlined section. She was chairing the 2S exam committee and would have to compile the whole thing after other teachers submitted other sections. She wanted to get the exams out of the way much earlier than she had initially intended because of the curriculum work Paul assigned on the research paper.

She was glad to have the time that afternoon to spend on the exams; it was work that she normally had to do at home. So she sat at her desk with the door locked and the lights off because she didn't want to have to explain to anyone why she was not downstairs. She was about to begin the 2S grammar section when she suddenly thought of the promise she made Jean to check out materials for her exceptional juniors. She found some excitement in the thought and unlocked her filing cabinet. The folders were stored in the bottom drawer, way in the back. She was wearing slacks so she sat on the floor to dig out what she thought Jean could use. The more she looked, the more she found. Some folders sent her to other drawers and by the time she finished she had ten folders stacked on the top of her desk. There was so much that she used to do.

As she looked through folders, for she couldn't hand them over without a last look, she remembered how students had reacted and performed when she used the materials. She had even kept copies of student work to use as future models.

One folder held *Love In Armor,* a prose allegory expressing lack of communication between a man and a woman and its effect on their relationship. How she once loved assigning that allegory for interpretation! She always did it second semester when she felt sure they were ready for that level of thinking, after she had trained them in the ways of allegory. She would wait a month or so after the short story unit and then hit them with the assignment, never mentioning the exact word "allegory," but alluding to it in the directions: In 200-250 words discuss this selection, giving its literal interpretation in your introductory paragraph. Go on to discuss its symbolic implications. Be very specific when speaking of symbols. Conclude your discussion with a critical evaluation of the author's intent. Does he accomplish what you believe to be his aim? If so, what factors in the selection have led you to this decision? If not, exactly where and how does he fail?

She remembered how carefully she had worded those directions, how she had attempted to be clear yet obscure, helpful yet challenging. She looked at the bottom of the sheet and saw that she had received the piece in college and kept it because it appealed to her. She read through one of the student papers she had reproduced for posterity and smiled as her eyes devoured it.

"The armor represents our fear of becoming involved with one another; it is the mask we wear to protect ourselves against life. So often today the words 'I don't want to get involved' are heard. People have lost their faith in other people. The people in this story are afraid to reveal their true selves, afraid to completely remove the armor, because emotional involvement can lead to pain. These two people refuse to communicate, refuse to bare their souls; they will not leave the security of the armor. When the author says at the end, 'I am not sure whether we shall ever lie together naked,' he means that he is not sure if they will ever really open up to each other, really communicate on a human level. The fact that they are happy when they embrace in their armor, or at least as happy as they can be while in armor, calls to mind the trend today among students of living together without thought of responsibility and of having sex without thought of love or commitment. Love can exist in armor, but it cannot thrive there, and chances are that it will decompose in the darkness."

Alyssa felt a lump in her scratchy throat. Cindy Sirouly. Where are you now, Cindy Sirouly? Oh, how you could write. Where are you now? Not in armor, I'll bet.

Two other folders contained advanced writing assignments that she couldn't use with sophomores. The other seven dealt with Greek drama. She reviewed the contents of each one, stopping often to read notes and assignments. Most of the material was her own, gathered and compiled and reproduced years ago. Some of it was left by Mary Gregory. The best of it, she decided. Mary was the most provocative teacher she had ever known. Mary's writing assignments, Mary's test questions, Mary's discussion, anything Mary conjured up was provocative and exciting.

The following is a description of Antigone. Discuss it from any viewpoint you wish. "No woman, they say, has ever deserved death less."

Why does the chorus change in composition from play to play? Sometimes the chorus is made up of old men, sometimes young men, sometimes old women or young women or a mixture. Why?

Discuss the concept of free will as it applies to Macbeth and Oedipus. Both men quarrel with prophecies. Is all human action fixed in advance? Does man have no say at all in his destiny? Is this what Sophocles and Shakespeare are saying? Is this what you believe? Should man reject his freedom to find out the truth? Should he give up the search and act like a dumb beast?

Discuss "The State vs The Individual" using *Antigone* as a basis for your discussion.

Discuss: Although the main problem in *Antigone* might be unimportant today, the discussions of the responsibilities of a ruler are as pertinent now as in ancient Greece. The moral and philosophical aspects of the play are universal.

In the last folder Alyssa found the notes she once distributed to students as an introduction to the unit: the Festival of Dionysus, definitions of the physical aspects of the Greek theater - cavea, skene, orchestra, eccyclema, periaktoi, deus ex machina; and a general description of the plays and play production, including music, choreography, cothurnus, chorus, prologue, parados, episodes, and stasimons.

And there, too, on the last page of notes was the Greek concept of Fate; she remembered what she used to tell students: the Greeks saw Fate not as one entity, but as three, as three progressive stages.

Clotho spins the thread of human life. Appropriately enough, Clotho means spinner.

Lachesis determines the length of the thread of human life; Lachesis means dispenser of lots.

Atropos severs the thread of human life; Atropos means inflexible.

All three are daughters of Themis, a Titaness, the goddess of justice and law.

Jean was also working in her room, only she didn't bother to lock her door. Alyssa traveled down the hall and dropped the folders on Jean's desk. "Have I got some goodies for you," she said. "Wait until you see some of this stuff."

Jean couldn't thank her enough. "There's mounds of work here. Are you sure you want to part with it?"

"When will I get to use it? We're locked in these schedules. Nobody wants to move around because nobody wants a new preparation. Maybe in 1990 I'll get another 3S section. If I do, I'll come knocking on your door to get this stuff back."

"By 1990 I hope I'm out of here."

"Yeah, me too. In the meantime, enjoy that class of yours."

"Thanks again, Matt."

The filing cabinet was still open when Alyssa returned to her room. She thought she would pull folders for upcoming units. She still needed to check on tests for the Shakespeare section of the senior course and the 2R poetry unit would begin after Thanksgiving and run until Christmas. 2S was finishing up *Silas* soon and she had to decide what work of literature to do next, but that depended on what she could get out of the resource room.

As she read tabs on folders she was struck by a disturbing thought. What she had given Jean was work that she couldn't use anyway because she wasn't teaching juniors. As she handled some of the folders that remained, she realized that the bulk of them were just as useless. There was so much that she used to do lying dormant, and so much more that she had prepared but never once used. She was pulling out the same old folders over and over again, using the same materials year after year, the same tests, the same study sheets, the same assignments.

She had once put students on independent study. She pulled that folder and looked inside. What topics they had worked on! The Literature of Cervantes; Sports Journalism; The CIA and *1984*; Communication Through Art; Individualism vs. Collectivism: The Philosophy of Ayn Rand; Effects of Soviet Censorship on Russian Authors; The History of the English Language. She remembered the excellence; she remembered telling a boy he had to cut his paper down to fifty pages because eighty was too much! Her fingers tightened around the edges of the folder as if it were a raft and she were drowning. She never even taught those students how to write a paper, just gave them a book of instructions and sent them off.

She found more. Essays by Russell Baker and Sydney J. Harris that she had intended to use for writing assignments. React to this! Agree or disagree, but do it intelligently, thoughtfully, accurately.

Once she had used a Russell Baker piece, the one about "shirtings," the one that expressed such delightfully humorous frustration over advertising and prices. Call it a shirting instead of a shirt and raise the price! She loved that essay. She loved Russell Baker's wit. But when she asked seniors to react to it, only one caught the tone, only one understood. She remembered how she had waited for the laughter. She intentionally made them write during class because she wanted to enjoy the laughter with them. It was just a writing sample she was after, the essay was light and funny and they would have little trouble with it. But only one student understood, the rest of the class was confused, befuddled, and then angry. What is this crap? they said. Is this guy for real? they wanted to know. It broke her heart. She couldn't just let it go, she had to explain, but it tore her to pieces. Explain Russell Baker? To seniors? Who would explain after graduation? And how sad, even after the explanation (as if, she thought, humor and wit can be explained) some of them still were of the opinion that the man was an idiot.

She started pulling folders, but not those she had intended to pull. She was attempting to extract everything that she hadn't used in the last three years, and she moved with a kind of pitiful vengeance. She amassed a pile that soon became top heavy and started to slide from the top of her desk to the floor. When she realized what she was doing, she stopped adding to the pile, but proceeded to pick up two and three folders at a time and to push them into the dented metal waste can at the side of her desk. She wondered if the can was too small to hold all of it, then saw that the folders were, of course, flexible, so she pushed and shoved until she forced it all in. The pile extended above the rim, but that didn't matter. It was all in there where it belonged.

The floor was littered with pieces of paper that had escaped the final journey. She gathered them up and paused to read the headline of a newspaper article that had sailed around the other side of her desk.

Johnny Can't Write Because Teacher Can't Teach. Why had she clipped and kept it? Masochistic tendencies? She crumbled it with both hands and stuffed it in with the rest. She felt another urge to continue through the file drawers, but couldn't bring herself to grab hold of another thing. The seriousness of what she was doing suddenly held her back; she felt a sudden fear that if she kept going she wouldn't be able to stop. She slammed the drawers shut, pushed the button to lock the cabinet, grabbed what she needed to take home, and left the room.

The parking lot was still full of cars, but she didn't care. The time she would put into grading the last two research papers and typing the 2R exam sections would more than compensate for leaving a half-hour early.

She thought about the meeting the department had had with Bassard before the report was written and submitted. Harry had been not only non-receptive, he was downright glacial. Well, he said, I saw two English teachers leaving early last week. He listened to all they had to say and that was his response. Then, she thought, we wrote the report and got no response at all.

But it's all my fault, this attitude of mine. I should be in there right now whooping it up on some committee. I should be changing my rotten attitude. I should go home and jog through the snow. The hell with the kids, the hell with exams, the hell with lesson plans and tests and Nettie NillyNellyNully. I should come here as if I'm going to a party. A masquerade. Only it's *The Masque of the Red Death*, damn it. One thing's for sure: I should stop thinking about it. No, I've got to stop thinking about it. I've got to stop.

II

- Len Straithe, Harry. Returning your call.

- Good morning, Len! Thank God for large favors! I've been trying to get through to you for three days! Nobody answers your phone! I told Brenda to keep trying though! Every half hour! Where the hell've you been?

- When it's warm I golf, but right now I'm bowling. The ball is easier to see in the snow. Why'd you want me?

- I've got a good one for you, one that you can really sink your teeth into.

- You think you do, huh?

- This one's real weird, Len. Right up your alley. Hey, I'll never forget what you did for us when that kid pulled that knife on me. Remember how you talked him out of my office? It was a work of art the way you handled that kid. Calmly. Quietly. Nobody ever knew it happened. I don't know where you get the patience for the work you do. It's good to know you're there when we need you.

- To keep things quiet, right?

- Right on, to borrow a phrase from the kids. Now, if you'll just hunt up the referral form I sent you, your girl must have filed it, Brenda sent it out three days ago, I'll fill you in further on this kid. The name's-

- Harry?

- What?

- Forget it.

- What do you mean, forget it?

- What's it sound like? Forget it means forget it.

- This can't be forgotten. It's too abnormal.

- So are a lot of other things that have been conveniently forgotten.

- How can you tell me to forget about it when you don't even know what it is yet? Find the damn referral form, would you, and stop giving me a hard time.

- Look, I haven't even had a chance to open my mail for the past week. Nothing's been filed for months.

- Your girl get sick or what?

- Sure, Harry. How about sending Brenda over?

- Well, I don't think I could spare Brenda, but maybe one of the other girls in one of the other offices. Christ, Len, I didn't realize you're without a secretary. No wonder you sound a little disgusted. The paperwork can get pretty nasty.

344

- The paperwork isn't the only thing. Do me a favor, Harry. I'll forget the secretary, you forget the referral. Call somebody else.

- Call somebody else? You're the school psychologist. Who else do I call?

- Wrong. I'm the district psychologist, Harry. Maybe you don't remember last June, but I'm sitting here still wondering where everybody went. There's enough work in this district for six social workers; they cut me down to two. And I'm all alone in this big office, Harry. I used to have three other psychologists and a part-time psychiatrist working with me. Now I don't even have a secretary. I trained a woman for six months, then she was pulled to help out in payroll. I got the message you called because the cleaning lady happened to be in here to answer the phone. I'm the only one left and though I might be able to manage a split in my personality, I haven't yet figured out how to send my body to more than one place at a time.

- Look, I understand all that. We're all up against it. I've been holding back referrals to you since school started, things that we can handle here, because I know you're buried. But this one's unique, Len.

- You mean you don't know what to do with this one.

- Well, of course that's what I mean! I'm no shrink. I know my limitations. I've got a kid who's spreading manure around this school and I'll admit I don't know how to deal with it.

- Manure? What do you mean, manure? Literally?

- Yes, damn it! Literally! I told you it's a weird one.

- Not if you look at it symbolically. Then it's not so weird, Harry.

- What the hell are you laughing at? And what do you mean, symbolically? I don't understand that at all. Depositing piles of manure all over this place seems loony to me. The kid seems loony to me. He needs help and lots of it. Professional help. He needs you. When are you coming?

- I'm booked solid. Sorry.

- You can't refuse to help this kid.

- I've got eleven grade schools, three junior highs, and the high school to worry about; that's three schools a day. I'm not kidding when I tell you I'm booked solid. You'll have to call some community service agency. Try to get help outside the district. Or doesn't that appeal to you?

- We take care of our own. YOU told me that once!

- It must have been during one of those discussions we used to have on public image. I'll admit I used to believe in the value of maintaining a low-keyed, controlled image. People panic at the word "drugs," they react negatively to "alcohol" and "premarital sex." The less the public knows, the better. But I've changed my thinking. Maybe it's better to stop the hype and roll with the truth. Maybe the public should know just exactly what's going on. Maybe if they knew, I wouldn't be the only living thing besides a Boston fern in this office. Maybe. Maybe not. Sometimes I think I need a shrink. I see kids with problems that would warp your head, Harry. I do what I can. And I'm telling you, I can't handle any more. It's only November and I haven't got five minutes to spare. I can't take even one more referral.

- All right. I'll give you two weeks, three weeks if you want or a month. I'll do something to keep the kid isolated. I suppose I could put him in ISSR or the reading lab until you get a chance to see him. But you have to, Len. What the hell kind of mind would make a kid carry shit around in a plastic bag?

- Maybe he's a budding coprophile.

- What the hell is that?

- Coprophilia is a sexual perversion. In order to be sexually aroused and satisfied the coprophile needs to play with excrement.

- Oh Christ, Len, do you really think that's-

- Chances are the kid's just looking for attention.

346

- Oh! Good! Good! That sounds better. That's not as frightening. So you'll take him then? In a few weeks? Don't feel rushed, I'll make do until you can schedule him in.

- No, Harry. You're going to have to make do until the end of the year. I'm not taking any more referrals. I am one person and I can't do any more than I'm doing.

- And I know as well as you do that you can't refuse a referral. Let's stop playing games.

- Maybe you're playing games. I'm not. If you think you can threaten me, forget it. If you want to put me on report, go ahead. If I get fired, it'll be a blessing. For me and for you. But you'll have to work fast to get your referral in first to my replacement. If I'm even replaced. There's rumor of that too, you know.

- All right, all right. No threats. I need a favor, all right? Just this once.

- The kid wants attention, Harry. Give him some.

- Len, you can't refuse. Len? Len!

Harold E. Bassard slammed the phone down then stared at the referral form on his desk. He read through it carefully. The kid's counselor had done a thorough job researching grades, IQ, behavioral history; Brenda had filled in the rest.

There had to be an out somewhere, and, sure enough, Harry found it. The kid's grades were atrocious; he never should have been promoted out of ninth grade. The junior high was notorious for social promotion. Harry read further. There would be no problem with the parents; they had refused to show up for a conference, told Brenda they didn't care if the kid lived or died. That was probably most of the kid's problem, his despicable parents. But despicable or not, they weren't going to challenge Harry's decision. He'd have to notify them, of course. He couldn't just send the boy back to junior high without notifying the parents.

III

- Mrs. Wrenkle, this is Alyssa Matthews at BCA. I'm returning your call about Bill.

- Oh, thank you. We're trying to contact all his teachers. We found out something over the weekend that has us horrified. I don't know if I'm more embarrassed than angry, or what.

- What is it?

- I was cleaning out his pants pockets to do the laundry and I found a great deal of money and some betting slips.

- Betting slips? He's a bookie?

- It took us all weekend to get the truth out of him. He's in with a group of kids taking bets on football games and from what he said, they plan to branch out into hockey and basketball soon. I'll tell you, my husband and I are appalled.

- I imagine you are. He's such a quiet kid. From my viewpoint, anyway. To tell you the truth, I think he's adorable. But now I understand why he's not doing his work. He's interested in other things. Lord, what they manage to get into. At least he's not selling drugs, Mrs. Wrenkle. You can be thankful for that.

- That's what we were afraid of. He swore up and down that they weren't into that. Of course he also finally let it slip that one of the boys has a connection for liquor. So as far as I can see, the drugs will follow suit eventually. I'm telling you, they're making a fortune.

- Have you notified Mr. Bassard? He really should know about this.

- I was afraid to, afraid that the rest of the gang would want revenge on my son. But Mr. McGuinness and Mr. Ruggles assured me that they would handle it discreetly. That's why I'm speaking with all Bill's teachers. I want you to know what's going on, but I'd also like you to keep it quiet.

- But of course. Bill won't even know that I know.

- Good. He's feeling mighty ashamed of himself right about now. We aren't that kind of people, Mrs. Matthews. We're trying to bring up our children the best way we know how. But it's so hard sometimes. Sometimes you don't even know what you're up against. How do you fight something if you don't even know about it? I waited until my husband left for work and the kids left for school this morning and then I cried my eyes out. What if we hadn't caught this in time? What if he were arrested? I don't want my son to have a record before he gets old enough to know better.

- But you did find out about it. I guess what you must do is concentrate on that. At least Bill is willing to admit he made a mistake; at least he's listening to you now and accepting your influence and your values. Some kids, no matter how well they're brought up, revolt against everything when they hit adolescence. Pity those parents, Mrs. Wrenkle.

- You're right. I hadn't thought of it that way. My son is still my son. He's not a stranger in my house. I don't know what I'd do if that ever happened, if he refused to stop doing what was offensive to me. What do parents do when that happens?

- I think they cry, Mrs. Wrenkle. I think they cry a whole lot.

IV

- Horace Dolby speaking.

- Hello, Mr. Dolby, this is Alyssa Matthews at Boesch-Conklyn. Lisa's English teacher. I was pleased to receive your note and I want you to know that there are more problems. Lisa is doing no work whatsoever. She can't even pass a spelling test. I don't know where to go from here.

- Well, I told her she had to straighten up and fly right and she promised me she would try. I know she's difficult. It's her attitude.

- You're exactly right.

- She's not being disruptive, is she?

- No, no, of course not. I don't generally have those problems with students. But if neither one of us can get her to do any work, she's going to waste the entire year.

- I know, I know. I've begged, I've bribed, and I've threatened. Her mother and I have tried everything we could think of short of whipping her. I just don't know what to do anymore. Do you have any suggestions?

- No, sir, I'm afraid I don't. But I will give it another try here. I'll talk to her again. You do the same on your end and I'll call you back in a week or so.

- Thanks. I appreciate all you're doing.

- We can only try, Mr. Dolby. We can only try.

γ

- Mrs. Romanoff, this is Alyssa Matthews at BCA. Raymond's counselor told me you wanted me to call.

- Yes, Mrs. Matthews. We're wondering why we aren't getting weekly reports on Raymond. We requested that it be done at the end of September.

- Of course. Your husband wrote a note on the deficiency report and sent it back. I remember it well. It was the only response I received.

- But we haven't heard from you.

- Mrs. Romanoff, I've been filling out weekly progress reports ever since. Raymond hands me one every week. I fill it out during class. Has he been showing you the weekly progress report form? It's a special form he picks up in guidance every week.

- Yes, he has, but English hasn't been on it. I asked him about it and he said you said you were too busy to fill it out.

- Well, that's true enough, but I never told him that. How the hell is he managing to get other teachers on that form and not me? Excuse the language, but I know I've been filling out that form for him.

- Listen, I'm starting to wonder what the hell is going on myself. And I'll tell you one thing: I'm going to find out. He's failing, isn't he?

- Right along. Wait a minute ... wait a minute. Something just occurred to me. Raymond's in my eighth period class and I think I've been filling out his form on Thursdays. I fill out so many every week that I can't be absolutely sure. But that would explain how he's doing it. Somehow he's getting an extra form every week, throwing out the one I fill out, then using the extra one the next day. That way I get the impression that you're being notified and he's off the hook.

- He told me another time that you said he was doing okay and there was no need to fill out the form.

- When that's the case, I fill it out anyway.

- I'm going to kill him.

- Well, you do what you must. But I'll tell you, he's not alone and there are kids here doing far worse.

- Are you defending him?

- Of course not. But I like Raymond; he's a good kid. Even though he's failing. I enjoy having him in class.

- That's good to hear. And I'm glad I didn't just let this slide. I'm glad you returned my call.

- Me too, Mrs. Romanoff, me too.

Alyssa hung up the phone and shook her head; she had made the call from Brenda's phone in the main office because only one faculty room had a phone with an outside line and that faculty room was further away from her study hall than the main office was. Brenda was chuckling. "Resourceful, aren't they?" she said. Alyssa mumbled agreement and ran out the door in an attempt to get to her room for third period on time. The note from Dick Ruggles had said, "Call Mrs. Romanoff between 8:00 and 11:00. She goes to work after that." More often than not, requests came through that way, as if she sat at a desk with a phone within arm's reach. One of the counselors had asked her once, "Do you make calls from home?" and she said, "Sure. Why not? It's easier than making them from here." Then she wondered why he had such a peculiar look on his face.

The bell for third period rang when she was halfway to class, but she stopped in the faculty room anyway for a quick slurp of coffee and a couple of drags on a cigarette. She was right into the heavy smoking again and trying to hide it from Jeff. She knew it wasn't helping her cold any, either. But she was addicted; she was addicted and she knew it and it calmed her nerves so she smoked. End of story.

She lectured to her seniors that day on the Shakespearean theater; it shouldn't have been necessary to do so. Every semester she hoped she could skip the fundamentals and get on with the plays. Every semester she required group work to get students to present their own introduction to Shakespeare, just a short one-day review of the basics as background. Sure, there were some who had never been exposed to Shakespeare at all, but she allowed for that with the group approach. Every semester she walked around the room amidst the embarrassment. A few students remembered that Shakespeare wrote *Romeo and Juliet*; one or two were proud to offer the revelation that the old man was born at that "on Avon" place; and occasionally a misplaced scholar would fill an entire piece of paper with information memorized the year before. She couldn't let them keep on believing that Shakespeare died in 1922, so every semester she ended up giving the lecture.

At one point during that third period in November she mentioned the fact that there is a symbiotic relationship between writing and acting, between writers and actors. Shakespeare, she said, had only words in his theater of sparse scenery and no lighting; indeed, atmosphere couldn't be accomplished by anything other than the dramatist's words. And the words needed to be voiced to give them life.

Someone asked the meaning of "symbiotic" and she stopped short. She had given the meaning of "genre" and "aesthetics" to her sophomore scholarship students the day before, with an explanation that the words had stumped her during a lecture once in college. She had been embarrassed by it and was trying to prepare them better.

But they were sophomores. What about seniors? Seniors and "symbiotic"?

"In a few short months you're going to be in college. I'm not trying to tell you not to ask questions when you're in college, but for God's sake get used to depending on yourselves for some answers. You should be able to figure out what 'symbiotic' means from the context, besides the fact that you should have come across the concept of symbiosis in biology or health. By now you should know enough to cross-reference the mass of knowledge in your heads. I know that's funny, it's real humorous to think there's nothing in your heads, but it's not only funny, it's false. I may be wrong, but if college professors are the same today as they were when I was in college, you're going to be mighty embarrassed if you ask the meaning of a word like 'symbiosis.' If you don't know what the word means, circle it in your notes and look it up on your own. On your own! Is the very idea revolting to you? If it is, you're in for a rude awakening in a few months!"

She knew she was hypersensitive that day. It was a week after she returned the graded research papers and the failures caused her to make repeated trips to guidance. One student thought her failing grade was unfair and bitterly complained to her counselor, who, she thought, could influence teacher's decision. Alyssa had been surprised that the girl failed because the girl had been a model student all along; but she could not pass the paper, it simply did not fulfill requirements set forth from Day One. Finally the counselor let it slip: the girl had previously submitted the paper to another teacher for another course, not an English course, and the student thought she would necessarily get another A whenever she submitted the paper, regardless of teacher or course.

"She sure fooled me," Alyssa told the counselor. "All that time I thought she was working diligently, and in the end that's all she did was retype a paper she already had. But that was no big crime. I suggest to students that they might be able to use the paper they write for me for another class. You have to be realistic about it, they do it anyway. It backfired on her, though, didn't it? Seeing that she won't talk to me about it — she's embarrassed as hell about it, isn't she? poor kid, she's probably never failed a thing in her life — would you do me a favor and explain to her that she needs to pay attention to course requirements? God, the footnotes in that paper were horrible." The counselor replied that he had already taken care of it. The girl had learned a bitter lesson, but still, a valuable one.

On another day after the papers were returned, Alyssa spent half her lunch period defending the failing grade on another student's paper. The mother had just popped into school with no appointment and Alyssa had just wandered into the senior office to deliver or pick up something or other. She knew drama was brewing when everyone was so ecstatic to see her. The secretary had been calling all over the school to find her, and with the new phone system, that qualified Doris for the Congressional Medal of Honor. And Lou Broglio was pacing back and forth in his office; his face broke into a broad smile as he ushered Alyssa in to face Mother and counselor.

Mother was on the offensive, demanding to know why her son failed after he worked so hard and so long. There was an unmistakable implication in the woman's tone that teacher was an idiot with little understanding and less skill. Defend yourself, the woman's eyes and bearing said, defend yourself, if you can.

Alyssa, who had been trying to spare her sore throat all morning, opened up and explained for twenty minutes why the paper failed. All of what she said was written on the paper and on the evaluation sheet returned with it. The paper was gorged with mechanical errors, footnotes were not in proper form, three-fourths of the paper was directly quoted, the bibliography was padded, the paper was too short, there was no outline ... on and on she went, and with each point she made, she was sure to point out that she, Alyssa Matthews, the teacher, had given sufficient instruction, had explained and verified, clarified and emphasized requirements over and over again, that if the student failed, the student failed, not the forever-damned teacher. At the end of her dissertation, Alyssa offered the woman an alternative that she never hesitated to offer anyone questioning her skill or her judgment: take the paper to the chairman of the department. Get a second opinion. If he thinks the grade should be raised, I'll work out a compromise with him. As it now stands, I cannot justify raising this grade. And I will not defer to the evaluation of another teacher; we all grade differently. The chairman of the department tries to be objective in such matters and judges each case according to its merits.

The woman must have been impressed with the teacher's defense, for she pursued the matter no further. The teacher would have liked the chairman to read the paper; Paul's standards were even higher than hers. That, of course, stopped many a referral from being made: there was always the chance that he would suggest lowering the grade. She had even argued with him once over that.

When she left the office, her throat raw and burning, Alyssa Matthews invoked God's blessing on all seniors who needed the intervention of their parents to get them through senior year. If they couldn't manage their own affairs by then, only the Lord could help them. While she intensely believed in the positive effects of parental guidance and concern, she nevertheless shivered at the appearance of armor-clad senior champions refusing, for love or pride, to abdicate the field of battle. Has a parent ever lifted sword and screamed a battle cry on a college campus? Does he not equate taxes with tuition? Or is there another darker reason?

She was saddened by the large number of students heading for college with no training in self-sufficiency. And she was disturbed by the unalterable fact that maintaining standards exposed her to attack while she never knew from what flank the assault would be made.

She gave her afternoon classes a reading period that day because her throat was so painful, and she tried not to smoke between periods because she was going through intermittent spells of lightheadedness. She also decided that the misery had gone on long enough, she just couldn't beat the damn cold by herself, she needed help. Jeff was on her back about it (When are you going to give in and see the doctor? For Christ's sake, I can feel your pelvic bones! You lose any more weight and you'll disappear!), and even Cassie Quimly exclaimed after school one day, "You look lousy! Don't you feel good?"

She called the doctor's office from Brenda's phone during sixth period. It took fifteen minutes to get through. "I'm sick," she told the nurse, "I've been sick for two months and I've tried everything I can think of to cure myself. I've been taking antibiotics and I've gone through about a gallon of cough syrup. But I'm still sick. I need an appointment." The nurse gave her one for the following week.

Later that day, in early evening, the nurse would call her at home with another appointment. The doctor wanted blood tests before he saw her. Alyssa made sure that the lab appointment was at 7:30 so that she wouldn't miss any school. And she smiled when she hung up the phone. The man was always thorough. Bless him, he was The Soul of Medicine. She always felt reborn after she saw him even though she was still sick. He was that kind of doctor; she called him Marcus Welby once and he roared. But he was almost fictional, she thought, a man apart, an artist. He was beautiful. She said that to the nurse once and the nurse was evidently upset by it. Within seconds, Alyssa realized why. The nurse was his night nurse and his night nurse was his wife. Lord, what a faux pas! "Listen," Alyssa said firmly, "when I'm sick, he's beautiful." Then both women breathed a sigh of relief.

Blood tests. So he wanted blood tests, so she'd go for blood tests. How could he possibly remember? He had so many patients. But she remembered. Mostly because she had been so frightened. Twelve years ago. What was it? Mono? Leukemia? God, she had been nervous about it. But that was twelve years ago when she let herself get hyper over illness. She was beyond that mentality now. If you worry about being sick all the time, you'd might as well be sick. Or dead.

He didn't remember. But she did. Mostly because it was such a relief when he called her with the results. Yes, he did that, he actually called his patients to ease their minds, he actually did things like that. When he called he was jubilant. "Alyssa!" he said. "Good news! Your blood is better than the average American female's! You're tired because you aren't getting enough sleep! Isn't that wonderful?"

Yes, it was wonderful, that first year of teaching, it was wonderful to know. And now he wanted blood tests again. Well, she would go. But she couldn't wait to see him, to tell him what he surely forgot. They would laugh about it, and he would see. The blood tests were hardly necessary. Hardly necessary at all.

EQUATIONS

Alyssa trudged along through the snow and into the hospital. She wore her heaviest coat, high boots, hat, scarf, and gloves. Jeff had taken one look at her and asked what she planned to do when it got really cold. She didn't bother to answer because she didn't have one, kissed him on the nose and left.

The hospital lab was on the second floor so she took the elevator; no sense in exerting herself so early in the morning, she'd climb enough stairs by the end of the day. She arrived at 7:15 and immediately recognized her mistake. The day shift started work at 7:30. She peeled off the outerwear and sat in the empty waiting room until a receptionist acknowledged her presence at precisely 7:30. At 7:32 a nurse opened an inner door and called her name. By 7:36 she was trudging her way back to her car, and by 7:48 she was having a slug of coffee and a cigarette in the faculty room.

She was in good spirits on November 20, ante meridian. Nettie NillyNellyNully was in homeroom — on time. And half of the study hall went to the library that day. She received notification from Bob McGuinness that some of the students who had never shown were either not enrolled in school at all, not scheduled for her particular study hall, or truant; he was working on the truancies. She spent some time during second period preparing a second list because there were more names to check out since she had sent the first one. She also filled out homeroom forms for direct notification to students she suspected of truancy from study hall.

She handed in the 2S exam to Paul that morning and felt free of one burden. She had literally begged one colleague to give her the last section she needed to compile the exam and was overjoyed when she found it in her mailbox earlier in the week. After she put all sections together, added directions, proofread the entire thing, and typed an answer sheet, the exam was ready to go.

Bonnie tagged along when she delivered it to Paul before homeroom because Bonnie was having a terrible time getting all the sections she needed to put the 2R exam together. She had to ask Paul to exert some pressure on other teachers. What pressure could Bonnie exert? And, as Alyssa told her, there were so many other pressures coming from so many directions that people resisted what

357

they could. Bonnie responded to that by saying she was waiting for Erica Vetterly and Al Rentsen. So Alyssa said, "Pardon my stupidity," and shut her mouth.

Alyssa found a note in her mailbox on November 20 that added to her good spirits that day. The note was from Hawkens. It said:

Curt Holbert is dropping your course, apparently because he failed his paper. Make the sign of the cross, then destroy this note.

Alyssa finished lecturing on Act I of *Hamlet* that day; she was pleased that most of her seniors were understanding and enjoying the play. Or so she thought. She would know who was meshed in mud when she gave the test on Acts I and II. She closed the period with Hamlet's words - 0 cursed spite/That ever I was born to set it right! - and translated for them: he's not too happy that his life has taken this turn, that he has to sacrifice all that was dear to him for this unholy revenge. It's a horrible mandate that he's facing; it's totally against his nature to fulfill it. After his emotional outburst with the ghost, after his violent promise to seek revenge, after his wild performance for Horatio and the guards, he calms down and sees a vision of reality. He doesn't much like what he sees. His life will never be the same. Everything he once loved is either dead or tainted or reduced to triviality. Can you understand his suffering even now when it has hardly begun?

At the end of the period Alyssa spoke with two students who were really into the play, then turned around to see Cassie Quimly's morose face staring her down. Cassie had taken her advice and solved the problem with Beth Whittsley; she was passing English again and even bragging about what a good teacher Mrs. Whittsley was. But she still appeared at Alyssa's door with personal problems.

Alyssa escorted her to a small room in the back of the library that offered some privacy because the resource room was inhabited. Cassie was more nervous than Alyssa had ever seen her.

"Something happened to me over the weekend," Cassie said falteringly. "I don't understand - it was - I don't know what it was." She went on to explain in bits and pieces: a girlfriend - best friend in all the world -slept over - music - bedroom - bed - a hug and a - kiss.

Alyssa's forehead wrinkled, her eyebrows dipped into a deep V. The girl was in agony, wringing her hands, barely able to push the words out of her mouth. But the words were in her brain, had been there festering for four days, and releasing them was obviously a relief to her. Knowing the consequences of extending the silence, Alyssa spoke to Cassie's bowed head after the girl stopped talking.

"Did it go any further than that?" Alyssa asked softly.

"No." The head didn't move.

"Did you want it to go any further than that?"

"No." Then after a pause, "I don't think so."

"Cassie, look up at me. There's no need for you to look at the floor. The floor's not interested in what you're saying, but I am."

Cassie looked up, her stricken face wet with tears.

Alyssa continued. "Now listen and listen good. Chances are that you are not what you think you are. First of all, teenage girls form friendships that are cast in cement. I had a best friend all through high school and we were inseparable. We listened to each other and shared everything. There are times when it's impossible to tell your mother something, even if you're really close to your mother, but you can tell your best friend anything. When you're in high school your best friend knows more than your mother, and most people between the ages of thirteen and twenty are quite certain that parents are the most ignorant creatures on earth. How does your girlfriend feel about what happened?"

"I think she liked it. I don't know, maybe not."

"But you were repulsed by it?"

"Not exactly. I felt ... funny. I don't know how to explain it. Then I was afraid. I moved away from her. I changed the record."

Alyssa wasn't too eager to dig deeper into that, so she continued to skate the surface. "Do you have a boyfriend?"

"No."

"Have you ever dated boys?"

"No."

"Why not?"

"No one asks me out."

"Have you ever liked a boy, wanted to go out with him, and would if he asked?"

Cassie smiled for the first time. "Sure. I've liked this one kid for two years, but he's always going with somebody else. He doesn't know I'm alive."

"Do you feel bad about that?"

"Sometimes."

"I used to feel bad about it too. Really rotten. I hated myself. My face, my body, my hair. My hair drove me crazy. I wanted it to flip up. Everybody else's hair flipped up. But mine, mine curled under. No matter what I did to it, it curled under."

"You? You didn't go out with anybody in high school?"

"No, I can't say that. I did date. But sometimes it was boys that I didn't like very much. Or boys who were really interested in somebody else. I remember one kid, he was sort of like the boy you like secretly. I adored him for a long, long time. He finally noticed that I was alive and he asked me out. We dated for a few months and I was in ecstasy. Then one day he stopped talking to me. That was it, he just stopped talking to me. That was the way he broke up with girls. It absolutely destroyed me. Now I can understand; how can a sixteen-year-old handle what many adults have trouble handling? But I'll tell you, I didn't understand when it happened; that little twerp broke my heart. I think of him every time I hear that song *50 Ways To Leave Your Lover*, and I wonder if he ever learned a classier way."

"I can't believe you weren't popular in high school. You're so pretty. You must have been a cheerleader."

"Are you kidding? I tried out once, was sore for weeks, and didn't make it through the first cut. I still get embarrassed when I think about it. If you ever want to see a clumsy ox, imagine me trying to jump gracefully into the air. An elephant has better chances. You know, dimwit, the more I see you this year, the more I realize how much passed through your skull last year. You know that saying, in one ear and out the other? Appearance vs. reality. Remember that? What you see isn't necessarily what's really there. Watch it when you form opinions without knowing what's under the surface. My adolescence wasn't exactly tragic, but I had my ups and downs. Like anybody else. I remember one thing that struck me my first year in college: all of a sudden people weren't categorized anymore, people were individuals. You know how it is in high school, who's good-looking, who's smart, who's athletic, who's popular, who has personality plus. Kids pigeonhole each other. When I got to college I felt free of all that. Maybe you will too. Lots of girls don't date in high school, Cassie. Is that what's really bothering you, the fact that boys aren't asking you out?"

Cassie's face darkened again. "Maybe. Maybe not. I just, - I just keep thinking about how I felt when she kissed me."

"Look, we've established the fact that you aren't necessarily interested in just girls, haven't we? I mean, how can you decide that you're interested in girls if you've never even dated a boy? It's very difficult for me to help you with this, Cass, because I don't want you to think that I'm telling you to go out and have sex with a boy just to see if it appeals to you so that you can then decide whether or not you like girls better. Do you understand what I'm saying?"

"I think so, but I still don't know what to do about my girlfriend. I was afraid, but before I was afraid I think I liked it. Maybe that's why I became afraid. Do you think that's why?"

"Probably," Alyssa said, realizing that she couldn't skate the surface any longer. "The fact that you liked it scared you. It wasn't just a warm hug and kiss between friends, it stirred you sexually. Now, I'm no psychologist, but I can't see anything so horrible in that, considering your age. It's too bad people don't reach puberty at age twenty-two when we'd be better prepared to handle it."

"Then I shouldn't have been afraid?"

"No, that's not what I'm saying at all. What I'm saying is this: you are too young to get involved in sex with a boy, man, girl, or woman. At the same time you can't be condemned for feeling the effects of your own sexuality, which is there regardless of all attempts to deny it."

"I'm getting confused."

"How's this: it's normal for you to become sexually aroused, but you have to practice self-control and refrain from having sex with anybody because you cannot at this point in your life cope with the emotional trauma that will surely accompany any sexual activity you are foolish enough to engage in."

"Huh?"

"Don't screw around, it'll mess up your head."

Cassie started to laugh." I understood you the first time."

"Then why-?"

"I like to get you going. I'd rather talk to you than anybody else, even my friends."

"I wonder sometimes how healthy that is. Don't tell me you fabricated this whole thing today just because you wanted some attention. I'll choke you with my bare hands. I'm having some problems of my own these days; I don't need to spend time entertaining you."

"Don't get mad at me, I'm not lying or anything. It happened, it really happened. I wouldn't make up something like that. And I still don't know what to do. Are homosexuals really that bad?"

"If you want my honest opinion, and that's all it is, an opinion, no, I don't think so. I don't think such a big issue should be made of homosexuality. It's gone from one extreme to the other. I don't like seeing them parade around with signs. And I think it's wrong to discriminate against a person just because he or she is homosexual. Some people think that homosexuality is abnormal, but who am I to say what's abnormal? I don't even know any homosexuals, or maybe

I do, maybe they keep their sexual preferences to themselves like most heterosexuals. It's a highly controversial topic and you might be interested in doing some reading on it. You ask these loaded questions and I have a hard time answering in twenty-five words or less. I don't think homosexuals are, by definition, monstrous people; at the same time, I am not encouraging you to go out and become one. And something else strikes me - I can't help but think that you and your girlfriend might not have this problem if it weren't for the fact that homosexuality has become as well-publicized as Coke and Pepsi. A French philosopher once said, 'There are many people who would never have been in love if they had never heard of love'. Do you think maybe that fits?"

"I think I don't want to be queer or gay."

"Well, if you think of it in those terms, you're passing judgment on those who are. There's supposed to be a physiological basis for homosexuality. There's certainly a psychological basis for it, as far as I can tell. I really don't know, I really don't know that much about it. Experts are still trying to figure it out. But I can tell you one thing for sure: You should not be consumed by such concerns now."

"But maybe I am. What if I am?"

"If you are, you should do what heterosexuals should do: put off sex until you're old enough to handle your sexuality. For God's sake, don't burden yourself with sex with anybody until you're mature enough to recognize the responsibilities involved and are able to deal with emotional upheaval. Enough adults have problems with sex; give yourself a break and wait. But I'm repeating myself again, aren't I? Has your mother told you about pregnancy? You're not of the opinion that babies drop out of the sky are you?"

"I know all that. My mother never told me anything, but you find out. I took biology, too. That's the chance you take with boys. But there's nothing to worry about with another girl. Is there?"

"Did your girlfriend tell you that or did you figure it out all by your clever self?"

"Girlfriend. It doesn't take too much figuring, does it?"

"Well, now I'm thinking that she's trying to seduce you. This is a little more serious than you've thus far led me to believe. I think you should consider cooling it with her, don't you? What's the matter? Do I sound like your mother now?"

"I knew you would say that. I knew it would all boil down to that. Well, she's my best friend. What am I supposed to do, stop talking to her?"

"You won't have to remind me never to tell you anything personal again."

"I'm sorry. That was a cheap shot."

"If you keep up the friendship you have two choices. Be friends with her, but tell her no sex; or be friends with her and have sex. You have options, don't you? And you've known them all along, you just bothered me today because you aren't mature enough to steer your own course. You were in tears a few minutes ago. What happened? Did I tell you what you didn't want to hear?"

"I'm sorry if I *bothered* you. I'll go now."

"Stop the crap. I'm not going to allow you to whip me with one word."

"Well, I can't tell my best friend to go fly a kite."

"Will you let her lure you into something that will affect you for the rest of your life, something that you can avoid if you want to?"

"No. She won't do that. I won't let her do that."

"You're sure? You can handle it if she tries to go any further?"

"Yes. But she won't. Maybe it's - maybe all of it's my imagination anyway."

"Keep me posted, Cassie. You know what I think you should do. I'm beyond helping you now. In fact I wonder if I haven't made the situation worse. It's very possible that you're making an elephant out of a peanut. And I've helped you do it."

"An elephant out of a peanut? Isn't that supposed to be a mountain out of a molehill?"

"Just keeping you on your toes. Sometimes I want to call the Roto-Rooter Man to bore a hole through your head. Maybe then you'd listen, maybe then something would sink in."

"I listen to you. You're about the only person, too."

"Because I can't do a hell of a lot about it if you don't. Right?"

Cassie started to laugh. "Yeah, I suppose so. I never thought about it that way."

Alyssa watched her walk through the library and out the door into the hall in awe, as always, of the girl's mood changes. She was a regular chameleon. If only she could change into an adult so easily. Alyssa wished she had a magic wand that would do the trick, then started laughing when she thought of how she'd use it. No doubt about it, she'd club her over the head and knock her out cold.

Before leaving herself, Alyssa stopped at the desk to check on a film she had ordered for the week after Thanksgiving. She was trying something different with the *Hamlet* films. She thought it would be more helpful to the kids if she showed each act after she covered it in class instead of waiting until the end to show the entire play. She knew the big pitfall of such a procedure; some students would quit reading if they could look forward to a film after each act. She normally showed the entire play after the unit tests because, as she told the kids, it wasn't a film course. And if students just watched the films, they'd never get through a quotes test. But she thought she'd try the alternate method anyway; maybe it would help more kids than it deceived.

She found out that the film was scheduled for delivery when she wanted it; as she turned to leave the room, she spotted a familiar face in a study carrel next to the checkout desk. She walked over, sat in the adjoining carrel, and peeked around the partition. "Is that a good book?" she asked. The boy was reading *The World According To Garp*.

"I don't know yet," the sophomore said.

"It's a little difficult to understand, isn't it?"

"Yeah. I keep trying, though."

She saw that he was only a few pages into it and was trying to figure out how far beyond the cover Garp's birth was. Half an inch? Maybe only an eighth? "You know, maybe it would be a good idea if you put it aside and try again in four or five years. Then you'll appreciate it."

The boy turned the book over in his hands. "It's a bestseller, but I can't understand what's going on."

"That's because it's a little beyond you right now. It is for adults. You don't have the experience to understand it yet. But do save it for the future. I read it over the summer and enjoyed it immensely. All through it I kept thinking what a fine line there is between comedy and tragedy."

"Yeah? It's funny?"

"I thought so. But it's adult humor, Ken. I wouldn't expect you to appreciate it."

"Guess I'll wait to read it. It's just a bunch of words now." He slid the book across the desktop, then said as it hit another book, "I should be doing vocabulary now anyway, right?"

"No, if you like to read, you should read whenever you can. I didn't stop to spy on you. I wanted to tell you I spoke with your mom this morning. She's subbing today."

"I know. I hate it when she's here."

"Why? You have nothing to fear. She doesn't follow you around, does she?"

"No, but I still hate it. What'd you tell her? I'm not doing so good, am I?"

"Well of course you are! I told your mom you're wonderful!" Actually, the word she used was "precious," but "precious" is for mothers, not sixteen-year-old sons. "What's wrong with you other than the fact that you bust 'em on me every day?"

"Aw. I always knew you liked it! Some teachers don't. Boy, some teachers get awful mad."

"But you just tease, Ken. You're not disrespectful or mean about it. I think you're fun, not offensive. And you know when to stop."

"Sometimes I do it to hide."

"Hide what?"

"My stupidity."

He floored her. She could see that he wasn't joking around. "What do you mean? You're not stupid. I just told your mother how bright you are. You've got personality and wit and you're a good solid student."

"Nah. I'm not a good student. Everybody else in that class gets nineties. I don't get nineties. They're all so smart. I don't think I even wanna be that smart."

"Boy, have I got a shocker for you. Everybody is not getting nineties. You have no way of knowing that, so I'm telling you. There are kids failing in your class, and there are kids getting nineties that don't work half as hard as you do. I know you work hard and your grades mean something, that's why I think you're a good solid student. Your eighties mean more than some kids' nineties. Furthermore, Ken, you are the type of person who will make it no matter what the odds are because you plug away regardless. I had no idea you felt inferior!"

"Yeah, that's it. An inferiority complex. Isn't that what it's called? I read that somewhere."

"That's what it's called, but you have no reason to feel that way. You are, in many ways, far superior to many other students. You should feel good about yourself. Don't turn into an egomaniac on me now. You won't do that, will you?"

He knew that she was teasing him. She left him with a smile on his face and thought about him on the way to the office to collect her mail. He was in the massive middle, between the seriously deficient and the exceptionally gifted. What a boost to his ego a special report would have been. She never would have known he thought so little of himself had she not approached him outside the classroom. It only took a few words, a few moments of her time, to boost the kid's morale, to influence his attitude.

It was so hard to tell who needed what and when. Some kids need gentle prodding, some need to be ridden mercilessly. Others respond to praise or encouragement or threats or deals. Putting the pressure on works wonders with some students, but backfires with others. Ideally, she needed to find out what worked with whom and then put it into practice. Just a few words and a few moments, but multiplied by ... how many?

After cleaning out her mailbox, she headed for the faculty room. When she walked in, Bonnie and Jean were in deep conference. Both looked up, and Bonnie handed her a sheet of notebook paper. "Would you read this and tell me what I'm supposed to do with it?"

Alyssa skimmed through the composition, but her eyes kept stopping and staring at strategic points. When she finished, she said, "It's pornography. What the hell are you assigning, Bon?"

Bonnie squirmed in her chair. "I know what it is. I only asked them to write on 'An Experience I'll Never Forget.' I thought I'd give them something easy in the beginning. It's a farce anyway, that class. They take the newspaper because they think it's easy credit and don't even know that the second half of the course is creative writing. Well, there's Mr. Creativity himself. How do I get poetry or short stories out of those kids?"

"All the creative minds, bar Super Stud there, are in upper level courses," Jean said. "They wouldn't be caught dead in your course, though they could benefit from it and give a lot to it."

"So what do I do with this paper?"

"You could charge him with plagiarism," Alyssa said as she handed the paper back. "I'm sure he copied it right out of an old copy of *Hustler*. That's not being published any longer, is it?"

"I don't want to talk to the kid about it at all."

"Don't blame you. And whatever you do, don't put a grade on it. Don't even fail it; even a forty means you accepted it."

"Jean told me that already."

"You can either just give it back to the kid and tell him it's unacceptable, or you can show it to his counselor. I think I'd show it to -what's the kid's name?-"

"Butte's the counselor."

"In that case I'd show it to Butte and to Lou Broglio. Lou's awfully good. He'll talk to the kid for you. That's how I'd handle it. That way you cover yourself in case the kid gets arrested for sodomy next week. Wouldn't it be cool if the police decide to search his bedroom for drugs and find this with a grade on it?"

"You trying to make me more nervous than I am?"

"You'd better handle this right," Jean said, "or you'll find out what the inside of an asylum looks like. Harry has been known to drop people like hot potatoes in much less severe circumstances. You know there's no backing here, not when the chips are down and there's a choice between your neck or some parent's goodwill."

Alyssa said, "Look, there's always the chance that the kid just committed an indiscretion. Let Lou find that out for you. When did you assign this paper?"

"I collected it last week. I just got around to reading some of them."

"Then you'd better get your behind down to the senior office. Now."

Bonnie took a deep breath and agreed. "This is just what I needed to make this a banner week. I've got a girl who's been truant off and on since school started and I just caught up with her on Monday. The parents are furious that they weren't notified sooner and I've got to meet with them after school today. I think I'm going to tell them if they can't control her, how the hell am I supposed to."

"You'd better cool down before then," Alyssa said.

"I know. I have to grin and bear it when Harry tells them I was negligent, but the school is doing all it can."

Bonnie left and, a few minutes later, Lainie walked in. Her first words were, "Would somebody tell me what gives these kids the right to deface this school?"

Alyssa and Jean looked at each other for a moment, trying to determine what she was talking about. Then Jean started to laugh. "Where have you been? This is the Renew-A-Hall program. The district doesn't have to hire painters if the kids do it! And can't you tell, the kids are bubbling over with school spirit."

"Bullshit," Lainie said. "They're slopping paint all over the place, and I think black walls are depressing. There's a big bull's-eye on the wall facing my room! What the hell is happening?"

"The kids are taking over," Jean said, the grin never leaving her face, "It's a communist plot."

Between fifth and sixth periods Alyssa checked with Bonnie and learned that Lou Broglio had agreed to help. Bonnie was somewhat relieved. Alyssa checked her mailbox again and found a notice from the central office addressed to all secondary teachers. The paper told her in no uncertain terms that she was required to send out progress reports for failing students in the middle of every report card period. She didn't waste any energy ripping it up; it sailed into the nearest wastebasket whole.

When she returned to the faculty room for her free period, she found Jean sitting on the decrepit davenport with Beth Whittsley. Beth was doubled over, her arms cradling her middle. Jean's face was as white as Beth's.

"She's vomiting blood," Jean explained. "As soon as she can stand up, I'm taking her to the emergency room. Would you notify the office? I'll be back for seventh period, but someone will have to cover her eighth period."

"And her seventh?" Alyssa asked.

"She has study hall. Be sure the other teachers know she left sick or some boob will report her for not showing."

Alyssa waited to help Jean maneuver Beth through the halls and out to the parking lot. They stopped on the way to check on Beth's class and to get her coat and boots out of the closet in her room. Hank Courtman showed up in the doorway and assured them he would take care of the class, which was sitting in stunned silence.

As she hurried back into the building, Alyssa made the obvious diagnosis. She had seen the symptoms before. She stopped in the office and told Brenda what had happened. Then all hell broke loose.

Who would cover Beth's eighth period class? It was too late to get a sub. Harry was out of the building. So were Dannemore and McGuinness. Lou Broglio was in charge, but she couldn't locate him. A secretary certainly couldn't fill in. What teachers were free eighth period? Brenda checked through the master list of teacher schedules and started calling. She couldn't get anybody. Teachers are reluctant to give up the one period they have free on such short notice. Teachers are unwilling to cover for colleagues in other departments. Teachers expect administration to solve such problems. Get somebody else. I've got kids coming in for make-ups. I've got tests to run off for tomorrow. I have a parent conference. Hank Courtman said: "I'm covering this period and it's hard enough. There has to be someone else." Get someone else.

Alyssa lost patience as she watched Brenda get more and more frustrated. She finally exploded. "I'll do it! I have a class eighth period, but I'll do it!" She pushed through the main office doors and back to the faculty room. Brenda was relieved that the problem was solved, and Alyssa was furious that Brenda had to deal with it to begin with. She wondered what it was like to have a normal job, a job that could be left without the sky falling in.

When she traveled down the hall to gather up Beth's class at the beginning of eighth period, she saw Lou Broglio standing in the doorway. She had planned to herd Beth's kids down to her room because she was too far away to keep popping in and out. But Lou was there.

"What happened to Beth? Brenda just told me she had to leave. I've been doing observations and I just checked in with Doris who sent me to Brenda. Did Beth get sick?"

"Very," Alyssa said. "Jean took her to the emergency room. She was in pain and vomiting blood."

"Ulcers? But she's so together all the time."

"Sure, Lou, aren't we all? It's the cool, calm, and collected ones who get ulcers. Some of us were discussing you the other day. We're wondering how much longer before you collapse in a heap. You're going to stay this period?"

"Brenda said she couldn't get anybody and you have a class. I'll stay."

"I don't know what Beth's plans are."

"That's all right. I'll ask the kids what they're doing."

"I always thought you were a brave soldier. I'm glad you're here. Dannemore would write her up for not leaving plans. Thanks, Lou, you're also saving my plans for this period. I wasn't too anxious to have two classes in one room."

She heard him say, "Okay, folks, quiet down. Mrs. Whittsley isn't here, so you're going to have to put up with me this period," as she took giant steps to get back to her room.

That evening she started calling the doctor's office at 7:00. Her appointment was for 7:30, but Doc always ran late; he invariably spent more time with each patient than he was supposed to. Call back at 9:00, the nurse said, he's about two hours late tonight. At 11:00 Alyssa arrived at the office with Jeff at her side. He wouldn't let her walk through an empty parking lot at that hour.

The nurse ushered her into an examination room, took note of her weight, then gave her a paper smock to change into. Doc had ordered a thorough check, it seemed. She sat on the examining table and waited for his brisk entrance. He always entered briskly, manila folder under his arm, the smile on his face lighting up the room beyond the stark white glow of the fluorescent tubes attached to the ceiling. He was well-groomed and fresh every hour of the day. She had seen him once in the hospital at 7:00 in the morning and she had seen him a number of times in his office after midnight. He was always alert and caring and spotlessly groomed. Jeff had asked him once how he did it, how he managed to keep such a pace with no ill effects. Jeff had teased: "I'd like some of what you're taking!" Doc rolled his head back and laughed. "No pill can do it for you," he said. "It's conditioning, there's nothing like conditioning." Alyssa expected the door to open, but when it did, she jumped.

"Alyssa! What's this I hear about you? Can't get rid of a cold?"

She didn't tell him that she felt better already, just seeing him raised her spirits. "I'm miserable," she said. "It started earlier than usual this year and I can't shake it. It's the same old thing, only worse. And my energy level is so low I have to push like hell to get myself to do anything." She added a dramatic "help!" and knew that she had said enough to get him started.

"Well, let's see what we can find out." He opened her folder and looked at a small pink slip of paper. She assumed that he was reading the lab report from the morning blood tests. Then he examined her ears, nose, throat, heart, lungs, abdomen. "Are you having any discomfort other than the head congestion?'

"No pain, if that's what you mean. But I'm coughing all the time and the sore throat comes and goes. I carry around a box of kleenex because the nose runs whenever it wants."

"You have ornade for that?"

"Yes, but I hesitate to take it, sometimes it makes me groggy. I can't go to school groggy, though maybe that would be better than the way I am going. I've also been lightheaded off and on and occasionally get a doozy of a headache. Not a migraine, aspirin usually takes care of it. Thank God I don't get migraines. I have a friend who does, split vision and all; they're no joke. I've taken sumycin off and on since I started feeling rotten, but that hasn't helped at all. And I'm slugging cough syrup right out of the bottle."

"You don't take it with codeine in it, do you?"

Codeine is El, she thought. "No. You stopped prescribing that one a few years ago."

"I thought so, but I wanted to be sure. I'd hate for you to get addicted to cough syrup."

"I hate taking anything as it is. I have to force myself to take pills."

"I know that, Alyssa, but medication is worth its weight in gold when it's properly prescribed and the patient follows directions."

"I should have you in to guest-lecture my kids."

"Well, that's the key to feeling better. I have people come in to see me for help who go home and do nothing I suggest they do, then come back complaining that I haven't helped them. I'm going to write you a prescription for Trinsicon. You're to take two capsules every day, one in the morning and one at night. As far as I can see right now, your only problem is very treatable. You're anemic, Alyssa. Your blood test definitely shows it and your symptoms are very characteristic of anemia."

She knew he would go on to explain just what anemia is; he always explained the details to his patients. Sometimes he drew little diagrams or used the charts and pictures hanging on the walls. He had models of the heart and lungs and other internal organs to use as instructional aids, as well as a vast bibliography to draw from if he thought patients could benefit from reading a pamphlet or a magazine or a book.

He told her that people are fond of diagnosing their own fatigue and listlessness as anemia, but the only way to tell for sure is with a blood test. He checked her records again and said that a normal count is twelve, hers had once been fourteen, which was exceptional, but now her count was ten-point-four. It hadn't lowered to crisis level, but she was feeling the effects more because her normal high seemed to be fourteen. She couldn't even beat a cold because her body's disease-fighting mechanism wasn't up to the challenge; anemia means lowered resistance to infection.

Furthermore, it was going to take some time to build up her defenses again. The hematinic he was prescribing would eventually do the job. Alyssa recognized the word. Somewhere way back in her schooling she had come across it. Chemistry. Hematite. Iron, it meant iron. Doc was putting her on iron pills; that made sense, wasn't it called iron-deficiency anemia? *But my blood's better than the average American female's! What happened? I didn't need a blood test! My blood's better than ... Was. Was. Was. What happened?*

She listened as he described the process of iron retention, then the process of iron loss in the human system. He fascinated her; whenever he turned from doctor to teacher, he fascinated her. She imagined him telling a terminally-ill patient, "Now this is what's happening inside you. The tumor is benign, but the cancer around it is spreading along this route . ." If she ever reached that point in her life, if she ever needed to be told she was dying, she would want to hear it from him.

He was saying: "The iron dissipates from the blood first, then the blood starts to draw it from other organs. When the iron is reinstated into the body, it builds up first in the blood and then goes to the organs. You're going to notice when you start the pills that a great deal of the iron you're trying to put in your system passes right through and out again. Don't panic when you see black bowel movements. It's just the iron coming out. But a little at a time it will replenish."

By the time he finished, Alyssa asked her question: How? How did I get this way? He could only speculate: not enough iron in her diet, women lose iron every month during menstruation, prolonged physical exhaustion. There are many causes for anemia and it's usually the result of a combination of factors

She had one more question: How long? How long does it take?

At least a few months. You don't become anemic overnight.

How about three years?

That's possible. But what makes you localize the time to three years?

The way Alyssa described it to Jean the next day, she started babbling then. "I was sputtering and muttering like an idiot. Somewhere in the mess I spit out something about five classes and three preparations. And do you know what that perfectly wonderful man said to me? He got the most confused look on his face and he said, 'Alyssa, what's a preparation?' He stopped me cold. What could I say? How could I possibly explain all this to him? And what could he do about it if I did?"

She left the office, told Jeff the diagnosis, and was as relieved as he was that nothing more serious was wrong with her. But she rode home in silence. Twice Jeff interrupted her thoughts, once to ask, "Are you sure you're telling me everything? You're not holding anything back, are you?" then again to make sure she was still alive next to him, "Is it all right if you fill that prescription tomorrow or should we go to that 24-hour drugstore that just opened up?"

She answered him with a "yes," a "no," and a "tomorrow's soon enough." Once in bed, she waited until he was dead weight, then slipped out of the bedroom and down the hall. The spare room was cold and dark, but she used a flashlight and knew she'd stop shivering once she found what she wanted and went downstairs. She worked in fear because if Jeff woke up enough to miss her, he'd be up looking to see if she was all right. She didn't want that. She didn't want to have to explain what she was doing. She had to do it, she had to see. And she needed something to fight with.

The next day Bonnie reported during lunch that she, too, had gotten little sleep the night before. She was too nervous to begin with and when she finally dozed off, she had a dream that woke her up again. She saw herself chained, in shackles, being stoned by angry citizens. She saw the blood pouring from her head and felt the pain as rocks hit her flesh. She didn't tell them that Michael was in bed with her while she was writhing in agony, and that he finally woke her up to smash the horrible scene. It was peculiar, this dream, because she knew she was dreaming, she knew Michael was next to her and could save her from it, but she could not communicate with him to do so. He was there but she was helpless to invoke his aid and so the horror was multiplied.

She told her audience that she awoke on her own, then, after an hour or so, fell back to sleep. In fact, Michael had left by then and she was terrified that the dream would return and she wouldn't be able to wake up on her own. But she was exhausted; no amount of willpower could keep her awake.

The second dream was different. Even comical. She told the other women: "I was dead. Beaten, battered, bruised, bleeding, hanging there like a piece of meat. And then my saviors came. You're going to really crack up at this. Letters to the Editor! Do you believe it? Piles and piles of letters to the editor saying that I was a good girl after all, a good teacher, a good citizen, a good human being. Too bad, the letters said, too bad she's dead, too bad she suffered, too bad, too bad. Maybe we made a mistake, maybe she shouldn't have died. And there were letters from my old students, letters saying 'she taught me all I know,' 'she taught me better than anybody else,' 'she taught me how to live and love and prosper.' But apparently there was one thing I didn't teach them. Every goddam letter was the same in one respect; every one read like a two-year-old wrote it. Now that I'm considering both dreams in the light of day, I'm terrified more by the second one."

Alyssa said something about hanging a sheet over The Maid, then added, "I wonder what's worse: being stoned to death or seeing a letter in print from an old student extolling your virtues in fragments and run-ons."

"There appears to be an equation there," Jean said.

Thinking that Bonnie's nightmares at least occurred when she was asleep, Alyssa pulled Jason Haywood out of his sixth period class. Jason closed his classroom door. Alyssa apologized for the rude interruption and handed him two sheets of paper. "I spent most of last night figuring all this out for you. I saw the doctor last night, I've been sick since the third week in September, and something has to be done or I'm not going to make it. I thought you could use some statistics. Isn't that what they're always after - statistics? Don't numbers mean more to them than anything else?"

Rosemary Cania Maio

"Sure," he told her. "Anything specific, any kind of data can be helpful. Right now they're hitting us with abuse of sick leave. You should see the figures on that. It's the same old crap: more people are out on Mondays and Fridays than any other day of the week."

"I do that on purpose when I'm trying to force myself to get over a two-week illness in three days. Do you know that I was out sick more days last year than ever before? I'll bet English teachers head the list for numbers."

"As a matter of fact,-"

"Christ, Jay, doesn't that tell them anything?"

"Yep. English teachers abuse their sick leave more than other teachers do."

"Can't they even consider the possibility that we're out sick because we are sick?"

"That would destroy their rationale. They're trying to reduce the yearly sick leave allotment."

"But all we've got for a longer illness is what we manage to accumulate."

"Don't worry about it. Chances are we'll maintain what we have, and we're trying to establish a sick leave bank for people who run out of days. We should meet in the middle on that one. You'll be interested to know that we've worked up a proposal for the English department. To tell you the truth, we were hesitating to work it in. But Paul's been on our asses and we worked out a way to at least give it a try."

"There's hope then?"

"I don't know if I'd go as far as to say that. There's no way they're going to increase staff, so get that out of your head. But maybe we can push through one of the other alternatives Paul supplied us with."

"Well, what you've got right there in your hands should help. I worked that up right out of my grade books, so it's no lie."

Jason looked at the information.

ALYSSA MATTHEWS BCA ENGLISH

PAPERS GRADED LAST YEAR:

Spelling: 2671 x 1 minute each = 45 hours

Quizzes: 692 x 1 minute each = 12 hours

Grammar tests: 786 x 5 minutes each (these are complicated) =
66 hours

Vocabulary tests: 1110 x 3 minutes each = 56 hours

Written work: 576 x 15 minutes each = 144 hours

Literature tests: 2230 x 15 minutes each(an average-some are
objective, some essay) = 558 hours

Research papers: 54 x 40 minutes each = 36 hours

TOTAL: 917 hours (that's 38 24-hour days plus 5 hours)

AS OF NOVEMBER 14, 1980, I GRADED:

630 spelling tests

195 grammar tests

200 grammar quizzes

195 vocabulary tests

420 literature tests

135 literature quizzes

150 essays

45 6-page papers (30-45 minutes each to grade)

26 research papers (30-45 minutes each to grade)

I duplicated and distributed: 2, 450 sheets for tests and quizzes
350 assignment sheets
2, 200 study guide question sheets

I have already used 8 different texts and will use at least 10 more
by the end of the year.

Alyssa said: "I may have made a mistake in math somewhere, but I started getting this together at 1:00 this morning. I think it makes a point, don't you? I mean, that's not including homeroom and study hall and attendance and department work, either. And one thing struck me like a ton of bricks: I'm not doing half of what I used to do with my classes. And there's another thing that's apparent in that list of papers I've graded so far this year: I vowed when our report was ignored that I was going to change my ways and do what I could. But I started this year the same way I've always started - like a maniac. I didn't even consider not assigning the big paper on *Tale* to my scholarship sections. Be sure to tell them, Jason, that this isn't even close to what I should be doing with my classes. My regents kids haven't written a thing for me yet."

"I don't believe you do this much work."

"You too? Maybe you should try teaching English for a year. You read our report. Does everybody need a crash course in reading comprehension around here? I'll tell you one thing: I'm slowing down. I'm half dead, and I don't know how to save the other half."

"Yes, you do, Mattie. We all do. We all know how to survive."

"You don't have to grade what you don't assign. Yes, I know. There are ways. It's just too bad that every one of them takes something away from the kids. They announce your name over the PA if your homeroom attendance summaries aren't in on time, but nobody gives a damn if you don't have time to prepare new lessons. It's insane, Jay, it's the height of insanity. And speaking of insanity, just what is the status of negotiations? Are we in for a strike or what?"

"I - don't know at this point. We almost reached impasse last week. The way it looks, we may by Christmas. We can't seem to agree on economic issues, what else? They cry declining enrollments and budget deficits. We know if we push too hard they can start a media blitz claiming that taxes will go up a million percent if they give us a raise. We haven't got much on our side. If we reach impasse in December, we'll hold off the strike vote until January. But I wonder about the effects of a strike."

"I'm ready to walk out now."

"Too bad the rest of the membership doesn't feel that way."

"Why? Don't tell me everybody else isn't fed up."

"Sure everybody else is fed up. But when it comes time for that secret ballot, people start thinking about their bills and their families. And remember, we're breaking the law. Some people can't handle that, they're afraid. It takes people with courage, people willing to sacrifice a hell of a lot, for a strike to be successful. We don't have enough of those people. And if everybody doesn't go out, we're dead. Everybody wants this union to perform miracles, but the number of people willing to fight isn't large enough to give us the support we need."

"But how much are we supposed to take? I believe in law and order, and I've always been a disciplinarian. But there's something grossly unfair about being at the butt end of a law that forces collective bargaining and prohibits strikes. It gives the other side a slight edge, doesn't it?"

"I think the rationale is that permitting public employees to strike gives the employees too much of an edge."

"Look, I'd hate to have my house burn down because the firemen are on strike, but you know even better than I how far beyond reason conditions have to get before public employees walk out. It's the last resort because we've got a lot to lose when we do it; the law made sure of that. The almighty public is protected and we can be dictated to as long as we aren't strong enough as a union to fight back. So we really have every right and no rights. Right? It's very profitable for them to delay settlement, isn't it? We're getting last year's wages. They'd have to be fools to settle fast.

"I think an employee should have the right to withhold his services when he starts feeling like a paid slave. I wouldn't hesitate a minute to go out if it meant I could look forward to a reasonable workload. And the way this district treats us, I'd walk out now for a nickel raise. I'm worth every penny they pay me and I like getting a raise. The way the public reacts, we're supposed to be poor and dedicated. Why the hell do people equate poverty with dedication when it comes to teachers? Well, I'm happier being well-paid and dedicated. I happen to like keeping my self-respect."

Jason was mesmerized. "How about going to the next session with us? I had no idea you were such a spitfire."

"I'm not. Believe me, I'm not. I just want to be left alone so I can teach. I don't want to get involved in any crusades. I want four classes again. I want fewer students. I want the insults to stop. I want to concentrate on teaching. Is that so much to ask?"

"Would you settle for the moon instead?"

"I had a crazy idea when I was gathering that data in the wee hours this morning. I thought of resigning in protest. Then I thought that maybe if the whole department resigned, maybe that would rattle somebody's sensitivities."

The color drained from Jason's face; the panic was unmistakable. "Don't you ever do that, don't think of doing that."

"There wouldn't be any public outrage, would there? Nobody would give a damn, right?"

"You'd be replaced in a minute."

"With someone at half my salary."

"Yes, m'am,"

"I know. And I think that's eating away at me more than anything else."

NOVEMBER 22, 1980

"This is pie time, all right," Alyssa said to Bonnie. She had intended to go to Bonnie's for the lesson in pie crust; she had wanted to visit Mrs. King and see the old apartment again. But she woke up Saturday morning congested, so she sent Jeff out for groceries and decided she'd better stay in all day. She called Bonnie and suggested the alternative, sensing that postponement would disappoint Bonnie too much. Bonnie rang the doorbell within the hour.

"Are you sure you're up to this today? You look terrible."

"I look worse than I feel."

"You sound worse than you look."

"I can't fight anything off, I guess. I'm on two iron pills a day, but I started them yesterday and it takes months to build up. It's like dieting; you can't take off ten pounds in two days after it took a year to put it on. I guess I'll be catching everything that passes by my desk for awhile; I'm of the opinion these days that teaching is literally hazardous to your health. Between what the kids carry around and the temperature extremes in that place, who can stay healthy? Something happened to the heat in my room yesterday and I froze."

"Is your study hall still without heat?"

"Strangely enough, yesterday it was comfortable in there. Maybe it was just warmer than my room. I believe in the theory of relativity. How's yours?"

"Still air-conditioned. I wear a coat. Whatever happened with that kid you had trouble with? The one with the foul mouth who got suspended?"

"Nothing much. He came back and got lost in the soup. I stay away from him, he stays away from me. I fight to keep my nerves under control when I'm in there. It's easier than keeping the kids quiet, though I still insist on that. You want to see the house before we start?"

Bonnie handed over her coat. "Yes, if you don't mind. I'm into houses lately. I still can't thank you enough for sending me to Mrs. King."

"After Mrs. King's, this isn't exactly a palace. Not yet. We're trying to do one room at a time, but it's so expensive, even with Jeff doing the work. Materials are enough to bankrupt you. Did I tell you Mrs. King helped us find this house? A friend of hers owned it. When the friend died, Mrs. King found out the house was for sale and told us about it; she thought we'd be perfect people to preserve it. It's over a hundred years old. Then she cried the day we moved out; hell, we all cried. But she said it was time we struck out on our own. She was right and we learned our first lesson fast. We were very careful to be sure that we could handle mortgage payments and taxes without choking ourselves. Then we got our first tax bill. Jeff hit the ceiling. It was almost triple the amount it was supposed to be. Come to find out, the house was reassessed on the purchase price and we couldn't do a thing about it. It has since become illegal to reassess on purchase price, but we and a lot of other people got screwed."

She took Bonnie through the rooms that were remodeled. The living room, she said, needed more decorating, but the essentials - walls, ceiling, woodwork, carpeting - were done. The dining room was complete except for table and chairs. Bedroom essentials were also new, but the area off the bedroom was under construction; Jeff's current project was possible because he had knocked out a wall to convert an adjoining bedroom into a dressing room, full bath, and walk-in closet.

"There are three other rooms," Alyssa explained, "one for a study, one for a guest room, and one for whatever. Some day we'll get to them."

As they traveled back down the stairs from the master bedroom, Bonnie commented on the obvious difference in woodwork from room to room.

Alyssa asked: "Which do you like better, stained or painted?"

"Stained, to be sure. I got used to it at Mrs. King's. I never thought much about it before, but since seeing her house I can appreciate the difference. You can see the grain in the wood when it's stained and it's beautiful."

"I like it stained too, that's why some of it is and some of it isn't in this house. When we moved in, all of it was white. It made me sick. I think it's horrible to cover up the inherent beauty of wood with paint. These moldings and doors are irreplaceable. You can't even buy wood carved like this anymore, or molding this thick. It isn't even available. The old craftsmen are gone. This staircase would cost two fortunes to replace, but I don't think you could find anybody to reproduce it at any cost. So I've been refinishing a little at a time. When Jeff guts a room to rewire, I strip the wood and refinish it."

Bonnie was incredulous. "You mean to tell me you put this finish on? It looks like it was born this way. God, that must be a lot of work."

Alyssa smiled. "It is. It's pure agony, but the results are worth it. I can't live with painted woodwork. Neither can Jeff, he hates it as much as I do."

"Why do people paint it? None of Mrs. King's is painted."

"There comes a time when it needs a coat of varnish if it's stained. Or, if you let it go too long, it needs to be sanded, stained, and varnished again. Like anything else, there's maintenance involved. Somewhere along the line somebody got tired of it and painted everything white. I wish I knew who it was, I'd choke him with my bare hands. Not that he's alive for me to do it."

"But you still have to maintain a paint job, don't you?"

"Sure, but nobody thinks of that. White paint also shows dirt and fingerprints more than stain does. There was a time when people didn't even consider staining wood, they just plopped on the paint. And in most true colonial homes the woodwork was whitewashed; remember Tom Sawyer's fence? Believe me, coat after coat of paint is very difficult to strip because the paint is in the pores and won't raise completely. Unless, of course, it's been on for sixty years and is twenty-five layers thick; then it chips and peels. Luckily, the wood in this house was stained and varnished before some moron painted it, so it's possible to strip it down almost bare. There always seems to be just a tint of color left, though. That's why I picked a dark stain for refinishing. It's Jacobean. That's the color. Do you like it?"

"Very much. It does look like Mrs. King's. Rich and deep. And it's so smooth. Like glass."

"That's tricky, getting it smooth. It takes a lot of time and patience, the whole process. I looked into quite a few ways to refinish before I settled on one. I tried it on the wood in the living room and was more than satisfied, so I've stuck with it. Jeff came home with the process one day; he got it from a contractor he knows, a man who still builds homes the right way. He's an old-fashioned craftsman and, as I found out, his process is worth the time and effort it takes. There are quite a few steps beyond the stripping. First you sand with fine sandpaper - that's extremely important. If the wood isn't perfectly smooth before you stain, it will never finish smooth. Then you stain. After the stain dries, you use sanding sealer. It's real goopy stuff, about the same consistency as butterscotch topping. You brush it on, let it dry, then use fine steel wool to rub the surface smooth again. I think that's the crucial step, that's what makes the finish like glass. Then you use a tack rag to clean the god-awful mess. Then you varnish. And believe me, varnish is tricky; you have to flow it on smoothly and keep a constant watch for drips. It's a lot of work, but good for big jobs. I don't know if I'd use it on a piece of furniture; there's another process for that, and someday I want to try it. But that calls for hand rubbing, and while I'm willing to work until the year 2000 to get all this wood restored, I'm not getting into hand rubbing. I use a brush for the stain."

"Aren't stains sometimes wiped on with a cloth? I remember seeing my aunt do that. I think she was doing a desk. Or maybe it was a table. Whatever it was, her hands were stained. That I remember. I can still see her cutting my birthday cake; I must have been very young, I asked her if she had been out playing in the mud. Weird what sticks in your mind."

"That's one of the reasons I don't use a cloth. I can't go to school that way and I hate gloves as much as a cloth. With both there's little control. Too much stain stays on the cloth, too little transfers to the wood, and it takes six applications to get the right shade, then you have to match it on another piece. And all my wood's installed. At least with a brush I can control where the stain is going."

"You didn't do this staircase, did you?"

"This staircase drove me mad. The spindles were nasty enough to strip and refinish, but Jeff had to reconnect some of them to the handrail and, though he tried, he just didn't wash all the glue off. Some of it dripped down after he thought he was finished with the job. If you ever want to pull your hair out, try to remove dried glue from wood. But I had to. Stain will not absorb into glue. It looked like it had the measles."

"I can't see any of it now. How'd you ever get it off?"

"Sandpaper. Coarse sandpaper and garnet paper. Once or twice I considered using an ax. It was hell because the glue was mostly up in here, where the spindle meets the handrail. But I did it, I got it out. Then I cleaned the whole thing with a tack rag and followed my steps: stain, sealer, steel wool, tack rag, varnish. Except for the handrail. No varnish there. Shellac."

"You're really something else. I'd never believe you did this kind of thing."

"Why not? You'd be surprised at what you'd do if the spirit moved you. When you want to do something badly enough, you learn. Sort of like ... pie crust?"

"I suppose so. If I ever want to learn refinishing I know who to look up."

"Ever try any needlework?"

"I know I hate to thread one."

"Did you notice the picture on the wall in the dining room?"

"The bowl of fruit? Yes, I did. It's beautiful."

"It's crewel."

"Cruel? It didn't look mean to me."

"Crewel embroidery. That's c-r-e-w-e-l. You never embroidered when you were a kid?"

"Oh, sure. I made a mess of more than one sampler. French knots. Yuk!"

"I never liked it much with the floss either. But crewel uses yarn in a variety of thicknesses. Come look at that picture again."

"Son-of-a-gun," Bonnie said as she studied the basket of fruit. "It is yarn. And it's not a bowl, it's a basket. It looks real. How long does something like this take to do?"

"As long as it takes. Everybody works at different speeds. That took me only a week, but I worked on it every day and I knew what I was doing because I'd done crewel before."

"I wouldn't mind spending time on something like this. The colors are so vibrant. It really warms up the room."

"Did you notice the large picture over the sofa in Mrs. King's living room?"

"The flowers? Yes. I remember thinking, *What a lovely painting,* but there was so much to see in her house that I didn't get a chance to concentrate on anything in particular."

"That's no painting. It's crewel. I made that for her for Christmas the last year we lived there. That framing gave me all kinds of trouble because the picture's so big. There's a small wrinkle in one corner that I absolutely could not get out."

"What a nice idea for gifts, though, something you've worked at yourself."

"There's nothing like it. It's like giving a piece of yourself. I used to make all my Christmas gifts. But I had to give it up, there's no time anymore. Besides crewel, I've done some needlepoint. And I used to crochet like a maniac; Jeff called the hook my fifth appendage. It's so fast once you know what you're doing. God, I used to do a lot of it, even in school during lunch. It calmed my nerves. Once I tried it during study hall; that was four or five years ago. I thought maybe some kid might figure out that there are many ways to use time constructively. The same day I found a letter in my mailbox telling me that I was negligent, that I shouldn't knit in study hall, I should supervise. That aggravated me to no end. I would have understood if the kids were hanging from the ceiling, but they were quiet and well-behaved."

"So now there's a letter in your folder saying you had to be told not to knit in study hall."

"Of course, I wasn't knitting, I was crocheting."

"Knit with needles, crochet with a hook. Even I know that."

"I was really upset over that letter. It's sitting there in my folder; anybody reading it would think I'm a real jerk. It's as if they want something on you. Just in case. I should have done what Jean suggested, write a note that I wasn't a knitter, I was a hooker. But I didn't see any humor in it at the time. If you'd like to learn crewel, I'll be glad to help you out."

"How do I get started?"

"Buy a kit. I've got some catalogs you can take to look through. Do you crochet?"

"No, but I used to knit a little. Very little, very long ago. But I think I'd remember if I tried again."

"Great! I'll teach you how to crochet, you teach me how to knit. I'd love to knit Jeff a sweater. Crochet is great for shawls and afghans, but I'm not too pleased with it for clothing, it's too thick and boxy-looking. Knitting is more flexible and natural, though I know it's slower than crochet. At least it will be for me when I start."

"It's a deal. We'll plan on it after the holidays. You know, that bit about knitting in study hall is real ironic. My workshop committee is looking into ways to make study hall more tolerable to students and teachers. We've already come up with the idea of offering craft classes taught by interested teachers or even students who are skilled at something. We're really excited over the proposal. I was grumpy as hell over the committee work to begin with, but we might make a difference after all."

"This is your first committee outside the department, isn't it?"

"Yes. Why?"

"Never mind. You'll see yourself. Or maybe I'm wrong. Maybe I'm getting too cynical for my own good. Or for anybody's good."

They moved from the dining room through the kitchen, which was an immense area, to the laundry room and first-floor bathroom.

Bonnie said, "When Jeff finishes the one off the bedroom, you'll have three baths in this house!"

Alyssa groaned. "Three toilets to clean. Three toilets for two people. It's a little nutty. Jeff says the baths increase the value of the house, but I think the inconvenience of one bathroom for seven people when he was growing up affected his brain."

They walked back into the kitchen which, Alyssa explained, was in dire need of remodeling, but would have to be the last project because of the expense. "We want to gut it and start all over again, just like the other rooms, but cabinets and appliances up the cost beyond what we can afford right now."

"It doesn't really look that bad now," Bonnie said. "You've got counter space too. I didn't have any at all in my old apartment. That's one of the things I'm enjoying now. Actually there's nothing I'm not enjoying in my new apartment. Have I thanked you for sending me there yet?"

"Forty or fifty times. How about some coffee before we start?"

"I'd love it, I was just rolling out of bed when you called."

Alyssa poured the coffee into huge ceramic mugs and arranged sweet rolls on a plate; she rarely served coffee without accompaniment, even if it meant pulling out the crackers and butter. She sat across from Bonnie at the oak table and continued to explain what she had in mind for her dream kitchen: cherry cabinets, an open brick archway, cherry beams, ceramic tile, embossed Formica, a huge island in the middle of the room with a stovetop and barbecue pit, sliding glass doors which would one day lead out to a patio, and lots of curves. "I want a round island and Jeff keeps telling me I want a hexagon. So I say no, round. And he goes nuts because wood doesn't bend too easily. Neither does Formica. He had a hell of a time curving that countertop you're enjoying. But he'll do it. By the time we're ready to do the kitchen, he'll figure out a way. He always does."

"Mrs. King adores him. And you. She talks about the two of you all the time. I make a point of seeing her almost every day. Isn't that odd? I know she doesn't need a keeper, but I feel better when I know she's okay."

"We got pretty close to her too. She's easy to love. I wouldn't mind living a long life if I could be as active and healthy as she is. She quote any Shakespeare for you yet?"

"How sharper than a serpent's tooth -"

"Oh, Lear. Of course. She identifies with Lear, you know."

"I got that impression. Did I tell you she was quarreling with her son the day I met her? I didn't know it was her son until she told me. What did she say ... something about a black heart."

"Oh sure, she always described him that way. And her daughter is worse. You won't see her until Christmas, she shows up once a year to torture the poor soul. But the son appears once a month; he's a real persistent devil."

"He looks so dignified. And he is handsome."

"Don't ever tell Mrs. King that. She told me once that he looks just like his father and I think that pains her deeply because his disposition is so ugly. He reminds her of Alex, has the same name as his father, but he's not at all like him."

"He must have been quite a man. Those windows leave me breathless every time I look at them. Sometimes I feel as if I'm living in a church."

"Or a shrine? That's what it is, you know, a shrine. Alex's workshop was in the attic and he built the house to accommodate the stained glass he finished but couldn't part with."

"There was a lot of it."

"Mrs. King always said if she hadn't stopped him, he would have started knocking holes in the house to accommodate more windows."

"She told me that. She must have been so proud of what he could create, though."

"Oh, she was. And is. That's why she fights with her son once a month. He thinks she should sell the house. Actually he's after those windows. They're worth a fortune, a large fortune. He's had a buyer for years, and that's usually the hard part in such things, finding a buyer willing to pay the price. But the old girl won't give in and there's no hope of declaring her incompetent to handle her own affairs. She's no Auntie Mame."

"I guess not. She's sharper than I am. Did you know her volunteer work three days a week is at the old folks' home?"

Alyssa laughed. "Did she tell you that those old people need some excitement in their lives?"

"Not yet. God, she's wonderful!"

"She's also a foster grandparent. I think that's because her rotten kids have rotten kids."

"She has grandchildren?"

"Four. And a few great-grandchildren. I don't know how many."

"How sad that is. She has family and she doesn't have family. Just like me."

"You going home for Thanksgiving?"

"No. I think I've finally resigned myself to the fact that I'm home when I'm here."

"Are you sure you'll be happy if you sever all ties, Bonnie? Life can be awfully lonely without any family at all. I know what you go through when you go home, but staying here alone might be worse."

"I think Mrs. King might adopt me, seeing that you and Jeff aren't interested."

"You two are good for each other."

"Seriously, Matt, I think it's about time I tell you because I have to tell somebody and you're the only person I trust enough." She hesitated. "You know already, don't you?"

"No! I don't know a thing! But I have to admit I've been wondering ever since you expressed a desire to learn how to make pie crust. I learned how to make pie crust for Jeff. Most men love pies. Most women wouldn't bother if it weren't for a man. So I figured you found your other half. When's the wedding?"

"Oh, you're insufferable! I've wanted to tell you for so long! The wedding's the day after school is out. Maybe the last day of school. We just hand out report cards that day, right?"

"If you can hardly wait, why not during Christmas vacation, or Easter? That would give you a few days to honeymoon. Or you could extend a weekend by taking your three personal days; of course, then you'd have to lie. I'm sure a honeymoon would be construed as recreation."

"What the hell is it about personal days? I've never taken any and I remember Lainie moaning over something or other last year."

"We can't take personal days for recreation or vacation purposes, it's bad for our image; the Board is suddenly very concerned about instructional time when it comes to our personal days. It's all right, though, when half my classes are out for 'family reasons' and I can't do anything worthwhile, or when they schedule those useless in-service days. The district doesn't grant any personal days directly before or after vacation periods on the assumption that we're extending vacation time. Joe Axelrod had a hell of a time getting a personal day the year his son graduated from college. The festivities coincided with Memorial Day weekend and they wouldn't give him Friday off because we were off the following Monday. Well, he didn't need Monday; he ended up leaving town after school and driving all night so he wouldn't miss the Saturday ceremonies.

"Lainie scheduled a trip to Hawaii last year during Easter vacation. We were supposed to be off Holy Thursday and Good Friday, remember? But we had to go to school those two days to make up snow days. I was out sick on Friday and got a phone call to verify the illness; I was waiting for them to ask for a note from my doctor, which I could have produced because I saw him that week, but wouldn't have. I would have grieved that one. They have no right to intimidate us that way. But I guess they have the right to do it in other ways; Lainie's plane left without her Thursday afternoon."

"They wouldn't give her the two days? Not even as personal leave? I can't believe I didn't know all that was going on."

"I can; I worked with my head in the sand for a lot of years. Lainie couldn't even get the time off without pay. She figured that losing two days' pay was cheaper than losing her trip. The trip was already paid for."

"You're kidding. She lost all that money?"

"You can't get your money back a week before the plane leaves. Prices for those excursions are based on the number of people going. She lost everything; it was that or lose her job. And she wasn't the only one. A lot of people who had trips planned were bitching."

"Well, in a way I can understand the district's viewpoint. Too many people taking off early can cost a fortune in subs and it's not the district's fault if we go over our snow day quota. But why wouldn't they let her go without pay? They'd make money that way; subs are paid peanuts. And the kids don't suffer any on days like that; we go berserk, but the kids have a grand old time, the ones that show up, that is. What could they have done to Lainie if she had just gone?"

"Nailed her to the cross. They can charge you with insubordination. You can be suspended or fired, pending a hearing which must be a real delight to go through. And, of course, you'd have to worry about what kind of schedule they'd slap you with for the next fifty years if you managed to win your case and keep your job. But it's nothing new; last year wasn't the first time it happened. It's happened before in a variety of ways."

"I remember how furious Jason used to get over union stuff when we were dating; he used to say 'intimidation' a lot."

"Intimidation and harassment; they're good at both. Ever since the Taylor Law. Jeff has done some work for his trade union and I've learned a little about how it works; the company and the union are adversaries, and they're at constant war. It's too bad, really. The Taylor Law forced us into collective bargaining and there are certain ailments that go along with it. Not that I'm complaining about the union. Can you imagine where we'd be without it, considering where we are with it?"

"Oh, sure. Eight classes and coaching after school."

"My pay has tripled since I started teaching and it never would have if it weren't for the union; my first day the starting salary was six thousand dollars. We'd be right back to that today if it weren't for the union. I could strangle them for getting us five classes, but that's the nature of negotiations, give and take. If they can only get us something to relieve the workload this contract, I'll be happy." Alyssa rose to pour more coffee. "So don't take personal days to get married because somebody will equate marriage with recreation!"

Bonnie laughed. "No chance. We can't do it during vacation, either. He's still in school."

"It has to be June, then. Is he in a college nearby? Graduate work? Most colleges are out in May -"

Bonnie moved her coffee mug for the refill. "Not college, Matt. He's not in college yet. He's a senior at BCA."

Alyssa poured with a steady hand. "Anybody I know?"

"Michael Ixion?"

A thought flashed in Alyssa's mind, something out of literature, mythology. What? "No, I don't think so. Not familiar at all."

"You'll meet him next semester. He's taking your course. I thought he should know how to write a research paper before he gets to college, and the Shakespeare will be good background. I told him he'll have an English requirement regardless of his major. I also told him to plan on typing his own papers even though he'll have a convenient proofreader!" She had been talking very quickly, as if the world were about to end and she needed to finish before it did. Then she took a breath and slowed her pace. "We met last summer at the mall. I had no idea he was in high school and he didn't know I was a teacher. He looks older than eighteen and I'd like to think I look younger than I am."

"What difference does it make?"

"None, really."

"Do you feel an age difference when you're with him?"

"Not at all. He makes better conversation than some of the college graduates I've dated. And I don't mean Jason. Jason is too much in love with himself and his bachelorhood; he's a damn nice guy, but I always felt he was parading me around as his latest conquest. Michael is the kind of man a woman marries."

"So you think of him as a man, not as a kid, not as a senior in high school?"

"From the minute we met. He threw me right into shock when he told me we worked in the same place, then proceeded to say he was a student. I went through an instant of disbelief, but only an instant.

The more I saw of him, the more I wanted to see him. I couldn't bear the thought of not seeing him again."

"I think that's called love. Age means nothing, especially if it means nothing to you and to him. But one thing's for sure. You have to wait until June."

"I get very nervous, you know. I don't want to be accused of seducing students. Weirder things have happened."

"They sure have. Just keep a low profile."

"Been trying to. We don't even speak in school. I don't want to jeopardize my job; I'll have to keep us going while he's in college. That's another reason why I'm not going home anymore. My father hasn't spoken to me in ten years, but I think he'd break the silence to tell me what a fool he thinks I am. I'm not up for that. I'm too happy right now to listen to his venom."

"Ten years? That's insane. I'd be so proud if you were my daughter. Have I ever told you how much I admire you? I've always admired your independence. It takes a lot of courage to do what you've done with your life. And you've done it alone. I've always had somebody looking out for me, my parents, then Jeff."

"I went against my father's wishes. I broke his law; he'll never forgive me for that. Nobody crosses him without paying for it. That's the way he is; he'll never change."

"It's too bad. Mostly for him. He's missing out."

"That's what I tell myself. But it still hurts."

"Of course it hurts. How could it not hurt? You're getting married and you can't share your happiness with your family? That's got to hurt. How does Michael feel about it?"

"It's hard for him to understand. His father is dead. He misses his father who's dead and I haven't got a father who's alive. That's the way it goes sometimes, I guess. Someday I'll take him to meet my mother, someday far away. In the meantime I'm a nervous wreck because I haven't met his mother yet."

"You haven't? Lord, I hope she doesn't give you a hard time. Mothers are very stingy with their sons under normal circumstances. Not that this isn't normal, that's not-"

"No, no, don't apologize. You're right. The woman lost her husband and Michael's been the man in the house ever since. He's her only son and has been an immense help to her and his sister. Why do you think I'm nervous?' Even if you disregard everything else, how would you feel if your son came home and told you he plans to marry an older woman the day after he graduates from high school?"

"I think I'd go right into orbit."

"So would I. And the woman went through hell when her husband died, she had to go through therapy to get over it. Michael says she's stable now, but how will she react to the news that I'm taking her only son away?"

Alyssa cringed. "Violently?"

"I hope not."

"I'm only kidding, Bon. He's not dying, he's getting married."

"Some mothers equate the two."

"That's true. Well, the only way to find out how she'll react is to tell her. What will you do if she's opposed?"

"Get married anyway. Neither one of us wants to do that, but what choice do we have? We can't wait four years for him to get out of college. That's definitely out. We decided that we'll go out of state if she won't sign for him."

"Sign for what?"

"Marriage license. Doesn't a parent have to sign if you're under age?"

"Isn't legal age eighteen in New York now? Check that out, I'm pretty sure it is."

"God, how I wish I was twenty again."

"I hate to ruin your theory, but what would that make Michael?"

"Before puberty. I guess that wouldn't work at all, would it? We have to deal with what is, I'm afraid. That's why I invited them all for Thanksgiving dinner."

"You did what? Without meeting her first? You've got more balls than the Yankees, Mason."

"Well, I didn't actually do it myself. Michael told her he's taking her out for dinner and she's expecting a restaurant. But he's going to take her to my place."

Alyssa shook her head slowly. "You're crazy. What if 'surprise-surprise' backfires?"

"Then we all have a lousy Thanksgiving. How else are we supposed to do it? I want to meet her anyway; she should see me. It would be worse if Michael tells her and she imagines an old dowdy type. Don't you think so? At least I'll be able to stuff a turkey leg in her mouth if she gets nasty. That's another thing I'm worried about. The turkey. I can't serve it raw, can I?"

"You've never cooked a turkey."

"Why would I cook a turkey for myself?"

"Oh, Christ, Bonnie. Couldn't you have invited her for toast and Jell-O?"

"Don't panic, there's a few days left. Don't you just drop it in a pan and shove it in the oven?"

"If it's frozen it takes two or three days to thaw, for one thing. And what are you planning to stuff it with?"

"A loaf of bread? Don't worry, I'll remove the wrapping."

"I'll give you a recipe before you go. I don't believe you've taken this on. We don't even have Wednesday off this year."

"I'm calling in. I haven't been out one day yet. As long as they're so sure we're abusing our sick leave, we'd might as well do it. There won't be enough kids to speak of anyway."

"People travel on Wednesday; it doesn't bother them to pull their kids out of school. I've had four kids tell me they won't be here because of 'family reasons.' One's going to be out the entire week after Thanksgiving so I had to write up her assignments last week."

"We have to do that?"

"You bet. If a kid requests assignments, we're required to supply them. You've never refused, have you? You could get your ass in a sling by refusing."

"I did once. The kid was spending the entire month of May in Europe with his parents. I didn't see why I had to do all that work because the kid was going on vacation."

"That has nothing to do with it. I know it stinks, but that's the way it is. The fact that we're required to supply work to truants aggravates me even more. Some kids wouldn't cut class if they knew they couldn't make up the work. Don't refuse to give assignments, Bonnie. Do it during class if you have to, but don't refuse."

"Is that a corollary to 'Never leave a class alone'?"

"I suppose so. Can you imagine the uproar if a kid ever hurt himself while he's supposed to be under your supervision? I never sleep well the night before the first day of school; I used to think it was excitement. I've come to realize that it's something else. Will this be the year some kid puts his fist through a window in my room and bleeds to death on the way to the hospital? Will this be the year some parent takes me to court? So far I've been lucky, but will this be the year … ? You know what? I wish we could get together just once without talking about school."

"Is Wednesday a good time to make pies?"

"The best. Then they're fresh. What kind do you want to make?"

"Apple, lemon meringue, chocolate cream, pumpkin, mincemeat, and blueberry. Do you think that will be enough? Maybe a banana cream, too, I love banana cream."

"Oh my God, you are crazy! You don't know how to make pie crust yet!"

Bonnie attempted to keep a straight face. "I'm trying to make a good impression, Alyssa. I want her to know that Michael will not starve to death once he leaves her house."

"Okay, chef-of-the-year. I've got lots of recipes you can take. But first the pie crust. And you're lucky you came to me. This oil crust is relatively easy."

"Who the hell else would I ask? Who else would take the news that I'm marrying a student so graciously?"

"Grace has nothing to do with it. I know you too well. Your head's been together for a long time. If you love somebody enough to marry him, it doesn't matter if he's ten, twenty-five, or fifty!"

"I hope his mother sees it that way. God, I'm a nervous wreck over meeting her. Turkey or no turkey."

"It'll work out all right."

"I hope so. I sincerely hope so."

Alyssa opened a drawer and pulled out a rolling pin. "Pie crust!" she said, waving the rolling pin in the air. Then she proceeded to give instruction as she worked through the recipe that was stamped on her brain.

"You put two cups of flour and one-half teaspoon of salt in a medium-sized bowl, mix it up and spread it out, don't leave it in a mound in the middle. Then you pour one-half cup of oil into a glass measure and one-fourth cup plus two tablespoons of milk into another small container. That's all your ingredients: a bowl of flour and salt, a cup with oil, and a cup with milk. Now you mix. And this is the tricky part. It's tricky because it's so easy. You cannot work this dough or it will be hard as a rock. This is what you do.

Quickly pour the milk into the oil and then the milk and oil into the flour. Do it fast, do not wait to pass go, do not collect two hundred dollars. If you stop and stare, the milk and oil will separate because milk and oil do not mix. You don't want the milk and oil to separate or even to have words. Watch while I do it and stop thinking of The Galloping Gourmet. See? Fluid motion. Did you notice that I sort of spread the liquid around in the bowl as I poured? Don't plop it in the middle. Now, very quickly use a fork to wet the ingredients until the mix holds together. It takes a few revolutions with the fork. See how it looks? Now throw the fork away and use your hand. Do not mix, mash, punch, knead, or otherwise assault the dough. Do not work it at all. Just take your little hand and push the dough together to form a ball in the middle of the bowl. You can turn it over if you need to, but do it with gentle swirling motions. See what I'm doing? Julia Child, eat your heart out. Now the dough is together and there's some flour left in the bowl. Forget the flour. Richard Simmons says, *Empty, empty calories*. It will never mix in now anyway. Sometimes when I make this, I clean the bowl right up, all the flour comes off the sides. That's ideal. But I used skim milk today. The recipe works best with whole milk. But you can use it with almost anything that's liquid and white, except, of course, milk of magnesia. I'm always out of milk and I often use evaporated; you know, out of a can. The recipe still works. Now. Take this ball, put it on the counter, cut it in half, and push the two halves into two balls. Look at the inside of that. It's beautiful. Nice and moist."

"Oh, yeah," Bonnie said. "Looks good."

"What the hell do you know? But believe me, this beats the shortening method. My mother used to cut the flour with the shortening for a few days before she got the right consistency. This takes about three minutes. But it still takes experience, Bonnie. You can't master anything without doing it. I must have made twenty two-crust pies before I got the top crust on right. I'm not trying to discourage you. Just the opposite. You've got to keep at it. Now's the fun part, and I am being facetious."

"The rolling pin?"

"Right. This is what it's for besides chasing your husband around the house. You have to roll this dough between wax paper. It's too moist and pliable to roll anywhere else, you'll never be able to pick it up. So you put a ball between two sheets, like this. Flatten the ball with your hand, then roll with the rolling pin out from the middle. Then roll in arcs until you get the dough as large as you need for your pie plate. Remember that it has to be round, or as round as you can get it. You're also supposed to roll the edges slightly thicker. I've done this for years and I still screw up now and then. But you'll find that this dough can take almost anything. It's flakier than a shortening crust in spite of what all the commercials say. Okay, now we've got a circle in between the wax paper. Now we've got to get it off the paper and on the pie plate. Watch carefully. This isn't magic, but there is some sleight of hand involved."

Bonnie watched as Alyssa peeled the top piece of paper away, then turned it sideways over the dough, covering half of it. Then she folded the bottom paper, with the crust still firmly adhered, over the top piece. Then she peeled half the bottom piece off the dough, flipped the dough onto one hand, and peeled the bottom piece of paper all the way off. She was left holding the folded dough in her right hand. Then she grasped the corner of the paper where the dough was folded over with the thumb and one finger of her left hand, released her right hand and moved it to grasp the other corner. And there was the dough, folded neatly in half over one piece of wax paper, the paper held in the air by Alyssa's fingers.

"Now you position half the dough over half the pie plate, loosen it so it will drop from the paper, then flip the other half over. If it tears, it mends beautifully. Just push it with your finger. And you can lay on a top crust the same way."

"You make it look so easy, the way you flip it around!"

"I was afraid of that. It is and it isn't. Be prepared for anything. If the dough is extra moist, you might have trouble getting it off the paper; if it's a little dry, it'll start peeling before you're ready for it to come off. There are a million things that can go wrong and they've all happened to me at least once. But there's one thing about this dough, it always bakes right and it's mendable. I had a top crust come off the paper too soon once and wrinkle on me. If that happens, you've got a problem. The dough tears if you pull on it. But if it doesn't tear too much, you can mend it or make strips. Or you can forget the top crust altogether and rub some flour, sugar, and butter together to make a crumb crust. If you want to learn to cook and bake, you have to learn to be resourceful. And remember that I've been handling this dough for ten years. I should be able to flip it around. I think I got good with it the day I stopped being afraid of it. You just have to keep doing it, even after you fail. At least this isn't too expensive to throw out if it turns out really bad. Come to think of it, that happened to me once. I must have mismeasured the liquids because I had soup. So I threw it out and started over. But some recipes are so expensive to make and/or so time-consuming that it hurts when you fail."

"I've got a lot to learn, haven't i?"

"Ninety percent of the battle is wanting to. And ten percent is keeping at it. I would suggest, though, that you limit yourself to two or three pies the first time around. Unless you have incredibly good luck."

"I plan to."

"That's the spirit; you're on your way to domestication. I've got recipes for all kinds of pies. I perfected a pineapple and I tried peach once. It was terrific. I'll try to fill you in on the pitfalls. No use you making mistakes that I've made and can warn you about. There are tricks to meringue and if you're serious about apple for Thursday, you'll have to use my recipe. It calls for white and brown sugar and plenty of cinnamon. If you use tart apples it'll be tastier than any apple pie you've ever eaten!"

"Okay, but I think I'd better make a menu and stick to it for Thursday. I never thought it could be this complicated to cook. My needs have been simple enough until now."

"It does depend on what you're cooking and if you're interested in learning more. It takes years to build up your repertoire. You can spend a lifetime learning how to cook and bake. Experience. Nothing like it. Once you get past next Thursday, you can look through my recipe files. There's thirty different kinds of cookies for Christmas, egg bread and candy for Easter, and piles of Italian goodies. Have you ever eaten a cannoli or tasted sausage bread? You don't know what you're missing. I also have the best no-crust cheesecake recipe on earth that calls for ricotta."

"That's Italian cottage cheese, isn't it?"

"I suppose you could describe it that way, though my grandmothers would be highly insulted."

"Are you Italian, Matt?"

"Very. Haven't you noticed my passionate nature? My maiden name is Grispelli. That's as Italian as Italy."

"But you didn't marry one. Aren't Italians as fussy as Jews about that?"

"Watch it, Mason, your WASP is showing."

"Wasn't that a legitimate question?"

"Unfortunately, yes. They used to be, and some still are. But my parents were more concerned over the kind of person I married rather than where his great-grandfather happened to be born. Of course, Jeff's mother is Italian and he used to sing 'I want a girl just like the girl-' to my mother every chance he got. I think she fell in love with him before I did. You know, it's funny, now that I think of it. When I went to college more than one person told my parents they were crazy to send a girl to school. You know, that old attitude that an education is wasted on a girl because she'll only get married anyway? And it wasn't that long ago - what? fifteen, sixteen years? Well, of course you know, don't you?"

"Sounds to me like they knew my father."

"I had a student a few years ago who was fighting her parents because they wouldn't let her out of the house to go to college. She was really bright and I felt just terrible about it, but I couldn't very well advise her to leave home. As it turned out, they agreed to let her commute to ACC."

"Adirondack? They didn't mind that she had to drive all that way?"

"As long as she was home nights, they didn't care. It was a shame because the girl was Harvard material; she used to come up with insights that floored me. But at least she got her foot in the door somewhere. I never heard from her again, so I don't know what happened to her."

"So my father isn't the only nut on the face of the earth, is he?"

"And Italian girls tend to be very family-oriented. She told me she couldn't possibly cross her father. To tell you the truth, I never would have crossed my parents either. Then again, they were never unreasonable. Had they tried they wouldn't have stopped me from marrying Jeff, that's for sure. Anyway, don't call ricotta 'cottage cheese' in front of an old-fashioned Italian lady, she might try to scratch your eyes out. And finish off that roll, would you? Jeff normally eats them six at a time, but he's trying to diet now so he can pig out for the holidays. If it's around, he'll eat it. Poor guy, between his mother and me he hasn't got a chance. It's a good thing he works hard or he'd weigh three hundred pounds."

Bonnie broke open the last roll. "I thought you'd never ask. These are really good. I inhaled the first one."

"I'll give you that recipe too. It's a yeast dough and you'll have to learn how to knead the right way. You have to develop a feel for it."

"You made these? I was about to ask where I could buy some. Where in hell do you find the time to do all this stuff?"

"Those I made over the summer and froze. I do that a lot. As far as finding the time, I used to be able to work in the kitchen half asleep. But it's getting harder. Maybe I'm getting old. I don't do needlework or crochet anymore, I haven't tackled any woodwork in two years. Maybe it's this anemia thing, I don't know."

Bonnie munched while Alyssa put on more coffee. When Alyssa sat again, Bonnie said, "I've been meaning to ask you something about Alex King's windows. Well, not all the windows, but the big one. I know she's Joan of Arc, but she looks like she's in armor in the middle of the fire. I haven't wanted to ask Mrs. King because I'm afraid she'll get upset if she has to dig up too much of the past. Why did he portray her that way? Her head is bare, and her hands are holding a cross, but she's not wearing clothing. I'm sure she wasn't allowed the protection of armor. Wouldn't it have heated up and roasted her anyway? It doesn't make sense."

"No, it doesn't. Not when you're looking for sense. You can't equate logic with art sometimes; logic had nothing to do with that window. It was a direct projection of the heart."

"Mrs. King did tell me that it was commissioned by somebody in France, but Alex stalled for time and made another window."

"Did she tell you the second window was a Madonna? A Madonna was safer, acceptable without question. Did you know he was native French?"

"No. King?"

"Le Roi. When he came to this country, immigration wanted to change it to Leroy. Obviously they didn't know any French, but he knew English, so he insisted on King. Leroy didn't appeal to his sense of aesthetics at all. He worked in New York City at a glasshouse for twenty years, making and installing plain window glass; the stained glass was always on the side. It was his first love and, from what Mrs. King told me, he learned the craft in France. He came to this country for the same reason immigrants have been coming for centuries: it was the land of opportunity. He thought he could have made a living with stained glass, but was disappointed. Louis Comfort Tiffany had a corner on the market; Alex was small potatoes. He took a job to live and dabbled with stained glass, selling a piece occasionally.

"When he and Dorothea married, he had quite a nest egg stashed away because he had worked for twenty years and spent little on himself. I can't help but equate him with Silas Marner at that point of his life. He must have been very lonely; Dorothea was his Eppie. She encouraged him to leave the job in New York and move upstate where, as she puts it, 'they'd have room to breathe.' That was in 1920 or thereabouts. She knew he was an artist more than a laborer, so she encouraged him to create. When the nest egg was gone, he went back to taking jobs in building construction to keep food on the table, but he never stopped making his glass and his windows."

"She told me he was a master of all trades."

"He was. He did a lot of work on the older homes in this town. If you look around, you'll see his windows here and there too. It must be quite a feeling to see pieces of yourself dotting the landscape, and to know that they'll be there after you're gone. By the time the Depression hit, they had two kids and Alex was in his fifties. By that time he had built the house and used to retreat to his studio to find solace in his craft. Mrs. King told me that she caught him up there once crying, but he quickly dried his tears and told her not to be afraid, that they would survive, that somehow he would find work. It must have been a living hell for a lot of people during the

Depression." She got up to pour more coffee. "I haven't answered your question yet, have I? I don't usually teach this way, I hope."

"No, no. Go on."

"Mrs. King told me all this in bits and pieces over eight years. It is fascinating, isn't it? The past usually is, people are. We all have our antecedents."

"You mean 'roots' don't you? I doubt if Alex Haley would have called his book *Antecedents* or *Predecessors*."

"Now your English Teacher is showing. Anyway, the Kings made it through the Depression and then Alex enjoyed a brief period of success. He made and sold more windows than ever before mostly because of family connections in France. He invested wisely and when he died he left his widow enough to keep her comfortable, apparently, for many years. He left nothing to the kids because he felt his first duty was to his wife. She had struggled with him all those years and the kids hadn't contributed anything to what they'd accumulated. Not that the kids were suffering any. Both were put through college, both had homes and families and were totally independent when Alex died. But that was when they turned ugly. I guess they thought he owed them more. They tried to contest the will, but got nowhere."

"Why do people think their parents owe them forever? I've got cousins who think that way. They've been milking their parents for years. My aunt and uncle are finally at the point in life when they should be enjoying themselves, but they're still supporting their kids who are married with kids of their own. And my lovely cousins are already fighting over who gets what when mom and dad kick the bucket. They have a fit if my aunt and uncle spend any money on themselves because it depletes what they've got in their will. The last time I was home I told my aunt to spend every penny she has and to have a good time doing it."

"Did your cousins run you out of town?"

"They wanted to; I had visions of tar and feathers. One of them told me to mind my own business, I was just jealous because my father disowned me and I wasn't getting anything anyway. What can you say to people like that?"

"Not much that matters. I believe that parents are obligated to their children only up to a point, then the children are obligated to return the favor. There's so much said about parents who won't let their children go, but what about children who won't release their parents from bondage? Shouldn't people get a break after raising a family? If they're lucky enough to be able to enjoy each other's company after the kids are gone."

"Michael's mother will never get the chance."

"That's what I mean. I used to get very aggravated every time Mrs. King was hurt by her son and daughter. There's an old Italian saying, I don't know it in Italian, but my mother always translated it this way: Watch out when you spit in the air because it just might hit you in the face on the way down. She always said it when she heard people with kids criticizing other peoples' kids. I think it applies to situations like Mrs. King's too. Sooner or later your own kids will treat you the way you treat your parents. Though I can't figure out what model those two took after. Mrs. King told me she first realized they were after everything when they tried to contest the will. They never would have dared if she had died first, and were shocked when she fought them. After she won she got the distinct impression that they were more than anxious for her to drop dead while the bank book was still fat.

"She told me that though she would have enjoyed seeing the world, she lost her taste for travel after Alex died; she said, and I'll never forget the barren look on her face or the flatness in her voice, she said that the Sistine Chapel and the Pyramids and the Arc de Triomphe ceased to exist, that she was blind and numb without him. I can understand what she meant. I'd stare at a picture of Michaelangelo's *David* before I'd travel to see the real thing without Jeff. Some marriages are like that. Maybe it's not healthy, I don't know. At any rate, Mrs. King didn't spend any money on trips, but when she realized what her kids were up to, she vowed to spend it in other ways. She's constantly pouring money into that house, remodeling and refurnishing; when we lived there, I started to wonder who was nuttier with the projects, she or Jeff. And believe you me, we got daggers from those two goldbricks; I'm sure they thought we were trying to weasel our way into the will. Now they'll be shooting dirty looks at you. Italians call it The Evil Eye."

"Just what I need. But you seem to have survived it and you're Italian!"

"You're right. You'd have to be Italian to appreciate The Evil Eye. I've tried for years and I don't even understand it."

"What do you mean? Isn't it some kind of curse?"

"Oh, sure, but it's- well, never mind, it's too complicated. I told you, I don't understand it myself. Where was I in the saga of Mrs. King?"

"The house ... remodeling ... projects ..."

"Ah, yes. Projects. As you know, we accomplished a great deal while we were there. She bought materials, we did the work; Jeff always says he served an apprenticeship there. When we bought this house he knew how to work on anything. And I was well-versed in how to live through the mess of remodeling. I think the worst of it, next to the months it took to finish the kitchen, was the time he broke through the roof for those skylights. I worried like hell that the sky would open up and pour buckets into my new kitchen or on my new bedspread, but Mrs. King was hopping up and down with nary a care. Those skylights excited her more than anything else we did. She used to wait for Jeff to get home from work so she could check on his progress. She'd catch him before he got to the door and ask because she'd never visit uninvited. In all those eight years she never knocked on the door. I used to have to call her and I did often, especially when we were remodeling."

"Didn't you come up with the idea for the skylights? I'm sure she told me you did because you thought the apartment needed more natural light."

"The old devil. Is that what she told you? I did say something once about the place being dark during the day, but I can't take credit for the skylights. She's the one who hunted through *House Beautiful* and *Popular Mechanics* for an answer to the problem. She came up with the skylight idea and then she and Jeff figured out how it could be done; every time they embarked on a new project they were like partners in crime. And I think she liked that particular effort because it was, in a way, similar to what Alex used to do; you know, knocking holes in the house and filling the holes with glass. Only he wasn't as crude as that. Have you looked closely at the images in the smaller windows? Some of them, like the ones around the front door, aren't particularly noteworthy, as far as the pictures go; all of them are exquisite examples of the art, to be sure, but some reveal depth of composition as well as simple accomplishment."

"Simple? Like making pies?"

"No, I don't mean simple as in easy, but simple as in pure. I think what I'm trying to say, and I'm botching it well, is that Alex King blended art with craftsmanship, he was artist and craftsman, and when that coalition is made, man glorifies his existence. There was something in Alex King the artist that forbade Alex King the craftsman from dealing in evil. Not a one of those windows depicts baseness, all are joyous interpretations of life. He thought Hieronymus Bosch was a madman. And he didn't restrict himself to religious themes either."

"The children playing in the field of flowers, the knight on his charger, the unicorn, the swans ... I have noticed secular subjects."

"And the Biblical ones were carefully chosen: the Resurrection, David in triumph over Goliath, Lazarus, the Holy Spirit over the head of John the Baptist. Alex King didn't have the stomach to deal with the Crucifixion. And that, to answer the question you asked eight hours ago, that is why Joan is in armor."

"He couldn't bear the thought of leaving her unprotected, in spite of the fact that she was."

"Exactly. Mrs. King told me that he was absolutely incensed the year Joan was canonized. That was 1920. Because, you see, he knew that she was martyred in the name of politics and power. Though attempts were made to fully blame the English for her death, French church authorities initiated her trial and she was convicted because she insisted on the validity of her visions and her visions were not sanctioned by the church. In all its pomposity, the church bureaucracy convicted her of heresy because she dared to claim direct spiritual contact without the required intervention of the church. She also flouted the customs of the times by wearing masculine attire, and it wasn't just any old pair of breeches and boots, she was fond of wearing splendid outfits suitable for knights. Can you imagine how all those men reacted to her audacity? We're having trouble today accepting women in coal mines and factories. She took over an army in the days when a woman was her husband's property."

"I don't suppose they issued a proclamation announcing the appointment of 'The First Woman Knight,' do you? That's what would happen today. At least way-back-when they were honest about their prejudices. We get the first this and the first that, but nothing beyond the tokenism. Some day I want to see a big headline that a woman made it for the second time. Or is that asking too much, am I being ungrateful? At least we aren't getting burned at the stake, not literally anyway."

"When Joan was canonized, Alex King was enraged at the sheer hypocrisy of it all. The church was five hundred years too late in deciding that her visions were legitimate. How could the church proclaim her a Christian martyr after the church had a hand in condemning her? He thought the Protestants should have claimed her."

"I never knew much about Joan, but the way it sounds she was reincarnated during the Sixties."

"I've read a little about her because I was so intrigued by that window. The thought occurred to me once that she was a psycho, but that's too pat, too convenient an assessment that our 'modern' minds indulge in. In spite of all the myth and legend, she was just a young woman taking on a role that was barred to women at the time and she suffered the Medieval consequences. She was defiant, heroic, clever, and articulate. Nobody can figure out when or where she ever learned how to ride a horse, yet she led men in battle. She was a virgin, she didn't even menstruate. She claimed divine inspiration through the voices of St. Margaret, St. Catherine, and the Archangel Michael. She was hell-bent, or I should say heaven-bent, to liberate France from British rule and to restore Charles VII as the legitimate king. And she did it. Then it all fell apart, not France, but her whole existence. It was as if she had served her purpose and was abandoned as no longer useful. The account of her trial wasn't published until sometime in the 1840's. That shed some light on what happened to her, but the myth still overshadows all else. She remains an enigma. She was nineteen years old when she was burned at the stake. Can you imagine that? She was terrified, poor soul. I'm afraid of the fire when I cook on my gas stove, afraid that my hair might swim down into it. Can you imagine being burned alive? Her executioner relented, too late of course, by saying that they should have put her out of her misery by killing her before she suffered too much in the flames. That was a customary procedure, but Joan wasn't so lucky.

"She almost saved herself from the flames, or at least she attempted to. She relented during her trial and promised to refrain from dressing like a man. But she fell back into old habits, excuse the pun, in prison; she also claimed to hear voices again."

Bonnie said: "It's remarkable, isn't it, that her ancient story is so modern? The best defense against a murder charge today is to plead insanity and profess to hearing voices. Maybe someday the church will canonize Son of Sam?"

"You may have something there. Maybe Joan was afflicted with some psychological disorder which was certainly beyond Medieval understanding and not a very useful theory for the church when it was trying to absolve itself from guilt by canonizing her."

"Excuse the underlying distrust of men in this question, but how did she manage to protect her virginity while in prison? Or didn't she?"

"There's a controversial story about that. Joan reportedly complained about being beaten and molested by the guards and there's something about a rape attempt by some English lord. Whether or not he succeeded isn't known."

"Why wouldn't he succeed if she was a prisoner?"

"That's one side of the question. The other is that he deliberately made the attempt to frighten her into making the fatal decision to don masculine attire again. Nobody really knows what happened to her in that prison. Whatever it was, she recanted on all the promises she made to her tormentors. She went so far as to say that she made the promises only out of fear of the fire anyway, and with that flagrant admission condemned herself."

"She came to prefer the flames over the prison, it seems."

"Certainly. Consider the fact that she had a perpetual sentence, no parole. I think I'd take death over being at the infinite mercy of prison guards in a Medieval prison. Is there a more vile and degrading way to force indignity on a woman than through rape? Maybe she wasn't raped, but I find that hard to believe and I'm not apologizing for any undercurrents of thought in that."

"No wonder Alex put her in armor."

"His compassion made him do it, his rage at what atrocities mankind perpetrates and then conveniently forgets or rationalizes. Joan burned before an audience of almost ten thousand people. Ten thousand people showed up in Rouen on May 30, 1431, to enjoy the show. I remember the day because it's our Memorial Day. Can you imagine gathering together family and friends on a beautiful day in May for the sole purpose of watching a woman burn to death?"

"Oh, I don't know, some of them probably planned on dinner afterward at a fashionable inn. It makes me think of Dickens."

"*Tale*? You bet. The blueflies. They paid to see the play at the Old Bailey just as they paid to be entertained at Bedlam. St. Mary's of Bethlehem. Such piety coupled with such despicable human behavior. It's sick commentary on mankind, that people are willing and joyful spectators at trials that promise a verdict of quartering and at insane asylums. Dickens couldn't resist making that point. I wish he were around today, he'd have plenty of material to work with. Anyway, just before Joan died she cried out the name of Jesus; then the flames were allowed to diminish enough to rake back the ashes to display her charred carcass as proof that the heretic was dead. The fire was stoked again to finish off the incineration. The authorities thought they had conducted a nice neat little burning that convinced everyone that she was mortal and she was dead. But it backfired. Somebody saw a dove fly out of the flames at the moment of her death, somebody saw her heart unscorched in the ashes, somebody said it wasn't Joan at all who was burned. It was a time of obsessive superstition and religious fervor to begin with; add that to the natural

403

inclination of people to believe everything they hear, especially if it's sensational, and voila! a myth is born."

"How grotesque. What a horrible way to die. I used to think the guillotine was barbaric, considering the spectacle it supplied during the Revolution, but it was merciful compared to fire."

"I think the worst part of it is that we never learn, mankind doesn't ever stop, man keeps committing the same atrocities. History repeats itself whether we learn and understand history or not. Given some time, man rebuilds his ignorance, his prejudices, his hatreds, and falls right back into barbarism. Think about it: the Inquisition, Salem, Hitler, Khomeini, Khadafi, Idi Amin, not to mention what we small folk do to each other every hour of the day. The Four Horsemen aren't apocalyptic, they're long-term employees of mankind. Unlike other mercenaries, they work for nothing, content to bask in the havoc and misery they engender."

Alyssa stared down into the dregs of her coffee, then continued when she thought of something else. "It's really weird," she said pointedly. Bonnie asked the obvious question and Alyssa reconsidered. "Well, no, it's not really weird, I'm just reacting to the coincidence. There's another fact about Joan that sticks in my mind; she left home without her parents' permission. And there was a conflict with her father; she was afraid he would try to stop her so she left without telling him anything and she defied him by refusing to marry a man he had picked out for her. There's evidence of a breach of promise suit brought against her by the man her father selected. She testified in court that *she* never promised anything. How that must have infuriated her father! She made a fool out of him when arranged marriages were mandatory. Then she rode off to war. You have to admit there's a coincidence entangled in there somewhere."

Bonnie started to laugh. "Oh no you don't. It's bad enough I dream of being stoned."

Alyssa grinned, then sobered. "Well, I'm not suggesting reincarnation, but the parallel is striking. Maybe I should shut up, I forgot about your dreams. God, maybe I've said too much already. I'm sorry."

Bonnie looked exasperated." Alyssa! Don't be ridiculous! My mind isn't that weak. In fact you've piqued my curiosity so much I'm going to stop at the library on the way home."

"Are you sure? Hell, a few days ago I told you to cover the window with a sheet and now I'm filling your head with the gory details."

"Don't worry about my head. It's perfectly all right. I asked you about the armor, remember?"

"You didn't expect an encyclopedic response, I'm sure."

"Believe me, I'm fascinated by it all. I can't wait to tell Michael; he's been staring at that window since I moved in. The colors mesmerize him, and he's moved by her face. It's so human, so real."

"You haven't been there long enough to experience the whole range of effects that light variations have on it."

"There's no effect at all at night."

"That's because the color draws life from light filtering through the glass. Reflected light deadens the colors, refracted light, light which passes through the glass, gives it a vitality, a beauty all its own. And you're in for a surprise. There is occasional luminescence at night. On a clear night with a full moon, the window illuminates, in varying degrees each month, depending upon the position of the moon in the sky. We used to watch and wait, watch and wait, to see just what would happen to it every month. But it's chancy. And speaking of chancy, I should warn you to watch out for the skylight in the bedroom."

"Why?"

"It's wise to leave the lights off when you're in there doing anything that normal people do in a bedroom at night. Like changing for bed."

"Whatever for?"

"Planes."

"Good Lord! I never thought of that!"

"Sometimes they fly low enough ... "

"Okay, okay, I get the picture. It might be handy if I were in the market for a pilot, but I've got all the man I can handle already. That's hilarious, though, an aerial Peeping Tom. My brain must be warped, now I'm seeing a guy holding on to the tail of a kite and floating off into oblivion."

"How about the Goodyear Blimp hovering in anxious expectation?"

When they both stopped laughing, Bonnie asked, "What exactly happens to the window when there's a full moon?"

"You'll believe all the stories about a full moon that you've tossed off as superstitious nonsense. But conditions have to be just right. The sky has to be clear, the moon has to be full and positioned at a certain angle in the sky. It only reaches that angle once a year. Hold on to your hat now. It's in the month of May."

Bonnie's eyes widened. "When she was executed? This is getting creepy. Do I want to know what happens to the window?"

"Jeff and I saw it only once and it astounded us both. Mrs. King has seen it many times and is quite sure that Alex intended the phenomenon. When the moonlight hits that window at just the right angle, the flames appear to be real, dancing tongues of fire that make you want to run for an extinguisher. The only thing missing is the crackling and hissing; Alex wasn't into audio. And, Bon, besides the flames, Joan comes alive. I don't know how to explain it, it's obviously an optical illusion, a *trompe l'oeil*; Mrs. King is convinced that he did it on purpose, that he did something to the glass. I don't know how he could have done it and prearranged the moonlight, but I saw it and Jeff saw it: Joan cries. She cries, Bonnie, we saw the tears running down her face."

"Mrs. King never mentioned any of that to me."

"She never told us either until we started noticing what was happening. Who could miss it in the bedroom?"

"In May, huh?"

"In May. Clear sky, full moon, and Joan burns again. I've never seen anything like it. Either the man was a genius or Mrs. King should be quoting Hamlet along with Lear."

"Which?"

"There are more things in heaven and earth, Horatio, than are dreamt of in your philosophy."

THANKSGIVING 1980

Alyssa was out of school the day before Thanksgiving, but not to bake pies as she too had planned; she called in sick because she was. She woke up with pains flashing through her stomach. She knew her period was due at any time and attributed the pain to that. She knew if she got going the pain would subside to intermittent stabs during the day, then vanish for a few hours, then reassert itself when she started to flow. Most months she'd grin and bear it; some months were worse than others.

But when she woke up that morning, she couldn't even deal with the thought of getting dressed and going to work, much less the activity. She was exhausted and she hurt and when she stood up next to the bed, the room started swirling around her. She was so dizzy she had to sit on the edge of the bed to keep her balance. She told Jeff she didn't feel well, then attempted to get up again. He told her to stay in bed and pulled the afghan up around her shoulders.

She waited fifteen minutes while he shaved, then crawled out from under the covers. "I have to call in!" she explained. "Before seven o'clock!"

He watched her feel her way out of the bedroom and down the stairs. She wasn't getting any better. Sure, the iron pills would take time, but shouldn't she be just a little better by now?

> This is a recording at the Board of Education designed for your convenience in requesting substitute teachers. At the sound of the tone, please leave your name, reason for absence, school, grade or subject taught, and dates of absence. Requests for specific subs cannot always be granted. Please speak at the tone ... now.

"Alyssa Matthews. Illness. BCA. English. Wednesday, November 26. Please tell the sub to follow emergency plans." She hung up the phone and crawled back up the stairs to the bedroom, stopping once to sit on a stair and drop her head between her legs. "We've got to get a phone up here," she told Jeff, then burrowed into bed.

She slept until two in the afternoon. When she woke up, her head was clear, she had her period, but no cramps. She showered and wondered how the sub was doing; the emergency plans were explicit and easily accessible, so she didn't worry much, but in her mind she was altering lesson plans for the following week and making a note to get poetry books for the 2R sections on Monday.

She decided what to fix for dinner, then mixed up some pie crust — two pies were better than none. It was too bad, really, she usually made eight or ten pies for Thanksgiving because she enjoyed giving them away. But not this year.

As the pies baked, she sat at the kitchen table and averaged grades, pleased that she had taken her grade book home the night before. She also had the computer sheets at home so she could bubble in grades and absences and be done before the December 3 deadline. The computer sheets had been late, good thing, or grades would have been due before vacation.

She used a calculator to average grades, a simple one because she only needed to add and divide. She thought calcs were a godsend for the time they saved her every six weeks. Not that she completely trusted her trusty calc; more often than not, Effie checked and rechecked anyway. Her averaging was complicated, it had to be, because she had so many grades.

Seniors didn't pose any problem other than the fact that the course was split into two ten-week sections and grades were issued every six weeks. Paul had turned into a storm cloud when that happened, when the whole school went from five-week marking periods to six-week marking periods right after the department instituted ten-week senior course sections. It simply did not compute. He was sure the maneuver was a plot to harass the department, and indeed it did. Harass and frustrate and anger. How to make two equal parts fit into three equal parts? Easy enough with loaves of bread, but impossible with Shakespeare and the research paper. Alyssa couldn't split two sections into three, no way, no how. She had to give primarily subjective grades for the first report, use the research paper grade as the basis for the second report, and save the Shakespeare grades for the third, which didn't do much to support the theory that the course was half literature and half writing. It wasn't fair, it wasn't fair at all. Two thirds of the final average was based on one half the course, one third was based on the other half. That bothered the hell out of her. But even more, she hated issuing the first grade. It was based on speculation; as much as she tried to make valid assessments, what did she really know as they worked on their papers? How many times she had to look in disgust at a good grade she issued for the first report, a good grade that was obviously a sham because the student's paper failed during the second report. It wasn't fair. It wasn't fair and it was maddening, but she had to live with it.

After she finished moaning and groaning over the discrepancy between first report and second report grades for seniors, she moved on to sophomores which were more complicated because she needed to compute averages for spelling and/or quizzes and/or vocabulary, then use those averages along with other major grades to compute the final average. It was the long way 'round, but the fairest; with sophomores, she could enjoy the luxury of being equitable. She didn't believe a student should fail just because he couldn't spell; on the other hand, a multitude of good spelling grades might raise the average beyond what a student was worth; the only way to give an accurate assessment was to weight the grades accordingly; averages are tricky, but she knew the loopholes and the dangers.

She averaged until Jeff pulled into the driveway, then finished later in the evening. The computer sheets could wait a few days; she had to do those when she was fully alert.

Thanksgiving Day passed with the usual fanfare. She and Jeff moved from house to house all day because everybody always said, "It's easier for you to come to my house, you don't have any kids." And Alyssa enjoyed not having to cook; she felt awfully empty handed all day though, with no pies to give. By late evening she and Jeff were starved, the natural consequence of overeating all day and returning home to find the cupboard bare. It happened every holiday. Alyssa was throwing together an omelet when the phone rang. She had been thinking about Bonnie all day, but hesitated to call her in view of the circumstances. If things went badly, Monday was soon enough to find out. She knew as soon as she heard Bonnie's voice that things had not gone badly, not at all. Bonnie was ecstatic, laughing and crying and rattling on with delirious joy.

"Mrs. Ixion - Mom - she told me to call her Mom, can you imagine? - Mom said that life is too short to waste time on foolish jealousies and petty grievances - those are the words she used, Matt, 'foolish jealousies and petty grievances' - isn't she wonderful? Wonderful and understanding and loving - I love her to pieces, and she loves me, and Michael loves us both, and we both love Michael, and everything is riproaring, screaming beautiful! - and you know what else she said? that she wishes she had met her husband sooner because they would have had more time together - isn't that sad? but true, oh so true, we were all crying there at one point - and she doesn't think it matters one bit that I'm older, she said I look seventeen and Michael looks thirty anyway! Isn't that a riot! and speaking of a riot, I have to tell you what happened to the turkey, the poor old bird hit the floor, I almost died - I guess I didn't get that string on right, you know, the one they give you to get him out of the pan in one piece? well, Michael had him in mid-air and he took a nose dive and landed like a kamikaze, got Michael's shoes full of grease - it was so funny, he had to clean the stuffing off his socks, we roared and it happened at just the right time too, it broke the ice, we were all staring awkwardly at each other up 'til then - Mrs. Ix- Mom bent over and pulled on a leg, the turkey's not Michael's, and when it pulled off easily she said, 'it's cooked, all right, let's eat!' and we all cracked up, then we scraped the rest of it up off the floor - thank God the floor was clean, I scrubbed this place like a maniac! and the pies, oh the pies were a big hit! I did have trouble with the top for the apple and made a crumb crust instead, and the damn blueberry ran all over the oven even though I managed to get the top on that one - what a mess I had! and I had to clean it up before I put the turkey in, you didn't tell me what a mess a blueberry pie can make! but they tasted fantastic! I went down and invited Mrs. King up for pie, she wouldn't come for dinner, I guess she had dinner company herself - God, we ate our hearts out all day! would you believe it, they just left, just now from two o'clock this afternoon? Michael wanted to stay awhile, but I shooshed him out the door, his mother took him by the hand and directed him out - I'm so tired I could sleep for a week, except we're all going shopping tomorrow, Mom, Andrea, Michael, and I - Andrea's my future sister-in-law, she's fourteen and a nicer kid you couldn't meet - she needs help with grammar so I'm going to give her some tutoring - I can't believe we hit it off so well, all of us - we're like a, well, not *like* a family, we *are* a family already! I'm so happy, Matt, so happy! Life is beautiful! I mean, wouldn't you say so if the turkey hits the floor and nobody really gives a damn?"

Bonnie went on and on while the butter browned in the frying pan and Jeff had to take it off the heat, while the eggs started to harden around the edges in the bowl, while Alyssa listened and added one more item to her list of things to be thankful for. Bonnie had become for her an odd compendium of many things: sister, daughter, protegee, colleague, friend. Sharing Bonnie's joy that Thanksgiving night did more for Alyssa's blood than the iron pills she was ingesting every day.

After teasing Bonnie by telling her to "invite them all back tomorrow for the clean-up," she hung up the phone and went back to the omelet. Her thoughts remained with Bonnie, though, and as she deftly folded the omelet in half she reflected on the happiness of her own life with Jeff. Bonnie was just beginning and, judging by her own experience, the best was yet to come. Love equals happiness, she thought. Love equals happiness.

DENIGRATIONS

Monday morning she was sick again. If she weren't at the tail end of her period, she would have thought she was pregnant, that it was morning sickness. Then she started running at both ends and decided that it was some kind of bug, maybe something that started with the dizziness the previous week. She had felt rotten all weekend, looked pale and drawn, but she had slept and she had eaten well. Maybe that was it, maybe she had shocked her system with too much good living; she had even cut down on the cigarettes.

There was no way possible for her to go to school; she had a hard time leaving the bathroom long enough to call in. The tape seemed to take a century as she exercised all the muscle control she could muster up while she waited for the sound of the tone. That call made, she rushed back into the bathroom and prayed for another brief period of control. She had to make one more call. Jeff left for work after strongly suggesting that she contact the doctor.

After she heard the door close behind him, she inched her way back to the phone to call Bonnie. "Tell the sub to use the grammar review sheets in the bottom left-hand drawer of my desk with the sophomore sections, and to give a reading period to the seniors. Also, remind first and fifth periods that they have a lit test tomorrow, and tell third period the test on Acts I and II of *Hamlet* will be Wednesday for sure. I'll be in tomorrow if I have to attach buckets to both ends."

It had to be some 24-hour thing, it had to be. It was no time to have to rely on a sub. Who could come in and pick up in the middle of *Hamlet*? Who could start the poetry unit with the regents sections and begin the vocabulary and grammar units with the scholarship sections? Not only was the possibility of a qualified sub immensely slim, but even an English sub would have a hard time teaching with no books or materials.

Sick or not she had to get in at least to prepare materials for a sub. The test on *Hamlet* was in a desk drawer, but there weren't enough answer sheets; she had planned to run them off today. Act III was too crucial, too complicated to let a sub botch it, the kids would be lost forever, she'd have to reteach it anyway.

She had planned on a writing assignment for the scholarship sections, a sub couldn't get to it in the filing cabinet. They had done

411

so much intense reading (some of them) so far, that she planned a breather: vocabulary and grammar and then *Our Town* the week before Christmas. The writing assignment was a break from literature evaluation, it was more in the line of an essay, they could be creative and personal; it was the kind of assignment some students enjoy. Even if a sub could get to it, nobody else could explain it adequately. She had to do that.

Before Christmas vacation. All of it had to be done before Christmas vacation. It went without saying for the scholarship sections; that curriculum was so packed every day counted. She had to finish *Hamlet* by Christmas in order to fit in *Othello* by the end of the semester. And the narrative poetry unit couldn't extend beyond Christmas vacation, she intended to begin *Tale* right after Christmas with the regents sections. Experience had taught her that those weeks in January and February, between Christmas and the February break, were the best time to teach *Tale*. The regents kids were more prepared second semester, more settled, better able to handle the reading in the heart of winter when most didn't mind being confined to the house. Some teachers taught *Tale* in May and she couldn't even imagine trying that. Even she would have a hard time concentrating!

There was entirely too much she had to do before Christmas vacation, sick or not. It was all in her mind as she dictated plans to Bonnie. A sub could fudge it one more day (how absurd to give seniors a reading period and the grammar review sheets were a good stalling tactic) but that was all. Beyond that, there was nothing a sub could do. That was another point she tried to make once with Jeff. "You're not indispensable!" he said. "Nobody's indispensable! When you're sick, you're sick. Let somebody else take over." It wasn't a matter of being indispensable, not really. If she suddenly dropped dead, someone else could easily take over. The extreme fit the cliché very nicely, thank you. Nobody's indispensable. Of course, who could argue with that? She also stopped trying to make him understand that it wasn't the extreme she had to deal with; it wasn't a matter of "letting" someone take over, either.

He had no idea what she was up against, no conception at all. Once, after they had enjoyed the efforts of a stand-up comedian's nonstop two-hour performance on TV, Jeff expressed amazement at the man's stamina. "How can he go on like that for two hours straight? He never broke his pace! It's amazing!" Alyssa, who had been laughing all along, suddenly became serious and said, "What the hell do you think I do all day? At least he can indulge in one tone of voice, he can concentrate on being humorous. How would you like to do that all day long, keep up the energy and excitement all day every day no matter what you're talking about? I have to make grammar and spelling palatable!"

But she believed in it: teachers are entertainers, frustrated singers, dancers, actors, comedians. She was a little miffed at Jeff's ignorance of that. But how could he know? Why should he care?

She spent most of the morning in the bathroom, sitting on the floor between spells of illness. If she left the room she'd only have to risk not making it back in time.

By that evening the worst of it was over. She felt limp and lifeless, but secure in the knowledge that it must have been a 24-hour flu. She told Jeff she was much better, but reserved the announcement that she fully intended to go to work the next day. "I'll see how I feel in the morning," she said. For one thing, he was not pleased that she hadn't called the doctor, and she knew he expected her to stay home another day.

The next morning she was still weak, but thought she was doing a good job of hiding it from him, until he gave her a sour look and told her she was hopeless. She assured him that she felt better than she looked and was relieved when he left for work. She needed one more run to the bathroom. Then she prayed that she wouldn't have to keep running from classes all day. Maybe it was colitis. Nerves. Nervous people get colitis. No. Couldn't be. Not with the vomiting. Some kind of bug. Virus. 24-hour virus. Calm down. Calm down, it's over now. Get dressed. Brush teeth. Slop some make-up on. Color. Need some color, that's all. Appearance vs. reality. Make do. Make do.

Grade book. For God's sake, don't forget grade book and computer sheets. Grades are due Wednesday. Tomorrow. If it's not 24-hour flu ...

Heavy coat. Heavy, heavy coat. Wind's blowing, whistling around the house. Coat, hat, boots, gloves, scarf. Snowing. Snowing, blowing ... what do you expect? December. Nothing stops nature from doing her thing. Mother Nature. Father Time and Mother Nature. Wonder why.

The car was frigid and she shivered in spite of the heavy coat, hat, boots, gloves, and scarf. The heat would start blasting through just as she turned into the school parking lot, it never failed. Her broom was still on the back seat; it not only pushed away glass, it was mighty handy when the snow piled a foot high on the car. This was going to be one of those days, it seemed. Unless the black sky portended other things.

She should have been home in a warm bed. She thought of that as she pushed her body against the force of the wind while walking into the building. Jeff was right, Jeff was always right, damn him. She had to fight to exercise those few steps from her car to the door of the school. She slipped once on the ice and almost dropped the computer sheets. She had covered them with plastic wrap for protection against the wet, but was afraid the wind might play an urchin's trick and send them flying across the parking lot, so she held on to them tightly, along with her grade book. Some things are irreplaceable, worthy of every precaution; some things you guard with your life.

She was not sick once she checked her mailbox and her desk, but sickened. The mess was vile. She didn't immediately blame the sub, subs try to do their best under difficult circumstances. She didn't blame the sub service, what did they know about any of it? They were concerned with procuring an adult body to inhabit the room in her absence.

Let somebody else do it. Sure. Why not? Somebody else had done it, all right. Somebody else had done it in spades.

The mailbox was jammed with notes and material that meant nothing to a sub, so it all rested dormant and cramped, wrinkled and folded and stuffed in the cubbyhole. Two books were in there usurping space; pulling them out caused an avalanche of paper which she scurried to catch in mid air, then collect off the floor. There was a note sticking out of one of the books; they were Gayle Fine's, she had dropped out of school. Alyssa didn't even consider seeing Hawkens to find out why.

The condition of the mailbox made her wonder what awaited in her room. She dropped off the computer sheets, left them on a desk in the main office, and dreaded the sight of her own desk. Halfway to her room she turned around, ran back to the office to get the computer sheets. It wasn't safe to leave them on a desk, she knew better than that, she had to give them to a person, to a breathing, living being. If they ever disappeared, there would be hell to pay; grades for the entire school would be held up while she waited for new sheets from the computer people, then did all that work all over again. What a stupid thing to do, leave them out in the open like that where they could be picked up so easily.

Brenda was in the office, taking off her coat. Brenda accepted the computer sheets and asked about Alyssa's health. Alyssa said something about "hanging in there" and made a U-turn back to her room. She unlocked the door with a great deal of trepidation.

The sight wasn't that horrific, it wasn't Auschwitz or Biafra or Roswell Park. But it was St. Mary's of Bethlehem, and she was not entertained.

Papers were strewn all over the desk. Drawers had been left open. Homeroom cards were all over the place, some on top of the desk, some orphaned in drawers; excuses were scattered here and there. In a moment of panic, she looked to see if the envelopes were still intact. They were, along with her class folders, thank God. Two different subs had been called. The first one hadn't caught on to the existence of emergency plans. Somehow he had missed the notes she left everywhere, absolutely everywhere — on the schedule sheet he received the first thing in the main office, on a card clipped to the homeroom notebook, on the envelope containing the plans in the top middle drawer of her desk. He must have been blind. And he probably complained to the office that she left no plans for him to follow. Damn. How could he have missed them? Every year she wrote it in big red letters: EMERGENCY PLANS - FOLLOW THESE PLANS ONLY IF NO OTHER PLANS ARE IN MY MAILBOX OR ON TOP OF MY DESK IN 418. The copy of her schedule that he followed gave directions to find the plans: EMERGENCY PLANS ARE IN AN ENVELOPE IN THE TOP MIDDLE DRAWER OF MY DESK IN 418. What was so difficult about that?

Nothing. And that was what he did all day too, then left a note that her classes were unruly. At least he took attendance, but she wondered how accurate that was. Later in the day she was to find out that he sat with his feet up on the desk during classes and told stories about his college days and his love life; the kids would fill her in, they always did. She used to request subs based on her own assessment, but with an ear open to what the kids said.

The second sub was a woman. She didn't bother to report to study hall second period, and she made it necessary for Alyssa to ask who was absent the day before in each of her classes. The second sub followed the emergency plans according to the note she left, and she did announce assignments as Alyssa had dictated them to Bonnie.

Neither sub was any good with homeroom attendance. Straightening out that mess was the first order of business; if she didn't get order restored before homeroom, she'd never be able to take accurate attendance herself. All the excuses for two days, and there was a pile for the day before Thanksgiving, had to be noted on both cards and then filed. She worked quickly to gather up the cards (why hadn't the subs followed the number system? it was so easy to do so, much easier than the mess they worked with, and she left directions); she put them in numerical order, then handled one excuse at a time. She wondered why the large cards weren't clipped in the notebook, there wasn't a reason on God's good green earth why they should have been removed. And she wrote slips as she went along because she anticipated requests from students.

Effie Efficiency had everything under control. Effie was in the saddle. Effie rode again. With a lurch and a leap and a yahoo!

As she worked, a multitude of questions popped into her head. Some cards were marked one way and excuses indicated something else; some cards weren't marked at all, but she found excuses anyway; some cards were marked, but she couldn't find excuses for them. She set aside the real mysteries to wait for the kids; the absence lists obviously couldn't be trusted, and she was having doubts about the sign-in/sign-out sheets. She found one name on one sheet, but no excuse. Maybe the excuse got lost, maybe one of the subs ate it for lunch, maybe it got thrown away, maybe it was hiding out in the piles of paper still tormenting her on the top of the desk.

There were notes to call parents, notes requesting homeroom attendance records, add slips for study hall (some students were adding days because they had passed swimming and didn't have to take it anymore), forms from guidance that had to be filled out by the end of the week, and the homeroom attendance summary that was due Tuesday, December 2, by the end of the day. Today. It must have been put in the mailbox the day before vacation. One more reason to get the homeroom attendance straightened out fast. The summary was for the month of November. State aid was based on the information supplied on the monthly homeroom attendance summary. It had to be accurate — number of full-day absences, number of illegal absences, number of times tardy. For each student in the homeroom during the month of November. Count across the line, note the numbers on the large card for each category. Then do the same on the small card and be sure the numbers are the same; well, shouldn't they be? Shouldn't they be exactly the same? If they're not, you're in a bushel of manure; if they're not, you'd better get cracking and check out the discrepancy. A student can't be absent on the large card and present on the small card at the same time, now can he? Or can he?

She'd have to do it later, take the materials to lunch or use her free period. She had to get those poetry books before seventh period, too, and run off the answer sheets for seniors before tomorrow. While she was in the resource room for the poetry books, she could sign up to take two sets of *Our Town* for the week before Christmas. Finish *Hamlet* with the seniors, vocabulary and grammar with a short writing assignment and *Our Town* with 2S, and narrative poetry with 2R. Before Christmas vacation.

Check on poetry notes, assignment sheets, final test; some poems are typed, not in the book, have to be duplicated. Some of it can wait a couple of days, but not the introductory notes. Need those today. Lunch or free period. Remember to take everything that needs duplication, do it all at once. If the machine is acting up today, I'll scream.

Three weeks. Three little weeks until Christmas. I can make it, it's not that long. Then two weeks, two full weeks to rest, to build up again. It's almost the end of the semester. Half over. I can make it, I have to make it. For *Hamlet*, if for no other reason. For God, King, Country, and *Hamlet*.

When she made the round of offices during sixth period to drop off, pick up, and inquire about, she found a form letter in her mailbox that admonished her for "failing to supply lesson plans as evidenced by the written testimony of a substitute teacher." She was warned against repeating the transgression in the future and reminded of the article in the contract that clearly spelled out the teacher's responsibility to make adequate lesson plans available at all times.

She showed the letter to Jean, then delivered it to Jason Haywood. He took it with a smirk and said that it was just another tactic. When she explained what had really happened, that she intentionally left emergency plans for emergencies, he shrugged and told her not to worry about it.

Jean told her the same thing, only in stronger terms and with examples. "We're damn fortunate that we don't have to hand in detailed plans every Friday for the following week. Some districts require that, with behavioral objectives and copies of all hand-outs. How would you like those apples? I know you didn't deserve to get your hand slapped, but things could be worse as far as plans go. Toughen up, woman! You're the victim of a minor injustice. Just don't think about the devils who never leave plans and never get caught, that's all. Don't think about them, and you'll be fine."

At 3:01 she looked out at her empty classroom and saw two poetry books lying abandoned, one on a desk and one on the floor. Two kids would be complaining about lost books the next day. As she picked up both books, her eyes strayed to a desk top which, like most of the other desks in the room, was covered with graffiti.

The haphazard oeillade was quickly followed by an urge for a closer look, for she saw her name in the midst of the testimony. At the same time, she was momentarily hesitant, afraid to look closer. She remembered when she was in the third grade, the time she wrote the note calling the teacher a mean, rotten old witch, and how the teacher found the note in her desk, and how she cried and cried after school because she was so ashamed; she hadn't meant it.

The desk top was particularly obscene. For how long? Was it that bad during open house? Had a parent sat there? The way it read, the whole place had an oral fixation, between the sucking and blowing and eating ascribed to various individuals, names not withheld in the interests of privacy. No expletives were deleted, either. And the florid text was accompanied by grotesque illustrations drawn by immature, artless hands. Alyssa was sure that the one sketch that dominated the rest through sheer size was not at all what it appeared to be, it definitely was not a thumb.

Then she saw: October 24, 1980 - the first time Mrs. Matt wore the same thing twice! She smiled and shook her head. The things they managed to come up with, the crazy things they noticed. If she could only get them to develop and use that awareness more constructively.

It was funny, really, because she had enough clothes to go a full semester without duplicating, the kids didn't catch on if she wore the same pants or skirt, but changed the rest of the outfit. She enjoyed the challenge of trying to wear something different every day; her clothes were as much a teaching aid as her voice.

She carried the two books to the front of the room and locked them up. She was glad that she hadn't seen anything worse on the desk, she knew it would have hurt her feelings. She still felt bad for her third grade teacher. At least it was a compliment, a compliment in the midst of all that obscenity. She never stopped to think that maybe the compliment was more offensive than all the rest, the blatant observation more revealing than the curious immaturity.

II

Jean sat and stared in disbelief. The small office was cramped with four people sitting in it. The only one who appeared to be comfortably perched was Dannemore; there was necessarily room to breathe behind his desk. He was leaning back in his swivel chair, his elbows resting on the arms, his hands locked together in front of his mouth. If he were reciting "This is the church, this is the steeple, open the door, and see all the people," he would have been at the steeple stage with his hands. But he wasn't reciting, he was listening. That was his job, to listen. Listen carefully and reserve judgment until the last words are spoken. Listen and remain silent. Then issue the verdict. Solomon knew how to do it.

Besides Jean and Dannemore, there was the woman and the young girl. In the small office their knees almost touched, for the three were sitting in the area before the bench. Outside the snow was falling furiously, Jean could see it from her vantage point better than the others. It was December snow, thus tolerable, even beautiful.

When she first walked into the office, Jean had commented on the desirability of a white Christmas. She had been surprised to see this particular mother and daughter in Dannemore's office. The call had come during her free period, she had looked at Alyssa in surprise and said, "I wonder what's up, the girl's one of my best."

Now she was staring not at the snow but at the mother. She was staring in disbelief because the mother was saying, "I don't want my daughter exposed to this filth. She comes from a good Christian home. There's no reason why she has to read obscene material in school. I want this stopped immediately."

Jean recognized the assignment sheet and looked at the student. "Michelle, do you think that's obscene material?"

The mother exploded. "How dare you ask her what is and what is not obscene? I make those decisions in my house. What makes you think she's old enough to know more than I do about such things?"

Jean chose to avoid the question; instead she held her ground and shot another volley into the air. "Mrs. Manse, have you asked Michelle for an explanation of that piece of writing?"

"You certainly have a way with insults, Mrs. Tevarro. And this is no piece of writing, it's a piece of filth."

Jean looked at Michelle; the girl was bursting. "I tried, Mrs. Tevarro, but she won't listen. What can I do?"

Jean tried again. "Mrs. Manse, your daughter wrote an absolutely brilliant interpretation of that 'piece of filth,' as you prefer to call it. She showed maturity of thought, a sensitive understanding of human relationships, and an ability to apply knowledge of concepts she's learned in class. You should be very proud of her writing and her ability to interpret and evaluate various literary forms. That is an allegory, Mrs. Manse, and you'll never understand it unless you interpret it correctly."

The woman's face contorted. "I don't care what you *prefer* to call it, it's still smut and you have no right to subject young minds to it. I'm interested in protecting my daughter, that's all."

"And I'm trying to educate her!" Jean tried to hold back, but couldn't. "So she won't turn into a narrow minded, ignorant adult!" She did manage to swallow back the last two words.

Michelle spoke fast. "Mom, an allegory has to be interpreted on the symbolic level. The literal meaning is not the essence at all, sometimes it's nonsense."

"Don't you lecture me, young lady. And don't you try to tell me that what is evidently here in black and white is anything other than lewd and lascivious ... "

You certainly know the vocabulary, lady, Jean thought.

"I'm sick and tired of sex, sex, sex, on the TV, in the newspapers and magazines; everywhere you look today, there's this unhealthy, disgusting attitude toward sex. My children should at least be spared of it in school. I do not appreciate being told that what I find offensive is nonsense. Especially by my own daughter. I have you to thank for that, don't I, Mrs. Tevarro?" She positioned the allegory for easy reading. "I ask you, Mr. Dannemore, is this nonsense? *I stroked her with my bare right hand ... she does it like somebody taking underwear off along with a garment ... I bare my other leg . . if I accidentally touch her bare foot with my bare foot, she jumps back right away . . once I even dared to open my breastplate, but when she saw my bare breast, she ran away in a hurry ... at that time I attributed it to the hair on my chest ... to be frank, we sometimes sleep in the same bed, we embrace each other ... we even want to get married in style and live together, but I am not sure whether we shall lie together naked.* This is nonsense? I don't think so."

Jean spoke before Dannemore. "Mrs. Manse, you've taken words and phrases out of context. How can you judge the entire piece that way? Michelle is right. The literal meaning is nonsense. You must consider the symbolic implications. You haven't even mentioned the armor; how could you miss it? You've ignored nine-tenths of what's there. The armor symbo—"

"I don't want to hear any more. I just want to be assured that my daughter will not be subjected to this kind of thing again."

Jean took aim. "What? What 'kind of thing' are you talking about? No more allegories? It'll take somebody bigger than you to stop me from giving instruction on allegories. You refuse to open your mind to this style of writing and feel justified in condemning it. How can you condemn what you know nothing about? Your daughter wouldn't do that! I've taught her differently!" Jean could see that she had gone too far; it was in the woman's face, which was contorting more violently than it had since the meeting started.

Jean said to Dannemore: "I think Michelle should be excused."

"No!" Mrs. Manse was almost out of her chair. "I want her to hear this. All of it! I hadn't intended for this to be a personal attack, Mrs. Tevarro, but it seems it must be. I know what kind of teacher you are, I know that you are overly permissive and 'modern.' I've heard Michelle talking to her friends about you. It's natural for youngsters to think that liberal teachers are a better influence than their own parents. I want Michelle to learn that you are not what she thinks you are."

Jean had no idea what the woman was talking about, but felt as if she were about to be ambushed. "Look, Mrs. Manse, don't you think it's better for students to face a wide range of experiences under the supervision of a teacher rather than to be let loose ignorant of the realities of life?"

"You make a mockery of that word, that word 'ignorant.' What makes you think you know what constitutes ignorance? Perhaps I do. Or is that just another word you throw around when it suits you? I happen to know that you practice no discretion when it comes to words. You use that word, that horrible word, in class. I know you do, I heard Michelle talking about it with her friends."

"Mother! What are you talking about?" Michelle was visibly angry. Jean looked at Dannemore and thought she saw his tongue hanging out. "I think Michelle should wait outside. If she doesn't, I will."

Dannemore moved forward in his chair and ordered the girl to leave. Michelle was not happy to do so. Dannemore settled back down again.

Jean focused on Mrs. Manse. "What word?"

The woman became a stick figure in the chair, wooden and immobile. "You know very well what word. The F word. I heard my daughter use that word and it horrified me. I heard her say that you used it in class. I think teachers like you should be barred from the classroom."

Jean was aware that she wanted to slap the woman's face, slap her repeatedly in an effort to bring her to her senses. But that was not the way. Jean was not aware that she replaced that physical approach with its verbal equivalent. "The F word? The F word! What word is that? Foreplay? Fornication? Father? Phooey? Flim flam? Or is it fuck? F-u-c-k? This may come as a surprise to you, but there is nothing inherently wrong with that word, Mrs. Manse, it's people like you who intensify the obscenity. Perhaps if you allowed those four letters to pass through your holier-than-thou lips, you'd realize that the world does not shatter when 'that word' is spoken. People create the evil distortions associated with some words and people can, with some intelligent effort, smash the facade and render those words harmless. I'm not horrified by the word 'fuck,' Mrs. Manse, not the word in and of itself. But I am horrified by some other words, words that do convey obscenity, words like 'genocide' and 'mind control' and 'bigotry.' Those words make my blood boil. What do you think of those words? Are they as bad as fuck? Pick one, pick the B word, and tell me, what's obscene, what's really obscene?"

The woman, who had been crimson, turned white. She jerked her head sideways to address Dannemore and said, evenly and victoriously," You see? She not only uses that word, she defends using it. Something must be done about this. Are you going to do it or am I?"

Jean watched Dannemore roll his chair closer to the desk, pick up his gold pen, and prepare to take notes. He was perfectly deadpan when he said, "Exactly what charges are you leveling against Mrs. Tevarro and what do you propose be done?"

Before the woman could respond, Jean did. She knew exactly what was happening and fought to control her anger. "Perhaps you should learn the facts before you level any charges or make any suggestions. Mr. Dannemore seems to have forgotten the facts in this case, which is certainly out-of-the-ordinary for him."

Expression flooded Dannemore's face. He stared at Jean but spoke to Mrs. Manse. "We are required to accept charges against any member of our staff. I promise a full investigation and a complete report. We appreciate your interest."

The woman smiled. "Thank you, Mr. Dannemore, for your support. I'd hate to think that the schools would ignore the sincere concern of parents for their children. I wish to charge Mrs. Tevarro with conduct unbecoming a teacher, with the use of profanity and obscenity in the classroom. She's not fit to influence the minds of young adults."

Jean sat quietly while Dannemore said, "And what do you suggest as a remedy?" A remedy. Jean was beyond anger and into curious. What would they do with her? (What's your pleasure, Madame?) Drown her in cod liver oil? Bury her in aspirin? A remedy. How foolish. They thought *she* was the disease.

The woman was saying," I know she's protected by tenure. I know all about tenure. I'm friends with the Holberts. Curt Holbert has been trying for years to get the tenure laws changed. I know I can't do much to get her out of the classroom for good; it's too bad because I do feel a responsibility to other people's children. As it is, I can only do something to save my own. I want my daughter taken out of that class immediately."

Jean felt the blow. "She'll never agree to that. She likes the class too much."

The woman rose to her full height, which was formidable. If Jean were an insect, Mrs. Manse would have stomped her into oblivion. "What makes you think Michelle has anything to say about it?" Jean was tempted to congratulate her for remembering the girl's name, but she was pushing on like a steam roller. "And isn't it pathetic that the only defense you can raise is based on the whims of a misguided seventeen-year-old? Good day, Mr. Dannemore. I'll leave this in your hands now."

"Wait a minute," Jean said, "wait one small minute. You listen and listen good. I'll take Michelle's intelligence over an adult's stupidity any time. You might just ask her what the circumstances were and what the class decided, with her very able help, the day we discussed the word fuck. My students know that they have a forum for discussion, not a license for profanity in my classroom. They know that anything goes and everything flies if they have something on their minds, they—"

The woman's head jerked. "There, Mr. Dannemore. She admitted it: anything goes in her classroom. She admitted it and I'm not listening to any more of this. If my daughter is not taken out of that class today, I'll be back."

Jean's jaw set up like concrete. "But, lady, do you need an interpreter? Look, I have five kids of my own and I—"

"You can corrupt yours in any way you like as long as you don't turn mine into perverts!"

Jean was stunned. The woman stomped out of the room and slammed the door. For a few seconds Jean still said nothing, she stared at Dannemore, who was writing frantically with his personalized gold pen. When he looked up at her she thought she saw a faint smile on his face, but decided it was her imagination. She stared him down and it was he who lowered his eyes first. She knew she had lost and she knew why. "You are a real, bona fide, dyed-in-the-wool, eighteen-carat-gold prick, Dan, and I want to thank you for letting that happen."

He didn't look up. "There you go again with that mouth of yours. Has it ever occurred to you that you have a filthy mouth and you offend people with it?"

"What's the matter? Can't you take it? Is my calling you a prick worse than what you just let that woman do to me? You know damn well that I'm not obscene or profane with my students, and the language I use with other adults is my business."

Dannemore looked up. "It's not your business. Not as long as you're a teacher; there are certain standards of professionalism that must be upheld."

"That's your theory. And there's plenty of people in this place who uphold your holy standards for all the world to see, but are the worst damn teachers on the face of the earth. Would you mind telling me how professional it was for you to sit there mute while that woman maligned me?"

"I happen to agree with her."

"Wonderful. So you think fuck is worse than bigotry, too. You are more dangerous than she is."

"I do not think fuck is—"

"Congratulations. At least you can mouth it."

"I do not think fuck is worse than bigotry, and she is the dangerous one. You heard her say she knows the Holberts. How would you like these charges to be brought up in public? I think I did you a big favor just now."

"You are warped. I'd enjoy the chance to spar with that self-righteous maniac in public. I'm assuming, of course, that the public has more balls than you."

"You would be crazy enough. Some day you may thank me, though, for handling this my way. Besides, the school doesn't need that kind of publicity. That's the last thing the school needs."

"Maybe it does. I've taught here for twenty years and I'm beginning to think that somebody should drop a bomb and blow this place into the stratosphere. Then everybody can study the entrails. You speak of 'the school.' What the hell do you mean, 'the school'? The building? The teachers? The kids? You? Have I hit the right chord yet?"

"You know very well what I mean. If all these tiny disturbances were made public, we'd spend all our time defending ourselves."

"Tiny? You call this tiny? I now have a reputation for being unfit to teach and you call it tiny?"

"You'll live through it. The way I'm handling it, it won't hurt you a bit."

"Oh. You aren't going to file that sheet of paper in my personnel folder?"

"Well, I have to do that. You know I have to do that. But it won't amount to anything. Not as long as you clean up your act a little."

"You're a real bastard, Dan. How's that?"

"Suit yourself."

"What about Michelle?"

"What about her?"

"I don't want to lose her. She's one of the best I've got. Students like her are hard to come by."

"You heard what her mother said."

"I'm going to fight to keep her."

"Oh, no, you're not. She transfers out today. It's bad enough you managed to turn her against her mother."

"I turned her against her mother? Why in hell did you allow her in here? You knew that woman came here loaded for bear. If it weren't for me, Michelle would have witnessed the whole disgusting thing. And believe me, nobody has to paint a picture for Michelle. She's too bright, she doesn't have to be told what her mother is. Don't accuse me of driving a wedge between them."

"Whatever."

"So I lose all the way around, don't I?"

Dannemore returned to his paperwork after saying, "That's the way it looks," and Jean knew she was dismissed, so she got up and left the office.

III

"I just had a long talk with Garson about some of the maniacs in this place. He was pretty disgusted, but in better spirits by the time he left."

"Why? What's up with Garçon? His film coming off its sprockets or what?"

Alyssa was disturbed by the comment, she had heard Jean commiserate with the media man often enough. "Well, the fact that everybody calls him Garçon has a lot to do with it. Especially when people use that tone of voice. He's just a little sick and tired of refereeing fights over equipment, that's all. What the hell's wrong with you?"

Jean told her in vivid detail. She finished the story by saying, "I've got a good mind to blow it wide open. If she wants a fight, I'll give her the fight of her life."

If anyone could fight to win, Alyssa knew, it was Jean. But it wasn't the notion of fighting that had her worried. And, in view of the circumstances, she was feeling personally responsible. "You told her it's an allegory? Are you sure you made that clear? I never had a single problem with that piece, though I'll admit I worried about it a few times. I get nervous every time I teach *Of Mice and Men*, and what's more bawdy than Shakespeare?"

Jean assured her that she had established sufficient groundwork, that she had received excellent evaluations, that she had enjoyed the best discussion period in all her years of teaching. "Don't you dare feel guilty for giving me that assignment. It was a raging success and I'm going to protect my right to use it in class if I have to spread that woman's ass all over town. Nobody's telling me that I'm unfit to teach. She also clearly accused me of raising perverts. The bitch."

"What?"

"I made the mistake of trying to appeal to her on a maternal level. I left myself wide open for her parting shot. How'd she put it? I can raise all the perverts I want as long as I leave her kids alone. How's that for a classic?"

"She should have had someone like you in high school, maybe her brain would've expanded beyond Neanderthal."

"Don't fall off the chair on me now, but she's a college graduate. Michelle told me her mother used to teach grade school. As I remember it, Michelle was pretty proud when she told me, and of course I sprang to the conclusion that daughter was a chip off the old block. Wrong again, Watson."

"She's not teaching now?"

"Apparently not. Michelle's the oldest; there are younger ones at home. Father's some kind of corporate executive. Must be nice to stay home with your kids; I never could. Bringing up five on one paycheck isn't easy."

"I don't see how it's even possible today."

"I couldn't stay home very long anyway. I had a strong aversion to diaper pails and baby talk. Besides the money, I always worked to keep my brain from rotting. I used to go nuts trying to keep my mind alive and functioning. You can't imagine what it's like to have five kids in seven years. I thought I'd go insane discussing formulas and rashes with other women. So I always came back to work. I had to or face extinction. And it wasn't easy. If it weren't for my husband, I never could have done it. But he knew that he would have eventually found me in a catatonic state with my head in a diaper pail if I didn't get out. Dominick always encouraged me to go back to work, but more than that he pitched in to help me whether I needed it or not, and he eased the guilt. And there's guilt; Christ, is there guilt. If ever husband and wife worked together, we did during those years. Sometimes it was hell, real hell; sometimes it was just a matter of relieving the guilt. The kids weathered it, they're healthy enough. And we're closer than a lot of families because we always had to make the most of our time together. If you ever want to see fur fly, try telling one of my kids that someone else in the family is no good. They'll rip your eyes out."

"Chips off the old block?"

"You can bet your life on it. You had Theresa in class, didn't you?"

"Her sophomore year. But we were just passing acquaintances then."

"This place is crazy that way. You can work with people for years and never get to know them because you don't share the same lunch period or frequent the same faculty room. This is the third year for us, isn't it?"

"Yes, and I must admit, Mrs. Tevarro, you are one hell of a lady to get to know. And we'd better enjoy it while it lasts, next year we may not be scheduled within fifty miles of each other."

"Did you ever have Dominick in class?"

"No, none of the others, only Theresa."

"Well, I tried to get Maria into one of your sophomore sections this year, but you were booked solid. I got her in with Bonnie, though, and she's enthralled with Miss Mason. Bonnie's come a long way since she started; I have to admit I wondered about her for awhile. I'm ashamed to admit that I was letting her looks influence my opinion of her. But she works damn hard and the kids think she's great."

"So do I. You can send Maria my way when she's a senior. Your twins are seniors this year, aren't they?"

"Yes. I remember the first time we put all five in chronological order for a picture. The girls are like bookends, with the boys in the middle."

"How old is Theresa now? I can't remember how long ago I had her."

"She's twenty-three; Dominick, Junior, is twenty-one; the twins are eighteen; and Maria's sixteen. So Theresa had Dom looking out for her, even though he was younger, and Maria has Vincent and Anthony as bodyguards. Sometimes they get to her. She came crying to me last week because they don't like the boy she likes. I guess they picked the kid up bodily and lifted him to the other side of the

427

cafeteria during lunch. I had a hard time keeping a straight face when Maria told me about it. I kept imagining what it looked like; my twins are large fellows. Poor Maria was mortified. I talked to the boys, but I don't think it did much good. Maria's the baby. It's an accident of birth, but the other four always took care of her."

"She'll learn to deal with it. And it'll get easier as she gets older. I have three brothers, so I know. And my mother always worked. We survived all right, none of us suffered any. In fact, I think we all turned out pretty independent because we learned that the world isn't out there to serve us. We looked after each other too, and I can remember a few times when I felt smothered by brotherly love. But I pulled a few tricks of my own."

"Listen, I didn't dare mention it to her last week, but poor embarrassed Maria forgot about the time she poured chocolate milk over the head of some girl her brothers had a crush on; it was an act of pure jealousy. She was in seventh grade, they were in ninth and had been falling in love with the same girl for years. Thank God they've outgrown that habit. Twins are an experience, believe me."

"I always thought that if I ever had kids, I'd want twins. I don't know why."

"I do. You don't do much of anything without wanting to do it just a little better than the way it's usually done. Right?"

"I suppose so, But that sounds so ... I don't know, it sounds hard and unfeeling when you put it that way. I don't think of having kids in the same way as I think of setting up my attendance register. Quite the opposite. As much as I love children, I know that loving children is a minute part of raising them. Maybe I've seen too much here. When I think of how emotionally draining teaching is, the way I care about other people's kids, I actually become frightened over how I would react if they were my own. I'd be one hell of a neurotic mother."

Jean nodded. "That comes with the territory. And the territory used to come before women had a chance to think about alternatives. Hell, not too long ago women had no alternatives. Women had babies whether they worked outside the home or not. Duty called. It was a waste of internal organs, a blight on society, a mark of shame; a woman was worthless if she didn't bear children. What the hell else was she put on this earth for? Men believed it and so did women."

"I know. I've hit up against that mentality. People are forever asking me what I'm waiting for; no, I shouldn't say people, it's women, other women mostly."

"I hope you tell them it's none of their damn business. That's the height of busybody crudeness."

"I have trouble with snappy answers to rude questions; it's not in me to return the favor. But the next time somebody asks me why I don't have kids, I'm going to smile sweetly and say, 'Why do you want to know?'. Maybe that will stop the insensitive slobs from asking somebody else the same thing. There are some women suffering like hell because they can't get pregnant, going through tests with and without their husbands, dying a thousand deaths every month because they see blood, and they have to put up with some moron who wants a blow-by-blow report to spread around the neighborhood along with the latest dope on whose husband's laid off and whose kid got thrown off the school bus.

"I do know what you mean about staying home, I couldn't put up with that crap either. Some women thrive on it, and some women stay home and rise above it. As for me and kids, I think I've put it off too long; I'm too set in my ways now, and so is Jeff. We've always been content with each other and with our lives. We never needed kids for the usual reasons people have them; we never felt obligated, thank God, because that's one of the worse reasons, and we never felt that there was a hole in our relationship that needed filling, another rationale that makes me sick, it just insures that the divorce will hurt some kids too.

"In my opinion, people should have kids only when they feel an overwhelming obsession to have kids, and the obsession is rooted in a pure heart. I think the purest parents on earth are people who adopt. And I think there would be fewer natural parents if more people thought about what the hell they're doing. I don't feel deprived because I don't have kids of my own. On the other hand, if I find out tomorrow that I'm pregnant, I'd be thrilled."

Jean said: "I think you'd make a wonderfully neurotic mother. You'd be a different person, you know, if you had a crew of your own at home."

Alyssa expressed facial agreement, but said, "So Maria will be footloose and fancy-free next year, the boys will be graduated and out of here. I'll bet she can't wait for that."

"She'll be free and I'll have two in college at once. There's twins for you. It's bad enough when you have to buy two of everything when they're young, but try to keep up with them when they're after cars and stereo equipment. They once had no qualms over sharing a girlfriend, but now I can't get them to share a car."

429

"And Maria will want one soon. Surely you treat the girls the same as the boys."

"You bet your ass I do. Nobody gets a car. An education, yes, everybody gets a crack at college or trade school or whatever. But if they want cars, they have to work themselves. I can't handle much beyond college costs, not with five of them. They understand. What I meant about the car was that I'm trying to convince the twins to pool their money to buy one car; they've both been working at anything that paid cold cash since they were ten. Those boys mowed more lawns and painted more porches and railings ... they had separate paper routes for years, and then got summer and part-time winter jobs where Dominick works. They're hustlers, they'll never starve."

"But, Jean, they'll slit each other's throat eventually; I don't care how close they are. Do you really think one car between two eighteen-year-olds will work without any blood spilling?"

"Wait up, Mattie. You haven't heard the plan yet. Christ, I'm not that dumb. You're mistaking trickery as stupidity. Dominick found a pair of cars, the same make, model, color, everything, on a used car lot a few weeks ago. He took both to a mechanic he trusts and found out they're both in excellent condition. Then he got a hell of a good price because cars are rotting on the lots in December. We can afford to buy one of the cars for the boys and we're trying to get them to buy the other one. Only they don't know that there are two; we plan to save the second one for a graduation gift. That way they both get cars, which would be impossible for them to do on their own. Sneaky, isn't it?"

"I have a feeling that such intrigues occur in your house often."

"Oh, we're always involved in something or other. Maria's in on the secret. In fact she's contributing a little of her babysitting money to the fund. I told her it wasn't necessary, that the old folks could come up with the dough, but she insisted. There's no problem among my kids over partiality, they aren't jealous of each other. I'm very proud of that. Maria won't expect a car when she graduates, but she's excited as hell over this plan for the twins. Theresa and Dom didn't get cars, but they had some scholarship help and they worked too, and eventually bought their own. It was easier then, college costs weren't so high. But when they started, I still had four and then three at home. Theresa is now totally independent financially, she got a fellowship to law school, and Dom is graduating this year. They all know that if they work to help themselves, Mom and Dad are more than willing to pick up the slack. The twins will be juniors when Maria's ready to go, and maybe by then, God-willing and if somebody wins a scholarship, we'll be able to get a big surprise for her. Maybe her own stereo system instead of a car, the way she loves music. And when the time comes, I may not even have to pay for it. The way my family operates, the other four will want to pitch in and do it for 'the kid.' That's what Dom calls her, 'the kid.' She'll be 'the kid' to him when he's 70 and she's 65."

"But they're beautiful! You've got a lot to be proud of."

"In spite of the fact that I'm raising perverts? I'd hate to tell you what I'd like to do with that miserable mass of protoplasm."

"Dannemore was no help at all?"

"Course not. He thinks I'm too mouthy for a woman. I offend his male ego. I don't care about him."

"Jean, I don't think you'd better do anything."

"Maybe you wouldn't do anything, but I'm different, Alyssa. I can't help it. People like that enrage me."

"She's dangerous."

"That's what Dannemore said, and it isn't any more appealing coming out of your mouth. Besides, people like that are dangerous by definition. And I'm not afraid of her. I know I'll never straighten out her mangled mind, but I'd like a chance to air the dispute in front of an impartial third party."

"Where the hell do you think you're going to find an impartial third party? Look what Dannemore did to you. I hope you're not considering Bassard, he sides with parents as a matter of course, and he does it with a knife to the back too. Where are you going? Not to the school board. You can't be that insane."

"What's so insane about that? If the board wants censorship, fine, but I think I'd have the bulk of the community on my side."

"Christ, Jean, you are off the deep end. What the hell are you talking about, the bulk of the community? Just who do you think will join you in this quest for Truth, Justice, and The American Way? Superman doesn't book into school board meetings."

"Wouldn't you support me? Don't you think any intelligent soul would? I don't expect Erica to jump on a white steed, but I'd expect you and Paul and Bonnie and Beth, if her ulcer could take it, and a hell of a lot of others in our department and in other departments as well."

"I'd love to, Jean, I really would. And I'd fight to the death with you, and believe it, it would be death. But don't expect an army of intelligent souls, you won't get even a handful of intelligent bodies. Would you stop and think for a minute? You don't fully comprehend just how dangerous that woman or anyone like her is. She'll command an army; all the nuts will crawl out of their holes and rush to her aid. You'll get massacred because the 'intelligent souls' won't think it too much of a sacrifice to give up one little assignment."

"But damn it, that's how freedom is lost, a little at a time. And it's not the assignment, it's the principle. Can we let narrow-minded ignoramuses tell us what to do? And I don't mean only teachers when I say 'us'."

"I know very well what you mean, you don't have to lecture me on principle. I saw a bumper sticker the other day that read, 'The Moral Majority Is Neither' and I can't agree more. But the fact remains that a vocal and persistent minority will make its mark, will ride herd over the complacent majority. Don't you read the newspapers? Something's happened to the concept of freedom in this country, the American people are of the opinion that they have the freedom to oppress each other. Think about it: public employees may negotiate but may not strike. The Moral Majority will graciously enlighten you on how you should think and what you should read. The Ku Klux Klan and The John Birch Society have taken all the shots for years, but there are plenty of other groups preaching self-righteous bigotry. Everybody's got an axe to grind and there's nothing wrong with that. Until they try to tell me that they're right and I'm wrong and I'd better submit to their way of thinking."

Jean gazed out the window and said, "Look at that, it's still snowing; we're going to be buried in it by nightfall." Alyssa told her to do a snow dance in hopes of a day off because of the weather. Jean went to the window, then spoke, with her back to Alyssa. "Do you really think it would get blown beyond control? That is what you're saying, isn't it?"

"Yes. Believe me, I'm at the point right now where I'd like to stick my finger in somebody's eye, too. I'm feeling pretty abused these days; every Monday I wonder if I'll last out the week. I'm sick and I'm so tired I could crawl into a cave and stay there forever. I keep pushing for the kids, they're the reason I put up with all of it. That woman is dangerous, Jean, she could incite a riot that none of us would survive. How would you like to attend an old-fashioned book-burning? What if it ever reached that level?"

Jean turned around. "It would kill me. I'd throw her in, you can be sure of that."

"I told you, I get nervous every time I teach *Of Mice and Men.* One year I got a call from a parent who objected to it. I offered an alternate to the student, but he had read the Steinbeck already anyway. He was a bright boy and I told him not to think less of his mother, that she was just concerned for him. But he listened to the class discussion and he must have wondered why she wanted him protected from it. That novel is the most successful piece of literature that I teach because the kids have no trouble reading it. I don't have to spend weeks on difficult language just to get them to understand the basic plot, I can concentrate on evaluation. And not one kid has ever gone through that book with me and decided that he wanted to emulate the coarse language or the lifestyle of those characters. They see the book as Steinbeck intended it to be seen. That mother leafed through it, saw a few offensive words, and condemned it. Or, even worse, she read the whole thing, didn't understand what she was reading, and condemned it."

"You never found out which?"

"No. I never asked. I was too terrified. We were a pathetic pair, she and I, both reacting out of fear. Sometimes I think we should have parents in class along with the kids. I have no trouble dealing with that book in class, the kids understand the loneliness and despair, the futile attempts to break out of a miserable lifestyle, the prejudice born of ignorance and misunderstanding; the kids empathize with George at the end, they see that he's in a worse fix than poor mistreated Lennie. What's it like to have to kill the thing you love for its own good? Can life put you into a more agonizing situation than that? At first they giggle and hoot over Curley's wife, but I change all that, they come to understand why she has the reputation of being a tart. Kids know all the synonyms for prostitute today, or rather, they think they know. I give them 'concubine' and tell them to beware if they're ever in a strange city and someone tells them they're in the red light district."

"It isn't certain that she's a prostitute, though, is it?"

"No. At least I don't think so. I think Steinbeck served his purpose by making the reader think so, the reader who's as unfeeling and ignorant as the men in the book. She wears red to draw attention to herself because she's as lonely as the men, but as a woman she's not allowed to have such feelings. Her quest for love - love, not sex - her yearning for a pleasant life are reduced to obscenity by the men around her because she's a woman, and women, decent women, aren't supposed to blatantly seek such things out of life. Steinbeck doesn't even give her a name. She's 'Curley's wife' through the whole novel; how's that for non-identity? Curley ignores her, but at the same time is violently jealous because it makes him look bad if she even talks to another man. She has nobody to talk to. I ask the kids how they would feel if they had nothing, no friends, no family, no love, no happiness in their lives. Then I tell them to go ahead and judge Curley's wife. There is so much in that book to make them think about their own lives and about people. If I ever have to witness Steinbeck or anything that we teach going up in flames, I'll never be the same again. It's bad enough reading about it happening."

"Steinbeck? Aren't you exaggerating just a little?"

"*The Grapes of Wrath* has been removed from school libraries in cities all over the country within the last few years."

"I'm using that next semester with my scholarship section."

"Then maybe it's a good thing Michelle Manse is out of the class."

"That's disgusting."

"I agree, but it may be a blessing in the long run."

"I've got a good mind to send that woman a copy of *1984*. That should be required reading for all the ignoramuses. That and *Fahrenheit 451*."

"Banned. Both."

"What?"

"Removed from school library shelves in cities all over the country, along with *Huckleberry Finn*, *Brave New World*, *A Farewell To Arms*, *The Catcher in the Rye*, *The Merchant of Venice*. Also, *The Dictionary of American Slang*, *The American Heritage Dictionary*, *Catch 22*, *Kramer vs. Kramer*, *The Godfather*, *The Thorn Birds*, and *Jaws*."

"I thought of teaching *The Thorn Birds* to a class of seniors when I read it. To be sure, it would have to be a very special class, more mature than most, like my juniors are. But banned? What the hell's happening?"

"So you liked it too? I thought it was highly sensitive to the problems of life, to the sufferings of men and women alike. It's beautifully written, passionate and profound, and made for discussion. But some people think it's smut. Do you remember the final words in that book?"

"Sure do."

"I'll never forget them either. We cause our own miseries and will never know enough to stop. God, I thought that was a powerful book. I devoured it. So did a hell of a lot of other people. But it only takes a small group of 'concerned citizens' screaming obscenity to knock it off the shelves. And it's not only school libraries, they're hitting public libraries and bookstores as well."

"Why don't I know about all this?"

"For one thing, the press doesn't cover every little instance. For another, you're too busy with your own life to concentrate on everything that's happening out there."

"You're right. I get to read a newspaper on an average of twice a week."

"The only reason that I'm so well-versed on the subject is that one of my seniors did a paper on censorship this semester. It was an eye-opener. I took notes. Do you want to see them?"

"Do I dare?"

Alyssa fished into the back of her plan book. "Here, educate yourself. Then decide if you want to seek out an 'impartial third party.'"

Jean reacted to the first item her eye hit. "My God," she said, "books were banned in ancient times? In Greece and Rome?" Alyssa told her to save the astonishment and read on. It would get progressively worse.

Jean followed the progression all the way from 399 BC when Socrates was put to death for corrupting the morals of youth to 1962 when a woman (religious, very religious) in Chicago was arrested for gluing shut a few hundred paperbacks in a crusade to protect the children of the community.

In addition to the rather well-known examples of Martin Luther and the Scopes trial, Jean skimmed over other examples that shook her. Every major writer in the world was, at one time or another somewhere in the world, for one reason or another, subjected to attack.

After winning three Pulitzers and a Nobel, the plays of Eugene O'Neill were banned in Boston and closed in New York. Sinclair Lewis was the first American to win the Nobel prize for literature; his novel *Elmer Gantry* was banned in the U.S. both before and after he won the prize. The works of Theodore Dreiser were banned in New York, Boston, Vermont, Ireland, and Germany. Hemingway has been banned and burned from Italy to Boston to Detroit to New York to Ireland. In 1962 books that even referred students to books by Hemingway were attacked by "Texans for America."

Mickey Mouse cartoons have been banned in Yugoslavia and Italy, and one was censored in the U.S. in the 1930's because it showed a cow reading *Three Weeks* by Elinor Glyn, a book which was banned in Boston in 1908.

In 1954 in Illinois Hans Christian Andersen's *Wonder Stories* was stamped "For Adult Readers" to keep such filth out of the hands of children. In 1933 a U.S. Customs official refused to allow books into the country because they contained obscene photos. The pictures were from the original fresco of *The Last Judgment*, thus the figures were nude. The customs official never heard of Michaelangelo.

When she saw Jean nearing the end of the information, Alyssa said: "That's only a small part of it. In recent years more books than ever have been suppressed. Here in the U.S." Jean let out a long, low whistle. "From Mickey Mouse to Michaelangelo. Unbelievable."

"I'm not only afraid of Steinbeck," Alyssa said. "I get the jitters with everything. *The Merchant of Venice*? By the end of that play, every kid I've ever had thought Shylock got a raw deal. There hadn't been a Jew in England in over three hundred years when Shakespeare wrote it. If anything, that play presents the perfect opportunity to discourage anti-Semitism. Have you ever heard of Island Trees?"

"No. Sounds like a resort."

"In 1976 the school board of Island Trees, Long Island, voted to remove books from school libraries and classrooms. There were nine altogether, and they included Malamud, Vonnegut, *Go Ask Alice*, *Soul on Ice*, and an anthology of short stories by black writers; I can't remember the rest. The books were attacked as anti-American, anti-Christian, and anti-Semitic."

"Let me guess- Malamud was anti-Semitic."

"Cute, huh? Five students brought suit against the school board, and the case has gone through litigation right up to the Supreme Court. I don't know where it's at right now. But one of the students was threatened by a board member, told that if the district won the case, the kid was going to be personally sued."

"Why can't people see that books aren't inherently evil, people assign that meaning to them. If we're allowed, we can educate kids enough so that they will be able to intelligently analyze what they read and decide for themselves whether or not it has any value. Lord knows there is raw pornography out there, but I'd like to think that an educated mind is a better weapon against it than anything else. And it's a personal weapon. Don't most of us start out by finding the dirty words and passages in a book and marking the pages? Kids will never stop doing that. It's our job to change that behavior, to replace it with intelligent awareness and an ability to make mature judgments. The answer is in education, not censorship."

"Bravo! You practicing your speech? I mean, it's beautiful and it's true, but how ready are you to open this can of worms? Maybe you should also know that in 1977 a school board in Indiana banned *The Bell Jar* and a group of senior citizens burned copies of *Values*

Clarification. Think about the uproar over *Little Black Sambo* lately, and consider the fact that *The Wizard of Oz* is still being attacked because it offers the concept of a 'good' witch."

"All right, enough. Enough. I was convinced when I hit the obscene photos from the Sistine Chapel, but you can't blame me for holding on. I still think the majority of people do not sanction censorship."

"Of course not. They're just quieter about it and unwilling to fight for books they don't know anything about. And after all, the censors are only interested in the welfare of their children. And they know all the loaded words designed to incite rebellion and hold off opposing forces: indecent, filthy, trashy, lewd, lascivious, immoral, harmful-to-minors, corrupting, pornographic, obscene, vulgar, profane. There are also movements in some states to make public the names of those checking out books deemed objectionable from public libraries."

"There's a Gestapo in this country!"

"There certainly is. And all is done in the name of freedom. They have every right to speak up and they firmly believe they have the right to deny freedom to others on the basis of their own moral, religious, political, social, or patriotic beliefs. Hell, look at the uproar Women's Libbers generated over Dick and Jane."

"That I remember. Gender roles. Some books make little girls feel inferior. I thought it was nitpicking. The theory was noble enough, but changing the books was overkill. A good teacher can use the book to generate discussion; the book isn't law, it's a springboard for ideas. I don't know, Alyssa; what if The Mother of the Year goes to the board over 'Love in Armor'? I won't comply if they tell me I can't use it."

"Island Trees also removed a book because it contained Swift's 'A Modest Proposal.' I guess they thought he was serious when he suggested eating Irish children. Where are we going, Jean, when people are ignorant of the nature of allegory and satire, when they can't distinguish irony and parody, when they have no desire to educate themselves, no intention whatsoever to understand? What do we do, hold classes on the village green, classes that attract no students? The only thing we can do is what we're doing, in the hope that we can eliminate some of the irrational ignorance before these kids leave our classrooms. Don't go public with it, Jean, you'll regret the move until your dying day. And I'm not telling you this only because I'm a coward, which, in this case, I undoubtedly am, but also because the repercussions will be vile for you. Do you want to be called a smut peddler? Your kids have already been branded as

437

perverts, do you want to put your family through a living hell? Just think about the way this community reacts to the word 'teacher.' And we're not alone here; teachers all over the country are in the same boat with us. If the board tells you to stop using 'Love in Armor,' for God's sake and your own, agree to stop using it. More than one teacher has lost his job over assignments."

"I'll say I'll stop and then I'll continue to use it. They'll never know if nobody else complains."

"Do you like sitting on a powder keg?"

"Much better than sacrificing my self-respect. Isn't it damned appalling to be placed in that position? But we are, aren't we?"

"All the time. Every minute of every day. You've only now realized that?"

"No, I've only now reduced it to simplest terms."

"Well, everybody had a good time telling me a while back, I suppose I should return the favor."

"What?"

"Welcome to the planet Earth, Jeanie-girl, welcome to the planet Earth."

JUBILATIONS

I

Report cards were issued Monday, December 15. The day report cards are issued is the day students choose to grieve their grades; students do not remember failing grades earned six weeks in the far distant past. Alyssa never refused to recompute a student's grade when a student expressed a desire for her to do so. In fact, she encouraged it because of the possibility of errors. She would take the time to write the student's grades on a 3x5 card and then to explain how she had come up with the final average. Not that she hadn't notified all her classes of the process, but because some kids aren't concerned until the boom falls or because some kids aren't physically in class when the explanation is given.

Sometimes she found errors in math when she recomputed. If the student had been deprived of one-half to two points, she wrote a note which the kid could happily carry home to his parents, and she made a note in her grade book to add the credit to the next average. Changing grades involved filling out a form and wasn't worth the time and effort for one-half to two points. More severe cases(when an 82 became jumbled to a 28, for example) demanded that she fill out the form to change the grade and remember to check the computer sheets the next time around to be sure that the grade was in fact changed. And, of course, she scrambled to write a note of apology for the poor kid to show his parents.

On December 15, in addition to justifying grades for a few students every period, she became aware of a colossal blooper that she had somehow managed to commit with the fifth period grades. She decided that she must have skipped an area on the computer sheet and made a mistake while bubbling. The last six students alphabetically in the class had received the wrong grades. After two of them questioned their grades, she became suspicious and checked on the other four. Sure enough, their grades were wrong. More investigation revealed that each had received an alphabetically previous grade. Alyssa apologized profusely and assured them that she would change all the grades to make it right. Some of the grades were lower than they were supposed to be, and, alas, some were higher. She felt bad about that as she filled out six change-of-grade forms during her free period after writing six notes of apology during fifth.

She was glad she had dragged in on the 15th. If she hadn't been there, the mistake might have gone undetected. Students have an uncanny ability to forget grades the day after report cards are issued. Of course, she had no idea that the 15th was to be the big day, either. The schedule established at the beginning of the year projected the exact day every six weeks, but nobody ever knew for sure how many days beyond the projected date report cards would materialize in mailboxes. Many teachers thought it slightly ridiculous that students were receiving grades for one report period halfway into the next; it threw many a wrench into the works of reporting chronological student progress. But that was The Law and The Way. Even those irritated by the system recognized the futility of trying to dictate policy to the Bubble God.

So why did Alyssa Matthews drag in on the 15th, if not for report card reasons? It had something to do with the fact that she hadn't dragged in on Thursday and Friday, December 11 and 12. She had contracted an old-fashioned cold again, and couldn't face the chilling temperatures outside or, as was again the case, in her study hall. She went on an antibiotic immediately, and hauled out the cough medicine again. She wrote out plans at home and had Jeff drop them off on his way to work. She was so sick she didn't care if Sad Sack went in to sub. By Sunday she was feeling well enough to start to worry.

She went in on Monday to "straighten things out" and to finish *Hamlet*, start *Our Town*, and check out which poems the regents sections were having trouble with. By the end of the day she knew she had made a mistake physically but at least she was there to write up plans for the rest of the week. And she found out from Jean, who had been out two days herself with a migraine, that their favorite sub was subbing again. Alyssa called the sub service from school because begging was wasted on cellulose, she had to plead with flesh and blood. She called in for Tuesday and Wednesday, giving herself what she thought was ample time to get over the latest infection that her body still was not able to fend off quickly and successfully. As it turned out, she had to call the tape during the night with a fervent request that the same sub be kept one more day. She dictated plans to Jean in the morning. Just in case.

She resisted Jeff's appeal to round out the week because she believed that it did make a difference if she went in on Friday. The thought of cleaning up after a sub in January made her more miserable than the thought of going to work sick. Besides, it was one day, only one day before a blessed two weeks off. She could tolerate one day.

It took her all day to straighten out homeroom attendance (summaries would be in mailboxes the day after vacation; it was the end of the December period) and she almost blew her cool during study hall when she got a call to hightail it up to her room to get Nettie NillyNellyNully's report card. Nettie had stopped her in the hall between first and second periods and requested the report card, which Nettie hadn't yet collected because she was tardy (8:40) on the 15th, absent on the 16th, 17th, and 18th, and tardy (9:15) on the 19th. Alyssa told Nettie that she wasn't in the habit of carrying homeroom materials around all day, thus she didn't have the report card, but Nettie could catch her in the room during third, fifth, seventh, or eighth periods. Alyssa was not about to turn around and trek back for Nettie NillyNellyNully.

Ten minutes into second period the phone rang. Joe answered it, then sent Alyssa up the stairs where she was casually informed of her duty to obtain the aforementioned report card pronto. Nettie was waiting in the junior office. Nettie was being excused from school at 10:00. Nettie couldn't wait until January to get her report card. That was unreasonable.

Alyssa hung up the phone.

Alyssa told Joe where she was going.

Alyssa walked back to her room.

Alyssa disturbed the class that was in session there.

Alyssa walked to the junior office.

Alyssa never looked at Annette Nieully.

Alyssa gave the report card to the secretary.

Alyssa walked back to study hall.

The study hall was livelier than usual on the nineteenth of December, 1980. Students are naturally hyperactive the day before any vacation. If it had been eighth period, Alyssa would have let them party with her blessings. But second period meant some students wanted to study for tests later in the day; therefore, a certain level of quiet had to be maintained. While she had plenty of her own work to do, Alyssa joined Joe in stalking the premises. It was the only way to keep the lid on. And they were alone with the job; Erica never showed.

It was during one of her trips down the aisles that Alyssa saw Angela (whom she secretly called Devila) LoGuasta pull a skein of yarn and a pair of knitting needles out of a paper bag. The yarn, both on and off the needles, was a welcome sight; Alyssa immediately

441

squashed the suspicion that Angela was finding it desirable to attend classes armed.

Alyssa walked to Angela's desk and tried to express interest quietly, so as not to disturb the entire room or encourage others to talk. Angela, who was consistently adept at doing both, said, "Just call me Madame Defarge." The words reverberated off the walls and the whole place, including Alyssa and Joe, cracked up. It wasn't necessarily true that everyone was familiar with the allusion, but that made no difference in view of the fact that Angela delivered the line in a sultry Mae West voice. Between the allusion and the voice, Alyssa felt a small hope that maybe there was something in Angela LoGuasta that she had never seen before.

After the room quieted down, Alyssa asked in a whisper, "What are you building?" She bent her knees and lowered her body next to the desk.

"Sweat-"

"Shhh ... Whisper, Angela. Please. People are trying to concentrate. That's a beautiful shade. I love lavender. And that pattern looks complicated."

Angela shook her head, then said softly, "No. It's not. It's just a variation of stockinette. It's a sweater for my mother for Christmas."

"Do you think you'll finish in time?"

"Oh, sure, I'm decreasing for the armholes now. I've still got a few days."

"What made you bring it to school?"

"Miss Mason told me I could teach kids how to knit next semester during study hall. I'm trying to drum up business."

"Do you think you could stand teaching me?"

Angela grinned. "Sure. But you'll have to learn to keep your mouth shut. Most of the time you have to count when you're knitting, and that takes concentration." Alyssa knew that although Angela was grinning, Angela was dead serious. It was an awakening for both of them.

Quite a few seniors were absent third period, which was expected. Alyssa used the time for make-up work. They had taken the essay test on Wednesday and the quotes test on Thursday, so Alyssa figured out who had missed what during the last few minutes of study hall. Some students needing to take one or both of the tests were in class, so she told the others to keep busy quietly She worked on homeroom attendance and planned to take both sets of tests home for grading. It bothered her that some students would have to do make-ups after vacation.

She was thankful that the sub had followed her plans to the letter and had been knowledgeable enough to teach. Effie wasn't satisfied with the piles of papers and notes left un-Effie-like on the desk and in the mailbox, but Alyssa was more than satisfied with the sub's handling of her classes. At their meager salaries, subs cannot be expected to take work home, read unfamiliar literature, study grammar, and grade tests. Alyssa never expected that of a sub. A long illness meant returning to sets of papers to grade along with the rest of the clean-up detail. But getting a sub who knew the literature, one who could actually teach any phase of the curriculum, was a bonanza that outweighed everything else.

Nevertheless, the sub had missed making some very important points in regard to *Our Town*; Alyssa knew how students react to the play, and was disturbed that their initial reaction had not been dispelled by the sub. They still thought it was a frumpy, outdated, corny, dull piece not worthy of their attention. She couldn't let them believe that, so she found some non-existent energy and went into her act. She had only forty minutes to change their minds and hoped that she could get through to most of them. She spent first and fifth periods giving a frenzied, impassioned, bravura performance and ended each time by saying, with genuine emotion: "Go home today and heed Emily's advice, learn from her suffering, try to see, really see, what's around you, see the things, the people, you love, and appreciate all you have. Wilder says that it's the common, ordinary, everyday aspects of life that we fail to appreciate, and those are our most precious possessions. You think the play is boring because you missed his message. Death isn't the tragedy. Emily is horrified when she views life from the position of one who has lost it. She inspires us to do better, to wake up and see how fortunate we are to be, merely to be, alive and able to hope and dream and love. Do you love your parents, or a brother or sister or aunt or grandparent? When's the last time you showed it? When's the last time you told somebody that he or she means a great deal to you? Are you embarrassed to do that? Why can four-year-olds do it with no trouble? Wake up, people! Thornton Wilder is saying that we're all a bunch of blind fools living our lives without appreciating what is most precious to us, and that is life itself, 'every, every minute of it.' Stop moaning and groaning and feeling deprived because mom says $50 is too much to pay for a pair of jeans!

"This is a good time of the year for you to consider the message in this play. You may think at times that I'm a dimwit, but I had you read this now on purpose. I thought it might get to you more now.

And I want it to grab you and hold you, if only for a day or an hour or the next minute. If it grabs you at all it will be with you forever, and then, far in the future, you'll have it to pull out again."

Most of them were spellbound. How she loved casting spells over them. When she knew she had planted the seed, she knew enough not to smother it, so she smiled broadly and with a wink said, "Who knows, if you go home today and tell your mother you love her, she may go into shock and buy you everything you want for Christmas!" They laughed, she laughed, and Thornton Wilder was justly served.

The regents classes were the worst to control, for they were at the end of the day. The kids were like jumping beans, eager to get it over with. Alyssa often thought about what grade school teachers must go through the days before vacations. If sixteen-year-olds can't calm down for the excitement, what are six-year-olds like?

Both classes knew they had to take a test on the poetry unit. The only way to maintain some sanity in some classes the day before vacation is to schedule tests. Units usually and naturally end at those times also, which requires that tests be given. The built-in problem, of course, is the absentee rate on those days.

Alyssa told her scholarship sections that she was foregoing the test on *Our Town*. "No," she said, "no paper either, have a happy holiday." But she couldn't do that with the regents sections. The poetry unit had lasted three weeks, that was too long, too much work to ignore. But she did ease up on them a little by giving the easier objective test. They exchanged papers and graded the test in class; she wouldn't have to take them home, and she announced that she would grade poetry charts after vacation. So the last two periods ran as smoothly as they could under the circumstances.

The plain truth of it is, if teacher has work planned and is determined to deal with it, most students will behave and do as they're told. At least, that was Alyssa Matthews' fortunate situation.

There was time left at the end of each period, so she used the opportunity to distribute copies of Frank Horn's "Kid Stuff." She said a few words, as time allowed, in explanation. She felt that the poem was appropriate because they had just studied poetry and because of the season. She liked the poem for what it said and felt that it expressed its message ecumenically. Though she never knew, she assumed that her students came from a wide spectrum of backgrounds and she taught with that in mind. Educating them did not mean changing atheist to Christian or Catholic to Protestant.

She was particularly aware of her own objectivity that day, her own intent to remain open minded; she had seen the letter Jean found in her mailbox sixth period.

You are hereby advised that objections have been raised as to the use of an article entitled "Loving Armor" by you in your classroom. This committee has reviewed the objections and the article and deems it necessary at this time to order the immediate removal of said article from the curriculum.

You are ordered to refrain from issuing said article to students in any way, shape, or form, neither for assignment nor lecture nor discussion purposes. This committee feels that such material is not conducive to the standard of education desired by this community for its children. Our children deserve instruction based on a high moral plane in order for them to develop into healthy, productive citizens. Said article is a threat to that development.

The Committee for Literacy, it seemed, had taken on another role.

"It doesn't matter what your religious beliefs are, or if you have none at all," Alyssa told her regents classes. "The message in this poem transcends religion." She explained the double meanings and the poet's use of capitalization, and made certain that they saw the message. By the time she finished with "Kid Stuff" for the second time, Alyssa was feeling the effects of the long day. Jeff had pleaded with her again, "You never give yourself enough time to fully recover! What are you trying to prove? What difference does it make if you're out one more day?"

What difference ...

A few cards were dropped on her desk by students during the day; she enjoyed cards. One of her seniors remained after class, pulled a wrapped package out of a bag and presented it with words of gratitude. Alyssa misted up, she opened the package immediately and told the girl she and Jeff would enjoy sipping the wine in front of a fire. The box was heavy, but Alyssa carried it to the faculty room fourth period. Jean was traditionally showered at Christmas, and Bonnie, who had no classroom for storage, had started a pile of acquisitions after homeroom.

The lunch crowd was sorely tempted to sample the wine. Lainie said it would be the perfect stimulus to get them through the frenzied afternoon; Jean wanted to invite Mrs. Manse in for a toast and a sip; Joyce uttered the possibility of spiking the sangria in her classroom, but she whispered in view of the fact that she was violating the NO PARTIES rule; Bonnie, who had been riding high on ecstasy since

Thanksgiving, didn't feel that anything could intoxicate her any further.

But in spite of the temptation, the wine remained sealed, as did the small package Alyssa found in her desk drawer at the beginning of third period. She put it in her purse and waited. The first mystery was no mystery because the box was tagged; Alyssa decided to forestall the second mystery.

She waited all day. As each period passed with no sign of the giver, she assessed the situation and decided what she would do if the face never presented itself. Her plan proved to be unnecessary, however. Immediately after the sounding of the bell at the end of the day, the face, with its supporting column, pushed its way through the hysterical mob rushing out of the room. Cassie Quimly forged in when everybody else was moving out.

She stood in front of Alyssa's desk, then moved to the back of the room, then paused to look out the windows, then moved up front again to sit at a student desk. She said nothing.

Alyssa played the game, then felt impatient stirrings, for she simply wanted to go home. She said, "Why have you been avoiding me all day? I usually see you three times a day, but today you were too busy?"

"No."

"You wouldn't even say hello when I saw you in the hall this morning. You looked the other way. Is that any way to treat a friend?"

"Aw, c'mon, Mrs. Matt. You must've found it."

"Oh-h-h-h, so that's why you made yourself scarce." She reached into her purse, pulled out the gift, and held it in the palm of her hand.

Cassie's face fell a mile. "You haven't opened it yet."

"I was waiting for you. And believe me, it was hard. I love to open gifts. Cass, why did you leave it and run?"

"I dunno. I was so afraid you wouldn't be here today. I worried about you this week."

"Don't worry about me, I'm all right. I just need a vacation. Were you afraid I wouldn't like it? Do you feel that way when you give someone a gift?"

Cassie thought for a few seconds. "Yeah, I guess I do. Can't help it."

"Yes, you can. It's natural to be afraid of rejection, but you should also consider the fact that anything you give with your heart should be received with as much love. I know it doesn't always happen that way. But if your gift is rejected, the receiver didn't deserve it to begin with. How about looking at it that way?"

446

"Yeah, that sounds good, but—"

"But it hurts too much anyway. I know. But that's the chance we all take when we give. It doesn't stop most of us. To tell you the truth, Cass, if this is an empty box, I'll treasure it forever. You should know me well enough to know that."

Cassie shrugged and said, "It's really not much. I mean, it wasn't expensive or anything."

"Cassie, whatever it is, it's everything." Alyssa fought with the wrapping and teased, "But you wrap the way I do! With more tape than paper!" Then she lifted the cover of the small box and removed the cotton square covering the contents. She fought to keep her eyes from filling with tears, which she knew would have been the case even if the box had indeed been empty; the last thing Cassie needed was melodrama.

"I love it. It's beautiful and I love it, and every time I wear it, I'll think of you. Thank you, Cassie."

She lifted the pin out of the box and blindly fastened it to the mandarin collar of the red velour dress she was wearing. "How's it look?"

Cassie was smiling and laughing. "Upside down."

"Oops, sorry about that. The little guy had enough trouble with one horn without being flipped over on it. Let me try again; it's hard to do this without a mirror." She adjusted the pin by feel.

Cassie said, "I noticed you like to wear things on your jackets, so I thought you might like it. It's not silver, it's only pewter."

"I'm so glad you noticed. And I love pewter; silver tarnishes, pewter doesn't. He's going to look smashing on a lapel."

"I had a hard time choosing, there were so many different ones. But I liked the horse. Even with that thing on his head."

"He's not a horse, Cass, he's a unicorn. You've never heard of a unicorn?"

"I dunno, I remember something about a horse with wings."

"That's Pegasus. He wasn't a unicorn. But a unicorn is also a mythical animal; no one really knows if unicorns ever existed. There are two schools of thought on it, of course; one says they did, one says they didn't. I prefer the myth."

"A myth like in mythology? Like the Gorgon's Head and the Loadstone Rock?"

"Hey! You remember that, do you?"

"You pounded *Tale* into my skull."

"Glad to hear it. Yes, the unicorn can be viewed as a part of mythology. He couldn't be captured, you see; he couldn't be captured

447

alive. He would impale himself in a tree with his horn if he were surrounded by hunters. He chose death over captivity. That's why he was considered to be such a prize. As the story goes, he was captured once. He loved and admired purity and innocence, so the hunters lured him with a virgin as bait. He was drawn to the virgin and sat beside her, resting his head on her lap. Then the virgin signaled to the hunters and the unicorn was taken."

"That stinks!"

"Sure does. But the unicorn still symbolizes a gentle spirit and purity and innocence."

"Symbolism, huh?"

"Yep, good old symbolism. Life's pretty dull without it, don't you think?"

"You English teachers never quit."

Alyssa laughed. "Thank you, Cassie, for my unicorn. I'll wear it proudly. Get your body home now, so I can do the same. I've about had it with this place, we all need a vacation."

"Merry Christmas," Cassie said on her way out the door. "See you next year!"

"Merry Christmas," Alyssa said. "Have a lovely holiday." Then she gathered up her things, donned her protective outerwear, and locked her classroom door on 1980.

Later that evening she read through the cards she had received from students. Though she had looked at them during the day, the looks were too hurried to matter. She sat at the kitchen table and spent some time soaking up the simple but joyous sentiments implied and expressed in the living pieces of cardboard. One of them said: To a really sweet teacher who I love very much and hope the best of luck in your many teaching years. I really enjoy being in your class because I learn so much every day. Hope to pass this year with a 90 in every class except Social Studies which is my worst maybe a 70 in that class! Love always …

They had a way of getting to her. And she felt particularly susceptible that year, that Christmas of 1980. One card was especially poignant. It was not unusual for students to give her cards quoting literature, and she always felt victorious when they did. The quote was beautiful enough, it stirred her emotionally.

> What can I give Him,
> Poor as I am?
> If I were a shepherd
> I would bring Him a lamb –

If I were a Wise Man
I would do my part –
Yet what I can, I give Him,
Give my heart.

C. Rossetti

The quote was enough to elicit the tears she had held back all day. But there was something else. The student, the student had done something that pierced her to the core of her being. The student had penned in the word "Amen" at the end of the quote.

II

The days off before Christmas afforded Alyssa a chance to complete errands postponed by her ill health. Not that she still had gifts to buy. Effie had taken over that department years ago. Effie decided that the Christmas rush was not at all appealing, therefore she kept The Christmas List and bought and wrapped gifts all year long with a hasty surge in September and October. By November 1, Effie was ready for Christmas gift-giving. The gifts out of the way early, Effie could then concentrate on baking thirty different kinds of cookies. Effie's cookie trays, which took six to eight hours just to assemble, were famous and eagerly awaited by family and friends.

Alyssa was behind in her baking that year, and she knew she couldn't catch up in the few days before Christmas. She was too meticulous with the mixing and the rolling and the filling and the frosting and the storing to torture herself by trying to do it fast and slipshod. Her cookies were works of art, every one handled individually with infinite care and patience. That was the only way to insure the beauty of the resultant trays; taste and texture were automatic requirements, along with visual appeal. Content and form, form and content. When she assembled the trays every year, she forgot the work and the exhaustion and the worry and the planning. When she saw the combined beauty of the different colors and shapes and sizes, she forgot the pain of work in deference to the joy of accomplishment.

But the few days before Christmas meant visits from family and friends, hectic last-minute errands. It was too late and too rushed a time to settle in her kitchen with flour and sugar and enjoy. She couldn't spread frosting for hours as she customarily did, with her finger, one cookie at a time, swirling and whirling the creamy stuff in

Rosemary Cania Maio

glossy patterns and peaks. It was too late and she didn't have the energy anyway. She was disappointed, but not as much as at Thanksgiving, for she had managed to bake and store eight or ten kinds of cookies. Those she assembled on trays during the weekend while admonishing herself to accept her own limitations for once.

Effie wasn't at all satisfied, of course, and it was Effie who couldn't keep her mouth shut every time a collection of cookies was offered. "I didn't get a chance to make too many this year," Effie said. Or, "I didn't make as many kinds as last year." Or, "Don't forget to take your cookies, I wish I had more to give you, but ..." Or, "I'm sorry I didn't make your favorite kind this year."

Monday morning Alyssa made some cookie deliveries that didn't require Jeff, then stopped to arrange delivery of Jeff's gift on Christmas Eve day. She was bustling out of the store when she thought she saw a familiar face looking at displays in front of the bookstore in the shopping mall. She walked over and when she was fairly certain of identity, peeked around the man's form and said, "Brandon, is that you?"

The man's head turned abruptly. In an instant, the face opened up. "Mrs. Matt! How are you? It's so good to see you again!"

She felt that he wanted to reach out his arms, as she, too, wanted to do. But neither did. "What are you doing these days?" she asked, wishing that she could remember when, exactly when, so that she could figure out the next question.

"I graduate this year. Then I'm committed to a firm in New York City. It's not the best of situations, I like living upstate. But it's a start."

"You always were an optimistic soul. You never once complained about anything." Then she remembered when. "And I was really piling on the work in those days. What did you end up majoring in?"

"Accounting."

"What? I thought for sure you'd be somewhere in the humanities end of it. You were so articulate and so skilled. I used to wait panting for your papers."

He laughed. "That was the most well-kept secret of the century. I couldn't bear to let you know I hated English."

"Brandon! I'm in shock!"

"But by the time I finished your course, I loved it."

"And that's the nicest thing you could have said to me today."

"Are you still there? Teaching, I mean."

"Yes, I suppose I'll be there forever and then some."

"You were one of the best teachers I had in high school, you and Mr. Cote and Mr. Axelrod."

450

"That's pretty prestigious company. I don't have enough years."

"Oh, and Mrs. Tevarro. I don't know where I'd be if she hadn't beat some sense into me junior year. She made me think about things, well, in much the same way as you did, only with her more of it stuck, I think."

"The brain of a sophomore is a slippery thing. You don't have to explain that phenomenon to me. And you ended up in accounting. Well, the world needs good accountants too. From the looks of it, you haven't completely forgotten your English training. It does my heart good to see you again in front of a bookstore."

"I'm buying gifts, just got in today. I love books, always have. Do you remember the time you brought that old, old copy of *A Tale of Two Cities* to class just to show it off? And those other old books too. I felt really special when you let me take some of them home to read." He started to laugh. "I kept them safe in my sock drawer! Isn't that a riot? God, I was serious when I was sixteen. But I was afraid something would happen to your antique books."

"They weren't antiques, Brandon. Old, yes. Valuable antiques, not really, not in a marketable sense, anyway."

"But you handled them as if they were the most precious things you possessed."

"Drama, Brandon, sheer and simple drama. A teacher's most effective instructional aid."

"Pretty good, I thought I had you fooled with my well-kept secret."

"Teachers do it every day. It's harmless enough. But it takes a lot of energy."

"I always wondered how you could get so excited over spelling and grammar. For years I figured teachers were just weird that way, then I had you and thought it was natural. Now you're telling me you faked it. How am I supposed to handle such disillusion, Teach?"

"No, simpleton, I never faked anything. The sincere feeling is there all right, it just takes an extra push to keep it riding the surface. But what do you care about drama anyway, you're into calculators and ledgers."

"You know, you'll be very interested in knowing what freshman accounting students are being told in colleges today. I'm involved in freshman orientation, so I know. First of all, they're told that the attrition rate for accounting students is extremely high, and it takes brains and persistence to make it in accounting."

"I knew that all along, Brandon. I've been teasing you, but I greatly admire scientists and mathematicians. Any function of the human brain delights me. I certainly wasn't attempting to insult you."

451

"Of course not. But there's been an enlightenment, a kind of marriage between science and the humanities. At least that's the way I see it. It makes me think of that short story we read, the one about the boy questioning man's mortality. He's afraid of death and no one can help him, not even a priest, and his mother and father argue because he's science and she's humanities. And the kid finds his answer himself by combining the two."

"John Updike. 'Pigeon Feathers.' "

"That's the story. The boy combines scientific observation with a love for beauty and his faith in God, and solves his problem. That's much more dramatic, I suppose, than what I'm leading up to, which is this: the second thing being preached to freshman accounting students is that the person who distinguishes himself in English has a better chance for success in the field of accounting than the person who has average or below-average English skills."

"Oh, I like that. I love that. That's dramatic enough for me."

"The more prestigious firms are swamped with applications. Sometimes the applicants are narrowed down to the point where the only basis for comparison rests in language skills. All are equally fine accountants, but the one who gets the job is the one who'll be able to handle complaints tactfully and write reports skillfully. That's how I got my job, Mrs. Matt; I was told that my ability to express myself raised me head and shoulders above the others. Competition is fierce with those big firms. Don't let anybody kid you, English is just as important to a mathematician as it is to a secretary."

"I had a kid tell me the other day that it didn't matter if he couldn't spell because he planned to work in an office and the secretary would have to do it, so why should he bother?"

"That's a terrible attitude. What's wrong with kids today?"

"Nothing any different than what was wrong with kids when you were in high school. I shock a lot of them when I explain that college math majors have to take English and that English majors have to take math. All students aren't like you were, Brandon. More's the pity, too. I'm glad everything worked out so well for you, and it pleases me to think that I played a small part in your success."

She basked in his smile. "Not small. Large." he said. "It was good seeing you again. Have a Merry Christmas."

"You too, and get in there and buy the place out. How's the ad go? A mind is a terrible thing to waste?"

He nodded and turned to enter the store, but didn't. Instead he jerked his body around, planted a light kiss on her cheek, and said, "My girl likes poetry. What do you suggest?"

"Anything by Rod McKuen. But look around, you never know what you might find!" The words trailed after him as he sped into the store and blended in with the horde of other shoppers.

Alyssa walked on with lighter step, anxious to make one more cookie delivery before she was due home to start supper. A few storefronts beyond the bookstore, she slowed again. She was almost sure she saw Jean. In a Mother-To-Be shop. She crossed over to the other side and couldn't resist when she was sure Jean's head was peering over the rack of maternity tops. Jean didn't see her when she said, "Well, you could've told your Mother Confessor that number six is on the way!"

"Heaven forbid!" Jean exclaimed, then turned, eyes rolled upward, hands raised in supplication, "Please, Lord, spare this miserable sinner!"

Other women in the store looked and giggled.

"Who are you kidding, Tevarro," Alyssa teased. "You'd love to hear the pitter patter to the potty chair again."

"Keep your alliteration to yourself. I'm at the grandmother stage right now, thank you. This store gives me the jitters to begin with, and I have to listen to you mangle a perfectly lovely little image."

"You looked as if you were thoroughly enjoying yourself. Can I help it if you transmit the glow of motherhood?"

"Well, the glow is secondhand. It's for another less fortunate than I." Puzzlement on Alyssa's face caused Jean to go on. "Every Christmas we sponsor a family that needs some help. It's bad enough to be down and out, but painful as hell at Christmas, especially with kids."

Alyssa was touched. "What a beautiful tradition. Where do you find these people? I know they're all around, but I'm sure you don't go knocking on doors."

"There's a variety of ways. I've gone through Catholic Charities and used the local Social Service Agency a few times. This year I made a connection through one of the nuns at church. I try to vary it every year. It is, by far, the best way to spend Christmas."

"It must be, just knowing that you've helped someone out. I'm going to speak to Jeff about it; we should be doing it, I think, seeing that we have no children of our own to buy for. We spend a fortune on each other. Some of that money could be put to better use."

"And I started because I have children. Years ago. I got fed up with their whining and crying every Christmas. The living room would be overflowing and they weren't satisfied, they always thought of what they wanted but didn't get. Or they'd fight over each other's gifts. They were spoiled rotten, and I had to do something short of child abuse. The first time we sponsored a family, I got them involved in the shopping. The next year they were on my tail at Thanksgiving to get started. I broke them of their selfishness. I made them sacrifice some of what they wanted, most of it's crap anyway, kids want everything they see, then ignore it once they've got it."

"Do you shop alone now?"

"Hell, no. They're all over the mall today. Dominick and I will come back tonight to finish up. This year's family has a set of twin boys, a set of twin girls, and one on the way."

Together they said: "Maybe two on the way."

Jean continued, "I always try to get a large family so the kids could split up and learn to handle money. One year the ages corresponded exactly, and my kids formed a coalition and informed me that they wanted nothing themselves. I wasn't too happy about that."

"One extreme to the other."

"Kids don't want to hear about happy mediums. But we worked through it all right."

"So you buy for the parents too?"

"Not really. We usually get some family gifts in addition to the stuff for the kids. Mostly food. I've been told that the father is laid off this year. That unemployment check doesn't stretch too far and I guess he's too proud to apply for food stamps, so I'm putting together some food baskets."

"But if they're too proud for food stamps, how do you get them to accept charity?" She was thinking of "The Sampler." She couldn't help it; the parallel was too striking. "The Sampler" by I.V. Morris.

"Oh, I don't. I have no idea who they are. Don't want to know. I'll deliver the goods to the nun and she'll take care of it. Christmas Eve. Listen, there isn't a parent on earth who would refuse gifts for his kids on Christmas Eve, especially when there's nothing under the tree and the gifts are tagged from Santa Claus."

"Is that what you do?"

"Sure. The nun gave me names, ages, and sizes. Besides toys, the kids can use clothing. Warm coats, hats, mittens, pajamas. Do you know how many pairs of pajamas a kid goes through in a year? Before you know it, those little toes are poking through the feet. And I make sure each child gets at least one book."

"It does sound like fun, Jean, the shopping, I mean. Next year you can give me a number to call."

"Will do. Gladly. Right now you can help me select an outfit for the brave mother. I thought that would be a good gift for the unborn, however many there are."

Alyssa agreed and told Jean about her conversation with Brandon Gilly as she provided a second opinion on what would be pretty enough for a woman expecting her fifth child.

III

Alyssa and Jean spent the holiday in typically Italian fashion: the big fish bash Christmas Eve, the visits, food, visits, food, visits, food, food, food Christmas Day.

Bonnie Mason spent the first Christmas since her childhood feeling loved and wanted. She delivered a gift to Mrs. King Christmas Day, noticed redness around her eyes, and insisted that she join the festivities two floors above.

Emanating from family ties and personal joys, the warm aura of Christmas enveloped them all in its seasonal arms.

Jean and Bonnie sponsored family partying for New Year's Eve, but the evening was its usual ordinary self for Alyssa. She saw no reason for celebration; she never had. It was a time to pause in grateful retrospection, that was true enough. But she never could dredge up much enthusiasm for noisemakers and party hats. It wasn't that she lacked optimism. It was something else, something deep inside her that made her wary of the unknown.

And so the season of light came and passed them by, the season of light with its attending warmth amidst cold, joy amidst sorrow, pleasure amidst pain. The eternal cycle moved forward with slow and steady pace and pulled them on.

455

BOOK THREE: An - TITH - e - sis

Testing ...

The kids were sluggish after vacation, and so was Alyssa. The only way to get them going was to light the fires of her own ambition and enthusiasm. She was looking forward to literature with all three preparations, literature five times a day. *Tale* with 2R, *Othello* with seniors, *Caesar* with 2S. Each required an inordinate supply of stamina, not to mention strong vocal chords. It was impossible to save her voice or spare her throat when she necessarily had to teach literature five times a day for weeks on end. She needed to wind up to peak level and stay there.

It didn't help that first week back when she attempted to unlock her room and couldn't because the door lock was jammed with glue. True, it was an innocent enough prank, she didn't take it too personally because other rooms were glued shut as well. But she had to handle homeroom attendance in the hall, take notes on a piece of paper, then transfer the information to the cards later in the day. She had to wait for a custodian to use a torch to get the glue out of the keyhole. He was adept with the procedure, bless him, and saved her from conducting first period in the hall. Once the glue was hot enough to run, the keyhole cleared; then the custodian gave her a lesson in how to maneuver the key in order to use the lock. "Force the key all the way in," he said, "then let up on it a fraction, just a fraction, and turn." She tried it a few times until she did it exactly as he said; he was right, the key wouldn't function any other way. He also told her to keep a tissue or a cloth handy for use whenever she pulled the key out of the lock. The glue would run for days.

In the same week, Beth Whittsley's room was ransacked. Excuses were stolen, books ripped apart, two windows broken. The worse thing though, as Beth explained, was the slimy sputum she found on the floor, on mutilated books, on the walls. It was disgusting enough to reactivate her ulcer, she said, in the hope that saying it would lessen the possibility. And the possibility was compounded by the fact that she had to move her classes to the auditorium while the mess was being cleaned up. When she found out it would be a week to ten days before the windows were replaced, she let loose with stronger language. Better to curse than to bleed.

It was a week to remember. Besides the glue and the spit, it was the week during which Alyssa became mired in far stickier stuff. Ann Brady appeared in her doorway one day during seventh period.

458

There was a mother in Ann's office, a mother waiting for the kill. Ann stayed with the class, while Alyssa, not pleased at having to leave, met with the parent. "It won't take long," Ann said. "Please go down there and see what you can do with her. I'm at my wit's end. It's too late to transfer him into a scholarship section."

Ann was right; the meeting didn't take long at all. Alyssa carefully outlined the student's progress, using grades and performance as a basis for her evaluation. She summed it all up with a strong suggestion that the student remain in regents. It would be highly unlikely that the student would be able to handle the vigorous regimen of a scholarship section, especially since he would be required to make up four months worth of work to begin with. How could he do that when he was such a mediocre (she said "average") regents student?

Mother said: He's Not Doing Well With You Because He's Bored.

Mother said: The Last Teacher He Had Challenged Him More.

Mother said: His Grades Are Low Because He's Not Interested Enough To Do The Little Work You Assign.

Alyssa's mind went into convulsions. Because she immediately realized that Mother Was Right. Why hadn't she caught it herself? It was as common as sin. Many times in the past she had encouraged regents kids to transfer into the upper level. But they had to be assessed and moved quickly in September. She thought about the boy who had transferred from a scholarship section taught by another teacher into one of her regents sections a few years back. As Mother was hurling barbs, the earlier boy's face popped into her mind. That time she recognized early that the boy was misplaced and literally pleaded with him to try scholarship with her. The other teacher had frightened him out of his wits. After she pressured the boy and his counselor (the boy's entire schedule had to be changed to get him into her one scholarship section), she finally got her way. The boy went on to win a Merit Scholarship his senior year. And now, this time, Mother was saying: He Needs To Be Challenged Or He Won't Do Anything At All. I Want Him In A More Difficult Class.

"Yes, perhaps that would be the best thing," Alyssa conceded. Why hadn't she caught it? Now she saw it all, all the symptoms: the boredom, the condescending attitude, the vacant stares, the erratic grades. She offered the use of one of her two scholarship sections. He could transfer into either first or fifth period with her. Her reasoning was simple: He was her mistake, her oversight, her responsibility. Another teacher should not be saddled with the duty of providing and grading all that make-up work. She had failed to see, failed to evaluate, failed. Her reasoning was simple, but she kept it to herself. It wouldn't have mattered anyway.

Mother piled on the excuses: He had a class first period with a teacher he loved (with a teacher who challenged him); the first period class couldn't be changed because it was offered no other time with the same teacher; he had lunch fifth period and his fourth period was another class he adored; besides, fourth period was too early for lunch.

Alyssa got the message. The words she swallowed back during the meeting were pounding in her head as she made her way back to 418, as she informed Ann of the decision, as she picked up the threads of her lesson. It's the price we're paying, she thought. It's the price of forced indifference and misplaced priorities. I care with every particle of my being, but I cannot do it all. What would you have said if I told you that? If I told you I looked at your son and did not see because I cannot do it all? It wouldn't have mattered, it would have made no difference. And rightly so. Because we both know that the boy is all that matters. Why should you care that I'm a victim too? That this is the first time I've lost a student under these circumstances.

By 7:00 Friday morning of that week after vacation all the radio stations in the area were announcing school closings. For those who are not winter sports enthusiasts, snow becomes the enemy in January. It must be fought. All the pushing, lifting, blowing, and redistributing is futile eventually, for the snow will not go away. It will increase at will as long and as often as the season permits.

Snow was falling Friday morning, but the reason for school closings was wind. Gusting and howling, the wind produced massive white-outs that caused zero visibility. Students quite naturally adore snow days. But no one on earth loves snow days more than teachers. No sub, no plans, no records (although Effie noted snow days on homeroom cards; what if a student were accused of being truant on a snow day?), no work, no worries. Unexpected nirvana.

Alyssa waited to hear the announcement over at least two stations (she never believed her ears when it came to snow days), then called Jean, who never listened to the radio at all in the morning. Jean was as thrilled with the news as Alyssa; snow days made the long stretch more tolerable. Alyssa said: "You know, there's something perverse in our thinking. We just had two weeks off and we can't wait for the week in February." Jean said that the perversity was not in their thinking and that five weeks was indeed a long time to go.

The next week provided some excitement along the way. As the press put it: TEACHERS AND DISTRICT REACH IMPASSE. STRIKE VOTE MONDAY. Alyssa read through the article, though she was familiar with most of the information from fact sheets distributed by the union. Rumblings predominated in all four faculty rooms right after vacation; people were growing weary of the wait, impatient with the old pay scale, anxious for settlement. BCA was the happy home of what the press called a "militant" faction. Agreement on the last three contracts had been stalled and stalled until the threat to strike was issued. Teachers at BCA were instrumental in rallying the troops. Even then, talks dragged on until the eleventh hour.

The article gave the history of negotiations with an emphasis on the recurring threats to strike. The article delineated the issues causing the current impasse with an emphasis on the union's demands. The article insured that the entire community fully understood that a strike would be illegal, that teachers would lose two days' pay for each strike day, that the union would face heavy fines, officials risk imprisonment, and everyone would suffer. Everyone. Especially the kids. And, the article glibly stated, the core of teachers pressing for a strike was "reportedly" based at BCA. Alyssa was irritated at the article, but that was nothing new. She was irritated not because it fulfilled the public's right to know what was going on but because of the way it was written. It was the same every contract. Teacher wanted too much, the district was only trying to hold the line. The glaring opinion was presented as fact not in so many words, but between the words, hidden in the spaces, absorbed in the newsprint. From now on, every article related to the contract dispute would offer the same information on the history of negotiations, the illegality of teacher strikes, and the penalties for striking. From now on every article would skillfully imply that teachers were the bad guys, that anyone who would leave his classroom, abandon his children for a picket line was not worthy to be entrusted with the minds of those children. Striking was illegal, thus a scurrilous and vile activity. Teachers should be better than that, teachers should rise above the common herd. Teachers are not mill hands or ditch diggers. Feature articles would make the appeal on the subliminal level, editorials would hammer away on the conscious level.

They want us to assume a prone position and do what we're told, Alyssa thought. They want us docile and dormant, mechanized and subhuman. Keep up the good work, folks, but don't complain. Don't raise a single cry or we'll crush you with an iron boot. Or with

461

newsprint. Well, I want a raise and I want better working conditions. And I'm willing to fight. They could call her a militant or anything else that pleased them; Alyssa Matthews was still strongly in support of a strike. What disturbed her more than money matters was the district's stand on issues directly related to the classroom. They wanted to increase maximum class size to 32; they wanted to leave the number of preparations open and at the discretion of the building principal; they wanted to re-establish bus and cafeteria monitoring duties for classroom teachers. Each item made Alyssa emit a roar of anguish; she felt as if she were being beaten about the head. How could they be so blind to reality?

"They're trying to eliminate the minimum-wage monitors we fought like hell for last time," Jason told her the next day. "It's money, pure and simple. Teachers constitute the bulk of the work force and they want all the services they can get out of us during the day. I'm going to be honest with you, Mattie; we never used that information you gave me on the papers you grade. It would have backfired for sure. They would have looked at it and said fine, that's just what we expect from our teachers. They would have turned it against us. If you're doing all that work, why isn't everybody? They don't give one damn about anybody's state of mind or physical condition. We're so many bodies that they have to pay, that's all. Maybe someday they'll realize that the quality of education is directly related to their teachers and nothing else. So far we haven't made a dent with that philosophy."

He went on to tell her that a study into the feasibility of establishing a Middle School for grades six through eight was currently on the agenda; it was a new approach being considered by districts all over the country. Alyssa exploded. "That means we get ninth grade here?!? Are they crazy?!? With all the damned decrease in enrollment we still don't have any empty classrooms! These halls are jammed now between classes! And who the hell wants to teach ninth grade? Not me. They'll have to transfer more teachers up here." It only took a second for her to figure it out. "Oh, Christ, that's why they want to open up the number of preparations. Jason, please, I can't handle four preps. Lord, what are they trying to do to us? They'll be able to lay off a few that way, though. Right?"

Of course, he said, of course. He had seen the projection: one English teacher could be eliminated in each of the three junior highs; and the redistribution would make it possible to close one elementary school. Hannah Boesch was shrieking epithets from the grave.

"When are the bastards going to hit us with a sixth class?" Alyssa spoke more out of bitterness than anything else, and lurched backward at Jason's response.

"They want to eliminate our free period. That's the first step."

"You won't agree with that, will you? Ever? Tell me you'd die first, or I'll march right down to the cafeteria, steal a knife, and slit my wrists this very moment."

"We gave them a flat no. But they'll try again. If they don't get it this contract, they'll try again next time."

"I can't believe it. How can they even consider such a thing?"

"Can't blame 'em for trying. If they give us a raise, they want to get their money's worth. Settling on economic issues isn't the problem, the problem is trying to get a better economic package without letting them take it out of our hides."

"And I used to think I deserved a raise because I was improving my skills as a teacher. It doesn't work that way, huh?"

Jason cracked up. "Not hardly."

She absorbed the double negative. "Six classes. Four preparations. No free period. Homeroom. Study hall. It sounds like something out of Ionesco, or Kafka. Or Poe."

"It won't happen. Not all of it. Not yet."

"Shit. Shit and shinola."

"Aptly put. For an English teacher."

"It's the 'not yet' that gives me the shivers. What are the odds for the vote? I'm sure you've been canvassing."

"It doesn't look good. If you remember, we barely made it last time. People get worn down going through this every contract. I honestly don't think we're going to get enough support."

On Monday of exam week the entire force of district teachers met and argued the pros and cons of a strike. Controversy arose as the result of differing situations. Conditions varied from school to school, from grade level to grade level. One teacher shouted that it was highly unprofessional and degrading to walk a picket line, so another angrily asked what could be more degrading than the treatment teachers were currently tolerating. One said that it wasn't fair for the kids to suffer; another said that they were already suffering. The only way was through peaceful negotiation; the only way was through violent upheaval. The district was traditionally hard line, a strike would only inflame the public; the district needed to be taught a lesson, a strike would show that teachers were concerned over educational policies and wanted a voice in determining those policies.

463

On and on it went. And the camps of thought, already established before the meeting began, became obvious. Grade school teachers weren't concerned over preparations; they weren't likely to be assigned more than one grade level (although at that point in the discussion a high school teacher took pleasure in hurling a wicked prophecy). Some teachers were only concerned with the percentage of increase in pay and shut off the fanatics shouting for a decreased work load. Workloads varied so much that some had no idea what others were bitching about.

The fight raged for an hour and a half. Someone noticed that it was 5:00, heeded the grumblings of an empty stomach, and moved that the vote be taken. A hand vote was not at all helpful. But union officials were prepared with paper ballots. By the time votes were cast, ballots counted and recounted, and the final tally ready, it was after six o'clock. Over half the group had left. That in itself was prophetic.

A simple majority was needed. Out of close to eight hundred votes cast, the simple majority to give the union some leverage was not reached.

"Do you believe it?" Jason repeated to Alyssa on the way out. "Do you believe it? Twenty votes? Twenty rotten votes."

Jean said, "Why the hell didn't you stuff the ballot box? I would have, there's too much at stake." She knew that a PERB official had counted the votes, but she said it anyway.

"For you there's too much at stake," Jason observed. "You heard old Miss Crummy state that she would never leave her little boys and girls out on the streets. That's her definition of dedication."

"What? Wipe their noses and pat them lovingly on the head? That's the way I treat my dog. That isn't necessarily education, even though she's been doing it for forty-five years."

"What is her real name, anyway?" Alyssa asked. "We always called her that too."

"That's it," Jean said. "I always thought she should be running a bakery, even when I was a kid. And she was young then, when I had her."

"Well," Jason conceded, "she's not the only one who won't even think strike. There are a few hundred others, young and old alike. I'd like to see all of them continue with negotiations now. All I know is I used to enjoy walking upright."

"It's not good, is it, being split down the middle," Jean said. "No matter how the vote turned out, that's not good."

Jason smirked. "Played right into the district's hands, we did. That's exactly what they want."

"Divide and conquer," Alyssa summarized. "It's as old as rope."

"What happened to Bonnie?" Jason asked, looking around. "I thought I saw her with you."

"She waited awhile, then left. I'll call her when I get home. She'll be disappointed. It's her tenure year and she voted to strike. Everybody's different, I guess. Each votes according to his own conscience."

Jean snickered. "Or his own bank book, or his own greed, or his own ambition or his own fear, or his own weakness, or his own strength. Must you be so damned *understanding* all the time, Matthews?"

"I'll have to catch Bonnie tomorrow," Jason interceded. "I saw her name on a list of possible lay-offs. I thought I'd warn her, so the letter won't be too much of a shock."

"Oh, Jay, she'll be crushed. What will they do, grant her tenure, then lay her off?" Alyssa moaned.

"That's better than denying tenure and firing her. It has to be one or the other. At least she'll have a chance for callback. But her name was last on the list, so she may be spared after all. Don't say anything to her about it, I'll handle it."

Alyssa hoped he didn't think he'd handle it over dinner. When she arrived home and told Jeff about the vote, he shook his head in a gesture of futility. "How can a union fight without the support of its members? That took the teeth out of any kind of strategy!"

Alyssa, who was getting used to futility, answered, "That's about the size of it. How much can a team accomplish by gumming it?" She was resigned to the fact: the English department report was ancient and worthless. It meant nothing, would prompt no action, had been a waste of time and effort. It was already outdated. Conditions were threatening to become worse, far worse, than those outlined in that silly report.

Testing ...

During exam week the temperature dipped below the human toleration level. Old Forge was making national news with readings of forty and fifty degrees below zero. The area was frozen in time, though time didn't congeal any. It was the kind of cold that causes the hairs in the nose to stiffen and prickle, the kind of cold that freezes exposed skin in minutes, the kind of cold that burns families out of their homes and kills old people unaware of the dangers of hypothermia. Warnings accompanied every weather report, and vulnerable humans panicked at the words "wind chill factor." It was a time to concentrate on survival.

The exam schedule, distributed the day of the strike vote meeting, incited some cries of discontent. Exam schedules always do. In January the small schedule required each teacher to proctor an average of three times. That was Alyssa's experience. She felt that three duties were fair enough. She knew that some teachers didn't get any, some were assigned one or two, but at least her three weren't four as some were assigned. Spread over three days, the half-day assignments still offered some time off. The state allowed classes to be canceled during exam days. In the absence of proctoring duties, a teacher was free, free, free! No wonder that some scrutinized the schedule to compare duties, to see who was where and when and how often.

Teachers were warned every year that presence in school on exam days was required, duty or no duty, because exam days were scheduled work days. It never occurred to anyone that hours spent at home on schoolwork throughout the year more than compensated for a day or a day-and-a-half off. Then again, not all teachers take work home ...

The unwritten, unspoken corollary to the warning was followed by almost everyone: If you don't report in, stay home, out of sight of the rest of humanity. Do not shop, do not ski, do not poke your head out the front door, do not venture out to the mailbox during school hours. Everyone knew the reasons: Grade school teachers became incensed when they knew high school teachers were getting time off during exams (even though they began later and were dismissed earlier every day of the year); and it was poor strategy, very poor strategy to let the public see teachers out and about during the school day, exams or no exams.

466

Alyssa was happy to stay home, especially with the weather the way it was. No amount of clothing was enough to shield her from the elements. Her three duties were spread out over two of the three days. She was scheduled for Wednesday morning and afternoon and Friday afternoon. Most times, people were scheduled for a half day on each of the three days, just to pull them in each day. She was happy that was not the case for her because she was feeling sick again. She stayed in bed all day Thursday, but wouldn't call in to release herself from the proctoring duties. It was ridiculous to request a sub, a waste of money; the practice was frowned upon in the office anyway. In case of illness, a teacher was expected to call the office so that another unassigned teacher could fill in. That did not appeal to Alyssa at all. Somebody would end up with another duty; it wasn't right to do that to someone else. And it was inevitable: the someone else would be called at home to hustle in for duty number four. She didn't want that to happen, so she sniffled and wheezed her way in. There was a minimum of talking required, and, for the most part, she was only needed for her gender. Each room was staffed with at least two proctors, one male and one female, in case a student of either sex needed to leave the room during the exam.

Wednesday morning she and Paul were scheduled together for the competency test in reading, but she spent most of the time in the room alone because Paul had to circulate to other rooms to make sure all was running smoothly elsewhere. He cursed a blue streak and apologized profusely at having to leave, but he had had no success in convincing the office that he couldn't run the exam and be assigned to proctor at the same time. Alyssa understood; it happened all the time. In June similar stupidities ran rampant.

She made it through the morning just fine; not a single boy requested bathroom privileges. And the room was small. She had only forty-five students to watch over. Her main concern all morning was the bubbles. She walked up and down the rows of seats and peered down on computer sheets to make sure students were filling in the circles completely with their number two pencils, to make sure they erased completely, to make sure they didn't inadvertently skip a section and throw off all succeeding answers. Paul had mumbled something about the answer sheets before he left, something about confusing the kids unnecessarily. Hand scoring was strongly suggested, so why were the kids subjected to computer sheets? Alyssa let him mumble on; she certainly had no idea why. And he was in no mood for what she was thinking: Ours is not to question why ... She wasn't even sure that she saw any humor in it.

467

There was one boy sitting in the front who had her in tears within fifteen minutes of the start of the exam. He worked with a fierce intensity. But for an interceding inch, his nose would have touched the desk top. When the point on his pencil snapped off, he carefully moved the pencil aside and picked up the piece of lead, which he held with the tips of two fingers, and continued to work. Alyssa watched him horrified. She quickly hunted through her purse, found two pencils, and lowered herself in front of the boy's desk. After a few seconds he became aware of her presence and raised his head. She explained with as much tenderness as she possessed that he could raise his hand to get another pencil, that he didn't have to use the broken lead. He seemed to understand, but fell back into old habits once she moved away from the desk. His back hunched, his head dropped, and his hand resumed its slow mechanical movements. Alyssa walked to the back of the room and stared out a window until the tears evaporated.

She met Jean in the faculty room for lunch, or rather, for the time allotted for lunch. "I'm going to blast the hell out of some kids come Monday," she told Jean after describing the pathetic sight she had just witnessed. Monday, the first day of the second semester, would be the perfect time for some new starts. "I've got so many kids wasting their God-given intelligence that it makes me sick. After seeing that poor child in there, I want to kick a few behinds. That boy has nothing to work with and he's devastating enough. But the ones who refuse to work with what they've got are an even bigger horror."

"Ah, but the state is taking care of all those problems with these exams," Jean said pseudo-innocently. "Here's the propaganda. These tests are designed to eliminate illiteracy in the State of New York. Haven't you read the manual? Never fear, the State Education Department is here." She tossed the manual across the table.

Alyssa had not had an opportunity to read the manual. Her copy was lost in a pile with other booklets, pamphlets, circulars, and manuals offering advice on how to teach, what to teach, and when to teach. If she studied everything in the pile, she wouldn't have any time to teach.

She knew the basics of the competency tests, Paul had conducted meetings to insure everyone's familiarity with the legal responsibilities of the schools and of teachers. But she hadn't read the manual. By the time she hit the tables on DAP (Degrees of Reading Power) units and the readability of prose, she wished she hadn't begun. It read like *Alice in Wonderland*. It read like The Ten Commandments. Sentences and whole paragraphs assaulted her.

She never noticed that she had two cigarettes lit at once, nor did she notice that Jean started smoking one of them.

She knew that the State Reference Point was the cut-off score identifying students in need of remediation. She also knew that the reading exam was issued in varying forms according to the readability levels of passages. So the business department was not alone on that, though it suffered continuously.

At one point Alyssa looked up at Jean and offered a subtitle for the manual: How The Bureaucracy Covers Its Ass. "If we were able to give adequate instruction, kids wouldn't need these goddam tests! Now I understand why Paul was shaking in his shoes last year when he ordered us to keep separate folders for kids who scored below 44 on the writing competency. At least we have one reading teacher to maintain the facade in that area, but we had to look as if we were fulfilling the mandate for writing remediation also. Paul set up a special filing cabinet in the resource room and was on our backs for months."

Jean asked for an explanation. She wasn't aware of the special irritations of sophomore teachers, just as they were not necessarily aware of hers.

"We had to remediate our own kids," Alyssa continued. "And after this afternoon's test, we're stuck again. Who else is going to do it? All the rhetoric about other disciplines being equally responsible for writing and reading skills is so much hogwash. Remediation is our burden. Last year I had seven kids who scored below 44, so I had to run off materials and keep special folders for those seven kids. It was a farce. It had to be a farce. When the hell was I supposed to find the time during the day to give intense individual attention to seven kids? I ended up assigning them the extra work and documenting all of it. I wrote notes right on the folders, giving dates and listing assignments, what was turned in and what wasn't, when I issued reminders and when they were ignored. It was an exercise in self-preservation. I didn't help any of those kids and I thought about every one of them as a casualty that couldn't be avoided.

"But I made damn sure I kept accurate records. I kept thinking that the time it took to keep records could have been, should have been used to help the kids! And Paul tried, he tried like hell to get us some time during the day to work on it, but you must know what a laugh that turned out to be."

Jean bummed another cigarette. "When did you resume this evil habit?" Alyssa queried.

"I just proctored with Al Rentsen. He's enough to make me take up chewing the stuff. He drives me up the wall. He stayed in the room a total of fifteen minutes during which he decided to take the exam. He thought he was being cute. I looked over his answers after he left for the fortieth time, and I had all I could do not to puke."

"Well, you'd better exhale before I tell you what the punch line was with last year's folder folly. We were notified at the end of May that there had been a mistake, that those kids had taken the wrong form of the test, that they had to be retested in June. Paul was breathing fire because the notification was received in February but took four months to trickle down to him. Now normally, one would figure that remediation certainly can't hurt, that more instruction is beneficial regardless. But there was nothing normal about that whole fiasco. The kids got nothing out of it, and I wasted a hell of a lot of time writing notes on folders. It infuriated me. But we were almost into June and I had too many other things to think about. I ditched the folders and forgot about it."

Alyssa picked up the manual again, thumbed through its pages indifferently, then slid it across the table. She stared at Jean, her face sculpted in stone, and said with marked intensity, "My regents classes haven't written a single thing yet. What do they think we are? How are we supposed to do it?"

Jean put out her cigarette. "Don't give me any more of these. If I start again, Dominick will wring my neck."

Bonnie appeared just as they were preparing to leave for the afternoon session. Jean made a trip to the bathroom because, as she told Alyssa, she was "flowing like a stuck pig again." Then Jean left for her assignment, but Alyssa waited for Bonnie to shed her coat and boots; they were both assigned to Study Hall A, along with two other teachers, for the preliminary writing competency exam. All students taking preliminary competency exams in January had either missed or failed them in ninth grade. On the way to Study Hall A Alyssa found out that Bonnie had been assigned five proctoring duties. She told Bonnie that she was a fool to put up with it, then relented when she realized why Bonnie was doing exactly that.

When they walked into Study Hall A they made an about-face for coats, and Alyssa cursed all the way because she should have known that the mausoleum would be cold. She stopped in 418 to pick up her box of kleenex, used one to clean the syrupy glue off her key, then met Bonnie, who had retrieved the coats, in the hall.

The other two proctors were in the large room when they made their second entrance. The second entrance was chillier than the

470

first. For some reason, the schedule had been modified. Alyssa was expecting Hank and Beth; when she saw Erica and Al, she wanted to run the other way. Four proctors were scheduled because the room was huge. Now there were two.

Ann Brady delivered the list of names of students taking the exam, along with test booklets and answer sheets. Alyssa made sure the list was in alphabetical order, inserting names of students added late in with the rest. Bonnie did the yelling to quiet down the kids, then Alyssa read names for seating. Bonnie watched carefully to be sure that desks were left unoccupied when the names of missing students were called. As it turned out, six empty chairs remained when Alyssa reached the end of the list. Six empty chairs and two standing students. She gestured to the students to find out their names, praying all the while that she wouldn't have to fit them in, thus move the whole room to accommodate them alphabetically. She rested when she heard their names; they were in another grouping. She checked the master list, then told them, "You're in the wrong room. Go to Study Hall C. And don't stop anywhere on the way, the test will begin soon."

The students left and four of her missing six appeared; three had reported to another room, one had obviously just made it into school. Bonnie seated them quickly.

Al Rentsen asked Alyssa why the big fuss over seating; Erica overheard him and rolled her eyes. She saved Alyssa the trouble of explaining that the answer sheets were numbered and alphabetical seating made it easier to keep track of answer sheets and missing students. Alyssa then entrusted Erica with the job of distributing answer sheets; it was best if only one person did it, to keep them in numerical order. Erica didn't miss the two empty desks, she left answer sheets in case those students showed. Alyssa gave Al a pile of scrap paper, and she and Bonnie split the test booklets. As they distributed the materials, Alyssa shouted orders," Do not open the test booklet until you are told to do so. Do not write anything on the answer sheets. I repeat: DO NOT WRITE ANYTHING ON THE ANSWER SHEETS!"

After all the booklets were distributed, Alyssa went through the computerized information section step by step. The usual problems ensued; students were confused over where to put letters and where to bubble. It was the most exasperating information section Alyssa had ever seen. Some of the boxes and bubbles ran horizontally, some ran vertically; she didn't blame the kids for their frustrated comments. It took thirty minutes to check around to see if everyone

471

was doing it right. Alyssa couldn't help equating the situation with a patient registering a high blood pressure reading after waiting five hours in the office. The kids were squirrelly already, and they hadn't even started the exam.

She quieted them down and directed their attention to the directions for the exam. She read through the directions, then explained again in her own words. Students were required to write a business letter, a report, and a composition using criteria supplied for each assignment. The directions on the cover of the test booklet were excellent, but they gave no warnings about the answer sheets. And Alyssa was frantic over the answer sheets.

She focused attention on the attached sheets of paper and directed students to separate the nine sheets into three equal groups. Each group had to remain attached, however, each group of one white, then two yellow sheets. It was pressure-sensitive paper, used for the purpose of getting three copies of each section. Each white sheet was clearly labeled to identify which part of the exam it serviced, so she pointed that out. She also stressed the importance of keeping the two appropriate yellow sheets evenly located under each white sheet, and of writing only when the other six sheets were safely pushed to the side. The paper would pick up anything written above it, that is, the yellow sheets would. The white sheets wouldn't, and if a student wrote up one section of the exam with the sheets for another section underneath, he would end up with two sections on the underlying yellow sheets.

"Please people, watch what you're doing," Alyssa pleaded, "because you cannot get more answer sheets. They are numbered, I don't have any more, and if you screw up we're both in trouble. Remember to deal with each part of the test separately, write your rough drafts on scrap paper, then transfer your final copies to the appropriate answer sheets. Right now put all the answer sheets in numerical order off to the side or in the desk. Get them out of your way until you're ready to write a final copy, then make sure that you have the proper sheets for each section of the exam. NEVER WRITE WITH MORE THAN THREE ANSWER SHEETS UNDER YOUR PEN! Now open your test booklets and begin."

As soon as the exam started, she moved to one side of the room and Bonnie moved to the other. Rentsen whispered that he'd be right back; Alyssa asked him to report the two absentees to the office, figuring that she'd get something out of him for the afternoon. As he bounded up the stairs, Erica settled in the back of the room with a newspaper.

One by one, Alyssa and Bonnie checked on students, making sure that the answer sheets were in proper order. Some students had pulled them apart wrong, some had them scattered all over the desk, some were already writing on them, totally ignoring the scrap paper. Some students were using pencils, which were mandatory for the computer section, but not acceptable for the writing, so those students had to be reminded that pencil was okay on the scrap paper but pen had to be used on the answer sheets.

Alyssa didn't dare sit down, and as long as she was up checking, Bonnie followed suit. Neither wanted to find out after it was too late that somebody messed up the answer sheets. Student after student was having a hard time doing it right. Some of the desks were absolutely filthy inside, and Alyssa understood when some students told her they weren't too anxious to touch gum and moldy food. She suggested that they keep unused, then used, answer sheets under their chairs. The desk tops were simply not large enough to facilitate proper organization of all that paper. As she walked the rows, however, Alyssa noticed that a few students were able to do it and do it well. Effie smiled broadly. She always did when she saw her own reflection.

Alyssa and Bonnie met once in the back of the room. "This is madness," Bonnie whispered. "How do they expect these kids to put up with all this malarkey? Learning to follow directions is one thing, but don't they realize that kids make mistakes? They can't even erase. That girl I was just with is almost in tears. I told her it's okay to cross out neatly with one line if she has to, but she's not pleased with that at all. She likes perfection, the poor kid; she got so nervous over the first error that she immediately made another one."

Alyssa was disgusted too; it was her first experience running the exam. She hoped she'd never have to do it again. "Some moron sitting in an office in Albany must have come up with this beauty. I can't believe that anybody who ever worked with sixteen-year-olds could have created this answer sheet mess. This is the salvation, though, this is going to solve our literacy problems."

"Tests, tests, and more tests. Why do they always think tests?"

"Somebody should issue a mandate to the state: No more mandates unless you come up with the cash to pay for the staff to implement programs to fulfill all your goddam mandates. But I'm looking for miracles and God's not making too many personal appearances this century."

Hands were up all over the room. Erica had floated away, Rentsen had never returned, so Alyssa and Bonnie took deep breaths and started circulating again. After an hour and a half, some students were ready to go. Bonnie showed Alyssa one exam she collected. The letter and the report were skimpy enough, but the composition was almost nonexistent. "He told me he ran out of words," Bonnie explained. "So I suggested that he try using some of them over again. That was an hour ago. I guess this is all we get out of him today." She wasn't happy about it, the boy couldn't possibly pass the exam. "How long are we here, anyway?" she asked Alyssa. "I'm pooped out already. This room's a killer."

"They get as much time as they need."

"You're kidding."

"This exam is too important to rush them," Alyssa said, aware of the absurdity.

"Oh, my aching feet."

"We can send out for a pizza at six."

"You can send out for anything you want at six."

"Don't you dare leave me alone in this crypt."

"Where the hell are those other two?"

"Napping? Skiing? No, I'm turning cynical. They must be shoveling out the parking lot."

"Right."

By four o'clock the room was clear of students. Most adults have trouble sitting in one spot for three hours; students get restless much faster than that. The exam was generous with time, but time was not a crucial factor after three hours. "Do they think it's all right for a kid to work seven hours as long as he passes this thing?" Bonnie asked Alyssa. "What the hell does that prove?"

"The kid gets a diploma, he can't sue the school or the state for an inadequate education, and he spends the rest of his life in low gear. I don't know, I don't know what it proves, Bon. I don't know what anything proves anymore. I only know that I want to go home. Will you deliver these to Paul? I wonder whom he roped into grading them this year."

"You're looking at her."

"Oh, yuk. Do you know what you're in for? Who's the third?"

"Beth."

"Good old Beth. She asks for it every time. But somebody has to do it. Have fun haggling."

"We get to debate every paper, don't we?"

"Every one. That's why there are three copies for each section. That's three sections per kid. Paul told me he sent the graded exams to Albany last June and half came back with the grades changed."

"Why don't they just do it there to begin with?"

"Who knows. Maybe they think we're lolling around with too much free time. When are you getting started?"

"Saturday. I invited Paul and Beth to my place. At least we can be comfortable while we argue. It's discouraging to know that some of them may be changed eventually, though. And there are so many fine lines to grading written work."

"Ah, but the time and effort is well worth it. Remember that you are being paid handsomely for your weekend work. Think about it every time you realize that you've just spent forty-five minutes coming to an agreement over one paper."

"I think that's an insult."

"What? A dollar a paper? Why, that's no insult, that's a disgrace! We made the editorial page on that one last year. A disgrace it was that teachers should be paid extra to grade papers. Grading papers is a fundamental duty of a teacher. We were ripped to shreds over a dollar a paper. Don't you remember how that editorial ended? It blew me right out of the chair."

Bonnie remembered. The editorial ended in a blaze of righteous indignation. She remembered the exact words because the ending was a repeat of the headline. It was a perfectly organized little piece of prose. The end summed up the central message very nicely, tied the essay up in a neat bundle. *What has happened to all our dedicated teachers?* the nameless author demanded with an inquisitorial voice.

"We're condemned at every opportunity," Alyssa said. "Someone should have had the moxie to answer that rhetorical question. Maybe someday, somewhere, somebody will. He'll have to scream bloody murder, though, before anyone listens. Nobody wants to know. Hell, if I weren't a teacher, I'd never believe it myself. Never."

Desdemona Be Damned

The window was deadened from lack of external light. The room was also steeped in shadows. One craved the forces of nature, the other the forces of man. Though the sky was starry clear and the lamp was within arm's reach, perception was inhibited by the obscurities of darkness. Both nature and man temporarily immobile, the darkness prevailed. Michael lay on his side in the bed, pondering the shadows. He had been on his back, but on his back he could see the stars through the skylight. Brisk winds had blown the snow away, clearing the view. It was a beautiful, sensual view, but he wasn't interested. Instead he turned on his side and faced the window.

The picture there looked like a cartoon, unimpressive after an initial view; in its entirety it was nothing more than a barrier separating in from out, an oeil-de-boeuf serving practical purposes.

He lowered his eyelids, then quickly raised them. The inner darkness harbored madness.

The bed felt prickly and irritating under him, as if it were violating his flesh with an even distribution of torturous instruments. His mind was swollen, feverish, covered with pustules. Body and mind coalesced into spasms of anguish. During one such spasm, he left the bed, left the room, seeking solace in mobility. None came.

He walked nude to the kitchen, opened the refrigerator door, and squinted at the sudden flash of light. He poured a glass of milk and carried it back to the bedroom. The bed repulsed him, so he sat in the chair beside it, sat like a shriveled old man holding his only comfort in life. His fingers were clenched around the glass with such pressure that the tips whitened. He couldn't drink, he couldn't move, he could only look at her. The desolation that he felt intensified as he watched her sleep. What agony it was that she was there sleeping, there, next to him, and still he felt desolate.

She hadn't been the same during the last few days, she had been ornery, short-tempered. She snapped at him when he left half his steak at supper, said something about expensive cuts of meat. He didn't tell her why he had no appetite.

He was losing her. He could feel it. He was losing her and he didn't know why or how. She had changed so suddenly, she had become another person. Isn't that the way it always happens? Something in her eyes, something in the way she looked at him during the last few days ...

It was unmistakable, she had grown tired of him, she was having second thoughts, she had ... found somebody else. He felt as if someone had forced a shovel down his throat and was scraping out his insides.

You're young, she would say, you're young and you'll get over it in time. You your whole life ahead of you. I was just your first love, there will be others, she would say. And he would die. It was as simple as that. He couldn't exist without her, he couldn't breathe without knowing that she was his. If she no longer loved him, the life would go out of him, drain away in rivulets like water after a heavy spring rain. He would never survive. Never.

She had to know that. Maybe that was why she was waiting, putting it off, prolonging the agony. Maybe she lacked the courage to tell him to get lost.

He suddenly became aware of the glass again. It was appealing, the thought of bloody fingers, the blood flowing through bits of imbedded glass. Visible mutilation. The best kind, after all. He set the glass down on the floor and resumed his watch, intent on studying her beautiful face. How could a face like that hide a demon? How?

Maybe there had been others before. He had seen the blood, but what of it? Perhaps he had been too naive to see the trick, the sleight of hand. Of body. She could have faked it. There are ways, there are always ways. Had she? Had she faked it, faked it all? He had seen the proof, seen her when she was unaware; he had heard from others, others who had no cause to lie.

Someone else. That was it. How could she? How could she be so shallow, so cruel? How could she destroy him so mercilessly? She had no right. People shouldn't have the right or the means to destroy other people. But if they didn't have the means, there would be no people.

She was stirring in the bed, changing position. Probably dreaming of her new lover. The picture of her in someone else's arms enraged him, his consciousness reshaped by grotesque configurations. If he had only known. If he had only known that she would change. But she had him fooled. Completely fooled, all along. If he had only known ...

It would have been the same, the same. She was too beautiful, too enticing, too clever. And he was too taken by such things, too young to know. He was the fool, he had let himself be used, and now he had to pay the price.

She moved again, her new position exposing her breasts. Arms arched above her head, hair tousled on the pillow, she looked like a goddess in repose, like the golden beauties poets speak of.

Michael Ixion shifted in the chair. His penis ached. It bothered him more than anything else that he had no control over his desire. Even now he wanted her. Even now he couldn't make the yearning stop.

Nothing in six days. She wasn't in the mood, she had too much to do, or she fell asleep. Tonight she fell asleep. She was that bored with it. With him. Over and over again she castrated him. How he felt the pain. The limb is in the trashcan, yet the suffering remains, illusion more terrible than reality.

He would tell her when she awoke to do it quickly, thrust the knife in him, the spot was marked and ready. He wanted it, had to have it, do it, do it quickly, then leave me to my martyrdom. I will wear the dagger, let the blood run with rust, and drink of it every moment for the rest of my life.

Her face was changing. The perfection was distorting, first around the eyes, then the cheeks and mouth. Her head bean to twist and buck in spasmodic contortions; her hands fisted then extended in quaking stiffness. He had seen it before. He remembered the tears, the joyful awakening, the soothing touches, the pressure of warm flesh. Now he was tempted to leave her, leave her to her own demons as she would feed him to his.

She was getting worse, her mouth agape with silent pleas, beads of sweat seeping through her skin. He spoke her name, knowing that the sound would awaken her. It surprised him that he still had some pity left.

She gasped and wrenched her way out of the nightmare. Upright and shivering, she threw her head back and inhaled great gulps of air. Then she looked at him and extended her arms. "Thank God you were here. Please, sweetheart, hold me so I stop shaking."

He didn't move, though he was shaking too. "An alarm clock would do just as well," he said tartly.

Her arms recoiled, flopped to her sides like two dead fish. "What? An alarm clock? You know what I go through when that happens. How could you say such a thing?" She was weak and confused. Why was he in the chair and not in the bed? "Baby, are you sick? What's the matter?" Why wouldn't he come to her? She felt as if she had changed channels and was in the middle of another nightmare. Was she awake or not?

"Don't call me 'baby.'"

She pulled the blankets up around her neck. She was awake, she was sure of it. And some strange being was sitting nude next to her bed. "You'd better tell me what it is, Michael. I won't let you play cat-and-mouse with my feelings."

"Your feelings? Your feelings? What about my feelings? Or don't I matter? Why do you keep me hanging around, anyway?"

"Hanging around? I don't know what you're talking about! Would you please stop speaking in riddles?"

Why was she making him say it? Did she enjoy hurting him that much? "You don't want me around any more. I know it. You haven't been hiding it very well. You don't even want sex out of me anymore."

It was true: She had been awake before and now she was asleep. It had to be. But who would startle her out of this one? And she was angry now. "Don't you dare put it that way, as if we're a couple of dogs. What the hell's gotten into you? Are you trying to get out of it? Is that it? If you are, you could do it more gently! And at a better time!" She was angry and she started to cry.

But he wasn't fooled by it; she wasn't going to trick him again. "Look, I know you've been sniffing around Haywood again. And you've been cold as hell all week. So I guess you've made the choice for me."

Sniffing around? He did think she was some kind of animal. Well, she didn't crawl to anybody, no man on earth made her cringe. He had his nerve accusing her and condemning her in the same breath. "I think you'd better go. Get out before you hurt me more than you already have."

He was enraged. "Hurt you? I'm hurting you? You're playing around with another man and I'm hurting you? What's that, some kind of new logic you're teaching?"

She screamed back. "I am not playing around with another man! And if you think I would do that to you, that I'm that kind of person, then I never want to see you again!"

"You're denying it, then."

"Yes, I'm denying it and I resent having to deny it."

"And I'm supposed to believe you. Well, I don't. I saw you huddled in a corner with him twice last week. Who knows what I didn't see."

She was beginning to understand. "We were not 'huddled in a corner.' And I will speak with whomever I please!"

"I overheard some kids talking in the locker room. They said you and Haywood are at it again. Why would they lie? They didn't know I

479

was listening. They didn't know that you stopped screwing me to screw him. Hell, I don't blame you. From what I hear, he's hung like a horse."

Bonnie was incensed, but more than that, she was saddened by his bitterness. "You think so little of me? I can't believe it, that you've turned on me this way. What makes you think that gospel is spoken in locker rooms? That's gossip, Michael, worthless gossip."

He wasn't ready yet to uproot the evil he had cultivated. "Then why have you been so cold all week?"

She wasn't about to make it easy. "Because of Jason Haywood."

His voice broke. "Why are you torturing me this way?"

She reached up to switch on a small light hanging from the wall. "Because you have to understand that things sometimes have another meaning. I don't ever want to go through this again with you. If you ever accuse me again, Michael, we're through. I will not spend the rest of my life living in fear of your jealousy. There's no reason for you to be jealous, no reason for you to imagine or believe that I would ever be unfaithful to you. I never slept with a man before you and I want only you. The very thought of infidelity is repulsive to me. That you accuse me of it is even worse. If we can't trust each other, we have no future together. I love you, Michael, but I won't let you abuse me."

He sat on the bed with her. She put her hands on his face, kissed him lightly, and continued, "I found out last week that I might have to take a lay-off next year. Jason's the union rep. He saw my name on a list. There's a chance that I won't be, though, a pretty good chance. I'll know by the end of February. I've been miserable all week because I'm frightened. A lay-off will ruin our plans. And when I tell you I'm tired, please believe it. I work hard all day. Sometimes I can't stay awake even for sex. It doesn't mean I'm not interested, sweetheart, it means I'm pooped. I read enough papers this weekend to fill this bed. Sex with you is wonderful, but loving you is even better. I like to equate the two, but I wish you'd realize that the love I feel for you doesn't diminish in the absence of sex. I love you, all of you, in and out of bed. And I waited a long time to find you."

Her eyes were filled with tears and so were his. He held her and spoke softly. "I guess I'm pretty stupid. Thank God it's not what I thought it was."

"Stop thinking, would you?"

He broke the connection. "Well, you're not very bright either!"

"What do you mean by that?"

"Why do you keep your worries to yourself? All this could have been avoided if you had told me what was bothering you!"

"I wanted to spare you."

"That's a laugh. I just went through the worst few days of my life. Thanks."

"I'm sorry. You're right. I guess we've both been screwed up."

"If you lose your job, I'll put off school for awhile, that's all. It's no tragedy."

"Oh yes it is. It is. I don't want that to happen. I want you to get an education. It'll work out. Don't worry about it."

"Why? So you can worry alone? Was it the same dream as last time?"

"No. No rocks this time. Just the vacuum. Nothing. A great mass of nothing. But terrifying. It happens when I'm overtired and anxious over something. I can't remember a time when I didn't have nightmares. It got worse when I left home to go to college. When I was a kid I used to sleepwalk. My mother had to hunt all over the house to find me."

"I didn't help your anxiety any, did I?"

"At least you woke me up. I'm surprised now that you did."

"It occurred to me not to. I'm sorry, angel, really I am."

"I'm going to buy you an alarm clock and make you look at it every hour so you never forget. And I want you to read something. A play. You'll have to read it next semester, but not until May or so. You need it now, my love. Remind me to give it to you before you leave tonight."

He pushed her back on the bed. "Any more assignments, Prof?" She pulled him down with her. "Kiss me you fool. And don't stop there."

"On one condition. We share our problems from now on."

"Agreed."

After a few minutes passed, they heard the sound of the plane. "Turn off the light," Bonnie said with a giggle.

"Why?"

"There's a plane passing."

"Who cares?"

"You like turning pilots on?"

"That's his problem."

"There are lady pilots now, you know."

"Then it's her problem. The rest of the world be damned, I've got my love."

"And Desdemona be damned too."

"Who?"

"You'll know after you read the play. She is damned, poor thing, through no fault of her own. Except that she's not strong enough to save herself."

"We saved ourselves."

"Yes. We did."

The sound of the plane became louder. The lovers looked up at the magnificent darkness pitted with spots of fire. The view from the heavens was reversed, but still, the same.

When the sound was directly overhead, Michael pulled the blanket over Bonnie, both of them laughing over his concern for her nakedness but not for his. Then, like two playful children, they waved their arms in great sweeping motions to acknowledge the unseen presence in the sky above.

A Teacher's Prayer Revisited

Second semester began with nearly as much confusion and activity as first semester. January is distinguished from September by a few months time and a sharp seasonal change, but within a high school, January and September are remarkably similar.

When Alyssa started teaching, the practice was to move students around in January whether they needed it or not. Therefore, it was necessary in those years to rewrite class registers and attendance books, to rework seating charts because, although she retained the same students, many of them were arbitrarily transferred from one section to another. She never knew why it happened. It just happened. Eventually, after years of it, somebody realized that the whole thing was rather foolish, it served no purpose other than to engender disruption and confusion, so the practice was stopped. That pleased many a teacher. It eliminated some of the work of starting anew in January by allowing students who were not starting anew to carry on smoothly. Carrying on smoothly is top priority in January. For teachers.

Alyssa expected to find her mailbox jammed on Monday morning. She had checked it on Friday when she reported in to proctor. She checked again before she left. She wanted to see her class lists before Monday morning, but they obviously weren't available yet. Apprehension motivated her, the same apprehension that accompanied her very first look at her very first class lists. That fear of what might be lurking in assignment folders never subsided in all those years.

There was no folder in January, just paper. She pulled it all out of her mailbox and glanced through the sheets on the way to the faculty room early Monday morning. Rage built as she walked.

The scholarship sections remained the same. Students who were failing were still listed. She hadn't heard a thing from parents, the notices she sent prompted no replies. Maybe parents never saw them. Maybe parents never saw report card grades. Maybe parents saw all of it. It didn't matter much, the kids weren't moving and she'd have to watch them fail the whole year.

The senior class was large. The thought of going through the research paper with another large class depressed her. Her energy level wasn't equal to the task. And second semester was make-it-or-break-it time for seniors. The pressure increased a

483

hundredfold second semester. Chances were that if she failed a senior, he wouldn't graduate. She had to be able to justify failures not only to the student but to herself.

When she looked over the lists for the regents classes, she felt the blood pounding in her head. Then she opened up the triple-folded study hall list and she thought her head would explode.

Jean was already pacing in the faculty room. Alyssa entered screaming. "I've got new kids in my afternoon classes! Where the hell did they all come from? I lost a few and was looking forward to smaller classes! Where the hell did these kids come from?"

Jean looked Alyssa full in the face and said pointedly, "Erica."

"What do you mean, Erica? A few of her kids manage to escape, but a mass exodus isn't allowed anymore. She has to keep some kids!"

"Oh, no, she doesn't. She's been promoted, the bitch. Erica is now in charge of remediating students who score below 44 on the writing competency. Give a cheer, Mattie! You won't have to put up with folders this year! Isn't it queer that you couldn't get time during the day to do it, and Erica now has all day?"

"Son-of-a-bitch."

"Erica-baby will fulfill the state mandate, whether she fulfills the state mandate or not. She has her own little room, her own little desk, and, I guarantee within a month, her own little TV. Bassard won't have to listen to any more parents complaining about her, she works with thirty kids one at a time three days a week, and we pick up her load of classes. Clever little scheme, isn't it?"

Alyssa was thunderstruck. "I suppose she doesn't have a homeroom either."

"Of course not. She's screwed up homeroom records for so many years, Bassard considers that a blessing too. Paul got her homeroom."

"Christ, he must be livid."

"I just saw him. He looks like an overripe tomato. He had no idea any of this was happening."

"Damn it, if Erica is no longer in the classroom, she should be replaced. We're now short one teacher!"

"Damn nothing. Or damn everything. It's all the same. I made that astute suggestion to Paul. He laughed like hell. She's still considered to be a member of the department, she still counts on the tally sheet."

"This is disgusting. Now I've got to get her kids through the final exam after she did nothing with them first semester! Son-of-a-bitch, this place is enough to make a sane man suicidal."

"Stop your bitching, at least you've only got a few. How would you like an entire class used to her methods?"

"What do you mean? Weren't they all split up? Who can take on a sixth class? Did they stick Paul—?"

"I now have her entire eighth period 2R class."

"What?"

"My senior section was eliminated. Somebody must have noticed I had only five kids last semester. The last I knew there were at least twenty scheduled for this semester. Lord knows what happened to them. It doesn't matter, nothing matters in this freaking hell-hole."

Alyssa lit a cigarette. "Have you checked your study hall list?"

"It's insanity. What else would it be?" Jean bummed a cigarette, lit it, and inhaled deeply. "There's something else. Paul just told me. We lost our room, the resource room."

"How could we lose the resource room? Where are all those books going?"

"They stay. But we can't use the room during the day any more because Beth and Hank have been moved in there. They were notified last week during exams that their rooms were being taken over by another department. I guess we're supposed to meet with kids out in the hall. And the only time we can get books now is before or after school. Classes will be in there every period."

"Another department needed rooms. Now we know where we stand in the hierarchy around here."

"Have you had any doubts? And we're in for worse. After that no - strike vote, we're in for worse. I'm getting out, Alyssa. The hand-writing's on the wall. Theresa's been after me to make a career change. She keeps sending me information on paralegals. They're something new in the field. I've been resisting because I'll have to take a big cut in salary. But I'm beginning to see that my sanity is worth it. Dominick is ready to support anything I want to do. I wanted to wait until the kids finish college, but by then I'll be a basket case. Or I'll have ulcers like Beth. I wish I could do what Jim Cote did. He found a job that paid more. But he's in the right field. Where the hell does an English teacher go?"

"It broke my heart when I read about Jim in the paper. Not because he left. I envy him for that, for finding something better. But it was so pathetic the way they let him go as if he had never been here. He spent twenty-five years of his life as an exemplary teacher and they accepted his resignation and crossed him off the list."

"They aren't filling his slot either. Whoever gets the chairmanship will have to keep a full schedule. Needless to say, nobody wants the

485

chairmanship. We folks with twenty or more years are too expensive to maintain. They're pleased when we leave for any reason. That's the only thing that curdles my stomach. I'll be doing the district a favor. But even that won't stop me."

"Christ, I'll miss you. You and Jim started together, didn't you tell me that?"

"Yes. He never took any maternity leaves, though. We used to joke about that. He teased me about losing pension time for biological reasons. We were two idealistic kids back then. I knew about his resignation last October. He told me in confidence the day we both found shit on our desks. Remember that? Jim, and Joe, and I. Maybe it happened to others. It was odd, all right. I still don't know who did it and I guess it stopped. I forgot about it. It didn't bother me really. It was inconvenient as hell, but not as offensive as that woman before Christmas. That letter took the stuffing out of me. I've been trying to forget about that, but I can't. I'm afraid now every time I assign something. I've been telling myself that the class is worth it, worth anything, my heart, my back, my brain. I've had to sacrifice more time at home than ever before, but I thought myself fortunate to get such a class now, when my own kids don't need to be tucked in at night and chauffeured around. I was enjoying the best experience of my career in spite of and because of the exhausting pace I've kept with that class.

"And now this. I can't keep up that pace with them along with a new preparation. I haven't taught 2R in fifteen years. Erica did nothing with them, so I'll have to teach two semesters in one. She would have passed failing exams in June, but I can't. What are the course requirements, anyway?"

"Three novels, including *Tale*, short stories, narrative poetry, vocabulary, grammar, spelling. The usual. I've got plenty of stuff you can use ..."

"No. You don't have time to go through that. I'll handle it myself. Everything else will have to slide. I'm resigned to that now. One way or another, they're going to make lousy teachers out of all of us. I'll make it through all right to the end. Then I'm kissing this place good-bye. They can find somebody else to dump on."

"How I wish I had twenty years in," Alyssa said. "I'd follow you out the door."

Alyssa passed by Erica's new room later in the day and saw Erica reading her newspaper in serene comfort. The room was small, it could accommodate only Erica, the newspaper, and ten student desks. When Alyssa passed by, none of the student desks were occupied. Alyssa vowed that she would take an alternate route for the remainder of the year.

What she dreaded most that first day of the new semester was second period. She wondered if she and Joe would have to go it alone. They had had little help when Erica was there, but at least she took the responsibility for some kids off their shoulders. Alyssa's list was unmanageable again. How she dreaded the walk to study hall! How she resented having to tolerate a repeat of the mess first semester.

When she arrived, the place was crawling with kids again. She wanted to tear her hair out. With all she had to do for her classes, she had to put up with this picayune crap. But the big surprise was Bonnie. Bonnie was there; Bonnie was Erica's replacement. Bonnie had been shifted from her afternoon study hall to the crypt second period.

But Joe wasn't there. Joe had been reassigned also. Maybe Bonnie was Joe's replacement. Either way, it was Bonnie and Alyssa, condemned to the pit together. Alyssa decided that first day of the new semester that she had no patience for study hall. Effie gave up the fight; it wasn't worth the toll it would take.

Alyssa gave Bonnie half the list of names. They both seated students who were there; neither had any desire to work on seating charts. They agreed that after the initial seating the whole place could blow up for all they cared. They would maintain a certain level of control, they would insist on quiet for their own sanity. But that was all. For the first time in her working life, Alyssa Matthews didn't care what was expected of her. She had no intention of sending names to the office, she hoped the whole place would cut so she wouldn't have to look at any of them, she wasn't spending time on attendance at all. She wanted to announce that she wasn't taking attendance so that they would feel free to make themselves scarce, but that was going too far with it. She wasn't that brazen yet.

A pinpoint of fear remained in the back of her mind. What would she say, what would she do, if someone requested attendance information on a student? What did other teachers do? Fudge it. Lie. There are ways. She couldn't extinguish the pinpoint of fear, but she responded to it in a way that never occurred to her before. She would blast anybody who wanted attendance records, lambaste him through the wall, scream that she couldn't handle it all. If anybody put her on the defense, she'd scratch his eyes out.

She would live with the pinpoint of fear as the weeks and months passed. She would slowly realize that no one else cared. It was common that truants weren't tracked as diligently in January and February as they were in September and October. It was common that nobody bothered with study hall unless teachers stirred up the muck by sending names. It was common to live through study hall every day the way the terminally ill live out their last hours. The end would come. Unfortunately with study hall, though, the end contradicted itself daily.

Bonnie was happy to be out of the air conditioning, but that didn't compensate for the chaos; her afternoon study hall had been much tamer. She told Alyssa that she too was afflicted with new students in her classes, Erica's students. She too was totally disgusted.

It was an auspicious beginning to second semester. During lunch Jean moaned, "Is it June yet?"

"Not yet," Alyssa answered. "But take heart, vacation's only three weeks away."

No matter what else happens to a teacher, be it fire or ice, famine, drought, illness, or death, a teacher must face classes of students. The primary duty remains regardless of any act of man or nature, in spite of all things, ephemeral and eternal.

Alyssa had to face five classes every day. She had to teach whether she felt like it or not. The kids had nothing to do with the forces wearing her down; the kids didn't deserve to suffer because she was suffering.

At first the doctor was pleased when he saw her the last week in January. The new blood test showed improvement. But when he looked in her eyes he saw something else. She was quiet, reserved, which was unusual. He asked if she was feeling any better; he believed in test results, but only up to a point.

She answered," I feel as if I'm fading from the face of the earth. My energy is gone. I'm burning out, Doc. I don't know how much longer I can last." She said it matter-of-factly, as if it were quite naturally the case. He said something about the kids, about how tough it must be to teach adolescents. She replied with lead in her voice. "It's not the kids. The kids are terrific. I've always been lucky enough to get good kids. The kids are no problem."

"But you're too young to be burned out," he said in astonishment.

She agreed because he was absolutely right, but she didn't have the will or the means to explain. And she forgot to tell him about her wrist. It had been aching for weeks and she walked out of the office without telling him about it. What was one more ache worth anyway? He wanted to see her again in March. If it still hurt then, she'd tell him about it.

The next week she caught the flu. With a temperature of 104 degrees for three days, she couldn't think much about anything else. Her eye sockets ached, every bone in her body revolted in pain. Even her skin was so sensitive she couldn't bear to touch it. After the fever left, she fought respiratory difficulties along with the aches. Actually, she didn't fight at all, she stayed in bed like a vegetable. There wasn't a pill that could help her, she merely had to survive it, it would have to run its course. That is the nature of influenza.

She was out sick for eight days. Because the fever hit so unexpectedly, she hadn't left plans for a sub. She forced herself to think and to write. She could hardly remember what she was doing with her classes, much less what she planned to do in the next few days. But the emergency plans were no help. Too many emergencies had rendered them useless. She wrote plans for the next five days. Three preparations, five days. In the throes of the fever, she couldn't remember where she was with *Tale*, and she had to remember. Had to. She closed her eyes and forged into her brain. It was there, the knowledge was there somewhere. Book II. Finish Book II. "Drawn to the Loadstone Rock." Test. Middle right-hand drawer of desk in 418. Begin Book III. Assign chapters 1-3, 4-6. USE STUDY QUESTIONS! Seniors. In library. When? Ask them, they have schedule. Ask Michael Ixion. Good student. He'll know. They're writing research paper. Help them. Help them. 2S. Can you teach *Merchant*? If so ... and spend plenty of time on Portia's "quality of mercy" speech. If not, grammar ... vocabulary ...

After her brain cleared a little, she wrote more plans and sent them in. She always kept ditto masters at home, so she wrote study questions for the sub to use as review with *Tale* and she devised a writing exercise for the scholarship sections. And she worried.

There were forms for college recommendations locked up in her filing cabinet, stamped envelopes ready for mailing. She had sent out six during December, four in January, and three more were waiting for her attention. What's the deadline, she always asked, what's the deadline? She knew she was a favorite with students for college recommendations. She wouldn't dream of refusing to do it. Of course, she always said, of course. And she made time. She wanted to be copious, had to settle for pithy, but couldn't refuse altogether. And there was always a deadline. A deadline. What if she didn't meet the deadline?

She was out for eight days. On the ninth day she returned in spite of lingering weakness and a chronic cough. How much longer could she stay away?

Rosemary Cania Maio

Three different subs had been called. The aftermath was gargantuan. It was impossible to figure out class attendance, though she tried. Homeroom was a maze she thought she'd never navigate. Student work was amassed in heaps, the heaps having no systematic order. It took her twenty minutes to separate 2R spelling tests from *Tale* worksheets. Somehow 2S materials were also mixed in the stew.

One sub had graded some spelling tests. Instinct told her to double check. Instinct was accurate; the grades weren't. Correctly spelled words were checked wrong, misspellings weren't checked at all.

Thus far, the heavy rope binding Alyssa Matthews' spiritual being had been snapping apart strand by strand. One by one, the taut twisted fibers, stretched beyond endurance, gave way, exposing frayed rawness. Spiritual hemp, once healthy and strong, deteriorates slowly but systematically. Once begun, the process is incurable, irrefutable, and deadly. It was during homeroom on that day in February, 1981, that Alyssa Matthews was assaulted by the horrific mental consequence of the frayed rawness.

She was attempting to handle homeroom when the phone rang. A student was wanted in the office. She went back to her cards. The phone rang again. A student was in the office, she was advised not to mark him absent. She went back to her cards. The phone rang again. Annette Nieully walked in late. Another student wouldn't move away from the front of her desk until he received absence slips validating absences since the beginning of the semester; he needed proof to show his gym teacher. Then she realized that while she was out three students had been granted late arrival privileges. That meant that they weren't absent just because they weren't in homeroom, she would get their attendance information from the junior office at the end of every week. She would have to transfer the information to the cards. At the end of every week. She was worried about her classes and she had to spend time on this garbage. Her mind revolted, the fever returned, far worse than the 104 degrees she had lived through a few days before. The final strand of hemp snapped with shocking severity.

I hate this. I hate it. I feel like an animal in a cage, pacing, pacing. Let somebody else do it. Let somebody else put up with this crap. Let somebody else put up with the demeaning insults. Anybody with half a brain can do this. I should be teaching. I'm here to teach, but I can't. I feel like an animal in a cage. I'm better than this. I'M BETTER THAN THIS!

She didn't teach at all that day. It took her the entire day to restore order and grade some papers. She gave reading periods and busywork to keep the kids quiet. That was a milestone in her career. She knew it. She knew she couldn't fight it any longer. She gave in to the unconscionable. Just as everybody else was doing.

Effie realized that not even her expertise was a weapon against such odds. But Effie wouldn't die, Effie was eternal. By virtue of its nature, the trinity remained inviolate. The trinity was One. How merciful separation would have been, how merciful.

The Allegory

The February vacation arrived none too soon. Alyssa finished *Tale* with the regents classes as she had planned. One day during class she realized that she was ignoring passages that she once thought worthy of explanation and discussion. Her book was filled with notes, but she no longer glanced at them. She had eliminated, passage by passage, most of the difficult teaching over the past few years. She now settled for the basic plot and she was ashamed.

She tried to get short story books for the scholarship sections the week before vacation. It was the first time she saw the resource room since classes had been moved in there. She couldn't believe the condition of the room. It was barely large enough for book storage and a few desks to begin with. After thirty desks were moved in, it made an anchovy can look spacious. Books were heaped in unordered piles all over the periphery of the room, on counters, shelves, even the floor. There was no way to tell which books were where, how many books of one title were available, or if titles were present in the room at all.

Beth was still half crazy trying to find her materials, which had been moved out of her old room and dumped in the midst of the chaos. Hank was furious because his filing cabinet was still in his old room, he couldn't get it moved at all. He was having trouble because his homeroom was in the old room, his classes in the new room. Nobody wanted to acknowledge the fact that he needed his filing cabinet for his classes.

Alyssa hauled books for two days. It took her twenty minutes to find sixty copies of the books she needed. Then she carried them, eight at a time because they were hardcover and heavy, to her room. She didn't have the strength to do it all at once, it was too many trips. So she made trips before and after school; she needed the books right after vacation; she wanted them in the room and ready. It was not unusual for her to play pack mule. Everyone in the department hauled books. And, remember, Alyssa Matthews used close to twenty different titles a year. The only books she didn't have to handle because the kids bought copies were two vocabulary books and two novels. The rest she moved in and out herself. She hated using kids. And she wouldn't use kids with the resource room the way it was.

She had gone to school in August to get grammar books. Over a hundred grammar books. She did it to avoid the fight for books the day before classes started. That was the usual time teachers took grammar books. The year before she had walked out without any because she couldn't stand the squabbling, the wild-eyed hysteria. People were afraid that the books would run out. So she walked out. The next day she went back to count out books in peace and couldn't get blue grammars for her regents classes. They were all gone. She had to take red ones. The exercises in the red ones were too difficult and too sparse for 2R, so she wrote dittoes all year. After that happened, she changed her strategy. She wouldn't wait for everyone else to finish, she would get there before they did. So she went in one hot, humid day in August and played mule. Her bones ached afterward and she sweated off three pounds, but she knew her grammars were safely locked up in her room for the first day of classes.

In February it was struggle enough to get short story books, but the struggle wasn't the worst of it. They were the wrong books. She knew they were the wrong books, but she had to use something. The new short story book for the scholarship sections was available; she had a copy at home. It had been there since September. She never lifted the cover. She had a choice in February: she could read and prepare fifteen stories during vacation, or she could use the same books she used first semester with the regents classes. She decided to use the wrong books.

She was sick over the fact that the book she had loved for years, *Short Story Craftsmen*, was no longer in print. The kids always bought those books, so the department had none. The more she thought about the simplicity of the stories in the regents text, the more displeased she became with her decision to use it. She still couldn't dredge up any enthusiasm over the new text, but she had to do something to make the unit tolerable to her sense of purpose.

The inadequacy of the unit bothered her through the weekend. She considered typing some of the stories on dittoes. She rejected that idea, though, because it would have taken her forever, the way she typed. But she thought of it, she thought of it.

She decided that what she had would have to do. Except for one omission. There was no allegory. She had to have an allegory.

Something in her stirred; she would one day far into the future realize that it was the rage, the rage that had grown monstrous, the rage that she had ingested for lack of proper disposal. She decided to write an allegory during vacation. She fought with it for the entire week, experiencing what she told many a student. *Writing is agonizing, gut-wrenching work.*

When she finished, she was proud. It was the first time in years that she had engaged in intellectual activity. Teaching no longer allowed such activity. And, as she intended, the allegory would afford an opportunity to give instruction on the nature of allegory as well as on a wide range of metaphors and allusions.

But it was not suitable for class. She decided that she would have to make copies of "The Man of Adamant" after vacation. Hawthorne's allegory on the Puritans, his treatise on bigotry would be far easier to use in class, though it was one of the most difficult stories she taught to sophomores.

No, as proud as she was of it, she couldn't use her allegory. It was far beyond the understanding or the appreciation of sophomores. No amount of explanation could change that. And she knew that she couldn't explain it to classes for another reason. It was too personal, too frightening; it revealed too much.

She showed it to Jean and Bonnie after vacation. Both were impressed with its significance. None of them knew that it was prophetic.

THE FALL OF THE HOUSE OF LLAH

The zookeeper decided that his charges needed

TRAINING IN SELF-CONTROL.

There had to be a way to muffle natural instincts without using maniacal force or abject leniency. A middle road had to be found between whips, which only prolonged adversity, and sugar cubes, which merely fed the illusion of passivity. He had tried both methods. The first provoked vengeance, the second spawned deceit.

He worked for years, trying one approach after another, carefully instituting, laboriously evaluating, then systematically rejecting each procedure in favor of some newly-discovered alternative. At first he worked alone. But as his duties multiplied, he found it more and more difficult to devote time and energy to his pet project. Something had to be done. He researched an answer to the problem.

DELEGATION OF AUTHORITY

What an easy solution. He immediately sought out the feeder and informed him of his new responsibilities. He never expected such a disgusting reaction.

What did he care about self-control? He supplied nourishment. His duties were predicated on natural instinct. Why would he want to suppress it? The feeder, not duped by the carrot of authority, refused delegation. The ingrate.

But not for long. The zookeeper would not tolerate such gross insubordination. The feeder would comply or the feed would be dispensed by someone else. Someone interested in progress. Someone dedicated to innovation. One thing was irrefutable: the feeder could be replaced.

But before he resorted to such a drastic measure, extremes being against his nature, the zookeeper traversed the middle road of persuasion. Just a subtle nudge in the right direction.

He requisitioned heavier feed.

He instituted periodic evaluations of technique.

He mandated minimum weight requirements for all species.

He increased the number of species.

He made the feeder carry water.

The feeder got the message. Repositioning his tail, he developed a sense of cooperation, a commitment to involvement.

While waiting for the feeder to break, the zookeeper continued his research into behavioral panaceas. He thought it most fortuitous that the feeder's change of heart was simultaneous with his discovery of the most thrilling procedure he had ever dug out of a book:

LLAH'S THEORY.

It was brand-spanking new. A breakthrough. The ingenious product of enlightened minds. What he liked best about it was its audacity. Llah's Theory espoused the institution of a communal arena for habitation, gestation, concentration, limitation, approbation, occupation, revelation, compensation, accreditation, and "restraint exercised over one's own impulses, emotions, or desires."

He could hardly contain his excitement. Intrigued by the criteria for implementation of the procedure even more than by the procedure itself, the zookeeper ordered the now-obedient feeder to construct Llah's Confinement Center. It was a new, daring concept in control. And it afforded the zookeeper an opportunity to experiment with his second great passion:

RESPECT FOR THE COMMON GOOD.

Under existing conditions, it was impossible to consider. But this new structure ... The more he thought about it, the more he could see a correlation. Developing self-control as a promulgation of reverence for the rites of existence.

Existence demands conformity. Where had he read that? No matter. He liked it. This was no place for rebellion. No jungle here.

The zookeeper gloried in the demands of construction. The feeder hauled the wood and stone, drove the nails, mixed the concrete. Casting a wary eye on the proceedings, the zookeeper insured strict adherence to blueprints and specifications.

When the feeder suggested more studs to strengthen the walls, he was told to keep his suggestions to himself. What did he know about this? When his skepticism focused on the instability of the roof, he stubbornly suggested additional bracing. This time he caught the zookeeper in a receptive mood. The modification was duly noted with assurances of consideration. And filed.

The zookeeper was attending the Annual Convention on Tactics to Tame the Truculent when the center was finally completed. The feeder's call intruded on the limpid buoyancy of lunch. Chewing on his seventh green orb of the afternoon, the zookeeper grew impatient as he listened to the latest in a long line of negative emissions. He was too sloshed to detect that the feeder's skepticism had turned to fear.

"It's madness," the feeder exclaimed, eyes riveted on the awesome structure. "It will never work."

"Nonsense. Stop gibbering like a fool. Of course it will work. It's theoretically sound. The risk factor is minimal. Negligible, in fact. Calm down. I'll be back in a few days. You might, in the meantime, consider widening your perspectives. It's your attitude that needs reworking."

Upon his return, however, the zookeeper was thankful he was standing in front of the massive rectangle alone. There was something wrong. He couldn't put his finger on it. And he couldn't admit it either. Now that the facility was there, it was unthinkable not to use it. As he stood staring at the universal confinement center, he came to one irreversible conclusion: He'd be damned if he was going in there. The feeder could do it.

Each day each species was herded into the common enclosure. Each was infected with false hopes of freedom during the process. A few attempted escape. But the bears were too slow, the hyenas too noisy, the giraffes too obvious, and the chimps too ignorant to make a successful break. Only the birds were able to soar away. The feeder let them go, thankful that he wouldn't have to put up with their antics along with the others.

Each night each species was segregated again. As the routine became established and inevitable, there were fewer attempts to gain freedom. This disappointed the feeder who began to wish they would all evaporate.

One day while involved in the tedious obligatory counting of heads, the feeder came up short. One mass of grizzle and bone was missing. He thanked the gods for the bestowal of good fortune and forgot about it.

Every day the scenario was repeated. The majority had come around. To some degree, natural instincts had been subdued. The giraffes stopped craning their necks, the bears became docile, the elephants refrained from shooting peanuts out of their trunks. The zookeeper was pleased with the progress of the experiment. It was only a matter of time before they were all trained in self-control, conforming to established rules and regulations. Harmonious cohabitation was not only possible but markedly preferable.

The feeder respectfully disagreed. While the majority seemed to be under control, a few heretics constantly fought to maintain individual freedoms, to display natural tendencies. And the heretics naturally influenced the others. Besides, the feeder couldn't help feeling sympathetic in those early days. Why shouldn't the chimps chatter and cavort in playful abandon? the hyenas laugh? the peacock fan? the tiger stalk? the leopard snarl? the snake hiss? the kangaroo leap? the zebra run?

But it didn't take long for his feelings to change. His benevolence was trampled on, mocked, and abused so consistently that he quickly hardened. It wasn't long before the feeder was disturbed by his feelings of contempt. He never thought he would feel this way toward them. He had enjoyed his contact with them before this. The rapport he had previously established with some of them engendered mutual respect which deferred conflict.

But the new ones were threatening his sanity. They didn't know him. He didn't know them. Under these conditions it was impossible to establish trust or friendship or even superficial understanding.

They began as adversaries in a game of wits and perseverance. He was being pushed to the limits of his patience and beyond.

They began to infect the others. Even a few that had once nibbled from his hand. That was when he used the whip. It shamed him afterward that he had become so enraged. But they drove him to it. Drove him to it.

As long as they were all required to participate in this insanity, he wasn't going to allow anyone to usurp his authority. Or mock him. Or defy him. He was running the show. As long as it ran. As long as they were stuck with each other.

TOMORROW, AND TOMORROW, AND TOMORROW,

Only a few rebels were left, disturbing the peace of the others, still undermining the feeder's control. He was growing weary.

CREEPS IN THIS PETTY PACE FROM DAY TO DAY,

Four devilish chimps, one disgusting hyena, and a kangaroo with a death wish. Begged. Threatened. Reasoned. Feigned indifference. Fruitless futility.

TO THE LAST SYLLABLE OF RECORDED TIME

Defiant as hell. Scorning the heart. Flouting the whip. Every day it was the same. Hopeless. Every day. Father, if thou be willing, remove this cup from me.

AND ALL OUR YESTERDAYS HAVE LIGHTED FOOLS

"You are not fulfilling your duties of supervision! Proper supervision would eliminate such problems! Here is Llah's Manual! Study it thoroughly!"

THE WAY TO DUSTY DEATH. OUT, OUT BRIEF CANDLE!

There went in two and two unto Noah into the ark, the male and the female, as God had commanded Noah.

Unbearable odious unrelenting stench.

LIFE'S BUT A WALKING SHADOW, A POOR PLAYER

And the waters decreased continually until the tenth month: in the tenth month, on the first day of the month, were the tops of the mountains seen.

Uncontrollable terrifying enervating hopelessness.

THAT STRUTS AND FRETS HIS HOUR UPON THE STAGE,

... stop that chattering laughter is not permitted here stop bouncing no wandering stop chattering no jouncing stop running no chattering ... every day ... every day ...

AND THEN IS HEARD NO MORE: IT IS A TALE

... stop caring stop trying stop pushing stop crying stop stop stop stop cease and desist. End this insanity.

TOLD BY AN IDIOT, FULL OF SOUND AND FURY

... the age of wisdom please respect the others ... the age of foolishness stop that jumping ... the season of light not malicious just puerile ... the season of darkness head smashed oozing under childish feet ... stop that chattering laughter is not permitted here stop bouncing no wandering stop chattering no jouncing stop running no chattering ... every day ... every ...

SIGNIFYING NOTHING.

Back to square one. The zookeeper cast a sour look on the wreckage. He decided that an investigation into causes of the disaster would be a waste of time. What difference did it make if the walls buckled causing the roof to fall, or if the roof collapsed taking the walls with it? Variable service to one table.

But his analytical mind was awakened when the rubble was cleared. There was something peculiar about the positions of the bodies. Panic would account for some degree of grouping. Evolved from fear, mass hysteria would account for some degree of violence. But there hadn't been any wild attempts to escape once the walls came tumbling down.

The bodies weren't anywhere near the exits. And they were grouped not in isolated clumps which would have indicated at least a cursory quest for safety, but in a single monstrously concentrated triangular battering ram.

Body after body was lifted and removed in the search for the feeder. He was finally located, released from one tomb only to be placed in another, a terror not unlike Roderick Usher's still etched on his flesh.

Now that he knew what had happened, the zookeeper initiated the obligatory evaluation. The experiment had failed. He had to determine why. He went all the way back to Llah's Theory, reading it again and again, looking for the weakness, the oversight. There had to be a hole in the original theory.

It eluded him for a long time. Until one day when he focused on the list of achievements promised by the proper use of the confinement center. There was a word missing. Glaringly missing, it seemed to him now.

Confrontation. The theory neglected to allow for confrontation. Never mentioned it. Never considered it at all. And neither had he. He didn't choose to remember the ambivalence that shadowed his first look at the completed structure.

Vowing to be more sensitive to such omissions in the future, the zookeeper concluded his evaluation, thankful that the whole matter could finally be put to rest. He was aching to forget this failure, to return to his research. He hated being mired in the past. He had already replaced the feeder and was anxious to chart new courses, explore new horizons.

Semper Fidelis

The school year is a predetermined series of unequal blocks of time: September to Thanksgiving, with Columbus Day and Veterans Day peppered in; Thanksgiving to Christmas; Christmas to the February break, with exams in between; February to Easter; Easter to Memorial Day; Memorial Day to the end. Each segment has its own characteristics, its own voice and volume and mood. The worst, by far, is the span of minutes between February and Easter. Though not the longest span, it is the most tedious, for it includes the month that pushes patience to its limits, the month that rubs the wound of winter over a grater. The month of March is the annual test, the cyclical challenge to the physical, mental, and emotional states of humankind. In 1981 there were eight weeks between the February break and Easter vacation; if the eight weeks were plotted on a graph, the bell would rest on its top, the abyss filled with the month of March.

One day during the week after vacation, Bonnie spent lunch in a fit of fury that no one could immediately talk her out of. Neither Alyssa, Jean, Joyce, nor Lainie could calm her down. The others were punch drunk, but it was Bonnie's first major slap in the face, so she was reeling from the pain.

"Why were we strung along for months? Why were we led to believe in possibilities when none existed all along? Why did he wait until we finalized the proposal to shoot us down?" She was asking old questions, old questions that required old answers.

Alyssa tried to be kind. "I had a feeling it would turn out this way. I tried to tell you before Thanksgiving. But you wouldn't have believed me then. You had to learn yourself."

Jean tried to be didactic. "Now you know firsthand what committee work means around here. Think about it the next time you're stupid enough to agree to serve on a committee."

Lainie tried to transcend both compassionate and instructional levels. "Screw 'em," she said. "Nobody else cares. Why should we?"

Joyce didn't try at all; she had been at a graduate course until 10 o'clock the night before and was too tired to do any more than shake her head.

Bonnie's committee had been told that craft classes were a threat to teacher image. Bassard put the kibosh on the proposal just as the committee was ready to submit it to the board. What would people think of teachers when they found out about craft classes during study halls? The board would throw a fit. Students should be studying during study halls, not having a good time; College Board scores were low enough. Were teachers being paid to teach knitting? The proposal was ridiculous. Absolutely not, Bassard decreed, public reaction would be devastating. His assessment came a bit late (though he thought it just in the nick), but it was accurate. The committee choked on its idealism, then shriveled and died. Soon after, Alyssa introduced Bonnie to Devila LoGuasta.

Alyssa's seniors were working(?) diligently(?) that last week in February. One day in the library one of them approached her with his thousandth question of the semester. He was a meek, docile young man, a wide-eyed perfectionist with a fierce desire to learn. He was researching food additives and having trouble organizing the massive amount of information he was finding; the topic naturally splintered every time he read a new article and Alyssa was trying to teach him how to eliminate extraneous information. They were both having a hard time of it because he became so excited over everything he found that he never wanted to toss any of it out. Alyssa was beginning to have visions of a three-hundred-page paper. And every time he found an earth shattering bit of information or worked himself into a frenzy over a structural technicality, he sought out his teacher.

Used to the constant picking at her brain, Alyssa tried to satisfy the student's need for encouragement and support, while, at the same time, she did something else that needed doing. She was walking around the room looking for students for attendance purposes, and he was following her every move. She listened with half an ear to what he was saying, with the intention of giving him her full attention as soon as she finished with the roll. But she was still aware of bits and pieces filtering in: experiments at a university, grinding chicken feathers into flour, cookies,—

Chicken feathers? Cookies? She looked at the student and said, "Huh?" He replied with intense seriousness. "The experiment was a success. They ate the cookies. Do you think I should include it? I'm not sure where to—"

She didn't even try to hold it in. Heads popped up in study carrels. The student smiled faintly, then gave in to the infectious laughter. "Flour out of chicken feathers?" she whispered incredulously. He shook his head up and down, he was laughing too hard to speak. She waved him over to the side of the room because they were disturbing the peace and she believed in a quiet library. They settled next to a table where another student in the class was working. The girl asked what was so funny. Alyssa explained and the girl giggled and said, "It must be contagious this week. I was a little crazy myself yesterday. I bought a stuffed animal and carried it around all day! It felt good to do something silly!" Alyssa agreed with the theory; then she gave the boy the help he needed (chicken feather cookies?) and went looking for the only student she hadn't yet seen that day. Gayle Fine.

She hadn't been surprised to see the girl's name on the list of seniors for second semester. It was simply another attempt; the girl was back, trying again. Her attendance was sporadic, as before, but at least she started at the beginning of the semester this time. Maybe with a little care she'd make it through. Alyssa found her alone in a corner in the back of the library. The girl looked and, Alyssa knew, felt like an orphan. The teacher sat next to the student and asked her how her note cards were progressing.

The class was a lively one, filled with quite a few vibrant personalities. Michael Ixion was one such delight. Alyssa started bragging to Bonnie about him during the first week of the course. "He's such a good student!" she said. "And, Bonnie, he's gorgeous! No wonder you fell in love!" Bonnie just beamed.

Anthony and Vincent Tevarro were also in the class, giving it vim and vigor. And, of course, there were the usual problem cases; the class was like any other class. But they were seniors; their needs were immediate. The needs of the good ones and the needs of the bad ones were immediate. No matter how she felt, Alyssa Matthews couldn't ignore the needs of Gayle Fine, Michael Ixion, the Tevarro twins, and the twenty-some-odd others in the class.

She met with seniors in the library four days that week. The one period spent in 418 started with an embarrassing drop in status. She took roll and directed students to prepare to take notes. She was planning to give instruction on bibliography form, but before she began, she wanted to check on something in her desk drawer, so she lowered herself to sit.

The chair wasn't there. She had moved the chair back when she entered the room. Study hall had been particularly unruly that day and by the time she arrived in 418 for third period she had smoked up a storm in the faculty room and was ready to throw all the desks and chairs through the window. She pushed at only her own chair, though, and forgot that she had moved it. When she suddenly disappeared from sight, the kids were startled and momentarily silent. Then someone said, "Where'd she go?"

503

Nobody moved forward, though a couple of kids stood up to peer from a height that allowed them to see behind her desk. One girl put her hands over her ears and said, her voice as tense as her body, "Mrs. Matt, are you all right?"

Mrs. Matt's tailbone was smarting, but after the shock of the collision, when she knew she was all right, she went into hysterics. Still sitting on the floor, she pulled on the small silk scarf that was stuffed in the pocket of her jacket, raised it above her head, and waved a signal.

The kids roared. Then she leaned to one side and peered around the corner of the desk and said, "This is the latest in teaching methods. Either this or I get replaced by a computer!" They roared again. The levity reduced her blushing to a pale pink; after she raised herself from the floor, she assured them that nothing more than her pride and her tailbone had been injured, and she went on with class.

Later that day a student from the previous year stopped her in the hall and requested help with an essay. The student was applying for a summer job as a camp counselor and needed to submit a writing sample with the application. The topic was "My Biggest Accomplishment in Life." Alyssa took the rough draft and promised to read it during the day; she hesitated a fraction of a second, then asked the girl when she was free for consultation. Seventh period, the girl said, so Alyssa told her to report to 418 seventh period.

The teacher read the essay during sixth, then sat at her desk with the student at her side during seventh. Periodically, she interrupted the conference to quiet down the class in the room with them. She had altered plans for the period to occupy their minds, but it took more than that to stop their mouths. She knew they recognized the ruse. They saw that she was busy with something else; the reason for the seatwork was obvious. But Alyssa didn't care. The thirty minutes that she spent giving personal attention to one human brain were thirty minutes of intoxicating rapture. The girl was a delight to work with.

With humor and exuberance, teacher and student discussed the special difficulties of writing. The student was far beyond average problems and into an advanced style of writing. When the teacher spoke of diction, clarity, balance, voice, and flow, the student understood. The teacher said, "Sometimes a short, concise sentence will suit your purpose, will create the impact, the effect, you desire. On the other hand, a short sentence might reduce a complex thought to simplistic nonsense. You have to think about the effect of structure, think about the flow of the words, and the way you want the reader to react. Consider the effect of placing phrases or words in various locations in a sentence because when you change the structure you modify the stress and the strength of the idea."

Images flashed through the teacher's mind, images of lessons and classes. She used to teach writing this way; this was the final lecture in a long series that spread through an entire year, a series that necessitated assignments at every step, papers that had to be evaluated and returned quickly; an effective series of lessons that took students from sentence to paragraph to essay, the way Mary Gregory used to do it, the way Alyssa used to do it. Before the flood.

"This sentence disturbs me," said the teacher to the student. "There's nothing wrong with it, it's grammatically sound, it expresses the idea clearly. But I don't like it here. It's dead. Maybe it's misplaced, maybe it should be here instead."

"I don't like it either," said the student to the teacher. "I rewrote it ten times, and I still don't like it. Maybe it isn't worth saving."

"No, wait. Try this. Sometimes an introductory participial phrase will give you just enough tilt at the beginning of the sentence to make it more interesting, give it some life."

"Hey, that's better! I didn't think to try that."

"Keep it in mind for next time. And follow your instincts," the teacher told the student because the teacher knew the student had all the right instincts to follow.

Alyssa remembered an observation about education that she had read in some journal long, long ago. It struck her at the time as the most astute definition of education ever devised by man. Teacher, student, book. Everything else is sheer nonsense, everything beyond a teacher, a student, and a book. As she discussed ways to create an impressive ending with the student sitting beside her, Alyssa Matthews simplified the definition even further. Teacher, student. She could do very well, thank you, without benefit of a book. Even a book is superfluous to the essence.

The student promised to revise and return for a final check. She was surprised when the teacher said, "Thank you for coming in. You made my day. I haven't done this in so long, I forgot what it's like."

"I don't understand," the student said. "Isn't this what you're supposed to be doing?"

Alyssa smiled crookedly. This girl always did hit the target. She was a dream to teach. But there was one lesson she couldn't possibly learn until she started working for a living. "I haven't done this in three years," Alyssa said. "It's become impossible. There are so many other things we have to do and so much constantly being piled on us that students have become last on the list of priorities. I don't like it one bit, but I have no control over it." She gestured at the restless class in the room with them. "You see what I had to do to find time to help you today. I won't stay after school anymore. I do enough work at home without staying here until all hours every night. If I didn't have so much non-instructional busywork to do every day, I could be helping students. But nobody wants to know about that. And students like you will make it through just fine; I really worry about the ones who can't write at all."

During eighth period the teacher made a pact with a student who had failed every test and quiz since the beginning of the year. In the midst of the jubilation over one recent grade of 70, she told the boy that if he continued to score at least 70 on all future tests, she would raise the failing grades already on the books for the current report card period. The boy agreed to try. The teacher was desperate to try anything to get him off his duff and working. Maybe if he had a taste of success he would change his ways. The following week he managed to squeeze a 68 out of a vocabulary test and wanted all the rights and privileges promised.

The following week offered anxiety and hope to a few teachers also. It was one week after Bonnie's bout with fury over the futile committee work. But now she was walking on air. The letters had gone out. She hadn't received one. She was safe for another year. Every year she accumulated strengthened her security within the system. So the theory goes.

The day she realized that others had received letters but she had not, she caught Alyssa between periods for a confidential sigh of relief and a bursting announcement. "I'm sure I'm pregnant," she said in the lowest of voices. "The doctor said an IUD is 95 percent effective, and, wouldn't you know, I caught the 5 percent."

"How sure is sure?" Alyssa offered. "Maybe you're late."

"I've never been late before. I'm as regular as the moon. I scheduled a test next week. But I'm sure. Maybe I'll cancel the test. Some poor rabbit will have to die. Do they still use rabbits? How would you like to walk around knowing you killed Bugs Bunny?"

"Does Michael know?"

"Not yet. I'll tell him soon. I figure I'm due at the end of October. I'll be able to come back to work after Thanksgiving."

"You've got it figured down to the minute, haven't you?"

"The only thing that worries me is the rest of this year. I may be waddling by June."

"The district frowns on unwed mothers in the classroom. Unless she's a kid, then she gets tutored. Maybe if you buy some baggier clothes —"

"That's what I plan to do. But If I start looking like the Goodyear blimp, we'll have to get married over Easter. I don't want to do that. It will make life too uncomfortable for Michael. I'd rather wait until he's out of here for good. We'll just have to wait and see."

"You're not considering other measures, are you?"

"Of course not."

"I didn't think so. It'll work out. Everything always does. In the end you'll have Michael, a baby, a job, and some peace of mind."

Bonnie said that right now she had three out of four, and right now three out of four were sufficient.

At 3:15 a.m. on Ash Wednesday, severe abdominal pain woke Alyssa out of a sound sleep and sent her doubled-over to the bathroom. Waste elimination was accompanied by waves of nausea and pain, perfectly-timed spasms that made her gasp in agony. When she returned to bed, the digital clock showed 3:34. She was incredibly weak, but waited until 6:00 to make the decision. When Jeff wasn't looking, she lifted the shade in the bedroom to look out. Snow was falling. It was snowy and cold and the thought of going out in it made her mind whimper for mercy. There were great heaps of snow all around, mountains threatening avalanche.

The bed was warm and comforting. The bed was sacrosanct, it was sanctuary. She burrowed under the bedcovers. When would it stop? When would she be strong enough to fight back? She was faithful with the iron pills; how long did it take to build up? Did she have to catch every germ that passed?

On Friday Cassie called during her lunch period. "Are you okay? I'm worried about you. You're out so much this year."

I'm okay, the teacher said. Just another virus. Just another cold. It will pass, it will pass. I'll live, I'll be all right, thanks for calling, good-bye.

By the weekend she was rallying back to quasi-normalcy. After she awoke from an afternoon nap on Sunday, Jeff relayed a message: "Call your mother. She's worried about you, said you haven't called her in over a week."

She trudged to the phone. "I'm sorry, Mom, that I haven't called. But I got sick again and it's getting embarrassing. I don't even want anybody to know. I guess my resistance is still down. But I'm so sick of being sick, Mom." She tried to absorb the soothing words coming at her through the wires, but she couldn't because she was crying.

When she returned to school Monday morning, she found that the sub hadn't taken attendance at all in any of her classes. She made a note of that fact in her attendance book in case somebody wanted records for those dates.

She also found an add slip for a new student in her seventh period class, a boy from Nebraska. The sub had accepted him. She knew she would have tried to refuse him sight unseen had she been in school. Seventh period was jammed. After she fumed all day over having to start a new student in March, she softened once she met the boy. He was polite, lively, and, according to his transfer record, an excellent student. Even if she could, she wouldn't throw him out. He was the stuff she was made of.

I've Got Those

Cynical,
Comical,
Acerbically ironical,
Dorothy
Parker
Blues ...

Let's see now. $1.59 for six ounces, $1.89 for nine-and-a-half ounces, $2.29 for eleven-and-three-quarters ounces. The big one is almost double the small one, so one big one is cheaper than two small ones. The one in the middle is the trick, that's what's supposed to confuse me. Or is it? $1.89 times two. $1.90 times two is $3.80, less two cents is $3.78. That's $3.78 for 19 ounces. Is that more or less or equal or— wait a minute wait one geometric minute. There are sixteen ounces in a pint (aren't there?), two pints in a quart, that's 32 ounces, four quarts in a gallon, the last time I looked, that's 32 times 4, 128 ounces in a gallon. $1.59 for six ounces. Six goes into 128 roughly 21 times. Twenty-one times? Twenty-one times $1.59? Thirty-three dollars a gallon? Good Lord, I'll drink water! They almost caught me, though, they almost caught me. If I hadn't ... uh, oh. I wonder how much water is by the ounce now that it's metered?

What's this? BIG SALE THIS WEEK ONLY! Three pounds for two dollars! Hah! I bought these last week at forty-nine a pound. Whom do they think they are kidding?

If apples are forty-three cents a pound, and there are six apples to a pound, how many pounds can a goldfish eat in twenty-two evenly spaced sittings spread out over seventeen days? And how much will it cost per cubic ounce?

At least a dollar. Everything is at least a dollar or multiples of a dollar. Ninety-nine cents doesn't fool this experienced shopper. I'm sharper than that. Redeem this valuable coupon now! Valuable coupon? Seven cents? A nickel and two pennies? What, pray tell, can I buy with a nickel and two pennies? Those species are extinct. The price went up thirty-eight cents in two weeks and they want me to redeem this valuable coupon. Is this what they call high finance? Maybe it's me, maybe I'm too dumb to figure it out. Maybe they are doing me a favor? Over my dead body, they are. Over my undernourished skeleton.

Supply and demand. I learned about that when my heart was young and gay. When the market is glutted with a product, the price goes down. When demand exceeds supply, the price goes up. Simple enough. So why is this box of crackers fifty cents more than it was last week? Are we in the midst of a cracker shortage? Have the oil companies taken over crackers? Do they think they can harass me with odd-even cracker days? Not me! I can live without crackers! We showed 'em when we boycotted beef, didn't we? We showed 'em all right! We had 'em on their knees! They stopped raising the price of beef. For a week. Or two. So what if it's more expensive now than it was before the boycott? So what? We showed 'em!

DOUBLE COUPONS! Hear ye! Hear ye! Morons, suckers, and fools! For one week only your coupons will be redeemed at double the value except for coffee coupons, you can only take advantage of this generous offer on one pound, AND only coupons with a face value of less than sixty cents will be doubled, AND coupons for free items will not be doubled, AND plan to stand in very long lines because our competitors are not offering this boon to the American housewife, we are the saviors, the balancers of your budget, we will make ends meet for you this week!

Bastards. Keep your fourteen cents. Every time they offer double value on manufacturer's coupons, every price in this store goes up. Is it worth it to them to pay people to change all these prices? Well, of course it is, stupid. Part-time. Minimum wage. No benefits. Rise up, Honest Abe! There's a new group a'callin! Maybe we can get the manufacturers to secede. If they can offer coupons and rebates, why, oh why, can't they lower prices? Blasphemy! Blasphemy! Pardon my wicked tongue, 0 Chairman of the Board.

Now how can they do this? Shortening, $2.19 with store coupon. It was $1.99 with no coupon last week. Look at this! After I took pains to neatly separate this square of newsprint from its flimsy surroundings, they raised the original price higher than it is in any other store within fifty miles. I know! I am A Comparative Shopper. And how excited I was! Seventy-five cents off! A veritable gold mine! I clipped with fiendish delight! I had 'em beat! Sucker.

Why, hello! How are you? I knew I recognized you a couple of aisles back!

And I've been avoiding you ever since. The face is familiar. From the Paleozoic Era. Or maybe the Dark Ages. Medieval mediocrity? Name, name, who's got the name? Please, Lord, a name. Just the right combination of letters, that's all I ask. How many combinations can be made out of 26 little letters? How much wood can a woodchuck chuck if a woodchuck could chuck wood? Last, first, it matters not. Looks like she's married. Let's see,— Ann, Abby, Alice, Barbara, Betty, Beth, Bertha, Beulah, Carol, Connie, Diane, Ellen, Fran, Gertrude,— damn. With my luck she's a Zelda. Or a Yolanda. Great. Now I'm going backward. Fudge it, Teach, you make yummy fudge.

How have you been? Fine! Yes! I'm fine too! Still teaching! Still at good old BCA! Yes, yes, still there! No, the place hasn't changed a bit, not a bit. You're married now? Oh, for ten years—?

The old gray mare she ain't what she ... The place hasn't changed a bit. You should only know how much the place hasn't changed a bit. I'm the metamorphic mutant; I'm withering away, brown around the edges, like the last rose of summer. Simile. Remember? Come, dear, let me change your diaper. You smell like hell. That's a simile with internal rhyme, sweetums. Mommy listened to her English teacher, Mommy listened and took notes. A simile is a direct comparison using "like" or "as." A metaphor is an implied comparison. Isn't Mommy the smart one? What do you mean, hell doesn't smell? Of course it does! It's rancid, putrid. The noisome odor of foul sleep. No, not the Bastille. La Force. The prison of La Force. Incarceration. Hell. What's the difference?

Oh, goody, now I get to meet the kid. An imp if I ever saw one. Does he always spit at strangers? Or just at strange teachers? That's it, I'll bet. He's in training for kindergarten.

And this is Jimmy? Hello, Jimmy! Can you shake hands? I guess he'd rather eat his animal crackers. Pulled them right off the shelf, did he? Couldn't wait to get home. Isn't that cute.

Atta boy! What this country needs is more assertive men! Born breadwinners. Pull 'em off the shelf and devour 'em, baby! Your world will never end with a whimper. But give it time. You'll resort to other measures: Is a scream better than a whimper? Really and truly? Meanwhile, back at the produce department, I still need a name.

511

I have your sister this year? Oh! That's right, I do! She's such a sweetheart!

Now I've done it. Now I've really thrown the acid into the fire. Or is it the fire into the acid? Let's see, first period, first row, first seat ... Oh, brother, now who's joining this clambake? I can't conjure up one little name and now there's a cast of thousands.

This is your mother? How nice. Glad to meet you, Mrs. — ah, — Bonsai? Yes! Of course! Mrs. Bonsai!

Bonsai? BONSAI? I've never had a Bonsai. Lord knows I'd remember a Bonsai. Or maybe not. My brain is rotting fast these days. Anemia is terribly common, but hardening of the arteries at 33? Wow. I'll make medical history. Fame, fame, fame. No fortune, but lots of fame, fame, fame. Got to try something to get out of this mess. Mix that fudge, Teach.

I'm sorry, but I'm having trouble with the Bonsai. Wasn't your name ... Ah! Ha, ha, yes! Well, I thought so! Harsnesczyniak. You don't pronounce the letters between the second s and the niak. Oh, mother remarried for the Bonsai. Life does get complicated, doesn't it?

Tricks. It's full of tricks. Can't Teach cover her ass well, though? And why not, with a BA in CYA and a Masters in Paranoia? What credentials. The fate of working-class America. Harsnesczyniak. Ah, Noreen Harsnesezyniak, third period, senior, second row, third seat. Noreen Harsnesczyniak cried real tears today. Great globs of goo streaked down Noreen Harsnesczyniak's stricken face. Only tragedy could jeopardize Noreen Harsnesczyniak's mascara. Poor dear. Poor suffering dear. Mom was rushed to the hospital for emergency surgery which prevented the completion of Noreen Harsnesczyniak's research paper. Can one be expected to finger the keys of a typewriter under such duress, such emotional upheaval? Poor, poor dear.

Student - 1, Teacher - 0. Tomorrow I will strangle Noreen Harsnesczyniak with ten bare digits, I will squeeze her neck until one of us turns blue. But not here, not here, Mom, not here in front of the fruits and vegetables. I wouldn't want the bananas to ripen from the blast. You'll find out soon enough, Mom, then you can show up in the office and roar that your cub got a raw deal.

It was nice seeing you again. And meeting you, Mrs. Hars— Bonsai. Pardon me? Jimmy? Yes, yes! I'll probably teach Jimmy. How old is he? Three? Goodness, yes. I'll look for him in a few years! Oh, no, of course not, of course it's not Harsnesczyniak. Brown? Plain old Brown. Good, good, I'll remember that. Like the singer. Easy, easy to remember. I'll look for him. How old did you say he is? Three? Three. Too bad we can't bottle all that energy, isn't it? Too bad. Well, good to see you. Bye now!

Three? I'll be dead by the time he reaches senior high. Or senile. Or both. Tomb. Asylum. Synonymous terms. Dig, dig, dig. Dickens knew. Three. He'll send more than twenty teachers to the loony bin before he gets a crack at me.

Good Lord, look at these prices. Too much even for an overpaid teacher. Wouldn't Dickens have himself a ball today? Oliver Twist in supplication before a grocery store manager; Fagin gleefully commandeering a ring of food stamp entrepreneurs; Scrooge paying illegal immigrants twenty-five cents an hour; the Defarges storming the White House. What drama, what plot structure. What irony. Two hundred years after the revolution, we're a chip off the old Mother Country. From The American Dream to No Expectations. Splendid.

Six dollars a gallon for laundry soap. Four dollars a pound for coffee. Oh? Only $3.89? Why, thank you, kind sir, thank you, thank you, thank you. I didn't know, I had no idea the price went down! Down! Imagine! Now if you could just do something about sugar?

Sugar. I said sugar. Shug—er. You know, the sweet stuff some of us like in our only-$3.89-a-pound coffee. Should a five-pound bag of sugar really cost $4.92? I mean, really, fellas? Fair warning! Don't hand me that shortage line, or I'll remind you of gasoline prices again! Why are there sufficient quantities of gas now that the price went up? Consumers of the world unite! They say we're the pigs, we want too much, we use too much, we eat too much, we burn too much, we waste too much. Big Joke. Why is there enough, always enough, for those who can afford to pay? Who is kidding whom? Who are the gluttons, anyway?

This lady in front of me, for one. She must shop once a year. Once every ten years. I've never completely filled a basket in my life. She has two and hubby is still making trips into the cornucopia for more supplies. Will it never end? Seven gallons of milk? Lord, lady, buy a cow. You'll have milk on tap. My feet hurt, I want to get out of here. Sometime this millenium.

Don't fight with the cashier, lady. You can't buy beer and cigarettes with food stamps. You have to buy food with food stamps. You have my sympathies lady, you and your steaks and roasts have the sympathy of my ground chuck. Stop bitching. I'm paying for both of us.

I just want to get through this line and go home. Why, oh why, do I always pick the slowest-moving line? They see me coming. That's it. I pick the shortest line. I'm no dummy. I always pick the shortest line. Then I watch the longest line move on by. Why is the shortest line the slowest line? Why? Why are blueberries blue? Why am I still standing here while that man in the funny hat who was twelve miles behind me in another line is walking out the door? Look at him! Look at him! He's wiggling his behind as if to say, Ha, Ha, I picked the right line, Ha, Ha, you didn't.

Ah, at last. At last, at long last. The conveyor. Move your bod, lady, so I can see what prices are being rung up. You never looked at the register, but I have to. Cashiers make mistakes, you know. Hard to empty this cart and look at the same time. Oops, that was supposed to be $1.88 not 1.89. No matter, a penny here, a penny there. Whoa. Wait a minute, Flash. That one was a little more than a little over.

Excuse me, but I think you hit $21.90 instead of $2.19. Would you check please?

Don't look at me as if you were a dill pickle. I can be a bowl of sauerkraut myself. Don't push me. I know you had a rough time with F.S. Brew, I know this is a nasty job, I know you never get a bag boy, but please, please, don't take it out on me.

I have to what? Go to the office? You'll write a voucher and I have to go stand in that line over there to get my money back?

To get my money back? Hardy-har-har. What makes you think you're going to get it to begin with? I may not look it, but I am a woman with brains. I have a college degree. Beneath this ordinary exterior lie the sinews of The American Woman. Would I be so foolish as to give you money because you made a mistake, then stand in another line to get it back? I should say not. How silly. What a ridiculous notion. Not me. You aren't catching me in this one. I Am Woman. Hear Me Roar.

Oh. Well. I suppose so. If it's store policy, I guess I'll have to, won't I? That line right over there? Certainly. It's not far to walk, not far at all.

Call in the Fifth Armored Division, secure the left flank, the right flank! Volley up the middle! Call in William F. Buckley, Jr.! Phil Donahue! Geraldo Riviera! Woodward and Bernstein! I can't even choose a line this time! Choice! Choice! Where's my freedom of choice!

That's right, lady, that's absolutely right. They're trying to discourage use of store coupons by making you stand in another line for a rain check. Of course they never have enough on the shelves! Of course they're trying to get you in the store! Now you have to come back with the rain check! Suffer, lady, suffer. Don't you know there are countries in the world that have no food at all? You can't even buy food in some countries, even if you have money. Here we are lucky, this is the most fortunate country on earth. Here, even if we can't afford it, we get to look at it! Aren't we better off, lady, aren't we?

You should be in my shoes. In my poor aching feet that chased a kid through two buildings because he lipped off at me, then left study hall without a pass. I thought he was going to plaster the wall with my flesh when I caught up with him. Thank God The Axe was in the hall and joined the parade.

Can this be? Have I reached the open window so soon, so soon? Where's the manager? I want to see the manager bound with ropes and chains with a foolscap on his head and fins on his feet. Now. Pass the thumbscrews. Lower the pendulum. Ready! Aim! Fire!

Is this any way to treat a customer? Can you honestly defend this asinine policy? I am mighty angry, lady, mighty angry. I'm ready to chew somebody up into little pieces and spit shrapnel at the glass in your automatic doors! Man the torpedoes! Full speed ahead!

Yes, m'am. The cashier made an error. It's circled there on the register receipt. You owe me $19.71. A check? Sure, I'll take a check. Of course I understand. You can't give me cash if all the cash just went to the bank to be deposited. Just five minutes ago? Son-of-a-gun. Well, I almost made it, didn't I? Ha, ha, ha, almost only counts with horseshoes. Right you are, m'am, right you are.

515

I wish I had a horseshoe. I'd wrap it around your neck, you old witch. Cackling over my misfortune. My car's misfortune. I wanted to buy gas with that twenty, you old biddy. No cash. What about that drawer my twenty is in? Now I know why people turn criminal. If I owned a gun I'd get my twenty back, yes indeedy. By the time I get out of here the banks will be closed and I can eat that check. I've always envied Scarlett O'Hara. But she didn't have to buy gas, now did she? Worrying about it tomorrow isn't such a good idea when the needle's at E.

Out. Out damned cart. Out into the fresh air. Yes, young man, you may help me with my damned cart, you are a mobile employee of this inflationary institution. Jesus H. Christ! What did you say? You like to help pretty girls? A parking lot proposition? You're insulting me, fella. If I were that kind of girl, you couldn't afford me.

Oh, I think you'd just like a walk in the fresh air. It's so noisy and hectic inside.

And the air is stale compared to you. Can't take a hint, can you kid? I'm thirty-three years old, you idiot! I'm a teacher! Isn't there a T emblazoned on my breast? No, no, forget the breast. Do not think breast. Forehead. I'm branded right above the nose. Do I think my husband would mind, would want to beat you up? Mind what, you mindless wonder? Thank God I parked close. Please trunk, don't stick. Key don't fail me now.

The same to you. Have a nice day.

May the pigeon of niceness fly up your nose, down your esophagus, in your ear, and up your arse. Did you have to touch my arm? Don't you know what Hetty Pepper did when she was pinched three inches above the elbow? Go, kid, take the cart and don't look back. Why me? Why do these things happen to me? A rolling cart Romeo. Lord, get me home. It's been a long, long day. Why me, Lord? Why me?

The best laid plans of mice and men,
Of mice and men ...

(music and lyrics by Burns and Steinbeck)

The second in-service day in mid-March was prefaced by fireworks, banners, and a parade of communiqués. The day was billed as The Way To A Better Attitude. Sensitivity training, group therapy, committee work, feedback, conflict resolution, every ploy known to civilized man was neatly scheduled for faculty consideration.

Check your preferences now! Hurry before quotas are filled! We cannot improve conditions unless everyone works at it! This is your chance to make a difference! Morale can be boosted through commitment! Come one, come all to the highlight of the year! Apathy is the enemy!

Neither Jean nor Bonnie nor Alyssa attended the festivities. They missed the central message of the workshop: Avoid the Yeah, but's! Down with the What if's! Think Positive! They missed the Grand Opening, that is. Posters and signs would show up on bulletin boards and walls all over the school within days. Every time she passed one, Alyssa would cringe and boil, cringe and boil. What a farce it was, what a colossal insult to her intelligence. The workshop couldn't give anybody time to teach, it couldn't reduce anybody's workload, class sizes, or responsibilities. It couldn't change school policies, no matter who ranted and raved, no matter how many committees were formed. How, then, could it possibly raise morale? Not mine, she thought, I need more than an appointment to a cheering squad. I need more than their goddam Think Tank. How dare they? Bassard's running around with a big smile, patting people on the back, playing court jester. He believes in surface. I call it hypocrisy. Think Tank. Air your grievances, get it off your chest, release those debilitating complaints. It's good for the spirit, good for the soul. Catharsis is good for the soul. Then go back to your classroom and open wide so they can stuff your catharsis back down your throat. Think Tank. Hypocrisy. Flaming hypocrisy.

She called in sick as she had planned to do, and was out for two days, the day before and the day of the workshop, because she was sick. The lightheadedness wouldn't leave her; periodically she had to stop in the middle of the hall or the middle of a sentence and close her eyes to wait for stability to return. The pain was still in her wrist, getting worse. She couldn't bend the hand back without feeling the pain. She felt limp and lifeless, but had felt limp and lifeless for so long that it was becoming the norm. She woke up tired in the morning, she was tired all day, she went to bed tired, and she woke up tired the next morning. She pulled unwashed stockings out of the laundry basket and wore them a second time without a thought. Washing her face before she went to bed became a dreaded chore. Getting to work was the prime accomplishment of each day, everything else was secondary. She had to go to work, had to answer the alarm, get dressed, make breakfast, fill the thermos, drive the car, get there, get there, every day. Monday. Tuesday. Wednesday. Thursday. Friday. There were kids, she had kids to care for, kids to teach. Kids. The kids wouldn't go away. The kids were always there. So she had to be. Had to be.

One evening she stopped and stared at herself in the mirror after washing the makeup from her face. No crows feet yet. Quite a few streaks of white, though, and in her dark tresses the contrast was striking. Too bad it wasn't a better distribution, she thought, then she could get away with it. Why are men distinguished-looking when they turn gray and women are just — old? Rounding the bend into middle age. Ridiculous. At 33? I'm not getting older, I'm getting better! If they'd let me, if they'd only let me.

The gray hair didn't deepen her depression any, though. It ran in the family. Besides, she had already reached that point in her life when she accepted her body for what it was. She would never have a flawless complexion, she would never be built like Marilyn Monroe, she would never have the glossy sheen and silky texture in her hair that she admired and foolishly chased for years. Her face broke out when she was nervous, before her period, and when she drank too much orange juice; her physique was slim, her breasts and her eyelashes stopped growing too soon; her hair frizzed when the air was damp. She couldn't do much about any of it, having little control over hormones, heredity, and humidity.

What caused her concern as she looked at her mirror-image was something of her own making. There were two symmetrical arcs chiseled above her nose. One curved to the left, one to the right. When she widened her eyes and raised her brows, they disappeared. But when she relaxed her face, they were there, etched by so many years of concerned looks. No wrinkles yet, but the curves of concern, symbols of solicitude, were there. She passed a finger over the spot and felt the indentations. How ironic that one day after they deepened enough, they would make her look permanently angry. Or was it ironic? Maybe that's the final response, after all, she thought. Anger.

Two days after the in-service day, she and Jean discussed the deterioration of their classes. Jean simply had laid it on the line to her scholarship section; she told them exactly what the circumstances were and made no apologies for the reduction of attention second semester. Her honesty with them gave rise to all sorts of questions and comments and served a purpose she hadn't considered. "Keep these things in mind when you get established in your lifetime work," she told them. "The more you do, the more you'll be expected to do. The harder you work, the harder you'll be expected to work. We all have limitations. Recognize and accept your limitations. The more you overextend, the more you'll be expected to overextend. It doesn't make me happy to tell you this, it shouldn't be so. But this is reality."

Still, she felt cheated. She didn't tell the class, she told Alyssa that she felt cheated. She thought she had herself convinced that it wouldn't bother her, but it did. There was so much to do for the new class, so many individual pains in the neck, that she couldn't arrange and plan for the class she loved. And besides the two, she had three other classes to keep rolling. It wasn't something that she thought about all the time, it didn't bother her all the time. Just once a day was the extent of it. Every day during third period.

Alyssa felt worse for Jean than for herself. Letting the rarely perfect class slip was torture. Of course, as she told Jean, she felt that all her classes were slipping, especially the regents sections. "The kids are starting to get obnoxious," she said most pathetically. "My seventh and eighth periods are going fast. I'm keeping a fairly tight hold on the scholarship sections and my seniors, but the regents kids have noticed that they're getting less and less of me. They know when the reins are loosened."

If the period isn't packed with meaningful activities, the kids take advantage. She knew that the first time she stepped foot in a classroom. Now she was keeping them occupied so she could grade papers during class, she was assigning less homework, she was letting them exchange papers to grade tests in class. That practice was loathsome to her. Grading tests in class was the lazy way, the cop-out; it let the kids form conspiracies, it allowed grades to become nebulous and inaccurate. But she was changing her ways. Grading tests in class was one of the methods of survival. Detachment was another. Detachment, the wise man said, learn detachment.

Once the kids caught on that she stopped checking faithfully on homework, more and more stopped doing homework. She still

519

lectured: "If you don't do the exercises, you aren't working with the words and you won't learn the meanings" and "If you don't read the assignment, you won't understand what I'm talking about the next day in class" and "You have to write the words to learn how to spell them." But she knew that if she didn't keep on their backs, they would slide into typical adolescent laziness. And that's just what was happening. There was no way around it; she could do no more than lecture. Lecture and watch them slip away. Because she knew that it would get worse. Research papers were due in a few days.

Her seniors were scurrying to finish in time. Most of them. Sally Mallone wasn't past note cards, nine in all, and she wasn't very concerned about it; the Tevarro boys were typing under the watchful eye of the family expert; Michael Ixion handed his paper in a week early; Joe Brissonson was making plans to bring in a car engine for his oral report; Brian Conneally was drawing illustrations for his paper and his report because he had an artistic soul. They were like flakes of snow, every one intricate, every one uniquely different.

The paper was due Monday, March 23. On Friday, March 20, Gayle Fine waited for the room to empty out, then stood in front of Alyssa's desk and said in a low voice, "I won't be here Monday. I'm having an abortion."

The teacher felt as though she had been hit by a wrecking ball. Her thoughts skipped rapidly from "My God, how much can this poor child suffer," to "Can't somebody get her out of that environment she's in," to "There's nothing I can do about it," to "Don't cry, for God's sake, don't cry, she doesn't need to see you cry."

"How long do you think you'll be out, Gayle? Have you any idea?"

She was looking past the teacher at the blackboard when she said, "Three days. If there are no complications."

The word streaked across the teacher's brain like chalk across the blackboard the student was looking at, with a high-pitched screech.

"Please call the school if you're out for more than three days. Leave a message for me or call Mr. Hawkens. Please, Gayle. Promise me you'll do that."

The girl focused on the teacher. "Okay. I will. I don't know when I'll have my paper, though."

"I don't care about your paper. I'll take your paper the last day of school if I have to. Right now I care about you." One step at a time. A child learns to walk one step at a time. A child with two healthy legs. "I'll see you next week."

520

What could she say? Good luck? Best wishes? Have a nice abortion? The best she could do, she thought, was to project beyond the nightmare. When it's over, come back, you have to take care of yourself, we all have to take care of ourselves.

The teacher raced down to guidance. Allan Hawkens was on his way to lunch, but she caught him in the hall. "As far as we know, she was raped," he explained dolefully, "but it's difficult to pry the whole story out of her. She doesn't want to talk about it. I'll keep tabs as best I can. I also told her to call me next week. Maybe she will, maybe she won't. There isn't much more I can tell you right now."

"I already know too much," the teacher said, wondering how she was going to carry on normally on Monday. Push it away, shove it into subterranean darkness. Detachment, learn detachment.

She passed by Jean's open door on the way to the faculty room and saw that Jean hadn't left for lunch yet. She waited for the students to leave, then walked in and spilled her guts. Jean told her what she already knew: "It's happening all the time, but we don't usually know about it. Child abuse, unwanted pregnancies, abortion, rape, incest, every indignity, every conceivable outrage. Man's inhumanity to man. Such a common theme in literature, such a commodity in life. We can't be all things to these kids. We can't be mother, father, priest, doctor, social worker, and psychologist. It rips me apart, too, when tragedy strikes one of them and I know about it. But tragedy is the risk we all live with, like it or not. You can pray for her, Matt, but that's all."

Jean's last statement was overshadowed by a presence in the doorway. Fourth period was well under way, so the living thing was sensed immediately by the two women. Dannemore stood framed by the door casing, the empty hall at his back, and, from the look on his face, a brick wall blocking further passage.

Alyssa took in his entire being with one glance and didn't like what she saw. His face was pasty white and his hands were in his jacket pockets, the fabric of the coat pulled and twisted by the pressure of clenched fingers.

Jean saw none of that. Once she sensed that it was Dannemore, she made hasty motions to gather up her purse to go to lunch. As she fidgeted, she said, "Slumming today, Dan? Or is this official business? You'll need reinforcements if you're here to cut off my tongue."

Dannemore didn't speak. He didn't move. He didn't twitch or blink.

Jean got up and slung the strap of her purse over her shoulder. She pushed in her chair, pulled a lunch bag out of the bottom drawer of her desk, and headed for the door. "Out with it, Dan-boy, I've got to gobble fast. Half the period's over and I need to bolster my strength for the p.m. How can I scream at Erica's misfits at the end of the day if I don't eat my Wheaties?"

Dannemore didn't speak. He didn't move. He didn't twitch or blink.

Alyssa, too, was silent and still. Jean finally saw all of Dannemore. "For Christ's sake, Dan," she said, "what's the matter?"

Total silence was not his forte, not when he was out for the kill, not when he was protecting the image, not when he was following up a complaint, stalking a transgressor of The Law.

His silence frightened Jean, who was more comfortable with discourse, any shade or degree of discourse. Her fear exploded into multifaceted terror when his lips started to move, when sound emanated from his mouth, when he said, "I just received a call —"

The Phone Call. The Phone Call at Work. The kids. Elderly parents. Who was hurt? Bleeding? Dying? Dear God, what's happened? He doesn't want to tell me. How bad is it? How bad can it be that he doesn't want to tell me? My children? A car accident? Did the house burn down? Did I put out that cigarette before I left this morning? Why did I start smoking again?

"— the phones are all screwed up. My number used to be the main office number, but now it's mine and the call came through to me, to my office. I — I'm sorry Jean, to have to tell you this; it was the emergency room at the hospital. It's Dominick, he's there, something happened to Dominick. I'm so sorry, I can't tell you how sorry I am."

Jean turned into a metal post. "I have to go to him. What did they say? What happened? They must have told you something more. Were they wheeling him into surgery? What the hell happened, Dan? Didn't you find out what the hell happened? Didn't you take notes?"

Dannemore didn't move. He didn't twitch or blink. But he spoke. "He's dead, Jean. Massive coronary. They said it was a massive coronary."

The metal post started to quake. "No. That can't be. He's strong as an ox. He's never had any problems with his heart. He's been more tired than usual lately, but that won't kill you, being tired. He must be hooked up to one of those machines, don't you think? I'll find him hooked up to a pump or something. He's in a coma, maybe. Tell me he's in a coma, Dan, please, please tell me he's in a coma ..."

Dannemore didn't speak. He didn't move. He didn't twitch or blink. But she saw the anguish on his face. She turned and looked at Alyssa; she said in a monotone, "He's gone. My Dominick is gone. He kissed me before he left for work this morning. He reminded me to make fish for dinner. It's Lent and I forgot last week and made meat. Spareribs. He loves spareribs. I told him to eat the spareribs, God would understand. We just celebrated our 25th. We didn't want any big party, we just wanted to be alone. We never stopped enjoying each other's company in all those years. Twenty-five years and five children. My God, the kids,—" She put a fist to her mouth and jerked her head around. "Dan, I need to find the boys and Maria. I don't know where they are this time of the day."

"It's taken care of Jean. They're waiting in the office. Give me your car keys and I'll take you to the hospital. I don't want you driving."

"Thanks, Dan. I need my children. In the office? Now. We'll go now. In a minute, in a minute."

She moved to her desk, jiggled the top middle drawer to get it to slide open, pulled out paper and pen and started to write.

Alyssa and Dannemore exchanged a knowing glance. Both were subverting their own suffering in deference to Jean's. Alyssa walked to the desk, saying, "Jean, I'll take care of that. You have to go now. Please."

Jean kept writing, her head supported by the fingertips of her left hand, the hand supported by the arm connected to it, the arm supported by its elbow resting on the desktop. Alyssa had to talk to the top of Jean's head. "Jean, please, please stop. You don't have to do this. It doesn't matter. I'll take care of it for you. Please go with Dan."

As she pleaded with Jean, another scene filtered through Alyssa's mind. Deja vu. Mary Gregory. The day her mother died. Mary Gregory shaking like a leaf in the wind, but writing plans for the sub. It happened during Alyssa's first year of teaching. The new teacher was impressed by the scene. And shaken by it. So this is what I'm in for, she thought at the time. This is what it means to be a teacher.

Why was there no testimonial when the Old Guard left? Why were they sent out to pasture without a word of thanks or praise? What happens to a society that sucks its people dry, then casts them off like so many worthless pieces of sewage?

Jean looked up. Her face was calm, serene, but her eyes were wild. Alyssa saw the wild despair as if the eyes had revolved in their sockets allowing an inward view. Jean looked down and started to write again.

Alyssa whispered to Dannemore, who was still rooted in the doorway, "Do something, Dan. Do something."

He walked briskly to the desk and stopped Jean's moving hand with his own. With great tenderness he took both her hands in his, then he said firmly, "Jean, look at me. We have to go to the hospital. Now. Get your coat on. Maria and Vincent and Anthony are in the office. They're waiting for you. Do you want to keep them waiting?"

He struck a responsive chord. Jean released her hands from his, got up, walked to the closet, slipped her coat off the hanger, bent over to get her boots. Something struck her then, something must have shot through her like an arrow through a paper target. She left the boots, dropped the coat, streaked past Dannemore and Alyssa to snatch up her purse and the brown bag from the top of the desk, then flew out of the room. Dannemore retrieved the coat and boots and chased after her.

Alyssa watched from the doorway as Jean maintained a steady lead all the way down the hall. After she saw them turn the corner for the stairs, Alyssa walked into the hall to pick up the brown bag. Jean had flung it to the side where it hit a row of lockers and dropped to the floor.

Alyssa was thinking of Dannemore when she threw the brown bag into the wastebasket in Jean's room. Dannemore was human, after all. On neutral ground Dannemore was as human as anybody else. She sat at Jean's desk and looked down. The illegible scribbles jumped up at her and her mind spasmed.

You can pray for her, Matt, but that's all.

Detachment, learn detachment.

Alas, poor Yorick. I knew him, Horatio.

I knew him, Horatio.

Alyssa started to cry. For Jean, for Gayle Fine, and for herself.

If he had had any say about it, Dominick Tevarro never would have died at the end of the week because he never would have put his family through three days and nights of his wake. After Jean picked out a casket and supplied the undertaker with her husband's favorite suit, shirt, and tie, the body was ready for the family Friday night. It had to be on display for public viewing on Saturday; Roman Catholic funerals are not customary on Sundays; therefore, the devastation was extended through the weekend.

Bonnie and Alyssa went to the wake on Sunday afternoon. The children responded immediately, but Jean seemed not to recognize them at first. Then she snapped out of her dream-like state and introduced them to Dominick's sister, brothers, and parents. As she was leaving, Alyssa looked back once again at the tableau of sorrow yet of strength: Jean flanked by five stalwart sentinels. The man in the coffin had done much with his short life. Alyssa was deeply touched and said a silent prayer of thanks that all the people she loved were alive and healthy. The day was coming, though. Only death avoids death. Living is a journey into the unknown. The merciful unknown.

Bonnie asked about the wailing in the funeral home. Not being Italian, she didn't understand. "That's The Chant," Alyssa explained. "I never learned any Italian, I'm ashamed to admit, so I don't know exactly what they were saying. But it's old-fashioned grief is what it is, just an expression of grief. My grandmother was a professional mourner years ago. She and a group of other Italian ladies went around to funeral homes to cry and chant for anyone who wanted the service. Not that they wailed for strangers; Italians lived in tight little communities forty, fifty years ago. I've heard all kinds of stories about The Chant, though. Once my grandmother and one of her friends thought they were doing some people a favor, but they were thrown out. So I guess they did get overzealous. The Chant is a leftover from the days when bodies were laid out at home, when the females of the clan shouldered the burden of mourning. Wailing about the deceased's life and accomplishments and virtues was a ritual of grief assigned to women. Italian men wouldn't cry, crying was an indignity for a man, so the women did it. The women cried and screamed and wailed and threw themselves on the floor. And they wore black. My grandmother wore black for ten years after my grandfather died. Then it took a hell of a lot of persuading to get her into navy blue and brown."

"Jean's not wearing black," Bonnie questioned.

"Times have changed. Even for Italians. It's my guess that she's not too pleased with The Chant either, but she's too distraught to care. She might not even be hearing it. Either that or she's allowing it out of respect for Dominick's parents. It has to be agony to bury a child when you're in your seventies. It seems such a distortion of the natural order of things. I understood a few words of what those old ladies were saying. Filio mio, filio mio. My son, my son. Jean may be tolerating The Chant for the sake of his mother. A wife is one thing, but Jean is also a mother. It has to be the world's worst misery to see one's child in a coffin."

Bonnie didn't answer. She crossed her arms in front of her body and rode the rest of the way home in silence. That evening both women clung fiercely to their existing happiness. Witnessing the sorrows of another hones the mind to hypersensitivity.

By the end of the following week Gayle Fine was not back in school, but Jean was. Alyssa checked with Hawkens on Wednesday for word on Gayle; he knew nothing and had no way of finding out what had happened. On Thursday he received a call from Len Straithe; Gayle was stricken with hysterical blindness, it would take time for her to work out of it.

After her husband's funeral on Monday, Jean reported in on Thursday. The shock hadn't worn off, the grief hadn't subsided, but, as Jean philosophized, the only way to fight the shock and the grief was to push on. Life goes on, Jean said in a steady voice. We have to learn to cope for each other, learn to rearrange and reconstruct for the sake of those still breathing. Dominick couldn't be resurrected. He was gone, the act was ended, but the drama played on. Life goes on with nary a care for the woes of man. Life goes on in hackneyed splendor regardless. "Never again will I tell a kid he's wrong to use clichés," Jean said. "I always felt it was a waste of time anyway, they aren't old enough or experienced enough to recognize a cliché. Now I know there's another reason. Life is full of clichés. Death is a cliché. How can we tell kids to avoid clichés?"

Thus she never reached the "Why Me?" stage. She plunged back into life fast enough to transcend the usual agonies of accepting widowhood. Her pain was private pain and she preferred to keep it that way. No one needed to know what he meant to her, how lost she was without him. No one needed to know that no other could take his place. She knew and that was enough. It would have been an insult to his memory to say that she could not live without him, for he was the one who supported her independence for so many years. She could live without him because she had to and because he had provided the understanding and the help that allowed her to work, to build her own bastion of defense. It wouldn't be the same without him, but she could go it alone.

She had to get the kids through school. That was the first order of business. The kids had to be taken care of. Then she would sit down and think about herself. The career change was out, of course. Maybe one day she would be able to swing it, but right now she needed all the money she could make to educate the kids. As she told Alyssa the day she returned to work, she would be hanging around for a few more years, at least until Maria made it through college. It was time to start anew, but not according to her own design. The cards had been dealt another way. She had to play with what she held in her hand.

One kink in the journey, one twist in time, had maligned the beauty. The day she returned to school, Jean Tevarro tore down the poster hanging in the hall outside her room. She had no desire to read a jolly exclamation-pointed AVOID THE WHAT IF'S!! every time she looked out the doorway.

Many were amazed at her speedy return to work, and a few indulged in snide comments. It was Daniel Mark Dannemore who blasted the pants off one such wicked-tongued female. "It's none of your business how she's handling her sorrow," he snipped. "Love and grief aren't gauged by a micrometer. You've got a lot of nerve accusing her of disrespect; you're just a vicious gossip. She has more courage than you could dig up in two lifetimes."

It was courage that bolstered Jean, courage and one other possession that she valued above all else. The sympathy card that Alyssa sent said it best, and Jean would carry it in her purse for a long, long time. She had read the passage before, but never before could it have meant so much to her. It was the passage about walking through life with God, the one that began, *One night I had a dream. I dreamed I was walking along the beach with the Lord and across the sky flashed scenes of my life. For each scene I noticed two sets of footprints in the sand. One set belonged to me, the other to the Lord.* It went on to focus on periods of time, times of pain and sorrow, when only one set of footprints appeared. And then the explanation, *When you see only one set of footprints, it was then that I carried you.*

Jean told Alyssa how much she appreciated having the passage to read during those times when she felt overcome. She showed her that she was keeping it handy. That was when Bonnie read it and said, "It's beautiful and very touching, and I envy you for being able to find solace in religion. Sometimes I wish I could, but I don't believe in a God."

"I had no idea you're an atheist," Alyssa said, surprised and more than a little sympathetic.

"It's not that organized, really," Bonnie said. "At least I've never thought of myself as an atheist or an agnostic. I have no feelings whatsoever about it. There was never any interest in religion when I was growing up, no God lived in our house, other than my father. I never went to church and I remember what he used to say about people who did. He called them hypocrites, weak-kneed individuals who needed a crutch to make it in life. It's funny, after reading this about sand and footprints, I can only think of the sign my father had on the wall of his office. It said, *Footprints in the sands of time are not made by sitting down.* He had me convinced for a long time that religion was for fools. I don't think that way any more, not about other people, but it's too late for me to sprout a sudden belief in something that takes years to nurture."

"It's never too late for God," Jean said. "You can walk into any church or synagogue and request instruction if you ever feel the urge. But it may be difficult for you, as you say, to sprout faith. I remember a course I took in college that was designed to stimulate critical thought about the existence of God and the function of religion. You must have run across the old slogans somewhere along the line: Religion is the Opiate of the Masses and Did God Create Man or Did Man Create God? One of my friends had a terrible time with that course; she felt as if all she believed in was being undermined. But the course didn't bother me at all. It was all very interesting and I learned a great deal from it, but no college professor was going to shake my faith in God."

Alyssa cut in. "That's why you may have trouble accepting any religion, Bon. Learning about the religion is all well and good, but none of that matters much if you don't have faith. Religion itself tends to be nonsensical and it's highly ritualistic. That's because man administers the religion. I've become pretty disenchanted with many aspects of my religion, simply because I'm not a kid anymore. But I won't ever lose my faith in God. Faith is a natural adjunct to religion; even if the religion becomes stale, the faith should remain."

"Forget it," Bonnie concluded. "My father taught me to believe in Man. Then he disowned me because I turned out just like him. I had no right to, you see, because I wasn't a man. I know the Bible, but it's just a big fantasy to me. Religious instruction wouldn't put a dent in my disinterest. As I said before, sometimes I wish I had something to fall back on, but I don't and that's it. So I have to depend on myself all the time."

By the end of the conversation, Jean felt sorry for Bonnie, Alyssa felt sorry for Bonnie, and Bonnie didn't feel much of anything. Bonnie viewed death as a natural end and sorrow as part of the human condition. There wasn't a thing any mortal could do about death, and dealing with sorrow was possible with or without Divine help. Michael's mother had done it one way, Jean was doing it another. In both cases, human strength was the key. Bonnie was sure of that. If one knows one's weaknesses, one can overcome them. She had been doing it for years. She didn't need any unseen father-image to get her through the rough spots. She needed only herself, her own determination and conviction. Twists of fate are twists of fate, that's all. And most of the time, twists of fate are spiraled by some human hand. All earthly things are controlled by earthly denizens. She was sure of it. We make our own problems and if we're smart enough, we can come up with our own solutions. That was her philosophy. In March, 1981, it was still serving her well. Had she been approached by a seer, she would have scoffed, like Caesar, and cast the prophet aside.

And so, the winds of March gusted and cut as they always do, with no concern for the plight of man. By the end of the month, Gayle Fine was nowhere in sight, Alyssa was halfway through the research papers because she was grading most of them in school, and Boesch-Conklyn Academy was heaving a collective sigh for the rapid arrival of Easter vacation, which was still three weeks away.

"So Much Unfairness of Things"

None of the research papers that were submitted failed. Alyssa knew that she had lowered her standards to get a few of them up to a bare 70, but the thought of disgruntled parents lurking in the senior office threw her into a frenzy. She had no energy for defensive tactics anymore. Noreen Harsnesczyniak's paper was better late than never, but two papers, Gayle Fine's and Sally Mallone's, were still outstanding the day Alyssa handed back the graded ones. Sally was attending class every day, ignoring the fact that she had overlooked a little something in the way of course requirements. She even gave an oral report based on the few note cards she had accumulated, which astounded the teacher, who made it clear that in no way would the oral report compensate for no paper. The teacher notified Sally's counselor that she was failing and why, and let it go at that. The teacher was not sending out any more progress reports or notices of absenteeism. She was expanding her methods-of-survival repertoire. The time she didn't take to fill out forms was put to more practical use: she planned lessons, duplicated materials, averaged grades, and graded tests. She took nothing, but nothing, home. She wasn't happy that the scholarship sections hadn't written a major paper since the one on *Tale*; she wasn't happy that the seniors wouldn't write a thing through the Shakespeare section of the course except for the final tests on the plays; she wasn't very proud that the regents sections still hadn't written anything at all. But she could do no more than what she was doing, and what she was doing was normal procedure for most of the other teachers in the department. Perfectly healthy people were having as hard a time as she. While she once listened in horror at what she thought were lame excuses for obliterating whole units from the curriculum, she now nodded agreement when Connie Baker exclaimed that she couldn't possibly fit in two novels and a short story unit by the end of the year. She nodded agreement because she fully understood, but she held tight to her last thread of pride. She wasn't that far gone yet. She still planned carefully. Maybe everything else was sliding downhill, but she was still faithful to the curriculum. She was covering everything. Everything except writing skills. And she had issued a warning about that.

... students will not be getting the individual attention so many of them need. The State of New York has mandated a minimum level of

writing competency for each of our students, and it is physically impossible for English teachers to give adequate instruction to fulfill that mandate ... not humanly possible ... though no one has expired from the strain ...

Her worst times, naturally enough, were in the classroom. Every set of eyes reflected a need or a want or a care; and she knew who needed, who wanted, and who cared. There were times when she wished she worked with sticks of wood or pieces of metal instead. One day in March, Ken Whistle, the boy who tried to read *Garp*, said to her, "Are you in a bad mood today? You look grumpy."

She was shocked. Ken-the-tease was serious. Was it that obvious? Was she wearing it around on the outside? Never in twelve years had a student said that to her. Never had she inflicted any kind of negative mood on her classes. Anger, yes. Anger over mass failures, anger over mass neglect of homework. Constructive anger. But grumpy? Unreasonable? Irritable? Never. They deserved better than that; if she had to get as good as Meryl Streep at it, she wouldn't subject her students to an uncomfortable classroom. Students don't learn from a grumpy teacher, tension has no place in a classroom. She twisted her face into a grotesque distortion to make Ken laugh. Then she smiled and said, "I don't get grumpy, but from what I saw of you yesterday, you do."

"Yeah," he said. "I was. I was real mean yesterday. I had a fight with my homeroom teacher."

"I knew something was up. You were growling. So I stayed clear. I thought you were better by the end of the period."

"I wasn't," Ken said. "I went to social studies and failed a test. After I studied all night for it."

The teacher became concerned, the curves above her nose deepening. "You have to learn to control your temper, Ken. It didn't make sense for you to fail a test because of your homeroom teacher, now did it?"

She felt like an idiot lecturing the boy on what didn't make sense, but he needed the suggestion and he didn't know what she was dealing with herself. She doubled her effort to be cheerful in every class, to give a bravura performance; she bantered with Cassie at least once a day; she ignored the possibility that some students were cutting class; and she concentrated on survival.

When a scholarship boy handed her a note from one of the coaches that explained his absence the day before, she swallowed her rage. The note requested that she excuse the boy from class because he was helping the coach with a project. What goddam project was more important than his English class? What right did the coach have to usurp her time?

But she let it go. She couldn't do anything about it except write notes to the coach, to the appropriate administrator, and to Bassard. What else was there to do? Complain to the Board? Call the boy's parents? Blow it so far out of proportion that sooner or later someone would tell her she was crazy? It was all over and done with when the boy gave her the note; he had already missed class. And it happened all the time, all the time, for a multitude of reasons. Students love to miss class. Who blames students for that? It's the teacher's job to make class so interesting and lively and provocative that students are anxious to attend. Who blames a student for wanting to avoid a dull, boring class? It's the teacher's fault. Isn't it?

She gulped down her anger and told the student that he had to take the quiz he missed. Immediately. "I can't take it today," the boy said indignantly. "I didn't study last night."

What was she to do? Make him take it and fail? What would that accomplish? Wasn't it better for him to study, to spend some time learning? Had he volunteered to help the coach to get out of taking the quiz to begin with? Did the coach think all along that the boy was simply missing study hall? In that case the boy should take the quiz and fail. But what if that weren't the case? The possibilities were exhausting; finding out the truth was exhausting.

"You will take the quiz tomorrow," the teacher said, "and you will never again miss this class because you have something else that you would rather do." The teacher was adamant and the student was on the absence list the following day. It took a week of scheduling and rescheduling before he finally made up one small quiz. All of it added to the seed germinating in the teacher's mind in March. How could she expect the kids to be more than they were when she was so diminished herself?

At the end of the month she went before school for another blood test because Doc wanted to know what was going on inside her when he saw her for the next two-month checkup. She looked away when the nurse inserted the needle into her arm to draw the blood; she always looked away, somehow it hurt less when she did. But this time it didn't hurt at all. She never felt a thing, not even the prick of the needle; she was surprised when the nurse raised her arm to hold the cotton in position. Already? she thought in astonishment. Then she said to the nurse, "Thank you. You did that beautifully. I never felt a thing!"

The nurse was dumbfounded, didn't know what to say. She had never heard a word of thanks before, and she needed a few seconds to sort out a response. "People don't realize that we don't enjoy inflicting pain." she said. "I'm always aware that there's a person connected to the arm I'm working with."

"You know what you're doing," Alyssa said. "That's why you do it well."

The nurse smiled. "It's nice to hear that. I know I'm good; I used to work on an IV team in a big hospital in Buffalo. We were specialists. It's agony for a patient to have to put up with an inexperienced fumble-fingers who keeps poking to find a vein. A patient shouldn't feel like a pincushion. People who need IV's are sick enough without going through that torture. And it's as devastating for a nurse to be told to do it when she knows she can't without hurting the patient. Some hospitals are advanced enough to recognize the problem and employ people specially trained for the job."

Alyssa assimilated the information and concluded, "But there aren't any like that around here, so you're working in a lab. Too bad."

The nurse's smile didn't fade. "Oh, no, it isn't. I'm happy here. The pressure is off. They had me spread so thin I cracked. When I started, I worked three floors and that was enough to keep me hopping. Within five years they cut the team by half and I had my patients plus emergency room duty. Then they were talking about assigning each of us to two or three surgeons every day. That was it. They wanted too much. I was responsible for my patients, and I couldn't care for them anymore. One day one of them died because her IV slipped out and hours passed before anybody noticed. If I had been making regular rounds the way I always did when I started on the team, that woman's life may have been saved. I've lived with that in my heart for a long time. I know it wasn't my fault, but I still think about it."

Alyssa was drawing parallel lines in her mind; she said, "What a shame that your skill isn't being put to better use. You could be eliminating pain for a lot of people."

"That used to bother me. But I finally realized that under those circumstances I was no good anyway. I burned out, right down to nothing, though, before I accepted what had happened to me."

Alyssa's eyes widened. Me, too. Will you see it under your microscope? Will the blood look charred? Is it in the blood as well as in the brain?

"My husband was transferred here to work," the nurse continued. "Then I had a baby. And now here I am. This is a nice little job. The money isn't at all what I was accustomed to, but there's no pressure here, no life-or-death responsibilities. That's worth more than money to me."

I envy you, Alyssa thought. How I envy you. But where can a teacher go? What can a teacher do besides teach? And it's still a shame, a disgrace that your skill is being wasted. It's an outrage that you are not respected and encouraged and doted on. An outrage. You. And me. And others of our kind. We offer gifts that are not only spurned but, worse yet, used to destroy us.

"How long have you been anemic?" the nurse inquired.

"A few months that I know of. I'm a teacher, and it's safe to say that most of my colleagues are walking around in an anemic state. It comes with the territory. I know what you mean when you say you burned out. I think I'm going through the same thing right now."

"Good luck to you, then; I'll have this count ready for the doctor today. It won't tell him much about your burn-out, I'm afraid, but he can treat the anemia based on it. At least you can be assured that you're not alone in either area. I thought I was some kind of freak there for awhile. But now I know it's common, very common. There are plenty of people in all jobs walking around like zombies."

Alyssa nodded. "It hits the superachievers, doesn't it? The ones who can't bear to be incompetent or lax or lazy. The ones who take pride in everything they do."

"Exactly," said the nurse. "Hey, you're not as bad off as you think. You know what's happening, anyway. I never reached that stage until I spent a few hundred on a psychiatrist."

"Oh, never fear," Alyssa said as she was leaving, "I still may need the shrink. Sometimes it's worse to know." By the time she saw the doctor that evening, she was so enraged that he served the purpose.

It was during lunch that she heard it, and it split the top of her head right apart. It was a simple declarative statement that roared through the department like wildfire. "That miserable excuse for an educator," Alyssa said venomously. "Can he be so ignorant? How can he even think such a thing? He started out as an English teacher!"

"Don't let that fool you," Lainie said. "I happen to know that Brenda corrects his spelling and makes sense out of his mangled sentence structure."

"That was the context of his words of wisdom," Jean explained. "He was trying to make the point that computers and technology are phasing out the need for language skills. He wants that new computer and I think he would sell the entire faculty to get it."

"I'd like to put him up for sale," Alyssa sputtered. "'English teachers are obsolete.' What an insanely stupid thing to say."

Jean shrugged. "From what I've heard, his speech was followed by more than polite applause. Paul was in the audience, ask him about it the next time you see him. But wait a few days, he's a little incoherent right now."

Alyssa was not thinking about her blood that evening when the doctor opened the door to the examination room. She gave one-syllable answers to his questions as he checked her heart, lungs, eyes, ears, nose, and throat. Then she explained the symptoms of the illnesses she had suffered since he saw her last. She was complaining about the pain in her wrist when she suddenly broke stride and said, "Doc, am I turning into a hypochondriac? I feel as though I shouldn't be here; you have really sick people to attend to. I feel as though you should be spending this time with a cancer patient or a heart patient."

"Are you feeling well, Alyssa?" he asked.

"No. I feel rotten. But the question is, am I sick?"

"You're not a hypochondriac. Old ladies who view a visit to the doctor as the social event of the month are hypochondriacs. People who are bored with their lives and have plenty of time to imagine exotic illnesses are hypochondriacs. You're too busy, too active to be a hypochondriac. You have little patience for illness. Right?"

She nodded and he continued. "But perhaps we should consider something else. Hypochondria, no. Psychosomatic, maybe."

Of course, she thought, of course. That was really what I meant. Psyche: Mind = Soma: Body. What's wrong with me? I can't even come up with the right word anymore? Why did I have to use a thesaurus to write that allegory? I'm regressing. I thought I was stagnant, but it's worse, far worse than that.

"Pain is very real, isn't it, even when the cause is psychosomatic?" she asked.

"Of course," he said. "There should be no shame or stigma attached to the need for counseling for psychosomatic illness. In fact, I believe that every physical disorder known to man has some kind of psychological cause or effect. The mind and the body are inseparable, they function together. Physicians who isolate one from the other are fooling themselves and doing their patients a great disservice and possible harm. Now, there are actually two terms to describe the concept, splitting the concept into two distinct areas ..."

Rosemary Cania Maio

Go, Doc, go, she thought. 'Splain it to me. How I love it when you turn teacher, when you want me to understand.

"... psychogenic illness actually originates in the mind. Diseases such as bronchial asthma, sinusitis, migraine, ulcerative colitis, and stomach ulcers may be caused purely or partly by emotional stress. The term 'psychosomatic' is more general in scope; it refers to any of the emotional overtones associated with a physical illness, and, as I said before, the emotional part of it may cause the illness, or it may be an effect of the illness. Purely physical disorders sometimes induce psychological symptoms."

Alyssa said," I have a friend who gets migraines that are so bad her vision splits. I have another friend who has bleeding ulcers. Both are teachers. And they're not the only ones with severe health problems. You wouldn't believe it. Walk into any faculty room at BCA and just listen. You'll be shocked at the disgust and discontent. Nobody's happy anymore." Except Erica. But she wasn't in the mood to get into Erica. "Conditions have reached an all-time low and there's no hope for an upswing. Any teacher who cares about students is under constant stress. And we're cursed and abused by anybody and everybody."

He was sincerely puzzled. "But teachers are professional people. I don't understand."

She felt helpless and helplessly inadequate. It was too dense, too involved to explain. But she had to try. She still knew that only another teacher could understand, but he was so naive she felt an uncontrollable urge to smash his innocence. "There's nothing professional about teachers, nothing at all. We have to fight and beg for a raise just like a mill worker, and when we get one we're hated because we're paid with public funds. People can't do a damn thing about federal and state taxes, so they take out their frustration on the local school budget. And the attitude of the public toward teachers allows the district to get away with intimidation that is so dehumanizing and degrading that I'm at the point where I feel like a piece of meat, a carcass on a hook.

"A friend of mine had to lie to take off the day before Thanksgiving because personal leave is barred before and after vacations. She knew she couldn't get personal leave or even leave without pay, though she had personal reasons to do so. So she called in sick. We're forced to lie and scheme. I'm ashamed to be a teacher; people look at you as if you're raping society every day. I went out for lunch last week and two people, bare acquaintances, raised their eyebrows and asked me why school wasn't in session

536

that day. I should have told them I outran the armed guards. I wonder if I'm getting paranoid. How's that for psychosomatic?"

He was sitting on a stool next to the examining table. As she spoke, gathered speed, then ground to a halt, she was aware of his intense effort to comprehend. The curves of concern. She hadn't ever noticed before, but there they were. When he listened, he listened with his whole being. "I had no idea, Alyssa. My children went through BCA and I thought they had the usual proportion of good and bad teachers. I'll have to admit, though, that my wife took care of school problems when they arose. I've always had great respect for teachers. Good ones. I shudder to think of the consequences if the good ones go bad."

She continued, "It would take a few days of constant talking for me to explain all of it to you, but you can take my word on this much: today the bad teachers are rested and healthy, and the good ones are dying a slow death. Tell me something, Doc. What would happen to the quality of your work if the government started assigning you patients, and you had no control over who or how many?"

"I've had many a nightmare at the thought of socialized medicine, Alyssa."

"But most people view socialized medicine as a panacea, a way to lower costs. Surely you've heard it all. Damn doctors charge too much. You can't get one when you need one. The public would love to see doctors put down a peg or two. Personally, I don't want a doctor who works an assembly line. I want a doctor who takes pride in his skill and knows he'll be compensated for it. I want a doctor who is genuinely interested in helping me, not one who stands with his hand on the doorknob while he mouths platitudes.

"If the government or the insurance companies ever regulate medical care, you and others like you won't last a year. Because you care, Doc. You care about your patients and you care about the quality of your work. How would you like to try handling your patients in groups of thirty? That's what I do every day, with five groups of thirty. Every one of those kids needs individual attention ranging from a pat on the back to intense and prolonged remediation. And I guess I'm back to psychosomatic again. Are teachers any less important than doctors? Am I crazy to think that training minds is as vital as the work you do?

"How would you like to dismiss your secretary, your insurance girl, your receptionist, and your nurses, then attend to their duties in addition to your own? Wouldn't that be absurd? A pathetic waste of your time and an insult to your skill? Well, that, too, is what I put up

537

Rosemary Cania Maio

with every day. I spend more time on extraneous duties than on classroom instruction. I once felt good about my job because I could do it well. It took damn hard work to do it right, but I'm not afraid of hard work. Now the hard work doesn't matter; I'm as organized as any human being could ever hope to be, and that doesn't matter either. For years I laughed at the stupidities of the system, but it's not funny anymore. The day my teaching was affected it stopped being funny. I should be getting better and better year by year. I've been at it only twelve years, I've got a lot to learn yet. But instead of rising to my peak, I leveled off, and now I'm sliding backward. It's only a matter of time before I hit bottom. I've always tried to be the kind of teacher I'd want my own kids to have. Is there something wrong with that, Doc? Am I crazy for feeling that way?"

"I'm beginning to understand the kind of stress you're enduring," the doctor said. "Have you thought of getting away from it for awhile? Perhaps if you took some time off you could get the rest from it that you need, you could stand back and reassess. Why don't you consider a sabbatical leave, Alyssa? You could go back to school, take some courses, revive yourself, get a fresh start, a new perspective. I think what you need most is a boost in self-image, an opportunity to feel good about yourself again. Then you can decide whether or not you want to return to teaching. Maybe you'll find something else more worthy of your talents."

He was beautiful. So beautiful and caring and concerned for her welfare. But Lord, Lord, was he naive. "What makes you think that I have all those options, Doc?" Alyssa asked.

"Why shouldn't you?" he queried.

"You're still under the assumption that teachers are more than common laborers. We're not. The district gives out two sabbaticals a year, and it's only because our contract stipulates that specific number. If it weren't in the contract, there would be no sabbaticals. As it is, the newspaper thinks it makes exciting headlines to notify the public just how much money is being foolishly spent on teachers who are on paid vacation."

"But a sabbatical is intended for professional reasons, for further study, for personal enrichment, all of which benefits the employer eventually."

"Sure, Doc. You know that and I know that, but nobody cares if teachers are stagnant as long as it's going to cost taxpayers' money to revive their interest in teaching. People on sabbatical get half their salaries and the district has to hire subs for the year. The public has no patience for sabbaticals. Why should teachers be granted such luxury when no one else has the opportunity? And, Doc, anyone fortunate enough to be granted a sabbatical has to agree to stay with the district for two years following the sabbatical. And even if I wanted to, I couldn't apply for a sabbatical for next year because it's past the deadline for proposals."

"Proposals?"

"A lengthy written proposal has to be submitted; the entire year has to be mapped out in advance with a detailed account of plans and a rationale connecting the purpose of the leave with the individual teacher's subject area. The proposal takes a considerable amount of work in itself, and it can always be rejected for political, personal, or God-knows-what reasons. I'll tell you something else, Doc. It's a good thing that the district is only obligated to award two sabbaticals a year. The way things are now, 99% of the teachers in the system would be applying for leaves next year if they thought they could get them with half-pay. There's no doubt about it, the world is full of disgusted, miserable teachers. And each reacts to the situation in his own way. I happen to be an emotional type. It's the first time in my life that I've felt rage, massive rage, and the frustration of not being able to do anything about it. The rage began when the system began tampering with my ability to teach. And there's nowhere to go, no one to complain to. You can't even imagine what it's like."

"Isn't there some other way you can get extended time off?"

"Oh, sure. There's personal leave, maternity leave, medical leave."

"Good. Consider any one of those then."

"I'm afraid to."

"Why?"

"Everybody's afraid to go on leave. One never knows what one will be subjected to when one returns. It's as simple as that."

"As simple as what?"

"Are you sure you can handle these horror stories all at once? Maybe this one should wait until next time."

"I'm holding up. Go on."

"Well, it happens all the time. A teacher returning from leave, any kind of leave may be stuck with a full schedule of poor classes, one or more classes that require new preparation, or may be reassigned to another school, or may lose his room. Do you know what it means for a teacher to float, Doc? No, of course you don't. Everybody assumes that one teacher and one classroom are natural twosomes. But it's not so, not so at all. It took me eight years to get all my classes and my homeroom scheduled in the same room. Eight years. Teachers fight and claw for a room, Doc. Don't believe all the propaganda about decreasing enrollments. The only part that's true is the fact that there are fewer kids each year. But it doesn't make a damn bit of difference on the inside of a school because staff has been cut so drastically that fewer kids have become more kids within the context of a classroom. And rooms are still at a premium. Teachers still float around all day to meet with classes in two, three, and four different rooms. Very often the rooms are on different floors and scattered across four buildings. If you're thinking right now that you do the same thing every day in the hospital, forget it. It just ain't the same. Teachers carry around tons of material within the course of a year; teachers use filmstrip projectors, films, the VCR, which is a monster to maneuver through the halls, and other media hardware. And there are snafu's every step of the way. One year when I was floating I had to use poetry books with three of my classes. I could get only thirty copies of the books, so I had to use them in class, the kids couldn't take them home. It would have been less of a problem if those three classes met in the same room, but they met in three different rooms on three different floors. So I had to haul those books every day for four weeks. Every September I'm afraid that somehow some way, I lost my room over the summer. I'm telling you, Doc, a teacher will sell his soul to get a room, any room. If I go on leave, only the Lord knows what I may have to go back to."

"All right, Alyssa. But perhaps then you'll be in a stronger frame of mind. And perhaps you'll decide not to go back. I want you to at least consider a leave. There's time for you to do that. And I would not hesitate to support your request for a medical leave. Emotional exhaustion is very real and just as devastating as any physical disease. You have both. I can't say that your susceptibility to illness and infection is psychogenic, though your frame of mind isn't helping any. You are physically as well as mentally worn."

"What's the verdict with today's blood test?"

He swiveled the stool to face the table on which he had placed her folder. "The count's gone down a fraction. Are you still taking the iron pills?"

"Religiously."

"Keep taking them. Two a day. And I'm going to send the nurse in to give you a shot of B-complex tonight. I also want an x-ray of your wrist. Which one is it?"

"The left."

"Okay. Call the office tomorrow for an appointment for the x-ray. I want to see you again in early May. But I'll let you know the results of the x-ray as soon as it's read."

"Thanks, Doc. And I hope something shows. I'd hate to think I'm imagining this pain."

"Imagining is not your problem, Alyssa. Reality is."

"And I've only given you an eighth of a teaspoon of it, Doc. There's oceans more."

The x-ray was scheduled for the next day. Late that evening the doctor called with happy news. "It's a calcium deposit, Alyssa!" he announced. "That's what's causing the pain. I want you to see an orthopedic surgeon for a more complete diagnosis. He can also prescribe treatment."

So it wasn't all in her head, it wasn't an evasive, intangible virus; it was something that somebody had actually seen. She thanked the doctor for the referral, feeling fortunate that he was a man who knew his own limitations and believed in specialists.

She saw the new doctor the following week. As she sat in the waiting room, she couldn't resist the sarcastic smirk that crept over her face. The office was dotted with the usual signs including one that proclaimed, PAYMENT IS EXPECTED WHEN SERVICES ARE RENDERED. The one that prompted the smirk, however, read:

Itemized statement	$2.00
Insurance forms	$4.00
Letter to attorney	$45.00

How curious, she thought, the smirk widening. The doctor feels he should be paid extra for paperwork. And he has a secretary doing it. Why can't I do the same thing, professional that I am? Teachers are professional people, aren't they? How about:

Homeroom cards	$2.00 per day per student
Attendance summary	$4.00
Letter to parents	$45.00

When the nurse called her name, the smirk was still on her face, and she chuckled all the way to the examination room, causing the nurse to give her a most peculiar look.

The doctor clipped the x-ray to a lighted board and showed her the calcium deposit. Then he felt it and made her feel it with the fingers of her right hand. There it was, all right. She saw it, touched it, and was satisfied.

How? she asked the doctor. How did she manage to build up too much calcium? Too much calcium, not enough iron. Weird. Weird insides. She drank very little milk.

He smiled. No, no, he said. Common misconception. The body deposits calcium in an effort to mend itself, not because of a surplus of calcium. You must have bruised your wrist some time ago. The pain developed slowly, didn't it? Intensified slowly?

Here we go again, she thought. Yes, she said, it developed slowly. But I never hurt my wrist that I know of. Unless I fell on it. A few weeks ago I fell; I may have broken the fall with this hand. But I already had the pain then. Maybe it was last year. I fell on the ice one day last year.

No, no, he said. You don't understand. Even if you did land on this wrist, that kind of injury will not stimulate this kind of body reaction. The calcium was deposited a bit at a time over a long period. It was deposited at this precise spot on the bone in your wrist because this precise spot was abused, either by one gigantic direct blow, or by repeated sharp hits to the same spot. He illustrated by pounding the side of his own right hand on his left wrist.

The patient understood. And she knew the futility of trying to convince the doctor that nothing like that ever happened to her. Surely she would remember if it had. The doctor offered two possible methods of treatment: one, surgery to scrape the calcium off the bone, or two, let's wait to see if the deposit dissolves itself. Yes, he said, many times it will go the same way it came, sometimes the process takes up to two years.

Cut it out or wait. The ultimate ultimatum.

Alyssa decided to wait. She wasn't anxious to undergo surgery, nor was the doctor anxious to perform it. She left the office with the pain in her wrist and hope in her heart. At least, as she told the doctor, the calcium had built in the one joint in her body that she used least. The pain would have been much more difficult to tolerate in her neck or shoulder or in a knee, ankle, elbow, or even in the other wrist, for she wrote with her right hand. The doctor was pleased that she was an optimistic sort, and as a result of his assessment of her personality, suggested that she wait six months to schedule another appointment.

Alyssa was struck by a thought when she left the office, a thought born of her almost obsessive interest in symbolism coupled with the imagery the doctor had used, that of repeated bludgeoning blows. As she contemplated the mysterious origin of the calcium in her wrist, she raised the concept to another level and wondered why her entire brain wasn't encased in a protective sac woven by some mending mechanism naturally contained in her physical self.

Suddenly Dickens popped into her head.

Sydney Carton, who cared for nothing; Sydney Carton, devoid of initiative, meandering through life in a lifeless state. Poor, miserable, luckless, lackluster Sydney Carton. For years she thought him to be the most pathetic of men, his final moment of usefulness too large a price to pay for living a wasted life, despite his famous contention to the contrary. Now she was seeing something else in the case of Sydney Carton. There was a sadder sight among legions of men, a sight sadder than a man such as he, a much sadder sight.

Alyssa planned lessons for the first two weeks in April very carefully. She wanted to use the time to catch up on vocabulary and grammar units with the sophomore classes before vacation. After vacation she planned to teach *Of Mice and Men* to the regents sections and poetry to the scholarship sections, then finish vocabulary and cover short units on letter writing, types and uses of reference materials, and library skills. Most of it would be hit-and-miss, and she knew the library unit was at the wrong end of the year. But she had to get into review before the end of May, especially with the regents sections. Time was running out for them; they would have to learn how to write a composition and how to answer a literature question during review. She was trying to figure out how to schedule the assignments so that she wouldn't have over a hundred compositions and over a hundred literature essays to grade all at once. Efforts to split due dates were futile to some degree. She couldn't allow one regents class more time than the other, for example, simply because students talk to each other. She had to keep it fair. As always, keeping it fair complicated her planning and increased the number of papers she had to grade. There was no way around it; she would have to give in and take work home at the end of May. The kids had to have some preparation for exams. She decided, though, that April was too early to worry about it; the scheduling could wait until May.

She started *Othello* with the seniors during the second week in April because the play is easier than *Hamlet* and she thought it could weather the week's vacation better. There was just about enough time left in the year to spend three weeks on *Othello* and five on *Hamlet.* She tried to stay calm over the mangled week before vacation, but once that week arrived, she tumbled into desperation. School was in session Good Friday, which insured mass absenteeism that day. The third in-service day was scheduled for Wednesday, which wiped out classes that day. How she resented the choice she was faced with for Wednesday: attend a function that she found utterly loathsome, or use another sick day. She chose to stay home and felt no guilt; the district didn't have to pay a sub for the day. The district made out better than she.

She showed a videotape to the sophomore classes that week before vacation. All four classes had already studied *A Tale of Two Cities* and she thought the videotaped version might be a timely review of the novel. It was also a good time to show a film because the week was shot anyway.

As she watched the film, she became more and more irritated. She understood that a book and a film are two distinctly different forms of communication. She invariably told her students," If you like a movie that's based on a book, be sure to read the book. The book is always better."

One of the most faithful movies she had ever seen was the one based on *A Separate Peace*, but even that had its changes. Students always noticed that in the movie Finny breaks the school's high jump record instead of its swimming record. "Maybe they couldn't afford an Olympic-sized pool," she told the kids. "It must have been easier to film a high jump. And it doesn't really matter what record he breaks, the point is the same: he doesn't want anyone to know about it."

Another change in the *Peace* film was Leper's curling into fetal position in the snow. That, she thought, was perfect use of the visual element of film. Instead of the dining room symbolism used in the book to indicate Leper's need for warmth and security, the film showed him in fetal position on the ground against the stark cold snow. It was a powerful scene, and she wondered if John Knowles had anything to do with it. She also wondered if he wrote the song about Hitler's balls that is not in the book, but is a horrifying aspect of the kangaroo court scene in the film, horrifying because it heightened the frivolity of an inherently frightening scene. Man's inhumanity to man. What we will do to destroy one another.

She enjoyed the *Peace* film, enjoyed showing it, because it was, in some respects, better than the book, simply because a film is a film and a book is a book. She particularly liked the shift from black-and-white to color in the beginning; it was a most effective way to emphasize the dramatic change in tone that exists in the book.

Though she never considered herself to be in any measure an expert in film techniques, she enjoyed explaining what she thought she saw, what she liked and disliked about films she showed her classes. What she hoped to accomplish was to instill a bit of awareness in the kids, just a small breakthrough in the way they viewed any film. Notice the camerawork, the long shots, the close-ups, the way scenes are presented, what's going on in the background, where your attention is focused, what kind of music you're hearing and how you're reacting to it. She taught one chapter in *Tale*, "The Knitting Done," as if it were on film, for she felt that it was perfect for camera shots. Remember that a film is directed toward your eyes and ears. In some ways it's easier to make a film than to write a book. Of course, when you read a book you should see and hear it as well as any film.

There was one deficiency in the *Peace* film, and it wasn't the fault of the artistry of the film; it was merely the one limitation of any film. Gene's blank stares were nonsensical to anyone not familiar with the book. How can a film relate thoughts? Mental activity cannot be logically conveyed on film. Audiences are too sophisticated to accept audio with no video. Characters do not speak with immobile lips in modern films. Therefore, she explained the one serious defect of the film: without reading the book, you'd never understand the full range of Gene's mental processes, the creation of evil in his mind, his anguish, his guilt, because his inner thoughts are revealed only when he is an adult, not while he is going through his misery. And so, she proudly concluded every time, the book is still better than the movie!

Sometimes, she knew, the movie had a lot of nerve calling itself by the same name as the book. For years she waited for a remake of *A Tale of Two Cities*. The old, old, old MGM version with Ronald Coleman as Sydney Carton would have been a joke if it weren't such a mutilation. Jerry Cruncher wasn't even in it; the Honest Tradesman deserved better than to be completely ignored, she thought. When she read that *Tale* was being filmed for TV, she felt the excitement she always felt at an opportunity to see flesh and blood characters. And what a story! As epic in scope as *Ben Hur* or *Doctor Zhivago*! A possible masterpiece! How would they handle the melodrama, she wondered. Dickens was so slurpy at times, a characteristic that she had long since forgiven him for, but one that would necessarily pose a problem to modern film makers.

The first hint that she was expecting too much came with the advance summary of the production. Two hours. *A Tale of Two Cities* in two hours. Impossible. Twelve hours, maybe. No way, no how, could justice be done to such an intricately contrived plot, to such flagrantly colorful and human characters, to such epic and poignant scenes, in two measly hours. She wished Dickens was alive to protect the integrity of his work.

She never saw the production when it premiered because she was too sick that evening to keep her eyes open even for two measly hours. When she used the VCR in April, she did it for all the wrong reasons, and she knew it. It was a way to entertain four classes for three days, a way to avoid teaching anything that she would have to repeat after vacation anyway, a way to avoid giving tests that would engender scores of make-ups. She rationalized well, though, and knew she could give justification for showing the film if she ever had to. Films are the highlight of any methods-of-survival curriculum.

As she watched the film, her mind ticked off the discrepancies. She had no control over the reaction; she knew the book too well, and she was still a novice at survival. Every discrepancy roared through her brain, along with jolts caused by student reactions to the film.

The carriage of the Marquis runs down Gaspard's child in Book II after the wine cask scene. Why did they put it in the beginning? And why are these kids laughing at that dead child?

Why is Defarge throwing that coin back at the Marquis?! Madame Defarge does it, damn it! She has more guts than the men! Didn't they read the book!

Oh,. how sad. No Recalled to Life and such a short scene between Lucie and Mr. Lorry. What an outrage! THAT Is Miss Pross?! Old and frail? No. No. No! Wrong! Who did the casting for this, anyway? Why didn't somebody read the book! Carefully!

Oh, this is disgusting. Lucy wasn't born when Dr. Manette was imprisoned. Wrong again. Miss Pross doesn't go to St. Antoine to get Dr. Manette. According to this mutation, she's entirely too weak anyway.

No, no, no. The two golden hairs are not from his little girl, his little girl wasn't born yet! The hair was his wife's! And his journal wasn't left behind in the wine shop. Defarge finds it when he ransacks 105 North Tower during the storming of the Bastille. Years later.

There's no pigeon shoot scene in the book. This serves the purpose of the argument between Darnay and his uncle, the Marquis? Dickens did it better. The Gorgon's Head.

Farewell to Gabelle? Barsad behind a tree? How silly. Gwillerman? Who the hell is Gwillerman? (Sorry, kids, I don't know either.) Good Lord, they rewrote the book. Gwillerman is Barsad's real name? They ignored Solomon Pross entirely. But that was an act of mercy compared to what they did to Jerry Cruncher. He barely exists. What a waste of a colorful character.

Carton berates Lorry for being a man of business, not interested in human feelings. This compensates for the lack of "business machine" dialogue in beginning? Like hell it does. Completely absurd here. By now Lorry has changed. Besides, how can Carton criticize Lorry?

Big deal. Madame Defarge shoots the governor of the Bastille pointblank in the gut. In the book she hews off his head. With her knife, "long ready" as Dickens says. I guess the book will always be better.

She watched the film four times a day and her aggravation accelerated with each viewing because she saw more and more misconceptions, mutilations, and outright lies each time. Some students also noticed, and the film turned out to be harmful to the understanding of many. She knew that those who had never read the book were learning the specifics of an entirely different story. She attempted to point out some of the discrepancies for those students who were aware that changes had been made, and let the others go. The book was complicated enough without further confusion.

Showing the film had been a mistake, an instructional mistake. The few students who were experts on the novel profited from seeing it, but the great majority simply sank lower into the depths of confusion. However, Alyssa applied her new approach, her methods-of-survival rationale to the activity. The film gave her three easy work days; therefore, it was worth something. Once she forced herself to believe that the harm it did was trivial, it would be worth everything. In fact, it would be priceless.

In addition to classroom irritations during that last week before Easter vacation, Alyssa also fought the nerve revolution that occurred every day during homeroom and study hall. Annette Nieully continued to be a source of daily rage, with Sharon Newcombe and a few others not far behind. And study hall was study hall, a waste of time, a cause of intense frustration. She despised having to go to study hall, detested the duty, abhorred it. Guerrilla warfare it was, and every day her nerves reacted accordingly.

One day she found another teacher, a sub, sitting at her desk when she arrived in study hall. She assumed that the sub was simply in the wrong location. After explaining that the despicable place was her responsibility during second period, she was surprised at the sub's refusal to move on. The sub explained that she was supposed to be there with her class because she couldn't get into her classroom, something about the room being painted. Someone in the office told her to take classes to Study Hall A. Alyssa was beginning to understand why the regular teacher stayed home for the day. But she was livid over what she was being forced to put up with.

Wasn't it bad enough in the pit without a class? And the sub absolutely would not move off the chair, she obviously believed in squatter's rights. So Alyssa sat at a student desk. For no more than ten minutes. She was wild by then, her insides steaming. Not only was it impossible to keep the study hall kids under control, but the sub was attempting to conduct a lesson with her students scattered all over the place. The stupidity, the absurdity of it rose like scum to the surface and threatened to drown Alyssa in a sea of phlegm. Rather than explode, Alyssa left, giving a small wave to Bonnie on the way out, leaving the sub the desk, the class, and the study hall.

She spent the period in the faculty room. By lunch time she was cooled off, but still needed to blow off steam. She was doing exactly that when the sub walked in, which gave her an opportunity to explain why she left in a huff; the sub was upset by the whole thing. Alyssa made sure the woman understood the real cause for her anger. She wasn't angry at the sub, she was angry at the moron who instructed the sub. She never found out which moron, for that information was superfluous to the point.

Something else was happening that week in relation to subs. Every morning public address announcements listed canceled classes. Students were advised to go to study halls. Nobody could figure out why. Were there simply not enough subs to go around? Or was the district simply trying to save money? At any rate, study halls were jammed with refugees, study hall teachers had no control over it, kids were going off to points unknown instead of to study hall and teachers left lesson plans for subs that were never called.

Canceled classes, previously unheard of in a public school, were a shock to the faculty. Nobody believed it was happening, but happen it did, and once begun, such procedures become fast rule, mostly because such procedures remain unheard of outside the walls of the building, or because those interested in educational matters are too far above to notice the scurrying of the ants below, or because nobody much cares about the day-to-day workings of a school until Mary or Joe is about to fail a grade. Even then Nobody focuses his wrath on One, not willing or able to manage an attack on Many.

The canceling of classes caused many a brain to swell; faculty rooms harbored many a bursting bubble. So that's what they think of us and our classes, is it? Why do we have to bother to leave lesson plans? They don't care if these kids are getting an education. Are we supposed to be afraid to call in sick now? Is that what they're trying to accomplish?

In the midst of the confusion that week before Easter, 1981, there was an undercurrent of excitement that ran oblivious to all else among members of the Class of 1981. Seniors were whispering in select groups, making phone calls, shouting coded messages across corridors; they had been anticipating since the first day of school in September, planning for a few months, and finally, finally, the date was set, secretly decided among those with social power over such things. The date was set and nothing, but nothing, would stop the Senior Class from exercising its right to Senior Skip Day.

No manner of rational argument could convince a senior that he had no right to skip school on some arbitrarily predetermined day in April or May. Yearly efforts to figure out which day was marked were futile, and students considered the yearly attempt to be part of the fun. What joy there is in hoodwinking authority. At first it was thought that the day was selected according to a backward count from the day of graduation, the number determined by the year. But 81 days before graduation put the date somewhere in the first week of March, and it didn't happen then. Actually, there was neither science nor math involved, it would happen according to the whimsy of a few student leaders; the rest fell in line willingly in the Holy Name of Tradition.

Senior Skip Day had become Tradition to a generation of students who no longer upheld the years-old practice of decorating the high school gym for the Senior Ball because the place wasn't elegant enough for their sophisticated tastes, and a fancy, expensive restaurant with banquet facilities was. Senior Skip Day became Tradition after the record player became obsolete and was replaced by high-priced live entertainment, and students considered dancing at a dance to be the queerest sort of bizarre behavior. Senior Skip Day became Tradition at the same time that graduation ceremonies became afflicted with gross signs of rudeness and disrespect, when students found it appropriate to wear bathing suits and cowboy hats, to jeer and shout obscenities, and to laugh and conduct jovial conversations during speeches by speakers who were attempting to convey a simple traditional message: The world is eagerly awaiting! Get out there and make a difference! You are our future!

Of course, seniors had all the answers. We're making our own traditions, seniors glibly stated when faced with criticism over Senior Skip Day. Other generations made their own traditions, why can't we? Had they researched any history, they would have said: We'd rather not swallow goldfish, you see, or jam ourselves into telephone booths or Volkswagens; we don't believe in sororities or fraternities. We aren't as silly as all that.

Senior Skip Day mushroomed into the highlight of the year, with seniors admonishing lower classmen that, no, they could not partake of the wine until they were of age. And the wine and the beer flowed with other intoxicating spirits, both liquid and otherwise, in a variety of locations. Each high school had its favorite spots; each grouping within each whole located itself according to taste, means, and station.

School districts attempted to stop the illegal activity after the fun seemed to be getting out of hand. Here and there students were sustaining injuries during party time, injuries which made spectacular headlines. The schools were at it again, loosening standards, losing their grip on discipline. Administrators started shaking in their shoes. But it was too late to nip the bud, for the bud had grown to a mammoth oak.

After a few drownings, a drunken brawl or two, and assorted other consequences of Senior Skip Day, it was deemed necessary to Do Something About It. School officials decided that it was indeed time to go public with the problem; it was indeed time for CYA. If some kid got himself too mangled, and the school hadn't made adequate attempts to discourage participation in the annual day of debauchery, there would be hell to pay, hell in the form of lawyers, litigation, and press coverage.

So the letters and press releases started to fly. The public was notified: Senior Skip Day Is Illegal. The School Does Not Sanction Nor Will It Condone The Practice Of Mass Truancy. Seniors Are Warned That They Will Be Subject To Disciplinary Action If They Are Willfully Truant From School On Any Day Designated As Senior Skip Day.

Administrators breathed a sigh of relief. The school could no longer be held accountable. And, after parents were already aware that Senior Skip Day was potentially dangerous and then notified that it was illegal, surely they would help the school to discourage the continuation of the activity.

How peculiar it turned out to be, how strange and unnatural. Senior Skip Day never lost a bit of its momentum, never changed in character, never skipped a beat in the rhythm of defiance. In fact, if anything, it gathered speed and puffed with pride. Once the school made it absolutely clear that students would need written excuses to cover absences on Senior Skip Day (the same required practice for any other day in the year) written excuses rained from the heavens with vengeful purpose and power. Students who chronically forgot excuses any other day of the year had that little piece of parental communication firmly in hand for Senior Skip Day; students who had never submitted a valid excuse in all their adolescent years supplied one for Senior Skip Day; administrators and teachers voiced the same reaction: This is impossible. How could a few hundred kids all be legally absent on the same day? Phone calls proved the impossible. Parents had written the excuses.

Then the school was faced with the real zinger: Was it fair to discipline the few students who failed to produce excuses because their parents refused to lie to protect them? Was it fair to reward deception and penalize honesty?

And so, Tradition reigned supreme. Why shouldn't a kid have a little fun his senior year? What difference does one day make? My daughter doesn't drink. My son drives safely. There's nothing wrong with an occasional breaking of the rules, as long as it doesn't get too far out of hand. Kids will be kids. They'll have to toe the line soon enough. So what? What can the school do about it? Whip you? You're not in prison, they can't do anything to you if I give you permission to miss school. Go ahead, honey, enjoy yourself, you're only young once, these are the best years of your life.

Thus and therefore, students who studied Shirley Jackson's "The Lottery" and C.D.B. Bryan's "So Much Unfairness of Things" during their sophomore year joined forces with the Traditionalists as if they had never heard of either short story. Alyssa Matthews was foolish enough to refer to both stories once when she attempted to convince seniors that Senior Skip Day was ridiculous. "Those stories don't have anything to do with us," was the response. "We aren't out to hurt anybody, and those stories are outdated." Alyssa, deeply disturbed that the lessons of literature were so ephemeral, protested to the contrary, but what did she know about such things? Everybody was blowing the whole thing way out of proportion anyway. Seniors knew what they were doing, they knew enough to be careful. Sure, they heard about the girl who drowned last year, the motorcycle accident, the boy who fell into a ravine, the house that caught fire. Sure. But those things happened Elsewhere. Nothing Like That Will Happen Here. And wasn't it foolish that stiff mortarboards were being replaced by Styrofoam just because of a few bloody foreheads?

On April 14, 1981, eight seniors showed up for Alyssa's third period class. But this year the district was well-prepared for Senior Skip Day; the night before, an article in the newspaper reiterated basic facts: seniors were not engaging in a school-sponsored activity, seniors without written parental excuses would be disciplined as truants, the school was not responsible for the behavior of seniors illegally absent from school. Letters had been sent to parents; phone calls would follow up the letters.

Teachers were instructed to penalize truants to the full extent of The Law, which was the most absurd piece of the puzzle, for it fit no space, it interlocked with nothing at all. The Law states that truants must be given every opportunity to make up work missed while truant. Truants cannot be denied instruction, truants must be allowed academic recovery. The most a teacher could do in the way of disciplinary action was to assign detention and/or a zero for the day's class work. But before he could do that, a teacher had to prove truancy. Can any puzzle accommodate a circular piece?

Teachers were faced with the same dilemma that the district washed its hands of; teachers were expected to do the dirty work because teachers were in the position to penalize honesty in the name of discipline. The pressure landed where it always does: on the head of the lowest man.

Very few teachers buckled, very few exacted punishment, very few were willing to play the villain after all the other villains were spared from wearing the title. But one consequence remained for the classroom teacher. When Alyssa Matthews met with the eight seniors who attended class on Senior Skip Day she had to deal with the consequence that all the other villains perpetuated.

"Are we going to have class today?" Brian Conneally asked.

"How can we? Nobody's here." Joe Brissonson observed.

"I'm under orders to conduct class as usual," the teacher said. "Would you like to see the official notice?"

"That's pretty stupid, isn't it?" said Michael Ixion.

"Sure is," said the teacher. "I'm also required to repeat the lesson for the rest of the class, no matter who is involved in Senior Skip Day.

I'd have to be pretty stupid to knock myself out today. Tell me, why are you people here today? Your parents won't lie for you?"

That was the general consensus among six; the other two simply weren't interested in Senior Skip Day. The teacher commiserated most with the minority.

Joe said: "It's not fair that some kids get away with being truant today. I mean, I'd be out there too if it wasn't Senior Skip Day."

"Stop letting out your secrets," Brian said to Joe.

"Well, it's the truth. Why are they making such a big deal out of one day? It's easy enough to skip school any other time."

The teacher tried to explain. "This one day is too flagrant, there are too many kids involved. Schools are legally responsible for students during scheduled school days."

One of the eight asked the next question, which sparked a series. "What are you going to do to the kids without excuses?"

"Nothing."

"Then why are we here? What do we get out of being here today?"

"Not much."

"You're not going to teach today?"

"Nope."

"Do we get extra credit for showing up.?"

"Why should you? For reporting to class? You're supposed to be here, remember?"

"So what do we do today?"

"Anything you like. You could read ahead."

"Can we leave?"

"Of course not."

"Why not, if we're not going to do anything? You can cancel class."

"You're here to begin with because your parents won't cover for you, and you want me to do it? Absolutely not. I don't have the authority to cancel class."

"Can we go to the library?"

"Stop asking silly questions."

"Why? Why is that a silly question?"

"Once you leave this room, you'll never make it to the library. Give me credit for some brains."

"What do you care if we skip out?"

"That's not the point. The point is, once you walked through the door, I became responsible for your whereabouts this period, and I haven't the authority to dismiss you from school."

"Are you saying that we would have been better off if we never showed up?"

"I suppose so. Then you would have been truant on your own without my knowledge. Strange, isn't it?"

"And you're not going to do anything to the kids who aren't here?"

"How can I? Most of them will have excuses. Is it fair to penalize the ones who don't? Besides, I'm not too anxious to spend a few hours tracking down the truth, especially when the truth will be a lie most of the time."

"How fair is all of this to us?"

"You can be thankful that you have the kind of parents that you have. I know that you don't appreciate them right now, but maybe someday you'll understand."

"Yeah, when we have kids of our own, right?"

"Maybe. Maybe not. Who knows? I'm sorry, but I can't sort all of this out for you. I wish I could. That's what I'm supposed to be able to do, isn't it?"

"But you can let us go. Nobody will ever know. We'll make ourselves scarce. Nobody will find out you let us go."

"What if you get stopped in the hall? What will you say?"

"We won't mention your name. We'll say we never came to class. But we won't get caught. We promise."

"You don't understand, do you? You're the ones who will get caught. You haven't lived long enough to understand that."

"Aw, c'mon. Let us go. We aren't doing anything today anyway."

"I can't. I wish I could, but I can't. What if something happens to one of you? I know you're all fearless, but I'm not. What if one of you gets hit by a truck while crossing the street? You ever think of that? What if one of you slips on the ice and slides in front of a bus? Why are you laughing?"

"We'll be careful. None of that will happen. None of that ever happens. It hasn't happened yet, has it?"

"Oh, to be young and fearless again. No, it hasn't happened yet. But if it does, I'm at fault for letting you out of this room. Can one of you tell me why today was picked for this foolishness? It's cold outside; there's still snow on the ground."

"The weather doesn't matter. Kids are partying anyway. You're getting old, Mrs. Matt."

"That I am."

"My cousin goes to a school that sponsors Senior Skip Day."

"That's crazy."

"No, it isn't. That way parents don't have to lie and nobody gets hurt. The school provides transportation."

"And those kids have learned that if you do something wrong long enough, you'll eventually be rewarded for it. And tell me, who gets to baby sit? Teachers?"

"Sure. It's kind of like a senior trip to the beach. Only it's during a regular school day."

"That's just ducky. Wrong wins out over right. No wonder you kids are screwed up. You're in school to get an education. If you want to play childish games instead, you should have to do it on your own time. The line has to be drawn somewhere. Sooner or later we all have to answer to somebody. You'd might as well learn that now."

"Right now all I'm learning is that it pays to lie."

"I know. This whole thing is as unfair as anything could be."

"So let us go! How about if you turn around and look the other way for a few seconds?"

"I can't. If anything happened to one of you, not only would I be legally responsible, but I would also have to live with it for the rest of my life. I know you think I'm being hyper and melodramatic, you people aren't afraid of the word IF. Somebody once said it's the biggest little word in the language. I've been afraid of IF ever since I started teaching. Try to see this from my end of it. I'm not anxious to feel guilty over somebody's paralyzed body. Thank you very much, but I'd rather not be held accountable for any accidental injury sustained by a student when he was supposed to be safe in my classroom. I'd never live down the fact that I could have avoided the tragedy. Sorry, folks, once you're here, you're here to stay. I won't sacrifice my sanity to give you a few minutes of freedom."

"A lot of other teachers excuse students all the time."

"I know that, and I think they're asking for trouble. It's a chance in a million that something tragic will happen, but even that's too risky for me."

For Alyssa Matthews and other teachers like her, Senior Skip Day was a dreaded annual reality. There was no way to be fair; equitable treatment was impossible. And there were the questions, always the questions, that no one but the classroom teacher had to face, questions requiring answers that mocked rational argument. Especially that one query, the one students never tire of and will attempt as long as the breed exists; that one query that prompted from some fearful souls an answer, ironically enough, in interrogative form. WHAT IF? Can such an answer be avoided by those who care?

Should it be? And if it is, who pays the consequences when the improbable reverses?

*... for there is a period in life which is called
the age of disillusion, which means the age at
which a man discovers that his honest
and generous impulses are incompatible with
success in business; that the institutions he has
reverenced are shams; and that he must
join the conspiracy or go the wall ..."*
George Bernard Shaw

Winter conscientiously maintained its control, mocking the frailties of man. The merciless defiance of March wouldn't subside, wouldn't submit to the inevitability of a new season. Through the first weeks of April, mountains of snow still harassed drivers at intersections, cold blustery winds still sliced through the thickest attempts at protection. The soul of the earth was still cryogenically entombed.

Marred by uncooperative weather, the last long vacation of the academic year was a disappointment to Alyssa. She desperately needed the rest, the time to rejuvenate before the last seven-week push to exams; but she also needed to open windows, to breathe the regenerative air of spring. The rites of resurrection were as remote to her as the rites of spring that Easter morning. She sat through the joyous celebration oblivious to its message.

By mid-week the third "last big one of the season" hit. High velocity winds battered the falling snow into massive prison walls. The white-out closed roads and businesses, grounded planes, and canceled all varieties of grandiose plans. Crucial endeavors were temporarily suspended by forces capricious and indifferent.

Jeff Matthews made a valiant early-morning attempt to clear the driveway, and almost succeeded before the city plow pushed more snow in than he had just blown out. He gave up then, for the winter had taken its toll; he cursed the plow, then called his boss. Work was almost at a standstill anyway. Building construction had slowed to a crawl, one natural symptom of a sick economy. Reaganomics had the country on its knees; it was a mere matter of time before the crippling disease would inhibit the use of any flexible joint, when all support would be terminated, and the patient would slither on an unemployed belly.

Jeff Matthews, who rarely missed a day's work for any reason, knew his boss wouldn't mind a bit; bad weather was a blessing when it cut the payroll. In fact, the man was celebrating; Jeff's was the third in what promised to be a long line of calls.

Jeff slipped back into bed, enjoying the unexpected comfort of a day off. He would fight the snow later, at his leisure, without the pressure of a time clock. How nice, he thought, how nice to be able to do that. Without pressure, the fight becomes tolerable, pleasant even. He stretched out in the bed, turned to face his wife, then gathered her up with his limbs. She awoke long enough to say, "Mmmmm. You feel good. Don't go away." Then she heard the relentless howling of the wind and murmured, "Don't go out in that today, hon. You need a break from it too. Stay home. We'll spend the day in bed. How's that sound?"

He thought that sounded extraordinary and was about to tell her, but she had already slipped back into sleep. It was noon before they both awoke again. She must have forgotten the earlier suggestion. In spite of his overtures, she left the bed. He heard the noises from the kitchen, smelled the evidence, and had no objections to pancakes and sausage. It was eating in silence that he objected to. Eating alone. Sleeping alone. Living alone. She was there, but she wasn't there.

The doctor said it was a form of depression. Good old Doc. He had tried to explain and to ease Jeff's mind. Jeff had gone to the hospital to find the doctor because attempts to get through to him at the office had been futile. No, he didn't want an appointment; no, he wasn't sick; he just wanted to talk to the doctor about his wife, she was the patient. She had him worried sick, but that didn't qualify him for medical attention, not the usual kind anyway. He realized finally that the only way to see the doctor without waiting two months for an appointment was to cross his path somewhere in the hospital. That was far easier said than done, however; Jeff stalked the halls one evening after his request that the doctor be paged was denied. Sheer determination pushed the worried husband from floor to floor, wing to wing, until at last, after interrogating every nurse he saw, he tracked down the one person who he thought could answer some questions.

The doctor was helpful and placidly frightening at the same time. "I doubt if she'll become suicidal, Jeff. She's made of stronger stuff, though right now her strength is diminished considerably. If the depression becomes more severe, though, call the office. Depression can now be controlled and abated through medication. Anti-depressants are a lifesaver for many people. She's not totally uncommunicative, is she?"

His mind still reeling at *suicidal* and *depression*, Jeff answered, "No. She talks once in a while, but mostly if I start the conversation. Otherwise, she stares into space a lot. When she's not sleeping. I tell you, Doc, that's all she wants to do is sleep and go to work. I know she's sick, she's physically exhausted. But she's a maniac over going to work. Then she falls asleep on the sofa after dinner and wakes up in time to go to bed. This has been going on since January. It's driving me nuts. I get stir crazy in the house all the time, but she won't budge. Nothing interests her anymore, nothing excites her, nothing except going to work gets her out of the house. She waited months for a trestle table and never cracked a smile the day it was delivered; I finished the bath off the bedroom, but she can't find the time to pick out wallpaper. I want to help her out of this rut she's in, but she won't talk about it."

"It's more than a rut, Jeff. She opened up to me the last time I saw her. She's going through a crisis, a personal crisis, and neither you nor I can help her through it if she doesn't want the help. I'd refer her to a psychiatrist if I thought she could benefit from one. I may still do that, but right now I think she's capable of working it out for herself. It will take time, of course, and she needs time first to get healthy again, then to work out her problem."

"She told me about the leave of absence. It was odd, though. When she told me about it, she obviously thought it was appealing, there was some excitement in her. But now she avoids the subject."

"That's all right. I'm sure she's thinking about it."

"Oh, no doubt. She's so damned intense, sometimes I want to shake her loose from whatever it is in her head that's caught her undivided attention. I'm starting to get jealous. She's my whole life, Doc, and I still think the feeling is mutual, but we can't go on this way too much longer or something is going to snap. Isn't there anything I can do to help her out of this?"

"The best you can do for her is to be patient. Does she slip in and out of the depressed state?"

"Constantly. When she's not sleeping, working, or staring into space, she cries. If I say the least little thing that strikes her the wrong way, she cries. And I can't figure out what the hell it was I shouldn't have said. The other night she went into withdrawal because I left some crumbs on the counter. We've been married a lot of years, Doc, and I've never known her to be this sensitive."

"What does this withdrawal consist of?"

"She clams up. I can see that she's upset, but she won't say what it is. I've never known her to complain over anything, but I've got a feeling she should explode. I feel like I'm living with a time bomb. Only she'll never explode. We've never had a serious argument in twelve years. I'm not complaining about that, but right now I wish she'd fight. I don't know what to do when she refuses to talk. I've been asking her 'What's wrong?' and she's been saying 'Nothing' for so long, I don't bother to ask anymore."

The doctor shook his head. "Don't stop asking. Let her know you care. But don't expect any answers, either. I suspect that she'll be this way until the end of the school year. Then, when some of the pressure is off, she should start to come out of it. Be patient. She'll recover."

"It is that goddam job that's done this to her, isn't it?"

Thinking about his own goddam job, the doctor replied, "She cares too much, attempts too much, worries too much."

"I've been telling her that for years," the husband said. "Maybe now she'll listen to me."

The doctor, whose office hours often extended until two o'clock in the morning said, "Don't count on it. Not yet. It may help you to know that her problem is not uncommon among people in the helping professions."

"I was beginning to think she loves her job more than me. It's like she doesn't want me around, I'm in the way, she has more important things to do, to think about."

"Don't take it personally, Jeff. I suspect that you'll be the element in her life that will shake her loose from the nightmare."

That sounded good to Jeff Matthews, who wanted to believe that he meant more to his wife than anything else in her life. As he sat before his plate of pancakes, he didn't dare mention that they weren't completely cooked. She murmured a weak apology, which included a statement that she wasn't doing much of anything right anymore, then looked at him with wet eyes, then looked away.

Jeff let the moment pass, finished drinking his coffee, then announced that he was going out to clean up the driveway and dig out the car. The wind had stopped. He knew it might whip up again; if he didn't take advantage of the periods of truce, the driveway would get beyond control. Alyssa offered to wield a shovel, which surprised him. "I'll be out to help as soon as I clean up here," she said.

He said: "I'm running out of underwear. Would you throw in a batch today?" He didn't see her face when he said the words, and if he had he would have been stymied. He moved her hair to kiss the back of her neck, then dressed and went out.

Alyssa finished washing the dishes, bemoaning the fact that they had to be washed whether the meal was edible or not; she left them to dry on the counter. Then she walked through the dining room, up the stairs, into the bedroom, and with every step, every deliberate step, her mind raced through the litany that was also deliberate, the litany that began months ago. She was too sick to move, and when she stopped moving, so did everything else. Jeff did nothing around the house.

Me. I do everything. If I didn't cook, we wouldn't eat. If I didn't buy groceries, I wouldn't have anything to cook. If I didn't clean, the dust would pile to the ceiling. I make sure the bills are paid, I run all the errands, I clean the bathrooms, I vacuum, I do the laundry. Me. I can't even be sick in peace. When I'm sick there are crumbs on the counter, dishes in the sink, clothes on the floor, and nothing on the table. Would it break his heart to do some of my work just because he would be saving me from doing it? My work. Why do I automatically call it my work? It's not my work; he lives here too. Why is housework synonymous with woman? I go out to work all day too.

She picked up the laundry basket and carried it downstairs. By the time she loaded the washing machine, she was into The Litany, Part II.

It's my fault. I've always done it all by myself. I wouldn't dream of letting him wash dishes. The perfect wife. I had to be the perfect wife, the perfect everything. He didn't know how, wasn't anxious to learn — can't blame him for that — so I did it all. And I won't ask. I will not ask. If I have to ask, I'll do it myself. What a disgusting attitude. But I can't help it, I can't. I know I shouldn't expect other people to be like me. But can't he see that I need help now? Can't he just do things to relieve me of having to do them? Isn't it pathetic that he doesn't know how to operate a washing machine? My fault. Mine and his mother's. What is it in women that makes them want to sacrifice themselves? Rampant maternal instinct? I don't want to do it anymore. But how do I stop? There's nobody to pick up my clothes, cook my meals, do my laundry. If I had a daughter I'd be teaching her to do it. But not a son, never a son. Women. We're our own worst enemies.

How can I blame him? He's out there doing what I won't do. But it isn't the same, it isn't the same as knowing you have to cook every day of your life, and clean the house every week, and wash clothes whether you feel like it or not. Modern conveniences. Women have it easy now, they just push buttons and the work is done by a machine. Which means that we now have an opportunity to get the washer, dryer, vacuum cleaner, oven, and stovetop going all at once after we get home from work. How convenient. Be thankful, kid, that you aren't going to the Laundromat anymore. Be thankful that YOU aren't going. A man's weird if he knows how to fold clothes, he's henpecked if he does housework. Maybe women were better off with a washboard and a broom, barefoot and pregnant, with neither hope nor ambition.

For the first time, she added a third segment to The Litany: I've got to stop this gunnysacking. Why am I doing this to myself? Before long I'll be wallowing in self-pity.

She looked out the window, saw that Jeff was doing a commendable job by himself, and decided to stay in. She pulled a package out of the freezer for dinner, and was irritated at having to do it. She no sooner cleaned up the mess from one meal when she had to start thinking about the next. She almost tumbled into Part I of The Litany again, but caught herself in time and left the kitchen.

The bedroom was a more comforting place, since she had spent two days scrubbing and cleaning the upstairs. Once she made the bed, the room was a pleasure to be in. She thought she would read awhile, and remembered a book she had borrowed from Jean a few months back, a Ludlum. She enjoyed Ludlum; he immersed her in another world, caused her to be involved in the lives of ordinary people cast into extraordinary circumstances. The author was being accused of extracting scenes from a file of past works, producing carbon copies, but the critics hadn't hurt his popularity any. People were still anxious to read *The Matarese Circle*.

The book was in the spare room down the hall. She remembered putting it there for safekeeping until she found time to indulge. She opened the door and entered the curtainless room. She felt the chill and fully intended to secure the book quickly, then return to the bedroom or, better yet, start a fire in the fireplace in the living room and read down there. But once she entered the room, she was hooked. It happened every time. One book led to the next, then the next, then to the next box or pile. The small room was not overflowing with books, but half of the floor-that-needs-refinishing was covered with three-foot stacks of volumes that she had carried herself, a few at a time, from the apartment to the old colonial in need of refurbishing.

She was an obsessive collector of books, a born bibliophile. One day Jeff would build shelving to house them properly, to give her easy access to titles. She used to fight her way through the mounds to find books to use in class, books to give to students, books for reference purposes. But no more. She hadn't entered the room to take out in a few years, only to throw in. What a shame, she thought in the midst of the wreckage, what a wasteful shame.

The Ludlum was lying atop a box labeled "College: Scrapbooks/Notebooks/Yearbooks." She set the novel aside, opting for non-fiction instead. Once she began, she couldn't stop. The Orphean reflex held her; she strained to accommodate the painful position, even revel in it, for it contained a deceptive element of sanity.

Familiar faces, places, events. Letters. Scholarships. The days when achievement was rewarded. Students are deceived. The world isn't made that way. Tuition, room and board, college fees. 1965. The new campus, still under construction, Rocky's monument. The arched, pillared, fountained, treed, unabashedly white, new campus.

Sorority. Sisterhood. Women in league with other women to grow, to serve, to learn. Over one hundred sisters then. Down to ten now, the last newsletter said. People don't join groups now, don't want to mass together and work toward common goals. The Age of Me took care of Greeks. Too bad. What's wrong with women sharing hopes, dreams, cares, joys, sorrows, blazers, and beer mugs? Part of the awakening, part of the preparation. But still, students are deceived ...

The days of disruption, of controversy, of sterility and fecundity, of assassination and police brutality; the days when students rioted, blacks rioted, and the old men who didn't have to fight or starve or face discrimination cried out for stability and control. Conform! they demanded with smoke bombs and bullets in unloaded guns. Where was the war anyway? Conform! You have no right to criticize! Men used to be willing to fight for freedom! Conform! This is the greatest country on the face of the earth! Love it or leave it! Fight for it! Die for it! Just don't criticize it. Eternal days. Only the minutes and the hours change, the days are sacred. Issues change. The world doesn't.

Courses. Notes. Papers typed with two fingers on an old pink clunker (Where did you ever find a pink typewriter?) with "e" and "a" problems. Literature. Writing. Science and math? Yuk. Student teaching. Closer to the dream fulfilled, the promise kept. *It's here, I know it's here. I remember it now, where is it?* When she found it, she wished she hadn't.

Jeff found her in the throes of her reverie. She never heard him come in the back door, shed his boots and coat, and wander up the stairs in search of her. When he entered the room, she didn't acknowledge his presence. She was sitting on the floor, surrounded by memorabilia, staring at a sheet of paper, and she didn't look up.

Accustomed to seeing her preoccupied by some unknown force, he teased, "A fine help you are." Then he felt the chill. "Why don't you open the registers to get some heat in here?"

She wasn't answering. "Alyssa?" Kneeling beside her, he lifted her chin and saw her tear-streaked face. "Honey, what's wrong?"

She still said nothing but buried her face in his shoulder. The tears kept coming, sobless tears, the fruitful river of the eye. Her Orphean Song had reached its crescendo, had pinpointed the site of the soreness, had raked it raw and burning.

He felt helpless and hated the feeling. "Isn't there someone you can talk to?" he asked softly.

"No," she said.

That evening, though, she talked to him. It was time to let it fly, to unload it on someone. Besides, she was frightened into it. Jeff left the house after dinner without a word of explanation, something he had never done before. She started a fire and watched the yellow flames leap playfully around the pieces of wood, watched until she was mesmerized by the intensity of the transferal. Wood to flame. Substance to nothingness.

Where is he? Where did he go? Have I become that difficult to live with? Yes. Would I blame him if he's out trying to find somebody who laughs? No. When's the last time I cracked a smile? Christmas.

She built a fire with utmost care, strategically placing newspaper, kindling, and small logs so that she might eventually enjoy the perfect blaze. She loved the beauty of a slow, perfectly balanced fire, a fire of symmetry and grace. She rarely achieved that kind of fire, but she avoided disappointment because she knew why. Too many variables; the size and shape of logs, the type of wood, the flow of air. Too many variables. This fire was as capricious as any other.

When she heard the key in the door, she jumped. When he walked into the living room, turned on the TV, and sat as far away from her as possible, she stared. When she tried to ask the question, she choked up. She was not good at interrogation, and she was afraid of possible answers.

An hour passed. She built up the courage to ask him to sit next to her on the sofa. He did. She leaned against him, then sat upright; he was too stiff for comfortable intertwining. She remembered when they used to sprawl together on the same sofa, oblivious to space restrictions, how they used to joke about getting rid of the double bed because a single was spacious enough the way they slept.

Now he was propped against the pillows at one end of the sofa, and she was just as comfortable at the other end.

"I'm sorry," she said to the wood burning in the fireplace.

"For what?" he said to Johnny Carson.

"I'm not very happy lately."

"No kidding. I wouldn't have guessed."

"You haven't been much help."

He clicked off the TV. "How am I supposed to help when I don't know what the hell is bugging you? I'll tell you what I think it is. I think you're bored, bored with married life, bored with me. I used to be able to make you feel good. We used to be married, remember? What's happened to us?"

"Please don't think that. I'm not bored with you," she said. Then her voice broke. "Don't put any more pressure on me, Jeff, ... Please."

"Do not cry, honey. Do not cry. We can't discuss this if you cry, or if you refuse to talk. You've got to stop turning me away, Alyssa. Do you know what you do whenever I try to talk to you? You fade away. Before I know it, you're gone, vanished."

She wiped her eyes with her fingers and fought to speak without quivering. "Where were you tonight?"

"Helping your father install a water heater. He asked me about it at Easter dinner, remember?"

"No, I — I didn't remember. I thought you might be out trying to find another wife, one who laughs and smiles and screws occasionally."

She started to cry, and he didn't try to stop her. Patience, the doctor said. Well, he would do whatever he had to do, but patience alone wasn't enough. He moved next to her, let her flow into his arms, waited for the water to subside, then began, "You can cry all you want, okay? We'll just take a break when you have to cry." She nodded against his shoulder, and he continued, "I don't want another wife, I want you back. Do you realize that the whole family's worried about you?"

"What whole family?" she sniffled.

"Both actually. Yours and mine. Your brothers pulled me aside Easter Sunday and wanted to know what's wrong with you. I've been through it with my parents and tonight you were the main topic of conversation at your mother's. I don't know what to tell anybody."

"Tell them I'm mean, moody, and hard to live with."

"That's just it — you're not. It's not you at all. Neither is the depression you fall into." After a period of silence he said, "Hey, you're fading away again."

"Sometimes I think I'm losing my mind. You ever wonder what a nervous breakdown is? I've heard about it, but I've never witnessed one. I wonder if it can happen if you think it might. I wonder if I'm going through one right now."

Rosemary Cania Maio

"If you're trying to scare the hell out of me, you're doing a good job of it. I can't stand to see you so unhappy. What the hell got into you this afternoon?"

She reached around to an end table, picked up the source of the tears, and handed it to him. "This did it," she said. He read by the light thrown by the old flames in the old fireplace.

Picture this ...

Newly painted walls
Enclosing bodies
All shapes and sizes
And faces.
Faces without names.
Why the tears Little Boy?
You bit his back because he kicked you because you poked him
    because he spit at you because you said ...
But now you're sorry
Sorry it all happened.
That's right — shake hands.
It will make a better man of you
Unless it happens again
And no one cares.

Look again and see
Valentines
Filled with love and friendship.
So much more than revolt and demonstration
In the world.
Remember to search for the Good
And spread it around.
You need those transitive verbs
And introductory "there"
But you need
So much more ...

Get rid of the gum!
Do Unto Others ...
Don't run in the halls.
Yes, you may get a drink of water.
No, you may not go to your locker.
Single file in the hall, SINGLE FILE!

Forgot your book? See you after school.
Must develop responsibility.
Must develop initiative, character, creativity, independence,
    good citizenship, manners, personality, respect for
    others, self-respect ...

So much more ...

The fog is clearing,
Faces have names,
Newly painted walls
Have meaning.

And there is
So much more
To Give ...

She was afraid he didn't understand, so the teacher explained. "I had to write a report two weeks after I started my student teaching. My college supervisor wanted impressions, reactions, criticisms, evaluations of assignments. He was responsible for eight of us assigned to different schools in the same area. I was his only English teacher. When he returned the reports, I could tell that he had had some problems evaluating mine. He never expected a poem; he asked me if it was that 'free verse' he had heard about somewhere. I don't think he knew quite how to deal with it, so he gave me a safe B. After all, it didn't really fulfill the assignment. Other people handed in pages and pages. I remember thinking, What did he expect from an English major, anyway?"

"It certainly is you," Jeff said. "I was never any good at figuring out poetry, but knowing the author helps."

"I'm no poet, and it's hardly great poetry. But it was the only way I could adequately express my impressions. I couldn't write a statistical thesis on procedures and theories. What did I care about how the school was run, who was running it, and why it was run that way? From the very beginning the kids were everything to me. That's all I saw in teaching. The kids. Kids with feelings, kids with needs, kids who had to be educated. Kids and a teacher. I felt overwhelmed with responsibility and I vowed that I would find another job if I couldn't make it in a classroom. It's like no other form of work. And I worked my ass off to prove I could do it. So much more to give. Christ.

There's nothing left. I'm depleted. I gave everything I had, and still they want more, more, more."

He read the poem again. "What's with the Valentines? In high school?"

Was it a lapse of memory? Or hadn't she ever told him? Perhaps it was both. At any rate, she was saddened by the fact that he knew very little, that over the years she had told him very little.

"Junior high," she said, "Seventh grade. The backbiting, kicking, poking, spitting episode really happened. After spending eight weeks in a junior high, I decided that I would never accept a position anywhere but in a senior high. You do remember how ecstatic I was when I landed a job at Boesch-Conklyn."

"Oh, sure. You worked yourself into the grave by November."

She ignored the remark; it was different when she said it. He added an element that she didn't like. "In the senior high you don't have to spend half of every class period shutting them up; at least, I never had to. I didn't want to discipline constantly, I wanted to teach. And I did, damn it, I did. For awhile."

She stared at the yellow flames, noticing every flicker, every tongue of fire assume its own shape, its own identity, then, in a matter of moments, change. She noticed intermittent flecks of blue blaze forth, then rapidly fade, consumed by the yellow, the common yellow, the usual yellow flames.

Jeff broke her trance. "Has it ever occurred to you that it's a job, just a job, that you should go there, do what you can in the course of a day, and collect your pay? That's all it is, honey, a job."

"No. You're wrong. It's more than that to me. I've been trying to look at it that way, but I can't. You don't know what it's like. You have no idea. You don't have to face classes of kids every day. How could you read that poem and tell me that it's just a job?"

"Because it's destroying you."

"I used to be so satisfied, so happy with it. I loved to teach. And now I hate it. It's my fault if my students don't learn, yet I couldn't maintain standards if I worked at it twenty-four hours a day, which I'll be damned if I do. No more overtime. Everybody bitches and moans over teachers' salaries, but nobody wants to talk about what we do outside of the classroom. I do enough work in ten months to make up for the other two. No more. They pay me for a hundred-eighty days, no nights, no weekends."

He thought she was coming around to his way of thinking, but then she added, "But who suffers because of it? The kids. The kids are getting a raw deal. And I have to look at the kids every goddam day."

He said, "I wish you'd start thinking about yourself, Alyssa."

Why wouldn't he understand? She tried feeding him some of the things she neglected to tell him all along. Homeroom, study hall, the immensely frustrating duty of tracking down truants, attendance policies, test make-ups, the favoritism shown some students by administrators; all in all: atrocities, absurdities, and abnormalities.

He held his ground. "If that's what they want you to do instead of teach, then do it! And stop fooling yourself. Nepotism and favoritism exist anywhere that two or more people congregate."

"You wouldn't be so hard line on this if you had kids in school," she answered. "If you had kids who were getting a crummy education because their teachers are burned out."

"Don't expect me to worry about nonexistent kids instead of you. I don't give one damn about the school system other than the outrageously high taxes we have to pay. And most people with or without kids feel the same way. Wake up, Alyssa. Parents send their kids to school because they wouldn't know what else to do with them during the day. Nobody cares about the quality of education when it means a higher tax bill. Why should you make yourself sick over it?"

"Because I've got to face my students every day. And because I don't want to be a lousy teacher. I used to believe that hard work and sacrifice and self-discipline could achieve anything. I did things in college that I'm still proud of. I figured out a way to make human figures on a float and I won first prize. I was a dumb little sophomore, new in sorority, and everybody thought, 'What the hell, we never win a prize anyway, nobody else wants to do it, let her do the work.' Well, I did it, all right. I didn't know the first thing about building a float, but I learned. I learned and I designed and I broke new ground. I figured out how to make faces, I was the first to use movable parts and a sound system. I won the goddam first prize trophy. It means a lot to me to be able to say 'I did it' with pride. And now I'm supposed to lie down and die. It's damned difficult for me to admit defeat."

"You're telling me."

"And I know there are consequences that have to be faced. I sacrificed my grade average in college because I couldn't indulge in student activities the way I did and keep up my grades at the same time. I've lectured my students about that. You can concentrate on only one passion at a time. Something has to suffer."

"And you're looking at it."

"What do you mean? You've had it pretty easy; I kept it going for a lot of years. And now I've had it. I can't do it all anymore. I don't want to do it all. We should have split the work around here a long time ago, from the beginning."

He gave her a puzzled look. "I do my share."

"Like hell you do."

"I have yet to see you pushing snow or cutting grass."

"That's only because by the time we bought this house I was beginning to wise up. If I started doing it, I would have inherited more chores on top of what I have to do because I'm the female. Would it break your heart to vacuum once in a while or cook?"

"I don't dare disturb your routine! I've always been under the impression that you have everything under control and don't want any wrenches thrown into the works."

"Bullshit."

"It's the truth; You're so damned independent! Why don't you ask when you want me to do something?"

"Why should I have to ask? Especially now? Can't you see that I'm exhausted? Every time I'm sick you don't see the dishes in the sink? Why do I have to ask you to hang your clothes?"

For the first time, he was speechless. She went on: "I know it's my fault. I've done it all for too long; you're used to being waited on. And if you think it's nasty to clean the driveway, you should try scrubbing the toilets. How about if you do the cooking? You start tomorrow and, whether you feel like it or not, you'll do it every day for the rest of your life. How's that for nasty?"

He found his voice. "I don't cook. That's one thing I do not do. You know that. I have trouble making toast."

She was still in hot pursuit. "What if I were just as bad as you? I'd still be stuck with the job, wouldn't I? And I'd be a rotten wife because women are supposed to cook!"

He reacted out of necessity and frustration. "Are you into that women's lib crap, Alyssa? Is that what's diseased your mind? You are tired of being married, aren't you?"

"No, God damn it! But now I know why I've been avoiding this conversation. You can't possibly understand any of it."

"What about your leave of absence?"

"What about it?"

"Are you thinking about it?"

"Of course I'm thinking about it."

"Have you considered taking it now?"

"What?"

"Now. Take it now."

"What do you mean, now? How the hell can I go on leave now? There's only May and June left."

"I think you need to get out of there now. Then, if you want, you can take next year too. You need the rest now. We can't go on this way."

She stared into the yellow flames. "Do I need the rest now because I don't want to do the housework by myself anymore?"

He didn't know what to make of her. This was what he wanted, he wanted to talk. He wanted an end to the silence. Well, he got it. Only he didn't quite know what to do with it.

The next day the weather cleared, Jeff was back to work, and Alyssa called Mary Gregory. They both agreed: It had been years, far too long, the years passed so quickly. Of course, Mary said, of course. I'd love to see you.

When Alyssa rang the doorbell, she felt a tiny bit awkward because of the long span that had separated them. But Mary smiled in the doorway, Mary immediately made her feel welcome and comfortable. Watching Mary move, listening to Mary's voice transported Alyssa back into the Orphean realm that she still refused to abandon.

Mary Gregory was a vision of retirement. Healthy and happy, she bubbled over with stories about her grandchildren, showing off their pictures with customary pride. It took only a few months to get her life in order, she told Alyssa, and after that she began to enjoy.

"You look wonderful! I'm so glad you're enjoying your retirement!" Alyssa said it once, twice, then a third time.

"And how have you been, Alyssa?" Mary asked. "Did you know you were my favorite? I couldn't tell you then, of course, but I can tell you now. I knew you had it in you, I knew all along. And you never let me down."

Alyssa smiled. "You were a sly old fox. I wouldn't have let you down, I would have died first. I never understood why you gave me a scholarship section my second year of teaching."

"I thought it was a good idea for you to get your feet wet right away."

"You almost drowned me."

"Oh, you survived. You learned to swim, to carry the metaphor one step further. Those first few years made a good teacher out of you."

"And now it doesn't matter, Mary. Good, bad, or indifferent, we're all rats on a sinking ship."

"I only know what I read in the newspapers; I'm not in touch with anyone still at school. But I'll tell you something, Alyssa, I knew this was coming. They were battering away to give English teachers five classes when I was there. I thought of all of you when it happened. How's Jean doing? I read about her husband. It was too bad. Mine's only been gone a year, you know. He retired one month and died the next. That makes no sense, no sense at all. But what can we do about it?"

Alyssa filled Mary in on Jean and Beth and Hank and Paul; she told her about Bonnie and Connie and other members of the department, including Erica and Al. Then Mary pursued, "How bad is it now?"

Thankful for an understanding ear, Alyssa let loose all that she had swallowed for so long; she spilled it, regurgitated it, spewed it, boiled, broiled, and baked it.

"Nothing's changed, has it?" Mary said dryly.

Alyssa's eyes widened. "Don't you think it's gotten considerably worse?"

"Of course. Yes. But the essence, Alyssa, is the same. The essence is in the attitude. I hit up against the attitude more than once. The employee should shut up and do as he is told. If it all turns to shit, then the employee should shut up and take the rap."

Alyssa started to laugh. "It still surprises me when you use that kind of language. The first time I heard you make an off-color remark, I went into shock. Do you remember that?"

"I certainly do. Whose mouth dropped open more, yours or Beth's? I should have started telling dirty jokes after that. You youngsters thought I was the Virgin Mary. I know you used to clean up the conversation when I walked into the faculty room."

"Remember how long it took me to call you Mary? I knew I had to give in when you started calling me Mrs. Matthews. But it was damned difficult. You had been my teacher, you were still my teacher. I had a hard time viewing myself as your equal. Do you remember what you said that day?"

"Not really."

"You said you were teaching *A Tale of Two Titties*. Beth and I still laugh over it; we couldn't believe you said it. We both figured that some day one of us would slip and say it during class."

"It hasn't happened yet, has it?" Mary laughed.

"No, not yet. But then, a lot of things haven't happened yet. I think you're right about the essence, Mary. But what do you do about it when it gets overwhelmingly offensive? And it's going to get worse before it gets better, if it ever gets better. I don't think we'll ever see four classes again, and the number of preps is up for grabs this contract."

"That's too bad. That's terrible, in fact. The very thought gives me visions of books, thousands of books, and people fighting over possession. Do they still hoard books the way they used to? God, that used to drive me wild."

"It's not quite so bad now. Paul has control over books. Or, rather, he had control before classes were scheduled in the resource room. He developed a system to promote a fair distribution. It wasn't perfect, but it was better than nothing."

"And nothing was what we had when I was there."

"Things were a lot simpler then, Mary. You should see the mess senior courses are in. The books for those courses alone would fill your living room."

"Still, Paul has done a commendable job working with the changes. I never could have done it."

"Of course you could have."

"No. I was too sick and too broken. It was time to leave. You always thought I was invincible, Alyssa. You still think so. But I wasn't, and I'm not. I didn't retire, I escaped. The walls were closing in on me, and I escaped."

"That's the way I feel now, as if the walls are closing in on me. I feel trapped. But I can't retire, Mary. What can I do?"

"You know what your options are. You can play the game or you can fold."

"Either way I lose."

"Either way you lose."

Alyssa was quiet for a moment, staring at Mary's perfectly white hair, noticing the permanent indentations above Mary's nose. "I still have your summer reading lists in my filing cabinet; we actually used to suggest summer reading. In fact, we required it for scholarship students. Remember? Between sophomore and junior year. Then we followed up on it in the fall. If we tried it today, some parent would take us to court and claim that we have no right to require work over the summer. No matter, anyway, I haven't used those lists, or any reading lists, in years. I remember how disturbed I was because I hadn't read everything on those lists. I vowed that I would read every one of those books; how could I suggest that students read books I hadn't read myself? But I never did. Then I vowed that I would update the lists because new books deserved to be included. Then I got the bright idea of devising a list of adult books to give to kids for future reference. I never did any of that either. I eliminated book reports altogether, that's what I did. Couldn't handle grading them. I don't talk to kids about books and authors anymore. I have no idea what they're reading or if they're reading. How I used to love it when a kid discovered Ayn Rand or Michener or any author who made him think and react.

"I've wanted to develop an entire unit on satire for years, and to come up with a better way to teach vocabulary. I can see what needs to be done, and I haven't got the time or the energy to do it. I'm barely getting through the curriculum. I stopped assigning papers. I have two scholarship sections this year and it's nothing but a curse because of the volume of paperwork. I had to stop their writing assignments because I couldn't grade all those papers. And you wouldn't believe the number of failing scholarship students. Sometimes I wonder if you did me a favor when I started teaching."

"I was waiting for you to see it."

"You know, don't you? I wouldn't be in this fix if I had been discouraged from the beginning. I'm not blaming you, how can I blame you? But the fact remains that I've known the best of situations. Remember the year you gave me a full load of scholarship sections, when a full load meant four classes and two preps? I was in heaven that year. I did more work that year than in any year following it, but it was work for the kids, teacher's work. Now I wish I never knew what heaven was like because hell is so much the worse by comparison."

"Did you come here today for an answer, Alyssa?"

"I suppose so."

"I can't work any miracles for you. The only thing I can tell you is put up with it or get out. It's too bad that you're so young. I was fortunate enough to be able to retire when the system broke me."

"Why do you say that? I thought you retired because you wanted to."

"Oh, I wanted to, all right. I had had it. I was tired of begging for crumbs and listening to petty grievances. I was just plain worn out. After my surgery, I was worse. But I wanted to get my students through exams, and I thought that maybe after summer vacation, after two months' rest, I might have made it through one more year. That's the way you get. One more year, you keep telling yourself, just one more year. That's what my husband said for three years, and look where it got him. I probably would have held on longer, too, if I hadn't gotten slapped around a little. Funny, I never looked at it that way before, maybe the kid did me a favor."

"What the hell are you talking about?"

"You never heard about it? That's difficult to believe, Alyssa. Rumors were flying like mad, I'm sure. Of course, it happened at the end of the year. And you used to work like an old horse with blinders on."

"Not any longer. Wait a minute ... You were on hall duty and some kid lipped off at you."

"Yes."

"But that's not all."

"He also slapped me across the face and sent me sprawling against a row of lockers."

"Oh, Christ. After your surgery?"

"Why not? He didn't know I had one breast cut out. Do you think he would have cared if he knew?"

"Hall duty. How I hated hall duty. I suppose you simply asked him where he was going."

"I did. He was in the hall without a pass. I asked him where he was going, he said 'None of your business, you white bitch,' I said, 'What's your name, you black bastard,' he hauled off and slugged me, I hit the floor, he walked away, and I retired. Maybe I should have been more professional; what do you think? Alyssa? Have I shocked you again?"

"I always hated hall duty, even worse than study hall. If a kid looked mean enough, I used to ignore him."

"Well, I should have ignored that one."

"Why the hell wasn't he arrested for assault? Or was he? No, the whole place would have known, I would have known when it happened."

"Nixon isn't the only one skilled in cover-ups."

Alyssa took a deep breath. "Harry."

"Exactly. Harry didn't see any sense in dragging me through the mud."

"What mud! The kid hit you!"

"I called the kid a black bastard."

"He called you a white bitch."

"Harry wasn't interested in going back that far. He claimed that I provoked the attack. I guess I did. Isn't 'black bastard' worse than 'white bitch'? Harry thought so."

"But the kid provoked you, the kid was defiant. Christ, you only asked him where he was going. That started it."

"Now you're really going back too far. That's all right, I tried it too. Harry said I must have used the wrong tone of voice to begin with."

575

"The Hairy Bastard struck again."

"Believe me, I wanted to kill that kid. But Harry wasn't at all eager to find out his name. Harry didn't want any waves. If I wanted to press charges, I had to do it myself and prove it myself and go to court myself. The school was not interested in riling the black community."

"I've had plenty of black kids, most of them were good students, and none of them ever misbehaved any worse than any other kid of any color. But I understand what happened and it doesn't surprise me in the least. Not now."

"That boy got away scot-free; in fact, in the few weeks left of school he strutted around like a peacock. He wasn't suspended, he wasn't even called to the office. Nothing. It disgusted me. About a year later, I saw his picture in the newspaper. He was busted for possession of drugs. He was probably selling in school, but nobody made that connection. Those were also the days when the administration was assuring the public that there were no drugs in our pure and holy school system."

"It's been going on for a long time, hasn't it, Mary?"

"Since the beginning of time, Alyssa. And there's no way to fight it or stop it. Oh, people may think they're beating the system once in a while, but that's illusion, pure illusion. The system regenerates itself, the system is never beaten."

"Well, Mary Gregory, my teacher, my model, my friend, we're finally equals. Aren't we?"

Alyssa gave Mary a hug and kiss good-bye and promised to keep in touch. Then she drove to an office building in the middle of town. The office she entered was bursting with activity; she responded to the same old questions and comments in the same old way. "Why sure! We're on vacation again! Teachers have it made! I wouldn't be off this week if I worked here! There's nothing like a teacher's schedule!" Nothing. She stopped at a desk in the back corner of the room, looked at Effie Senior, and said," I'm taking you to lunch."

Effie Senior said: "Honey, lunch was two hours ago."

"Then I'm taking you for coffee."

"I just came back from my break."

"When you take a break, you go the bathroom. And you worked through lunch yesterday. I'll take you for yesterday's lunch."

"How'd you know that?"

"Are you my mother or aren't you?"

"Honey, have you flipped out?"

"Get your fingers off that freaking adding machine, would you? You're making me dizzy. How can you do that without looking?"

"Experience. Nothing like it."

"Yeah. Right. Well, are you coming with me or not?"

"Okay, if it's a fast one. This report has to go out today. By four o'clock."

"We'll go right next door, Ma. I need to talk."

"I figured. Believe me, nothing less would pull me away right now."

The coffee shop was empty, the waitress cordial, the coffee hot. Alyssa lit a cigarette, shoveled the sugar, dumped the half-and-half, then stirred and stirred and stirred. Her mother lit a cigarette and stared and stared and stared, then said, "Do you think that's mixed yet?"

Alyssa looked up. "Ma, when did it hit you? When did it happen to you?"

"Maybe you should go back to mixing your coffee. That was dull, but much less confusing."

"I'm sorry. My thoughts are ahead of my mouth. Your job. When did you first realize you hated working?"

"Did I ever tell you that?"

"Not in so many words. But I saw the signs. I didn't know they were the signs at the time, of course. But now I know. Besides, right now I can't handle one job, one house, and one husband. How the hell did you do it with four kids? Dad was never much help because of the weird hours he worked. You used to get home at six o'clock and have to cook for six. I get out at three and I can't manage cooking for two."

"Honey, I hated working and I loved working. For most people it's a love-hate thing. Last week I lost two girls, but I still have to get out the same amount of work. I'm disgusted as hell over it; the responsibility falls on me. It's my fault if the work isn't done. So I do the best I can. What doesn't get done, doesn't get done."

"Just don't let them see that you'll do it all, Ma, or you'll never get your two girls back. But you're lucky you work with paper. You should have kids to worry about too."

"It's getting to you, isn't it? Dad and I are worried about you, and Jeff is frantic. Do you realize that?"

"Oh, sure. Last night I told him he should be sharing the cooking. If you thought he was frantic before, you should see him now. He can't figure me out. I'm tired of being Little Miss Do-It-All, Little Miss Perfection. All my life I've been out to please somebody else:

teachers, you and Dad, Jeff, my employer, my students. There was always somebody I wanted to be proud of me. Well, I'm sick of it. I'm sick of proving myself all the time. But that's something I have to deal with; you can help me with something else. Tell me what you did when you started hating your job."

"Not much besides giving your father a hard time and giving myself headaches. Once we started sending you kids to college I straightened up a little. Actually it was before that. I got into the habit of changing the living room whenever I started feeling overworked. That helped a lot."

"How?"

"I had to keep working to pay for it. That's the name of the game."

"How long have you worked?"

"Almost thirty years."

"I'll never make it, Ma. It's so damned unfair. Either I lower standards to go on, or give up and get out. If I stay I'm a prostitute, selling myself, marketing myself; if I go I waste my training, the education you worked so hard to give me. I've got too much into it now; I'm handcuffed to it. And I'm angry. This should not be happening to me; I've done nothing to deserve this. Am I wrong to want some satisfaction from my job? I used to be willing to work my tail off, but I found out where that gets you. I feel like a fool. Why are the incompetents rewarded while the fools get more work to do?

"I worked myself into the ground, and it's my problem; I can't teach the way I used to, and it's my problem; I used to love teaching, now the whole process is a farce, and it's my problem. I'm a glorified clerk. I wouldn't mind if I was supposed to be a clerk. Right now I'm even jealous of your job. You've got too much work, but you don't have kids to teach on top of it. That's what I've got, Ma. I can't do it. A lot of teachers have given up and I know I have to give up trying. I already started, and it's against every principle I possess. I'm selling out myself. Isn't that prostitution?"

"I had an argument with one of the girls in the office last week. She was badmouthing teachers something wicked. I usually keep my mouth shut, I get aggravated enough without asking for more. But she pulled my cork. First of all, she blames the school every time her kids get in trouble, which is often. It's always the school's fault — the school's too lenient, the school's too strict, the school's too indifferent. The story changes to fit the circumstances. Last week the shit hit the fan again; one of her kids was sent home for using foul language and knocking down his teacher. Well, she bitched for half an hour; she had the whole office in an uproar. The school was no good, the teacher was no good. Then she got into teachers' salaries and all the vacations. Then she wanted to know why she had to go home and lose half a day's pay because some teacher's feelings were hurt."

"Some people are really warped when it comes to their kids."

"That was when I exploded. I told her if she thought teaching was so profitable and easy that she should get her ass to college and try it out, but I doubted if she would make it through because she's so damn stupid. Then I told her it's her fault her kids are monsters, that teachers shouldn't have to put up with kids like hers, and that she should go home and teach her nine-year-old some manners, it was about time he learned to be civilized."

"Hey, Ma, I didn't know you had it in you."

"She hasn't talked to me since."

"Well, it takes more than one tongue-lashing to get through to some people. She'll never change."

"But you have, haven't you?"

"Ma, I used to be an excited, enthusiastic teacher. I thought that was the only way to teach. I enjoyed going to work. It was satisfying. It wasn't perfect, I never expected it to be perfect. But it gave me a sense of achievement, it justified my existence. I need to be productive. I don't have kids of my own, and teaching filled that void in my life. What am I supposed to do now? Get pregnant fast?"

"Is that what you want?"

"You're forgetting that I need a rest. Having a baby doesn't quite fill the bill."

Mother and Daughter sat and sipped and sat and sipped, filling an ashtray as a matter of course. I'm going to tell you a story, Mother said. And Daughter listened.

Once upon a time there was a little girl. The little girl was three years old. One day she was outside playing and she heard music coming down the street. She knew what the music meant. Ice cream! The ice cream truck was on its way! How the little girl loved ice cream!

The little girl ran to get her father because she was sure he would get her an ice cream cone. She pulled and tugged at his hand and said, "Ice cream, Daddy, ice cream!"

The little girl's father pulled her back. He didn't say anything because he couldn't; he didn't walk to the street because he couldn't. He knelt down next to the little girl and held her in his arms. He loved her more than anything else on earth. She was his princess, his only child, his beautiful daughter. But she was only three years old; how could she understand what was in his heart?

The little girl started to cry. She wanted an ice cream, just an ice cream. It was as simple as that. Why was her father picking her up and carrying her into the house? Why was her father crying too?

"You were three years old and Dad was twenty-three. I'll never forget the look on his face when he carried you into the house. I heard the bell from the ice cream truck and I knew what had happened. He was laid off and he didn't have a nickel to buy you an ice cream. I'll never forget the tears in his eyes. For years your father said, 'A nickel, one lousy nickel, and I didn't have it.' It broke his heart. But it gave him a determination that's kept him going since. You know he doesn't make much money. But he was so thankful to get a job that didn't threaten a lay off every few months that he stayed."

"It never bothered him that you make more money than he does, did it?"

"It all goes in the same pot. I was lucky enough to get a job that allowed me to work my way up. He wasn't. But we always felt that we were working together, for the same reasons. And we wanted better for our kids. That's why we sent all of you to college. There's nothing new in the theory. Don't most parents want a better life for their kids?"

"That's another thing bothering me. You educated me to be a teacher. You deprived yourself to send me to school. Don't deny it. There are lots of things you don't have because you've been putting kids through college for the past fifteen years."

"I won't be disappointed if you quit teaching. Is that what's on your mind today? You think Dad and I will be ashamed of you? Didn't you just say you're tired of the burden of making people proud of you?"

"Yes, I did, didn't I? And yes, that's what I'm afraid of, making you ashamed of me."

"For all that education, you still have a lot to learn."

"I've lost my sense of direction, Ma. There was always a path to follow. Suddenly I'm standing in the middle of the freeway and the road's been whisked out from under me. The traffic keeps roaring by, but the road is gone, and I'm in the middle of nowhere."

"How much does your job mean to you?"

"It means independence, self-sufficiency, a pension, health insurance, a paycheck,—"

"Sounds to me like you've found the road."

"With a lot of other jobs that is the road. But not with teaching. I can't limit it to just that. Teaching isn't just a job, it's a commitment to other human beings. My job does not mean everything to me. Were you trying to get me to say that it does and shock myself? There's no shock because it's not so, it never was so, and never will be. But the way I do my job means everything to me, and I'm being forced to do it poorly. I resent that. I want to tell somebody that I'm better than they're treating me, that I'm leaving because of it, and that they damned well ought to feel a sense of loss when I go."

"But there's nobody to tell, nobody who will listen, and you can and will be replaced very easily."

"You do know what I'm talking about, don't you? Haven't you ever wanted to scale the wall? Haven't you felt like screaming 'I won't put up with it any longer'?"

"Of course. Many times."

"And you stayed on for your kids. For the little girl who wanted an ice cream. That's why most people stay."

"You learn to close your eyes, seal your ears, and collect your pay."

"For me that means watching kids learn nothing. If I want to survive myself, I have to ignore two thirds of my students. Why am I being punished because I want to do my job right? What good is an education if it leads to this?"

"Working for an employer is no different for you than for anyone else, Alyssa."

"Oh, brother, Ma, you just said a mouthful."

Alyssa drove home with her head full of Mary Gregory and her mother, two mothers really. Each had given her the means to an end. Neither was responsible for the souring, the disappointment. Had her life gone another way, perhaps the collapse would not have occurred. Maybe she was too happy, too content, to begin with, and now she was paying for it.

One thought superseded all others; it churned to frothy foam in her head, it filled her entire being, it was a product of her bitterness and anger. She wanted more than anything to scale the wall. She wanted to go on to something better, to something more honorable, then look back and say, "You had me once and I was good; but you abused me so I left. And it's your loss, your loss, not mine."

But she knew the thought was futile. Even Mr. Gessler, who held on to Principle, was engaged in futile effort. His own death mocked him. Quality is better than quantity. So what? He lost; they won. They. Who are *they*? What is *society*? Where is *the system*? Massive intangibles, limitless, omnipresent, and omnipotent. How many people have wanted to scale the wall? How many, out of fear, allowed it to imprison them instead?

Alyssa was afraid. If she didn't work, what would she do? But that was the long run, she reasoned. She didn't have to think about that until later. A leave of absence was probably the right course to take. But that frightened her too, for many reasons. When she arrived home she went to work to research one of the difficulties that she could foresee. When she was sure that she had her figures straight, she set the facts aside for later. After dinner she tried to ease into another discussion with Jeff.

"Thank you for putting your clothes in the laundry basket instead of leaving them on the floor," she eased, knowing full well that she shouldn't have to thank him, but telling herself that it wouldn't hurt.

"I'm willing to try," he said. "How about you?"

She looked him in the face and started to cry. He waited. She said, the tears dripping through her voice, "I spent the day looking for answers. There aren't any answers, there's just more questions."

"Where did you go today?" he asked.

She told him.

"So you're taking your leave," he concluded.

She hesitated, then said, "It's not that easy. I don't think I can."

Now what? he thought. Now what's brewing in your brain? "Why not?" he asked.

She showed him the piece of paper. "We can't possibly afford it. I figured it all out. I added up the bills for a year — everything — taxes, mortgage, insurances, utilities, plates for the cars. I figured out how much I'll have to set aside every week out of your pay to cover the bills. It doesn't leave much for groceries, gas, and odds and ends. We spend a fortune on gifts throughout the year; I didn't add that in at all. The way it figures up, there won't be any extra money and we won't be able to save at all."

"So what? We'll go to the bank when we have to."

She cringed. Why, oh why, did she manage everything herself? "We've only got a few hundred in the bank, not enough to cover taxes for a year."

"Where the hell did it all go?" He wasn't angry, just puzzled.

She thought she detected anger. "Would you like to pay the bills from now on? I wish you would, then you'd see where the money goes."

"It didn't all go out for bills. And I know you don't squander money. Don't be insulted, I'm not questioning you, I'm simply amazed."

"You wouldn't be if you'd think about it. We went down to nothing when we bought this house, then we went on a restoration binge. You've said yourself that the house eats better than we do. It never bothered me to spend as fast as it was coming in, I figured I'd" — her voice broke — "work forever."

"Well, all right, if that's the way it is, that's the way it is. We can get by for a year."

"But I just told you, we can't! The way everything keeps going up, those figures will be useless in six months. And you don't know what groceries cost."

Now he was angry. "Why did you do this, Alyssa? Sometimes I wish you would let loose and be haphazard and happy like the rest of us mortals. Do you have to be so goddammed efficient all the time?"

Effie bristled. "I thought you'd want to know what we're in for if I go on leave."

"You're telling me that we can't live on my pay. There are men raising families on the same amount of money! Why can't we make it?"

"I'm telling you that it's not going to be easy. I thought you should know ahead of time. I'd hate to lose this house; we worked too long to get it."

He realized then how much a victim of the weakness she was, that without strength even thoughts terrified her. He said, "To tell you the truth, I'd sell this house in a minute to see you healthy again. This house and everything in it mean very little to me next to you. We don't have to worry about feeding and clothing kids; we've only got ourselves. And we've scrimped before. We did it to buy this house. You used to giggle over the fact that we were broke most of the time."

"That was different. We were broke because the money was in the bank. It was there in case of emergency. That's a different kind of broke."

"And now we're involved in a different kind of emergency. You've developed a warped sense of priorities. You come first, your health, your well-being. Everything else is secondary. That's the way I see it, and I wish you'd fix your head."

If only there weren't so many disconnected ends, she thought. Too many ends, not enough space to reconnect. She projected herself into the future and saw her new identity: Alyssa Matthews: Full Time Maid. Jeff was offering all he could and she loved him for it. But he wanted her to find contentment in being less than she was.

"You're fading away, Alyssa," he said. "What's the matter, are you afraid you might like staying home?"

"Yes," she whispered.

The weekend approached and she was still melancholy. Talking about it hadn't solved anything, had only made her more confused, more unhappy. She agreed to go to a movie Saturday night, then suggested dinner instead, then tried to plan both, then burst into tears because she couldn't decide which movie, which restaurant, or which should come first.

Jeff chalked up the evening as another typical Saturday night and went to bed early. When she joined him he was lying on his back in the darkened room and staring at the ceiling. She slid next to him, wanting desperately to be held, to be cradled and stroked and soothed. She wanted him to say, "It's all right, baby, it's going to be just fine. I'll take care of you. You're hurting now, and I understand, and it's going to be all right." It didn't occur to her that he had already said it.

He didn't move. She recoiled and turned to face the other way, thinking: how much was he supposed to take? He was miserable too, and she made him that way. She knew that her moods determined his. The hell with the laundry and the cooking and the housework. She needed more than that from him. She used to get more than that from him. But not now. Now she curled into fetal position and cried herself to sleep. The little girl had grown; no one else could pay the price of the ice cream. The price was high and she had to pay it herself.

Sunday was a dreary day, dull and sickly gray, but warm, almost into the sixties. When the gray sky opened up, rain instead of snow came pouring down.

"At least rain doesn't have to be shoveled," Jeff said.

Alyssa answered, "God help us if all this water causes floods. And what if the temperature drops all of a sudden? We'll be skating to work tomorrow. Ice terrifies me."

Jeff was about to comment on her infernal pessimism, but stopped short. Such a comment would undoubtedly annoy her. He wondered if there would ever be a time when he could speak freely to her again without risking tears, silence, or indignation.

Her melancholy increased as the day wore on. She was thinking about poetry books, *Hamlet*, and two regents classes that hadn't had any instruction in writing yet. She was thinking about individual students and how many had to make up tests because the end of the fifth report period was a week away. She was thinking about the massive amount of work that had to be done by the end of the year.

How could he suggest that she go on leave now? He didn't know what some kids go through when they lose their teacher. Trauma, that's what. As inadequate as she viewed herself, she was still better than a stranger. If circumstances were different, if she had to have surgery, if she dropped dead, then someone else would have to take over. But she wasn't dead yet and nothing else could make her abandon her students.

Agreements

One

The last week in April brought with it a sharp change in the weather. The temperature soared into the seventies with shocking severity, winter was replaced by summer with no intervening season to ease the transition. Rapidly melting snow caused flooding, heavy outerwear gave way to sandals and shorts, and the heat continued to pour into classrooms despite thermostats and human discomfort. Students and teachers alike bemoaned the arrival of good weather as soon as vacation ended. Student absenteeism soared along with the temperature. So did teacher cynicism.

On Monday over half the faculty at BCA were greeted with letters questioning their certification and threatening their dismissal. The place was filled with disgruntled, disgusted teachers, enraged teachers. How could so many be accused of not being permanently certified to teach? Was it possible that so many certificates suddenly disappeared out of personnel folders at the central office? Bonnie promptly made another copy of hers and sent it to the appropriate administrator; Jean Tevarro wrote a note on her letter and sent the letter back. The note said: I was permanently certified fifteen years ago. If you don't believe it, it's your problem. If you want another certificate, send to Albany for it. If I'm supposed to be frightened, forget it, it didn't work. Joe Axelrod ripped up his letter; so did Alyssa Matthews.

Everyone knew it was harassment even before Jason Haywood spread the word that the contract was very nearly ready for a ratification vote. In the middle of the week a meeting was called. The negotiating team suggested another strike vote if the membership didn't ratify the agreement. But the results were inevitable: Big Brother was watching, his tactic involving certification only one in a series of intimidations. The meeting was just as emotionally charged as the strike-vote meeting had been; the vote was just as close. When it was all over, the contract was ratified by twenty votes.

"Well," Jean said on the way out, "we have ourselves a token raise that's supposed to compensate for a good reaming. Class size is now 32. Two at a time they'll work up to 40 before we know it."

"That retirement incentive has me irritated," Alyssa said, too exasperated over the increase in class size even to talk about it. "Do you know how that's going to look in the press? I guarantee the headline will be ninety-nine percent dollar signs. Why should teachers be paid a bonus to retire? I wonder if anyone will bother to explain that they won't be replaced with bright, eager new ones."

"There aren't any new ones," Bonnie added. "They're going to be biting their elbows for teachers in a few years."

Jean commented on the fact that not a single student teacher in any subject had entered the hallowed halls of BCA in the last five years. "Anybody interested in reviving the Future Teachers of America?" she asked facetiously.

"It makes me sick to think that they're so anxious to get rid of experienced teachers purely for economic reasons," Alyssa concluded.

"It's just another way to force people out," Jean observed pragmatically. "Actually it's a nicer way than what's been going on for years. Plenty of people have been pressured out by a year of sudden floating or a sharp change in classes. That's hard to stomach after thirty years' experience."

"Those threats always exist, don't they?" Bonnie said. "I thought when I had enough years in I wouldn't have to worry any longer."

"Not on your life," Alyssa advised. "Those letters we received this week were meant to perpetuate the undercurrent of fear. You won't read about those letters in the newspaper, not that it would do any good if you did. It's very subtle intimidation, very clever. The district can always say that it's merely running a check, that it's insuring the competency of its teachers. Besides, money makes better headlines, so steady yourself for the shock waves over the retirement bonus. The way the unemployment rate is climbing, more and more people are jealous of anybody who has a job, much less a raise and a retirement bonus. If I were 55, I'd take my bonus and run. I would have been much happier with no raise and four classes."

"Well," Jean said even more pragmatically, yet more facetiously than before, "let's look at the bright side. We didn't lose our prep period and we don't have six classes."

"Hoo-ray, hoo-ray," Alyssa drawled. "Add that to 'the number of preparations is at the discretion of the building principal' and drink your poison like a good girl."

"They wouldn't dare give us more preparations," Bonnie said.

Alyssa easily dashed the hope. "Well, if we lose a few people to retirement, and if we get ninth grade at BCA, and if they lay off a few junior high teachers, whoever is left will have to teach whatever classes there are, nine through twelve, three levels of each."

"That's a lot of 'ifs'," Bonnie said. "And more lay-offs don't necessarily mean junior high teachers. Some of them have more years than I have. I'll go first. But that's still a lot of 'ifs'."

"Your problem," Jean said, sarcasm dripping from every word, "is that you have not benefited from your in-service training. By now you should feel that 'if' is cowardly, a threat to your happiness, a detrimental influence on morale." Jean started to laugh. "Hey! Maybe they sent us those letters as a test to poll morale!"

"They wouldn't want us too happy," Alyssa said wryly. "I can't believe the hypocrisy. Do they think we're idiots, that we can't see through all of it?"

"Next year should be a real circus," Bonnie said.

"We should have gone on strike," Alyssa mused. "We should have stayed out until class size was reduced, along with our workload. It stinks that grade school teachers are getting monitoring duties again. Next time around they'll stick us back in the halls."

Jean said: "That's the way it's done. Divide and conquer. We're too many factions. When it comes time for a vote, people weigh what they get against what they lost, and what they lost against what other people lost. Sooner or later it's going to get beyond anybody's tolerance and this district is going to see a strike that will make Haymarket look like a picnic. Then the community will scream at us. It's the same old story, we're damned if we do and damned if we don't. But the discontent is building; someday it's going to blow, and nobody will be willing to understand that the insurrection brewed for years."

The three women walked out into the afternoon sun and commented on the oddness of it all: sun, heat, and mounds of still-melting snow.

Two

Bonnie saw the ladder propped against the side of the house as she rounded the last corner; within seconds she also saw the small figure slowly ascend. She parked the car quickly and ran up the sidewalk, not wanting to startle the old lady, but still, wanting to get her attention.

"Mrs. King," she called out. "Get down from there! You shouldn't be up on ladders!"

The old woman peered down. "I'm quite comfortable, dear. Don't be alarmed. My last dizzy spell was hours ago. I just have to see how much deterioration the winter caused. I do this every spring."

Bonnie held her breath as Mrs. King went up two more rungs then stopped to scrutinize the windows on either side of the ladder. After she apparently saw what she wanted to see, she began the descent, carefully placing one foot, then the other, on each rung of the ladder. When she was three from the ground, she faltered, and Bonnie ran toward her.

"Not to be alarmed, dear," Mrs. King said in a tiny voice, as she closed her eyes and bowed her head. "It will pass quickly. I know enough to stop moving when one hits. It's old age, that's all it is. You have to learn to live with it. Put up with it, I always say. A hundred years from now I'll never know the difference. There. It's gone. You can relax now. I won't be splattering all over the sidewalk."

"First of all," Bonnie said in her best teacher voice as the old lady completed her journey to the ground, "you should never climb a ladder without someone watching the bottom; secondly, you have no reason to be doing this yourself, I told you Michael would be happy to do whatever needs to be done by a man and that includes climbing ladders!"

"Now, now, don't lecture me, dear. I've heard every lecture conceivable to man, and I've given every one too. There isn't much you can tell me that I don't know or have decided to forget."

Bonnie considered how attached she had become to the old lady, but didn't want to burden either of them with sentimentality. "You forget that lecturing is my business," she said, smiling. Then she added, as matter-of-factly as she could, "Have you seen a doctor about those dizzy spells?"

Mrs. King shrugged. "Oh, pooh! At my age seeing a doctor is a little foolish, don't you think? How long can a person live anyway? I wouldn't expect you to understand, dear, you're too young. But when you're 83, the prospect of being 93 isn't all that exciting. Come into the house now, I have something to show you, my bonny lass!"

In the kitchen Dorothea King made a grand sweeping motion with both arms and said, "There it is! Isn't it lovely?"

Bonnie issued exclamations as she listened to Mrs. King extol the virtues of her new microwave oven, thinking all the while that some store was missing out on one hell of a good saleslady.

"How I love newfangled gadgets," Mrs. King concluded. "Just give me buttons, levers, and lights, and I'll be your friend forever." She started chuckling, her eyes were dancing, and she said, "It finally happened, one of them came around, it finally happened, and now I can die in peace."

Bonnie didn't understand. "You're awfully intent on dying today. I wish you'd change your mind, I rather like having you around."

"Oh, thank you, dear, thank you. But there comes a point when life is more to be feared than death. Sooner or later something in you must give way, must simply wear out, and then you're in for it. You think about that more and more as age creeps up on you. Eventually you see every day as a reprieve from illness, and you wonder if the next day will be the one, the fatal one, the one that's the beginning of the end. I've always prayed for a quick death. Who wants to linger in pain and know it's coming, but not know when?"

Bonnie was becoming alarmed; in all the times she visited the old lady, never once had she heard her speak of death. Now she was so ... excited about it

Mrs. King continued. "My daughter was here today. She brought me my new toy. She's had a change of heart because of something one of her own children did to her. Isn't that the way it goes? The mother remembers that she has a mother. That's the way the world is made. And it finally happened. I've been waiting. We didn't bring them up that way, you know; we didn't teach them to be selfish and heartless. I never wanted to will this house outside of the family to keep it intact. I knew if I waited long enough, if I lived long enough, I would see the day when one would repent. Today was the day. Today the prodigal child returned and there is rejoicing. My daughter returned and promised that these windows will never leave this house. And that was all I ever asked."

Dorothea King smiled faintly, then closed her eyes and slumped to the floor.

Bonnie went into a panic, caught the body just in time to prevent the head from striking the handle of the refrigerator on the way down, then gently lowered the old woman because she couldn't hold on to dead weight very long.

Bonnie knelt on the floor, never once concerned about her own condition, and started to cry. Can we will ourselves dead? Is it that easy? Is the mind as potent a weapon as razor or a gun? Can a person die from an overdose of love or hate or contentment or anger?

On her knees Bonnie whispered, "Dear God, dear God," and groped for something else to say because she used the words simply as language, the invocation hollow and useless. "She's not dead, don't let her be dead," she said to no one.

Pulse. Breathing means life. She attempted to feel a pulse in both wrists. Nothing. Behind the ear lobes. Faint, very faint, but there. Just as she was about to dash to the phone, Bonnie saw a steady rise in the chest. She jumped up, wet some paper towels and applied them to Mrs. King's forehead. The eyelids started to flicker, then opened suddenly.

"Welcome back," Bonnie said, her voice flooded with relief.

"How long was I out?" Mrs. King asked weakly.

"Too long. I'm calling a doctor and I don't want to hear any objections."

"You won't, dear," Mrs. King said as she sat up. "But you'll have to hog tie me to get me there."

"Why won't you help yourself? What if this happens when no one is here? You almost hit your head!"

"Oh, but it has happened when no one was here. Sometimes I wake up in the oddest places! But today the good Lord put you here for a reason, didn't He? Everything happens for the best, and my time hasn't come yet. When the Lord wants me, He'll take me. None of us can escape that."

The philosophy frustrated Bonnie, but she knew better than to try to fight it.

Mrs. King said: "He wants me to see it one more time. One more time before I die. You'll see it too. It's been years since conditions were just right; Alyssa saw it only once, you know. But this time it will happen, I know it will, I can feel it. He took metal and glass and he created a living thing. I asked him once how it felt to harness the forces beyond man's control. He said, 'Magnificent, magnificent!'"

Bonnie helped the old woman to her feet, tried to make small talk for as long as she could, then issued a dinner invitation.

"You want to keep an eye on me, don't you?" Mrs. King concluded accurately. "How about if we have dinner here so I can play with my new toy?"

"Are you sure you're strong enough?"

Mrs. King laughed. "Stronger than two of you!" Then, very seriously, she said, "You can't watch me every minute, you know. When it comes, I'll be alone. It's the same coming and going, just you and the Lord. Don't worry about me. I have all I want now to die in peace. Most people aren't so fortunate. One more time, though. In a few weeks. It's about the middle of May this year. Alex's legacy."

Mrs. King did not offer further explanation and Bonnie did not require any, for she remembered what Alyssa told her about the window months ago. Bonnie often stared at the colored glass and wondered why such things were no longer produced by humans, why the world no longer engendered artistic genius on the level of a

Michaelangelo or a Shakespeare. What human qualities push the artist on to achieve the impossible, to satisfy self-imposed obsessions, and to risk all in the process? Ambition? Self-sacrifice? A willingness to suffer? Blind determination? A separate vision? She didn't know. But the more she looked at the window, the more she admired the man who created it, admired him without ever knowing him, or his motivations, or his particular bout with life. The thing he created transcended all else.

The world would be poor indeed had Michaelangelo been less willful and Shakespeare less ambitious. But how long can the spirit of civilized man prosper by depending upon the splendors of the past? Why have centuries crawled by since the greatness of a Chopin, a Beethoven, a Van Gogh? Is the world too intent on creating an easier existence, so intent, in fact, that it has replaced art with technology and eliminated its artists and craftsmen in the process? What is the eventual fate of a society that repeatedly contributes to the death of Mr. Gessler?

Bonnie often contemplated the special significance of the old windows, old but immaculately kept; as Mrs. King told her during dinner, however, the old windows were slowly deteriorating from the constant assault of the elements.

When Michael arrived in early evening, Bonnie had him move the ladder around the house to inspect the windows according to the old woman's directions; he looked for the opaque white covering caused when moisture on the glass interacts with gases in the air to form a corrosive alkaline solution. Once the shiny outer skin of the glass is permeated, the corrosion begins to eat through the glass, pitting it and wearing it thin.

Michael hesitated to tell the old woman what she already knew: the process of decay had begun, the windows were corroding from the outside. But his fear of depressing her was unfounded, for, as she explained, modern restoration techniques were superb. She had done her homework: "The oldest windows in the world are being not only expertly restored but also protected from future decay by external glazing, the installation of clear plate glass beyond the colored glass. The colored glass is mounted in a new metal frame, then the plate glass is set in place three inches away in the original groove. The space in between allows free flow of dry air from within the building, thus eliminates moisture and its harmful effect on the stained glass.

"I explained all of this to my daughter today," Mrs. King said with excitement. "She agreed that in the event of my death the restoration would proceed on schedule. I'm leaving enough money to pay for it, and I've already contacted some excellent men in New York. When the restoration and the glazing are completed, then and only then will she consider selling this house. I'd rather that it be kept in the family, of course, but if a stranger will care for it better, so be it. The only stipulation I insist on is that these windows are never removed."

Michael said: "Your daughter agreed to that?"

"Oh, yes," the old woman said. "We had a lovely reunion today, and she promised to do all I asked. Now I can die in peace. My burden has been lifted."

Three

"I don't believe it either," Bonnie said to Michael after they left Mrs. King for the night. "I hope she gets something in writing, but I can't very well suggest that to her. I wish we could afford to buy this house."

"Maybe in a few years," Michael said. "If I go to work right away and we save as much as we can."

"You're not going to work, you're going to school. You've been accepted and nothing on earth is going to interfere with your education. Where do you think you're going without any training?"

"I could sell cars or wash windows. I don't know. Something. Anything. By the time I get out of college, we'll be broke and the mortgage rate will hit thirty percent. It's almost eighteen now."

"Why are you so interested in mortgage rates?"

"We were talking about it the other day in class. Axelrod got us going on it. My generation has no hope of ever owning a home, not anybody who's average middle class America or below. Even the upper middle class is being priced right out of the market. Kids starting out today haven't got a chance. We're beat before we start. Is it any wonder that kids in high school don't give a damn about anything?"

Bonnie was disturbed at his frustration. "But we're better off than a lot of people," she said. "We can be very comfortable here while we're working toward our goals. In the long run we'll make out fine. Ten years from now you'll regret it if you don't go to college."

"I'm not so sure of that," he protested. "And I'm beginning to have my doubts about this place. If Mrs. King dies, who knows what will happen?"

The thought worried Bonnie too, though she didn't voice her concern; Michael was unusually sensitive, and she didn't want to deepen his mood. She was worried about all kinds of things. They would have to keep two cars on the road as long as he commuted to school and she to work; gas alone would eat into a third of her weekly check. But the apartment was cheap and she was getting a raise. "We'll deal with it a step at a time," she told him.

In the bedroom she fussed her way into a nightgown, with her back facing him, lest he comment again on her great success in the kitchen and the consequences of eating too much of her own good cooking. Then she let out a small shriek when he kissed her neck. "What in the world are you growing on your face?" she demanded. The short stubble was so blonde that her eyes hadn't noticed what her skin now felt. "What do men usually grow on their faces?" he answered with a silly grin.

"Why?" she asked.

"I want to see what it will look like," he answered.

"Why?" she asked.

"Why not?" he answered.

"I hate it already," she said. "Do you have to?"

"No, I don't have to, but I want to. It'll soften up when it gets longer."

"In the meantime you can kiss alone."

He nuzzled into her neck and she shrieked again. She couldn't understand why he wanted to cover his handsome face with a hairy growth. "I like it when you shave," she said, laughing and pushing him away. "My tender parts can't take prickles."

"Ah, but when it grows out, you're in for a treat," he teased.

"I doubt it. But come back in a month and we'll find out."

He offered to shave under those conditions, but she said, "No, do what you want, just don't grind the little beasties into my flesh." She added that she hoped he would tire of the novelty quickly.

Four

Bonnie spoke to Alyssa about Mrs. King the next morning, expressing more concern over the woman's change in attitude than over her fainting spells. Alyssa offered little in the way of suggestions, other than to say that age was probably the prime factor in all of it. By the end of the day, Bonnie was so embroiled in a crisis of her own that she forgot about Mrs. King altogether.

The crisis began with simple hunger pangs during lunch. More and more lately, Bonnie wasn't satisfied with a sandwich and a piece of fruit in the middle of the day. While she was desperate to keep her weight under some kind of control, she also was aware of the importance of eating enough to properly nourish herself and her baby. She took to drinking milk instead of coffee and juices instead of soda. Beer and alcohol were definitely out; she wouldn't even sip a glass of wine for fear of harmful effects. She ingested nothing medicinal, including aspirin for a headache. If she didn't get nervous, she wouldn't get a headache, thus she wouldn't require aspirin. It worked. For a long time. Until that day she decided to go to the cafeteria during fourth period for an ice cream sandwich to supplement her lunch.

Perhaps if she hadn't heard the kid call her name in the noisy lunchroom, perhaps if she had ignored him and continued through without altering her route, perhaps if she had exited by another door, she would have avoided the entire experience.

Was the kid acting on a dare? Was he trying to impress his friends? Was he out to win a bet? She didn't know. She didn't know either what made her stand there and demand his name. That was sheer courage — or was it simply shock reaction? Or simple stupidity? As she made her way out of the maze of bodies and tables, then through the halls to the office, she continued to hear the raucous laughter and see the leering faces; the laughter and the faces followed her as they had followed their lewd leader.

The boy looked no more than a boy, with a young face, an immature baby face; sitting in the chair, he looked eight years old. When he caught her eye and gestured her over, she didn't know what to expect. She didn't know him nor any of the others at the table. But she assumed that he had some kind of question, he recognized her as a teacher and he was about to ask her if they were on assembly schedule or when the next day off was. She never expected to hear what he said, what he threw out at her from that eight-year-old face with all the right lascivious inflection: "Hey, baby, my balls are dragging for a chance at you, how about a fuck?" She froze. She froze solid, but she said, "What is your name?" He gave it proudly.

Somehow she steered herself to the main office; by the time she left the office and reached the faculty room, the ice cream sandwich was dripping, her entire body was trembling, and she was a mass of anger and fear.

When she told the story, Jean exploded and flew out the door. Alyssa did her best to calm her, but it was most difficult in view of Bassard's refusal to get involved.

"Exactly what did he say?" Alyssa demanded.

"He told me I had several options for disciplining the kid myself. That was it. I told him the kid's sitting in the lunchroom right now, and I really thought he'd stomp over there and grab him by the collar. But he sat back in his chair and told me to 'exercise my options.' I can't believe it. I never want to see that kid again. Am I supposed to give him a vacation in ISSR or what? Will three detentions convince him that he shouldn't plan to act out his fantasies? If he gets away with saying something like that, what comes next?" Bonnie's eyes welled with tears.

Alyssa was furious. "Bassard probably figures you asked for it. He's notorious for that. Take it easy, Bon, if anybody can get through to him, it's Jean."

Thankful that they were alone in the room, Bonnie said, "I'm worried about Michael. If he ever finds out about this, he'll kill that kid, and I'm not exaggerating. Please, please, keep it quiet, and tell Jean to do the same."

"Of course, Bonnie. You've got to calm down. You're not doing yourself any good. You'll have a nervous baby that'll cry all night and you won't get any sleep for the next three years."

"Stop trying to cheer me up. I keep seeing that kid's face. I'm afraid this baby may have an unwed mother and a convict father. No doubt about it. Michael will go after that kid with his bare hands."

"Well, tell him he has as much a responsibility to his baby as he has to you, and he won't do either of you any good behind bars."

"I can't. He doesn't know about the baby yet."

"What? How the hell have you managed to keep that from him?"

"He thinks I've gained weight because of all the terrific recipes you've given me. I'm really not that pregnant-looking yet."

"But what are you waiting for? Don't you think he should know?"

"I thought it would make a nice wedding gift. I don't want him to feel pressured into anything."

"I still think there's something screwy about your sense of timing."

"He worries too much, Matt! He's worried about money, he keeps saying that he should go to work instead of to college. If I tell him there's a baby on the way, he'll have something else to worry about. I can spare him a little longer."

"What do you mean, spare him? I think I know him pretty well. He's a positive thinker, he'll be more excited than anything else. I never showed you his essay test on *Othello*, did I?"

"No, but he did. He came a long way on that one. You're only his teacher, you don't know all of him."

Alyssa didn't get a chance to pursue the subject because Jean came bursting into the room. "It's all set," she said, almost, but not quite, out of breath. "The kid's down there now, Harry is suspending him for three days. When he returns with his parents he has to be prepared to promise he'll never speak that way to a teacher again. In the event that he continues, charges will be brought against him in an attempt to place him in a juvenile detention center. Now things are as they should be: you can relax and the kid is down there being threatened." Jean took a deep breath, then said with conviction; "I can't stand it when the victim is penalized for being the victim."

"How the hell do you manage these things?" Alyssa asked.

Jean raised one corner of her mouth. "I told Harry that within one hour I'd have every woman in this place so incited that by the end of the day he'd have a stroke from all the angry females breathing fire at him. He got the message."

Bonnie thanked Jean for her helpful intervention and tried to steady her still-pounding heart. It was nothing, she told herself, nothing after all. Michael need never know about it, it was over.

It was nothing and it was over.

When The Juggler Misses

"This is your easy time, isn't it?"

Someone said those words to Alyssa Matthews one year in the middle of May and the teacher went into convulsive laughter; then the gross ignorance of it reduced her to nonsensical giggling. But every year thereafter she remembered the question, the declarative question, and every year thereafter the laughter subsided a fraction at a time, then by leaps and bounds.

In May, 1981, she wasn't laughing a bit; in fact, she was wondering if perhaps she had some exotic disease that stopped the corners of her mouth from turning up. Why not? Her head was still congested most of the time, her wrist still ached, and she had developed an annoying twitch in the lower lid of her left eye. It was peculiar; the twitch was not visible from the outside, but she felt it fluttering constantly.

In May, 1981, she was giving the performance of the year every day third period. Keeping second semester seniors enthusiastic over *Hamlet* took the patience of Job and the skill of all seven Muses. Seniors like to think they've already graduated by May 1. Teachers hate to see anybody blow it during the last lap. It makes for an interesting race: seniors prone on the track, teachers pulling and tugging, hoping to extract one final lunge to the finish line.

May was also the month for poetry. She had fallen into the habit of saving the scholarship poetry unit for May; it had something to do with flowers and sunshine and the poetic voice. She enjoyed teaching poetry in May, even poems about war and death. The poetic voice was the poetic voice. How could she have known that it had grown hoarse?

There were plenty of books when she signed up for them in September. Paul laughed at her when he saw she was projecting into second semester so early. "You're amazing!" he said. "Most of us don't know what we're teaching next week, and you're planning for May! I can't stand it!"

But in May there were no poetry books for her to carry eight-at-a-time to her room. In May there were no poetry books at all in the resource room. And she was of no mind to poll the department to find out where they were. The short story unit had been a mutilation, why not poetry?

She scoured her files to find typed copies of poems she used to supplement the usual unit, and never mourned the inaccessibility of the books. She was so tired of distributing and collecting books that she decided she was blessed.

She changed her mind about the blessing when she had to fight the machines to make copies of the poems she had. She did think of eliminating the entire unit; she thought of it more than once, but she couldn't do it. She knew that most students hate poetry; one of her objectives was to instill an understanding that might lead to appreciation. She was quite realistic about it, as she was with all forms of literature. She didn't expect every student to love everything; she did expect every student to try to understand. Then she hoped for the best as far as appreciation was concerned.

When she taught poetry she tried to give as much of a survey as she could, hoping that somewhere along the line even the staunchest hater-of-poetry might get interested enough to say, "Hey, that's not so bad." She tempted them with narrative poetry and lyric poetry, nonsense verse and haiku, didactic poetry and satirical poetry. She worked to be vivacious, somber, sarcastic, silly, musical, depressed, enlightened, or whatever else she needed to be in order to transmit the poet's message or the poet's frame of mind or the poet's perception. Some of it dented a few skulls, some of it flew into the stratosphere. She never emphasized the relationship between content and form more than when she taught poetry. She fiercely defended figures of speech and poetic techniques whenever students complained that learning about simile and metaphor, alliteration and onomatopoeia was a waste of time. She would argue: "How can you possibly understand what a poet is saying if you can't analyze how he's saying it? The beauty of poetry is in its construction, in its sound, and in its meaning."

There was a time when she required that students spell terms correctly too. She learned how to spell *onomatopoeia* in eighth grade. But requiring them to spell required her to spend more time grading and deducting points, so the practice went the same way as so many others.

Teaching poetry that May was as frustrating an experience as a teacher can have. She looked at blank stares for days; she graded work sheets in despair. Most students were at a complete loss when asked to determine the basic thought in even the simplest poem. Poems that had offered no special challenge to students in the past were grumbled over in a sea of disinterest; students who had been quick to understand all along were still forging ahead, but the others had progressed very little since September. She remembered when the poetry unit had been the ultimate test of analytical thought, when the year's work paid dividends at the end. Now the end was a natural result of something else.

One day in an effort to make herself and her students taste encouraging success, she distributed copies of a small poem she was sure would be easy for them to analyze since it was written by a seventeen-year-old girl. After lectures on form and poetic techniques, worksheets on the same, and classroom evaluation of much more difficult poems, the little gem would be understandable to almost everyone.

How disappointed she was. In the middle of the exercise she realized what the grades would be like, so she decided that she wouldn't collect papers for grading. One boy, an unusually perceptive boy, called the poem "obscure." She was crushed. "You'll never learn anything without being challenged!" she responded, still clutching to the noble theory in spite of the fact that the poem should have posed no overwhelming challenge.

Why couldn't they determine what the poem meant by considering the title, the form, the imagery? She asked all kinds of questions in addition to the questions on the worksheet which were devised in a particular order to help them derive a meaning. But they couldn't pinpoint it, they couldn't summarize in their own words the simple message of the author: that someone hurt her, left her, and was proud of having done it. Even after the teacher gave an evaluation, some students couldn't see it. In May, 1981, the teacher was hearing students still use the word "stupid" to describe works of literature, a habit she once was able to discourage by Thanksgiving.

STUDENT: This is stupid.

TEACHER: Why are you calling it stupid?

STUDENT: Because it's stupid.

TEACHER: Did you read all of it?

STUDENT: Yes. And it's stupid.

TEACHER: I will not allow you to call it stupid unless you can tell me why.

STUDENT: I don't know why. But I know it's —

TEACHER: Stop using the word "stupid." Now tell me what it is.

STUDENT: Uh,— I don't know.

TEACHER: Try harder.

STUDENT: Confusing. That's what it is — confusing!

TEACHER: Hard to understand?

STUDENT: Yes.

TEACHER: Does that make it stupid?

STUDENT: Yes, — to me.

TEACHER: If I eliminate the confusion and you still think it's stupid, will you work on why you think it's stupid?

STUDENT: I'd rather just think it's stupid.

TEACHER: Of course. That's the easy way out. But you will not stoop to that. I will not allow you to call it anything unless you can explain why.

She used to joke about it; she used to say, "If a sophomore were barred from using the word 'stupid,' he'd lose fifty percent of his vocabulary." She used to roll into class and announce gaily, "Have I got something stupid for you today!" She used to tease, cajole, wheedle, and trick them in addition to the serious teaching because she despised the attitude and pitied the ignorance that engendered such a reaction.

But in May, 1981, she heard scholarship students call poem after poem "stupid." And some of them were still under the assumption that *Our Town*, *Julius Caesar*, and assorted other works of literature fell into the same category.

Alyssa complained to Jean about it, about the inevitable fumbling of the juggler when one too many balls was added to the act. She saw the doctor again in May, neglected to tell him about the twitch under her eye, and put off making a decision about a leave until the summer. She told Jean about the leave and accepted her encouragement. "You've never had a break from this schedule since you were five years old," the older teacher said. "Have you thought of it that way? Take some time for yourself, Matt. Get out of this hell-hole for a year. It'll do you a world of good."

Every day, more and more, the thought was exhilaration. She couldn't even imagine the month of September without school; her life had been governed by the absolutes of first semester, second semester, and summer vacation for so long that she thought and spoke in those terms, she planned her life according to those terms, she was incarcerated by those terms.

One day Paul knocked on her door to tell her how he had tentatively scheduled her classes for the following year, and she was thrown into confusion. Her mind screamed No! But she wasn't sure yet, she couldn't tell him for sure. Still, she felt she owed him some kind of warning, so she said, "Paul, I may not be here next year. I've been so sick this year and so exhausted. There were times when I thought I needed a psychiatrist. I have to get away from it for awhile." Her voice broke and he reacted with emphatic surprise. "You can't let these kids or this place get to you, Alyssa!" She swallowed hard and said, "I know, I know. That was always my philosophy. But something gave way, Paul." "Well," he said lamely, "if you need a rest, that's understandable." She said, "I do, I really do." When the schedule was finalized, she saw that he had maintained her usual assignments. She never spoke to him about the leave again, nor he to her.

Throughout the month of May Alyssa Matthews was one person by day and another at night. In school she maintained a facade of normalcy for the sake of her students; at home she reverted to the sullen, morose, problem-ridden person she really was. At home she avoided confrontation, for she had no energy for confrontation; all her energy went into the days. Jeff was still trying to pull her out of it, but when he expressed concern over her smoking ("How is it possible for you to smoke a whole pack between periods? Do you chain during lunch?) or suggested that she get her hair trimmed because it was growing wild, she put him off with superficial replies and empty promises.

She never put off Cassie Quimly, though. Cassie was still making appearances, but not as frequent nor as intensely desperate as in the past. Alyssa decided that Cassie's personality was evening out, that Cassie was growing up, and Alyssa was glad for that. The mere thought of helping Cassie through another crisis was debilitating. As it turned out, teacher and student went through a subtle reversal in roles. Cassie sensed a difference in the teacher and poked around just to cheer her up. The teacher became the one with the face, the ever-changing face, the one who needed to laugh or to cry or, it seemed, the one who needed diversion. Cassie hardly knew herself that she sensed a change in her favorite teacher, until the day she asked, "You're not very happy here anymore, are you?" and the teacher gave her an honest answer. After that, Cassie did her best to elicit a smile or a clever comment on any number of subjects, as long as the subject was not in any way related to school. She initiated a rather lengthy discussion on homosexuality, palimony, and Billie Jean King one day, a discussion which lead the teacher to believe that earlier sessions had done some good. And Cassie chased down the hall after the teacher one afternoon with a newspaper clipping which had her in gales of laughter.

Some people in California claimed to have bred a unicorn, using "an ancient secret for unicorns," as if the composition of the mythical beast had been found in some newly discovered medieval recipe file. What they had produced was a goat with one horn; a one-horned goat who dined on oyster crackers; a one-horned, leash-trained goat named Lancelot (what else?) who earned his keep by responding well to training and by drawing gawkers amazed at the abnormal protrusion in the middle of his head. Even better, Lancelot didn't just stand there, he was clever enough to heel, lie down, jump through a hoop, take a bow, and tap dance to "The Star Spangled Banner."

Of course there were two schools of thought about Lancelot, who was doomed to live as a freak or as a celebrity, depending upon which side won out in the end. His "naturalist" creators cited the "responsibility" of "scientists, romanticists, and idealists" to protect the legend. Such a gross manipulation of contradictory terms was mindboggling, never mind the pretentious assumption that the legend needed protection. And Lancelot's masters were intent on patenting the process, evidently inspired to fill the world with "the message that wonder and beauty and hope are available, and if you work hard enough you can have them." Lancelot, the one-horned goat, was the epitome of wonder and beauty and hope; imagine what a whole flock of Lancelots would mean. Cassie's reaction was simple but profound. "How can they call a goat with one horn a unicorn? There's more to it than that!"

The teacher pointed to the pin on her lapel and said," When you gave me this, you didn't know what it was, remember? Now that you know, you can't be fooled into believing that a goat can be a unicorn;

you know that one horn doesn't give life to the legend. But the people who don't know are easily fooled. The best way to protect a legend is to leave it alone. The best way to profit from a freak is to display it. Whether or not you're fooled depends on you, on what you know and how much you're willing to find out."

Cassie thought she might have gotten a laugh out of the teacher over the one-horned goat, but the teacher thought that the article was sad commentary on the state of the world. Men were taking pot shots at a President and a Pope, starting wars all over the globe, embracing aggression "in the interests of national defense," and using natural resources as instruments of power, but somehow, in her heart, she felt that man's willingness to call a goat a unicorn was worse, far worse.

Besides *Hamlet* and poetry in May, Alyssa was involved in wrapping up the year's work with the regents sections, then getting into review. Jeff was not too happy when she started taking work home again. But it couldn't be helped; she told him she had no choice, which only made him angrier. There was absolutely no time in school to grade the papers and she had four classes that had to write a composition and a literature essay on final exams. They had to be given instruction and they had to practice, which meant she had to grade papers.

In the May, 1981, issue of the *New York Teacher*, Alyssa Matthews read an article by Albert Shanker discussing the latest report on education by sociologist James Coleman. Coleman had been reporting on education in the United States since 1966, and, Shanker pointed out, Coleman had been misinterpreted every time. The current Coleman Report, Shanker further pointed out, did not condemn public schools and praise private schools as was the popular notion of the day; the current Coleman Report differentiated between good and bad schools regardless of type. In 1966 James Coleman was of the opinion that socio-economic factors alone determined the success or failure of students in schools, that the conditions in the schools had little influence on student progress. The current Coleman Report seemed to be an effort to repudiate one interpretation of the 1966 dictum.

How enlightening, Alyssa thought, that Coleman found it safe to acknowledge the influence of academia on a child's intellectual development, that he was able to adjust his original contention that students from poor homes necessarily did poorly in school, that class size and other conditions within the school had little to do with quality education.

How enlightening, she thought, that Shanker found it necessary to point out that the most recent Coleman Report was being misinterpreted, that Coleman was not saying private schools are better than public schools, but simply that any school which enforces discipline, requires that high standards be instituted and met, exerts pressure on its students, and rewards achievement not existence, is a good school.

How enlightening, she thought, that Coleman meant what he meant when he meant it, changed what he meant when he decided he really meant something else, and all along the way was misinterpreted by experts; that Coleman made headlines every time he said what he meant, changed what he meant, or thought he might have meant something else; that his interpreters made headlines every time they interpreted or misinterpreted; and that any interpretation of the current report castigated schools for lowering standards, reducing the quality of education, and tolerating intolerable student behavior.

What fun to criticize, Alyssa thought. How easy to point the finger, to generalize, to make sweeping indictments. And why wasn't anyone paying attention to Richard Bossone? In the same issue of the magazine Richard Bossone, University Dean for Instructional Research and Professor of English at the City University of New York Graduate Center, described the conditions under which teachers were required to teach writing skills as woefully inadequate: too many papers to grade, not enough class time, too many students.

Alyssa wondered what would happen if the Big Boys descended from the heights long enough to see the shape of things at eye level. Let's change places, Boys, let us underlings beat on your heads for awhile. I guarantee you won't like it down here, but you will learn to dull your hatchets and qualify your statements. We need help down here in the nether regions, Boys, help, not theories and interpretations. We know the WHY down here, Boys. Anybody care to descend into the abyss?

In May her own particular abyss was deepening. Quite a few students, regents and scholarship alike, never completed the writing assignments; she was beyond begging at that time, so she never saw a preview of the writing of some before exams. She told them that they were missing out on a chance to find out where they were making mistakes, and let it go at that.

By the time she finished grading the papers that were handed in, she was surprised, not so surprised, and despondent, not necessarily in that order. Among the scholarship papers, students who wrote well to begin with were still writing well, students who were mediocre were still mediocre, and students who wrote poorly still wrote poorly. She got what she expected from the scholarship sections, though she was a little surprised at some of the students who failed to submit one or both assignments.

She also expected almost anything from the regents sections, but some of what she saw turned her stomach. They used another language. She expected spelling errors, but what could she do about massive distortion of words, words that weren't even words? She circled and underlined: fer, certin, stoped, comming, thier, sujesting, had went to, had wrote, autmaticly, he don't, trapd, missary, compisition, brang, stoled, everone, dose, wounderful, worpt, doomful, eaisly, exsist, groce, peice, writting, kepted, broughten, mentaly retarted, auther, phine, sain, and vonurable, among others equally bad or worse.

She read: The choice of words are well chosen.

She read: He lead me to belive furtor he had stanima by the way he took charge of everyone esle's actions and helped them uphold thier duties.

She read: What ever happen to the Good old Day's is what people say now day's. For instance rember when ga's was 30¢ a galon and only cost about 7 dollar's to fill up the tank. That frist car you had that took you any every where. Rember when those Kids use to read comic books' and go to the Satday Matnease just around the corner Well those day's are gone will probly never return. Now Day's who can afford theose comic book's 50¢ a book thats out ragous. Those Satday matnasies you would be very luky to find them they are so sacersh its unreal and nearly imposible.

She read: The authors purpose may be to make you feel sympathize with Curlerys' whife. Who went throw torter marrid. In the novel of mice + men Curleys whife had made her misteak by marry Curly and alway's listeun to people and belivin them even throw they were lying. Another misteak is that she alway's wantid attenion and She didn't care who she got it from and She had alway's flittred with other men to.

She read: First the bad things that wan't on. Some of the kids got in fights with kniefs. This still goes on in some placeses. The kids distroyed things that was not there's. The cops had to try to calm thing down between rumbuls. Some of the words were pritty cool prices were a lot lower than they our know. The movies were maybe 25¢. You could get in by popcorn and see a double feather.

She read and knew that she had never before seen such writing from regents level students. Some papers were so close to being completely illegible that she had a hard time reading them at all. Over two thousand years ago Chinese boys had to drink a dish of ink for carelessness in writing. In 1981 a student told his teacher: "So what? I'll learn how to type. Or, better yet, I'll pay somebody to type for me."

Even the good regents students hadn't had the necessary help with writing skills to allow her to recommend anyone for a scholarship section the following year. It was an end-of-the-year practice she used to enjoy. But not this year, this year inadequate writing skills disqualified students who were otherwise capable and qualified. The juggling act had finally taken its toll, and she felt worse for her students than for herself.

Alyssa Matthews was particularly sensitive to what she was reading in the press in May, 1981. The New York State Board of Regents was inordinately concerned over instituting strict controls for licensing of teachers by 1984, and with streamlining the hearing procedure for teachers to save school districts time and money. The Court of Appeals, the state's highest court, ruled that letters of reprimand could be placed in a teacher's personnel folder without a hearing even though such letters "could have some adverse effect on the future employment chances of teachers and could be used later for disciplinary action."

The New York City Board of Education was involved in a major recruiting drive to fill vacancies after having laid off 15,000 teachers five years earlier. The insolvent Boston school system was completing the year under court order. In the Logan Heights section of San Diego, 18 miles from the Mexican border, high school students were receiving "paper credit" amounting to twenty-five cents to attend six periods a day, not to exceed five dollars a month. The ninth grade president said, "I definitely think they should keep the program, but I guess they should, like, make it up to fifty cents. Some kids are getting just a little tired of twenty-five cents." The school principal cited the high cost of truancy in his defense of the program, which was described by a multitude of critics as quackery, bribery, blasphemy, and brilliance. The principal was called realist, idealist, and mountebank.

There was also a "new" trend, a "new" force in school districts advocating that special programs be established for gifted and talented children. The "new" task forces were insisting that removing gifted students from classes for extra attention in supplemental areas was the best way to adequately challenge those students.

Furthermore, they advocated in-service training to indoctrinate teachers into accepting such pull-out programs. Classroom teachers were not skilled enough to handle the needs of gifted children, they needed in-service training in order to understand how pull-out programs worked so that they might support those programs.

That one made Alyssa Matthews see red and curse a blue streak. "If they take these kids out of classes for one more goddam reason, I'm going to start running a Film Festival all year," she told Jean. "They can take their rotten in-service training and stick it where it doesn't fit! Now we're not capable of teaching gifted kids! I used to get work out of gifted kids that these people wouldn't even understand. I know how to challenge gifted students, I did it for years with terrific results. Now one set of bastards has made it impossible for me to do it, and another set wants to farm out my job! Son-of-a-bitch. I'd like nothing better than to be able to take care of my own gifted students! What the hell is wrong with these people? Why doesn't somebody advocate some new programs that will let us teach again? Son-of-a-bitch. I've got kids who could have done great things this year if I had had the time and energy to challenge them. Christ, Jean, look at what happened to you. Where the hell is it all leading? Are we eventually going to be so involved with tracking down truants, keeping attendance records, and monitoring, that we won't be able to care about teaching at all anymore? Will we be using the same plan book year after year? That's what they're doing to us!"

She popped her cork often during May, 1981, but she spewed molten lava one day when she was alone in the faculty room. It was during sixth period, Jean was running errands, and Alyssa was leafing through a newspaper left by someone earlier in the day. When she saw the illustration, she was immediately offended; when she read the words, she was repulsed. It was as heinous a condemnation as she had ever seen, an insult not only to teachers but to students as well. The cartoon showed a big-nosed, droopy-eyed, long-faced student dressed in graduation gown and mortarboard. The question was: ALTHOUGH THE STUDENT PASSED EVERY COURSE WHAT DID THE TEACHERS FAIL TO DO? The answer was: FILL IN THE BLANK. And the blank was a dotted line running into one oversized ear and out the other.

She said nothing to Jean about the cartoon, she closed her mind to it, because, in the midst of the molten lava, one thought surfaced: Get used to it. Get used to it. Get used to it. Or get out.

Act II

Scene. The same. Except the piles of paper and the tins of fluid under the side altar are gone.

When the curtain rises, JEAN and ALYSSA are sitting and smoking; they smoke continuously, sharing one very large, overgrown lighter. BONNIE is fussing with the duplicator, which won't start up. She checks the wiring and the wall outlet, then pushes the lever to start the machine. Nothing happens. She removes the master from the roll, makes a few adjustments here and there, replaces the master, and hits the lever again. Nothing. LAINIE enters and sits.

Frozen in time, the CHORUS is equipped with newspapers and peepholes in their blindfolds, vision restricted to reading only.

LAINIE: Don't waste your time, Bonnie. It died two days ago.

BONNIE: Can you fix it?

LAINIE: Not this time. It needs a repairman. And a thorough cleaning.

JEAN: Forget it. It's May. Maybe by September ...

ALYSSA: Would you care to take bets on that?

JEAN: Not especially.

            (BONNIE sits.)

ALYSSA: What were you trying to run off?

BONNIE: A test.

LAINIE: There must be a machine working somewhere.

BONNIE: Who cares. I'm not running my ass off today.

609

ALYSSA: Go to the office and use the zerox. Just be sure nobody's looking.

BONNIE: Maybe later.

JEAN: Just don't get caught.

LAINIE: Yeah, they may flog you with a wet ditto. You'll be purple for life.

JEAN: Worse yet, they may dock you for it. Or write you up. Black copies cost money.

BONNIE: Shit, I think I'll just cancel the test. I've had enough aggravation for one year.

JEAN: Is it June yet?

ALYSSA: Where's Joyce today?

JEAN: Giving orals. She's on a hell of a schedule this month, testing before and after school, during her lunch and free period.

ALYSSA: One kid at a time ...

JEAN: She was bitching this morning over no-shows. She's a nervous wreck; the oral is ten percent of the final, some kids fail because of it. And she's got exams herself this month, for those two courses she had to take.

ALYSSA: Did you understand what she was telling us that day after vacation?

JEAN: That attack she had? Sure. Nerves, plain and simple.

ALYSSA: That's what I thought it was too.

BONNIE: But she said she was completely calm when it happened.

JEAN: That's exactly when it happens. You think you're okay, then your whole body starts to shake. It's delayed reaction is what it is. And it scares the hell out of you. She thought she was having a heart attack, which made it worse, of course. At least when I get a migraine I know why; it happens immediately after I get aggravated.

LAINIE: I don't know how she made it through this year. Can you imagine having to evaluate kids when you aren't any too good at the subject yourself?

BONNIE: Have you been reading the newspapers? The consensus is that the quality of education has been eroded by unqualified teachers.

LAINIE: Maybe that triggered Joyce's nerve attack. I avoid newspapers. I value my sanity. I don't need to read things like *He who can, does. He who cannot, teaches.*

ALYSSA: Shaw?

LAINIE: Yeah, the old fart really put us in our place, didn't he?

ALYSSA: Not really. Do you know anything else about the old boy?

JEAN: What's there to know?

ALYSSA: Context, for one thing. His life, for another.

JEAN: Don't tell me the poor fella was misunderstood and misquoted while he counted his money.

ALYSSA: Yes and no. He had disciples and critics, then and now. I researched Shaw once. He was called a devil, a fool, an illness, and an old fogy when he was alive and writing. He was controversial and he loved it because he was obsessed with effect.

JEAN: I never studied him. I should know better than to condemn him on the basis of one quote. Still we do it, huh?

BONNIE: I haven't read much about him either, but I do find it peculiar that his followers are called Shavians, though I suppose Shawettes wouldn't work.

ALYSSA: Shaw called the proletarian a prostitute; he said the proletarian's fate is "the only real tragedy in life: the being used by personally minded men for purposes which you recognize to be base." I used that quote in a paper once when I was too young to appreciate it.

LAINIE: Didn't he think that teachers were part of the working class?

ALYSSA: What do you think he was? He believed in being irritating, in startling his audience; he liked to deal in contradiction. That was his technique — grate on peoples' nerves or don't bother to say anything at all. And he wanted to change the world. He was a teacher, all right, and he failed to do what he wanted most. The paradox of his career was that he had so much fame but so little influence.

JEAN: Poor fella, maybe we should weep for him.

ALYSSA: He'd rather you cursed him, dead or alive.

(The women freeze. The CHORUS comes alive.)

1st CITIZEN (reading a newspaper):

REGENTS APPROVE TESTING OF PROSPECTIVE TEACHERS

ALBANY – New York's Board of Regents voted at their April meeting to require new prospective teachers to pass an exam before they could receive either a provisional certificate or a license to teach in the State's public schools. The amendment to the Commissioner's Regulations becomes effective on Sept. 2, 1984, after which all teaching candidates must pass an exam.

Separate exams will be given for each certification area including administration and supervision. The Regents envisioned about fifty different tests.

3rd CITIZEN: Well, this is fine and dandy for new teachers, but what about the ones in the schools now? Why aren't they being tested? Some of them stink. They should have to pass a test or get thrown out. I think that's fair enough.

6th CITIZEN: Just exactly how bad are the teachers we've got if the State thinks these measures are necessary for the future?

12th CITIZEN: *FIFTY* different tests? Who pays for *fifty* different tests? And what guarantee is there that all those tests will produce good teachers?

(The CHORUS freezes. The women come alive.)

LAINIE: Did you see that movie last night about the teacher?

JEAN: *The Violation of Sarah McDavid*? I caught parts of it. Enough to switch stations.

ALYSSA: You should take up reading newspapers and avoid TV, Lainie. I read the summary for that show: Nagging questions about school security, administrative competence, and the responsibilities of the public. Then I avoided the movie; I'm depressed enough without seeing that. It was a wasted effort, anyway. Or did something change this morning that I'm not aware of?

LAINIE: Well, I saw it and it was terrifying. But it probably got poor ratings. People don't want to think about the job hazards of cops and firemen, much less teachers. How about you, Bon? Did you see it?

BONNIE: Hell, no. I'm still shaking over that rotten kid in the cafeteria. Maybe it's my imagination, but I've seen

613

> him in the halls and sometimes I think he's stalking me. The last thing I need is to see a movie about a teacher who's raped.

JEAN: Do you want me to go back to see Harry?

BONNIE: No, Jean, thanks. There's nothing to charge the kid with. I haven't seen him much in the last few days. I think he's getting tired of the game.

JEAN: Just don't stay alone in any room at any time.

BONNIE: Don't worry, I don't and I won't.

ALYSSA: And never tell yourself that it can't happen here.

(The women freeze. The CHORUS comes alive.)

12th CITIZEN (reading a newspaper):

FRESHMAN CHARGED IN TEACHER DEATH

April 10, 1981 — A 16-year-old freshman at Braxton High School in Buffalo has been arrested and charged with first-degree manslaughter in the death of his math teacher, John Smith, who died from injuries suffered while breaking up a fight between the youth and another student on March 15. The freshman, Louis Doolen, was suspended indefinitely by the superintendent of schools. The other student, an upperclassman who was on out-of-school suspension, should not have been on school grounds; he has been referred for additional disciplinary action.

Doolen allegedly punched the teacher. The 42-year-old teacher struck his head on a locker. Mr. Smith taught his classes the rest of the day, but collapsed later at home. He was dead on arrival at Community Hospital of multiple head fractures. If convicted of the manslaughter charge, the youth could face a sentence of 8 to 25 years in prison.

Mr. Smith is survived by his wife and four children. School officials said Mr. Smith was "respected and loved by the kids." More than 400 attended his funeral services.

The Board of Education said 346 assaults on teachers have been reported so far this school year in the entire district, compared with 157 reported for the school year ended last June. They wished to stress the point that Braxton has a "below-average incidence of violence."

(The CHORUS freezes. The women come alive. LAINIE rises and walks to the door.)

LAINIE: I'm going down to check my mailbox. Can I pick up and deliver for anyone?

JEAN: Bring back some Black Flag. These ants will be crawling up our legs pretty soon.

ALYSSA: And some disinfectant. God only knows what's breeding in the filth in here.

(LAINIE says, "Right, ladies!" and leaves.)

BONNIE: Shall we try again with a petition?

JEAN: In May? Don't waste any ink.

(BONNIE walks to the window, opens it, saying "I wish you two would quit your evil ways.")

ALYSSA: It's a lousy habit. I wish I could quit. But once you start, even quitting isn't forever. Right, Jean?

JEAN: I swore I'd never start again. I feel like a big kid. If Dominick were here, I wouldn't be smoking, that's for sure.

BONNIE: How can you do it when you know it might kill you? The odds aren't in your favor, are they?

JEAN: We smokers learn how to rationalize with the first puff. There are a lot of things that can kill you. Everything's hazardous to your health these days, even tampons. I can't stop using tampons.

ALYSSA: I don't want to stop using tampons. I hate feeling my insides gush out. Now it's risky to use tampons. What the hell isn't risky?

(BONNIE sits. The phone rings. She answers it, but there's no one at the other end. She repeats "Hello" then hangs up.)

BONNIE: Toxic Shock Syndrome. It's a scary name, all right.

JEAN: Yeah, it's got the tampon business scared out of its wits.

ALYSSA: I wonder what women used in ancient times. What was life like Before Pads?

JEAN: Messy. Didn't they use pieces of cloth? Has anyone researched the history of women, B.P.?

BONNIE: What's there to research? It was a mark of shame in every civilization of the world throughout history. Some women have only started talking to each other about menstruation in the last ten years. I doubt if the subject is discussed in hieroglyphics.

JEAN: I wonder if Cleopatra had cramps.

ALYSSA: Or Liz Taylor, for that matter.

BONNIE: Or Mata Hari when she had a hot one on the line.

ALYSSA: Queen Elizabeth?

JEAN: My mother still refers to it as "coming sick."

ALYSSA: My grandmother asked me that once! I guess I didn't look too good to her and she said, "Did you come sick today?" My mother had to translate, I couldn't figure it out.

(The phone rings. BONNIE answers it: "Hello! Hello? Hello, hello, hello!" Then she hangs up.)

ALYSSA: Have we got a phantom caller?

BONNIE: Seems so. Somebody's dialing this number.

JEAN: If Paul calls for me, I'm not here. I've been ducking him all week. The Sons of Italy are running a writing contest. I'll be damned if I fool around with that this late in the year. I feel bad for Paul because they're on his back for entries, but I can't read any more papers this week.

ALYSSA: He came begging to me this morning. I told him I'd try, but I won't announce it to classes either. They put us on the spot with those writing contests; we average two a month starting in February. If no kids enter, we look bad and Paul has to take the heat.

BONNIE: It's a shame, really. I'd love it if one of my kids won something, and contest sponsors are only out to do honor to everybody involved. But they don't realize what we're up against here. I announce every contest and I never get any response from the kids.

JEAN: You're supposed to offer some incentive. Kids do nothing extra today unless you dangle extra credit in front of their noses. And then you'll only get one or two.

BONNIE: I won't do that.

ALYSSA: Neither will I. Life rarely offers extra credit for anything.

JEAN: Unless it's maybe a retirement bonus.

ALYSSA: That's a bribe.

JEAN: Case closed.

BONNIE: Some kids think that extra credit means instead-of credit. Paul should refuse on behalf of the department whenever these people approach him with more work for us to do.

ALYSSA: Are you kidding? He can't do that.

BONNIE: Why not? We're up to our ears in work. Why are we so involved in hiding that fact? Why can't somebody come out and say it? Maybe we should stop beating around the bush and stop pretending and stop saving face. Why are we constantly trying to convince people that we'll try to do what we can't do?

JEAN: Because we're afraid. What other reason is there? Paul has people screaming at him all the time. Last year there was that woman crusading for a speech contest. You remember her, don't you? She was in here three days a week ordering people around because she had Bassard's blessings and she was obsessed with seeing her name in the newspaper. I almost told her one day to go find a job if she was bored and to leave us alone. The only reason I didn't tell her off was out of sympathy for Paul. He had to listen to her, take orders from her, and usher her around.

ALYSSA: The community pays our wages and expects us to be at their beck and call. If we blatantly refuse, we're in for it. Paul starts every year by telling us to protect ourselves, and that's the best advice he can give.

BONNIE: Well, maybe it's about time for the truth.

ALYSSA: The truth means a big fight, and I'm too tired to fight.

(The phone rings. BONNIE answers it. Nothing. She slams the receiver down. LAINIE returns and distributes mail.)

LAINIE: Exam schedules, ladies!

JEAN: They're awfully early this year. What can this mean?

ALYSSA: Isn't this cute? Tomorrow I'm supposed to notify these kids to show up for tests — one never showed in September, one left in October, and the third dropped out in January. Oh, look — here's Nettie's millionth excuse. How exciting.

JEAN: If you want excitement, start reading the exam schedule. Somebody's really into thrills and chills this year.

BONNIE: It doesn't make any sense to do this.

ALYSSA: What the hell—? How can we run classes and give exams at the same time?

JEAN: We've had at least two days for school exams for the past fifty years. What the hell happened?

LAINIE: We didn't use any more snow days than we should have. Somehow we must not have enough instructional days. What a zoo this is going to be.

BONNIE: It doesn't make any sense to do this.

(The phone rings. BONNIE lifts the receiver and immediately slams it down again.)

JEAN: Wait a minute. Wait a goddam minute. The dawn is breaking. Think about it. Think real hard. And be sure to avoid any what if 's.

ALYSSA: Oh, shit. Those goddam useless in-service days. Look at this insanity! *Teachers with scheduled exams may opt to proctor their own exams or teach remaining classes on these two days. Substitutes will be hired to fulfill either teaching or proctoring duties.* Why is it now so easy to hire subs after classes have been canceled for months? Subs can't answer questions during exams, what do they know about our exams? Christ, this is going to be a two-day abortion.

JEAN: Well, we're in some kind of luck. The sophomore English exams are scheduled during regents week. Not that we can teach those two days.

There won't be any kids because they'll be taking other exams.

LAINIE: Look at this. Joyce has exams Thursday morning and Friday morning, classes both days, and her exam grades are due Monday morning. Clever, very clever. What's she supposed to do on Friday with the kids who take the exam on Thursday? Has she got any choice but to grade exams at night and all weekend?

JEAN: I wonder how many asses are being protected by this stupidity.

BONNIE: It's senseless, utterly senseless. I thought last year was bad enough, when we had to conduct homeroom in the morning and in the afternoon on school exam days. What the hell was that for? Kids had to report only if they had exams, and attendance was taken in exam rooms.

ALYSSA: It gave the illusion that school was in session, I guess. Taking homeroom attendance means the day counts as instructional-time. Pretty asinine, if you ask me. I ignored the whole thing. I was home grading exams; I wasn't about to run back here for that foolishness.

LAINIE: None of my kids showed up. And nobody wanted a report anyway.

JEAN: The kids know a farce when they see one. And speaking of farces, anybody know what the blockbuster finale is in our series of workshops?

ALYSSA: Why the hell don't they cancel that and give us at least one school-exam day?

LAINIE: What's the last one on?

JEAN: Are you ready for this? Half the day will be spent on organizing a district-wide committee to improve communications with the superintendent and the Board; the other half will be dedicated to stress, stress and burn-out.

ALYSSA: Shit. Shit and shinola.

BONNIE: Son-of-a-bitch! They've got me scheduled to proctor right after my exam! When am I supposed to grade papers?

JEAN: You'd better go raise a stink or you'll be up all night.

BONNIE: They're not supposed to schedule proctoring for a day and a half after you give your own exam, are they?

JEAN: That has been simple courtesy and common sense for a long time, but it ain't written anywhere. They probably did it to me, too, only I'm not looking to find out right now.

ALYSSA: I feel like we died and went to the Twilight Zone. This year cannot end fast enough.

(The women freeze. The CHORUS comes alive.)

1st CITIZEN: (reading)

BELL URGES STIFF TESTS

WASHINGTON, April 9 (UPI) – Schools should require students to pass tough comprehensive examinations as a means of "quality control" before promoting them from key grades and allowing them to graduate from high school, Education Secretary T.H. Bell said today.

Asserting that most school systems in this country have become "academically flabby," Mr. Bell said, "When performance is measured, performance is improved. We need quality control."

Several school associations and parent groups favor increased testing but the nation's largest teachers' union, the National Education Association, opposes the idea.

Mr. Bell said that automatic promotion robs students of an incentive to learn. Critics of the education system say that a lack of firm standards is one reason why the test scores of today's students are lower than those of previous generations.

12th CITIZEN: I've said it before and I'll say it again: Quality control is as important in education as it is in business. If strict standards are set, a better product will emerge.

6th CITIZEN: The key to quality is accountability. Schools must be held accountable for the failure of their students. If schools were threatened with loss of aid or decertification, you'd see a change, a big change. I say make schools accountable.

9th CITIZEN: Of course the union is against the idea. The union's looking for less work with more pay. Do you expect a union to be interested in quality?

12th CITIZEN: Pushing kids from grade to grade is wrong. This Bell guy must know what he's talking about. Even the President is worried about our educational system. There's something wrong, very wrong, with our schools and our teachers.

(The CHORUS freezes. Forever. The women come alive.)

LAINIE: Hey, look at this. Look at this, will you? We've just been notified that our competency tests have been declared invalid by the State! So many teachers wrote to complain about errors on the test forms that they've all been voided! Why the hell can't they decide these things a little sooner? I've been a maniac all year for nothing! Christ! All those goddam charts and records, all that scheduling and rescheduling!

ALYSSA: Does it really surprise you any?

LAINIE: Why do they do these things?

ALYSSA: It'll never stop. Administrators will administrate, subordinates will subordinate, and never the twain shall meet.

JEAN: Is it June yet?

BONNIE: Soon, Jean, soon.

ALYSSA: I wonder how many doubles we'll have, seeing that there are no provisions for doubles with school exams.

JEAN: What? Where'd you see that?

ALYSSA: Page three.

JEAN: They can't make us take care of our own doubles! How are we supposed to do that?

LAINIE: Just do it. Bitch all you want, but do it.

BONNIE: I've got a feeling there will be some triples this year. What agony for a kid to have to take three exams in one day.

ALYSSA: So what? The kids don't matter, we don't matter. As long as we can fake 180 days of instruction, the assembly line is running smoothly.

LAINIE: Kids are bouncing in and out of class so much this month, the entire month is a waste of time.

JEAN: Some school districts are experimenting with a shorter school day, starting earlier in the morning and releasing earlier in the afternoon.

ALYSSA: I wouldn't mind that. I'm here early anyway.

JEAN: It also means a thirty minute lunch and shorter class periods. They're doing it to accommodate after-school sports programs.

LAINIE: Ah, yes ... priorities. Where would we be without the bus schedule, the cafeteria schedule, and extracurricular activities?

(Suddenly there's a rumbling in the squawk box on the wall. Then music blasts out of it.)

SHOVE YOUR CLASSES

ALYSSA: What the hell's going on?

BONNIE: Somebody's trying to start a riot.

JEAN: I heard some kids talking about doing this ...

SHOVE YOUR BOOKS

JEAN: ... and I tried to explain that it wouldn't be too appropriate.

LAINIE: They're flying high today over yearbooks.

ALYSSA: Don't remind me. Did you see the quote they used from Dickens?

BONNIE: It was the best of times, it was the worst of times; it was the age of wisdom, it was the age of foolishness It was a beautiful choice. Too bad they billed it as a poem.

ALYSSA: A poem by Charles Dickens. Astounding.

WE HATE ANY TEACHER'S LOOKS

BONNIE: I never taught *Tale* as a poem. Have you?

ALYSSA: Not me. Did Dickens write poetry?

BONNIE: Not that I know of.

ALYSSA: Where did we go wrong, I wonder.

SCALE THE WALL TO SAVE YOUR SOUL

JEAN: Somebody better pull the plug on this disgusting song; it's making me sick to my stomach.

LAINIE: Maybe they want this to replace "Pomp and Circumstance."

ALYSSA: Just pray the senior class doesn't get to vote on it.

WE'RE ESCAPING MIND CONTROL

(The music stops. But not forever.)

BONNIE: Aren't we working on a dignified graduation this year?

ALYSSA: Too bad we're not working on a dignified exam schedule.

JEAN: The public sees graduation; the public does not see the exam schedule.

ALYSSA: Case closed.

BONNIE: Sometimes I feel like I want to break out of this place.

JEAN: Forget it. The deus ex machina broke down last week.

(The phone rings. BONNIE lifts the receiver, replaces it, then lifts it again and drops it so that it dangles off the table.

The phone rings again. The women stare at it as the curtain falls.)

King's Legacy

Dorothea King was excited, as excited as a child about to attend a party. She ignored the pressure in her head, the feeling of faintness. No time for that now, she thought, no time for that now. The night was clear, the moon was full, conditions were perfect; the time had come for one more viewing, one more chance to see the spectacle. Next year would be too late, she'd never live that long. She knew it; in her heart and in her mind she knew that her time of death was fast approaching. And she didn't care to postpone it. She'd had enough of one world and was looking forward to the next. She had no doubt that Alex was there, in the next world, waiting for her. She had not a single doubt about that. There was that period early in her bereavement when she wished herself dead just to be able to join him, but that passed because she was not able to do what was necessary to end her own life. When she made more of an adjustment to her husband's death, she resigned herself to the fact that he was dead and she was alive and only the Lord knew the day when they would be reunited. Now that day was fast approaching and she welcomed it.

But she would see his legacy one more time, see what he left in this world to herald his solitary existence. Dorothea King called Bonnie Mason on the phone and said in hushed tones, "It's time, dear. I'll be up later in the evening, after it's completely dark. The moon should be positioned just right tonight."

Bonnie Mason answered politely, saying that any time was fine with her. She was tired, and for that reason sent Michael home early, but she was also curious. The window had begun to show its personality, the flames seemed to be building heat nightly, flickering, yet not flickering. She was not sure how much of the effect was her imagination. But she was sure that something was happening, that external light in the midst of darkness was giving life to the stained glass in a way that was not possible during the day.

Since Alyssa had stimulated her interest, Bonnie had read more about Joan's life and death. She decided that religion had given the young girl an opportunity to break away from the confines of her gender, then religion proceeded to destroy her. Joan herself said that her parents kept her "in great subjection." Joan reasoned that her "voices" gave her the right to disobey. Bonnie reasoned that Joan was born in the wrong century, though her problems sounded typically adolescent in any century. She was a victim of the times and quite possibly mentally ill.

When Mrs. King called, Bonnie was working with a crochet hook and yellow yarn, trying to maneuver her wrist the way Alyssa showed her. She wasn't too pleased with the results yet. Her stitches were uneven and jagged. But one good thing about crochet — it could be ripped out easily enough. Alyssa's words gave her some encouragement: "You have to develop a rhythm, a flow of control. Once you know what you're doing and do it enough, you'll be consistently good at it. But you'll never be good at it if you don't keep trying." So she kept on trying. She started the third rip-out when she heard the tiny knock on the door, the inside door that Mrs. King had never approached before for reasons of privacy.

Bonnie peeked into the bedroom on the way to the door, and what she saw made her rush to let Mrs. King in.

"She's burning," Bonnie said blankly.

Mrs. King smiled an enigmatic smile. "Of course she is, dear. It's a resurrection of sorts, don't you think? Now why don't you put some water on for tea? I'd suggest popcorn, but that's a little tacky." She was laughing softly as she walked to the bedroom.

"Is there time?" Bonnie asked. "I mean, will I miss anything?"

"No rush. There's no rush. We have a few hours, you know, and you will see the diminishing for another week. Together we have most of the night. Don't hurry, dear. It never makes sense to hurry when you consider what we're all hurrying to."

Mrs. King was sitting in the chair in the bedroom when Bonnie served tea. And the window was ablaze. The artist had created a perfect fire to begin with. Now, as it raged violently, Bonnie thought she heard the crackling and hissing, thought she smelled the glowing embers, thought she felt the intense heat. One sense had taken control of the others.

Dorothea King sipped her tea in a radiant glow, as if encased in the fiery illumination. "Isn't it wondrous?" she murmured. "And he protected her, out of pity he protected her. What a kind and gentle man he was. He was a woman's man. How it saddened him that she had suffered so horribly. He wanted to spare her, but how could he? He was too late, centuries too late. How sinful when cultures revile beauty and create horrors that can never be undone."

Mrs. King fell silent, her eyes fixed on the mandala. As the women watched, the fire continued to rage, but the blue-gray mass in the midst of the flames began to intensify, to protrude, it seemed, beyond the flames. The armor and the form within it became the overpowering force, the eternal message. The glass was dead and yet it lived through the capricious spirituality of light. Colored images lived through luminous illusion.

Bonnie watched the spectacular sight in awe of the third dimension, the color, the beauty created in a kinetic paradox, where no beauty existed to begin with, centuries ago. For Joan had nothing to isolate her flesh from the flames. She felt the fire for an eternity before she expired.

Then Bonnie wasn't sure that she was seeing right. She blinked once, twice, and a third time to clear her vision. Then she was still not certain that she wasn't being tricked into seeing what wasn't there. Not that it mattered. She concentrated on the face, the placid, sorrowful face crowned by a cap of short-cropped hair. The eyes in the face drooped, the lids closed, and the tears trembled down. Sparkling bits cascaded to the hand-held cross.

"She's crying," Bonnie said in a whisper, expecting a response from Mrs. King. There was none. Bonnie glanced to the side, saying, "How did he do this? How was it possible?"

The old woman must have fallen asleep.

"Mrs. King?"

Bonnie went to the chair and touched the old woman's arm. "Mrs. King? Are you all right?"

Maybe it was too much remembering, too much for her to take. Had she fainted again? With her eyes open? Bonnie spoke her name one more time, then lifted an arm from the arm of the chair. That was when the body creased and fell into folds. Then there were two women crying; one was dressed in armor, one was not.

Bonnie dragged into work the next morning without benefit of sleep, but what she lacked in energy she made up for in choler. "I called an ambulance," she told Alyssa, "then I thought I should call somebody in the family. She told me she made peace with her daughter, so I went downstairs to find a phone number. I was frantic. I found a note on the wall next to the phone that said to call her daughter in the event of her death! I'm telling you, she planned it! I think she just willed herself dead and that was it! Anyway, I called the number she left and her daughter told me that if she died I should call for a hearse! She wasn't at all interested in seeing her. I told her I had already called an ambulance and she got angry, told me I could pay for the ambulance because I called for it and it was unnecessary to call an ambulance for a corpse. That's what she said, a corpse! I told her I wasn't qualified to certify death, for all I knew her mother might have been in a coma, and I'd be happy to pay for the ambulance. Then I hung up on the bitch.

"By that time the ambulance was in front of the house. I ran out to direct the men up to the apartment. When we got to her she was still crumbled in the chair. The attendants tried to revive her, then put her on a stretcher. They were so fascinated by the window I had to remind them a couple of times to hurry. But I guess they knew that hurrying wasn't necessary.

"I followed the ambulance to the hospital and waited for somebody to tell me something. I knew she was dead, but I didn't want to believe it. I waited for two hours before a doctor finally found me. Only he was looking for next-of-kin. I felt like an idiot all of a sudden, like I had no right to be there. I gave the doctor the note I found next to the telephone and left.

"I spent the rest of the night sitting on the bed and staring at that window. I felt as if I had been orphaned. I never felt that way when I left home. It was different. I sat there until this morning because I couldn't sleep knowing that she had died in that room. She said she wanted a peaceful death. Well, she got it, all right. But I wish she could have heard her daughter's tone of voice. Or maybe it's better that she didn't."

That afternoon as she rounded the last corner and traveled down Brickstone Street on her way home after school, Bonnie saw the ladders leaning against the house. They looked like flying buttresses, like some medieval attempt to keep the structure standing upright. Had Mrs. King contracted the restoration to begin today? It seemed so. There were men on the ladders.

When she parked in front of the house, Bonnie saw the awful truth and was sickened by the sight. The glass was gone, the colored glass was no longer framing the front door. Protected from the weather by the porch, the stained glass on the first floor was not deteriorating like the rest, it was in excellent condition, it was easiest to remove. Men were working along the side of the house, following the line of the porch, removing another window, replacing it with wood.

As she walked toward the house, Bonnie heard a man say, "Any of you guys think you're an artist? If I can get some pictures painted on this plywood, I won't have to buy windows before I sell this museum."

The man was standing in the grass. He wore a brown business suit. Bonnie recognized him immediately. She had seen him the first time she saw the house, when she first met his mother. He was laughing and joking with the workmen. Bonnie wanted to shove his laughter and his jokes back down his throat. She wanted to open the earth under him and watch him sink into hell where he belonged. Bonnie Mason experienced a deep, overwhelming hope that she was wrong in her beliefs. There didn't have to be a heaven, but there had to be a hell. This man had to be punished, somehow, somewhere, sometime, he had to get what was coming to him. This man and his sister. Bonnie found pleasure in conjuring up a hell to accommodate them.

She walked up to the man and said venomously, "How can you do this when you know how much she loved this house?"

The man said, "Are you the tenant?"

"Yes."

"You have until the end of the month to get out. The large window will be the last to go, after you leave. If you aren't out by then, you'll be sorry." He looked the other way, as if to dismiss her.

"You can't threaten me. You owe me a month's notice."

"I don't owe you anything," the man growled. "Let's get that straight right now. You don't have a lease, your agreement was with the old lady, and I'm not obligated to you for anything. You'll get out or you'll find your belongings on the curb."

"You can't take that window. It belongs in this house."

The man laughed. "Who the hell are you to tell me what I can't do? Look, face it, your cheap rent days are over. My mother was a fool and you reaped the benefits. Now she's a dead fool and it's my turn."

"You're an evil, vicious, unfeeling bastard. I loved your mother and that's more than you can say. If you take that window out of this house, you'll -you'll — a curse should fall on you!"

What could she threaten him with? How does one threaten the devil? How could she defend the dead? She felt helpless and foolish, and the feeling increased her rage. "You must know why that window should stay in this house! Did you hate your mother so much that you'll make a mockery out of her last wish!"

"Look, lady, go on up and start packing and get your ass off my property. I don't have to listen to you. That window is worth two hundred thousand dollars. You'll never see that much money in your whole life. But I will. Nothing's going to stop me, least of all you."

"I saw it last night. Your mother died in that room watching it. Are you made of stone?" Bonnie grabbed the man's arm. He pushed her away and hissed, "So my father thought he was Walt Disney. That was his problem. He lived his life the way he wanted, and I'm living mine the way I want. And it's none of your business. Make yourself scarce. Get out before I throw you out."

Bonnie backed away for fear she would try to kill him. "Where is she?"

The man was thoroughly puzzled. "Who?"

Bonnie spoke each word as if each were weighted with concrete, "Your mother. Where is your mother?"

The man's patience was wearing. He screamed, "She's dead!"

Bonnie yelled back, "Which funeral home?"

The man calmed down. He looked at his watch. "She was cremated an hour ago. You can have the ashes. As soon as you get the hell out."

Bonnie's face contorted. She screamed, "You burned her! You bastard, you burned her!" Then she flew at him, pummeling with her fists.

He hit her once, in the face, which sent her down in a rush of pain. It felt as if his fist had knocked her head off.

The man screamed at the workmen, "You saw it, you saw it, she attacked me! I was defending myself!" Then he straightened his tie and looked down at her. "I'm telling you one more time," he snarled, "get out! If you don't, I'm calling the police. And don't get any ideas. I've got witnesses to this."

Bonnie had no ideas, she had no thoughts. The pain shooting through her eye and into her head precluded ideas and thoughts. Somehow she lifted herself from the ground and walked around the house to the back entrance. As she passed the front door, she was aware of people inside the house. Two of them passed by her. They were carrying something out. She couldn't see out of one eye, but the other one took over. The two women hurried past her, and, despite the pain, she had a thought. It was too late, though, to do what she wanted. They were too fast. At the very least, she wanted to trip one of them. They were carrying the microwave oven.

Bonnie spent another night without sleep. Her eye was swollen and purple. But the painful eye was nothing compared to what she had to contend with when Michael saw her. She was terrified that he would do something irrational, so she talked through the pain to convince him that it was her fault, that she provoked the punch. Anything, anything to calm him down.

Michael kept screaming, "He's an animal! What kind of man would do this to a woman! He's an animal! Somebody should rearrange his face a little so he can see what it feels like! I wonder how he'd like to fight another man!"

631

Bonnie let him rage, then took advantage of the times when he stopped to catch his breath. She finally made him understand that she just didn't want any more trouble. "We'll have to go apartment-hunting," she said ruefully.

"If we need more time, you can stay at my mother's," Michael offered. "She won't mind."

"I'd hate to do that, but if I have to, I have to. What a lousy mess this turned out to be. It was so perfect, so beautiful, and it all turned to shit. It's not fair, not any of it." She stopped there because she didn't want him to see just how heartsick she was over all of it.

"Well, this settles it, I'm getting a job," he said. "We won't be able to pay high rent and heat bills if I'm in college."

Bonnie's good eye flashed anger. "I finished off my loans last month. We'll borrow the money to get you through school. And I don't want to hear any more about it!"

He saw that she was in no mood to argue, so he let her be, but he had made up his mind and nothing would change it.

She convinced him that she would be all right if he left her alone. Then she sat on the bed holding a cold pack against her eye, which was swollen shut and every color of the rainbow.

The flames in the window started to flicker. She watched the flames and she looked at the chair and she thought she would go mad with grief and rage. She couldn't stay in the bedroom. She fled to the sofa where she found the yellow yarn and the crochet hook. By the time the sun came up, she was up to the armholes on the little bunting.

The next day she was the talk of the school. The lunch crew heard the truth and by the end of the day, Jean quipped, "Maybe you should call a general assembly. There are some awfully malicious tongues in this place. I've told a couple it's none of their business, but that hasn't stopped the wagging."

Bonnie told her classes she had had an accident and she didn't care to elaborate. Her quest for privacy in a public place was futile. What people didn't know for sure, they fabricated in a spirit of vindictiveness, as if their right to know was being violated. Speculation lead to more speculation which inevitably became rooted in the darkest, richest soil.

A beautiful, young, single woman with a blackened eye had to mean one thing — her lover was beating her up. One proponent of the theory went so far as to check out the victim's car in the parking lot to rule out accidental injury. Many an eyebrow was raised and many a snickering comment attributed the bruise to a run-in with a door.

Bonnie fully expected to be called to the office, but Bassard was conferencing out of town and the assistant-in-charge was out of sight playing appropriate administrator on a higher level.

From lack of sleep and the constant barrage of questions, comments, and sly looks, Bonnie's nerves were raw by the end of the day. Alyssa offered sincere apologies. "I sent you there," she said. "Now I wish I had kept my mouth shut. It was a big mistake." Bonnie replied that she was a big girl, she made her own decisions, and how could anyone have known it would end the way it did?

And so the daughters of Night, Clotho and Lachesis, worked with steady hands, while their sister Atropos sat poised and ready to strike the next fatal blow.

Roy G Biv

RED

The shiny red Volkswagen put-putted its way down city streets as if it had never known the indignity of being multicolored. In its restored state, it looked brand new. It even sounded bright and shiny. And proud.

"My brother did a terrific job on this old wreck," the driver told the passenger.

"Yeah, I'm gonna be as good as he is someday," the passenger said with a grin.

"I still can't believe it! You got accepted, you really got accepted! Colleges must be pretty desperate to accept you!" The driver laughed as he shifted into third gear. He had been teasing his friend about it for a week. It *was* possible to fail your way through most of high school and still get into college.

"Well, I ain't gonna be no doctor," the passenger said. "But I don't wanna be no doctor neither."

"Why do you talk like that? You're no dummy. You don't have to talk like that."

"It's just easier, that's all. I know how to talk right when I have to. I was pretty good in class that time, wasn't I?" He puffed with pride.

"Yeah, you were. Even the girls were asking questions. I think Mrs. Matt liked your report better than mine."

"Oh, I dunno. You were pretty good, too. Those pictures you drew were terrific."

"I thought it would go better than it did. About half way through I was boring myself."

"Nah, you weren't boring. I always fall asleep just before lunch." He shot a playful punch at his friend. "How about this Shakespeare stuff? It must be easy for you."

"Well, yeah. I've been reading it since ninth grade. *Hamlet*'s not so easy, though."

"Christ, I never saw it before. I thought Shakespeare was for you geniuses. It's another freaking language! Hell, I failed Spanish four times."

"Then why did you take the course?"

"My old man forced me into it."

"How is old Archibald?"

"In shock. Also mad because he can't go to college with me. He tried to arrange my courses for me already, he called on the phone. They told him I had to do it. I can't wait to go, to get out from under him."

"I can't wait either, but not because of my parents. My mother's crying already, but she'd cry if I didn't go, so I guess it's better for her to cry because I am going. You aren't failing English, are you? You have to get out of high school before you get to go to college."

"Hell, no. I don't know what I'm doing when she throws those quotes at us, but I know the stories pretty good. It's too bad we can't read those things after they're translated into English. They're better than soap operas. I really got into that Yago guy. He was one villainous bastard. And clever. Boy, was he clever. I almost wished he got away with it."

"E-AH-GO. Not 'Yago.' He got away with too much as it was."

"Whatever. The big tough guy was pretty stupid, if you ask me."

"He wasn't stupid, he was too much in love and he didn't know anything about women. He could fight wars, but he knew nothing about human relationships."

"Love turned him into a pansy."

"Did we read the same play?"

"Hey, Mrs. Matt said that Shakespeare has lasted for centuries because there's so many ways to look at it. I happen to have my own way of looking at it."

"Pardon me. What do you think of Hamlet?"

"He's an even bigger pansy."

"He's a lot more complicated than that."

"Yeah, but it all boils down to one thing. He's queer."

"But he probably slept with Ophelia and he might subconsciously want his mother."

"So?"

"What do you mean, so?"

"So he's AC/DC. I still think he's queer! Besides, *queer* has more than one meaning."

"Pansy doesn't."

"Oh, yes, it does. You think about it."

"Did you drink beer for breakfast?"

"Gotcha goin', didn't I?"

The shiny red Volkswagen put-putted into the faculty parking lot. The driver maneuvered it into a space that wasn't a space, just an unassigned spot, half blacktop, half grass.

"Look at the glass all over this lot," the driver complained. "If my new tires are sliced, I'm going to sue."

"Sue who?" the passenger asked.

"I don't know. Somebody. Why do kids get away with being slobs?"

"You don't like beer, you think nobody should like beer."

"I do like beer, I don't like slobs. There's a difference and you know it. What the hell's with you today? You're awfully argumentative."

"Say what?"

"You're arguing a lot today."

"Not arguing. Practicing for college."

The driver of the shiny red Volkswagen didn't tell his friend what he was thinking. Some things cannot be crammed in at the end.

ORANGE

Gayle Fine dropped out of school and, it seemed, off the face of the earth on May 6th. Alyssa Matthews hardly noticed. The month of May was so pitted with distractions and disturbances and disruptions that she was in a frenzy trying to keep track of the students she had; she x-ed out Gayle Fine in a matter of seconds and wished the days remaining until the end could have been so easily dispensed with for everybody else.

Students were out of classes almost every day for one reason or another. Tennis, baseball, and golf pulled kids out of afternoon classes and teachers were advised to check lists in the appropriate class office to determine legally appropriate absentees; California Achievement Tests cut into class time for three days, as did advance placement exams; students still went to music lessons, released from academic courses to do so, as they did every other month; students still left during the day for doctor and dentist appointments.

In May assemblies ran wild; in May some students were in assemblies, screaming and catcalling, more than they were in class. Sophomores had an assembly, juniors had an assembly, seniors had four assemblies. Student elections were held in May, requiring more assemblies; students were excused from study halls to vote, and a small core were excused from classes to administer the proceedings.

The Junior Prom and the Senior Ball wiped out two Fridays in May; two fire drills in one day mangled a Thursday; and the Red Cross obliterated a Tuesday with a highly successful blood drive.

"It's certainly commendable that so many kids are interested in giving blood," Jean observed. "But why the hell do they have to do it during class time?" Many a teacher wondered how many adolescent humanitarians would show up on a Saturday or after school on a week day. But the blood drive made excellent press; frustrated teachers trying to wrap up the year's work and prepare for exams rated a far distant second to excellent press.

Some few students were academically inclined in May; they were in the minority, but they were the ones at whom teachers directed lessons.

May was also the popular time for panic. Panic can be highly constructive in November or February; unfortunately, "early panic" is a contradiction in terms. One evening in early May, Alyssa received a phone call at home from a concerned parent. The concerned parent wanted the lowdown on her daughter's failing grades. Daughter was a scholarship student. Teacher had sent form after form home and had never heard a thing. Teacher had talked to the student and offered her an exorbitant amount of time to make up work not completed because of absence. Liz Fan had missed two thirds of the first semester, was tutored, but did no work. Parents were notified again and again. In May Alyssa Matthews had to rehash all of it over the phone one evening after dinner. Mother was politely on the offense in May; Teacher was politely on the defense, as always.

In the regents classes there was little seriousness during review, but there was ample joking, playing, and sleeping. Vocabulary review prompted one student to ask the meaning of the word *immense*; once apprised of the meaning, the student quickly selected the word as a synonym for the vocabulary word *diminutive*. Another student selected *imperiled* for *prodigious*. Still another looked at *galore*, pronounced it *gory*, and thought it meant *hypersensitive*. Another thought *fragile* meant *expensive*. And so it went. After hearing the correct pronunciation of *hyperbole* umpteen times during the year, students were still saying *hyperbowl*. The teacher had a correction to the IE rule as she had taught it earlier in the year; newscasters were pronouncing *sheik* the way it was supposed to be pronounced, which threw it into the long A exception to the rule. But she never bothered to mention the change.

She sent out one truancy notice in May, something she hadn't done in months, because she couldn't help but see the cumulative darkening of skin on a student who hadn't been absent all winter, but was strangely ill on warm sunny afternoons in the middle of May.

637

Rosemary Cania Maio

Parents never responded to the request for validation, and the girl bronzed beautifully by Memorial Day.

Students left the building at all hours of the day, sometimes even before entering; little groups congregated on the grass, in the parking lots, and within the federally-funded campus area. No one sat in the gazebos for, alas, the gazebos had long since lost their charm. Too many winters had cracked their cherubs and demolished their foundations. The gazebos were scheduled for removal.

It seemed, however, that the future held additions for the faculty at Boesch-Conklyn. Or so it was assumed by teachers who found in their mailboxes what was called an In-Service Needs Assessment Survey. The lunch crew in the fourth floor faculty room had a good time getting disgusted at the absurdity of the questions. Responses were requested on a scale of one to five:

1-not at all 2-slightly 3-moderately 4-quite a lot 5-very much
And the questions were strictly hilarious:

1. Do you think it is important for general educators to receive training regarding the education of exceptional children?
2. Do you feel prepared to work with disabled children in the school setting?
3. Do you think your colleagues are well-prepared to provide education for the handicapped?

INDICATE THE DEGREE TO WHICH YOU WOULD LIKE IN-SERVICE TRAINING FOR EACH TOPIC LISTED BELOW.

4. Disabilities / Handicapping conditions
5. Handicapped students in the public schools
6. Law and education of exceptional children
7. Resources
8. Support services
9. Classroom management
10. Committee on the Handicapped - Role and responsibilities
11. Individualized / Adaptive instruction
12. Philosophy / attitudes
13. Mainstreaming / least restrictive environment
14. Individualized Educational Program (I.E.P.)
15. Student self-concept
16. Counseling students
17. Community-based services for the disabled

INDICATE THE DEGREE TO WHICH YOU WOULD BE LIKELY TO PARTICIPATE IN IN-SERVICE TRAINING IN EACH SITUATION

18. Training conducted on a voluntary basis, on your own time.
19. Training conducted during release time.
20. Training conducted on a non-credit basis.
21. Training conducted on a credit-granting basis.
22. Training conducted in a single session workshop format.
23. Training conducted in a multiple session format.
24. Training conducted by district personnel.
25. Training conducted by out-of-district personnel.

"Do they think we're morons?" Jean observed.

"Worse than that, they think we're bored," Alyssa observed further.

The women proceeded to fill out a single response sheet with an unbroken answer series of '1'. Then they wrote in TEACHERS WITH ENOUGH WORK TO DO on the name line and sent the sheet out to the appropriate bureaucrat.

Eventually, after the final tally, word would leak out to the public that teachers weren't interested in professional growth nor were they willing to engage in progressive activities on their own time; teachers were too complacent to learn something new.

In short, dedicated teachers were a thing of the past.

YELLOW

There it was, glistening in the sunlight, a temptation if there ever was one.

"I'm not asking him for the keys," said the driver of the shiny red Volkswagen. "He's got a memory like an elephant. Besides, I don't want to get in trouble. I did last time."

His friend persisted. "Look, pretty soon we won't ever see each other again."

"How do you know? Maybe some day you'll be a world-famous mechanic and I'll design a new kind of garage and we'll need each other."

"Nah, it doesn't happen that way. We gotta make hay while the sun shines, and it's shining today. C'mon, who cares anyway.

School's almost over. You're on the certified list, why should you worry? I'm the one who's squeaking through."

"I'm not asking, so forget it."

"You don't hafta ask, man. I've got a key if you've got the balls to use it. It's home in a drawer, let's go get it."

"You're crazy. How'd you get —?"

"It was easy. Your brother made two and I kept one. Let's go get it. Haywood will never know. His room's around the other side. We'll come right back, he'll never miss it."

"I'll think about it. Maybe later."

"Yeah, yeah, maybe later. Like the other night you got up the nerve to talk to those two broads after they left. Maybe later the sky will fall in, too. You gonna live the resta your life saying 'maybe later'?"

"You're crazy, you know? You want to steal a car and you're telling me I'm chicken."

"What? Steal? Never say steal! Are we planning to keep it? Course not! We'll have it back before he ever knows it's gone. Steal? I'm not that stupid. Look, you owe me another five. Remember? You said we'd hit a hundred before we graduated. Hey, man, I'll drive if you don't want to. I'm pretty good with a stick. How about it? We'll get ourselves something to remember when we're too old to do anything else but remember. What'll you have to remember about high school except that you were a good little boy?"

The driver looked at his friend, then started up the shiny red Volkswagen and headed out of the parking lot. His friend, elated beyond words, hooted and yelped his excitement.

The yellow Corvette sat waiting in the parking lot, glistening in the sunlight.

GREEN

The tree had been there in the field for over a century. Once during its early years it was attacked by morning glories, the vines twisting and turning around the sapling, choking off its growth. The farmer noticed what was happening and cleared the vines away to save the tree.

Another time disease consumed the leaves, stunted the branches, threatened imminent extinction. The farmer's grandson, who learned about such things, stripped the cancerous growth away, administered the proper medication, and saved the tree.

It grew in succeeding years to massive breadth and height. Trees nearby were uprooted during hurricanes, struck by lightning and diminished in size, and toppled by the ax; but not this tree.

This tree, once made healthy and strong through the efforts of Man, was spared disfigurement through the capricious mercies of Nature. This tree split the sky, its roots burrowed down to the center of the earth.

This tree stood eminent and immobile, stood lonely and awesome in the midst of the field no longer plowed, the tree and the field long since forgotten by Man and by Nature.

BLUE

Beth Whittsley's hands were shaking as she marked homeroom cards and wrote excuses. One of her students noticed and asked what was wrong. The teacher said, "The world's gone crazy," and kept on writing.

As soon as homeroom was over, the teacher raced down the hall because she had to tell somebody before it ate away too much of her insides. She found Alyssa Matthews smoking in the faculty room and she unloaded the whole story in a low, hysterical voice.

"I've got a kid who's failing, a senior; he's been failing right along and I've been sending reports home. His attendance has been erratic, but I've never been able to prove truancy. I sent notice after notice all semester and never heard from the parents. Last week the kid decided he wanted to pass the course because he found out that if he doesn't he can't graduate. I've been giving him chance after chance to make up the work and he hasn't done it. Two weeks ago I gave him another chance and he blew it again. He's handed me every feeble excuse you can imagine. Last week he couldn't take a test because he had to go home to get his gym clothes.

"I finally got fed up and told him it was too late to make up work from January, that I wouldn't accept anything, that he should have thought about graduating a little sooner. He's been in my room every day since then screaming that I have to give him another chance, that I can't stop him from graduating. He came in four times in one day to argue about it and I had had it with him, so I told him to stop harassing me because my mind was made up.

"I figured that I was within my rights, that there has to be a cut-off point somewhere, especially since he never made an effort to do any work and I documented every move he made and every move he didn't make all semester.

"But he wouldn't take no for an answer. He came in one night after school and started in on his whining that it wasn't fair, why was I so hard on him, why couldn't he get the same chances as everybody else. That blew my mind.

"When he saw that I wouldn't budge, he started to get nasty; I was a lousy teacher anyway, why did I have the power to ruin his life, his parents would see to it that I lost my job. Well, I blew sky high. He was screaming, I was screaming, and I finally ordered him to get out and never come back. As if I had the authority. His parting words were: You can lick my ass, bitch.

"He upset me so badly that I spent two sleepless nights trying to decide what to do. Two days ago I saw Lou Broglio about it. He went wild and told me to write it up for disciplinary action. I thought that might be useless this late in the year, but he informed me that I should put my side of the story in writing in case the parents tried to brand me incompetent so the kid could graduate. That was enough to scare the life out of me, so I wrote it up.

"This morning Harry called me in because the parents are incensed, the parents are getting a lawyer; they advised me to get a lawyer. They want a hearing! They want to put me on trial! Me! They want me to take a lie detector test! Can you believe it? They're out to prove that I was after their son. My integrity is suspect.

"I told Harry that they can all go to hell, I'm not submitting to any lie detector test and I'm not showing up at any hearing. They can get all the lawyers they want. But I'm scared, Matt, scared out of my mind because these people have the power and the connections to stick it to me good."

Until now Alyssa thought she was hearing another typical senior-in-May horror tale, but she was beginning to sense a special significance.

"Who is this kid?" she asked.

Beth shuddered. "Curt Holbert. Ever hear of him? He's taking double English this semester. That was another one of his excuses for not doing any work."

"So it finally caught up to him," Alyssa said. Then she went on to explain what she meant, all the while thinking that she might very well be in Beth's shoes if Curt Holbert had taken her course second semester instead of first, all the while feeling the twitch under her left eye worsen.

INDIGO

"This is the way to travel, man! Some day I'm gonna own a whole fleet of these mothers! I'll specialize in Corvettes!" The young man settled back in the seat.

The yellow Corvette contradicted its low profile as it moved sleekly along city streets, stopped for lights, and slowed for children; it was, already in its journey (indeed, from the very first twisting of the key), conspicuous and daring.

"Put your seatbelt on," the driver said to the passenger. "We'll be out of the city soon. Then I'll open her up and we have to get back. I still don't like this."

The passenger shifted in the seat, but made no effort to fasten his seatbelt. "Don't worry so damn much!" he told his friend. "We're only missing an assembly. I was planning to skip out anyway. Who cares about the Air Force Band? As long as we're back for third period, we got nothing to worry about."

"I'm going to throw this key out as soon as we get back."

"Go right ahead. I got no use for it. Hey, you gonna be bitchy for this whole ride?"

The driver didn't answer. He was not comfortable at all. He did not know exactly why he had given in to such a lamebrained scheme. But he had gone this far, he would see it through and be done with it. Chances were excellent that Haywood would never know.

Unless he decided to go out for breakfast. Highly unlikely.

But what if he was called out for some reason? Maybe he had a sick mother who was dying. What if she died this morning and he had to leave?

What if some kid got sick and had to be rushed to the hospital and Haywood just happened to be in the hall and he offered to — No, no, no. Highly unlikely.

Everything would be all right. Haywood would never know.

What if somebody saw the car being driven back into the parking lot in the middle of the morning, what if that somebody was another teacher who reported Haywood for being out of the building?

What if another car took the parking space! Dear God, what then? What—? Oh, stop it, stop making up stories. Relax and drive. Relax and stop worrying. This is supposed to be a joyride, remember?

The driver headed the bright yellow Corvette toward the outskirts of the city, toward the road rarely traveled. He hardly knew how fast he was increasing speed because his mind was focused on the end

643

of the journey, the parking lot. He saw the bright yellow Corvette making the turn onto the street leading to the parking lot and his foot pushed to 65; he saw the bright yellow Corvette traveling down the street to the parking lot and his foot pushed to 75; he saw the bright yellow Corvette entering the parking lot and his foot pushed to 85; he saw the bright yellow Corvette safely parked, glistening in the sun in the parking lot, and his foot pushed to 95.

Suddenly he was totally aware that the bright yellow Corvette was under him and around him. Then he heard the siren. "Holy shit!" he yelled to his friend above the wind noise. "Look behind us!"

The passenger did. "It's the cops, all right," he yelled. "No! Wait! It's not the cops, it's the fucking State!" He shot a look of panic at his friend. "Jesus Christ! We stole this car! They're gonna say we stole this car!"

The driver felt a fear unlike any he had ever known. This was not like cutting class and getting caught; this was not like failing a test or even a whole course; this was not kid stuff. This was the big leagues.

How would he ever explain this? He saw himself calling home for bail; he saw himself standing before the judge. He saw his mother's face. And he pushed down on the accelerator.

He was sure he could do it. A Corvette had to have the power to outrun a State Police car. He watched the road as best he could in between furtive glances at the rearview mirror.

The passenger watched the needle move. 100. 110. 115. 125. His eyes glazed with fear, he swiveled to look back. "We're losing him!" he screamed. "We're losing him! Slow down! For Christ's sake, slow d—!"

The State trooper was once again amazed at the absurdity of a high speed chase. He always got his man, no matter what kind of car he was driving. For one thing, there was the license plate; for another, sooner or later the chase would end, it couldn't go on forever. Very few drivers could outmaneuver him, and he was never very discouraged by speed. Once the car was within his sight, he simply drove fast enough within reasonable distance to keep the car within his sight.

How could he miss on this one? Where did the driver think he was going? As a matter of fact, the trooper slowed on purpose to get the driver to feel a false sense of success so that he, too, would slow down. It was getting a little out of hand, but those Corvettes were notorious for it. The trooper sincerely believed that all cars should somehow be prohibited from reaching speeds beyond 70. That would solve a multitude of problems and still allow speed traps. That way the highways would be safer and money could still be made from speeding tickets. If he really had his way, cars would be unable to travel faster than 55, but that was neither practical nor profitable.

He paced himself behind the yellow Corvette and waited. He slowed to 80, shut off his siren, and waited. Sooner or later the car would have to pull over to the side or reach some point in the road when the road would take over. Where the hell did the driver think he was going? Sooner or later he would have to realize that he wasn't James Bond, that his car wasn't equipped to emit an oil slick or to revolve a machine gun, that the trooper wouldn't disappear in a puff of smoke. Did he really think he could play the chameleon in a bright yellow Corvette?

The road started to curve slightly; it was a broad curve, not remotely related to a hairpin; the curve required a miniscule turning of the wheel, then a steady consistency. The trooper knew the curve well, as he knew the road, every bump, every indentation, every shadow. The road was straight for miles, then it ribboned into a wide, innocuous curve, not a dangerous curve, for it was not an inherently dangerous road, as some roads are.

In a split second the trooper saw the yellow Corvette approach the beginning of the curve, then, with a graceful unbroken surge, continue along the path it was following, though the path was no longer there. When it hit the field, it flew into the air like a giant wingless yellow bird, violating unfamiliar space with ease, as if some primeval force had rendered it powerless, had somehow taken control from below and lifted it, body and soul, to the heavens.

The trooper skidded to a stop as the airbound Corvette made contact with the tree in the field. He saw the impact; the top of the car was severed from the chassis, the chassis squeezed together accordian-style. Something flew out the passenger door, then the car dropped to the ground and burst into flames.

The trooper immediately called for emergency equipment, then ran across the field, but not with much hope for the driver. The car was engulfed in flames and the driver was in it. But the passenger had been thrown clear, the trooper was sure of it. He ran to within sight of the body, then stopped. He covered his face with his hands, took a few deep breaths, and turned away. There, next to the severed top of the car, was a young man's head. The body was a few feet away.

Though he had seen his share of grisly accidents, the trooper wasn't hardened to it. He knew he'd never be. He walked slowly back to the patrol car because his legs felt rubbery; he stopped twice along the way to vomit in the field. As he waited for help to arrive, he wondered how long it would be before he could wipe this one from his mind.

VIOLET

"That's impossible," Jason Haywood said, "my car is in the parking lot. There's been a mistake."

Bob McGuinness told him not to argue and to get himself to the office right away. When Jason saw the trooper, he realized the seriousness of the charge.

Jason Haywood had a lot of explaining to do. There was no doubt about the fact that the car had been stolen, that is, that he hadn't given permission for its use.

The trooper had names. One was found on a sheet of paper in the shirt pocket of the boy who had been decapitated; his wallet verified the identification. The other name was in a book, a paperback edition of *Hamlet*, that had been thrown clear of the car upon impact. McGuinness had checked that one out; the boy was nowhere to be found in the building.

Jason Haywood verified the second name; the two boys were known friends, they had used his car earlier in the year with his permission. But not today, not today! Jason Haywood wept. If they had only seen him before they took the car, he never would have let them go. He had driven the car in for one reason: he had an appointment at a garage after school. The car wasn't running right, he wanted it looked at. Something was wrong with the steering wheel, the steering wheel had developed a dangerous tendency to lock into position.

Jason Haywood sat in the office until he got hold of himself, then he asked for a sub; there was no way he could face a class.

Bob McGuinness made a fast phone call. "Get back right away," he told Harry Bassard. "The roof just caved in."

The trooper left the school with the information he needed to notify next-of-kin. It was not his favorite duty. The first name sent him to insurance offices in an old building on the outskirts of the city. The boy's father was alone in the office; he turned into a raging maniac when he heard of his son's death. He demanded details: Who was driving? Whose car was it? When did the accident happen? Where did it happen?

When the trooper left, the man was still screaming, "Somebody's going to pay for this! There's something wrong here! My boy should not be dead! Somebody's responsible, I tell you!"

The trooper avoided telling the man about the condition of the body. He would find that out soon enough and someone else could listen to his bellowing. The trooper wondered if the man was incapable of sorrow, if he reacted to everything with anger. Some people were like that, the trooper knew. He had seen every conceivable reaction, ranging from a catatonic trance to an immediate suicide attempt. Some people hid their anguish with anger, some people hid their anger with anguish. He had come to expect anything as initial reaction. Archibald Brissonson's initial reaction was not a shock to him at all.

When he rang the doorbell of the modest home just a few blocks from the school, the trooper was once again expecting anything. When the woman opened the door, a look of panic crossed her face. The trooper spoke quickly after she invited him into the house, after he was sure she was the person he had to see. He said: "I'm sorry to inform you that your son Brian was in a car accident this morning. He's dead, Mrs. Conneally."

Helen Conneally's head started to shake violently. "No," she said firmly. "No. No. No. Someone else. It was someone else. Not my Brian. My Brian is graduating, he's going to college, he's making something of himself. In fact he's due home soon. He always comes home right after school, even now when he's old enough to do what he wants. He knows I worry. When he was a child he always let me know where he was because he didn't want me to worry. You wait, you wait right here and you'll see, he'll be here soon, he'll be driving up the driveway in his red Volkswagen. You'll see, you'll see you're wrong. Somebody else. Too bad, too bad somebody had to die, but not my Brian,—"

"Please, Mrs. Conneally, we're sure." How could he tell her now that dental records would have to be used for the final verification, that her son's body had been burned beyond recognition?

"No!" she screamed. "I said NO! You're lying! You're lying! You have to be!" She started to cry and to whimper, her hands covered her face, her head never stopped moving back and forth, back and forth. Then she sank to the floor.

The trooper had seen massive grief before, but it never failed to move him. He helped the woman to her feet and into a chair, then went to find a neighbor to stay with her.

647

Helen Conneally sat and sobbed. Through her tears she saw the open closet door in the hallway. Hanging in the closet was the graduation robe she had pressed that morning.

"It's all right, Ma. I know you hate to iron. I can wear it with a few creases in it," Brian had said.

"Not on your life," she told him. "I'll get it ready early. You graduate from high school only once you know!"

He was her second-born, her middle child, the one who was supposed to feel left out, neglected. Never, never had he felt neglected, she saw to that; always she made sure he felt as loved as the other two.

She walked in a trance to the hall closet. She tore the robe from the hanger and clutched it to her bosom in a ferocious embrace. From across the street, the trooper heard Helen Conneally screaming her son's name.

Kaleidoscope

The next day the evening paper devoted most of the second page to the accident. Only a few lucrative ads and two other less sensational accident reports shared space with the tragic deaths of Brian Conneally and Joe Brissonson. The two seniors received more coverage in death than they would have had they lived to graduate. A large picture showed the wrecked, charred, almost non-existent car. One article gave the who, what, where, and when in minute detail.

Jason Haywood did not escape scrutiny. He was placed in an awkward enough position. How could he disclaim responsibility for the tragedy without maligning the character of the dead? But at least he had truth on his side. Yes, he said, the boys had driven the car before with my permission, but no, not this time, this time they took the car without my permission.

Are you saying that they stole the car, Mr. Haywood?

I'm saying that they took it without my knowing about it.

How could that be, Mr. Haywood? Can the car be started without a key? And what about the key found melted into the ignition?

I don't know where they got that key. I still have my own keys.

Really, Mr. Haywood? You're not lying, are you, to protect yourself? Those poor boys are dead, they can't defend themselves, now can they? Isn't it easy for you to brand them as thieves, easier than taking the blame for their deaths? What about the key, Mr. Haywood, what about the key?

Jason Haywood went to a great deal of trouble to ready witnesses to testify in his behalf. He was with people every minute that morning and if he had to, he could summon those people to testify that he never gave up his car keys. Of course, a good attorney would shoot holes in the attempt easily enough, but Jason Haywood was feeling pretty desperate.

Under the large picture and the who-what-where-and-when article, there was another headline which read:

PARENTS CHARGE SCHOOL WITH NEGLIGENCE
Demand Full Investigation Into Deaths

There was a thirst for the fifth 'W.' Archibald Brissonson said, "I want to know who's responsible for the mutilation of my boy. He wasn't a thief and no one's going to call him a thief as long as I'm

649

alive. I'm suing the parents of the driver, I'm suing that Haywood creep, and I'm suing the school district. Somebody's at fault and I damned well want to know who."

Helen Conneally and her husband weren't into lawsuits yet. But the woman was hysterical in her quest to know why it happened. Especially since it never should have happened. Brian should have been in school at 9:30 in the morning. He should have been safe in a classroom. Why wasn't he? Hadn't she gone to a great deal of trouble in the fall to notify the school that she wanted to know whenever he was absent? Where was he supposed to be at 9:30 in the morning and why wasn't he there? Why? Why? Why? Helen Conneally wanted to know why she was suffering the agony of a closed casket, the misery of looking at a picture, his graduation picture, propped on top of the box holding what little was left of him. Helen Conneally would scream in her sleep for the rest of her life, and she wanted to know why.

"Why do they print pictures of only the most horrific accidents?" Jean asked no one in particular the next morning.

"To scare people?" Bonnie offered. "Maybe they think that showing the gruesome details will prevent future accidents."

"Nothing prevented this one," Alyssa added.

"I think it sells papers," Jean concluded. "I think people actually enjoy seeing a mutilated car because they can say 'how terrible, how terrible' and feel good that it happened to someone else. There's so much tragedy in the papers every day that we've become immune to it. As long as it happens to somebody else."

"Poor Jason," Bonnie said. "I wouldn't want to be in his shoes right now."

"Poor us," Jean corrected. "Jason's problems are small compared to what somebody else in this place is going to have to contend with. Those boys were supposed to be somewhere. I hope whoever was responsible for their attendance in the morning has a large collection of notices."

Joyce turned pale. "Thank God I didn't know either one of them. I never keep copies of the notices I send home. It's just more paper to keep track of. I always figured that the copies in the guidance offices were enough."

"Start saving your copies," Jean advised. "I wouldn't want to have to depend on someone else's files if my job were at stake."

"Do you think it's that serious?" Bonnie asked.

Jean replied: "Of course it is. After last night's paper, every teacher hater within fifty miles will be screaming for blood. Teacher's blood. Somebody was negligent, with the Conneally boy anyway. When I read that his mother called the school for daily attendance reports, I had a vision of somebody hanging from the nearest tree. It all depends on what Harry turns up. If the kid was truant for the first time the day he died, then who can be blamed? But if it was an ongoing thing and the parents were never notified, somebody is in one hell of a lot of trouble. Technically, the same is true with the Brissonson boy. His father wants somebody on the rack and that's all there is to it."

"I had Joe Brissonson last semester," Bonnie said. I liked the kid a lot, but believe me, he was no angel. He slipped in and out of here all the time. He certainly didn't deserve to die for truancy, but I can't see how they can pin the blame for his death on the school."

"Not the school," Jean corrected. "The school will come out of this smelling like a rose. Some teacher is going to get it, but good."

"I had both of them third period," Alyssa said softly, "and I don't know what's worse, the sense of loss that I feel or the terror of knowing that if they died during third period, I'd have to whip up a defense. I'm damned tired of being a truant officer."

"We all are," Bonnie said. "Was there ever a time when it wasn't part of the job?"

"There was a time when it wasn't three fourths of the job, if that's what you mean," Alyssa answered.

There was a sharp undercurrent of fear in each of the faculty rooms. Some teachers were able to eliminate themselves from the investigation easily enough by virtue of the fact that they had classes first and second periods and neither of the boys were enrolled in those classes. The teachers who worried were the ones who had the boys in classes, and the ones who were assigned to study halls first and second periods.

Allen Hawkens found his office door unlocked the morning after the press coverage of the accident. Bassard was waiting for him.

"Cancel your appointments for this morning," Harry said. "We've got an investigation to conduct. The pressure is on, Hawk. I had phone calls until midnight last night."

"I don't like it, Harry. It's a witch hunt. Why aren't they satisfied with Jason? He's suffering enough. He was in here crying yesterday. He does feel responsible, though he swears he never gave them a key. It doesn't make sense that he would have, since he knew the car wasn't safe. Isn't it bad enough that those two kids are dead? Why do we have to dig up dirt to bury somebody else?"

651

"We've got no choice," Harry said. "We can hardly refuse to investigate, can we? The public pays our salaries. This is a public institution. Can we refuse to do what the public requests?"

"When was the last time the public was in here offering some support, Harry? The public is only interested in what it can get out of us, in what we owe, in what we aren't doing right."

"That's why we always have to emphasize the positive, the good we're doing, our accomplishments. When something like this happens we've got to appease quickly and start all over again, because the public forgets the positive in an instant."

"How far is this going to go?"

"That depends on what you find. I'd like to be able to tell these people that no one here was irresponsible, that those boys died because they made a fatal mistake."

"And what if I find out otherwise?"

"Then we have to release the truth."

"I don't like it, Harry."

"The knife is twisting in my gut too, Hawk. I'd like to protect my people above all costs, but I can't in a situation like this. I'm damned proud of most of this staff. But I have to do things that I don't like and resign myself to the fact that somebody's going to hate me for it. We've got no choice in this, Hawk. If we don't come up with something, Brissonson will be in here with a fleet of lawyers and the Conneallys will spread their sorrow so thick it'll run all the way to Albany. Mrs. Conneally is the one who has the real justification for an investigation. Can you blame her for wanting to know why?"

"Who can explain death, Harry? Will her son be resurrected if she knows why?"

"Would you care to go to the media with that rationale?"

"How soon do you want names?"

"As soon as you have something. It shouldn't take long."

Hawkens pointed to two folders on his desk. "I pulled them as soon as I heard what happened."

"Have you checked them out yet?"

"No. I thought about putting a match to them on the way in this morning. But that wouldn't help any, would it?"

Bassard rose to leave. "Then you'd have to take the rap for not keeping accurate records."

"You'd let that happen too, wouldn't you, Harry?"

"What goddam choice do I have?" Bassard said in anger. "I'm dispensable too, you know. We can all be replaced. Now get to it and bring me facts. I want facts, in writing with signatures. I want proof, real proof, and plenty of it. This is no time to try to protect anybody's hide."

"Anybody's, Harry? Odd you should say that."

"Self-preservation is man's strongest instinct."

"You can say that about any animal."

"I can do without philosophy right now."

"Right now you want facts. Okay, Harry, I'll dig up your facts. That's part of my job, following orders and digging up facts. As soon as I know, you'll know."

Bassard left the office. Allen Hawkens stared at the two folders on his desk.

Detachment, the wise man said, learn detachment.

Chances were slim that no one could be held accountable for the whereabouts of the two dead seniors. Especially the Conneally boy. Allen Hawkens hoped he would find proof that would clear the teachers responsible for his attendance.

The counselor realized that what was in the two folders might destroy at least one, and possibly more than one, teacher. Charges of negligence, dereliction of duty, irresponsibility, even insubordination could be leveled against anyone who failed to notify Helen Conneally of her son's absence from class after she called to request reports. That was the kicker. The woman was a concerned, caring parent. The counselor knew he had notified all the boy's teachers of the mother's request. Thank God he had kept all the copies of those notices.

What was in those folders? Who might be thrown on the sacrificial pyre? Who might be displayed in the market place, the cynosure of all eyes, wearing the Scarlet Letter? Who?

Allen Hawkens wondered as he began to sift through scores of pieces of paper, paper of varying size and shape and color. As he started to piece the information together, he fought back the chilling possibility that the search might even lead him to himself. Under those circumstances, detachment was difficult. Practically impossible.

Jason Haywood ran into the building and through the halls; he was breathless when he waved to Brenda and bounded into Bassard's office.

Harry swiveled around in his chair to see Jason swing his arms into the air, throw back his head, and announce joyfully, "I'm off the hook! Thank God, I'm off the hook!"

"What do you mean?" Harry asked cautiously.

"Mrs. Conneally called me last night. Her son, her other son, Bernie, distinctly remembers making two keys for my car last fall. I asked Brian to do it for me. Bernie also distinctly remembers that Joe Brissonson pocketed both keys. From the way Mrs. Conneally was talking, she never liked Joe Brissonson much and told Brian to stay away from him. Too bad Brian didn't listen. She thinks Joe kept one key. She can't imagine Brian doing it."

"How can you prove that?"

"Brian gave me one new key, or Joe did. I never saw two new keys."

"But that's still your word against — whose?"

"Look Harry, it's enough for Mrs. Conneally. She believed me when I told her I got one key from the boys that day. I wish I could go back and do it over. I never should have sent them out."

"It was a stupid move," Harry said dryly. "What does Brissonson say about this new theory?"

"I don't know and I don't care."

"He's not going to accept any of it, especially since it paints his son as the villain. You've got to be able to prove it, Jay."

"Well, maybe I can prove it. Paul Haust and Joe Axelrod were in the faculty room with me when the boys brought the car back. I was pretty angry because they kept the car out so long. Paul and Joe knew that I had only one extra key. The boys returned my key ring and one unattached key. I put the unattached key in my wallet. I wanted it to begin with for my other set of keys, the ones to my Chevy. I wanted two full sets as a matter of convenience. I explained all that to Paul and Joe and they said I was worse than a woman for wanting to be organized. So I have two witnesses that I received one new key and Bernie Conneally knows there were two. That leaves one unaccounted for. And, Harry, I don't give a damn which of those kids kept it and used it two days ago. I only know that one of them did and it's been hell ever since for a lot of people."

"I guess you're off the hook, then. But not totally, Jay, not completely."

"I don't know what you mean."

"Oh yes you do. I've spoken to you a number of times about it and you never wanted to listen. Stop trying to be pals with your students. You may think it's all right for them to call you by your first name, but such familiarity makes kids think they have special privileges, that they can take liberties. Would those two boys be dead today if you hadn't allowed them to drive that car to begin with? Are you really off the hook, Jason?"

"Legally, I suppose I am. That's what I'm so thankful for. Other than that, I know what I've let happen. Not intentionally, certainly not

654

intentionally. I'm an optimist, always have been. I never think that the worst will happen. I guess I've learned my lesson. Deep inside I feel responsible for those two kids, not that I would have done anything different at the time. I didn't think there was any harm in letting two kids enjoy a ride in a Corvette. How could I have known that they would die because of it? I'm sorry it turned out the way it did, and I'll live with some guilt for the rest of my life. But my wanting to be friends with my students wasn't the only factor in that accident and you know it. What's wrong, Harry? Have I disappointed you? Were you counting on me to be the scapegoat? Are you desperate to pin the blame on anybody because the heat's on? Well, forget me. You'll have to find somebody else to throw to the dogs. That's what you need right about now, isn't it? A piece of meat to throw to the dogs?" Jason didn't wait for an answer. He stormed out of the office, disgusted with the whole sorry affair.

Harry Bassard was disgusted too. He hadn't thought of it that way, a piece of meat. But he supposed that was exactly what he was doing: sitting there, waiting for Hawkens to deliver a choice cut on a silver platter to throw to the hounds. It was disgusting. He hated it, every bit of it. But he had no choice, he simply had no other alternatives.

Brenda walked in and left the morning edition of the newspaper on his desk. "This time we made the front page," she said. "Someday I'd like to see scholarship winners on the front page."

"Hold all my calls this morning," Harry directed. "Tell them I'm busy with the investigation or in conference or anything you like."

"May I say that you left town?"

"You may not," Harry growled.

Brenda left quickly, aware of the consequences when he growled, when he wasn't in the mood to be pleasant. He looked at the front page.

BOARD SUPPORTS INVESTIGATION INTO DEATHS

The article included statements from the superintendent, the principal, and board members, who promised a crackdown on truancy, stricter attendance procedures, and a new district-wide policy to coordinate rules and regulations in all the schools.

Curt Holbert, Sr., said: "Parents like Helen Conneally should not be afraid to send their children to school, afraid that they will not be notified of absence. Youngsters today will try to get away with anything if they know it's possible. It's the school's responsibility to set a standard for behavior and to police its ranks to insure consistent enforcement of regulations. The climate set within the school is the single most important factor in keeping students interested in attending classes. Secondly, of course, we need a strict system of disciplinary controls to discourage students who insist on cutting class. The Board is presently working with building principals to establish a comprehensive code for attendance in all the schools. The tragedy that occurred this week will not happen again."

You bastard, Harry thought, you silver-tongued lying bastard. I wish I had a recording of what you told me last night: *Wrap it up fast, Harry, you've got 24 hours to quiet this down. I don't want a riot at next week's Board meeting.* Attendance code. We can't enforce the one we've got and the one we've got was updated last year.

There were two more articles on the front page related to the accident. One was headlined: FATHER DEMANDS JUSTICE; the other: NEW EVIDENCE CLEARS TEACHER. Harry skimmed both, then saw another smaller article underneath: FATHERS FIGHT IN FUNERAL HOME. The story must have been picked up late, or, Harry was certain, the bit of sensationalism would have been given priority over the rest. According to the write-up, a bitter feud had arisen over which dead boy had stolen the car, a violent argument that lead to a fist fight.

The principal sat alone in his office and waited. He looked at the clock. Another hour, maybe, and it would be resolved. The hook was empty and waiting. Like it or not, Harry Bassard had to face the possibility of hanging somebody on it.

Alyssa Matthews was worried sick. She didn't discuss her fears in the faculty room because she knew if she heard her own voice say the words she would start believing in possibilities. There were possibilities, of course. She had both students in class. What terror she experienced when she first heard about the accident. Then, when she recognized the names, her mind went into trauma so great that every nerve in her body became agitated, her head started to pound, her pulse quickened, and she started gasping for air.

While she attempted to feign control in the faculty room with her reasoning that the boys hadn't died during third period, therefore she was free and clear, she knew that her reasoning was flimsy. Her contention that she didn't have to "whip up a defense" was sheer bravado. She had already done exactly that. Only it was no defense. Not with Joe Brissonson, anyway. Brian Conneally had missed class only once, and she had a copy of the notice she sent home. She was not negligent with his attendance. But Joe Brissonson was another matter. She had wondered about the legality of his absence slips more than once. But she never questioned him about them, she never checked with his homeroom teacher or his other classroom teachers to figure out if he was cutting class or not. And there were plenty of empty chevrons in her attendance book after Joe Brissonson's name, plenty of times when he was absent and she never saw an excuse.

But that was true for a large number of the students in her classes. She absolutely could not check out every single absence every single day. Not one teacher in the whole school could do that.

The current crisis, however, was having a profound effect on every teacher in the school. Teaching was indeed secondary after accurate attendance records and an extensive filing system for copies of everything, but everything, in writing. Teachers promised themselves that, in the future, first things would be handled first.

And so, because she had stopped sending out forms after she became fed up with it second semester, Alyssa Matthews was among the small number of teachers experiencing trauma at the word 'investigation.' Then, of course, there was the other thing. At least she could show attendance records for her classes. The other thing was something else. When she thought about that, she went into hysteria.

Allen Hawkens compiled information on the Brissonson boy first. The folder was bulging. The kid spent more time out of school than in since ninth grade. But poor attendance seemed to be his only transgression. He was disciplined for truancy again and again, but never had he been involved in any other kind of trouble. As far as Hawkens could see, enough reports had been sent home to deter any attempts by the father to successfully carry out a lawsuit against the district or anyone at the school. Joe Brissonson's history of truancy was well-documented. Reports were sent out by his first and second period teachers as recently as four days before the accident. If Archibald Brissonson claimed he had never seen any notices of alleged truancy, the school could beat him with sheer volume.

Nevertheless, Hawkens now wished he had had the foresight to send notices out by registered mail for chronic truants. Maybe the Board would be interested in instituting that procedure in spite of the cost. Of course, that would put counselors in the position of being responsible for determining who was chronic and who was not. That would make counselors more accountable for mistakes, oversights, and inaccuracies. Thanks, but no thanks. Hawkens decided to keep his suggestion to himself.

Brenda knocked, then opened the door just a crack. "Mr. Holbert is on the phone," she said with a grimace. "I can't get rid of him. He called three times and he insists on talking to you. What can I do, short of hanging up on him?"

"Put him through, I suppose," Harry grumbled. He waited for Brenda to return to her desk, lifted the phone receiver, pushed a button, and heard the raspy voice that never failed to irritate him.

"Anything yet, Harry?"

"No, Curt, nothing. Nothing yet. I told you I'd let you know as soon as I know. Please keep in mind that there's every possibility we're blameless here."

"What do you mean, Harry? Brissonson's out for blood and the Conneallys want an explanation. Are you telling me you're fucking up this investigation? If you are, I'll handle it personally and you can be damn sure it will be all over by the end of the day."

"Calm down, Curt. The Conneallys will get their explanation, but I can't promise blood for Brissonson. I should know something soon. I'll call you back."

"Remember, Harry, immediate suspension. I contacted the rest of the Board this morning and the feeling was unanimous. I want this thing laid to rest in tonight's paper. We'll worry about formal charges and hearings later. Maybe we can negotiate a resignation. That would be a cheap way out for the district, less bad publicity for the teacher. What do you think, Harry? Of course, if we have to, we'll follow through with the hearings. But it seems to me that whoever is guilty will want to avoid hearings. Incompetence is incompetence. Negligence is negligence."

"Right, Curt," Harry said mechanically. "But perhaps no one was incompetent and no one was negligent."

"If I find out you're protecting somebody's ass, Harry, you'll be faced with suspension too. This is too serious to play around with. I'm warning you, don't try it. By the way, I'm waiting for that waiver for my son's graduation. Send it to my office. I'll get it signed in executive session next week. And send me every copy of that damned broad's lies too. She had a lot of nerve accusing my son. I still want to go after her."

"You won't, though, will you, Curt? Remember, that's part of the deal. You'll leave Beth Whittsley alone."

"You may think she's God's gift to education, Harry, but you don't know the stories my son's told me about her."

"You'll forget you ever heard her name, Curt. Is that clear?"

"Are you threatening me, Harry?"

"I wouldn't be so foolish. I just want to be sure you'll keep your word."

"My word is sacred. I never go back on my word. But I wouldn't be disappointed if she turns out to be the one we're looking for. Has that occurred to you, Harry? Kill two birds with one stone. Nice and convenient."

"You may not get any birds at all."

"If that's the case, I want details. Whatever the case, I want details."

"You'll get details as soon as I know details. I'll call you back."

"Okay, Harry, just call the superintendent. I'm in his office. You can tell us both at the same time."

Rumors were flying like shrapnel. By the end of first period, various stories were circulating through the halls, in and out of faculty rooms, and in the general vicinity of the offices. Secretaries were whispering among themselves, teachers were speculating, and students were avoiding instruction by initiating discussion on the accident and its aftermath.

One story claimed that a coach had already been indicted, another that the two boys had been involved in homosexual liaisons with Haywood, a new twist that satisfied those bored with the three-day-old drama. Still another story claimed that Harry blew up in a fit of rage because somehow it was proven that he was responsible.

The truth of the matter was that by the end of first period, Allen Hawkens was still taking notes and making copies of pieces of paper. By the end of first period he knew that one teacher was in trouble, unless that one teacher could come up with her own evidence to prove otherwise.

Brian Conneally was supposed to be in study hall second period. He had been signed in by the teacher in question, but there was no indication that notices of absence had ever been sent home. That was odd because Brian had been absent during the semester as evidenced in notices sent by his classroom teachers.

Hawkens gathered up what he had, walked to Bassard's office, closed the door after he entered, and started with Joe Brissonson; then he began the much easier second history. "Conneally was clean as a whistle," he told Harry. "Never truant, never disciplined for any infraction of the rules. He was a model student. Except, of course, for the forged excuse last fall."

"The one he tried to pass off to Joe Axelrod?"

"You already know about it?"

"Joe brought in a summary of his records on the boy this morning. He wanted to be sure he was cleared."

"Even Joe's running scared on this one. What would you have done if Joe screwed up, Harry?"

"Stop quizzing me and get on with it."

"Well, it's really very simple. Brian Conneally was supposed to be in study hall second period. I have no way of knowing if he was all semester or not. I suggest that you question the teacher who signed him in."

"Why was he signed in?"

"He had a schedule change. He was going to take a course with Jim Cote second period. After Jim left, there was no course, so I sent Brian to study hall."

"Which one?"

"Study Hall A. Bonnie Mason signed him in. There's the copy of the add slip. You'll have to talk to her about attendance records. And, Harry, there's a big chunk of irony in this."

"What's that?"

"Brian was in Study Hall A first semester. He made a big deal out of telling me he wanted me to send him back to the teacher he had then. You can see who it was on the add slip. Bonnie crossed out the name and wrote in her own."

Bassard looked at the add slip and cursed when he saw the teacher Hawkens originally sent Brian Conneally to.

It was Erica Vetterly.

"Exams are a few weeks away, people! Please stop talking! All of you must have something to study."

Alyssa waited a few seconds to give them an opportunity to settle down. When they didn't, she continued in the monotone that she had developed months ago to keep herself from erupting again. She found she could tolerate second period if she used the monotone, shut her eyes and ears to some of the shenanigans, and avoided watching the clock. It was only forty minutes out of the entire day. If she kept busy with her own work and ignored the irritation she felt, the time passed quickly.

"Stop talking and get to work. That goes for everyone. Angela, shut your mouth or I'll move you to the other side of the Earth. Greg, I just gave you an assignment, get started on it!"

The teacher ignored the dirty looks and began grading the set of review sheets she had carried with her. When the phone rang, she jumped. She cast a look at Bonnie, who was also visibly startled by the noise.

Both women were thinking the same thing.

Alyssa was aware that the study hall began to liven up as she walked to the stairs. Any interruption whatsoever caused the talking to start again. Bonnie issued a firm "Stop talking!" and Alyssa climbed the stairs. Every step was torture.

The phone was no longer covered with the old sweater that once muffled its call to attention. Now when it rang, the sound reverberated off the walls and ceiling. It kept ringing every few seconds while Alyssa made her way to it. The sound threatened to split her head apart.

She lifted the receiver, took the message, and felt the color drain from her face. Her legs weakened and she closed her eyes to stop the room from swirling around her.

She headed back down the stairs, and when she faced Bonnie, she could hardly speak the words: "Harry wants to see you. And your study hall attendance records."

Bonnie stiffened. "Why?"

"I don't know. Brenda didn't say."

Bonnie panicked. "We don't have attendance records, Matt."

"I know," Alyssa said. "I know."

"Nobody's bothered us for records all semester. Why does he want records now?"

Alyssa didn't answer. She didn't have to. Bonnie already knew. They both already knew. What neither could imagine was how, how could it have happened?

Harry stared at Bonnie in disbelief. "What the hell happened to you?"

"I was walking around on my knees in the dark and I connected with a doorknob."

"You're right. It's none of my business. It must hurt like hell, though."

"It does, Harry. Why did you want to see me?"

"Well, you'll have to go back for your records. I told Brenda — didn't she tell you to—"

"There aren't any records."

"Don't tell me that, Bonnie. Please don't tell me that."

"I'm telling you what most study hall teachers would tell you. You know what study halls are like. Even people with records couldn't swear to total accuracy. The whole thing's a farce and you know it."

"Farce or not, right now you need something, anything, to defend yourself."

"Against what?"

"Brian Conneally was in your study hall."

"No, he wasn't. I never saw the kid in my life. I may not be keeping attendance, but I started to, in the beginning, and I know my regulars. I do have a few pages of signatures from the first few weeks when I had them sign in every day. That kid was never in my study hall. I saw his picture in the paper and I didn't recognize him."

"Wonderful. Just wonderful."

"What are you getting at, Harry?"

"You don't remember signing in Brian Conneally."

"No. I told you. I never saw the kid."

"Well, you did see the kid and you signed him into your study hall on February 2. Here's a copy of the add slip."

Bonnie looked at it, not realizing that it was being offered as Brian Conneally's death certificate, not ready to accept it as her own. "A copy. Where's the original? Locked in the safe? In with the diplomas and exams? Is it that precious to you? What's happening? Are you trying to pin responsibility for that accident on me? It wasn't my fault! It wasn't!"

"Wait a minute," Harry said. "Follow this through with me, okay? Brian Conneally had to be assigned somewhere second period. His parents are interested in knowing where. This piece of paper put him in your study hall. There's no doubt about that; you not only signed the slip, you crossed out the name of another teacher and wrote in your own. You just told me the kid never showed, so obviously you never reported his truancy, his parents never knew about it, therefore they never had a chance to do anything about it, and his mother is going to say that if she had been notified the kid would be alive today. Do you see what the problem is?"

"Whose problem! Yours appears to be solved!"

"Jesus Christ! Do you think I'm enjoying this?" He stood up and started pacing. "I had every hope that you'd show me proof that the kid was in study hall every day except the day he died!"

"Do you know how many kids cut study hall every day, any period of the day? Why should I be nailed to the cross for it?"

Harry stopped pacing, sat, and spoke slowly. "Because this kid died."

"And it's my fault."

"Yes, God damn it! Can't you see it?"

"And if he hadn't died, nobody would have ever known the difference. Where was he first semester?"

"In study hall."

"With Erica, right? What the hell do you think he was doing first semester, Harry? Why don't you get her in here, she's the one who trained the kid! You can pull in any teacher in this place who has a study hall and find out that there's some kid who was signed in and forgotten about!"

"That will not prove anything!"

"That will prove everything!"

"Bonnie, look, I'm really sorry that it turned out this way for you, but I have to tell you, you're suspended pending further investigation."

"What?! You're crazy, Harry! What further investigation? Suspended? Jean Tevarro had to come in here and threaten you before you suspended that kid who was obscene with me a few weeks ago! And now you're suspending me? What is it? Is somebody threatening you again?"

Bassard's face set. "It's out of my hands. I no longer have control over any of it. Please believe that. I can't do anything for you. Not without something to work with, and you can't give me anything to work with. It's out of my hands now. I'll supply you with a letter of recommendation if you want one to apply for work in another district. That's all I can do for you now."

Bonnie turned into a mass of anguish and fury. "Do you know what I went through to get credentials for this thankless job? I put myself through school. I've been tolerating the indignities of this job because I put everything I own into it. Where am I supposed to find another job? There aren't any jobs! Am I supposed to run and hide? Move to another State where my reputation for being incompetent won't follow me? What the hell is wrong with you? You'll brand me, then write a letter of recommendation? You're a goddam hypocrite and you make me sick. What if I tell the press you offered to write a letter of recommendation? You wouldn't like that, would you?"

Harry squirmed. He never thought she'd be dangerous, but she was backed into a corner. He had to change his strategy or be trapped himself. "I'd deny it, of course," he said calmly. "I was only attempting to help you where I could, Bonnie."

"I should have kept my mouth shut and then used it against you. That's the way the game is played, isn't it? I'm just not devious enough to play to win. Well, what happens now? Do I leave immediately? Am I too tainted to walk these halls, or what?"

"I don't think you're in any frame of mind to meet with your classes."

"Thank you very much, Harry. This black eye is nothing compared to what you've just done to me."

He was relieved when she left. He made the phone call and agreed that it turned out to be much easier than expected. No hearings were necessary, no muss, no fuss, no bother. The Board simply had to deny tenure and the case was closed. Without tenure, Bonnie had no rights, and the Board could deny tenure without explaining why. That fact gave Harry Bassard an idea, which he strongly suggested. Perhaps the Conneallys would agree. But he was told by his fellow Keepers of the Public Trust that the story had to be released, the public had to know what happened, the transgressor had to be named.

At the end of second period, Alyssa sidetracked to the office. Bonnie's ominous disappearance had her in a frenzy. Harry couldn't have kept Bonnie all period. Or maybe he had. Or maybe something had come up and Bonnie was still waiting to see him. At any rate, Bonnie's books and materials were left in the study hall. Alyssa had to find Bonnie, for more than one reason.

Harry's door was closed. Bonnie was nowhere in sight. Alyssa asked Brenda. Brenda stopped typing and said in a low voice, "She's gone. I'm typing the press release. Oh, Alyssa, it's terrible, just terrible."

Alyssa read what was already typed on the page and said, "I have to see Harry."

"No, he doesn't want—"

But Brenda was too late. Alyssa was already through the door.

"You can't do this to Bonnie," she said with conviction. "It isn't fair and you know it."

Harry was sitting at his desk, his head in his hands. He looked up. "Whatever it is, it is. I can't do anything about it. It's out of my hands."

"Stop playing Pontius Pilate. There's got to be something you can do. I'm in that study hall and I don't have attendance records either. So we lie and say we do. So what? Or we say that he was never put into a study hall, that his scheduling got screwed up somewhere along the line. You know damn well that happens all the time."

"If we say that, the counselor gets accused of negligence for not following it up."

"Why can't we admit that it's impossible to do every God-damned thing we're told to do?"

"We have to stick with the truth and the truth is that Bonnie never reported Brian Conneally's truancy. If she had, it would have been stopped. It's as simple as that, Alyssa. Your name is not on the add slip, Bonnie's is. We can't lie, we can't lie to the public and expect to get away with it."

"That's where you're wrong, Harry. We've been lying for years, this whole place is one big fabrication for the public. We're all guilty of perpetuating the hype. We've been lying so long that even the truth is a distortion. Bonnie is one hell of a good teacher. The kids respect her, she knows her subject, and she works her ass off. What more do people want from us? Doesn't it matter that Bonnie is good in the classroom, that she's a fair and enthusiastic teacher?"

Harry didn't answer. Not fast enough, anyway. Alyssa lost control and shrieked, "God damn it, Harry, answer me! Does being a good teacher mean nothing around here?"

Harry looked the other way and said vacantly, "You'd better leave or you'll be late for class."

After she did, he closed the door and locked it.

Michael Ixion was already in class when Alyssa arrived. She took him aside and said, "Bonnie was just fired. You'd better go see how she is. She'll be needing some moral support. Tell her I'm going to do something for her, I don't know what yet, but I'll check with the union as soon as I can."

"What happened? How can they fire her? Christ, nobody found out about her and me, did they? How do you—?"

"No, no, Michael, it's not that. Bonnie told me about you two a long time ago. Nobody else knows. They're making her take the rap on Brian Conneally. She'll explain when you see her. Just tell her I'll see what I can do and let her know."

By fourth period, the entire school was buzzing. An announcement over the p.a. during third period canceled Bonnie's classes for the remainder of the day. Her students were told to go to study halls, which filled Alyssa with massive rage. Study hall teachers had no idea who was supposed to be in Bonnie's classes. The announcement was no more than an invitation for her students to cut class and get away with it.

By the end of the day, Paul Haust received his orders. No sub would be hired to cover Bonnie's classes. There were only three weeks of instructional time left. The department was expected to fill in, teachers would have to give up their free periods on a rotating basis to handle the load. The chairman could grade her exams. And Bonnie would not be replaced the following year.

Alyssa tried all day to find some small hope for Bonnie. But everywhere she turned, she hit up against the same brick wall: Bonnie didn't have tenure.

Jason said it didn't look promising for the union to be able to do much, but he also said he'd go as far as he could in trying. Jean was also pessimistic about Bonnie's chances for a reprieve. "They've got her," she said sadly, "just as they might have gotten any one of us. Bonnie picked the short straw, she picked the piece of paper with the inkspot on it. It could have been any one of us."

Bonnie won the lottery. Alyssa thought about that on the way home. She thought about Shirley Jackson and the short story that was a terrifying reminder of man's refusal to abandon ritual, even when the ritual is barbaric. Must the tradition of human sacrifice be perpetuated among civilized man?

She thought about the film that was an exact replica of the story. Every time she showed the film, she worried. She knew that parent groups all over the country had attacked the film as being too violent for adolescents. But that never stopped her from showing the film or assigning the story. The message was too crucial, and the violence was an integral part of the message.

What could she do for Bonnie? There had to be something. Jean suggested mobilizing the entire faculty. "We're branded as militant," she said. "Now we've got something of our own to fight for. We don't need the rest of the district, though we'll take any support we can get. Next week we'll start the ball rolling. It's useless now, with a three-day weekend coming up. But we can feel people out at the in-service day on Tuesday. Maybe we'll get a chance to picket this year, after all. We can't sit back and let this happen. If we do, we deserve everything we get from now on."

The thought of revolt appealed to Alyssa. She'd picket for Bonnie. But it was more than that, more than just Bonnie. It was Mary Gregory and Jim Cote. It was the aura of fear, the threatening atmosphere, the constant barrage of insults. She was filled with so much rage and disgust that she no longer felt exhausted. Purpose had once again entered her life.

Bonnie lay mute and motionless on the bed, wondering how all of it had happened. In one week her whole life had been turned upside down. Everything she worked for, planned for, hoped for, was gone. The bottom had fallen out. In one week.

What was she going to do without a job? She'd never teach again, not after the campaign to ruin her. Page two was filled with it.

Did they have to print the boys' pictures again? Was it really necessary to emphasize how good-looking and healthy they once were? Was it crucial to elaborate on their plans for the future? Was it critical that she be hated for spoiling those plans? Did no one think that she, too, had plans?

No doubt about it. She was the culprit. Bonnie Mason saw her own name in a headline and even she was convinced of the credibility of the heinous act of negligence she was convicted of. Mrs. Conneally insisted that her son never would have died; she was pleased that action had been taken to exact severe punishment on the responsible party. It would not restore her son, but, she said, at least justice had been served.

Archibald Brissonson also expressed satisfaction with the results of the investigation. He admitted that while his son may have been the one with the key, the other boy was driving, so the decision to take the car must have been a collaboration. He also felt that the ultimate responsibility for the accident rested with "Miz Mason."

Bonnie read his statement in horror. He turned over to the press the note she had sent him first semester. There was no harm in it then, it saved Joe from an ugly scene, it saved her a phone call. She didn't want to talk with the man, so she sent a note. She lied, of course, to save Joe from his father's wrath. She wrote that she had made a mistake with his attendance, that her records were faulty; it wasn't a very large sacrifice to make, and it paid off. Joe was never truant again. He raised his grade and passed the course. She was proud of him. So what if his father thought she didn't know what she was doing? The student was the only one who mattered.

How ironic. What horrible irony. Now Joe was dead and his father was using the note as proof of her incompetence. She had condemned herself without knowing it. And she should have known better. More than once Alyssa had warned her: "Never put yourself on the line for a kid. Do all you can to help, but never, never, never put anything in writing that even remotely resembles a statement of your own failing. They'll hang you with it."

She never really thought that was possible. Until now. Now she saw what could happen, and it was too late. Her name was plastered all over page two. Somehow they had managed to get her picture, the one that was in the yearbook. She wondered if Harry had supplied it, or if they simply cut it out and reproduced it. She wondered why no reporter showed up at her door, then realized that she never gave the school a change of address after she moved. That was a stroke of good luck, along with the fact that her phone number was also unlisted and unknown in the office. She was sure that if they had been able to contact her, the yearbook picture would have been rejected in favor of one showing her bruised face.

As it was she felt like a freak in a sideshow, on display at thirty cents a ticket. She knew she would have to move out of town, go somewhere else where she might be able to find work without being gawked at and whispered about. But not teaching. She never wanted to see the inside of a school again. That was what she told Alyssa when Alyssa called. She didn't want any picketing. She was adamant about that. No more publicity. She couldn't bear any more publicity.

Michael had agreed to move away. They needed to find another place to live anyway, why not somewhere else? They could both try to find jobs and take it one day at a time. Bonnie was heartbroken that his college plans had to be postponed, but she could no longer fight it. Michael stayed with her all day, through the tears and the anger. She sent him home in late afternoon to catch his mother before she read the newspaper. Both returned in the evening to offer love and support. Mrs. Ixion went so far as to offer her home and whatever financial support she could muster up.

Bonnie was thankful but embarrassed. She had always made her own way. Accepting charity was not to her liking at all. That evening Bonnie was served with an eviction notice reminding her that she had one more week to vacate the apartment.

It took some fast talking and feigned frivolity before she convinced Michael and his mother that she would be fine if they left her. She joked about her notoriety right up to the minute she closed the door. An hour later Michael called and she forced lightness into her voice. She needed some time alone, some time to try to sort it all out, to convince herself that everything would be all right, that she was strong enough to live through it. It had happened, it was over, and she had to stop reeling from the blow.

She lay mute and motionless on the bed, couldn't stop looking at the window and seeing herself there. Martyrdom: what a curious thing. No. Alyssa, please, no demonstrations, it's bad enough now. I don't want any more of it. I know I never should have written that note. I know. I made mistakes and I'm paying for them. But no more, please, no more. They can do whatever they want with me. Nobody can help. Nobody. He would be alive today if I had reported him, you know. Probably both would be. It wasn't intentional, I didn't do it on purpose, but I did it, I did it —- but it *wasn't* you, don't you understand? —- it *wasn't you*— it *could have been, but it wasn't!*

It was me. And everybody knows it was me.

Leave me alone. Just leave me alone. I'll be fine. I'll get over it. I'm leaving town. I don't know what I'll do. I can always waitress. After the baby is born, maybe I'll stay home. If I have a home to stay in. I don't know, I don't know yet. Funny, isn't it, how important a job becomes after you lose it? Everything else becomes pretty trivial, all the complaints, the disgust, the discouragement. Having the job to begin with is the only real significance, keeping it the only real duty. And you need them more than they need you. It's dangerous to lose sight of that. You're nothing, nobody, to them. They don't care if you live or die. What was it Jean said about clichés? She was right. It's every man for himself, it's dog eat dog. Erica knows, and she's right. She's the smart one, the smartest one of all.

No, Michael doesn't know about the baby yet. How can I tell him now? Things are bad enough now. Not now, I can't tell him now. How much can he take at once?

What a difference a week makes. Where are you, Dorothea King? Nowhere? Nowhere with Alex? Do you know what your children are doing? Are you feeling as helpless as I am right now? Or does it end with death? It should, it must, it must end with death. It has to end sometime, it can't go on for all eternity. There has to be peace somewhere.

Where did you go when you left this room forever? Are you with your God? Did He welcome you to a better place? How can I believe? You were a strong woman. Can I pray to you for strength?

Sleep. I need to sleep. Help me to sleep. That's all I ask. No one can undo what's been done, I can't ask for that, but I can ask for strength. Strength and sleep. I need to sleep, to forget for awhile.

She closed her eyes and felt her body relax, the weightlessness becoming more and more pronounced as she drifted into semi-conscious sleep.

The sphere materialized around her, and she knew what it was, and she tried to pull away, but she didn't possess the fortitude, and so she melted into it, into the mist, the damp, dank, ebonied vapor seeped through her, rotting her flesh, causing it to turn rancid and leprous, ridden with consumptive sores, oozing a milky white substance. The stench of rotting flesh, the sight of her own decomposition, threw her into familiar terror. But she knew, she knew, and again she fought to awaken. And again she was swallowed into it, deeper and deeper, until only the terror remained.

Then suddenly all of it cleared, the vapor solidified into one form, the form covered by a black hooded robe, and the form began to beat her.

669

You don't need to go to college to get married and have babies.
Are you a Mrs. or a Miss or one of those liberated mongrels?
Exercise your options for disciplinary action.
That window is worth two hundred thousand dollars.
You can have the ashes, as soon as you get out!
Those boys are dead because of you!
GET OUT!
You're suspended pending further investigation.

The man was shrouding her in his black robe, suffocating her under its weight, when she heard the tiny voice: Come with me, my bonny lass, come with me. The man was gone, and she answered: Where? Where are you? Can you help me? But the tiny voice didn't respond.

A bullet-shaped object, burning, a headless corpse rising out of the flames; another, blackened, speaking through charred lips: Look what you have done, WHAT YOU HAVE DONE! Horrible, grotesque shapes, some with searing green eyes, some with pointed ears and fangs, all with bloody hands and mouths, screaming at her, ready to rip her to pieces. She was pulled toward the fiery mass amidst the screams — My Child! My Child! Murderer! Murderer! You Murdered My Child! — pulled shrieking to get away — No! No! Don't make me see! Why must I see? The flames, the flames, protect me from the flames! Why must I burn? Why must I see? She struggled to pull away, but they held her, the flames parted, and she saw a child, a fetus, burning. No! Not my child! Not mine! Let it be born! Wake up. WAKE UP! I can, I can. This is not real. This is not. Run, run from it. Crawl away, then run. There. I can, I can. Oh, no, no, the flames, the flames are all around me. The flames are real. I feel the heat.

Come with me, my bonny lass.

I will, I will, but the flames—?

Push through them. Push your way. He gave you armor, remember? He took pity on you, long ago. Push through the flames. The fire can't hurt you. Push, my bonny lass, push.

And she did. And the walls of hell cracked and split, gave way to consciousness, then followed her to eternity.

The woman ran up the sidewalk and around the back of the house. She stopped short when she saw what was left of the window. It must have been a horrible sight before the body was removed. Broken pieces of glass covered the ground, sparkling pieces of jagged color mixed with torn strips of lead.

She looked up and saw the gaping hole left in the house. Why did we leave her alone? Why did we believe she was stable?

The woman was in shock. She had heard the news on the car radio. She didn't want to believe, but now she saw and she had to.

Michael should have stayed with her. He wanted to, but she was so independent, so sure that she wanted to be left alone. Michael wasn't anxious to leave and returned soon after. The woman knew that, she heard him slip out of the house.

She had no way of knowing that he hid in the shadows until the crowd dispersed, the investigators left, that he saw and heard everything.

She was worried because she didn't know where he was, what state he was in. On the way to work she heard it on the car radio, and she changed direction immediately.

Now she surveyed the shards of glass and felt the old cloud descending upon her. Once before, shock over death had almost destroyed her. But not now, she couldn't let it, she had to find Michael.

The woman's thoughts were interrupted by sudden awareness of a pointed yet distant sound, a hum, a low-keyed extended hum. She walked to the back door, opened it, and followed the hum up the stairs to the apartment. The inside door was opened wide and from that vantage point she saw the source of the hum, an alarm clock on the dresser in the bedroom. She walked into the room, shut off the alarm, and turned to leave. The human form huddled in the middle of the bed startled her so violently that she gasped, then used both hands to stop the scream rising in her throat.

The razor was still in his hand. He held it limply. His head was tilted, eyes turned up, staring at the sky. Blood was streaming down his face onto the pillows he cradled in his arms. One hand clutched a mass of yellow yarn.

The woman spoke in a whisper. "Michael? My God, Michael, what have you done to yourself?" She moved toward him slowly and took the razor from his hand. She was not afraid. She knew he would not be violent, that the violence was spent, that what he now had to overcome was worse than violence or anger or grief, though in the process of renewal he would battle all three.

She heard voices in the back of the house, male and female voices. The male voice was bellowing, "How do I sell this! I'll sue to get my money!" The female voice answered in acid tones, "Who, you fool? There's nobody left."

The voices were lost to the sound of an airplane passing overhead. Michael's body started to quiver with the first rumblings, the quiver intensifying as the noise hit its peak. By the time the sound of the plane diminished, Michael was rocking wildly and there was the sound of footsteps on the back stairs.

Thankful that she knew the alternate route out of the apartment, the woman quickly pulled her son upright and lead him down the front stairway and out of the house. Michael held her hand and followed obediently.

Bonnie's body was flown to Maine the same day that Joe Brissonson and Brian Conneally were buried. Half the senior class and a large number of underclassmen attended the funerals, or, rather, half the senior class and a large number of underclassmen were out of school that day. While close friends were sincerely grieving the first casualties of the Class of '81, many students untouched by the tragedy used the occasion as an excuse to cut classes. It was not a difficult thing to mastermind. No one was taking attendance at the funerals.

Memorial Day

The shopper is standing in the check-out line in a daze. The cart is in front of her, but she hardly knows it is there, its contents thrown in absentmindedly. Certain rituals have to be maintained. Food. Clothing. Sleep. Milk and bread are necessities of life. Consumable items have to be replaced. Some consumable items.

The shopper is wearing a lavender-flowered dress, her favorite dress, one she wore when she wanted to feel as soft and feminine as the garment. She often selected clothes to fit her mood or to modify it. Today she is attempting modification. She rarely wore a dress when she didn't have to go to work. That was going to change, she decided. Going to work was not the focal point of her life, it was not worth her undivided attention. Her work was not worthy of her heart. It was possible to give too much. She would never do it again. She would be stingy with her heart. Putting it into her work had been foolish and naive, a vestigial notion from childhood. She was a child no longer. She had crossed the threshold. Loss of innocence. Such a common theme in literature.

Jeff's words pulse through her brain: People go to work for the money, the paycheck. Don't expect to get anything else of value from your job and you won't be disappointed. Change your attitude and collect your pay. Start thinking about yourself. Do what you can and forget about the rest. Don't ever make your job more important than anything else in your life. I know you want to be the best you can be, but that's impossible, isn't it? So admit it. Nobody cares about you. Except me. I care about you, and you've forgotten I exist.

She finally agreed with him. There was no doubt that education was in for far worse in the next few years. Aid would diminish even more drastically, more programs would have to be cut, along with staff. School districts would be saddled with more mandates from the top to insure quality, while the quality oozed out the bottom. Taxpayers would pay more and more for the continuance of less and less. She couldn't fight it. She couldn't save education. But she could save herself. Her new creed was a step in the right direction: Forget that you want to touch someone's life. Forget that you need to develop skills. Forget what you think is important. Forget the welfare of the kids. Forget about valid tests and fair grading and extra worksheets. Forget all that and concentrate on survival. Yours.

Suddenly angry words filter through the daze, snapping the shopper into awareness of place and time. One woman is stacking items on the conveyor belt, the other is waiting behind her. Their conversation is spirited.

"What was she doing in a classroom anyway?" the stacker-of-items says. "Teenage pregnancy is bad enough. What kind of example was she setting? What the hell is going on when teachers are having bastards? She should have been thrown out a long time ago. There's more to it than what's in the newspaper, I'm sure of that!"

The second woman says: "It's common knowledge she was in school with a black eye. I think somebody did her in. Maybe she was desperate to find a husband and tried to rope the wrong guy. Who knows? You're right, there's more dirt in what happened there. At least she's not in a classroom any more. I'd scream bloody murder if my kids had a teacher like that. But how do you know? How do you find out these things? It sickens me to think that somebody like that is allowed to work with impressionable kids."

The shopper in the lavender-flowered dress hears the words, feels a surge of emotion, recognizes the futility of the feeling, decides to leave the cart where it is, and starts walking out of the store. Someone shouts, "Hey, lady! You can't leave this here!"

Alyssa Marie Grispelli Matthews hears the shout and knows it is directed at her. But she's not chained to the cart. So she keeps walking.

Printed in the United States
745000001B